P9-CQI-660

Honour and the Sword

Honour and the Sword

A. L. BERRIDGE

MICHAEL JOSEPH
an imprint of
PENGUIN BOOKS

MICHAEL JOSEPH

Published by the Penguin Group
Penguin Books Ltd, 80 Strand, London WC2R ORL, England
Penguin Group (USA) Inc., 375 Hudson Street, New York, New York 10014, USA
Penguin Group (Canada), 90 Eglinton Avenue East, Suite 700, Toronto, Ontario, Canada M4P 2Y3
(a division of Pearson Penguin Canada Inc.)
Penguin Ireland, 25 St Stephen's Green, Dublin 2, Ireland (a division of Penguin Books Ltd)
Penguin Group (Australia), 250 Camberwell Road, Camberwell, Victoria 3124, Australia
(a division of Pearson Australia Group Pty Ltd)
Penguin Books India Pvt Ltd, 11 Community Centre, Panchsheel Park, New Delhi – 110 017, India
Penguin Group (NZ), 67 Apollo Drive, Rosedale, North Shore 0632, New Zealand
(a division of Pearson New Zealand Ltd)
Penguin Books (South Africa) (Pty) Ltd, 24 Sturdee Avenue, Rosebank,
Johannesburg 2196, South Africa

Penguin Books Ltd, Registered Offices: 80 Strand, London WC2R ORL, England

www.penguin.com

First published 2010
1

Copyright © A. L. Berridge, 2010

Map artwork by Stuart James

The moral right of the author has been asserted

All rights reserved
Without limiting the rights under copyright
reserved above, no part of this publication may be
reproduced, stored in or introduced into a retrieval system,
or transmitted, in any form or by any means (electronic, mechanical,
photocopying, recording or otherwise), without the prior
written permission of both the copyright owner and
the above publisher of this book

Set in 13.5/16 pt Adobe Garamond
Typeset by Ellipsis Books Limited, Glasgow
Printed in Great Britain by Clays Ltd, St Ives plc

A CIP catalogue record for this book is available from the British Library

ISBN: 978-0-718-15544-5

www.greenpenguin.co.uk

Penguin Books is committed to a sustainable future
for our business, our readers and our planet.
The book in your hands is made from paper
certified by the Forest Stewardship Council.

From all that terror teaches,
From lies of tongue and pen,
From all the easy speeches
That comfort cruel men,
From sale and profanation
Of honour and the sword,
From sleep and from damnation,
Deliver us, good Lord!
                    – from 'A Hymn' by G. K. Chesterton

Acknowledgements

I must apologize to the people of Picardy, not only for dumping my fictional Saillie smack in the middle of the Forest of Lucheux, but also for landing them with so tempestuous a son as André de Roland. I have tried to find names authentic to both place and period for my fictional characters, but if any of these appear to reflect badly on a genuine family of the time, then I apologize unreservedly to their descendants for a similarity which is both unintentional and coincidental. The real personages, however, are written as history shows them to have been, and require no apology from me.

Many of those I should thank most are long dead, for the best sources on seventeenth-century France remain the vast number of contemporary memoirs. I would still have been lost in this wealth of material without the guidance of many members of the Society for French Historical Studies, and in particular Robin Briggs (author of *Early Modern France 1560–1715*) and Dr David Parrott (author of *Richelieu's Army*), whose generous personal help and encouragement I can only acknowledge with astonished gratitude. I am also much indebted to Ken Mondschein for advice on historical fencing, and to David Reid of the St Albans Fencing Club for guidance on practical aspects of the art. Thanks are due also to the many friends who helped with the different languages, and in particular Clare Cox, who polished the lyrics of '*Le Petit Oiseau*'. Anything impressive in this book is down to these experts; the mistakes are entirely my own.

I am also very grateful to those who gave invaluable feedback and advice in the actual writing, especially Julie Howley, Janet Berkeley, Michelle Lovric and Harry Bingham of The Writers' Workshop, my agent Victoria Hobbs, and my editor Alex Clarke. Thanks also to Mervyn Ramsey and Laura Rawling for their inspiration and encouragement, and finally to my husband Paul Crichton, without whose faith and support *Honour and the Sword* would never have been written at all.

Editor's Note

Even the dead can speak.

It is not from me the reader will learn the story of André de Roland, but from the recorded voices of those who actually knew him: a handful of letters, the memoirs of a parish priest, the journal of an adolescent girl, and the transcripts of interviews with a soldier, a merchant, a blacksmith, a tanner, and a stable boy. These interviews are the first in a series conducted by the young Abbé Fleuriot, and appear to be surprisingly frank. The reader should remember, however, that while it is possible for a speaker to reveal more than he knows, it is not only the living who can lie.

In order to render the oral material accessible to a modern reader, I have adopted an informal approach to the translation, and substituted modern English idioms for those of seventeenth-century Picardy. The content, however, is bound to remain alien. André de Roland was anachronistic even in his own times, genuinely believing 'honour' to be something which ought to affect his behaviour and play an integral part in his daily life. The reader will not need me to point out the danger of this, nor is that my responsibility. The dead may speak; it is the job of the historian only to see that they are heard.

Edward Morton, MA, LittD, Cambridge,

April 2010

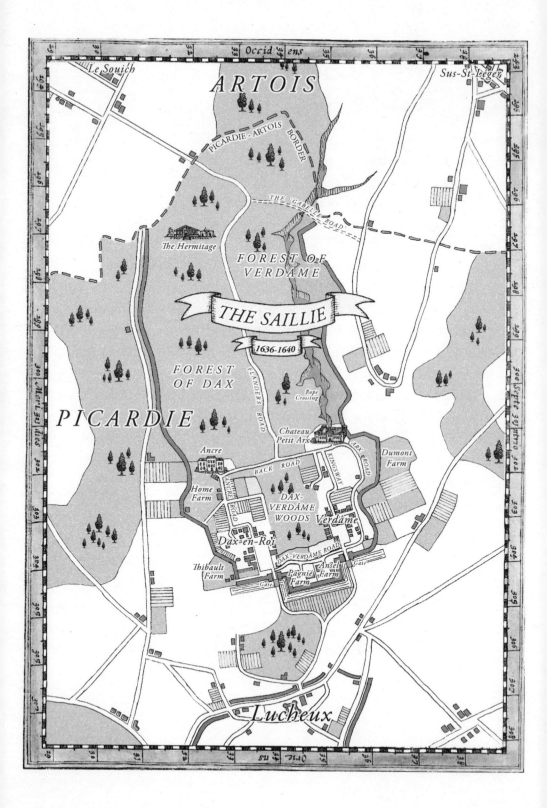

PART I
The Boy

One

Jacques Gilbert

From his interviews with the Abbé Fleuriot, 1669

You can trust me.

No one knew him like I did. Not that bastard Stefan for a start, you don't want to believe a word he says. You don't need him, you don't need any of them, except maybe Anne later on. I'm the only one who really knows.

I knew him from when he was tiny. My Mother was his nurse up at the Manor, and sometimes she'd take me with her so I saw a lot of him even then. They had all kinds of interesting stuff there, like a real clock in the hall and a tapestry with all pictures of stags on it, and a great big gong on the landing. Sometimes we'd see the Seigneur himself, and he was always kind, he used to give me sugared nuts which he carried round in a little silver box, and sometimes he'd ruffle my hair and call me a fine boy. More often it was just me and Mother in the boy's room, and sometimes she'd sing to us, which was nice, and sometimes she'd make me play with him, which wasn't. He wasn't really André back then, he was just a baby that cried a lot, because I was jealous of him for taking my mother away and sometimes used to pinch him when she wasn't looking.

I saw more of him when he was older, because he was the Seigneur's son and I had to be nice to him and trot him around the paddock and answer all his stupid questions beginning 'Jacques, why . . . ?' It was always 'why' in those days. It was only much later he started asking the really hard questions, the ones that begin with 'if'.

But it wasn't a proper kind of knowing in those days, just sort of knowing the shape of him and the things he did and said. I was only the stable-master's son and he was André de Roland, he'd be Comte de Vallon when his uncle finally got on and died. But I did use to watch him, because if your own life's a bit crap you can get a lot of entertainment out of watching people with better ones, and anyway I thought he was funny. He had this awful temper back then, he'd shout and wave his arms about, and sometimes even stamp. He never did it with me, of course, he was always polite with servants, it was only being ordered about he couldn't stand, or people telling him things he couldn't do.

What I liked best was watching him fence. I know peasants don't have anything to do with swords, but there was no harm in looking, it's like there was a bit of glass between him and me like a window and I was always safely on the other side. I think he knew I watched him, but I don't believe he minded. He hadn't anyone of his own kind to play with, his mother just used to drift round looking beautiful and never having any more children, and Colin's dad said it was a black disgrace, they ought to have a spare in case anything happened. He didn't say what 'anything' meant, but I knew, my own little sister Clare had died that year.

It was a pity for the boy, though, and I think it made him lonely. That makes me feel bad now, him being lonely and me just watching him being it, but that's as much as I wanted in those days. I remember one time when he sort of reached out and smashed the window between us, and it got me one of the worst beatings I ever had.

It was one afternoon when they were looking for him all

over the estate. That happened a lot actually, most days you'd hear someone yelling 'André!' round the place, he was never where he was meant to be, that boy, just never. But this time it was important because the new Baron de Verdâme had brought his children to meet the Rolands, and there wasn't a sign of André anywhere. I just went on mucking out the stables, then I dug the fork back in the straw and there he was, curled up at the bottom trying to hide. I gaped at him, but he got his finger up to his lips, and I heard César, the Second Coachman, go by calling him, and I didn't say a word.

It's natural, isn't it, it's instinct. You stick together against the adults, though I'd have been fourteen then and him only eleven. So I never said a thing, I just went on working round him, but he wouldn't keep quiet, he started up gabbing, then someone was coming and he was trying to burrow back under the straw, but it was the Seigneur himself at the door and we were caught.

It was terrible. The Seigneur kind of lifted him up, got him out of the stables and standing on the cobbles in front of him, all with just a look. It was a belting look, that one, very powerful. The boy inherited it, so I should know.

Then he really laid into him. Not the way my Father would have done, it was all just what he was saying, how the boy had let him down, let his whole family down, embarrassed his mother, failed as a gentleman, and shamed them all in front of their new neighbours. I could see the boy getting white in the face and his lip starting to tremble, then his father got even angrier and said in this terrible voice 'You will not cry, André,' and the boy swallowed it back and stuck his chin out and said 'Yes, Sieur.' There were times I wondered if my own Father really loved me because he beat me so much, but I remember thinking in a way what the Seigneur was doing was worse.

Then he turned to me and said 'As for you, young Jacques . . .' and my heart jumped I was so frightened, but the boy leapt in at once and said it wasn't my fault because he'd ordered me. The Seigneur looked at him then, and I saw he really did love him after all, but that didn't stop him giving him another bollocking for putting me in an impossible situation, which was apparently even worse than being rude to the Baron. Then he packed the boy off to apologize, but I saw Father watching on the other side of the track, then I knew I was really in trouble and felt sick.

But the Seigneur was nearer. I was standing in the doorway clutching my hat and rubbing and pulling at it, and my hands were all sweaty and I wished I was dead, but he just leant forward and said 'You did quite right, Jacques. A gentleman never tells.' That was an odd thing to say, but I knew he meant it kindly, so I tried to smile and say 'Yes, Sieur,' like the boy did, and he reached out and tousled my hair. Then Father was suddenly there next to me, apologizing for what I'd done and saying he'd deal with it now, and the way he was saying it was like telling the Seigneur to piss off.

The Seigneur said not to worry, it was his own boy caused the trouble and he hoped my Father wouldn't be hard on me for it, but Father just bowed and looked him right in the eye, which you're not supposed to do with nobility, you're meant to look at the ground or your boots or something, then he stuck his hand on my shoulder and said 'He's my lad, Sieur.'

I could never understand how Father didn't get sacked or flogged, because quite apart from the drinking he could be really rude sometimes, but instead of ordering him hauled off to have something horrible done to him, the Seigneur just looked at him a minute then turned away. I watched his

6

boots walking out of sight, then Father took me into the stable and beat the shit out of me.

Nobody beat André, of course, that window was round him all the time like a bubble nothing could get through. I remember crawling home that afternoon, bruised and aching all over, and seeing him sitting by the sunken garden with a girl, deep in conversation like there was no such thing as a stable boy trudging past with a black eye and ribs that were purple for a month. That would have been Anne, I suppose, it was the first time they met, but I wasn't thinking about that at the time, I just wanted to get home to Mother and tell her it wasn't my fault.

I avoided him after that. He caught me at the stables next day to say sorry, and I just mumbled it didn't matter and wouldn't look at him, and after a while he went away. He still came hanging round asking questions sometimes, but now I just said 'yes' and 'no' till he left me alone. It was better that way.

Until the night the Spaniards came, and everything changed.

This is when it really began, the summer of 1636. This is when it gets really hard, what you're asking me to do. I can remember all right, I remember all of it, but I understand what was going on in a way I never did at the time, so I'm sort of seeing things wrong and not what they were really like at all.

If you want the truth as it really was, then don't ask me to remember. What I've got to do is forget. I've got to forget everything I know now and feel now, and everything about what happened later. I've got to go back to being what I was then, that hot night in July when the Spaniards came.

Père Gérard Benoît

From his André de Roland, A Personal Memoir,
privately printed in 1662

It was yet within the octave of Peter and Paul in the year of Our Lord 1636 that the Spaniards came to our village.

The seigneuries of Dax and Verdâme, or the 'Dax-Verdâme Saillie', as they are collectively known, lie to the north of Lucheux, and thrust as a finger into the territory of Artois, at that time in the hands of the Spanish Netherlands. The villages had long been part of Artois themselves, and indeed are still bulwarked on three sides by the now famous Dax-Verdâme Wall, constructed at the time of the uprising in Flanders against Philippe le Bel. This hastily assembled fortification is unusual in its extent, encompassing even a portion of the major farms within its perimeter, but boasts neither flanks nor bastions, nor is even of considerable height, standing in places no more than six or seven foot above the moat. Yet frail a defence as it seems, this Wall had still a significant part to play in our history, as my readers shall learn.

By the time of which I write, however, the Saillie had long been absorbed by conquest into Picardie, and although the Wall remained, its Gates were ever open and its people enjoyed the freedom of the realm of France. So the villages prospered, especially that of Dax-en-roi, where I have the honour to serve as parish priest. It may seem a false modesty to ascribe the name of 'villages' to so large an area, but the northern part is entirely given over to a thick forest which extends well over the border with Artois, its steeply rising slopes and great east gorge rendering the land impractical for building.

The Dax of 1636 was a contented community. The Chevalier

de Roland kept his own Household Guard, so we had only a small militia to feed and billet, and while the *gabelle* or salt tax imposed a grievous burden, our crops made us largely self-sufficient, and the visitor could find here no trace of the poverty to be seen in so many villages of our kind. Verdâme was in other case, its Seigneur having died without issue and its new Baron being unacquainted with the needs of a rural population, but its little businesses still thrived, and starvation had yet to come there.

Yet there are dangers other than these, and so we were about to find. The previous year our King Louis had declared against Spain, so that our northern marches now lay directly on the borders of a hostile country. Since by reason of our history Artois was the one side our Wall did not reach, we had already been exposed to raids and skirmishes from this direction, fortunately repelled by the valour of our Seigneur, but the events of 1636 proved of far greater significance than these.

The Spaniards came in the early hours of the morning, and this time they came in force. Mindful of their previous reception, their first target was Ancre, the Roland estate, surmising that by cutting off the head of such resistance as they were likely to meet, they would incapacitate the entire body. Otherwise they would surely have opened their attack on the village itself, which they could not have known to be so empty of soldiery because of the *gabelle* riots at the Market in Lucheux the day before.

It was Gabriel Lange, sexton of this church, who roused me about two of the clock to warn that the Night Watch reported a large body of cavalry approaching us from the Flanders Road, which bisects the forest. There were, it seems, too many to challenge, but the Watch reported the first part of the force had already turned west towards the gates of

Ancre. I immediately sent Gabriel to the taverns to alert the militia, and myself began the tocsin, as Jehan Bruyant, our bellringer, was unfortunately indisposed after a late night at the market.

Jacques Gilbert

I remember the heat. I had a headache, and the flies were bothering me, the horses were all sweaty and snorting, and the straw was dry and prickly against my skin. My back was hurting because Father had beaten me about something, so I had to sleep on my stomach, and it was pissing me off because I wanted to think about Colin's sister Simone who I'd kissed a few days ago in the lumber room of Le Soleil Splendide, but I needed to be on my back for that, if you know what I mean.

I was fifteen.

I was sleeping in the stables because Father had taken Mother and the children to the Market at Lucheux, and we'd had problems lately with horse thieves. I'd got an arquebus just in case, but it was a rusty old thing, and they're stupid guns anyway, because most people aim with their eyes not their groin. At least it was a firelock, which was something. I wouldn't have fancied pissing about with a slow match in all that dry straw.

I was woken by gunfire. It was raining hard and I thought maybe I'd been hearing thunder, but the Général was going bonkers in his stall, and he was an old warhorse who always went crazy at the sound of guns. Then high and clear above it all I heard the distant bell of the tocsin and knew it was a raid.

I don't know how long it had been going on, but I'd only

got one leg in my breeches when the door banged open and César came crashing in. He must have been working late in the coach-house, and was already fully dressed and clutching a nasty-looking scythe.

'Come on,' he said. 'It's the Manor.'

He was stamping about impatiently while I hurled my boots on, he just couldn't wait to get out and start killing people.

'Spanish, from the look of them,' he said. 'Whole troop. Have you got . . . ?'

He stopped when he saw I'd already hauled out the arquebus and was groping for the powder flask.

'That's good, that's something, but we'll need my pike against the cavalry.'

Cavalry. My fingers were fumbling, I was spilling the powder, the ball slipped out of my hand, I lost it in the straw and reached for another. His hand came clamping down on my wrist and held it still for a second.

'Steady there,' he said.

I took a deep breath, and finished loading. Then I slipped the strap over my head, the flask in my coat, the bullets in my mouth, stuck the ramrod under my arm and I was ready. I felt like a bloody packhorse, but I was ready.

'All right,' he said. 'Stick with me and you'll do.'

I followed him out into the rain. He was a bit mad, really, César, but I was glad he was with me, because I'd never fought before. I'd been bundled off to the woods in the last raid with Mother and Little Pierre, but César was a soldier, he'd only retired after La Rochelle.

The bells sounded louder outside. We took the right-hand fork in the track, down the carriageway that led to the rear courtyard. I don't think I was scared, not really, I mean we had the Seigneur, and he was indestructible, he could beat anyone. I think actually I was excited. There's something in the sound of gunfire that makes you breathe faster and run towards it, it's like you just have to. I remember when we reached the last bend I realized the shooting had stopped and felt disappointed in case we'd missed it all, but César only ran the harder, and his face was grim.

We pounded on down to the apron, the slapping of our boots suddenly louder as we hit the wet flags. There were noises from inside the Manor now, screams and yelling and what sounded like the clash of swords; it all came through the windows, which were open in the heat. Another crashed open right in front of us, and in the light of the flambeau I saw someone scrabbling out, a woman in a long white chemise, her movements clumsy and desperate. She was running before she even got properly upright, and as she lifted her head I recognized Mme Panthon who ran the kitchens, scary Mme Panthon who bawled at me when she caught Marie giving me a cake at the kitchen door. Her hair was loose and wild, her mouth was open and no sound coming out, she saw us and stretched out her arms as she ran. A bright yellow flash cracked in the darkness of the window behind her, a wad of something flew away from the side of her head, her face seemed to turn black, but her legs still ran on two more paces before she dropped in a heap, spattering a spray of water from the stones. Her nightdress was all bunched up round her body, I could see her naked legs.

'Don't stop!' panted César, running past me. 'Don't stop!'

I hadn't realized I had. I tore my eyes off Mme Panthon and ran blindly after César, on across the apron, past the bodies of two of the Household Guard, one on his face, the other staring up at the sky with all black shiny stuff spilling out of his belly, on without stopping and down the carriage-way sweeping round the side of the house. I could hear hooves, there were horses galloping behind us, I yelled back to César and ducked off the drive into the bushes while I struggled to bring up the gun. My hands were damp and I panicked the powder might be too, then saw César had slipped on the wet flags and was still on the drive. I jerked myself forward, but he was up and skidding towards me, then the horses came hurtling round the bend.

There were two of them, Spanish light cavalry, with huge red Burgundy crosses flapping on their cloaks, laughing and waving their swords as they galloped. They saw César at once, and rode whooping towards him. He could have got to the bushes, we could have taken them on together, but he stopped running, that stupid, gallant old man, he stopped and turned to face them, that scythe gripped fast in both hands. I was fumbling the gun up again, trying to tilt the barrel high enough to point at a man on horseback. César struck out and hacked into the first, but as he followed through, the soldier behind spitted him right through the body with his sabre. I fired at last and got him, but the horse kept going, and César was dragged with them a few paces before the soldier slid off and César crashed on his face on the wet ground.

I knew the shot would bring someone, so I stayed in the bushes a moment, struggling to reload with hands that were shaking as well as wet, and trying to ignore the pain in my balls where that bloody gun had kicked me. Something moved above me, a man leant out of a window in the middle storey, and for a moment my heart leapt, because those were the Seigneur's apartments, and if the Seigneur was there everything could still be all right. Then I saw he was a bearded man in a helmet, wearing a scarlet sash diagonally over his black coat like a bad wound, and I knew he was the enemy.

That's when I realized it was over. The Spaniards were in the Seigneur's own rooms, and I didn't see how they could be if he was alive. What's more, the man looking out didn't seem like he was in the middle of a fight or anything, he looked like he had all the time in the world. There was screaming going on somewhere behind him, but it clearly didn't bother him. He just peered out at the darkness, then shrugged, said something to someone behind him, and left the window.

I went to César and turned him over, and unbelievably he was still alive, though there was a trickle of blood coming out of his mouth. His face was covered with mud from the drive, and torn where he'd been dragged along the stones. I tried to wipe it with my sleeve, but my hands were still shaking and I was making it worse. He opened his eyes and saw me, and I felt terrible because I knew it was all my fault for not getting the gun up quicker. He tried to speak but couldn't, then his eyes went out, and I knew he was dead.

More screaming was coming from upstairs in the house, and now there was laughter as well, and a horrible kind of rhythmic chanting I didn't understand. I tried to close César's eyes, but my hands had wet mud on them and I remember I left dark smears on his eyelids. I didn't try to wipe them off. I was suddenly afraid to touch him any more because he was dead.

I crept back to the bushes to get out of the light from the torches. There was banging and crashing all over the house, but nothing that sounded like real fighting, just a lot of soldiers having a good time. There was screaming coming from the servants' quarters downstairs, women shrieking and men laughing, and I thought of Fleurie and Marie and felt really sick. There was nothing I could do. I couldn't stop any of it, I just stood by this stupid box hedge, shaking like a kid and doing nothing.

After a bit I cleared my head and started to edge along the laurels towards the front of the Manor. I wasn't thinking of fighting any more, there obviously wasn't a defence left to join, but I was hoping the front might be clear and I could escape into the woods behind the dairy.

But it wasn't. When I peered round the corner I saw horses and a couple of Spanish soldiers guarding them, though they seemed to be more interested in what was happening indoors. They were talking and laughing and looking towards the courtyard doors, then one wiped his mouth on his sleeve, tugged at his breeches, and strolled inside.

I daren't risk it. I left the laurels and was just crossing back to the first box hedge when I heard a sort of slithering from the house, then the hard thump of boots and a ring like iron on the flags behind me. I jumped like a rabbit, swivelling the gun round so fast César would have been proud, but the terrace looked empty, there was only a sword rolling to a standstill on the drive. Then something moved under the ivy, a small figure sat itself up in the light of the flambeau, I saw a white face with a lot of floppy black hair and realized it was the boy. It was him, I mean. It was André.

I guessed he'd climbed from a window, but the Spaniard at the front had heard him too, he came belting round the corner, blade raised and ready, a tall black-clad soldier slashing down with his sword at a little kid of twelve. The boy dived to one side, but he wasn't trying to run, he was scrabbling across the drive to retrieve the sword. He snatched it up fast, but it was too big for him and his balance still off, the soldier grabbed his collar, dragged him round, and drew back his sword for the lunge.

I fired. I'd forgotten the kick on that gun, and it walloped me straight back into the bush. I scrambled up fast, but there was just the boy standing bewildered, looking out into the dark like he was wondering where the shot had come from.

A black heap on the ground beside him proved at least I'd shot straight.

I showed myself and tried to call out in a kind of loud whisper, which is impossible actually, especially when you've got bullets in your mouth, but they'd have heard the shot indoors and someone could come any second, so I waved my arms around and sort of hissed 'M'sieur, m'sieur!' He stood staring like his wits had gone, which I suppose was reasonable now I know what happened in there, then suddenly jerked himself towards me, running across the drive on to the lawn, that stupid long sword trailing behind him on the grass.

I yanked him right into the heart of the bush and clamped my hand tight over his mouth, just as three soldiers came charging round the corner. He was wearing this bright white shirt I was terrified would show through the leaves, so I covered him with my body and pressed his face hard down, but he was wriggling away and my hands were wet and slippery, I was scared I couldn't hold him. The bush was rotten and almost hollow inside, but we were still making it rustle, and the soldiers only feet away, looking at the body of the man I'd shot. Then he bit me, right in the hand, but I didn't dare yell, I just clenched my teeth and forced him to face me till I saw recognition in his eyes and felt him relax. I took my hand carefully away from his mouth, and turned back to watch the soldiers.

They were looking round to see where the shot might have come from, then caught sight of the other bodies further up, which were César and the first two soldiers. One went to look, but the others peered fearfully out into the dark and I realized they were more scared than I was. They were in the light and totally exposed, they hadn't expected attack from outside the Manor, and they couldn't know there was just me and the boy, and our only gun discharged with no time to reload. When the horses started kicking up and neighing round the front, they all jogged back to stop them wandering off, but I think the truth was they just didn't want to stay out there another minute.

Neither did I. As soon as they disappeared I pulled the boy up on his feet and squeezed us out from the bush. I gave up the idea of escaping from the front while those soldiers were there, and led him back towards the bank instead. If we climbed that, we'd get on to the upper bridle path and the stables.

But as soon as he realized I was leading him away from the Manor he stopped dead and let go of my hand.

'No,' he said, and shrank back into the bushes. 'We can't leave the others.'

I crouched down beside him and started to reload the arquebus. If there was still a defence going on somewhere I was going to need it.

'The Seigneur . . .' I started.

'They've killed him.'

I think I knew that anyway, but hearing it was awful. If the Seigneur was gone, there was no hope at all.

'My mother's dead too.'

There was something funny in the way he said that, though I didn't know why. I went on loading, I didn't want to look at his face.

'The Guard?' I asked.

'They're all dead. What about the militia? Has anyone gone for the militia?'

'They don't need to,' I said. 'Listen.'

He cocked his head, then seemed for the first time to hear the tocsin, which was still ringing urgently from the village. I was surprised he hadn't heard it before, even with the rain.

'They must know,' I told him. 'They'll be here any minute.'
'How long has that been going?'
'Ages.'
'Then why aren't they here?'

I remember what it felt like as that sunk in. He was right, of course, you can ride from Dax into Ancre in ten minutes, five if you gallop.

The Spaniards must have got there first.

Père Gérard Benoît

The militia were mustered in haste, but as I relinquished the bells to younger hands and proceeded on to the Square, it became clear to even the most sanguine among us that the road to Ancre was cut. The enemy could by this time be perceived by the movement of horses down the Ancre Road, which runs for a mile between the village and the estate. Barriers were speedily constructed, yet we had perhaps fourteen of the militia to man them and had to call upon our own folk to fill the broad gaps between. Our blacksmith, Henri Lefebvre, took the lead among the civilians, and himself took a musket, assisted in the business of loading by his son Colin. Our ranks were further augmented by the return of some of our people from the Livestock Market, among them Pierre Gilbert, the Ancre groom, and Martin Gauthier, the chief verderer, whose devotion to our Seigneur was so great he had needs be forcibly restrained from rushing to his rescue against the entire Spanish cavalry. It is pleasant to record that some of the Verdâme men also elected to remain with us in our extremity, most notably their village tanner, a man named Stefan Ravel.

Yet there was little reliance to be placed upon so slight a defence as this, and I accordingly dispatched Gabriel's son to plead for aid at Lucheux and convey the intelligence to M. de Rambures, Governor of the citadel at Doullens. He had but just departed when there came a young soldier on foot from Verdâme requesting help of our own Seigneur. It appeared there had been an attack there also, but the Baron was from home, and had only a small ceremonial Guard at the best of times, so the Château had fallen with scarcely a shot fired. The young family of the Baron was believed to be imprisoned within, so this soldier had been sent of his officer to beg help from Ancre in repelling their invaders. He had run all the way through the woods without even shoes to his feet, for there had been no time to dress.

This young caporal was in fact the famous Marcel Dubois, who was later to cause such a stir among us. He was perhaps eighteen years of age at this time, but his devotion to duty was such he would not even permit me to dress his feet, which the stones of the roads had used sorely, but was determined to continue to Ancre as he had been ordered. Only the first movements of the Spanish cavalry against our northward barricade convinced him that help from that direction was not to be thought of, but at this realization he merely loaded his musket and went to the barricade himself. He had failed in the defence of Verdâme, he said, so must lend us his aid in what looked to be the last defence of Dax.

Jacques Gilbert

'No one's coming,' he said. He looked back towards the Manor, and there was another burst of screaming and yelling, then a huge loud crash, like furniture being overturned and crockery breaking. His face was suddenly desperate. 'There's no one but us.'

19

Then he was scrambling to his feet, grasping that ridiculous great sword, and I realized with horror what he was going to do.

'You'll be killed,' I said.

He looked at me, and I saw he was every bit as scared as I was, his eyes looked huge and his breathing was ragged. But he looked back at the Manor and said quietly 'I must,' and I understood he had to, though of course I didn't know why, not back then. He hefted his sword in his hand, glanced back at me and said 'Coming?'

There was only one possible answer to that, which was 'no'. It was completely mad, a kid with a sword, and me with a gun which would maybe get one Spaniard before the other fifty pounced on us while I was reloading. I gaped in shock, but he only nodded like I'd said yes, took three quick breaths, stepped out of the bushes into the open and started to run towards the Manor.

I had to stop him, I'd got no choice, he was bloody twelve years old. I was up and pelting after him, swinging the gun as I went. I caught up with him at the terrace, clonked the barrel down hard on the back of his neck, and brought him sprawling down flat on the stones.

I thought I'd overdone it, or maybe he hit the front of his head when he fell, because when I dragged him back into the bushes I saw he was quite unconscious. I tried not to think about the penalties for knocking out the son of your Seigneur, but at least he was breathing, his chest was moving up and down. It felt strange being able to look at him with no one to yell at me to keep my head down, but I did now, and thought he looked a mess. He was pale, with a tangle of long black hair like mine, and one side of his face was bruised and badly scored. He was just wearing nightshirt and breeches, his boots weren't done up right, he was grubby with earth and scratched and grazed all over. The only pretty thing about him was those long dark eyelashes, which made him look sort of young and innocent.

Which just goes to show how wrong you can be. When I put his wrist down my hand felt sticky, and I saw red traces in the creases of my palm. I uncurled his hand and saw that some time that night it must have been soaked in blood. It was over his sleeve too, and not all the patches on his front were mud like I'd thought. I wondered just what had happened in the Manor before he'd climbed out of it.

But I couldn't worry about that, not right then. Our only chance of escape was the horses, which meant getting to the stables before the Spaniards did. There was no sign of the boy coming round, but I couldn't carry him up the bank, not with ten pounds of gun already round my neck, so I stuck his sword under my arm, climbed up half backwards, and actually dragged him. I felt bad because we were going through nettles and brambles and stuff, but it was the only way.

He started stirring before I got to the top, so I whizzed him up the last bit, then laid him down gently on the path and sat back warily because I didn't want him biting me again. He lay a second, sort of twitching, then his eyes opened and at least he knew it was me. There was this awful moment when I saw him remembering his parents had been murdered, but he didn't cry or anything, he just looked away a moment then asked what had happened.

I said 'You got jumped,' which was true enough.

'How?'

'There was another soldier on the terrace.' That was a bit less true, but I had to say something. 'It's all right, I dealt with it.'

He didn't say anything, he just reached out his hand and got hold of mine, and then I really felt like shit. I had a horrible fear he might go and kiss me, because they do that kind of stuff, nobility, but just at that second I heard hoof-beats below us down to our right, there was cavalry coming up the drive to the Manor. I don't think the boy heard it, he was still gazing at me sort of moistly, so I slammed his head down quick and said 'Horses!'

'Is it the militia?' he asked.

It wasn't. It was more bloody Spaniards, sweeping up towards the Manor like it was their home and we were the bandits hiding outside. They drew up before the courtyard gate, and this young officer stood upright in his stirrups and raised the arm nearest us with a sword in it. He waved it about like a baton, directing little parcels of men off round the estate to surround the Manor and check the outbuildings. I didn't know it then, and it wouldn't have meant much if I had, but that was my first sight of d'Estrada, the Capitán Don Miguel d'Estrada himself. There was something odd about what I was seeing too, something not quite right, but of course I missed it, like everything else that was really going on round me back then, or at least everything important.

'They're coming up here,' said the boy.

There was a bunch of them trotting gently round towards the apron at the back, they were bound to see the carriageway and if they followed it they'd come right to the stables and us.

'Horses!' I said again, and turned and ran for the stables. The boy was hard behind me as I belted inside.

It was warm after the night air, and smelt like home. I threw open the stalls and urged the horses out, then grabbed Tonnerre, because he was the most valuable, a great black Mecklenburg stallion and the Seigneur's own warhorse. I got a halter on him, but didn't waste time with a saddle, I just threw his blanket over his back and led him straight out, looped the halter round a post, and ran back for Duchesse.

There was the boy trying to put a halter on Tempête. I should have bloody known it, he loved that horse, but the gelding was too temperamental, I'd have trusted him less than any stallion I ever knew.

I said 'No, take Duchesse, she's safer,' and quickly threw a halter on Perle. She was mild enough to let me lead her, and even if she wasn't the best of the mares her foal would follow her anywhere, and the foal was Tonnerre's.

When I turned round, the boy was still standing by Tempête.

He said 'What did you say to me?' There was moonlight coming in through the open door, and his face looked different, sort of harder. His eyes had narrowed, they looked like the slits in the donjon at Lucheux.

I said 'You can't ride Tempête, take Duchesse.'

'You don't tell me what I can do with my own horses.'

It was unbelievable. The Spaniards were two minutes away, there wasn't time for one of his tempers now. I nearly told him so, but then suddenly what he'd said sunk in with a thud. 'My own horses' he'd said, and he was right. His father was dead and he wasn't the Seigneur's son any more. He was the Seigneur.

I said quickly 'All right, do what you like, but I couldn't ride him myself, not bareback, I'm not up to it.'

I turned away to grab my blanket, and make a bundle of it for the gun and some oats for the horses. I had a bit of bread and cheese up there too, so I took that along with a bottle of apple brandy which Father used to hide under the rafters and didn't know I knew about. I ran out into the yard, and there was the boy standing by Duchesse. He looked mutinous and thoroughly pissed off, but he was standing by Duchesse like I told him.

I gave him a leg-up, hurled myself on Tonnerre, took Perle's halter, and signalled the boy to follow. The loose horses were blundering about in confusion, bumping into each other and half bolting, but we weaved our way through towards the fork in the path. The right was the carriageway down to the Manor and about a million Spaniards, the left was where the bridle path wound on up to the north of Ancre and the Forest of Dax. I reached the fork and saw horsemen starting up the carriageway towards us.

Duchesse whinnied behind me, and I turned to see the boy half sliding off her back. The stupid little bugger, he was still clutching that sword in one hand, and actually trying to lead Tempête with the other, he'd got nothing to hold on with and was slipping off towards the ground. I fought back to him through the milling horses, but I'd only got one hand to support him, I was holding Perle with the other, while crushing the gun and my bundle against Tonnerre's neck to keep it on.

'Let go of him!' I shouted, struggling to drag him back up. 'They're coming, let go of the halter!'

He turned his face to me, pale and desperate and sheened with rain. Down the carriageway I heard someone shouting.

'Then the sword, drop the sword!' I said.

He shook his head furiously. 'It's my father's.'

There was a flash below us, then the sharp crack of a musket. I hauled him back high against Duchesse's neck, screamed 'Come on!' then tried to turn Tonnerre, but we were blocked in by the loose horses, I couldn't get through, Mai was in front of us, rearing and rolling her eyes white in panic, and the poor old Général was backing into me, trying to turn towards the guns, desperate to get back to his old place in the cavalry lines.

Another horse loomed beside me. I swore at it, then realized with shock it was grey and black, a horse I didn't know, and when my eyes went up there was a man on him, black and red, and his arm high in the air. Something white was striping down towards me with a sound like whipping air, I tried to jerk back, but another blade whistled in between us, there was the sharp ring of steel as swords clashed just inches from my nose. I dug in my heels, driving Tonnerre back, and there was the boy on Duchesse, one hand screwed in her mane, the other slicing down with his sword, the rush of it changing to a hard squelch as it bit into the Spaniard's neck. The man was screaming in my face, he was veering back, his arm coming up, an open white palm with fingers splayed in panic, he was falling away, he was gone.

I closed my eyes, yelled again 'Come on!', got my head down, urged Tonnerre to the gallop and rode like mad down the other fork. There was no time to look back, but the sound of hooves told me the boy was following, and at least I knew he'd let go of Tempête.

There was more shouting below us, and the neighing and stamping of horses, but no more shots, and I couldn't hear anyone else coming after us. I suppose they were too busy trying to round up the loose horses, which were a lot more valuable than we were, after all. Perle was still up with me, and the foal tangling its long thin legs as it skittered desperately after her. I risked a glance behind and saw the boy was keeping up too. He was twisting his head to look back for Tempête, but he still had that sword in his hand, and the blade was dark with what I knew was blood.

We kept going. We followed the bridle track where it circled the rear gardens below us, and went on to the northernmost part of the estate and the back meadow. There was rougher land there, where trees had been cut down for building, and it was fringed directly by the main Forest of Dax. As we finally reached the tree line it was just starting to get light.

I slowed down Tonnerre, and let the foal catch up to Perle, which was a mistake, because he was under her belly and suckling in a minute. The boy came up more slowly, and stopped to watch us. He looked even more bedraggled now it was lighter.

'We'll need to lie up in here for a while,' I told him. 'Let things die down. We'll go back down when it's dark, and find out what's happening.'

He nodded like it didn't matter much, looked vaguely about him, then stiffened suddenly and stared towards the estate below. The rain was making a kind of gentle mist, but through it I could see a plume of dark smoke sort of rolling and coiling into the air in thick purple waves. I followed it down to the dark shape below, where I saw more smoke and little flashes of bright orange flame.

They were burning his home.

He didn't say anything. He just looked at the fire for a long while, and his face had no expression at all. He didn't get angry, he still didn't cry, he just watched. The air round us was shimmering in a strange way, making little shadows pass over his face, like something was on fire behind that too. That was fair enough. It was his whole world going up in smoke down there.

What I didn't realize at the time was that it was mine too.

Two

Stefan Ravel

From his interviews with the Abbé Fleuriot, 1669

I don't know what you're talking to me for. Oh, don't give me that balls about the pursuit of truth, you'll be after canonization before you're done. All you want to hear is how perfect he was, and I'm afraid, M. l'Abbé, he fell a little short of that.

Not that I knew him back then, the night the dons came to Picardie. I'd somehow survived to the age of nineteen without having set eyes on André de Roland, and can't say I was breaking my heart over it. I didn't much care for nobility, not what I'd seen of them. I'd joined my brother in the army at fifteen, and come across enough officers who treated men worse than horses to last my humble lifetime. My brother died in the army, as it happened, Abbé. He died there.

So when the old man dropped dead in '35 there was no one but me to go home and take over the tannery. Verdâme wasn't the nicest place to live back then. The whole village had been sold with the title to this du Pré bastard, who upped all the rents he could, and charged everyone the earth for using the mill, the wine-press, the bake-house or just about everything except breathing. But I wasn't a peasant, Abbé, I was safe from the worst of it. I was a skilled artisan, and I was getting by.

And then the dons came. Christ, yes, of course I remember, there'd been a bunch of us at the Lucheux Market, and there we were sweeping home through the Dax Gate only to find ourselves in the middle of a battle. Not a real one, no officers, no order, nothing but a bunch of civilians weeping and wailing and running out the Gate with their little handcarts, and a few stouter folk desperately flinging up a barricade across the Ancre Road. Well, what's a man to do? I wasn't going to save my home by running away from it, so I went with the others to the barricade.

It was all very amateur. We had civilians with scythes and reaping hooks, and behind us a priest trying to ward off the danger by saying prayers. At least we had a militia sergeant, and when he heard I'd been in the army he gave me a wheel-lock musket, and stuck me in the front by a young Verdâmer in the uniform of the Baron's Guard. That's right, Abbé, Marcel. He seemed a nice, well-brought-up lad, but there wasn't much time for conversation right then, I was busy checking my musket action and getting the damn thing loaded. I'd only just got it comfortably on the rest when there was movement in the dark and the sound of pounding hooves, and there they were, cuirassiers charging us down the Ancre Road.

The press of men behind me slackened a little, and I had a nasty suspicion some of our civilians were trying to back away. Our sergeant kept his head. He watched the bastards thundering closer, he knew as well as I did those breastplates can resist a ball at anything other than close range, and only when they were nearly on top of us did he give the order to fire. It was a good, tight volley, a great crash of sound, and through the smoke we heard the screaming of horses, the shouting of men, and the thud of bodies hitting the ground.

It was over a year since I'd stood in the line, but the drill comes back pretty quickly in that situation, and I was legging it to the back before the echo even died. I'd forgotten the rest of it, though, the bitter smell of smoke, the roar in your ears, the instinct that reaches for your powder the second your hand's off the trigger, I was only just in with the ramrod when the second rank fired. There was still a third, but the sergeant called them to hold, he knew once they discharged we were stuffed, we weren't up with the reload. The cavalry saw us waiting, thought better of it, and backed off to regroup. Some of the civilians cheered, but not me, Abbé, I'd seen it all before. I knew what they'd do next.

And they did. They'd mustered more men for their next assault, so they halted just out of range, then sent up the first group with levelled pistols. It was only the bloody *caracole*, and us a sitting target with three thin ranks to beat it. On they came, blasted their pistols at us and skipped back out of range while the next lot took their place.

The sergeant divided our ranks into two, so we could raise six rounds to cover the reload, but it couldn't last, men were dropping all round. Next time I reached the front there was only Marcel and one other man beside me, a hard-faced bugger in a fancy coat who was Steward of Ancre itself. He wasn't even that for much longer, the bastards fired the same time we did, and blew a hole in his chest I could have stuck two fists in. I was over his body and off for the back, Marcel limping beside me. His hand was clutching his thigh, while between his fingers pumped out thick, red blood.

I grabbed Giles Leroux from the second rank to take his place and yelled at Marcel to leave the line, but he only grinned and shook his head. Smoke-blackened face, wide smile and eyes as bright as hope, poor lad, just burning to be a hero. 'It's all right,' he said. 'They'll give up soon.'

Did they buggery. A murmur ran along the ranks in front of us and I saw something nastily familiar rumbling down the Ancre Road towards us. Field guns, Abbé. Artillery. We were fucked.

Père Gérard Benoît

Our sergeant saw that all was lost, and ordered the civilians to flee while he took upon himself the business of military surrender. I was rejoiced to see the young Marcel Dubois escaping into the woods with a companion, for his gallantry deserved a better reward than to be made prisoner of the enemy.

Many of our folk had already quit the village with such goods as they could carry, but others had nothing in their lives but the homes and businesses they were now required to leave. Some ran for Verdâme, in the hope the assault might have spent itself there; some concealed themselves in the Dax-Verdâme woods which divide our two villages; others barricaded themselves in the illusory safety of their homes. Many sought sanctuary in our own church of St Sebastian, crowding the building to the extent I found it hard to re-enter, the more as some had brought their livestock, and the aisles were filled with pigs and chickens. I nevertheless sought to comfort the people with the saying of Mass, but was scarce halfway through the service when a loud crash announced the opening of the west door, and in the next moment a great body of soldiery came thrusting into the church with levelled firearms and drawn swords.

The people cried out in alarm, but I only raised my voice the higher and continued the Mass, in the hope the soldiers would respect the sacrament. In this I was at first justified, so that while they came roughly enough among us, they did not seem set on violence, but contented themselves with gathering up the livestock while demanding money of the congregation. Some, indeed, wrenched from the walls such poor ornaments as our church could boast, and one was so blind to his own soul he reached out to the very chalice in my hands, before a better-educated colleague, aware the consecration had already occurred, struck down his arm, saying 'The blood of Christ, man,' and averting this most terrible blasphemy.

All this while I continued the service, and the people kept their eyes upon me and their voices steady in the familiar responses as if their lives depended on the action. The soldiers stood irresolute while the service proceeded, but as at last the *'Ite, Missa est'* was uttered, they stirred and looked about them as though awoken from a spell. Seeming to become aware for the first time of women amongst us, one reached out to the beautiful Mme Gilbert, while another seized the youngest daughter of Mathieu Pagnié, a maid but eleven years old. At once his fellows plunged eagerly into the crowd, competing to secure the youngest and most attractive women, and all was in uproar as men fought to protect their wives, and parents their children. In vain we appealed for restraint in the house of God, but as Pierre Gilbert wrested his wife from the hands of one trooper, another thrust forward with a pike to spear him to the wall.

The boom of the west door as it was flung violently open shocked us all into silence. There stood in the entrance but one man, yet at sight of him the soldiers immediately lowered their weapons and became still. The man stepped forward within light of our candles: a tall, slim figure, elegantly dressed, with a broad scarlet sash slung carelessly over his breastplate, and atop his helmet the red cockade of Spain. That this was a Capitán was evident from the page who now stepped from the shadows to his side, and as he advanced down the aisle, the escort which filed after him numbered the full eight of a *maestro de campo* himself.

The soldiers parted in respectful silence to let them pass. Those who still clutched evidence of their looting now furtively laid it down, and one man who held in each hand the legs of a struggling chicken attempted to bestow them discreetly on a bench behind him, but the affrighted birds made such haste in effecting their escape they collided in mid air with much squawking and flapping of wings, so that feathers flew all about us and into the very face of the advancing Capitán. He paid no heed, but continued on his way, pausing only at sight of the soldier who had hold of Suzanne Pagnié. He still spoke no word, but only looked in the face of his trooper until the man bowed his head and released the girl to her anguished father. Others about him immediately relinquished their own captives, and I rejoiced to find we were fallen at least into the hands of a gentleman.

My faith proved justified, for on reaching the sanctuary the Capitán removed his helmet to salute the altar, then turned to address the people. He announced himself as the Don Miguel d'Estrada, and said there was no need to be afraid, for we were come under the protection of the Cardinal Infante of the Spanish Netherlands. He urged the people to disperse to their own homes, assuring them of their safety as long as no further resistance was offered and all assistance and co-operation given to the forces of Spain. His men would require billeting and maintenance, but we would be otherwise unmolested.

He made us a curt bow as if to retire, but fear for our Seigneur emboldened me to ask the fate of our people at Ancre.

He turned to me a face of such strain it was with a sense of shock I realized he was but a young man, of perhaps not even one and twenty.

'I'm sorry,' he said. 'I understand there was resistance and my men had no choice. By the time I arrived there were no survivors.'

Our world darkened, and all within hearing bowed their heads. I fear my voice trembled as I asked 'None at all? Not even the child?'

He had been in the act of turning away, but my words arrested him.

'Child?' said he, and his manner seemed more attentive than before. 'The Chevalier de Roland had a child?'

Jacques Gilbert

We spent the whole bloody day hiding in the forest, and it was just awful.

It was raining for a start. We went deep into the woods to get shelter off the trees, but the rain had still drizzled through and everything was dripping wet. I dried off Tonnerre and Duchesse with their blankets, but hadn't got one for Perle, so I used mine and hoped she'd keep the foal warm by nestling up to it, which she did.

The boy cleaned his bloodied sword on the grass, then sat against a tree, hugging his arms round his knees. He was soaking wet and shivering all over, so I offered him my blanket but he just shook his head. I showed him it wasn't that damp after rubbing down Perle, and really it wasn't, though it was perhaps a bit hairy, but he just waved it away and went on sitting in silence.

So I fed the horses, then got out my bread and cheese for the boy, but he wouldn't take that either, I guessed he'd never seen black bread before. I didn't feel I could eat if he didn't, so I wrapped it up again and stood with my stomach rumbling.

I couldn't even think of anything to say. I'd never talked much to him except for answering his questions, but he wasn't asking anything now, he was sitting looking miserable as if he knew.

What made it even harder was him being a different person, because now he was Seigneur. I didn't mind nobility, not the way Father did, but when they were around you had to behave nicely, and not scratch yourself or fart or anything, and you had to be very careful what you said and did. So I just stood there, because of course I couldn't sit unless he said so, and he wasn't saying anything at all.

I had an inspiration, and offered him the brandy bottle. He sniffed it and looked a bit doubtfully at me, so I nodded encouragingly and he tried a little sip. Then he coughed, looked at the bottle more thoughtfully, and had another. He passed the bottle back, but when I took it he noticed my bitten hand. I tried to hide it, but it was too late.

'Let me see,' he commanded.

'It's nothing.'

'Let me see.'

I showed him, and it was a bit of a mess actually, he'd practically gnawed it. It was throbbing too, but I didn't feel I could complain, I mean he was the Seigneur, he could bite every peasant in the village if he wanted, even if it was a rather odd thing to want. But he tore a strip off his nightshirt, soaked it on the wet leaves, and cleaned the wound himself, then wrapped another strip round like a bandage and said 'There!' like it was all better.

Things felt easier after that, so I risked asking if I could make myself comfortable. He said of course, so I walked deeper into the forest and grabbed the chance to eat some bread where he wouldn't see. I had a good belch too, and yawned and stretched and scratched my legs where the wet breeches were itching, everything I couldn't do in front of the boy.

It had stopped raining when I got back, but the boy was still sitting against that tree, looking soggy and sullen. The bruising on his face was coming up black now, like someone had clobbered him good and hard, there was dried blood by the corner of his eye, and his ear was just a mess.

'How did that happen?'

He ignored me, but I remembered his parents had been killed and his house burned down, and maybe it was reasonable he didn't want to talk. So I just passed him the bottle, took the strip of linen he'd used before, and crouched down to clean his face.

At once he put up his hand to shield his cheek. 'No, it's all right.'

'I'll just clean it,' I said, and made another dab at him, but his hand snatched up and caught my wrist, and he'd got the strongest grip I'd ever known. I felt helpless and humiliated, and maybe that's why I said what I did, which obviously I wouldn't if I'd thought about it. I said 'I let you do mine.'

He stared at me in shock, and that's when I realized I'd also given him '*tu*', which is about as good a way of committing suicide as I know of, I mean you don't *tutoyer* your Seigneur, however young he is. I closed my eyes.

His fingers slowly relaxed and let go of my wrist. After a moment I heard him say 'All right.'

I couldn't understand why he was letting me off, but certainly wasn't going to ask, I just got on and cleaned him as best I could. He didn't flinch at all when I was doing it, not even when I wiped round his battered ear, it was like he was determined not to show any feeling at all.

He just said 'Thank you,' then 'Why don't you sit down?'

I realized he genuinely didn't know I was waiting for permission. I sat down quickly and he passed me back the bottle, but I didn't like to drink much because I saw he was watching me. It's like he was expecting me to say something, but I couldn't think what.

I began to feel uncomfortable. I'd like to have gone off again, but couldn't keep pretending I needed to crap, he was going to start worrying there was something wrong with me. I tried suggesting he get some rest, and laid out my blanket all invitingly on a pile of bracken, but he said he didn't think he could sleep. In the end there was only one thing for it, so I just kept passing him the bottle and waited for results. It wasn't the real thing, that brandy, just distilled cider M. Thibault used to make on the quiet, but it was good strong stuff and I didn't think the boy could hold out against it long.

After a bit he started to talk. He didn't say anything about what had happened, he just talked about the future and getting the estate running again like nothing had changed.

I said 'But the Spaniards have destroyed it all, haven't they?'

He looked down his nose, like I was a bit of snot hanging on the end of it. 'I can rebuild. I have resources hidden here, I don't need to worry about money.'

I'd never heard anyone say that before, I mean you don't, do you? But he seemed to mean it, so I asked casually if he was going to live in Dax or stay in Paris like his uncle, who used to spend all his time at court before he got the pox and lost his nose. I didn't say that about the pox, obviously, we all had to pretend we didn't know about that, I just said 'like M. le Comte', and he understood.

He said 'I told you, we'll have everything back the way it was before. You'll still have your jobs, Jacques, there's no need to worry about that.'

I tried to look like I hadn't been, but he only nodded importantly and said everyone was safe, but us especially because his father had made him promise the groom's job was Pierre Gilbert's for his lifetime, and mine afterwards if I wanted it.

That was interesting. I passed the brandy and asked why.

He said 'I don't know. Maybe your father saved my father's life or something?'

I didn't think so somehow. If my Father had come across the Seigneur drowning in a river he'd have been more likely to chuck a rock at him than pull him out.

'It doesn't matter anyway,' he said dismissively, 'because now you've saved my life, so I'd look after you myself.'

I felt guilty for a moment, then remembered I really had saved him when I shot that soldier, so it was perfectly fair after all. I passed him the brandy and he drank my health, then I took it and drank his, and thought this was all right, actually, this could be good. I saw me telling Colin how I'd sat and drank with the Seigneur and we'd toasted each other, I could say 'my friend, the Seigneur'. I could say that to Simone too, and maybe she'd let me kiss her again. Maybe she'd let me do more.

He asked if I did want Father's job when he gave up, and I told him no, I was going in the army at sixteen, and he brightened because he was going to be a soldier too. He said we'd go and kill lots of Spaniards together, hundreds of them, and maybe France would actually invade Spain, then we could go and burn their homes down for them and see how they liked it. Then we'd come home to Dax to make sure the Manor was all right and the village being looked after, then we'd go and fight some more. Then he said he felt a bit funny.

I said 'Have some more brandy.'

He took another gulp obediently, and asked if I'd enjoy a life like that. I said I wanted to get married and have children too, maybe a little girl like my sister Clare. I told him all about Clare and what it was like when she had her fits, I think perhaps I was a bit pissed too. He still listened carefully, watching my face like what I was saying was really important. I'd never had anyone listen to me like that before.

He said 'I've got to get married at fourteen and have at least two sons right away. My father did say I could marry Mlle Anne, the Baron's daughter, but Mother says I can't because her family's nobody.'

He'd forgotten they were dead.

'Do you like her?' I asked.

He started pulling up tufts of grass with his fingers. 'Well, she's a girl, of course, but not as silly as most of them. She doesn't giggle.'

I said cautiously 'She sounds all right.'

'She was sensible,' he said. 'I made her sit on the grass and she got green stains on her dress, but she said it didn't matter, the stripes would disguise it. She said a dress you couldn't sit down in was no good at all.'

I thought of my Mother's dresses, the light blue for day and the dark blue for Sunday. I said 'I think she's right.'

He threw down the tufts of grass like he didn't know why he'd pulled them. He said 'It doesn't matter really, I've only met her once, that day when they all came, and I hid in the stables and Father . . . and Father . . .'

He tailed off and looked round, like he was expecting to see his father standing in the woods beside us and couldn't understand why he wasn't. I shoved the bottle at him quickly, because it looked for a moment like he might actually cry, which would have been awful. He took it like he didn't know what it was, then drank again and looked at me.

'She was all right,' he said. 'I liked her. She had pretty hair.'
Then he had to go into the bushes and be sick.

I washed his face again with water I got off the trees, and next thing I knew he was curled up in a ball in the wet leaves, fast asleep. I wrapped him up in the hairy blanket, and sat back to relax for the first time in hours.

Anne du Pré

Extract from her diary, dated 3 July 1636

There was a battle last night, and I think the Guard are all killed. When they brought us in here I saw two of our soldiers dead on the landing, and one was our nice Sergeant Lebriel who used to do the trick with the three coins. We did not see Marcel, but Florian says he was probably killed downstairs. He also says I am not to speak of him as 'Marcel' because that is too familiar, but if the man is dead defending us I don't see why I can't be allowed to say his name. And Sergeant Lebriel is really called Raymon. Florian doesn't think I know that, but I do.

I wish I knew what had happened to the servants. The fat guard with the big lips says they are all run away except for Françoise, but the screaming was quite dreadful last night and I am not sure I believe him. Jeanette says I am not to think about it, I must stay calm and brave until Papa rescues us, but I am finding it quite difficult.

I am so grateful Jeanette came. She went to the Capitán *herself* to get permission, and will ask if she can come every week. She said she used to be a lady's maid when she was a little girl, and surely the soldiers must let us have somebody. I hope she is right. I managed to dress Colette myself this morning, but she said I was clumsy and did not lace her hard enough, so I will need someone to teach me.

At least we are in Mama's apartments, and that is comforting. Papa has had nothing changed, so everything smells of her lavender as if she is still alive and watching over us. We have things to do too. A nice elderly guard who looks like an untidy owl fetched us what we needed from our own rooms, so at least I have my embroidery. I have this book too, and am determined to keep a proper journal. Colette says nobody will read what a twelve-year-old child writes, but I notice she has looked over my shoulder twice since I started. If she does it again I shall write 'Colette is a fool' in very large letters.

The senior officer came this afternoon, a Capitán called Don Miguel. He said it was likely we would soon be exchanged for Spanish prisoners, but whatever happened we would be protected, because neither Spain nor the Holy Roman Empire made war on children.

Perhaps it was the word 'children' to which my brother objected, but he certainly responded with unusual haughtiness, saying 'It doesn't seem to have bothered them at Ancre. We heard it was burned down.'

'Did you?' said the Capitán gently. 'From whom, I wonder?'

'It doesn't matter,' said Florian quickly, for we did not wish to get Jeanette into trouble. 'But you've killed André de Roland, haven't you? How do we know you won't kill us?'

The Capitán did not answer for a moment. He was standing at the curtain, playing with the tassel, and I thought perhaps he was angry at Florian's directness, but he was still smiling when he turned, so I thought myself mistaken.

'No,' he said. 'We haven't killed him. Tell me, Monsieur, would he be a suitable companion for you here? Or might his age make that inappropriate for your sisters?'

Florian was amused. He said André was only twelve, and

he had no fear for us in his presence. The Capitán agreed André looked young, then asked if we would say he was as dark as his father.

I realized suddenly he had not seen André at all, and was merely attempting to learn what he looked like. That must surely mean André is free and they are seeking him. I said quickly that indeed no, André was very fair, rather like a plump, blond cherub, and stared hard at Florian that he might not contradict me. I tried to catch Colette's eye too, but she was watching the Capitán (who is rather handsome) and burst out laughing at what I had said.

'Who *are* you thinking of, you silly girl?' said she. 'André is slim, with long black hair, I remember him very clearly.' There was a long silence, in which Colette looked at our faces and said 'What?', then the Capitán came over and stood by my chair. I was a little nervous, but he merely said I was a clever and loyal girl, but I must not worry because no harm was intended to André. Then he left us, with Colette bursting out in recriminations that she was not to know and we ought to have told her.

Florian does not seem overly concerned at what we have done. I think he does not like André anyway, because he showed surprise that Florian had only just begun to fence. Papa explained the Rolands are Sword Nobility, and we must be friends with them because they have been noble so much longer than we have, but I think it is all very silly and I do not wish to marry André, whatever Papa says.

I don't think he would wish it either. We only met that once, and he didn't seem to want to be there at all. He joined us very late and covered in straw, and when Papa asked him to show me the rose garden he took me round the corner and gave me a display of fence instead. He rather annoyed me by saying what a pity it was girls weren't allowed to do anything useful of that kind, so I put a grass snake in his pocket when he wasn't looking. I wished I hadn't afterwards, because we sat and talked, and he didn't laugh when I said I was sometimes lonely. He said he had a friend who worked at the stables, and looked defiant, as if I might criticize him for playing with a servant, but I only said I wished I had someone like that, and he looked so kind and sorry that I quite forgot the snake. I think he found it just as we were leaving, because he put his hands in his pockets then took them out again rather quickly, but he only looked at me thoughtfully then thrust his hands back inside to show he wasn't bothered. I can remember exactly how he looked as we drove away.

I hope they do not catch him. But we have given them his name, his age, and his description, so I do not see how they can fail.

Jacques Gilbert

I had to wake him in the end because it was dark and time to go. He didn't say much on the journey, and sat on Duchesse's back like a sack of wet corn.

We came back through the forest in case there were still soldiers around, and emerged from the woods behind the Home Farm. Everything seemed quiet and safe. In the distance I could see light from the farmhouse, so it looked at least as if M. Legros was all right. I hoped the boy might let me leave him there, but he said no, we'd go to my cottage first to make sure my family had got back safely from the Market.

We went quietly as we could down the lane, but saw nobody the whole time. The only sounds were the sleepy clucking of chickens in the farmyard, the jagged barking of a fox in the woods behind us, and the gentle *clop-clop* of our horses' hooves. Then we turned into the Ancre drive and there was candlelight coming from my own cottage, so I knew Father was home and everything was going to be all right.

I was looking forward to seeing Father. It wasn't often he could be proud of me, it was my little brother who was better at everything, but even Father was bound to be impressed this time. I'd saved the Seigneur's life, I'd saved our jobs and future, I'd saved us all from starving, he was going to practically hug me he'd be so pleased.

I went in front to warn them, but they must have heard the horses because I'd hardly reached the yard when the door opened and Father came out, peering into the dark to make out the shapes. It was odd seeing him when he couldn't see me, he looked almost menacing. He was an impressive-looking man, my Father, maybe not that tall, but with huge broad shoulders and brawny arms.

I said quickly 'It's only me.'

Father stopped. 'Only you.' He glanced back at the cottage, then came on softly towards me.

'You've got Tonnerre,' he said, his eyes brightening. 'And Perle and the foal. Quick now, into the barn with them before anyone sees.'

I said quickly 'Look, Father, it's André de Roland.'

The boy joined us on Duchesse and Father stared in shock. There was an awkward sort of silence, then the sound of running feet and here was Mother rushing out of the house, her hair flying like a great golden cloak, and her arms stretching out like she couldn't reach me quickly enough. I grabbed her to my chest, her hair soft under my chin, and that familiar smell of crushed roses rising up from her shabby old dress. I'd been so worried. She ought to have been all right at the Market with Father, but with Mother you could never be sure, not the effect she had on men. Only here she was, safe and warm and babbling in her usual way, saying she'd thought I was dead, she'd heard everyone was dead, it was all so terrible, she didn't know what we were going to do.

I disentangled myself, and saw Father still staring at the boy like he didn't know who he was.

I said again 'It's André de Roland, Father. I've been looking after him.'

I gestured proudly as he dismounted, but that was probably a mistake. He was covered in mud, blood and scratches, with that wounded ear, and a big bruise coming up on the back of his neck where I'd hit him. His expression was groggy with hangover, his nightshirt had all bits torn off it and a sick-stain on the collar, and his breeches were covered in horsehair from my blanket. It maybe didn't look like I'd done a very good job.

Mother gasped and opened her arms wide to hug him, which I suppose was natural since she'd been his nurse so long, but Father stuck his hand out fast to stop her.

'No, no, Hélène,' he said, like he was reproving her, except when he was really reproving her he used to yell, and sometimes he'd hit her as well. 'You must remember this is our new Seigneur.'

Mother stepped back like the boy was hot, but he didn't look cross, just a bit tight round the face. He turned stiffly to my Father and said 'I owe your son a great deal, Pierre. He saved me from the soldiers.'

Mother looked at me all glowing, which was lovely. Father did give a sort of smile, but there was something odd about it I couldn't explain. He said 'Then we must hope he can keep doing it.'

The boy was quicker than I was. 'The soldiers are still here?'

'I'm afraid so, Sieur,' said Father. 'This isn't a raid, it's an invasion. They've taken over the Saillie, and the talk says half Picardie's overrun.'

My stomach did something strange, like that gun had just hit me again. I looked at the boy, but he was just standing still, his face getting paler and tighter, his hands curling into little fists.

He said 'The village. Have they hurt the village?'

I thought of my friends, of Colin and Robert, then I remembered the screams in the Manor and thought with sudden terror of Simone.

Father shrugged. 'It's not bad, Sieur. There's been no burning, only a few men lost in the defence. I'm afraid your steward was killed.'

The boy's eyes were very wide. I could hear his breathing.

Father smiled. 'Perhaps, Hélène, you might take our new Seigneur inside. I expect the poor lad will be glad of food and warmth.'

He bowed as the boy went past, but the smile was still there and it looked even broader. I followed him to the barn with the horses, feeling like nothing was safe or made sense any more.

Father lit the candle, and I saw Rosalie and Jolie were already there, both harnessed up and even with panniers on. Then I understood.

'You were going to leave?' I got a dull ache of misery in my chest as I pictured myself coming back here and finding they'd all gone without me.

'We thought you were dead,' said Father, taking the halter off Tonnerre. He was having trouble looking at me, and I realized how upset he must have been. 'The Manor's full of burnt corpses, the curé had us go over it. We thought you were dead.'

I looked at the panniers and saw they were stuffed with bundles. There was a candlestick poking out of one of them.

'But they're not our horses, that's from the Manor, it's the Seigneur's.'

'Oh for God's sake,' said Father irritably, grabbing a sack to fill the manger. 'He's Seigneur of nothing, he's a pauper like the rest of us. It's every man for himself and I've a family to think of.'

I started to rub down Duchesse. I was finding it difficult to take all this in, it was easier just to do something I knew.

'What will André do?'

'Starve, I expect,' said Father, and chuckled. 'It's that or work for his living. I'd like to see him labouring in the fields for a bully like Pagnié, wouldn't you?'

I didn't think I would much. I said 'He won't need to do that, he's got money.'

'In Paris, yes,' said Father. He finished the manger and took the sacking over to Tonnerre. 'But how's he going to get there, boy? Walk?'

I thought that was stupid, I mean he'd got six horses, they were right in front of us. I said 'He's got money here in the Saillie, he said so, lots of it.'

Father paused. 'Has he?' He started to rub down Tonnerre, but seemed less brisk than usual, like he was thinking. 'Has he indeed?'

We worked in silence for a moment, with nothing but the brush of sacking, the swishing of tails, the snorting of Tonnerre, and the slurping noises of the foal suckling Perle. Then Father started to whistle. He whistled a lot, my Father, he was brilliant at it, he could do '*Bransle des*

Chevaux' with all the twiddly bits, and I loved that best. It was '*La Pernette*' he was whistling now, but it still made me feel better, like everything was normal and somehow coming right.

The cottage looked all right too when we went in. Blanche and Little Pierre were tucked up in bed and there was soup simmering on the hearth like this was an ordinary day. I thought the soldiers might have looted it and smashed things, but I suppose they'd been too busy killing people to bother.

Ours was a nice house. You'll have seen it from outside, of course, but all the Ancre cottages are properly built with stone flags on the floor and good big fireplaces, and they're even divided into two rooms. Ours was the best, because it's built on what used to be the edge of the Home Farm, so there's this cobbled bit outside like a courtyard of our own, and a well at the back for water, and we had that spare barn next door for when the horses were sick or foaling and Father wanted them near. I slept in there myself back then, because there wasn't room in our bed for five.

The boy looked comfortable enough. Mother had got him settled by the fire to wash his face and comb the twigs out of his hair, and he was sitting laughing up at her and calling her Nelly, like he did when she was his nurse. It made me feel those days were back and we were all sitting together in the boy's closet and any minute the Seigneur would walk in and give me a sweetmeat and call me a fine boy. Then I saw the way Father was watching them, his face all closed up and those faded blue eyes hard as grey slate, and my bad feeling came back with a whoosh. By the time we sat down to eat I was so tense I was hardly even hungry any more, which was a shame because it was good soup, there were actual bits of rabbit floating in it.

Mother did her best. She smiled at us sort of bravely and said 'André says the soldiers won't stay long, Pierre, our troops will drive them out.'

The boy nodded gravely. 'They'll never get past Doullens or the border forts. Monsieur le Comte will certainly fight. We'll turn them back and drive them all the way out of the Saillie.'

There was a long silence. It sounded good to me, but I wanted someone else to be convinced as well.

'No doubt, Sieur,' said Father politely. 'But of course there might be a long delay before we're relieved. What will you do until then?'

The boy said easily 'Oh, the curé will take me in.'

'Naturally,' said Father. 'But the Spaniards are already looking for you, Sieur, and I hear they have a description. They will wish to make you hostage, like the family at Verdâme.'

The boy looked shocked. 'They've made the ladies prisoner? Mlle Anne?'

'Oh, they'll come to no harm, Sieur,' said Father smoothly. 'They are in much the safest place, and will doubtless soon be exchanged home. Nobody could blame the Seigneur if he made such a choice himself.'

The boy sort of bristled with outrage. 'The Rolands have never been prisoners, never.'

'Quite,' said Father. He drank more soup and watched the boy over the spoon. 'The Seigneur will need to hide.'

The boy looked doubtful. 'But if they've got a description . . .'

Father laid down his spoon. 'What if you pretended to be a peasant among peasants? What if you hid in my own family, here at Ancre?'

That was a really horrible idea. I hoped the boy would

throw a temper at the mere suggestion, but he just rocked his chair back from the table and considered.

'I don't know,' he said at last. 'You think I can pass as a peasant?'

He was sat carelessly stretching out those long legs of his in that way nobility have of taking up more room than anybody else. He was all clean from Mother washing him, and his skin seemed dazzling white, he made me feel brown and leathery just sitting next to him. His hair was falling in all neat waves, his hands and nails were perfect, his eyes bright and challenging, his voice sort of oozing authority. He couldn't have looked less like a peasant if he'd tried.

'Of course,' said Father. 'Cardinal Richelieu's agents pass as all manner of things in their way of business. If the Seigneur pleases I'm sure he can be whatever he chooses.'

The boy nodded thoughtfully. 'It might be dangerous for your family.'

Father shrugged nobly. 'Only if we have much contact with the soldiers. Of course, we'll all have to work for them if we can, even Hélène. Perhaps they'll need people to wait on them.'

The soup went into a cold lump in my belly, and I think I maybe choked a little. Mother's face had gone grey and frightened, and it twisted me up inside. I found myself turning desperately to the boy, but he just pressed his hand on my arm and stood up.

He said 'We can't let Nelly wait on soldiers.'

'Our employment is gone, Sieur,' said Father sadly. 'I can't let my family starve.'

'No one's going to starve' said André sharply. 'I won't have it. You're still employed, Pierre, and so are all the Ancre staff. I have enough money to look after us; there'll be food from the estate, the soldiers can't take all of it. It's only right I should be paying when you'll be looking after me.'

I saw the relief in Mother's eyes, and the panic slowly eased round my throat. I should have known Father would find an answer. He loved us, he'd got to keep us from starving and save Mother from being near soldiers, and he'd found a way to do it all. All right, it meant we'd got to have the boy with us, but I told myself it needn't be too bad, it wasn't going to be all like today. I wouldn't need to see much of him, he was my parents' problem now.

They started working out arrangements, so I finished my soup and let them get on with it. Mother was fretting of course, she was worried the bed wasn't big enough, but then the boy said casually the best thing would be for him to sleep in the barn with me.

This time I really did choke. At least Mother argued against it, she said it wasn't fitting to put the Chevalier de Roland in a barn, but the boy pointed out he'd spent last night in the forest and the barn had got to be better than that. Father was concerned about the lack of protection, but the boy said I'd be there, wouldn't I, and I'd protected him all day.

Father looked at him when he said that, then back at me, and he seemed oddly satisfied about something. He said of course the boy should go in with me if that's what he wanted, so Mother shut up and stopped arguing. Nobody asked my opinion, of course. Nobody ever did.

So Mother looked out a blanket then we showed the boy the barn. It wasn't that big and the wood rattled a bit, but it was really comfortable, with hay bales you could sit on like chairs, and a ladder to the upper level so you didn't have to sleep with the horses. There was even a grain hole at the back which was sort of like having a window, and you could always shove straw over it if it got cold. Mother started making up a bed for him, so I left them to it and went back to the yard to wash, hoping the cold water would help me clear my head.

Then the back door creaked, and there was Father watching me.

'All tucked up and comfortable, is he?' he asked.

'He's in bed,' I said, drying my hair on my shirt.

'Is he awake?'

'Oh yes,' I said bitterly. 'He'll probably be awake all night.'

'Good,' said Father. 'See you make the most of it.'

I looked at him blankly, because that's just how I felt.

He sighed, then stepped out into the yard and sat down on the edge of the well to talk to me.

'Come on, boy, it's simple enough.' He patted the rim to show I was meant to sit next to him, so I did. It's a very small well, so we had to squash up close. His face was so near I could see the little red veins round his nose Mother said came from working too hard.

He spoke softly, the way people usually do in the night air. 'It's all up to you now, boy. Play this right, and we're made.'

I thought he was mad.

'No, no,' said Father. 'It's Jacques saved his life, Jacques can protect him against the whole Spanish army. Trust me, he likes you'.

I started to say that was bollocks, then remembered the way the boy had put his hand on my arm. I looked at Father, and he nodded gently.

'Use it, boy. Be respectful, call him "Sieur", handle him right and it won't be the Seigneur running Dax, it'll be us. Now do you understand?'

I remember staring at the cobbles and noticing how bright the snail trails looked in the moonlight. I remember the rough stone of the well digging in through my breeches and sting-ing where Father had beaten me. I remember how close he was, and the warmth of him coming right through my damp shirt.

I said 'Yes.'

'Good boy.' He gave me a little wink, then got to his feet and padded back to the cottage.

It was quiet in the barn when I got back. The horses were nuzzling sleepily after their long day, and it made me feel like I was still in the Ancre stables and had dreamed the whole thing. Then I climbed up to the top level, and there was the boy sitting on a red blanket looking brightly at me and I knew I bloody hadn't.

I remembered what Father said about being polite, and knew I hadn't been, not very, so I took a deep breath and tried. 'Have you everything you need, Sieur?'

He looked at me, and it was like the little light in his eyes slowly faded.

'Yes, thank you. I have everything.'

I looked at him sitting in his tatty nightshirt on Clare's old blanket in the straw. Beside him were his breeches all folded up neatly, and his boots laid carefully beside them, and the sword nearest him so he could reach out for it if he wanted. That was all he owned in the world now. I felt sorry, because even I had more than that. I had a Mother and Father for a start.

But it's impertinent to feel sorry for nobility, so I dropped my head quickly and asked if he wanted any water or anything, and again he said no. I couldn't think of anything else to be nice to him about, so I said to call if he wanted me, then just sort of bowed and went to my own blanket in the far corner. It was still damp and hairy, but I didn't care, I was just too tired.

I dreamed about Clare. I had a nightmare about the day she died, when she just didn't come out of the fit at all and nothing we did made any difference. I was holding her like I always did, then she gave this great twisting leap and lay still, and Father said 'She's quiet now, isn't she? She's quiet.' Then I felt her getting colder in my arms, and I looked at her face and her eyes were open like César's were, and as I'm waking I think 'He's another, he's another I ought to have saved and didn't.' And I'm awake now, but it's like the dream's still going on, because I can hear these odd sounds, like something banging faintly against the wall, a sort of thrashing in the straw and the noise of stifled breathing, and someone really is having a fit, then I'm fully awake and realize it must be the boy.

I move so fast across the barn I trip over my boots. He's clinging on to the wall, his fingers digging into the boards like he's trying to hide, and his breath's coming out in hard little gasps. His eyes are screwed shut, and he doesn't even know I'm there. It's not a fit, of course, he's only crying, or would be if he could make himself let go. I guess he's afraid of making a noise, of me hearing or anyone knowing, because he's the Seigneur and must not cry.

I want to help him, but know I can't, it would kill him to realize I've even seen. I tiptoe away and creep quietly back to my blanket. It's hard, but I keep reminding myself he's not really a child, he's the Seigneur just as much as his father was, and I've got to protect his dignity.

I'm hesitating all the same. I'm remembering the way he looked when Mother put her arms out to him. I'm remembering when he almost cried in the woods and I just shoved the brandy bottle at him. I turn round to look back, and suddenly know I can't just leave him.

I go back. I reach out and unpeel him from the wall, which

is difficult actually, like trying to get a leech off when it's still sucking. I turn him towards me, making soothing noises, and next thing he's made a dive towards my chest, he's clinging on to hide his face in that instead, his fingers digging into my shirt like he's trying to burrow his way right through me. I find I'm putting my arms round to shelter him, and as soon as he feels himself being held safe he takes in this great long jagged breath, and at last he cries.

It sounds like it's being ripped out of him, it's tearing up through his throat in these awful broken sobs. I hold him, and find I'm rocking and murmuring to him like it's Clare all over again. Then I move to put my back against the wall, but I'm still holding him and telling him it's all right and all that bollocks, and my shirt's getting wet with his tears, but somehow I don't mind. Gradually he gets quieter, but I go on rocking and whispering, and he's relaxing and getting heavier, and at last I sit back and just hold him. We stay like that a long time.

Then my collarbone starts to hurt where his head's resting, and I look down and find he's gone to sleep in my arms.

That's too much, it really is, I mean he's going to go mad when he wakes and finds himself like this. Then I look down at him again, and he's peaceful at last, and his face is relaxed as I haven't seen it all day. I rub my cheek against his hair, and he just makes a funny little noise and sort of digs in harder.

So I think 'Sod it'. I nudge his head down off my collarbone into the crook of my arm, rest my head back against the wall, and go to sleep.

Three

Jacques Gilbert

I woke at dawn with a stiff neck, but the boy was gone. For a second I was relieved, it meant we needn't say anything about last night, then I realized there was no sign of him at all and even his sword had disappeared. I didn't stop to put my boots on, just hurled myself down the ladder and belted outside, fear banging hard inside my chest.

There he was, strolling across the cobbles, unconcerned as a sparrow and swinging his sword in casual salute. The panic drizzled out of me and I could suddenly smell the warmth of my own sweat. I wanted to yell at him 'What the fuck do you think you're doing, don't you know it's nearly daylight and there might be soldiers around?' but obviously I couldn't, and in the end I just said 'Oh.'

He nodded gravely at me, and dragged something out of his pocket. 'I thought I'd better fetch this.'

His hand was grey with earth like he'd been digging, but gleaming on the palm was a little pile of gold coins. I couldn't believe it. They weren't even écus, they were bloody golden louis.

'Is it enough, do you think?' he said. 'Just for the next few days?'

It was enough to keep a family for a year. I swallowed and said 'I think so,' then followed him into the cottage in a kind of daze. I didn't even ask where he'd got it from, what mattered was he'd got it, and no one was going to starve.

It certainly made Father happy. He went straight to M. Thibault's to get wine, and I heard him whistling all the way to the gate. Mother was happy too; M. Legros sent round eggs and ham and cheese from the Home Farm and she couldn't decide what to cook first. Little Pierre went for the curé, and he was even happier, he practically sobbed over André and went down on his knees to give thanks for his deliverance. I hoped he'd say it wasn't fitting for the boy to stay with us, but he didn't, he only talked a lot about the sacred nature of my trust, which obviously meant that if anything happened to André the person to blame would be me.

But I didn't see how to protect him, I didn't think it could be done. They stuck him in old clothes of my Father's and talked about him passing as a peasant, but that obviously wasn't going to work with him strolling about like he owned the place, which of course he did. The best thing would be just to keep him in the barn, but he wasn't going to agree to that, and I couldn't exactly make him.

He had to come out the next day anyway, because we had the funerals at the Ancre chapel, and I couldn't ask him to miss those. I thought it was safe enough, he'd just be one ragged figure in a crowd, but even then he insisted on standing out. When the curé tried to usher him in he just stopped and said 'I can't go in now, I have to follow the biers.'

The curé blinked nervously. 'But, Sieur, the Don Miguel d'Estrada is there himself, come to pay his respects.'

André's mouth went tight. 'These are my parents. It is my duty to follow them.'

Poor Père Gérard. He sort of cringed and said perhaps the Seigneur wouldn't mind leaving his sword outside and pretending he was a serving boy rather than the Roland heir.

The boy considered. 'Very well. Jacques and I will carry candles together, and no one will know.'

I didn't like that idea much, if he was caught I wasn't sure I wanted to be right beside him, but I did sort of understand how he felt. Gabriel and his men were just getting the biers off the trap, the bodies all covered in black cloth so no one could see them, then I remembered the fire and guessed why. The boy's eyes followed the bundles and his face was so taut it looked painful. He didn't cry, of course, it's like he'd done it that once for always, but I knew how I'd have felt if it had been me.

I said 'We'll go in together.'

So we carried candles and followed the biers side by side, but he still didn't look right, he couldn't help it, he was walking firmly and upright, he looked sort of dignified. Then I saw a young man dressed in black and gold sitting right at the front, and my stomach jolted as I guessed that was d'Estrada. We were going to walk right by him and the boy was on his side of the aisle.

He bowed his head in respect as the biers passed, but we were just behind, his head was coming up and the boy right in front of him. I'd got to do something, anything to make him look away. I jerked my hand with the candle in it, saw d'Estrada's eyes flick to the movement of the light, then had an inspiration and wiped my nose on my sleeve. His head recoiled at once, then the boy was safely past and so was I. I could see Colin looking sniffy with disapproval, but the curé gave me the loveliest smile and I knew he understood.

No one else did. D'Estrada left straight after the service, but then the boy went into the vault to do the handing over of the ring, and when he came out everyone crowded round him bowing and taking their hats off, and M. Gauthier actually went down on his bony knees to kiss his hand. They kept calling him 'Sieur' too, and I had to go round saying 'No, no, he's meant to be a peasant, we're to call him André,' but no one listened. Colin was impossible, but then he would be, you'll understand when you meet him. He just said 'It's not right, Jacques, not fitting at all, Bible says everyone should be in their place.' I couldn't blame him really, everything about André was just screaming nobility, no one could mistake him for anything else.

I'd got to teach him. By noon there were soldiers already drifting back into Ancre to see if there was anything left to steal, so I kept the boy in the barn and suggested he start learning how to be a peasant.

'Well, if you like,' he said, puzzled. 'I'm ready.'

He wasn't, he wasn't anything like bloody ready, it was virtually impossible just getting that sword off him for a start. I finally got him to understand that conquered peasants don't carry swords and he'd get caught in a second if he did, but he still wouldn't let me near it.

'I'll hide it myself,' he said. 'A gentleman shouldn't allow anyone else to handle his sword, it's a matter of honour.'

I wondered if that applied to cleaning it, but thought it better not to ask. I just watched as he carried his sword to the hole in the rafters and stretched up to put it inside.

He couldn't reach. I waited for him to ask me, but he just went to the other wall and started to roll a hay bale across instead. His face was red with the effort, but he'd got far too much pride to let me help him. He got it there at last, stood on it and solemnly stowed his sword next to the arque-bus.

'There,' he said, stepping down a bit breathlessly. 'Now we're done.'

I hesitated.

'What?' he said impatiently. 'I look right, don't I?'

It was the way he sounded. He spoke too loudly, like he didn't care who heard him, he spoke too nicely, with all proper words and no patois. I suggested nervously that if there were soldiers around he maybe wouldn't mind not saying anything at all.

He sniffed. 'Why on earth would I want to speak to a Spaniard?'

'Quite,' I said quickly. 'Good. Now maybe just a bit of work on the way you move.'

I walked up and down the barn so he could watch how I did it, and he looked at me aghast.

'That's ridiculous. You look like an old woman.'

I thought that was rude actually, since I was just showing how I normally walked, but I suppose he'd never noticed. I coaxed him into trying, but it was hopeless, he'd start out right but just got taller with every step. At last he got fed up and just stopped.

'This is stupid, I'm not doing this. If there are soldiers around, I can always sit down.'

I felt suddenly uneasy. 'Well, yes, but you'll have to stand if they talk or anything, you've got to show respect.'

He was stretching his arms, but stopped in mid air. 'I've what?'

I recognized the tone, and saw his eyes were getting narrow, but I had to explain, this was something he'd just got to understand.

I said 'You know, lower your head, don't look at them. I mean they've conquered us, we've got to be submissive.'

He looked at me in silence for a moment, then spoke very quietly. 'I don't mind outwitting the Spaniards, that's part of war. But I am never going to submit to them, and you need to understand that right now.'

I didn't dare answer. He nodded dismissively, announced he was ready for lunch, and started calmly down the ladder.

I think that's when I started to realize what I was really up against. The problem wasn't his voice or his walk or anything like that, it was what was inside his head. There was nothing I could do to change him, I'd been stupid to think I could. The only way to keep him safe was make sure he never saw the soldiers at all.

But that was impossible too. They were still all over the estate the next day, but André wanted to go riding and couldn't understand why I wouldn't let him. We'd moved the horses back to their own stables, which had already been searched and stripped bare, but it was madness to think of trotting them along the bridle path in full view of the Manor.

He said 'I don't care. They're my horses and I want to ride them.'

I said 'No, I'm sorry, we can't.'

Quite suddenly he went mad. One minute he was standing there normal and almost reasonable, the next he was red in the face and shouting. 'Don't you dare tell me I can't do something, don't you ever dare tell me that.'

I said desperately 'I'm only saying it's not safe because of the soldiers.'

'The soldiers!' he said. 'You think I'm scared of the soldiers?' He started stamping up and down, he even kicked the wall. He said I was making him give in to the enemy and he was never going to do that, never, not after what they'd done.

I'd seen him lose his temper before, I'd actually thought it was funny, but there was nothing funny about it now. I looked at him slamming about with rage and hitting out at nothing, and at last I understood what was really at stake.

I'd been trying to stop him being taken hostage, and worried about getting in trouble with the curé, but I knew now none of that mattered. I couldn't keep him away from soldiers, I couldn't change him, and I couldn't begin to control him. He was going to give himself away in seconds, when they caught him he'd fight, and I knew what would happen then.

They'd kill him. They wouldn't just take him hostage, they'd kill him, and probably the rest of us too.

Colin Lefebvre

From his interviews with the Abbé Fleuriot, 1669

You don't want to take too much notice of what Jacques says. Hear him talk back then you'd think looking after Seigneur was the last thing he wanted, but I knew better, I knew Jacques through and through. Family were being paid good money, not to mention the favours they'd be getting when Seigneur came into his own again, advantages were obvious. Wouldn't have suited me, got to say, I'm an independent sort of chap, but looked like a chance for poor old Jacques, and I'm not the man to grudge good fortune to a friend.

And he was a friend, old Jacques, we'd been close all our lives. That'll sound strange maybe, me being the blacksmith's son and him only a stablehand, but there, he was an amiable lad, never say he wasn't. Always thought we'd end up together, him and me, sitting in the Quatre Corbeaux, sharing a jug of cider of an evening, getting old together. Seigneur coming put paid to all that. Put paid to a lot of things.

Not that we weren't glad of him being there, things being

what they were. Spaniards weren't going to stay for ever, stood to reason, and village like ours needs a Seigneur. No other heir but André; if something happened to him we might get sold off like had happened to Verdâme, we needed him kept alive.

And Dax wasn't safe. Spaniards were looking for him, men checking everyone went out the Gate, yes and searching them for letters too, in case someone was writing to the old Comtesse in Paris. They searched the curé's cottage, ransacked all the good houses, turned both the Thibault and the Pagnié farms upside down, even searched the church, and when old Hébert tried to stop them messing about in the crypt they beat him with musket butts so badly he died in three days. D'Estrada didn't like it, went and apologized to the curé, but the man was dead, nothing to be done, those Spaniards meant business and no mistake.

They were looting too. D'Estrada said not, but some of his officers weren't above it, that Abanderado de Castilla, nasty piece of work, he let the men do whatever they pleased. You know what July's like, waiting for harvest, winter stores as low as they get, everyone on tight belts, and now we'd got Spaniards booting their way into people's homes, taking food right off the table.

'You get on up to Ancre,' said my dad. 'Bad times in the old days Seigneur'd throw open the tithe barn. This one's got money, he'll help out. Folk can buy food in Artois, there's plenty going in Sus, bit of cash is all we need.'

So I went. Wasn't for ourselves, you know, Forge was busy enough, even if mostly farriers' work by rights and none of it reliably paid, but there were others in real need, and people look up to the smith, he's got a duty to the community. So I upped and went to Ancre, and Seigneur helped out right away, gave me cash to divide with the curé, see no one starved.

Only right and fair, but you won't catch every seigneur acting like that, not by a long way.

Strange set-up all the same at Ancre. Food was good and plenty of it, they sat me down and poured a bowl of soup I'd swear had beef in it, but the rest didn't feel right at all. There was our Seigneur dressed in a shabby old shirt of Pierre Gilbert's, breeches held up with string, clogs on his feet, total disgrace. Old Gilbert was plain loving it too, never been the loyal type, he was smiling all the while like the kitchen cat.

Still, it seemed safe. I was just thinking I'd tell my dad he'd no need to worry about the Seigneur, I was thinking it right that moment, when we heard a cart rattling past down the Ancre drive then suddenly a bloody great crash.

Everyone shut up fast. Shouting and swearing outside, all in that Spanish, couldn't understand a word. The young one, Little Pierre, he upped and looked through the window, said there's soldiers outside and a wheel come off their cart.

Didn't seem much to me, seeing I saw Spaniards every day, but I looked over at Jacques, saw he'd turned dead white, scared half out his wits. His dad was quicker, on his feet right off, ordering Madame into the back room. 'Now, Nell,' he was saying, 'Now.' I understood that all right, Jacques' mum was something, wasn't a man in the Saillie didn't feel it. Wasn't much doubt what the Spaniards would do to her, and she knew it, out and in the back room with the little girl in a second.

But Jacques was just as panicky. 'You too, André,' he was saying. 'Go on, quick.'

Didn't see the need myself, Seigneur looked scruffy as the rest of us, but Jacques pulling at his arm, trying to make him hide. Seigneur shook him off, stayed right where he was. He said 'I don't run from Spaniards.'

Too late anyway, there was the door crashing open and in came Cabo Mesía. He was one of the nastier ones, I did a buckle for him just the day before and he never paid a sou. He looked at us sat round the table, checked the bowls were empty and nothing for him to steal, then grunted and jerked his thumb outside.

Gilbert's up at once, but the Seigneur didn't move. Sat with his spoon in his hand, looking at Mesía insolent as you like. Gleam of gold on his hand too, and I knew what that was, that was his father's ring. Jacques saw it too, shot out his hand, grabbed the Seigneur's and pulled him to his feet, and when he let go the ring was gone.

Didn't have much French, Mesía, ignorant type, he just said 'Out,' and jerked his thumb again, so out we went, the lot of us, Jacques pulling the Seigneur like a mule that won't go.

Jacques Gilbert

I knew what he'd do, and how they'd react, I knew exactly how they dealt with resistance. I remembered the flames at the Manor, I heard the screaming in my head, I thought of Mother and Blanche and the fear was like a kind of roaring in my ears. I was pulling the boy so hard I was almost dragging him.

The fat cabo came out with us and jerked his head at the wheel. Colin said 'Right you are, Señor Mesía,' all sort of hearty, and moved to get his shoulder to the cart. I tugged at André, but when he saw what was in the cart I heard him suck in his breath. It was all stuff from the Manor, all of it, bits of furniture, one of the tapestries, and right on top the old gong. It looked sort of sad and pathetic lying there, I could feel the boy's anger without even looking. His hand started to pull out of mine, but I yanked it back hard, I hissed at him 'Please!'

Father and Little Pierre joined us, and we heaved the cart up together. André didn't push at all, but with Col's broad shoulder taking the weight no one seemed to notice. Two soldiers rolled the wheel in place, the cabo signalled us out, and the cart jolted back down again, the cabinets sliding about with a bang and a cloud of dust. I let out my breath in relief and finally let go André's hand.

The cabo grinned in satisfaction. 'Well,' he said. 'Well.' I think he meant 'good', but his French was crap. He turned to the boy, reached out his hand and actually patted his cheek.

André wrenched away in outrage, his face white and his eyes blazing with insult. The cabo took a step backwards, the smile dripping off his face like melting fat. I was willing the boy hard in my head, I was begging 'Look down, look humble, please, for God's sake look *down*,' but he didn't, he was glaring right in the man's face. One of the soldiers laughed, and the cabo flushed, his eyes went small and hard.

I was talking, I was almost babbling, I said 'Don't mind my brother, he's simple, he doesn't understand,' but it was no good, the cabo strode forward and walloped the boy smack on the head, sending him sprawling on the stones.

I couldn't seem to move, I remember an odd little pulse banging away high on my forehead. Then André rolled over, slapped his palm hard on the ground and began to clamber up. The look on his face was of sheer cold fury, he was going to fight, he was going to get us all killed. I was down beside him so fast I cracked my knees on the cobbles. I snatched desperately at his hands, cold, muddy fingers in mine, I held them like I was helping him up but kept my eyes on his face like I was hoping he could read me, I was whispering so hard I was almost sobbing, 'Please, André, please, they'll rip the place apart, they'll find my Mother, please, my Mother.'

His face changed. Something went out of it, and for a second he looked as dead as César. Then there was a little flicker in his eyes, his mouth tightened, he pulled his hands out of mine and stood.

I stayed on my knees, my hands pressed on the stones, hardly daring to look up. I remember peering fearfully up through my hair and seeing André just standing in front of the cabo, but he wasn't moving, he wasn't fighting, and after a long moment I saw him lower his head and look at the ground.

The cabo gave a short laugh like a grunt, reached out and tousled the boy's hair, then said something to the others that made them all laugh. The boy stood where he was, and they moved past him and jumped back into the cart, lots of loud laughter and creaking of wood, then the crack of a whip and the cart lurched off.

The boy's head was up in a second, but he didn't look at me, he didn't look at any of us, he just spun round and stamped into the barn. Colin stared after him, slack-jawed with shock, he'd just seen the Sieur of Dax knocked flat by a filthy Spaniard and doing nothing about it. Then he turned and looked reproachfully at me like it was somehow my fault.

Father said 'Better go after him, boy, he'll be kicking the walls again.' Then he actually grinned.

I went into the barn. He wasn't kicking the walls, he was standing quite still on the top level, his hands thrust deep in his pockets and his head right down. I climbed cautiously up the ladder, but he didn't shout or anything, he kept staring at the straw, and I saw the side of his face was flushed.

I said 'Thank you.'

'For what?' he said. 'Letting an enemy soldier pat me like a dog?' He lost control suddenly and smacked his fist against the wall. 'Like a fucking *dog*.'

I'd never heard him swear before. 'But you saved my Mother.'

He jerked his head back. 'All right. I know.' He stepped back from the wall and threw himself down on his blanket. He said quietly 'Like a fucking dog,' then turned his face to the wall.

I don't know why, but I felt like shit. This was what I'd wanted, I'd found a way of controlling him, but something I liked had sort of oozed out of him, and I was almost sorry it was gone.

He wasn't much better next day. He thought he'd do some fencing exercises in the barn, so I got his sword down and he never told me not to. Then he did his exercises and I watched him like in the old days, but it wasn't the same, his heart wasn't in it. At last he just stopped and sat hopelessly in the straw, and I looked at how slumped he was, and thought he really did look like one of us now, he could have just been one of us.

Then I heard this strange droning sound in the distance, which gradually turned into the moaning noise of M. Gauthier singing one of his horrible hymns. He never sang any of the cheery ones, he liked things about the corruption of the body and the worm of sin, he seemed to find them encouraging. I suppose if I'd had a body as nasty as M. Gauthier's I'd probably have been the same.

I said brightly 'That'll be M. Gauthier coming to see you.'

The boy sighed, got slowly to his feet, and followed me down the ladder.

The gamekeeper came striding in with a sack over his shoulder and his horrible dog at his heels. I used to find him quite scary, M. Gauthier. He was very tall, about a hundred years old, and filthy. He had a huge head, enormous ears and terrifying eyebrows which jutted right out from his face and had spiky wispy bits like the antennae on a beetle. The dog was like a kind of smaller version, only even smellier, and as far as I could work out it was just called 'Dog'.

M. Gauthier snatched off his hat and bowed, like the boy was receiving him in a salon at the Manor, not dressed in rags in a straw-filled barn.

The boy said dully 'Good morning, Martin. What can I do for you?'

M. Gauthier said there'd been a party went round the Manor the first day to see what could be retrieved after the fire.

'Yes, I know,' said the boy, his arms clasping themselves round his body like he was cold. 'The curé told me.'

'The curé!' said M. Gauthier, and grinned horribly. 'The curé collected valuables for your future, Sieur. I was looking for things you might like now.' He lifted his sack and dumped it on the floor with a thud.

The boy let his arms slide slowly back to his sides and knelt down to open it. I looked over his shoulder while he felt around inside and brought out the contents one by one. It was an odd collection, but the boy was fascinated, he got more alive with every thing he pulled out. First came two blunted swords he said were fencing foils, and then a rapier wrapped in soft linen: his father's dress sword, the mark of a gentleman and the *noblesse d'épée*. Then there were books, there was paper and chalk, a quill pen and a bottle of ink. There was a hard little rag ball for a game called tennis, which he used to squeeze to strengthen his fingers for fencing. Then there was a little wooden horse all charred from the fire which he seemed specially pleased to see, he actually touched it to his face. I used to have one like it myself which the Seigneur gave me one day as a present. I called mine 'Héros' and played with it a lot till Father threw it at Mother during a row and it broke.

Next came a flat metal thing with hinges, which had pictures of André's parents inside, joined together to make like a sort of book. The boy sat staring at it, like if he breathed it might go away. Then he went over and hugged the gamekeeper and just said 'Thank you, Martin.' He even kissed his cheek, which I wouldn't have done, you never knew what might come off.

There was one last thing in the bottom of the sack, and when the boy dug right down he came up with his father's scabbard. He turned it solemnly over in his hands, then looked up at M. Gauthier and said 'I will wear this one day, Martin. I really will.'

'Course you will, Sieur,' said the gamekeeper, blowing his nose in a revolting handkerchief. 'Course you will. Maybe you'd like a pistol too?'

We stared. He bent down to yank the empty sack out of Dog's fangs, and said casually 'When we were going round the Manor, a few of us just happened to collect up weapons from the dead soldiers. They're under the dairy floor. Just for when you want them, Sieur, that's all.'

André's hands stilled on the scabbard. 'You think it'll come to that?'

'Oh, our army will drive them back, Sieur,' said M. Gauthier. 'La Capelle, Le Câtelet, Corbie, we'll hold them.'

The boy went on looking at him.

'Ay, Sieur,' said M. Gauthier. 'I think in the end it'll come to that.'

The boy's eyes seemed to gleam in the darkness. 'Good,' he said. 'Good.'

I didn't think it was good at all, I didn't see a bunch of peasants being able to do much against a whole Spanish army no matter what weapons we gave them, but it didn't seem worth worrying about just then, we'd got armies out there fighting our battles, they weren't going to need the help of people like us.

The idea of it still made all the difference to André. He forgot all about being miserable when M. Gauthier had gone, he spent ages arranging his possessions carefully round his blanket, his books in a neat pile, the tennis ball in a nest to stop it rolling away, his picture propped up so he could see it all the time, and when he'd finished he stood back and nodded in satisfaction, like that was his home.

Then that evening he got out the foils and said it was time I learned to fence.

For a second I almost stopped breathing. It was something I'd always wanted to do, ever since I'd started watching him all those years ago, but I knew it was only a stupid dream.

I said carefully 'André, I'm a peasant.'

He studied me with his head on one side, like he was seeing me for the first time. Then he gave a little nod, put down the foils and picked up his cloak instead.

'Come on,' he said. 'There's something we need to do.'

I was a bit nervous following him, because it wasn't really dark yet, there might still be soldiers around, but he didn't head for the Manor, he strode across the paddock towards the Home Farm and led me to the back of the barns where the beehives were. It wasn't somewhere people liked to hang about in daytime, but it was all quiet now, just a sort of gentle buzzing coming from the skeps like the bees were all snoring peacefully. The boy walked straight past the trestles to the stone wall at the back, bent down and started working away a rock at the bottom, then reached into the hole to drag out a large wooden box. I glimpsed another in the darkness behind.

I knelt down beside him. 'What are they?'

'My father hid them here after the last raid.'

He slid off the lid then peeled away the cloth underneath, and I saw a great heap of jewellery glistening softly in the gloom. When he dug inside there was a tinkling sound like coins as well, and the whole pile moved and slithered under his hands. I remembered people saying Mme de Roland wasn't actually noble, that her father had been a big financier and was worth millions. I tried to think what the box would be worth, then remembered there were two, and my brain just gave up.

The boy handed me a ring with a big stone. I'd never seen one close before, but knew it had to be a diamond. When I tilted it to the sunset it broke into thousands of splinters of coloured light, painting little rainbows over the pale stone of the wall. I made to pass it back, but he shook his head.

'It's for you.'

I gaped at him. 'Why?'

'Because you saved my life, I suppose. It's usual.'

He was so matter of fact I found myself believing it, but it felt impossible all the same. I said 'This was your father's.'

'He never wore it, that's why it's in here,' he said. 'But you ought to have some sort of ring if you're my aide.'

I thought of M. Chapelle, who'd been aide to the old Seigneur. He was a real gentleman, with fine clothes and flowing hair, who wore big hats with white plumes. Then I thought of me, Jacques Gilbert the stable boy, and I had to laugh.

'Why not?' said André. 'It's the job you're doing, isn't it?' He reached for my hand and thrust the ring on my finger. 'There. You're not a peasant any more, you're my aide.'

71

He meant it. He wasn't just giving me a diamond worth more money than I'd ever seen, he was making me a whole different person. I remember staring at the ring on my grubby hand like it was my whole future in this one shining stone.

He dug out more coins for me to give Father, then we just put the boxes back in the wall, rolled the stone back and walked home. He never even mentioned the ring again, he just talked about my starting to fence tomorrow like it was normal, and this time I said 'Yes'.

I couldn't wait till morning to tell Father, so as soon as the boy was asleep I sneaked outside and went to the cottage. Mother was already in bed, but Father was sitting at the table with the dregs of a bottle of wine.

'Up late tonight. What's he got you doing now, telling bedtime stories?' He chuckled to himself and shoved the bottle towards me. 'Here, have a drink, you'll find it helps.'

I said 'He's given us more money, look.' I put the coins down on the table. 'He's got lots of it, enough for years and years. Whatever happens in Dax, we'll be all right.'

He stretched out his hand and brushed the coins towards him, then put them in his pocket. 'You've seen it?'

I'd never lied to my Father. I said 'Yes.'

'Ah,' he said. 'Where is it?'

It was very quiet. There wasn't a sound from the other room, not even the rustle of straw. The wind had dropped, and the night birds had gone silent. It was like there was nobody in the world except the two of us.

I said 'I don't know.'

I could hear the candle flickering. Then Father's chair creaked as he leant forward.

'You don't know?'

I said 'It doesn't matter anyway, does it? He'll keep paying us.'

He breathed out hard suddenly and stood up. I felt him walk past me, and turned to see him standing at the window, looking out into the dark.

He said 'That's nice of him.'

He wasn't understanding. I got up and went over, I touched his sleeve and held out my hand to show the ring.

'Look. If I hold it near the candle you can see it sparkle'.

He lifted my hand with the tips of his fingers, then let it drop.

'And what did you do to earn that?'

'Nothing. It's like you said, that's all. I think he likes me.'

He glanced at my face. 'And you, I suppose you like him too?'

I said 'He's made me his aide. Like being a gentleman.'

'God in heaven,' he said, jerking round suddenly. 'Is that what you want?'

I found myself stepping backwards.

'Look at you,' he said. 'Strutting round, showing me your jewellery. Lying to your father, paying me money –'

'It's not me,' I said. 'It's not my money, it's the boy's.' The edge of the dresser was biting into my back.

'"The boy!"' he said. 'That's the Seigneur to me.'

'He's André,' I said. 'We're all to call him . . .'

'That's the Seigneur!' he shouted. 'That's our lord and master!'

He rounded on me, eyes burning, hands coming up, I shut my eyes. But nothing happened, and when I opened them again, he slowly dropped his arms down to his sides and just looked at me with this awful defeated expression.

He said 'And you like him.'

He turned away as if the sight of me disgusted him, then swung back suddenly, his fist shooting out in this white blur and smashing into my face, my head cracking back, the dresser

73

cutting into my back as it ground past me, and I went smack down hard on the floor.

He looked at me lying there.

'Yes,' he said, and his voice was quite calm suddenly. 'I'd say you're a gentleman all right.'

He walked back to the table and blew out the candle. I heard his footsteps start again, the creak of the door to the other room, then the little thud as it closed.

I was alone in the dark, with an ache in my jaw and the taste of blood in my mouth.

Four

Colin Lefebvre

Forts fell one by one, we had news of it every day. La Capelle, Bohain, Vervins, Origny-Sainte-Benoite, Ribement, even Le Câtelet. Early August and the Spaniards were on the Somme, with only Corbie to hold them. Then mid-August Corbie fell and the road to Paris was wide open.

Things weren't good in Dax. This was August, right, harvest coming in and soldiers letting us do it, but when it was done they moved in like locusts and took the lot. Left enough for the farms to keep going, but no more. People hungry every-where, don't know what we'd have done without the Seigneur. Couldn't come into Dax himself, but Jacques did, came once a week to see my sister, brought us cash every time.

Couldn't last, though, couldn't go on that way for ever. More than five hundred Spaniards in Dax, same in Verdâme, just about doubled our population, not to mention less land to feed them, lot of our crops being outside the Wall. Mostly hops and barley, on account of us making beer for the region, but lot of the sheep out there too, and that was meat we needed. Looked like being a lean winter and no mistake. Lean times for everyone till the Spaniards left.

But they weren't going. Usual thing with an invasion, right, they come in, do their stuff and move on. Those left behind bury their dead, rebuild their houses and get on with their lives, just the way it is. But not this time. This time they're not just billeting men in our homes, they're taking over the old building used to be the original Roland home, the one with Le Soleil Splendide in one wing and storehouses in the rest, they're taking over the whole thing, extending the back, and turning it into a dirty great barracks. They're even taking over the old steward's house, say it's for a new governor from Spain. 'It's the Wall, that's what it is, Col,' said my dad. 'The Wall's a good defence for them, they're trying to make us part of Artois, you mark my words.'

Some talk of fighting and throwing them out ourselves, others saying no, that's the army's job, like we pay taxes for. Some sense in it too, our own troops were moving at last, driving them back from Compiègne. 'Wait it out,' everyone's saying, 'Wait it out, they'll be here any day.'

But days came and went, and those of us who remember the Chevalier Antoine start thinking there's maybe another way. October comes, and every day there's more and more of us looking toward Ancre and the Seigneur.

Jacques Gilbert

The boy was clutching eagerly at every scrap of news, working out how long it might take our army to get to us and boot the Spaniards out. I was almost as desperate myself. Being Occupied didn't bother me as much as it did André, but I knew if our troops didn't come soon the boy would want to fight.

It was all he thought about. Even teaching me fencing wasn't for fun, it was all about killing Spaniards and doing it for real. He showed me how to twist and turn and jump to stop someone stabbing me. He showed me how to use a cloak in my other hand to distract or block him, and how to get in close and grab his sword-hand. He chalked an outline of a man on the barn wall and demonstrated the different ways to hit him, all of which had horrible Latin names but all seemed to mean killing the other man stone dead. Then he got M. Gauthier to bring me a real sword from his cache, a proper battle one like his own, strong and edged from point to hilt. It was a beautiful sword, with a guard like a golden cage to protect my hand, but I knew it wasn't for me to wear and look important as André's aide, it was there for me to kill Spaniards.

It was the same with everything. He treated me quite differently now I was his aide, he spoke like we were almost equal, but everything was about grooming me to fight. He talked about things to do with honour, he was even teaching me to read, but all his books were about chivalry and stuff and people standing up against horrible odds. My Father thought it was very funny. I knew he was sorry about hitting me that night, he never even mentioned it again, but he still couldn't take any of it seriously. He might have done if he'd known what it really meant.

I understood why the boy felt strongly, I knew what the Spaniards had done to him, or thought I did. I knew he had nightmares, he'd toss and moan in his sleep, arms thrashing about to fight someone who wasn't there, breathing hard and painful, face pale and damp with sweat. It was still madness to think of resistance. I knew he could fight, I'd never forgotten the way he hacked down that mounted Spaniard, but I remembered the rest of it too, him running back into the Manor to fight a hundred soldiers by himself and me having to knock him out to stop him. He'd only turned thirteen that August, he'd got no sense, let him loose in a battle and he'd be dead in seconds, and half the village along with him.

I did my best to talk him out of it. I said we'd still be all right if our troops didn't come, the soldiers wouldn't need such a big garrison when they saw we were docile, there'd be enough food to go round, they'd stop bullying us and settle down. André just sniffed and said it was a matter of honour, and there was never any arguing with him about that.

What really didn't help was M. Gauthier. He kept bringing us stuff like sword belts and baldrics, he watched us fencing and even got us to try it on horseback like soldiers in a real battle. He didn't seem to realize he was encouraging the boy to do something that wouldn't just kill Spaniards, it might be the end of all of us in Dax.

He brought some venison to the cottage one day, so I grabbed him on his way home and begged him to leave the boy alone. I said 'It's dangerous, M. Gauthier, you're making him want to fight the Spaniards.'

He grinned at me and I had to look away to avoid seeing his teeth. 'He doesn't need any encouragement, lad, that's the man he was born to be.'

The rest of us weren't, but I suppose he only cared about André. I said 'But he could get killed, M. Gauthier, don't you see?'

He stopped to wait while Dog did something disgusting in a ditch. 'Not the Chevalier André. Don't you know what he can do? His father was the finest swordsman in Paris, and this one's better, his father said so himself.'

I did know, actually. The boy had this way of sensing what I was going to do before I did it, in all these months of fencing I'd only ever touched him twice.

I said 'It's not that, it's just what he's like. I've seen him, he'll do something stupid and get himself killed.'

M. Gauthier was silent a moment, and looked at Dog enjoying his crap. 'Well, if it has to be, it has to be,' he said philosophically. 'There's worse things than that.'

I couldn't believe it. 'Like what?'

He glanced at me in something like surprise. 'Shame, lad,' he said. 'Shame. Haven't you learned that yet?'

He smiled kindly at me as Dog emerged triumphant from the ditch, then tipped his hat and strolled away.

Colin Lefebvre

Things looked up that November when our army retook Corbie. Imperial troops withdrawing all over, thought we'd only got to wait and they'd all be out of France. But oh no, end of the campaign season is all it was, Spaniards racing each other home to get the best winter quarters, and our own troops not much better. Week passes, then no more Spaniards coming through, all sitting tight in La Capelle and Le Câtelet and waiting it out till spring. More to the point, they were sitting it out in Dax-Verdâme as well, and not just till next year. First time in my life the Dax Gate is shut, soldiers are knocking holes in our Wall and sticking bloody great cannon to point out of them, and it looks like they're here to stay.

People started talking. People saying this was it, we were on our own, no one coming to help us now. Some said lie down and accept it, there were towns changed hands twice already in this war, but no one happy all the same. D'Estrada doing his best to control the troops, decent man in his way, but soldiers are soldiers, no matter what flag they fly. People being robbed, some getting raped, lot getting beaten, and where there was resistance there'd been a few killed.

The Verdâmers cracked first. Nothing much, nothing big, just a soldier killed now and then and maybe his gun stolen. Rumour said it was a caporal in the Baron's Guard who'd escaped the surrender at the barricade. Rumour said he was being helped by the Verdâme tanner, man called Stefan Ravel. Nothing to do with us, no one in Dax involved, but the Spaniards didn't like it, things turned ugly all round.

It started with the Pagniés' pig. November's killing time in Dax, and Pagnié always had cider for them as helped. So there we all were, right, butchering it up nice and neat, then in come the soldiers and carry off the lot. Old Pagnié pleads with them, says he needs to feed his people through the winter, but the cabo just takes up the pig's testicles, throws them in Pagnié's face, and says 'Here you go, you can all share that.'

Word got round fast. Thibault farm were butchering too, so they took warning and did it that very night, all very secret and quiet, sent it out in little parcels; we had some of the guts salted away ourselves for making andouillettes. So when the soldiers come swaggering in to take the meat there's nothing but an empty table and the testicles arranged tasteful on a plate. Soldiers went mad. Robert's dad taken out and beaten, then the cabo says 'Well if we can't have the pig we'll take the sow instead,' and they took Robert's sister into the barracks and had her all night. Poor little Agnès, not much above thirteen, we could hear her screaming through the walls. Wouldn't have happened if d'Estrada'd been there, but he was in Verdâme that night, that de Castilla in charge, for all I knew he took part in it himself.

D'Estrada wasn't happy when he got back, had his men flogged and de Castilla reprimanded, but he couldn't do more. Old Père Gérard pleaded for order, but d'Estrada said he couldn't blame his men for being rough, said it came of people taking pot-shots at them, said it made them touchy. He said 'You keep your own folk in order, *mon père*, then I'll be able to do more with mine.'

Not a bad type, d'Estrada, but he didn't know Picards.

We're not like those madmen in Gascony, we'll bend a while if we have to, but we won't take bullying and we won't be made quiet. There was no more talk of lying down and taking it after that, no talk of anything but fighting.

There was only one answer for it, same as there's always been, and my dad told me straight. 'Up to you, Col,' he said. 'You're the man for this, seeing as you know them. You cut on up to Ancre and see the Seigneur.'

Jacques Gilbert

As soon as I saw him I knew this was it. We were fencing in the back meadow with the swords that afternoon, and the moment I saw Colin toiling purposefully up the bridle path I knew what he'd come to say.

I couldn't really blame him, because it was a dreadful story. I knew Robert Thibault, him and me and Colin went round a lot together in the old days. I didn't really know Agnès, but I'd dreamed about her sometimes, and now I couldn't even do that, it felt sort of indecent. But the boy seemed even more upset than I was, which was odd, I mean they weren't people he knew. He stood with his face turned away all the time Colin was talking, prodding his sword savagely into the grass. When it was over he just stared at the ground and said 'Right then. That's it, isn't it? It's time to fight back.'

I felt a kind of dull ache of acceptance. 'How?'

Colin started talking enthusiastically about all those who'd be willing to fight, and of course it was all people our own age or not much older.

'Haven't we any veterans at all?' asked the boy. 'No one who knows how to go about something like this?'

We hadn't. There was M. Gauthier, of course, and Jacob

Pasle the woodcutter, who was even older and had shaky hands with all brown spots, but that was about it. I said bitterly 'It won't be much of an army.'

André looked at me. 'We'll manage somehow, we'll learn. But we've got to fight them, Jacques, we've got to show the bastards, that's what really matters.'

I thought our surviving mattered a bit too, but he wasn't in the mood to hear it so I kept my mouth shut. We just packed up our swords into the bundle of firewood we carried them about in, then set off back to the cottage with Colin.

We were just approaching the top of the bridle path when we heard crashing and banging from down by the Manor, and looked at each other in alarm. The soldiers had finished looting Ancre months ago, and we liked it that way, it meant we could ride the horses and fence in the meadow, we didn't want them coming back now. We crept carefully to the edge of the bank and peered down.

There was a cart on the back apron, and it looked like the same we'd stuck the wheel on. The two soldiers dumping a slab of marble inside looked like ones we'd seen before too, though there was no sign of that fat cabo, I was glad to see, he wasn't someone I wanted to run into again. Then I looked at the horse harnessed to the cart and forgot all about the cabo and anything else, because it was the old Général.

I loved that horse. He was a huge German-bred beast, the Seigneur used to say he was the best warhorse he'd ever had, but he got a bit of shrapnel in his eye at Casale and had to be retired afterwards. He didn't understand, the poor old Général, I remember the look on his face when the Seigneur went riding off on Tonnerre instead, and the desolate little whinny when he saw them disappear out of sight. He was old now and confused in the head, but he was still a warhorse inside, he didn't know how to be anything else. And there he was, harnessed to a cart by Spanish soldiers like he was just some scrubby workhorse from the Auvergne, it made my heart sort of burn.

'Look what's in the cart,' whispered the boy. 'Look.'

I couldn't tell at first, they were just big square slabs of marble, some black and some white, then a picture swam into shape in my mind and I recognized the hall floor at the Manor.

'They'll be for their barracks,' said Colin knowledgeably. 'They're extending it at the back.'

'And what about the dairy?' said the boy. 'Suppose they take the flags there too?'

I'd forgotten the weapons, but the boy hadn't, he looked half frantic.

'We've got to get them out,' he said. 'We've got to do it now.'

I explained we couldn't stroll in and start digging up the dairy floor while the Spaniards were sitting practically on top of it, but he only said all right, we'd come back and do it at night.

'Ah, but where will you keep them?' said Colin. 'We're talking about iron and steel here, Sieur, needs looking after, needs to be inside and dry.'

That was typical Colin, he went droning on about rust and stuff, but the boy just flapped at him to shut up and said 'The barn, we'll put them there.'

I only just didn't shudder. I asked what he thought the soldiers were going to do if they found us sitting on a whole armoury of guns, they'd kill the lot of us and burn the house down.

'Risk you might have to take, Sieur,' said bloody Colin. 'Don't know what else you're going to do, and that's a fact.'

I could have brained him. I think the boy felt the same, he just said coldly 'You find the volunteers, Lefebvre, I'll provide them with weapons when the time comes.'

'Right you are, Sieur,' said Colin, all huffy. 'I'll do my bit, you can count on me.' He picked himself up off the grass and went on down the path, oozing outraged dignity through the stiffness of his back.

I started to get up myself, but the boy pulled me back down. 'Wait a bit,' he said. 'Let's see if they're going to just take the hall and leave it at that.'

I didn't see how they could possibly take more than the hall floor in one go, I mean this was stone, it was going to take them days to shift. Even as we watched, the soldiers dropped in a last slab then hopped on the cart themselves, and I knew they were finished.

'Maybe when they've gone,' said the boy. 'Maybe we can . . .'

I stopped listening. The lead soldier flicked his whip and I saw the Général heave, but it was too much for him, poor beast, it was too much for any horse. The soldier flicked the whip again, and I heard him shout, the voice drifted right up to us and it sounded full of swearing.

I said 'They can't, they can't expect . . .'

The soldier jumped off the cart in a temper, went up to the Général and brought his whip down *crack* across his flank. The Général shied away, and the whip lashed down again, the Général neighed shrilly, the soldier's arm was coming up, and somehow so was I, I was on my feet and running down the bank, I'd got to stop him, I couldn't bear it. I slithered and fell down the last bit, but I didn't care, I was up and on the apron and running towards the cart.

The soldier on top lifted out a musket, and I guessed they'd got jumpy about their fellows being killed in Verdâme, but when he saw it was just a stupid unarmed peasant, he said something to his colleague, laughed and put the gun back down.

The one on the ground ignored him, he was raising his whip again, the Général snorting and trying to back away. I panted up and tugged the man's sleeve, I said 'Please, Señor, don't hit him, he can't do it,' but he wasn't listening, he just swung round violently, then there was this tearing pain shrieking through my belly, I was folding myself in two, sucking in air in great whoops. He'd punched me in the guts.

He didn't even look, he turned and whipped the Général again, and there was nothing I could do, I might have been in fucking Germany. Somewhere in my head I heard running feet, but they didn't seem to matter, there was a kind of fierceness screaming inside that forced me upright, I was reaching out and grabbing the bastard's hand, wrenching the whip right out of it, I was saying 'You leave him alone, you hear me, you leave him *alone*.'

He shoved me back, he was tugging the sword out of his belt, then behind us came the explosion of a musket. The Général screamed and reared, I turned and saw André pelting up with a sword in his hand, he'd got his bloody sword, no wonder the man fired. But he'd dodged the ball, he was charging straight on, and for the first time since I'd known him I thought he looked frightening. The man on the cart did too, he was trying to reverse the musket and use it like a club, but André was up to him, reaching up and grasping the barrel, and I remembered how strong his grip was, he just twisted it out of his way, his other hand coming round, and in it the sword.

Something was hacking down at me, I only half saw it, but I'd fenced long enough to know to spin on the back foot as the soldier's sword slashed through the air where I'd been.

I knew the next move, I was leaping forward on his inside line, I got both hands to his sword arm and tried to wrestle the blade away, but he was too strong, he clenched his arm to tighten his elbow round my neck. Behind us the Général was rearing and kicking, then one of his hooves came swiping through the air, my man ducked in panic, and I didn't even think, I swivelled and punched him with everything I had, and the back of his head went down *crunch* against the hub of the wheel.

I'd killed him, I knew it, his eyes rolled up and he was making gurgling noises in his throat. Behind me came a cry and a thump, and I looked round to see the other man on his knees, André standing over him with a sword that was bloody halfway to the hilt. I looked back at mine, and he was sliding to the ground, still making choking noises, then stuff dribbled out of his mouth and at last he went still.

The cart lurched, and I saw the Général slumping down on his front knees. I was up to him in a second, I'd got my knife and was sawing at that bloody crappy degrading harness, but it didn't help, he just slumped further, his nose was almost in the dust. I was on my knees and stroking him, and I think he knew me, he gave this last little whinny, then a white film went over his eyes and stayed there and I knew he'd gone. My tears were falling hot on my wrist, but I wasn't sad, I was almost elated. He'd never wanted to die miserably in his stall, the Général, he'd wanted to die in battle, and he had, he really had.

There was a little tinkling sound behind me, and I turned and saw the boy looking down. He'd got two bandoliers slung over his shoulder, and I knew he'd been spoiling the dead. I didn't care, I'd got this savage kind of gladness boiling up in me, I said 'We beat them, didn't we? We beat them.'

He reached out and touched my arm. 'We outnumbered them,' he said. 'You, me, and the Général.'

He understood. He didn't think I was stupid to fight over a horse, he bloody understood. I felt strong suddenly, I remember standing up and saying 'You're right, André, you were right all along. We've got to fight these bastards, it doesn't matter if we lose, we've just got to fight.'

He bent to clean his sword on the coat of the nearest corpse, and my mind turned over and realized what he'd done. He was thirteen years old but he'd seen me in danger and come to save me, he'd just killed a man without my even looking. 'Silly,' he said. 'We've already started.'

Five

Stefan Ravel

Oh yes, I'd been busy. It wasn't only André de Roland who didn't like being invaded, you know, there are other kinds of heroes in this world.

Marcel was one of them. I'd been nursing him at my tannery since the night at the barricades, and he turned out quite a little firebrand, desperate to continue his own private war. It was a matter of honour, of course, as you'd expect when it's something unbelievably stupid. He'd failed in his duty to defend the Château, he'd allowed his patron's family to be taken prisoner, and the shame of it needed to be wiped out. Honour, Abbé? It kills more people than plague.

Me? Oh, there's nothing heroic about me. I rather doubted an army of two could achieve much against a thousand, and suggested we'd be better off nipping over the Wall to join our own troops. And who knows, Abbé, maybe we'd have done it if it hadn't been for the accident.

It was a lone trooper, who came looking to steal leather to make himself a nice buff jacket. I told him there was bugger all left, his mates had nicked it, I said '*Nada*, you understand? Now fuck off.' But well, he couldn't take a hint, he went poking and prying about, and next thing he'd turned up Marcel's uniform coat, which unfortunately he recognized. I'd have talked my way out of it, but there was Marcel in the breeches that went with it, and the trooper knew he'd caught himself a stray enemy soldier. I thought he'd be off for his sergeant at once, but no, he turned out to be an even worse bastard and said kindly he wouldn't report us as long as Marcel agreed to 'be nice' to him.

No, I wasn't shocked, Abbé, I've seen the Italian disease in our own army, and Marcel was an attractive lad, young and blond, just the type they like. But willing's one thing, unwilling quite another, so when the filth dropped his breeches I gave him my graining knife in the guts. Messy, I grant you, but effective.

We still had a little problem in the form of a corpse on the premises, but Durand helped us with that one. That's Philippe Durand, local butcher, a sweet-tempered man, but he didn't like thieving and liked bullying even less. He came round, butchered the body fit for a banquet, then I carried it out in sections and dumped it in the lime pit. It took weeks to rot down, but at least the stink of decomposing don kept looters away from my tannery for quite a little while.

It didn't deter Giles Leroux. He was the Verdâme verderer, used to go to the livestock markets with me and Durand, along with Martin Gauthier and that pisshead Pierre Gilbert from Dax. He was round next day, saying 'I hear you're killing dons.'

'Says who?' I said.

'Says no one,' said Leroux. 'But Durand and I want in, Ravel, so bear it in mind.'

Marcel was right after all, it looked like we had the makings of an army. Durand was a champion longbowman, and Leroux a first-class shot, they were both good fighters who'd stood with us at the barricades. Then Durand brought along Bernard Rouet from the vineyard, who was a top crossbowman if otherwise scarcely human, and that brought us up to five. We ambushed a few pissed soldiers who were stupid enough to wander near the woods at night, and then we'd the guns to look for a few more.

I considered Gauthier, a mad old bugger but soldier through and through, but unfortunately he had one weakness I couldn't ignore: he used to lick the arses of the Rolands till you'd think they'd be red-raw. Oh yes, Abbé, he'd told us all about young André, son of his father, retainers lining up to die on his behalf, but the kid was thirteen and nobility, two things I rather thought we'd be better without.

But there was one thing he told us about his young Sieur that caught Marcel's interest, and no doubt you can guess what. And we knew something else he hadn't mentioned, the name of the man rumour said distributed money for him. An unattractive personality, as you'll know by now, but we thought he might be dim enough to look kindly on men who'd stood alongside him at the barricades.

We thought we'd put it to the test, that night in November. And yes, Abbé, from your rather singular point of view, that's the night my life starts to become interesting.

Jacques Gilbert

We couldn't do much to hide the bodies. The boy said it didn't matter, the Spaniards would think it was those people from Verdâme, they'd never imagine it was miserable peasants like us.

But the Manor would be even less safe from now on, so we waited till dusk then sneaked across to see M. Gauthier. He'd crawled over every inch of the forest stalking; if there was anyone who could find a new hiding place it was him.

I'd never actually been inside his cottage before, and it was pretty horrid really, it was sort of rancid. He had a dead deer and what looked like stoats on the floor, and a couple of pheasants hanging on hooks which from the stink ought to have been eaten last week, but he said no, they had to be hung till the necks rotted and the bodies fell off, that's how you knew it was time to cook them. We nodded politely, then tried to find somewhere to sit that wasn't underneath them.

The boy explained, and M. Gauthier nodded wisely then sat in silence to think. I listened to Dog crunching bones and tried to close my nose against the smell.

'There's the old Hermitage, Sieur,' said M. Gauthier at last. 'Secret enough, aye, and big enough for your horses too. There's a stream, you'd have water. It's very deep in, mind, maybe three miles, you'll want to think about that.'

I didn't want to think about it at all because of having to slog there twice a day to do the horses, but right then nothing seemed to matter as long as we could fight. The boy just said 'The deeper the better, so the Spaniards won't find us,' then looked at me and grinned.

We loaded up the horses with straw from the Home Farm, then tied them up behind the wash-house while the three of us crept furtively to the dairy. We didn't really think there'd be soldiers hanging round after dark, but we couldn't be sure, we hadn't expected them this afternoon either. M. Gauthier made us both wear our swords.

I'd always liked the Ancre dairy, it was cool and airy with whitewashed walls. I used to stand in the doorway watching Fleurie making butter, her eyes flicking up at me sideways through her hair, her hands moist and slippery, and everything feeling fresh. It wasn't like that now. There were filthy boot-marks and a pungent smell like the soldiers had been using it to piss in. The big churn was gone, the stool was on its side, the trestles had collapsed, and there was broken pottery crunching under our feet along with sticky grit where the salt crock had smashed. Something soft caught at my boot, a trail of muslin unravelled like a huge bandage. I remembered watching Fleurie making cheese, measuring out the muslin, then placing the strip between her little white teeth and ripping it clean off with one jerk of her head. I remembered her keeping her eyes on me all the time she was doing it, and how it made me feel. But now the muslin was blackened and disgusting, and Fleurie was dead.

'The floor looks all right,' said the boy.

We went to the far corner where there was a slab you could tilt to slide your hands underneath. M. Gauthier and I prised it out between us, then the one next to it, and now there was a white sheet exposed, with the gleam of dark metal and polished wood showing underneath. Behind us the boy gave a faint sigh of relief.

We laid the top three muskets in the sheet and wrapped them into a bundle. Under the next sheet were two pistols, but the boy was just lifting out the first when I heard a distant rattle of shingle and realized someone was crossing the drive.

M. Gauthier was by the window in a second. The boy didn't seem to have heard, he was still taking out the second pistol, but I touched his arm and indicated the window, and he was on his feet at once, sliding his sword out the scabbard in the same movement. I fumbled out my own, but it felt awkward and unfamiliar, like I'd never handled it before.

M. Gauthier came back from the window.

'Four,' he whispered. 'And another waiting on the grass.' He put a hand on the boy's shoulder, pushing him gently down by the milk cans, and signalled me to crouch next to him. He was too tall to join us, so he just sort of stood and melted himself into the shadow of the corner. If the soldiers went past the door they wouldn't see anything, and I couldn't think of a reason in the world why they'd actually come in.

Then suddenly I could, and an odd flush sort of rippled through me as I realized how stupid we'd been. Those men we killed, someone was bound to have missed them and come looking, they might go through the whole Manor before they checked the apron. I was praying desperately 'But not here, not the dairy, please don't come in here.'

But they did. We could hear them as they came up the track towards the wash-house, then took the fork to the dairy. M. Gauthier bent low, left arm flung out to protect the boy. He was unarmed, but he was big, and those huge long arms looked ready to tackle anything. I told myself we had surprise on our side, there were only four, and we had André, who could surely take two out by himself. I was confident I could get one too. I was sixteen now and bloody strong, I'd been fencing six hours every day since July and thought I ought to be a match for a single Spanish foot-slogger. Then I remembered it wasn't enough just to hit one, I'd got to stick the blade right in him, and I'd never done that in my life. My hand started to feel sticky on the pommel, and the tip of my blade was wobbling.

The darkness by the door thickened and shapes appeared in it. They came forward, closing the door behind them, and the little patch of moonlight narrowed to a crack. I heard their boots crunching on the debris, then an exclamation, and knew they'd seen the floor was up. There was a faint metallic rasping and a pale flash of light as one of them drew a sword.

I shifted position to spring up, but my boot nudged a milk can and it rocked back into the others with a great clang. The men jumped round, but M. Gauthier was already leaping forward and grabbing the one in front. The boy was right behind him, smashing at someone with the heavy pistol, then

I heard the clash of steel as he engaged the one with the sword. I was on my feet and dodging round him, there were arms and elbows everywhere, something soft bashed against my shins, then I was clear and the fourth man right in front of me. I jerked up my sword, but he exclaimed and jumped back, he was in the crack of light from the door, and then I was yelling 'Stop, everyone, André, stop!' because it was only bloody Colin.

For a second nobody moved. Then Colin stepped back a pace and pulled the door wide open, letting moonlight flood into the dairy.

André was standing very still, the point of his blade against his opponent's throat. Half a second later, and he'd have killed him. The man he'd hit with the pistol was on his hands and knees on the floor.

M. Gauthier looked into the face of the man he was throttling, then shoved him away with an oath.

'Durand!' he said in disgust. 'Philippe Durand!'

I peered in the gloom, and saw it was. Everyone knew Philippe, the butcher from Verdâme, he was fat and jolly with a huge grin that showed his missing front tooth. He and M. Lefebvre had this big rivalry between them in the archery competitions, like the May Day contests weren't so much between Dax and Verdâme as between Lefebvre and Durand.

André didn't take his eyes off his own man. He said simply 'Friends of yours, Martin?'

'I'm not so sure about that, Sieur,' said M. Gauthier, glowering round at them all. 'But I know them. The one on the floor lodges with a friend of mine.'

'And this one?' said André, looking thoughtfully at the man on the end of his blade.

'That one,' said M. Gauthier, and spat on the floor. 'That's the so-called friend, Sieur. That's Stefan Ravel.'

So here it is at last, the wonderful moment in my life when I first came face to face with André de Roland. Three loud cheers, and bring out the brandy.

Not that I saw much of him at the time. He was rather smaller than me, Abbé, and you'll appreciate I was having to carry my chin a little high. When I peered down his blade all I could see was the steel of his guard and these dark eyes regarding me coolly over the top. So, no, I wasn't hugely taken with him. For one thing, he took his time getting his blade out of my neck, just to make sure I understood he'd beaten me. Oh yes, Abbé, of course he had, but I didn't see why I should give him the satisfaction of admitting it, so I stared right back and gave him a nice smile.

I said 'Take that fucking blade out of my throat or I'll break your back.'

Something sparked in his eyes, and for a second his blade twitched against my skin. Then slowly the hilt lowered to show more of his face, and I saw him smile back.

'I should like very much to see you try.'

I knew who he was then all right, there wasn't a peasant in the world spoke like that. I didn't need Durand gibbering with shock, saying this was the local Seigneur himself, I knew what I'd got here without that. I merely observed I couldn't be expected to see who I was talking to while I was stuck with my nose pointed at the ceiling, and if he'd have the goodness to get the fuck out of it I might be able to converse in a more civilized fashion.

A toss-up, I grant you, Abbé, but it paid. The kid lowered his sword and stepped back, and I got my first proper look at him. He was a scrawny little thing, scruffy clothes, hair all over his face, and grubby as a street urchin.

I said I was delighted to make his acquaintance.

Jacques Gilbert

Stefan hated him on sight.

He was pissed off at being beaten, of course, he just kept staring at the boy, and I didn't like his look. But M. Gauthier seemed quite comfortable, he just said 'What was that you were saying, Ravel, about our Seigneur being too young to fight?' then creased himself up in wheezy laughter.

The last man came shuffling in while all this was going on, no one I knew, just a shabby little man in a stupid woollen hat pulled too low over his forehead, who looked round nervously then tried to hide himself among the milk cans. André waited patiently for them all to settle, then leant arrogantly against the cheese bench, folded his arms, and said 'Well, gentlemen, would somebody care to explain?'

Colin started blustering, like he always does when he's scared or in the wrong. He said the men had come to the Forge that evening, he told them we wanted the weapons hidden and they'd volunteered to help.

'Tried to ask first,' he said. 'Went round the cottage myself, checked the barn, not a sign of anyone. Thought it better not to wait. Thought you said it was urgent.'

He sounded all injured, so the boy said he quite understood and thanked them for their trouble.

There was a little silence, then the one who'd been on the floor gave this discreet little cough behind his hand and stepped forward.

He said 'I have to confess we had something of an ulterior motive.'

André liked frankness. 'What was it?'

The man looked at him very directly. He was nice-looking, blond, sort of fresh-faced, and really not much older than us, probably only about eighteen. There was something clean about him too, a sort of innocence that made him seem younger. Just looking at him made me feel old and scabby and cynical.

He said 'I hoped you might lend us some of your weaponry. We want to raise an army to fight the Spaniards.'

I suppose we should have guessed, but it felt like a miracle all the same. Then he introduced himself as Caporal Marcel Dubois of the Verdâme Guard, and that was even better. He wasn't a kid like us, and he wasn't just a farm labourer who wanted to fight, he was a proper trained soldier who'd been in battles and knew what he was doing. The boy looked at him like he was the Archangel Gabriel.

Stefan Ravel

It was quite a change, Abbé, he was all over Marcel as if they were long-lost brothers. When Marcel told him I was a soldier too, he clasped my hand and actually gave me a great big smile.

I gave his hand a really tight squeeze, just to show I hadn't forgotten the way he'd been looking at me a minute ago, but his smile never faltered and he gave me one fuck of a squeeze right back. So I thought 'all right,' and really put the pressure on till his eyes glazed. He didn't make a sound, I'm glad to say, just gritted his teeth and glared, but when we let go I noticed him rubbing his hand under cover of

97

his cloak. Someone else saw him too. The silent young man standing beside him took one look at André massaging his fingers, then turned his face towards me and for the first time our eyes met.

Jacques Gilbert. Well now, Abbé, what would you like me to say about young Jacques? The stupid stable boy, devoted nursemaid, loyal companion, gallant soldier, take your pick. But what I first saw in his eyes was something a great deal more primitive than that. Ownership, Abbé. Possession. He had his hand on the kid's arm, and the look on his face was saying 'Keep off' in every language you'll ever hear.

It wasn't very effective, unfortunately. André had obviously decided we were now all bosom friends, and insisted on proper introductions whether Jacques liked it or not. He knew Durand, of course, and remembered he'd personally crowned him King of the Bird last May Day, which made Durand flush pink with pleasure. Rouet was a social challenge to anybody, I'm afraid, but he muttered away respectfully enough, and backed off at the first opportunity, lurking in a corner and cracking his knuckles with nerves. Me, I leant against the wall in deliberate imitation of the kid, and watched the little pantomime with considerable amusement.

It served a purpose for all that, because now the kid was promising us everything. We could have the weapons, we could borrow his horses, he had a hideout in the Forest we could use, and he was pretty sure he could find us a number of volunteers too. All very nice, Abbé, all very helpful, except for one little snag.

Marcel saw it right away. 'Forgive me, Monseigneur, but surely you will want to use some of these things for your own forces?'

'My forces?' said young André. 'We haven't got any, that's

why we're so pleased to see you. Now you're here, we can build up a regular army.'

Marcel gave that apologetic little cough of his. He'd a few nervous habits like that, Abbé. He used to bite his nails as well.

'It would be better to keep our forces separate, Monseigneur. M. Ravel and I are professional soldiers, and we'll want to run our own army.'

'Of course,' said the kid, surprised. 'Of course you must run it, I wouldn't expect anything else. I only want to join it, and fight like anybody else.'

Marcel hesitated, so I knew it would have to be me put the boot in.

I said as nicely as I could 'Look, you're the bloody Sieur of Dax, aren't you? Surely you can see that's not possible.'

Jacques Gilbert

M. Gauthier bristled at once. He growled 'Watch your mouth, Ravel,' and went and tried to loom over him, which was a bit difficult actually, because he was really big, Stefan, he sort of dominated everything around him. Even now when he was leaning against the wall, he had his legs apart and his left hip thrust out, and that great naked sword clanking on his belt, it's like he tried to take up all the space he could. He can't have even been that old then, he was maybe only nineteen, but he made you feel like he was older, like he'd seen everything in the world and pissed all over it.

'You remember who you're talking to,' said M. Gauthier.

Stefan smiled cynically. 'You see? How can we have the Sieur of Dax in the army if we're not allowed to talk to him

99

like anyone else? How are we going to give him orders? And if we do, would he take them?'

I felt my heart sort of sinking, because I could see his point. I couldn't meet his eyes, and neither could M. Gauthier, he just muttered and looked away.

André didn't seem bothered. 'In the army one takes orders from all kinds of people. My father served under a German mercenary at Casale. There's no shame in it.'

I could see Stefan's lip curling at that phrase 'all kinds of people', but it was M. Gauthier who got in first.

'It's different, Sieur,' he said urgently. 'That would be a man of senior rank to your father. M. Dubois here is only a caporal. You are Chevalier, you are an officer, you cannot take orders from a caporal.'

The boy shook his head. 'In this army he'll be Capitaine. I can take orders from a capitaine, can't I?' He smiled at Marcel, and Marcel smiled back. It felt warm and friendly, you could see them liking each other.

Stefan ruined it at once. 'And I'd be Lieutenant,' he said. 'How do you feel about that, my young Sieur? Take orders from me as well, would you?'

'Even you,' said André, looking him right in the eye. 'I give you my word.'

Stefan gave a short grunt like a laugh, but Marcel said quickly 'He's right, Stefan, we should all swear. We're forming an army, we should swear ourselves in.'

We did it all properly and formally, we dug out a sword for Marcel and all swore allegiance as volunteer soldiers in his army. Then Marcel swore to lead us fairly and justly, all the usual bollocks, and kissed the sword, which I bet he wouldn't have if he knew they hadn't been washed or anything, they'd just been taken off dead men and bunged under the floor. Stefan had to make the same oath, and he did it somehow without being struck by lightning, but he never took his eyes off the boy, and I didn't like his smile.

Colin Lefebvre

Jacques ought never have allowed it. Sieur of Dax agreeing to take orders off a thug like Ravel, absolute disgrace. Anyone could see Ravel was a troublemaker, he might have been one of them Croquants we'd got insurrecting round the country. Talked like a rebel and smelt like a tanner, and got it in for our Seigneur from the start.

But Seigneur was so red-hot to fight he'd have taken orders from Gauthier's dog. Keen as keen he was, insisted on unpacking and loading the weapons like everyone else. Friendly too, even saw him trying to make conversation with that dimwit Rouet, and that took some doing, the man only had about three words in him and they were 'crossbow', 'bolt', and 'cranequin'.

One funny thing though, tell me what you make of this. Durand was digging out the last bits from the cache when up he came with this dagger. Beautifully wrought it was, lovely bit of steel, proper bloodied up from something but the Roland crest on plain to see. So Durand offered it the Seigneur, right, and Seigneur's face went suddenly tight-white. Took that knife like it would burn him, backed right away from the hole, and next thing I saw he was outside, wiping it as careful as if it was a baby, making the blade bright and clean again on the wet grass.

Yes, I saw that too. I knew it was André's knife, I'd seen it in his belt in the old days. I guessed he'd had it with him that night at the Manor and stabbed someone. He'd never told me anything about what happened in there, he never talked about it at all, but I knew he'd fought someone, I remembered the blood on his sleeve.

He didn't say anything now either, he seemed all right after he'd cleaned it, and when we set off in a great file in the dark I could see his excitement coming back. There were eight of us now, we really did feel like a proper army. The tramping of feet, the snorting of horses, the clatter of muskets and jingling of swords, the muttering of men's voices, he was sort of breathing it in and loving it.

It was just as well really, because M. Gauthier was right, it was a bloody long walk to the Hermitage, especially with all those guns to carry. He took us up to the back meadow, then plunged confidently into the darkest part of the Forest with the rest of us floundering behind him like baggage mules. I couldn't see how he was finding his way at all, but he talked us through it and made us notice landmarks as we went, like a tall tree with a spiky crest we had to head for till we hit the stream. It's funny how that stuff comes back to you, I could take you there right now.

The Hermitage stood in a clearing in the middle of a dense patch of trees, and you could still see the slimy dead trunks where the wood had been taken to build it. The air was very still, and the atmosphere close and heavy, even at night. It was unbelievably quiet, except for a distant kind of soft rushing sound I guessed must be the stream.

There were three buildings. The Hermitage dominated

everything, huge and dilapidated, but there were two smaller outbuildings on one side, which M. Gauthier said were more solid and would do for our stables and armoury. We tethered the horses and went forward to explore.

'I thought the Hermitage itself might make a good base for you, Sieur,' said M. Gauthier. 'You could have a hundred men in here.'

It was certainly big enough, but I didn't like anything else about it, it looked like something out of a scary story for children. It was all made of planks of wood, and what struck you first was that it was totally green. There was soggy-looking moss all over it, the walls as well as the roof, and the far end was choking with ivy.

'It'll maybe need a bit of work, Sieur,' said M. Gauthier. 'But I'm sure we can make it right in a couple of days.'

There were rickety steps onto a kind of wooden stage, which had pillars supporting the front end of the crumbling roof. Marcel put his foot on the first step, and it cracked under his weight.

'Well, maybe a week,' said M. Gauthier.

The wood creaked damply underfoot as we followed Marcel up and through the open door. It took a minute to adjust my eyes to the total darkness, but I was already aware of the swirl of space around me. I took a tentative step forward, but something squelched under my boot, and I nearly slipped over. M. Gauthier caught me before I fell.

'Careful now,' he said. 'There's maybe a few toadstools.'

There were thousands. As the picture became clearer, I could see them stretching away in front of me like a field. Above them was just nothingness, this dark, empty space which took shape at the far end with a kind of raised plat-form. The roof was held up by dark pillars that seemed to be growing out of the fungus like giant stalks. I put out a hand to steady myself, but snatched it back at once. The wall was cold and furry with mould.

'It's perfect, Martin,' came the boy's voice behind me. 'Just perfect.'

Marcel obviously thought so too, he couldn't thank the boy enough. 'There's everything we need for an army here, Chevalier, absolutely everything.'

I thought we probably needed men as well, but kept my mouth shut because André was almost glowing. It was extraordinary really, I'd been with him every day for months and months, but it wasn't till we were standing in a freezing forest in the middle of the night discussing how best to kill lots of Spaniards that I really saw him happy.

Stefan Ravel

Forgive me if I throw up.

Oh, come on, Abbé, the way they all fawned round him turned my stomach. Durand was distressed with himself for having the temerity to offer the kid a dirty knife, Rouet watched him with his mouth hanging open like this was the baby Jesus himself, and Lefebvre called him 'Seigneur' every other word. Even Marcel balked at calling him André until the kid insisted it was a kind of *nom de guerre* and no disrespect in it at all, at which Marcel declared we should all do the same, and he was 'Marcel' and I was 'Stefan' for the duration.

Ask yourself, Abbé, ask yourself what the kid had done to earn that respect. He'd got himself out of his home alive when all his servants were murdered, but that was just about it. Oh, and one other thing. He'd got himself born into the right family.

But I'm a fair man, and the kid wanted to be a soldier. Naturally he'd need breaking first, but I'm good at that, Abbé.

I'm very good indeed.

Six

Jacques Gilbert

The first thing the bastard did was make us clean the Hermitage.

M. Gauthier didn't mind the filth much, it probably made him feel at home, but André hated it. I watched him with his lips tight shut scraping the crud off the walls, shivering with the effort not to be sick. But whenever Stefan poked his head in to see how we were getting on, the boy just said 'Fine,' and went on scrubbing. Stefan smiled sarcastically, then went back to oiling weapons in the warmth of the outhouse.

At least Colin was recruiting people in Dax, so we weren't on our own long. First Jacob Pasle the woodcutter came to chop up trees with M. Gauthier, then Dom and Georges the under-gardeners turned up to help inside. Georges was a bit of a pain at first, he kept chucking toadstools and clowning around, but Dom explained he'd only been five when their parents died, and said 'He's had no one to show off to, Sieur, do you see?' When we went back in and saw Georges had stuck a big toadstool on his head, the boy laughed and clapped, and Georges looked like someone had given him a present.

I was glad Dom was with us. He was dark and slender where Georges was plump and fair, and I'd always thought him wise and kind in a dreamy sort of way. I saw a lot of him in the old days, because I shovelled shit out of the stables and Dom took it away in a cart to spread on the gardens. He called me his 'Brother Shit-Shoveller', and looked at things differently from anyone I knew. I'd look at the horse manure and see a pile of shit, but Dom would see flowers blooming and vegetables ripening. He didn't even seem to mind the Hermitage, he went scooping up great armfuls of fungus, humming gently to himself as he worked.

Next came Robert Thibault, but I'd expected that after what the soldiers had done to his family. I'd always looked up to Robert. He was strong and handsome, and his dad was second biggest tenant farmer in Dax, so when we played soldiers he was always capitaine. He was kind though, as long as you remembered he was in charge. Once when Bruno Baudet was beating me up about something Robert came and stopped him, he stood with his hands on his hips saying 'Jacques is my friend, and if you hurt him you'll answer to *me*, do you understand?'

I watched him being introduced to Stefan and even from a distance I could see Robert wasn't keen. When he reached me he said 'Hullo, Jacquot, that man's a bloody tanner, you could smell him in Abbeville. What are we supposed to be doing?'

I told him and he sniffed. 'Fuck that. I came here to fight dons, I'm not cleaning out bloody stables.'

At that moment André rushed out of the Hermitage and was noisily sick in the bushes. Robert shut his jaw with a snap, rolled up his sleeves, said 'On the other hand . . .' and walked purposefully into the building.

Most of the Dax men were like that. Marin Aubert, the baker's son, hairy Bruno Baudet from the mill, Simon Moreau from the Quatre Corbeaux, Edouard and Vincent Poulain, the mason's sons, none of them liked the idea of menial work, but when they saw their Seigneur doing it they joined in like it was their idea of a holiday. Stefan watched them all and smiled.

Others saw it differently. Next day we were replacing the rotten wood when that enormous Bettremieu Libert came up from the Home Farm. André was staggering along with this great load of timber, but Bettremieu had it off him in a second, saying reproachfully in his mangled French 'You don't do that, Sieur.'

'Yes I do,' said the boy. 'When it's for the army, I do.'

'No,' said Bettremieu calmly. 'Not when Bettremieu is here to do it for you.' He nodded firmly and carried the wood up the steps without another word. He never did say much, Bettremieu, which was maybe just as well because he was Flemish.

But with people like him along we started to make real progress. Clement Ansel and Luc Pagnié brought us straw from their dads' farms, and the Hermitage started to feel warm and comfortable. The walls and pillars had been scrubbed so hard the wood was almost white, and we'd even uncovered a window under all the moss, which let in the daylight and made the whole place feel bright. Colin made little tin holders to stick candles in, and we wedged them at intervals all round the walls. After dark it looked almost like a church.

The weapons outhouse still needed a lot of shoring up and rebuilding, but Marcel had been putting the word round Verdâme and we had loads more volunteers. We'd already got Philippe and Bernard, of course, and Stefan also brought in Giles Leroux, chief verderer for the Baron's estate. We were a bit shy of him at first, because he was older than the rest of us, maybe even thirty. He had a brown, lean face with hard cheekbones, and looked like an intelligent fox. He seemed to be an actual friend of Stefan's, but I suppose he had to be, I mean the local tanner's got to be on good terms with the keepers. They didn't seem close though, Stefan would just say 'Leroux' and Giles would say 'Ravel', then they'd reach out and sort of smack hands together in a hard grip, and push against each other like rams fighting. It looked really tough and manly, and I watched them closely to see how it was done.

Some of the other Verdâmers were a bit sneery, like that cowman everyone called 'Pinhead' because he had a huge body and the smallest head you ever saw on top of it. When he saw us struggling to lug turfs up to the Hermitage roof, he and his friends perched on a pile of logs to jeer at the Sieur of Dax working like a day labourer. André was seething, he dropped his turfs with a great thud and started to climb down, but luckily Giles came by before he reached them and said he wanted to 'borrow' them a moment. They all swaggered off after him, and when we went to feed the horses we saw he'd got them mucking out the stables. Giles didn't say a word, he just flicked his hat casually over his eyes and grinned.

We could have done with more like Giles. We'd a few veterans like Jacob, who could load and fire a musket twice a minute however shaky his hands were, but otherwise it was like I thought, the volunteers were mostly young and inexperienced. I understood their fathers couldn't be spared from their work, but Marcel and Stefan were obviously concerned too, and as soon as the base was finished they held a proper meeting to start things off.

It was impressive seeing the Hermitage filled with men for the first time, we had to pick our way over loads of legs to find a place of our own in the straw. I'd no idea we were so many, but there had to have been at least sixty. With them all talking at once it sounded like two hundred.

Marcel put that into perspective right away. He stood on the platform at the far end, and told us we'd got maybe a thousand Spaniards in Dax-Verdâme so we didn't have anything like enough men or arms to drive them out yet. Our job was just to harass and kill as many as we could so the Spaniards couldn't turn the Saillie into a fortress against France. He said 'One day our own troops will come. It's up to us to see Dax-Verdâme is ready for them.'

People started cheering with excitement, but then Stefan stood up and it started to sound real instead. He said we'd got to form ourselves into units of six for training, then we'd stay in them for guard and stable duty as well as what he called 'actions', which seemed to mean killing people to nick their guns and powder. We could pick our own units, but since this was the Occupied Army of Dax-Verdâme they each ought to contain people from both villages.

The whole place turned into a livestock market in a minute, with everyone milling around trying to find friends to form a unit. I grabbed Colin and he managed to grab Robert, and M. Gauthier practically trampled about twenty people as he thundered across to join us. I looked round for Philippe as our Verdâme member, but he'd been snaffled up already, which wasn't surprising considering he was such a good archer. So Marcel brought us over this young man all dressed in tatty silk and lace, and said he'd better join us because nobody else wanted him. I could understand why. He was thin and weedy with watery eyes and bony little wrists sticking out of his sleeves like sticks. He also had the most appalling cold, his nose was dribbling and he had to keep wiping it on this hard sodden ball of a handkerchief. He whispered his name was Jean-Marie Mercier, then sneezed all over Colin and went bright red with shame.

We'd just started to organize our first training session when

Stefan came strolling up, and I saw he was starting to smile. He really did have the slowest smile in the world, Stefan, it took about five minutes to get all the way there, by which time there was usually nothing in the world left to smile about.

'This your unit then, is it, André?'

'Yes,' said the boy firmly.

Stefan's smile just kept on growing. 'Chosen a leader yet?'

'Martin Gauthier,' said André. 'He's much the most experienced.'

Stefan's smile reached its peak. 'We can't ask the Sieur of Dax to take orders from a verderer.'

André dismissed that. 'I'll take Martin's orders, I respect him.'

'That's nice,' said Stefan genially. 'Martin Gauthier isn't going to order you into danger, is he? I can see why you like the idea.'

M. Gauthier moved so quickly he was just a hairy blur. He got his hands on Stefan's shirt-front in a second and actually shook him. 'You dare imply that, Ravel, you dare even hint our Seigneur's a coward, I'll wring your evil neck.'

André cried 'Martin!' but Stefan was already reaching out a big hand and just shoving M. Gauthier back and away till he had to let go.

'Oh, come on, Gauthier, I'm only saying you're too loyal to be the slightest good to him, and I rather think you've proved my point.' He brushed off his shirt like M. Gauthier had left dirt on it, which actually he probably had, then looked down at the boy. 'This really what you want, is it? Someone who'll let you run the whole thing yourself?'

The boy was simmering with anger. He knew Stefan was right, but he couldn't have had anyone be as rude to him as this ever, he looked like it was choking him. He said in a kind of strangled voice 'I won't take orders from anyone else.'

'Oh, you will,' said Stefan. 'You'll take mine. We've decided I'm going to lead you myself.'

I thought 'oh fuck'. The boy went very still, which was sort of like him saying 'oh fuck' as well. M. Gauthier just stared at Stefan in impotent fury.

'You'll still get to lead, Gauthier,' said Stefan. 'I've a unit of estate men over there who need your experience.'

André's head was up at once. 'Martin's staying with us.'

'We're too many,' said Stefan. 'Gauthier's going, and that's that.'

André's mouth tightened and his eyes narrowed into little green slits. I hadn't seen it for months now, but I knew exactly what was coming. Stefan had pushed it too far.

Stefan Ravel

He blazed up at once, the whole routine, head up, hand on sword hilt, he was as predictable as a gun dog and a lot less effective. His voice got shriller and his face redder, and at one point he even stamped. All over the building people turned to look, and that was all to the good, I thought they'd find it edifying to see their heroic little Sieur make a champion fool of himself. So I let him ramble on till he ran out of breath, then told him I was sorry but it was an order.

It stopped him like a blow to the chin. He wanted his gamekeeper, but he wanted to fight even more. He couldn't bear people to see him back down to a humble tanner, but he couldn't bear to break his word to Marcel. I watched him fighting it, then at last his eyes dropped and I knew I'd won. More than that, I'd always win. He wanted to be part of our army, but if he didn't take my orders he was out.

He did it with grace, I'll give him that. He told his game-keeper he was sorry but I was right. Gauthier said 'Sieur,' and trotted off to the other group at once, but he gave me one of the filthiest looks I've ever seen, and I've had a few over the years, Abbé, as I'm sure you can imagine.

I can't say I was that bothered. I was doing what I had to, that's all. Hardly my fault if it happened to be fun as well.

Jacques Gilbert

Colin and Robert were wide-eyed with shock. They didn't like seeing their Seigneur humiliated by a tanner from Verdâme, and it didn't help hearing Pinhead and his mob jeering away in their corner. I tried to explain there was nothing shameful in what the boy was doing, it proved it wasn't a game, him dressing like a peasant and letting us call him 'André', it proved he was really going to be like one of us. But it was difficult because I didn't like it myself, there was a bit of me wanted to say sod the army, let's kick Stefan's head in and go home.

I tried saying that to the boy on the way home. I said 'You don't have to take it, you don't have to be in their stupid army at all. You've done everything the Seigneur needs to do, you've given them the base and the weapons, you don't have to muck in like everyone else.'

'Don't I?' said the boy, kicking savagely at dead leaves. 'You think I should let other people fight my battles for me?'

I did actually, but knew him well enough not to say so. I said cautiously 'You mean it's a matter of honour?'

He paused a moment, then reached out his arm and pulled

it through mine, just like I was another gentleman myself. 'Yes,' he said. 'I knew you'd understand.'

But I didn't, and I know that now. I didn't understand at all.

Jean-Marie Mercier

From his interviews with the Abbé Fleuriot, 1669

I knew they didn't want me. Why would they? I was nobody.

I'd perhaps been somebody once. When there was still trade with Artois my father built up a thriving business, buying the best of the Flanders cloth, having it made into fine garments in our workshop, and selling it on for a profit at Lucheux. That all ended when the war came. We kept going a little while, but then the Spaniards invaded and stole everything we had left, and times had become very hard. I knew I wasn't dressed properly, but they were the only clothes I had, you see, the ones I'd worn in the old days.

I wasn't even a very soldierly person, but I did just want to do something like everybody else. We'd used Stefan Ravel for leather in the old days and I hoped he might be welcoming, but he called me 'Mercier' and seemed to think my volunteering was rather funny. I might have just gone quietly home again, but Marcel found a unit to put me with, and then it was too late. It was the Sieur of Dax's own unit and they had hundreds of friends they'd like to have had, instead of which they were forced to take me.

We met next morning at the old hunting lodge in the Forest of Verdâme, which Marcel was planning to turn into a second base for emergencies. I was anxious to arrive early, so I'd been there quite a while when I heard chatter and laughter then saw Jacques coming through the trees with André himself. I suddenly wished I'd come later, but it was too late to hide so I said hello and tried to smile.

They said 'hello' back and sat down beside me, but I couldn't think of anything to say, and the silence was awful. I remember I had a little chill at the time, and was afraid they might find me irritating if I sniffed.

Jacques said 'Aren't you cold?'

I was rather, because my clothes weren't very suitable for January. I tried to say I was fine but André actually took my hand and said 'You are, you're freezing. Jacques, he's freezing.'

He began to take off his cloak, but Jacques wouldn't allow it and started to remove his own. I tried to protest but Jacques showed me he was wearing a thick woollen shirt underneath, so I gave in and let him wrap the cloak around me. André smiled in satisfaction, and a wonderful warmth began to grow inside me like a glow.

Colin and Robert joined us soon afterwards, but that was all right too. Colin was a little difficult just at first, but when he saw André was anxious to include me he really became quite kind. Robert was charming from the first. He'd brought some apple brandy to warm us up, and gave me a sip for myself. Everything felt very friendly, and by the time Stefan arrived I was beginning to think the army might be all right after all.

He started us on gun drill. We were working with half-muskets because you can use them without a stand, but they were still rather heavy, and Stefan showed us how to use branches for support, or prop up the barrel on a rock if we were lying down. André was a little awkward at first, because he was younger and perhaps less strong, but Stefan was really quite beastly about it. He tried to make us all laugh at him, and said dreadful things like 'For Christ's sake, André, it's a gun, not your bloody knob.' I'm so sorry, but he really did talk like that. I thought he was very coarse.

I hoped it might be better when we went on to loading. A wheel-lock misfires terribly easily, so you need to be careful to load it properly, but Stefan said we needed to do it quickly as well. In the proper army we'd have pike to protect us, but without them we were what he called a 'Forlorn Hope' and very vulnerable. Our best chance was to keep some men loading and passing fresh muskets to the front line, but if we were caught unloaded we'd have to protect ourselves with the empty guns.

Robert said 'How?' He never seemed very intimidated by Stefan, I thought he was terribly brave.

'I'll show you,' said Stefan, and grinned. 'You do this.'

He reversed his musket and clubbed down viciously at André's head, only stopping short at the very last second. André quite flinched in shock.

'You beat the bastard's brains out, that's what you do,' said Stefan. 'Oh, sorry, André, did I scare you?'

It went on like that all morning. When we tried loading ourselves, Stefan stood right over André, yelling 'Too much powder' or just 'Faster!' until poor André's hands were shaking so much he spilt his powder on the grass. Stefan was horrid. He said what André had wasted could have saved a man's life.

I know it sounds ridiculous, because of course Stefan was a professional soldier, but he honestly did seem quite determined to bully André.

As soon as it was over I went straight to Stefan and told him to leave the boy alone.

He was sitting watching the rest of us pack up the guns, and didn't even bother to look up. 'What's the matter, scared I'll make him cry?'

I said 'It would take more than you.'

'If he doesn't like it, he can always leave, can't he?'

'He won't do that, you know he's desperate to fight.'

'Then I'm doing him a favour,' said Stefan. 'He needs a lot of toughening up before he's going to be ready for that.'

I couldn't think of an answer and he knew it.

'You look after yourself, stable boy,' he said. 'Leave the kid to me.'

The boy shrugged it off, he said it was just Stefan teaching him discipline and he could handle it, but the next day we did pike and that was even worse. We were using great long poles to practise with, and the boy just wasn't tall enough to work them properly. When we started trying to knock a man off a horse, Stefan deliberately made André try first so we could see how bad he was. He himself was the rider, and the boy made a desperate effort to sweep him off, but lost control of the pole, slipped and went flat on his face. Stefan almost fell out of the saddle laughing.

Colin was red with fury, Jean-Marie was nearly crying, but it was Robert who lost his temper. He threw down his pole and said 'This is stupid. Of course he can't bloody do it, he's shorter than the rest of us.'

Stefan smiled. 'Pick up the pole, Thibault.'

Robert glared at him and folded his arms. He never seemed

that scared of Stefan, he used to say he was only a smelly tanner and if he didn't start treating us better then he'd just leave.

The boy scrambled quickly up on his knees, and said 'Please, Robert, it's all right.'

Robert looked at him in confusion. He couldn't let his Seigneur get pushed around by someone like Stefan, it went against everything he believed in.

'Please,' whispered André.

Robert lowered his eyes, then bent and picked up his pole.

'All right,' said Stefan, amiably. 'But if André wants to stay in the army with the rest of you, he's got to do the same as the rest of you. Right, we'll try that again.'

There was this awful silence. The boy climbed slowly to his feet and I handed him his pole. He wiped the earth from his face with his sleeve, and walked into position. His expression was grim.

Stefan went off round the corner on Duchesse, then came cantering back towards us. This time André didn't even try to sweep him off, he just leapt out in front of Duchesse and thrust the pole right at her eyes, making her rear in fright. Stefan was thrown clear off her back and smack on the ground, and the boy had the pole across his throat in a second.

I didn't dare laugh. We all watched in silence as Stefan picked himself up and brushed the dirt off his clothes. The boy stood back and waited, looking nervously defiant.

Stefan walked over to him and looked down with an expression I couldn't read. Then he said 'All right, good enough,' and turned away.

That's when I realized how close to cracking the boy really was. He came back to the barn that night, and just sat on his blanket thumping his fist against the wall and saying

'That bastard. That bloody bastard.' I knew he was only hanging on for the chance to kill the enemy, and had the feeling if it didn't happen soon he'd go and kill Stefan Ravel instead.

The last day we were doing sword drill. André would have been brilliant at that, of course, so Stefan said he didn't need it and made him clean muskets instead. The boy didn't complain, he just sat miserably working away and trying not to watch the rest of us enjoying ourselves, but when it was over Stefan had a go at him anyway and said two guns weren't done well enough, a fouled musket could cost a man's life in action.

He picked up the dirty muskets and slung them at André. 'There you go. Get those strapped to your back, run round the base ten times, then report back to me.'

Nobody moved. We were all staring at André, and I knew this was it. Then he bent down, picked up the two heavy muskets and looked Stefan full in the face.

'All right,' he said, and actually smiled. 'All right.'

So I strapped him up and watched him set off, the guns banging up and down on his back all the way. I knew he was going to be black with bruises.

'What's he done?' said a voice behind me.

Giles had turned up for duty with his own unit, and was leaning against the Hermitage wall with Philippe. I told them the boy hadn't done anything, it was just Stefan being a bastard, and Philippe smiled sadly through his gap tooth and patted my shoulder.

'I know, M. Jacques, I know. Our poor Ravel.'

'Poor *Ravel*?' I said, suddenly furious. 'What about poor André?'

'Of course,' said Philippe hastily. He never liked any kind of row. 'But he's a troubled soul, young Ravel. A bad experience in the army, I think. Something to do with his brother. We have to make allowances.'

I tried to feel sorry for Stefan, but it was no good, the minute I pictured him I just wanted to smash his face in. I said 'No we bloody don't. Wait till M. Gauthier hears about this, he'll kill him.'

'I expect he will,' said Giles calmly. He was wadding up tobacco leaves to chew and didn't look at me at all. 'And then we'll lose our best soldier. Do you think that's what he wants, that boy out there?'

André was coming round again. He seemed lower to the ground, his knees were buckling, but he was still going, pounding along, head down, seeing nothing but the Spaniards he was earning the right to fight.

I looked at Giles but he was chewing his tobacco and apparently enjoying it.

I said 'I won't tell M. Gauthier.'

Giles looked up at me and the brown skin round his eyes crinkled into a smile.

'You'll do, soldier,' he said, tipped his hat and strolled away.

Stefan Ravel

I don't know where you get your ideas from, Abbé, but you're wrong this time. There was nothing personal, it was all for the good of the army. The kid was holding up better than I expected, but I knew there was a weakness somewhere, and only hoped I'd find it before it did too much damage.

The dons decided otherwise. We'd ambushed two patrols that last week, but it seemed the bastards were starting to work it out, and our last attempt brought a load out from hiding at the first sound of gunfire. That big Flamand, Bettrem-ieu Libert, he took a ball in the arm, and we were lucky to get the team out alive. It might have been an accident, but Marcel sent Gauthier and Leroux out scouting the fringes next day, and they both reported groups of these pickets camping out in the woods, poor frozen sods, just waiting for the sound of our next ambush. Marcel and I discussed it, and thought we'd have to find another way.

So when the little Sieur of Dax came panting back in to me that afternoon with a back that resembled a child's hoop and a look that would have exploded fireworks, I just said 'Very good. You'll sleep well tonight, young André, and be fine and fresh for tomorrow.'

He looked at me warily. 'Tomorrow?'

'Yes,' I said, lifting the first musket off him, which was tricky since it seemed to be adhering to his shirt with sweat. 'We're doing a silent action tomorrow, sword and pike, no guns. I thought our unit might be right for the job, but of course if you're not up to it . . .'

'I'm up to it,' he said at once, his back straightening with a creak you could have heard in Lucheux. 'You know I am, Stefan, I'm up to it.'

And do you know, I really thought he was.

Jacques Gilbert

André was quiet that morning. He hardly spoke through breakfast, and Mother thought he might be sickening for something. She leant forward to put her hand on his fore-head, but he only took it firmly and said 'It's all right, Nelly, I promise.' She looked at him uncertainly, but he patted her hand and gave it back, so at last she said 'Dear André,' and sat down. Father got up and slammed noisily outside.

They didn't know, of course, they'd got no idea what we were really doing. We were supposed to keep the army secret from our families, and most of us probably did, but that morning I found it hard. It isn't every day you deliberately set out to kill someone.

We walked to the Hermitage and found the others in the same kind of serious mood. Even Stefan was different, he spoke almost gently as he ran through what we'd got to do. It was reassuring in a way, but in another it made everything feel more serious, and I know I was getting twitchy when at last we set out through the forest. We'd heard rumours about pickets listening for us, and the leaves seemed to crackle under my boots with every step.

We were on the Back Road, which had the Dax-Verdâme woods to the south and the Forest of Dax to the north, and Stefan had picked a section inside a kind of bend so we were out of view from either direction. The trees came right up to the road, and there were four with branches at exactly the right height. It looked perfect.

Colin and Jean-Marie took a tree either side and looped their rope over the branches to trail across the road between them, then we covered it with dead leaves so the patrol wouldn't see it till it was too late. Stefan and Robert were in bushes further along, armed with home-made pike, then it was me and the boy with swords. We had the muskets loaded and stacked together beneath the signal tree, but they weren't to be touched unless it was that or die. Stefan had a bloody great pistol shoved down his belt as well, but when Robert mentioned it Stefan just said it was his 'safety' and stared him right out.

We had the dullest part, the boy and me. Our job was to

raise a second rope after the riders went past, so they couldn't escape back the way they'd come. Stefan did say we could join the others once the men were safely on the ground, but I didn't fancy that much, I didn't like the idea of six of us hacking at two people on the ground, not even Spanish soldiers.

Giles sauntered up, reported there wasn't a sign of a picket for a mile in either direction, then climbed expertly up the signal tree to watch for the patrol. Everyone settled carefully into their positions, and that was it, we were ready.

Half an hour later we still were. I hate waiting anyway, and that rope-thing was the worst. The first few minutes are fine, you're all excited and expect it to be happening kind of now. Then it gets boring, and your arm starts to ache from holding the rope still so as not to mess up the camouflage. Then you start to think about what could go wrong and what you'll do if it does, then the nice clear instructions you started with get fogged, and you realize you've been daydreaming and maybe missed the signal, and your hand twitches and you have to look round to see if anyone's noticed.

I couldn't even talk to the boy because he was on the other side of the road. He was lying facing me, so I winked at him, and he winked back then mimed going to sleep with boredom. I felt a little laugh bubbling up inside. Then he did an imitation of a disapproving Stefan, and I couldn't help it, I started miming back. I did Pinhead, I just hunched my shoulders and let my mouth flop open and he was giggling so much the rope started to twitch.

The voice of Stefan came out of a bush like God. He said 'Pack it in, you two, it's not a fucking game.'

That made us even worse, but then I heard Giles speaking above us, and he was saying calmly 'Here you go, boys. Two.'

I lowered myself back down into cover. My hand had stopped shaking, and I found I was calm.

There were hoofbeats coming from Dax, and when I peered upwards I could see the horses, a nice little cob in the lead, then a bloody great warhorse with ragged hocks. They were quicker than I'd thought and in a second they were past. The rope jerked in my hand and I knew the boy was ready even if I wasn't. I pulled and we brought the rope up neatly between us.

I looked ahead to the others, and saw the horses skittering and falling into confusion as the rope shot up before them. The cob was caught tight across the breast, it screamed in fright and reared, the man struggling to hold on, then he was down, and Colin and Jean-Marie were on him, Colin's axe sweeping high in the air. But the second rider was too far behind, he's seen what's happening, and he's turning, dodging Stefan, he's going to get back, and he's coming straight for us and our rope. We brace ourselves for the impact.

But he's seen it in time, he's swerving and bringing the horse right into the woods to go round us. He's one fuck of a rider, the horse is panicking but he's got control of it, he's coming round and right at me. Robert's dashing in front, pike held high like the boy did it, but the Spaniard thrusts forward, it's the big warhorse, he aims straight at Robert and rides him down. Somehow I'm moving, I have to, that's Robert on the ground, those great hooves ready to smash his skull with one blow. I've got the bridle, I've got the horse, I'm calming it, but the rider's pulling against me, his other hand's coming round, there's a pistol in it, and it's aimed at me.

Then the boy's beside me, I hear him yelling. He gets hold of the man's leg, and the rider's twisting to bring the pistol round to him, but just for half a second the armpit's exposed under the cuirass, and that's all the boy needs, his hand's round with the sword, he's using the leg to hoist himself up, and he's up and lunged, sword arm straight to the blade, and the point's sheered right in that tiny space under the armpit, right in. The rider's collapsing, and I help the boy pull him down, but he's not dead, the boy stuck him at full reach but it's not deep enough, and I finish it with my own blade in his throat. I'm so afraid of not lunging hard enough I push right through till the guard's against his chin, there's hot blood pouring over my hands, and I withdraw quickly as he crashes the last foot to the ground.

Then Stefan's there, hands bloody where they've finished off the lead man, and he grabs for the bridle to catch the loose horse, which is about to bolt with fear. Horses can't stand the smell of blood, and I begin to think I can't either. It's all over me, and it smells like the Forge, it smells like hot iron. I'm panicking, then I look up and face the boy, and he looks pale but sort of peaceful, and suddenly I feel all right too. He cleans his sword on the grass and smiles at me. We did it. We killed one. One.

Robert was trying to sit up, and we went to him at once. The horse hadn't trampled him, but he was rubbing his head and looking a bit sick. Stefan took one look, shoved me out of the way, ran his hands expertly over Robert's head and neck, then forced him to look in his eyes. After a moment he nodded and said 'That was a brave thing to do, lad. Nearly cost your life, but it was fucking brave,' and Robert, who didn't need any praise from a smelly tanner, smiled up at him, and some of the stress went out of his face.

Stefan grunted in satisfaction. 'Rest a minute and you'll be good as new. You can thank young Jacques it's not worse.'

I watched him with oddly mixed feelings. This was Stefan, I hated his guts most of the time, but I think I'd have died to win his respect, and just for that moment I had it, and it made me feel seven feet tall.

Giles' voice came suddenly from the tree. 'Infantry. Quarter of a mile.'

Stefan straightened. 'How many?'

'Six or seven,' said Giles. I could see him on his branch, leaning casually against the trunk and chewing tobacco.

Stefan sighed. 'All right, lads, wrap it up. Quick as you can. Thibault, stay where you are but keep low.'

We knew what we had to do. The boy ran to retrieve the ropes, Colin started to drag the first body into cover for spoiling, while Stefan and Jean-Marie went into the road to clear away traces of the struggle. I led the horses back into the forest out of earshot of the road, tied them to trees, then ran back to help the others.

I'd only got about halfway when I heard the shot.

Colin Lefebvre

Poor old Mercier. Clumsy sod at the best of times, and face it, this wasn't one of them.

They'd just got clear of the road when the infantry appeared round the bend. We crouched down low, quiet as mice, while they marched past. Robert still out there, but huddled low in undergrowth, they never saw a thing. Then Ravel upped and signalled, me and Mercier went to get the second corpse, and that's when it happened. Must have had a pistol in his hand, must have been lying in his palm, and Mercier moving him triggered it off.

Shocking sound at close quarters, pistol shot when you're not expecting it. We were all stuck like statues, infantry only yards away.

'Run!' yelled Ravel. '*Run!*'

It was an order, right, so I turned to leg it, but there was Mercier with his gob open, not moving at all. Ravel was out in the open, gone back to help Robert, and the infantry already dashing back round the bend. They were pike, this lot, well trained too, straight down and level with the weapons and charging at Ravel. Then suddenly there was the Seigneur himself, wasn't running away, not him, coming out the trees, heading right for the pike from behind, drawing his sword as he came.

'Run!' yelled Ravel again, shoving Robert hard for the trees, but Seigneur ignored him, charging the soldiers before they can turn and form up properly, too close for them to do a bloody thing. Thing about a pike, right, it's twelve, fourteen foot long, not much use when there's someone a foot away stabbing with a sword. Seigneur had one in the back before they even knew he was there, and whipping out at the next like it was all one big game.

Ravel turned back himself, dragging out his pistol. André fighting a second man now, but this one blocks the sword bang with his pike, others dropping the pike and snatching for their swords. Ravel fired and brought one down, but Seigneur in trouble and no mistake. Dodged the pike and wounded his second man, but had to whirl his sword to keep the others away, and one thrusting right at him. Movement from the tree line, and there's my poor old Jacques . . .

Jacques Gilbert

. . . running at them with my sword out, yelling as loud as I could, trying to make them look, anything to get their eyes off the boy. Three minutes I'd left him, just three minutes, and he was fighting the whole Spanish army.

There was a pike coming at me, but I knew how hard they were to control, I got my left hand on the shaft to thrust it away. I kept running forward, my hand scorching down the wood, the soldier was wide open and my sword coming at him, I didn't even lunge, the point slithered into him like butter. I felt the weight of his body on my blade, it was bending, I had to pull out fast before it broke. He was scream-ing, but I heard the boy's voice over it, he was shouting 'Yes, Jacques, yes!' then '*Down!*' just like it was the two of us on the back meadow, and I didn't think, I ducked without look-ing and felt a pike slice past my head. I looked round for the boy, but his blade was locked against a pike, someone else was thrusting behind him, and I couldn't help, my soldier had his sword out and at me, then the crash of a musket from the signal tree . . .

Jean-Marie Mercier

. . . and the man behind André crumpled to his knees. I reached for a second gun, while Jacques threw himself at the next soldier and Stefan grabbed the shaft of the last man's pike. I aimed at his back, but Colin was there first, spearing him savagely from behind. Poor Colin, he probably felt terrible at having set the pistol off in the first place, but it honestly wasn't his fault, it might have happened to anyone.

I turned the barrel towards the others, but André had finished his man and was turning to help Jacques, only Jacques was pulling out of his own and they were every one of them down. I lowered the gun and looked at the man I'd shot, his feet scuffling in the leaves for ages before he finally lay still.

I felt a little uncomfortable, but behind me Giles said 'Nice shot, soldier,' and when I turned round he gave me the nicest smile.

Stefan picked up his pistol, panting slightly, and glared round at us as if we were the enemy. I could hear the faint sound of hoofbeats approaching in the distance.

'*Now* will you fucking run?' he said.

Jacques Gilbert

We left the others at the first foresters' road, and ran all the way home. We were so out of breath when we hurtled back into the barn we couldn't do anything but bend double and pant, grinning at each other like a couple of idiots.

We'd fought side by side and I hadn't let him down. Between us our unit had killed nine, and it was the most of anyone, the best ever. The boy was elated, he kept pacing up and down thrashing his sword about, I couldn't even get him to sit down. In the end I just squashed him on to a hay bale and fetched a jug of wine from the cottage, but when he helped himself he'd got hands like Jacob Pasle, the cup was going *dink-dink-dink* against the jug as he poured. He gulped it back in one go, wiped his mouth with his sleeve, put down the cup and let out his breath in a long sigh. He was happy.

So was I. I'd fought before, of course, but then I'd been defending myself, this time it had been the Spaniards having to fight for their lives, it had been their turn to be frightened. I thought César would have enjoyed that, and Mme Panthon and all of them at the Manor, and Robert's sister and all of them since.

I said 'I bet your father's proud of us now.'

There was a long silence, then the boy said 'Mmm.' He

was still lying back, but I thought the light had sort of faded off his face.

I wondered if it was wrong to remind him of his father. 'At least we're hitting back, aren't we? It's like putting things right.'

He was quiet again, and I wondered if he'd heard me. He'd do that sometimes, just go off in his head and not come back till I stuck myself right in front of him.

But he'd heard me this time. After a moment he said 'Doesn't make up for everything, though, does it?' then rolled on his side to face the wall.

Seven

Anne du Pré

Extract from her diary, dated 10 February 1637

The soldiers downstairs are angry, we can hear their raised voices through the floor. I think really they are frightened, and I am glad of it.

I am still sorry for Don Miguel, who truly does seem a kind man. He visited today to enquire after our well-being, and I would have liked to tell him about the food, but Colette says we are at the mercy of the men here and must not risk upsetting them. She may be right. This morning the Slug came on duty still in his outdoor clothes, and he was wearing that beautiful pleated brown coat Josef was so proud of. Florian says it proves nothing, Josef perhaps ran in only his nightshirt, but I cannot believe he would have left that coat behind. There is also a tear in the back, I saw the line of lumped stitching where a hole must have been, and Josef would never have been so careless. Dear Josef, who would not so much as kill a mouse in the kitchen that day, and told Françoise only to let him know when it was gone. I think Colette is right and these men are capable of anything.

However, Don Miguel was as kind as ever, and even brought with him a chess set so that he and Florian might play. It is so good of him to do that. My poor brother, I sometimes worry about the way his mind is wandering, but he can still be sharp at chess, his face takes on quite the old look and for an hour or so he is Florian again. Don Miguel seemed quite puzzled how to beat him when that servant of his arrived with the news.

He is very jolly and friendly, the servant called Carlos, but he was not in the best of moods tonight. He spoke in Spanish, of course, with no idea that I understood him, but he said there had been eight of their men killed and the ninth likely to die from wounds within the night. He said the man claimed his assailant had been a very young man with long black hair who was exceptionally skilful with a sword, and Don Miguel sat up so abruptly he almost upset the chess board. He said 'André de Roland, Carlos, what did I tell you?'

They said no more in front of us, Don Miguel conceded the game and left, but it was enough for me, it is still enough now. All this time Colette has said André must have escaped to Paris and cares nothing for us, but I now know for certain that is not true. He is out there. Somewhere outside my window he is out there and fighting back.

Carlos Corvacho

From his interviews with the Abbé Fleuriot, 1669

Oh no, Señor, call me Carlos, I'm more than happy with that. My Capitán used to call me Carlos. That's the Don Miguel d'Estrada as was, Señor, a most amiable gentleman. I'd only been an ordinary corselete in his company, but he took to me from the first, and when his personal servant died at the Dax barricades I was the natural choice to take his place.

Oh bless you, no, I'm quite comfortable in French. Most men in the Army of Flanders pick up a little, but it was that much easier for me, you understand, my poor mother being half French herself. Tragic it seemed to me, two Catholic countries fighting each other instead of standing together against the heretics. Tragic.

Still, it's all behind us now, isn't it, Señor, and very nice to be back at Ancre. Got it all back looking beautiful, haven't they? Just the way it was. Not that I saw much of it myself, you understand, I was mainly outside the Manor that night, hardly went in at all, but the men that did – well, they talked, Señor, it's only natural.

But it's not old Carlos you want to know about, now is it, Señor? My gentleman now, oh he was a one, people stepped out of his way on the streets of Madrid. The 'Lacemaker' they used to call him, did you know? He'd have been sixteen then, still only a young abanderado in our company, which is what I think you call an 'enseigne', is that right, Señor? It was only his second duel, but his opponent was afraid of his reputation, and turned up in the biggest shirt you ever saw, sleeves like young sails, or so they say, hoping my gentleman would be deceived into missing his body altogether. He wasn't fooled, Señor, not our Don Miguel, but attacked the shirt as if he were, reducing it to ribbons till it resembled nothing so much as fine Venetian lace. 'Ah!' says my gentleman. 'So there is a body under all this finery. Let us see if there's a heart as well.' He then proved there was by stabbing the silly fellow right through it. Oh, he'd wonderful wit, my Capitán.

But he was a kind man underneath. There were men in our company complained he wasn't hard enough, there ought to be more reprisals, but that wasn't my Capitán's way, he used to say it was a poor lord who murdered his own servants. You need to understand, Señor, this occupation business didn't come natural to him. He was a soldier, the very best, he ought to have been back campaigning, not stuck in this dunghill with a pack of rebellious peasants. But that's the way it goes with politics, isn't it, Señor? There'd been a little trouble over his killing a friend of the Conde-Duque's in a duel, so here we were stuck, and nothing to be done but make the best of it until a proper governor could be found to take over.

But we had to tame the natives first, and that didn't look like happening just yet that winter. We'd lost a few men before, nothing too serious, but then nine men down in this single day and things started to look different. There was this one fellow managed to speak to the surgeon before he died, and we didn't like what he said at all. Oh, you know about that, Señor? Now, you'll forgive my asking how?

No, no, not in the least, I'm very happy for the Señor to keep his secrets, I've nothing to hide. Yes, it's true, my Capitán thought one of the attackers might be de Roland. Oh, we knew about him, the padre told us he existed, the hostages gave us his description, we knew he was about somewhere. He wasn't in Dax, any nobleman would have stood out like a blister in a place this primitive, but he might be hiding in the woods, seeing as they stretched for miles and no hope of searching them without a full *tercio* with nothing else to do for months. We weren't that bothered at first, he was only a lad and not much harm in that, but now we started to wonder if letting him escape wasn't the worst mistake we'd made yet. As my Capitán said, occupied villages generally come to heel fast enough, but if there's a leader left over from the old regime, who knows what kind of resistance they might stir up?

Poor de Castilla was in real trouble now. Oh, I'm sorry,

Señor, I'm forgetting you don't know about him. Not that he was important, not in the least, he was only the abanderado in the raid on the Manor. My Capitán had given orders most particular the family wasn't to be harmed in any way, seeing they're of real value as hostages, and first de Castilla lets the lady escape by suiciding herself, and next we find out about this child he swears blind he's never seen at all. My Capitán was a little suspicious of his story, felt something about it didn't seem right, but it was no more than truth, Señor, I can testify to that myself. None of our men so much as broke into their apartments, and as for the child, there wasn't one of us saw him, not one. Why do you look at me like that, Señor? We were never in those rooms at all, not until it was over. There's no one alive says different, is there?

No, my Capitán had no reason to doubt it, only that he never much cared for de Castilla. Very old family there, father at Breda, but poor as peasants and he'd a very unfortunate manner. He liked to swagger round the place, bully the men to show what a fine dog he was, you know the type I mean. He was forever picking on the *nuevo rico*, I don't know your word for it, Señor, the rich officers with no breeding. My gentleman was already looking for an excuse to transfer him to Verdâme.

Not that it mattered now, Señor, bless me, we don't want to waste your time on *him*. What mattered was young de Roland was loose in the Saillie, and from the look of it going to turn out more trouble than we'd ever dreamed. My Capitán sent his description round again, but more than that we couldn't do.

'For the moment,' said my Capitán, and to my surprise I saw he was smiling. 'You've never fenced, have you, Carlos? Let them think we know nothing. Let them get confident. Sooner or later they'll give us the opening we need.'

I got pissed that night.

I didn't mean to, I only went into Dax to check Colin and Robert got home all right, but they were both celebrating in the Corbeaux and of course I had to join them. Everyone there guessed I was involved because they all knew André had to be, so people kept buying me cider and treating me like some kind of hero.

After a while I began to feel like one. When it got late I went across to see Simone, and when I left I felt better than a hero, because now I was a man, I was really a man at last. The sky felt huge, but so did I, I felt like I was part of everything, instead of just an ant crawling over the surface.

Of course I was just drunk, I know that now. I remember finding myself sitting by the side of the road giggling at nothing, and knew I must have fallen over. I was still staggering when I finally reached the cobbles in front of my cottage, shoved the door open and stepped inside.

I hadn't realized how late it was. The candles were on their last inch, the fire was low, and there wasn't any steam coming out of the pot. My parents were still at the table with Little Pierre, but Mother looked weary and slumped, and when she turned her face towards the door it felt like it cost her a lot of effort. Then she smiled and said 'Hello, my darling.'

Father grinned at me, his face glistening in the firelight. 'Sweet Jesus in Heaven, look at the state of it.'

I moved carefully to a chair, while Mother got me some soup. I said 'Has André had his?'

Father's face clouded. His eyes went like stones when you take them out of the stream and they stop being pretty, they just go on being stones. 'Been and gone.'

'Was he worried about me?'

Father gave an odd little grunt. 'Not him. Your Mother's been worried sick, but I don't suppose that bothers you, does it, boy?'

Mother said 'It's all right, darling, André said you'd had a hard day, he quite understood.' She put a bowl of tepid soup in front of me, but there was hare in it and the fatty smell made me feel sick. I reached for the wine instead.

'What kind of hard day would that be exactly?' asked Father, watching me pour.

I said 'Hard,' and drank the wine.

Little Pierre laughed. 'Playing with your swords again? I've seen you in the back meadow, it's just games.'

I thought of the games we'd played this afternoon. I said 'You don't know anything, just shut up, you don't know.'

'I do,' said Little Pierre. 'I know real men went out today to fight for Dax. While you were playing at soldiers, they went and killed a dozen Spaniards stone dead.'

The room seemed to be going further away. There was just this bowl of soup in front of me making me want to throw up. I heard my own voice saying 'It wasn't a dozen, it was nine. And we didn't mean it like that, it just happened.'

Everything went very quiet. I wondered if I'd actually spoken or if it was just in my head, but when I looked up they were all staring at me and I knew I had.

'You're lying,' said Little Pierre, but he didn't really think so, his eyes were wide.

'I'm not.' I dug out my handkerchief and slammed it on the table. The blood was dry now, but it was still thick and sticky where I'd wiped my hands. 'Me and André fought today, we fought with our swords side by side.'

Mother whispered 'Jacques . . .' but couldn't get any further.

Father threw back his head and gave this great, loud laugh that hurt my head. 'You and André? I might have known.'

'We're soldiers,' I said stupidly. 'I can use a sword and everything.'

'And what does a stable boy like you want with a sword?'

'I'm not a stable boy, I'm a soldier. I'd have been going in the army this year anyway. This is like training for that. André and me, we'll be going in together.'

'You won't need a sword then, boy,' said Father. 'A pike or musket will be good enough for you.'

'It won't, I'll be in the cavalry with André. I'm his aide, aren't I?'

'When the Occupation's over?' His voice was almost kind. 'When he's back living in the Manor or staying with the Comtesse in Paris? Still be his aide then, will you?'

The room felt too hot suddenly, it was starting to move round and round, I put my head down in my lap. Mother sat beside me, stroking my hand and making anxious murmuring noises.

'Don't fuss, Nell,' said Father's voice. 'He's pissed, that's all.'

'He's upset,' said Mother.

'He's pissed.' I heard the scrape of his chair as he stood. 'Aide to the Chevalier de Roland, drunk as a stablehand.'

Little Pierre laughed.

I saw Mother's hand take my cup and pour the wine back in the jug. The material of her dress looked smooth and clean, I thought it would be nice and cool to lay my head against, and behind it was my Mother's softness and comfort and that smell that was like roses. I reached for her, and she leant forward to stroke my hair.

'And why not, Pierre?' she said. Her voice sounded louder,

maybe because I was hearing it through her chest. 'Who says my son can't be a gentleman?'

'Oh, don't be a fool.' Father's voice was sort of amused, but there was something hard in it I didn't like at all. I dragged my head away from Mother and tried to look at him, but he was only pouring more wine.

'It's not foolish,' said Mother. 'André's taken such a fancy to him, you know he has. He might have him educated. With a little help, why couldn't Jacques . . . ?' Her voice was trailing away even as she said it.

Father gave a soft little laugh. 'Not kind, Hélène. Not kind to get his hopes up. The poor lad's beginning to forget who he is.' He picked up the cup and brought it over to me. 'Here you go, boy. A little more of this, and you'll start to remember.'

Mother made an infuriated noise and smacked the cup out of his hand. The pewter crashed and rolled noisily on the stone, and the wine slooshed out in a great red puddle on the floor. Father looked expressionlessly at it, then cracked Mother hard against the face, making her stumble backwards against my chair. I closed my eyes.

'Clean it up,' said Father. 'It'll stain.'

I'd got to get out. I pressed my hands on the table and managed to clamber to my feet. Father was telling Little Pierre to go to bed, and I knew it was only just starting.

'Don't forget your trophy,' said Father.

He nodded towards the handkerchief. It looked disgusting and horrible, I picked it up and threw it on the fire. The smell as it burnt was filthy, and I only just made it out the door before I was sick.

I crouched on the cobbles, sucking in deep breaths of night air. I'd walked over this yard feeling happy and excited, a man and a hero, and now I was nothing. I'd sicked up what felt like my whole guts, but there was still this cold weight somewhere like undigested porridge, something sad and aching inside my chest. I forced myself up and staggered back to the barn.

The boy was already asleep. One hand was sticking out of the blanket, and I saw how brown and rough it was now, the nails nearly as scuffed and broken as mine. But I knew it didn't mean anything, it was only on the surface. The ache inside me grew heavier as I started to understand just how very stupid I'd been.

It was still there in the morning, along with the most appalling headache. I rolled myself up in my blanket and didn't even put my head out when André got up for his fencing exercises. I just wanted to be dead.

When I woke again he was back. He was pacing up and down making the boards creak, and as soon as he saw me moving he was right there.

'Are you ready for breakfast?'

'I'm not hungry.'

'Neither am I.'

I peeled my eyelids open to look at him. He was wearing his sword, and that puzzled me. He'd never done that in daylight, it was too risky. I wondered what had changed.

He said 'The fire wasn't lit when I went out. I want to make sure everything's all right.'

I got myself up fast. I knew exactly what would have happened, and didn't want him charging in and making it worse. Father had been very careful about that kind of thing since André came, so I hoped he had this time too.

But he hadn't. Mother was nowhere to be seen, it was Father salvaging the fire, and only Little Pierre at the table, eating his bread in silence. Father looked up and gave a little grin when he saw how ill I was, but he winced when I shut the door so I knew he wasn't much better himself.

The boy didn't seem to notice, he only wanted to know about Mother. I kept my head down while Father said she was just tired and wanted to be left alone, but when we heard a noise from the back yard André was out and gone before I could stop him.

I went straight after him but of course I was too late. He'd found Mother at the well, he'd seen the black eye and bruises and was already asking what happened, who did it? I could see he was furious, his face was white with it.

Then Father was standing in the doorway looking at us, and we all went quiet. André faced him with his chin up and I knew he knew.

'Who did this?'

'It was an accident,' pleaded Mother.

'Who did this?' the boy asked Father, and his hands were bunching into fists, though he must have known my Father could break him in two. 'What kind of coward would do a thing like this?'

Father's face twisted and he made a sudden move forward. Mother cried out, but André just took one step back on his left foot and drew his sword.

Father stopped. The sword wasn't pointed at him, it was just there, but the boy's hand kept it totally steady. Then slowly Father smiled. He leant against the doorway, and took a bite out of the hunk of bread in his hand.

'Sieur,' he said, and at the sound of his tone the boy brought the sword up into the *en garde*. 'This is your house and your property, I and my family owe you our duty. But there is one thing you cannot do, and that is to interfere between husband and wife. That, Sieur, is only for the good God.'

He chewed his bread slowly, watching André with bright, malicious eyes. He was like a bull in his own territory, and the boy had blundered into the wrong field.

André knew it, and after a moment he sheathed his sword. Then he lifted his head and said 'I acknowledge your right, Monsieur. What I question is your decency.'

He practically spat the word, but Father only smiled again.

'I am required to look after your horses, Sieur. I am not required to be decent.'

The boy stared, wrong-footed and weaponless. He turned suddenly to me, the question glaring out of his face, but I couldn't do anything, I just gave a sort of shrug. There was a moment's awful silence, then he slammed his way past me and out of the yard. Father looked after him with satisfaction.

'Firmer hand on those reins, boy,' he said, just like when I was breaking Tempête. 'That's all he needs. You'll see.'

He tossed his last piece of bread in the air, caught it neatly in his mouth, grinned at me and strolled inside, whistling '*La Pernette*' as he went. I looked wretchedly at Mother, but she only smoothed her hair with shaking hands and went in to Blanche, who was whimpering somewhere indoors. I didn't follow them, I didn't want breakfast, I just wanted to be on my own. That horrible gnawing feeling was back from yesterday and it was getting worse.

I trailed round to the front, thinking I'd just stay out of the way till it was time to go to the Hermitage, but as I came round the corner I saw André standing in the yard in front of me. He was head down and scowling with his hands thrust hard in his pockets, and as I stopped he gave a savage kick at the barn doors, making them bang and rattle. After a second he did it again. Then he lifted his head and saw me.

I've never felt such contempt from anybody, not ever. It sort of stabbed into me, it made me shrivel inside, right where the bad feeling was. I ducked my head to get away from it, I couldn't bear to look. I just wanted him to say what he'd got to say and get it over.

But there was nothing, only silence, then the scrape of his boots on the cobbles, and the awful finality of his footsteps as he turned and walked away.

Stefan Ravel

I knew we were in for trouble right away. He came stamping through the door with Jacques creeping behind him like a dog that's been whipped.

I didn't let it deter me. Marcel and I both knew it was decision time for the young Sieur of Dax, even if we disagreed on the right way about it. Me, I'd have had him flogged like any man in the real army, but Marcel wouldn't countenance such a thing for a gentleman. He said persuasively 'There's no need, Stefan, there's really not. Words will hurt André more than a whip, you won't need anything more.' So I sent the rest of the unit outside for sword-drill, dispatched the sidekick on to the roof as look-out, and took the master aside for the bollocking he so thoroughly deserved.

I gave it to him straight. I pointed out he'd disobeyed an order in the face of the enemy, and that was a hanging offence.

I'm rather good at insolence, Abbé, but I had nothing on André de Roland. He said 'We beat them, didn't we?'

'I told you to run.'

He sniffed. 'I don't run from Spaniards.'

'You do when I order it. You run like bloody hell.'

He shook his head. 'You don't understand. It's not something I can do.'

You'll note it was something scum like myself could do with ease.

I said patiently 'I don't need to understand you, André, this is the fucking army. You gave your word to obey orders, and the first time in action you broke it. You're young, and I'll allow you one mistake. But no more, ever. From now on you're in the army on my terms, or you're not in it at all. Understand?'

He scowled as if he'd like to have had me taken out and flogged, but I went on staring until he finally lowered his head.

'All right,' I said. 'Now pick up a foil and get out there with the others.'

He did it, but he slapped his sword against his boot as he went through the door, and I rather sensed I wasn't finished with him yet.

Jean-Marie Mercier

André did seem to be rather angry that day. He was really quite terrifying in the bouts, and even when he was sitting out he produced that little ball he used to carry about with him, and sat kneading and squeezing it so hard I was afraid it might burst.

Stefan continually glanced round at him, but sword-drill was one activity when it was simply impossible to pick on André because he was so much better than anyone else. I think perhaps that's why Stefan ended the bouting and explained the weak points in a soldier's armour instead. He made a lot of the fact the officers were better protected than the men, and I was quite sure it was all directed at André. André didn't say a word.

When it came to the demonstration we naturally expected Stefan would choose André, but he didn't, he chose me. I was horrified, because I'm honestly not very good with swordplay, and I thought Stefan knew that. I did try, I tried my very best, but really I think I was quite dismal.

Colin Lefebvre

Never saw such a shambles. Ravel started laughing at him, goading him to try harder, and poor Mercier going redder in the face all the while. Seigneur wasn't happy, I could see. Perched on this fallen tree, sword swinging dangerously, swish-swish in the long grass, looked like trouble to me.

Mercier begged Ravel to let him stop. He said 'I'm no good at this, you know I'm not. Couldn't one of the others try?'

Ravel swore at him something shocking. Mercier never liked that, never, always very careful in his own speech, and now Ravel calling him names he'd maybe never even heard. Looked for all the world as if he was going to cry.

Ravel thought so too. He said in disgust 'For Christ's sake, if you can't be a soldier, at least try to be a man.'

Then *bang*, there was the Seigneur suddenly on his feet. Didn't yell, didn't stamp, just walked up to Ravel and said 'No.'

Stefan Ravel

I took one look at him and knew he'd snapped. A pity, after all he'd taken on his own account, but here he was throwing it away for that wretched little Mercier.

I told him to shut up and sit down.

'Not until you apologize to Jean-Marie.'

Poor Mercier was in a real panic now. He said 'It doesn't matter, it doesn't matter,' but it was a little late for that.

I told André I was giving him an order.

He said 'Don't you try to hide behind that, Ravel, that's bloody cowardly.'

That's when it stopped being professional. I'd had a bellyful of his arrogance already that day, and I'm afraid I lost my temper. I told him he was pretty cowardly himself, insulting people when his position kept him safe from retaliation.

He looked me right in the eye. He said he had no desire to hide from anything, he was happy to abide by the consequences of his actions. He stood there looking noble and heroic, his birthright shimmering round him like some kind of halo.

'Good,' I said, and knocked him down.

There was a shocked silence, then oh Jesus and Mary, all chaos broke loose. There was a crash and clatter from the Hermitage roof, and I thought 'Hullo, here comes the bodyguard.' Lefebvre protested, Thibault sprang to his feet, and Mercier actually tried to pull me back. I batted him away with one hand, but then André yelled 'Leave it, Jean-Marie!' and I turned and saw he was getting up.

All credit to him, he was getting himself up, and looking fucking determined about it too. He straightened up, leant against a tree, and began to push up his sleeves. Mercier stood back obediently, but looking confused and frightened, which I could rather understand. It was obvious to us all that André was going to fight.

It was quite ridiculous really, but I'm an obliging man, Abbé, and when someone asks for something that desperately I don't have the heart to refuse. So I shoved up my own sleeves and prepared to give him another lesson.

Jacques Gilbert

I was down off that roof so fast I hurt my ankle landing. I didn't give a stuff about guard duty, I knew the relief would be in soon anyway, I just had to get to the boy and nothing else mattered.

I ran up to them and grabbed hold of Stefan's arm, but André stuck his hand out and said fiercely 'Stay out of it, Jacques.'

Stefan jerked his sleeve out of my hand without even looking at me. André turned again to face him, he turned back to Stefan and shut me out.

All I could see was his back, all mud and grass on it where that bastard had knocked him down. I'd come to help him, it was my job to help him, but he just said 'Stay out of it,' and turned his back.

Stefan Ravel

The kid came at me with his fists up, but it was sadly amateur, and I had difficulty keeping my face suitably grave. He aimed a punch at my guts, which I thought was probably all he could reach, so I went to block him, but next second he'd swung up and got me clean on the jaw, and God help me if I didn't nearly go down with it too.

My own fault, Abbé, I should have remembered he was a swordsman. He'd feinted like a fencer, and caught me out like a novice. If he'd followed through right away he could have had me on my back, but no, he was waiting like a gentleman for me to get my balance before he had another go. So I weaved about as if I was still groggy, then gave him a quick jab in the belly to wind him, followed up with a two-hander on the back of the neck, and down he went flat on the grass.

Jacques screamed at me to stop. He was red in the face with rage.

I said 'Relax, kid, it's finished anyway.'

'No, it bloody isn't,' said André, and I saw he'd got up again.

I really didn't want to hit him any more. I don't know what kind of man you think I am, Abbé, but it seemed to me he'd been hurt quite enough to make the point.

I said 'Yes it is, kid. You're beaten, that's all.'

He was still coming towards me, and I was a little wary, because I knew he was stronger than he looked. That last one certainly ought to have kept him down.

He said 'How can I be beaten if I don't give in?'

I said sadly 'Like this,' and dropped him with a neat little crack to the side of the head. For the first time he let out a yelp and I knew he was really hurt.

At once Jacques came tearing at me. Mercier was one thing, Jacques quite another, he was a powerful lad and boiling with outrage because I was hurting his pet. I sidestepped and he only grazed me, so I reached for him while he was off balance, but then it was André yelling 'No!' and the shock made us both stop and look.

He was struggling to his feet, which ought to have been impossible. His mouth and ear were bleeding, one eye was swollen, but he was using the tree to haul himself up, and he was only looking at Jacques, no one else.

He said 'Please, Jacques, no.'

They were staring at each other. I wanted to say 'Excuse me, this is my fight actually,' but I doubt they'd have even heard. Then Jacques turned away looking baffled, and

148

the kid managed to stand himself straight and face me.

I said 'That's enough now.'

'It's not,' he said, and came at me again.

I wouldn't hit him, I wrestled him instead, but he wriggled his arm away and whacked out at my nose, a good hard punch which actually rather hurt, so I'm afraid I swore at him and pushed him back down.

And again he got up.

That's when I knew I was fucked. I didn't dare try to knock him out, I could break his neck without even thinking about it, but the bugger was quite prepared to go on till I killed him.

I got him by the elbows and held him firm.

'Enough,' I said. 'I'm not going to fight you any more.'

He tried to headbutt me, and I only just dodged in time. He fought like a *gamin*, that one, I'm only surprised he didn't bite. I said 'Pack it in, will you?'

'All right,' he said breathlessly. 'As long as you apologize to Jean-Marie.'

For a second I wanted to knock him right back down again and fuck the consequences, but there was something about him, something about the glint in his eyes, and all I know is suddenly I was laughing.

'All right,' I said. 'If it means that much to you.'

I went over to poor Mercier, who'd gone the colour of pork fat, gave him my best gentleman's bow, and told him I was sorry, which really perhaps I was. André put me in a temper, and I oughtn't to have taken it out on harmless little Mercier. Then I returned virtuously to André and said 'Satisfied?'

He grinned at me and nodded, but he was looking a touch wobbly for all that.

'Good,' I said. 'Now we'll talk about the army.'

He looked wary again. 'The army?'

'Forgotten that, hadn't you?' I said. 'I ought to throw you out this minute'.

'I know,' he said. Green, green innocent eyes, like a meadow with fucking lambs frisking over it. 'But you won't.'

'No,' I said. 'I won't.'

He looked right at me, as if he could really see me. Then he raised his voice and said 'I was wrong to call you a coward. I think I was wrong about a lot of things. I'm sorry.' He held out his hand.

Well, well. The *amende honorable*, and not forced at that. I took his hand, Abbé, I don't see anything hypocritical in that, and I didn't crush it either, we'd got a little beyond that now. But he stumbled as I released him, so I whipped my arm under his elbow to support him, and looked down at the bloody mess I'd made of his face.

'Why?' I said, as softly as I could. 'Why, you silly bugger? For the son of a Verdâme merchant?'

He was still dazed. He half shook his head, then said simply 'Someone who couldn't hit back.'

Tragic, really. I'd found his weakness now all right, and it was about as bad as it could be for a soldier. Oh, I may have made a mess of his body, Abbé, but someone else had done a first-class job on his mind.

Eight

Jacques Gilbert

I took him home.

Mother was alone in the cottage so I brought him inside. She stared in horror, then ran and wrapped herself round him so I couldn't see her face. 'Oh, André, it wasn't . . . ?'

He lifted his head quickly from her shoulder and said 'No, no, it was an accident.'

That seemed to frighten her even more, but he couldn't say anything else without mentioning Stefan, because he just couldn't lie, the boy, he never could. So I lied instead, and said we'd had an accident with the horses. My parents knew we'd got them hidden away somewhere, so I said the door blew shut with the boy inside, that Tonnerre started kicking, and I only just got him out in time.

Mother's face calmed a little, but she still hugged the boy close and said 'Oh, my darling,' and he let her. Then she started rocking him against her, and her face was like she was dreaming or something, and she started humming '*En passant par la Lorraine*'. Everyone at Ancre knew that one, it was a favourite of the old Seigneur's. Mother used to sing it to André when he was tiny, and sometimes she'd sway his little feet along to the '*Oh, oh, oh, avec mes sabots*' bits, and he loved it. I wondered if the boy remembered too. He rested his head comfortably against her chest and closed his eyes.

Then Father came in.

The boy jerked away at once to face him, but Father took

one look and was immediately all concern, so I understood we were going to pretend the morning had never happened. I told him the story about Tonnerre, and he lectured me on being careless with horses, but I thought it was somehow giving him pleasure to see the boy all battered, and when he reached out to his face to get a better look, André pulled away without a word. I felt my sad, hollow feeling coming back like a memory.

Mother got the boy cleaned up and I took him back to the barn, but the feeling just came along with me like it was there to stay. I wondered if fencing would help, but the boy wasn't up to it, he was still wobbly and sick. I wondered if I ought to read to him, but I looked at all those books about honourable people doing honourable things and just couldn't face it and hoped he wouldn't ask. He dozed off after a while, so I went back to the cottage because I needed a drink.

Father was already having one, and as the jug was full I knew it must be at least the second. That usually meant trouble, but when I drained the first cup Father poured me another, and when I filled his pipe he took it from me with a hand that was somehow gentle, and said 'Thank you, lad.' There was something in his face I hadn't seen for years.

I drank the wine and watched him sort of furtively, but I wasn't imagining it. He even passed me the tinder box for his pipe like he used to, and nodded approvingly when I sparked it right first time. He started to whistle '*Bransle des Chevaux*' half under his breath, and I found myself remembering things that went back to when I was little. Sometimes when there was no one around we'd play horses, he'd sit me on his shoulders and run all the way down the bridle path, then put me down and walk into the cottage all sedately like we'd never been running at all. Mother used to look at him suspiciously, and he'd smile and look innocent, but he'd be whistling '*Bransle des Chevaux*' all the while, and sometimes when I caught his eye he'd wink. I looked at him now and the picture was so clear I half expected him to wink again.

He reached out a finger and pressed the tip of my nose. 'Big eyes,' he said, and smiled. Something warm flooded over me inside. The dull aching feeling sort of went and hid in a corner so I could forget it was there.

Mother sat watching us, looking nervously happy. Father poured her some wine, and she actually had a sip and smiled as if she liked it.

'That's right,' Father said encouragingly. 'Drink it up. Let's celebrate getting your favourite son back. No more dreaming of being a gentleman now, is there, Jacques?'

Another picture came up to shut out the ones of me and Father, a picture of André's face as he'd looked that morning by the barn door. I screwed up my eyes to get rid of it and said 'No.'

Mother gave a high-pitched little 'oh' of disappointment. 'But why, darling?' she said. 'You haven't fallen out with André? You seemed all right this afternoon.'

Father gave a short bark of laughter. 'Of course they did, nobility will put a face on anything. You think he wants it known he took a beating from the son of his groom?'

My cup sort of jumped in my hands, it slopped wine all over the table. Mother stared at me, then back at Father.

'But that was the horse,' she said reasonably. 'Jacques told us. It was the horse.'

'Horse!' snorted Father. He took a gulp of wine and looked at her impatiently. 'Oh, for heaven's sake, if Tonnerre had kicked him that hard, he'd be dead.'

I said 'I didn't, it wasn't me, I didn't touch him,' but Father stopped me.

'Of course you didn't. But next time you tell that story, have the sense to keep your hand out of sight.'

I looked down and saw my knuckles were grazed where I'd punched the side of Stefan's jaw. I opened my mouth to explain, then I met Father's eyes and he just nodded.

'It's all right, boy. He drew on your father, didn't he?'

Mother was aghast. 'You didn't, Jacques? How could you, that little boy?'

Father said patiently 'He's not a little boy, he's thirteen and he's nobility. In another year it won't just be swords, it'll be women as well.'

I drink more wine. It's sort of numbing that ache inside, I can understand why Father likes it so much.

'Don't talk like that,' says Mother. 'Nobility are people, same as us.'

'Oh, maybe in the beginning, you can turn a child into anything if you get the bringing up of it. Look at our Jacques here, he's his father's son, isn't he?'

Mother looks at me throwing back the wine and turns away quickly. I close my eyes and drink and try to bring back the nice pictures I'd had in my head, only now they won't come.

'But André's too old for that,' Father says. 'We'll need to be careful from now on. He won't talk, but he'll take it out of us if he can.'

'Of course he won't,' says Mother, and her voice sounds hard and angry. 'As if André would ever do anything to harm Jacques. Look at everything he's done for us.'

'Oh, for Christ's sake,' says Father, and his good mood's gone out like a snuffed candle. 'The brat's never done anything that didn't suit himself. People like us, we're nothing to him, we're less than one of his horses.'

The pictures are back, only this time they're different. The boy this morning, saying 'I'd like to make sure everything's all right.' The boy laughing and clapping at Georges with his stupid toadstool in the Hermitage. The boy trying to put his cloak round Jean-Marie. We weren't nothing to André. We weren't.

'I'm sorry, I won't have it,' says Mother, and I have to come out of my head and look at her. This is my Mother, who always needs a man to tell her what to do, but here she is standing up to Father all by herself. 'I know you're annoyed about this morning, but André was only trying to protect me.'

Father says quietly 'It's not his business to tell me how I can treat my own wife.'

'I was his nurse,' says Mother. 'And this is his house, isn't it? We work for him.'

'Thank you for reminding us of that,' says Father, and walks over to where she's sitting. I want to scream he's getting dangerous, but then I look at her face and see she knows. She knows, but she's fighting him anyway.

The boy running back into the Manor to fight a hundred soldiers by himself. The boy fighting Stefan when he knows he hasn't a chance. The ache inside me is almost unbearable now and I drink more wine to deaden it.

'Taking sides against your own family, Nell?' says Father, and starts playing gently with her hair.

'It's not a case of taking sides,' says Mother, trying to move her head away. 'It's about what's right.'

But it is, it's all about sides. Me talking to the boy about honour and him thinking I understand. Me sitting here now, getting credit for having beaten him. Me sitting back while Father bullies my Mother right in front of me, like he knows I won't do anything because I never do.

'What's right is standing by your husband,' says Father.

He winds her hair round his knuckles, drawing her closer.

Me standing by and watching while a big man beats the shit out of a boy I'm meant to be looking after.

'It's natural for me to be fond of André,' pleads Mother. 'I nursed him for five years.'

'Yes, you did, didn't you? With my little Pierre back here crying for his mother, you were always over at the Manor with the Seigneur's brat.'

Me sitting in the boy's room while Mother sings softly, '*Rencontrai trois capitaines, avec mes sabots, dondaine, oh, oh, oh . . .*'

She says 'We needed the money.'

'You didn't do it for the money. You don't now. What is it, Nell? Is he getting old enough to be interesting?'

'That's disgusting.' Mother wrenches her head away and stands up.

'I agree.' He's blocking her way to the bedroom. 'It's filthy. Fawning over another man's child under my roof. How do you think that makes me feel?'

She turns wearily to face him, pushing her hair out of her eyes. 'It should make you ashamed.'

Shame. I know what that is now all right. Shame.

'No, you don't give me that,' he says, and seizes her by the arm. 'You to talk about shame?'

She's crying out, he's dragging her towards him, and suddenly it's easy and there aren't any choices to make at all, I realize I've already made them.

I stand up and say 'Stop it.'

It doesn't come out deep and manly, it's actually a bit squeaky, but it makes my Father look round all the same, and his expression is so surprised it's almost funny. Then it clouds over and isn't funny at all.

'Shut your bastard mouth and get out.'

Mother cries out in protest, then it's a sudden sob of pain because he's twisting her wrist. I can't take it, I'm yelling 'Stop it, I won't let you!'

He really does laugh at that, a great loud rumbling laugh from his chest. Then he goes quiet and looks at me with something like pity. 'Stick to hitting children, boy. It's all you're good for.'

'I didn't,' I say, and the relief is wonderful. 'I never touched him. Why would I?'

'Why?' says Father, and there's no pity about him now, his eyes look almost hot. 'Do you really want to know?'

'Pierre!' says Mother desperately. She pushes in front of him, but he shoves her aside, hand up to smack her, then I'm moving, I've caught his arm, and pulled him right round to face me. He shakes free and his fist's coming up, so I hit him in the face, and I've knocked him down.

I've hit my own Father.

Everything goes silent as he stands up. He wipes his mouth deliberately with the back of his hand, but never takes his eyes off my face.

'You poor, stupid bastard,' he says.

Then he's on me. I try to defend myself, but he's just hammering into me and I can't seem to stop him. I'm young, I'm strong and fit, but he's bigger and heavier, and it's some-how hard to hit him, it's hard to see my Father's body and drive my fist right into it. And I'm not André, I'm not this unbeatable force, and when he's got me down I bloody stay down, and now he's kicking me, his boot in my belly, my ribs, my thigh, and Mother's screaming at him, then Blanche starts crying and I can hear Little Pierre too, and finally he stops, and everything's going quiet and dark.

Mother's footsteps, her feet in front of me, and her voice, very low, 'Please, Pierre.' Father's soft laugh. 'Look at him,

Nell,' his voice says. 'And that other one in the barn. Not very impressive, is it? Why can't you stick to your own kind?'

There's a pause, heavy footsteps, and he's gone.

Then Mother's cradling my head and saying I mustn't listen, he doesn't mean it, and it's all her fault, but I can't bear it, I push her away. My body hurts all over and I want to be on my own.

But I can't be, of course, not these days. I stagger out on to the cobbles, and there's the boy pelting towards me, barefoot but with his sword in his hand. He stops short then runs to me in horror. I shove him away and say I'm all right, leave me alone. He looks past me at the house, and his face goes very cold, and his grip tightens on his sword, and he's striding towards the door. I've got just enough strength left to grab his arm to hold him back.

'No,' I manage to say. 'He's gone, he's gone out. He won't hurt her any more tonight.'

He looks at me, and believes me. But I'm staggering so much I can't stand, my ribs are squeezing me, and I can't breathe through the blood in my mouth and nose, it's all bubbling, I can't breathe. Then his arm's round my shoulders and he's lowering me to the stones, and I hear him say 'Wait there,' and I do, because I can't do anything else, and it feels good just to let go and let someone else take it. I hear him go to the house, he's calling 'Nelly!' loudly and clearly like he's the master of the house just come home, and it feels safe, it feels like someone's in charge and I'll be looked after, and then everything goes black.

When I come round I've got Mother on one side and the boy on the other, and they're getting me into the barn, and Little Pierre's there too, looking mutinous with a basin and cloths. Then Mother's getting my shirt open, and it hurts, and the boy's saying he thinks I've got a broken rib, maybe two, then someone's giving me water and I close my eyes.

I must have slept, because next there were voices murmuring and someone prodding me, then there was M. Pollet the barber strapping up my ribs and M. Merien the apothecary doing something nasty with leeches on the inside of my arm. I struggled to sit up, and said 'Where's André? Where's André?' but the boy's voice said 'It's all right, Jacques, I'm here,' and I strained up my eyes and saw him holding a candle for the doctors. He smiled like everything was all right so I lay back down and told myself it was.

It was really quiet. I could hear M. Pollet's breathing as he finished the strapping, and an odd clicking in M. Merien's throat as he checked his leeches. I've often wondered about leeches. I'd see the doctors fishing them out of the jar, and wonder if they picked the same ones each time that got all the blood, and if there were like tiny starved leeches at the bottom that never had anything.

If there are I think I've got them all, they're taking for ever. M. Pollet says conversationally 'Having quite a little party there, aren't they, Monsieur? Been drinking anything nice?' and his eyes are bright and twinkly like he knows.

M. Merien's insisting on examining André's injuries, and the boy's hating it, of course, he doesn't need doctors fussing over him, he's not helpless like me. M. Merien's moaning about leaving things too late, he says the ear should have been seen to long before, but the boy's just saying 'Damn your impertinence, it's my ear, isn't it?' and I smile to myself because that's André, that's what he used to be in the days when it was all so much simpler and no one expected anything of me except to know what to do with horses.

When I next wake up we're alone. It's dark and silent outside, everything feels still, and I know it's the middle of the night. I can see the boy sitting a few feet away watching the door. His sword is close by his hand and I know why. He's wrong, though, Father won't come here, not now. He'll be sleeping it off somewhere and be fine in the morning, he always is. Maybe he'll be sorry, maybe he'll even forgive me. I can't think what I'll do if he doesn't. I've got nowhere else to go now, there's nowhere I belong.

I sit up and find actually my body feels better. Maybe my ribs aren't broken after all, or maybe the strapping's helped, but I can move and it doesn't hurt much. My nose starts bleeding again so I reach for one of the cloths beside me, but then André's there, coming to help like I'm a baby can't even wipe my own nose. I tell him to leave me alone.

He almost smiles. 'I let you do mine.'

I try to laugh at him, but it all goes wrong, and something terrible's happening, blood and snot is coming out of my nose and I'm shaking all over. Sixteen years old, and I'm crying like a kid.

He reaches out to comfort me, and I can't stand it, I shove him away. He kneels back obediently, but the cloth's still in his hand, he's just waiting his chance.

'Don't,' I warn him. 'Don't. It's stupid.'

'Why?'

'There aren't any Spaniards here, you don't need to pretend with just me.'

Blood went down my throat, I had to jerk my head back again, and before I could stop him he was holding my head and wiping me.

'Hold still,' he said.

I needed to talk, and he was wiping a bloody wet cloth over my mouth. I waited till he took it away to rinse it, then said 'You're not supposed to look after me, it's just stupid.'

'Is it?' he said mildly.

'You know it is. I'm your servant, and I'm only nice to you because I'm paid, it's stupid to pretend anything else. I mean it's best to be honest, isn't it?'

'Yes,' he said after a moment. 'It's best to be honest.'

I said 'It would be stupid to be any different, I mean what would I do when you went away?'

'Who says I'm going away?'

'When the Spaniards leave. You'll be going home, won't you?'

He was swirling the cloth round in the basin, making faint little circles of pink. 'Yes, of course. But I always thought you'd be coming with me.'

I stared at him. Mother said that, but then it sounded ridiculous, and suddenly it didn't, it was sort of obvious. Then I remembered everything else, and a cold weight settled back inside me.

I said 'You won't want me, not when you've got proper people round you again, you'd be ashamed. I'm not like you, it's stupid to pretend I am.'

'No, it isn't!' He smacked the cloth down into the basin, splashing up little drops of water on the straw. 'We've managed all right, haven't we? We do the same things, there's no difference that matters.'

I remembered the contempt on his face. 'That's not what you thought this morning.'

He lowered his eyes. 'I should have understood.'

'You understood. You despised me because I didn't stand up for my Mother.'

He started wiping again. 'You protected her tonight.'

I risked a snort. 'Didn't do any good, did it? I mean look at me.' He did, but I suddenly found I couldn't meet his eye. I stared at the straw and said 'He kicked me while I was lying on the ground.'

André's hand left my face. I raised my eyes cautiously and saw him sitting back on his heels with an oddly confused expression on his face.

'What does it matter what he did? What matters is what you did.'

'You mean I tried."

'So?' he said. 'Isn't that better than nothing?'

'Not for you,' I said bitterly. 'You just had to win that stupid fight with Stefan, even if it killed you. Well, it's not like that for real people. I tried to be you tonight, I tried to be a hero, but all I get is the shit kicked out of me and everyone fussing round me like a baby.'

'You still did the right —'

'No, I didn't,' I said. 'I fucking didn't. You can sit there giving it all that noble stuff about standing up for things, but we're not all like you, André, we can't all be bloody heroes.'

'Don't,' he said. 'Don't.' His hands were gripping the sides of the basin, his knuckles all shiny white.

'Then stop pretending you understand!'

'But I do,' he said, his voice so quiet I could hardly hear it.

'No, you don't,' I said savagely. 'I'd like to see you feel all noble and honourable if you couldn't even protect your own mother.'

He stood up so suddenly he kicked the basin. 'But I didn't!' he said, and now he was almost shouting. 'I didn't, did I, and now it's too late!'

Instantly his face went taut with shock, like it was me who'd said it, not him. Then he made an extraordinary noise and turned violently away, slamming himself against the wall.

I remember hearing the Dax clock striking four in the distance. I remember hearing it while my heart slowed back to normal, and this awful heavy sadness came with it as at last I understood.

I said 'I'm sorry.'

He didn't answer. After a moment he turned round, but he was too far from the candle for me to see his face.

I said again wretchedly 'André, I'm sorry.'

He glanced up. 'You've done nothing to be ashamed of. Only me.' He leaned back against the wall and slowly slid himself down till he was sitting on the straw.

'Will you tell me?'

'If you like,' he said. 'It doesn't matter now.'

We sat quiet a moment, then his voice began to talk. He took me right back to that hot night in July, back when I was sleeping in the Ancre stables with the straw prickling me and the horses restless, and César still alive in the coach-house next door. He never looked at me the whole time he was talking. He rested his chin on his knees, looked straight across to the other wall and spoke to that instead.

He said he'd woken to the noise of a musket being discharged nearby. He wasn't scared at first, just interested and excited, so he sat up in bed and listened. He heard running footsteps on the Gallery and stairs, then more shots, some of them outside, and realized it was a raid.

He scrambled out of bed and opened his door. It was dark on the Gallery, but someone was bringing a lamp from the other wing, and he could see shapes of people moving about, servants and some of the Guard. He wandered out among them, then saw his father running from his apartments calling for M. Chapelle. The Seigneur was bare-chested and putting on his coat as he ran, but as he reached the stairs he saw André standing there in his nightshirt, and stopped to tell him to go back to his chamber at once.

'He didn't seem worried,' said the boy. 'He was grinning

at me, and when Chapelle reached him he just clapped him on the back and said "Let's try a bit of steel instead," and they ran down the stairs together. At the bottom he looked back up at me and called out "And bloody stay there!" He was laughing. He looked happy and alive, he was almost shining with it.

'I hung on the rail, I wanted to see. But Camus, one of the Guard, he pulled me away and said "Come on, Mondemoiseau, the Sieur wants you back in your room." I told him I wanted to watch, but he said "Please, André, don't give me any trouble now, I've your mother to see to as well," so I went back to my room and he closed the door. I still wasn't frightened, because my father was there, but I put my breeches on just in case and stuck my knife in my belt. I was just getting my boots on when I heard more running footsteps and somebody stopping outside. Camus' voice said "All right, André, it's only me," and then I was alarmed because he sounded scared. Did you know him, Jacques?'

I thought he'd forgotten I was there.

'He was so funny. He had a woman in Doullens and another in Beauval, and neither of them knew about the other. The one in Doullens was a widow with a nice little house, but the one in Beauval was a blonde and he couldn't decide between them. Poor Camus. He used to throw dice to help him choose, but whenever it came up for the one in Doullens he always found a reason to throw again.'

He was quiet a long time. I wondered if I ought to say something, but then he started again, and he was talking a lot quicker now, like it was falling out of his head and into his mouth and he'd got to get rid of it quick.

'There was fighting on the Gallery, I heard it, swords and men shouting, some of it in Spanish. Then my father was there, somewhere in the other wing, I could hear him. He was calling the men, but there were no more footsteps and I don't think anyone came. Then there was the clash of swords right outside my door, and I knew Camus was fighting. I had to help him, I started to open the door, but he pushed it shut right in my face. I didn't want to distract him so I waited while the fighting went on, swords and little panting noises, feet slipping and stamping on the boards, then a great thud against the door, a sword point flashed through and stuck there, and someone was crying out. I tried to open the door, but it was blocked by something heavy and the screaming was hoarse and agonized. After a moment it stopped and I tried the door again, but it would hardly budge, it took ages to open it enough to squeeze past. I got out at last, and there was Camus, he'd been thrust clean through and pinned to the panel like an insect.

'I came out then, as I should have done fifteen minutes earlier if I'd been any kind of man. I came out, and I wasn't looking to do anything brave even then, I was looking for my father. I ran for his apartments, but all I could hear was my mother, and she was screaming. Screaming. It wasn't just noise. There were words. She . . .'

He stopped again. I glanced at him out of the far corner of my eyes, and he'd stopped looking at the wall, he was watching an ant climbing up his leg, he watched like it was the most important thing in the world. He picked a bit of straw, pointed it at the ant like a sword, and stared in fascination as it took hold of the blade.

'She was begging,' he said at last, but seemed to stick at that, he couldn't get past it. The ant let go of the straw, and he brushed it off his leg and went back to looking at the wall.

'There were only dead men on the landing, three in our uniform, but the others in black, all in those helmets with red plumes. The antechamber door was slightly open, and I pushed it and went in. There were dead soldiers everywhere, all of them enemy, there wasn't one of our own, but when I picked my way through the bodies I saw my father lying in the middle of them.'

He'd got his arms round his knees, but now he moved them up round his body like he was hugging himself.

'He was right by the doorway to the bedchamber. He'd been protecting my mother, stopping them going in. I counted five. He killed five just in this one room before they got him, and even then the wound was on his back. I knelt down beside him, I think I hoped he might just open his eyes and tell me what to do.

'My mother was still crying in the other room, she was begging them to stop, but there was no one answering her, only laughter. I knew what I had to do. I had to kill as many as I could to avenge my father, and I'd got to save my mother from what was happening in that room. I knew what it was, of course, or at least I knew the word for it. So I pulled out my dagger and went to the door.'

He made it sound really matter-of-fact, like it was what anyone would have done.

'There were six of them,' he said. 'Three just standing by the bed, and two holding my mother down, one each side, they were pressing her arms down, and holding her legs apart. The last man was between them.' He stopped and swallowed suddenly.

I said quickly 'You don't need to tell me this, don't tell me about this.'

He nodded vaguely, but I don't think he actually heard.

'She saw me,' he said. 'She turned her head to the door and called out my name. I went to her, I tried, I tried to get to her, but they stopped me, they were grabbing at me, and

166

I slashed out with the dagger to keep them off, and I got one, Jacques, I cut full across his face, then one was in front of me and he wasn't armoured, only leather, so I pushed the knife right deep in and out again, it stopped him and I got past. I made it up to the bed, but the others caught me, I tried, I wasn't strong enough, there were too many, and they seized my arm and twisted it and I dropped the dagger, then one of them punched me, and I fell back and banged my head against the wall.'

It must have been a hell of a punch. I remembered how badly bruised his face was, how swollen and black he'd been round his ear.

'Two came after me with their swords drawn, but one by the bed said "No," he called out "No" and something else I didn't understand, and they put their swords away. He was an officer, Jacques, an enseigne, tassets and a red sash. He ought to have been stopping it, not joining in like some rutting animal.'

'At least he stopped them killing you.'

He shrugged. 'I suppose they'd had orders. They'd have done it otherwise, I know they wanted to. They were angry because I'd stabbed their friend, and I think I must have killed him, I got the knife in really deep.'

I thought he must have too. I remembered his arm being soaked in thick blood right up to the elbow.

He said 'They dragged me off the floor, they held me tight between them. The officer told them . . . he said to make me . . . they turned my head towards my mother, I tried to fight but they . . .' His hand went uncertainly up to his hair. 'They held my head up, they made me . . . they made me . . .'

They made him watch.

'They found it funny,' he said. 'They should have killed me. It would have been better.'

He sat back and closed his eyes. When he started speaking

again his voice sounded calmer. 'There was a shot outside. I hoped it might be the militia come at last, but the officer went to the window and said there was no one there.'

I said 'I think it was me.'

'Was it?' he said. 'I thought it was the militia. But it helped. The officer stayed down that end of the room watching, because it was still going on, Jacques, it was going on and on, and now they started up this awful kind of chanting, emphasizing every thrust, it was animal and vile and I had to stop it. I wrenched myself towards them, I almost got loose, and the nearest one holding my mother came with arms spread to stop me, and I saw her hand come down off the bed and pick up my knife.'

There was a silence. Then he said 'They didn't kill her. She did it herself. I saw her. She saved herself because her son couldn't.'

I tried to think what it would be like to see your own mother kill herself. I remembered watching the boy cleaning that knife on the wet grass.

He said 'The officer was furious, I think he knew he'd be in trouble. They forgot about me, they let go, and I didn't wait, I turned and ran.'

I said 'Of course you did, there wasn't anything else you could do,' but he looked at me blankly as if he didn't understand what I was saying.

He said 'I needed a sword. I couldn't fight them with nothing, I needed my father's sword. I ran into the anteroom, and bolted the door behind me to buy time. I knew where my father's sword would be, I bent down and tried to take it from his hand. His grip was still firm, I had to loosen his fingers, but they were warm, and when I looked at him his eyes were open. He was alive.

'He shouldn't have been. He was cut wide open, he shouldn't

have been breathing at all. But he looked at me and knew me, he said "André." He looked agonized, he looked frightened, I've never seen him . . .'

I tried to imagine seeing my own father frightened, and couldn't do it. I couldn't imagine it with the Seigneur either, it just couldn't happen.

'The soldiers were at the door, they were shoving against the bolt. My father said "Run." I said "No," and he said "Run, or it's all for nothing." I said "I've got to have the sword," and he understood and smiled at me, and his fingers relaxed, and he let me take it. No one else, Jacques, he wouldn't have let anyone else in the world take his sword but me, and when I had it in my hand he said "Now run," and there was blood dribbling down his chin.

'The soldiers were hurling themselves against the door, thudding hard against it, they daren't let me escape now. My father forced himself to sit up, the blood was pouring out, he shouldn't have been moving. But the top bolt fell off, the door was bursting open, the soldiers piling up behind it.

'And my father stood and threw himself into the gap. He didn't even have a sword any more, he only had his body, but he threw it at them anyway and cried at me to run, and then he was stumbling, they were pushing him back, and I did run, Jacques, I ran down to the drawing room and climbed out of the window, and they didn't catch me because my father held them up long enough, he saved me, and he died all alone in that room because his son left him and ran.'

He stopped abruptly, and his hands crept slowly back around his knees. He was still staring at the wall and it was safe for me to look at his face. I think I expected him to have changed somehow, to look like someone this awful thing had happened to, but it was already done by the time he first came to me, and the only person changed was me, because now I knew.

I'd got to say something, I'd got to at least try. I told him it was stupid for him to go blaming himself, he'd done more than anyone else would, and it wasn't his fault it hadn't been more, because he was only twelve years old.

He said 'What matters is they both died in agony and all I did was watch.'

I said 'It was their choice, wasn't it? Your mother wanted to die, and your father gave his life to save you.'

He nodded. 'They died honourably, didn't they, both of them? And I'm left alive to carry the shame of it.'

'There's no shame in surviving, it's what they wanted, isn't it? I bet your father was really happy he didn't die just lying on his back but standing up and fighting to save his son.'

Tears trickled slowly out from under the boy's eyelids. He didn't even wipe them away. 'And that's what I want too. I don't want to be this, I don't want to be me. I can't go on watching other people suffer when I ought to be helping them, that's where the shame is, that's what I can't bear. I wanted to be like my father.'

I said 'But you are. I was in the Corbeaux last night, and everyone was saying so.'

'Killing soldiers, that's all. It's not enough, Jacques, it doesn't undo any of it.'

I said 'It could do. Those soldiers, the ones who did it, they'll still be here, won't they? We could find them and kill them.'

'I wouldn't know them if I saw them. It was dark, they wore helmets, the only one I saw properly was the officer. It could be any of the soldiers who've come to use our well, that could have been them with the cart that day, it could be bloody any of them, any soldier I ever see.'

The horror of that hit me like a hammer. I remembered the hate in his face when he'd stared at that cabo, and how I'd made him let the bastard pat him while he stood and lowered his eyes.

I said 'It doesn't matter, you're still fighting them, aren't you? You did everything you could, and you're still bloody doing it, you ought to be proud.'

He gave a hard little laugh. 'I tell myself that every day. I tell myself I tried.'

I felt a complete shit. 'I didn't mean that. It's not the same.'

'No, it's not. You saved your mother, I didn't save mine.'

I shook my head and wished I hadn't, it sent a sort of stab through my ribs. I said 'I was scared to even fight my own Father. But you, you went in to fight all those soldiers on your own. You're a hero, you must see that.'

He jerked forward so hard he knocked the basin right over, I watched the pink water soaking away into the straw. 'All right,' he said. 'All right then, what does that make you? I couldn't have done what you did. Not without a sword in my hand. Never.'

'André . . .' I said, and stopped. No one had ever looked at me the way he was looking now. I'd dreamed of my Father looking at me like this one day, I'd dreamed of it even when I was awake, but he hadn't, he'd never, no one, ever. 'André . . .'

He nodded gently and sat back. 'Trying's got to be good enough, it's all there is. How would you feel if you hadn't?'

I remembered how awful I'd felt while I was sitting letting it all happen, and how much better when I was up on my feet. I tried to recapture that aching feeling I'd had, but found to my surprise I couldn't, it had sort of broken up and gone, there was a kind of warmth growing there instead.

I looked at him again and he actually smiled. The tears weren't dry on his face, but he smiled.

He said 'So stop calling me bloody stupid.'

We sat in silence, but it was a nice silence and went on for a long time. An owl hooted somewhere, and the boy's head slipped down off the wall. He was asleep. It didn't hurt me, and I didn't move him. His head was on my shoulder like it belonged there, like it always had.

I knew it was true what I'd said. I thought of the Seigneur dying on his feet, and there was a kind of fierce pride burning up in me because he was the Sieur, and it's what I would have expected of him, he was everything I always thought he was, and I'd loved him. And André was the same. He'd fought six soldiers on his own, and he'd have gone back if his father hadn't stopped him. He was the Seigneur's son. I don't just mean the title and all the other stuff, I mean he was the son of Antoine de Roland in every way there was. And here he was, sleeping beside me in the straw like I was part of it too.

As I was drifting off to sleep, I found myself remembering a day when I was very little, and Mother was bringing me back from the Manor. The Seigneur walked a little way with us, and I was tired, and Mother held my hand and the Seigneur took the other. They walked me between them, and I felt like the safest person in the world.

PART II
The Soldier

Nine

Père Gérard Benoît

As spring warmed into summer, the hopes of our people rose. A year had passed since our Occupation, a new campaign season was upon us, and there were once again French armies abroad in Picardie. The success at Landrecies stirred all hearts, and the investment of La Capelle rendered them almost feverish with excitement. Our conquerors clearly shared in the sense of anticipation, and began forthwith a great work of fortification, not only extending the height of our Wall, but also erecting a watchtower on the roof of their barracks, the better to spy the advance of the French troops we expected daily for our relief. Yet no one came. The siege of La Capelle proved prolonged, and autumn was well advanced before the fortress once more reverted into French hands. Armies withdrew into winter quarters, the campaign season was over, and another year of Occupation was begun.

Yet for all the heaviness of our hearts, the evils of Occupation proved less than fear had made them. Some indications of unrest had made the Saillie a less attractive prospect for colonization than perhaps the Spanish had hoped, and there was no further sign of either the importation of new citizens from Flanders, or the arrival of our long-threatened governor. Dax-Verdâme continued under the rule of Don Miguel d'Estrada, whose government was as fair and peaceable as circumstances could allow.

The André of this period was a charming gentleman of

fourteen, but grown a little rustic in his manners and sorely in need of contact with his own kind. I saw him more regularly at this time, for he visited me weekly for the purpose of his neglected education, but he was not, alas, a scholar by nature, and while his progress in the Spanish tongue was rapid, his Latin did me little credit. Madame la Comtesse contrived to send books for his improvement, but while he displayed considerable acumen in his study of martial strategy I was less sanguine as to his progress in the arts. He was enchanted by the old-fashioned *Amadis de Gaul*, but his reaction to a translation of *Don Quixote* was to hurl the book against the wall of my cottage and say he wished he might throw the author after it.

These lessons were abruptly terminated by the events of the following spring. The little signs of unrest I had already remarked began to swell, and rumours now circulated freely among us of an Occupied Army formed in our very midst, which was not only in communication with French forces outside, but also assailing and frustrating the enemy within. It was whispered abroad that the Sieur of Dax had followed in the spirit of his family's tradition and was leading a great body of men for the succour of his stricken people.

Stefan Ravel

Oh, for Christ's sake.

Look, the kid was fourteen. He was in the army all right, but we didn't let him lead anything back then, I wouldn't have trusted him as far as I could spit. Yes, he was turning into a fine soldier, I'll grant you that, he did what we told him and did it well, but he still had those ludicrously romantic ideals and he was a disaster with a musket. The nearest we let him get was loading for Jacques, but he was happy enough with that, he was happy with anything as long as we let them do it together. St Roch and his dog had nothing on those two.

Oh, it's true people talked about him, but what do you expect? You want to lift the morale of a bunch of backward villagers, you're not going to do it by talking about a brave caporal and a tanner from Verdâme. Word got round the Sieur of Dax was playing, and we had volunteers crawling out from every stone. We even had women. That appalling Simone Lefebvre was one of them, and there wasn't much doubt what she was after. She'd heard Jacques was going to stay with André after the Occupation, and was all over the poor bugger like a blanket. Oh, some were maybe genuine, but you can't make a soldier out of a woman, Abbé, they're too unpredictable. There was only one I'd any time for and that was Margot from the Dax bakery, big tough lass who could heft a musket like a man and swear like one too. The others were only fit for loading, so we let Giles Leroux train them, which was as good as having a fox drilling a bunch of chickens. Christ knows how he did it, he was thirty if a day, but he was the biggest stoat this side of Abbeville, wiped the eyes of all our young glory boys where the women were concerned. He never showed so much as a blink of interest, but turn your back for five minutes and there'd be another bandy-legged bint staggering cross-eyed from the undergrowth and Leroux back teaching them like he'd never moved.

Still, we were doing all right. We'd a well-trained little army, and were picking off enough stray dons to keep the bastards from moving in themselves. We were also keeping communication open with France. Both Gates were shut now, but we got people in and out, Abbé, we managed all the same. We had siege ladders hidden in the forest and the back of some of the orchards where the Wall was lowest, but when we needed to take out horses as well as men we had one other little secret up our sleeves.

We called it 'the *gabelle* road'. It wasn't much, Abbé, just a single-track path deep in the Forest of Verdâme, but it was a way out of the Saillie without going through the Gate or climbing the Wall. On the east side the Wall stopped short in the woods because of the gorge, and there was this one place, only one, where there'd been another kind of landslip and the gorge was so shallow a horse could cross it and trot clean into France with the dons none the wiser. It was the perfect way for people to ride out of the *pays de grande gabelle* to buy salt at a twentieth the price, and bring it back in without bothering those inquisitive militia at the Gates.

The *gabelle* road really came into its own now. We used it for trade we didn't want the dons near, such as André flogging off jewellery, or our trips to buy gunpowder from the garrison at Lucheux. But its real function was communication. The Poulet Noir at Lucheux acted as a staging post, and the owner took in letters for us and passed on our own by the next coach. Courier duty wasn't the most exciting in the world, but it was worth it to keep in touch with the war outside.

That's what we wanted most, Abbé, news of the war. We got it locally from a bald-headed lunatic called Arnould Rousseau who worked as chef in the Dax barracks, but he could only tell us what the regular soldiers knew, which was frequently bugger all. So we used to pounce on any Spanish couriers we spotted prancing down the Flanders Road, swipe their dispatches, then pass them on to d'Ambleville at Doullens, de Rambures having died the year before. I doubt anyone ever acted on them, least of all that prize goat Châtillon, who had the Picardie command that year, but at least it was a calling card, a way of saying 'Don't forget about Dax-Verdâme.' We still didn't have enough of an army to boot the dons out, and our only hope was help from outside.

André wanted more of course, and Marcel wasn't much better, he was forever wanting to redeem his honour by rescuing the hostages from the Château Petit Arx. Oh yes, they were still there, the King being in no hurry to give away important prisoners for the children of a jumped-up banker. André would doubtless have been desperate to help fellow nobility, but a rescue was rather out of the question, since the Château housed officers from both garrisons, and was more heavily guarded than the Bastille. That still mightn't have deterred the lad from trying, so I made good and sure to keep any news of the hostages' plight well away from him. What our soft-hearted little gentleman didn't know wasn't going to hurt him, and it wasn't going to get the rest of us killed either.

Jacques Gilbert

I was happy that spring, the spring of 1638.

Things weren't the same at home, of course, but I'd sort of got used to it by then. My family never talked about what happened that night, it was just accepted that when the Occupation was over I'd go with the boy, and no one ever questioned it or asked why. But obviously it couldn't happen yet, so it was a bit like saying goodbye to someone then finding they're still there.

We didn't actually see that much of them. The barn was our home now, and we only went in the cottage for meals or to see Mother when Father was out working at the barracks stables, which he did as a way of paying taxes. We could have gone at other times if we wanted, there'd never been any open breach, but it felt uncomfortable all the same.

What really hurt was the way things were between me and Father. I hoped for ages he'd forgive me, and I really thought he might, because I knew he loved me really, I'd seen it in his eyes that night when he'd looked at me in the old way I remembered. I'd have given anything to have him look at me like that again, but he never did. I don't mean I regretted what I'd done, I never doubted I'd made the right choice, but it was just a tiny sadness singing away at the bottom of things that never quite went away.

I didn't go back to the cottage at nights any more, I used to take wine across the drive and visit M. Gauthier instead. He was always pleased to see me, I'm not sure he ever went to bed at all. Of course he was getting very old now, his cough was disgusting and his teeth kept dropping out. There was one evening I found him rummaging around in his soup for one of them before deciding he must have eaten it in mistake for a lentil.

The truth is I liked him. We'd sit and drink together, with Dog curled up on the floor gnawing at dead animals, and I felt sort of comfortable. He was very wise, M. Gauthier. He knew everything about the Rolands, he'd known them what seemed like for ever. He'd talk about them quite openly now, because I was a family retainer like himself, he even referred to the Comtesse admiringly as 'the old bitch'. He'd tell me stories about her and the others, and you could tell he'd loved them all. It was our own Seigneur he'd known best, and there was one evening he told me all about him, how he was his mother's favourite and did everything she said, but at last he broke away and went to the siege of La Rochelle.

'I was with him then,' said M. Gauthier wistfully. 'Me and César. But you never saw a soldier like him, young Jacques, you never did. Surrounded on all sides, Buckingham coming at us from the sea, and my Chevalier walking among us like all that mattered was his breakfast was cold. Never mind the rights and wrongs of it, it was bloody murder, and every one of us in the front line, but my Chevalier, he went in the thick of it every damn day, and came back at night with that glow in his face, my Chevalier.'

He was silent a moment and I knew why. Big fat tears were dropping off his face and landing on Dog's back. At last he said simply 'Ah well. Young André is your Chevalier now. Mind you bring him safe home, like I did mine.'

I felt responsibility landing on me like a hayrick. I said 'I don't know how, M. Gauthier, I don't know enough to look after him.'

He cocked his head at me. He had a way of doing that that was just like Dog, they got more like each other every week that passed.

'You know enough,' he said. 'There's only three things nobility need, and young André has them all: honour, courage, and the use of the sword. Keep him that way and you won't go far wrong.'

That didn't help much. 'But the honour stuff, he's going to need someone his own kind to help him with that, isn't he?'

I stopped because he was laughing. He had this alarming wheezy laugh, like a creaking gate just before it falls off its hinges.

'Ah, lad,' he said, wiping his eyes on his sleeve. 'A man's not a dog to be trained that way. The seed of honour's in every man, ay and woman too, and up to him if he lets it grow. Even Stefan Ravel has it in him, and one day he'll maybe find it if he looks.'

I never liked to disagree with M. Gauthier, so I kept my

mouth shut and pretended to pat Dog, which was a mistake, because he slobbered on my hand then tried to rape my leg. It was always doing that, that dog, especially if you wore bucket-top boots, it thought you were something exotic and exciting.

'Nay, lad,' said M. Gauthier, hauling Dog off me and smacking his nose with his soup bowl. 'It's maybe true honour's expected of nobility while for you and me it's a choice, but there's no man can escape his own judgement, and you know that same as me.'

I watched Dog trying to lick the soup off its back. 'I thought that was shame.'

M. Gauthier refilled his bowl from a foul-smelling pot on the hearth. 'And what's shame but the door to honour? Pity the man without it, young Jacques, for he'll never amount to more than that dog.' He flashed his broken teeth at me and started up singing one of his depressing hymns. It was a belter actually, the one about his wounds stinking and his loins being full of a loathsome disease.

Still he taught me a lot, M. Gauthier, he helped me prepare for when we finally went to Paris and were with proper nobility. That was really going to happen one day, I knew that now. André used the *gabelle* road couriers to send letters to his grandmother, and she wrote back that of course I was welcome whenever he came. She didn't know much about me, we didn't dare identify my family in letters the Spaniards might get hold of, but she knew I was André's aide and that was enough. At least I hoped it was. She could be quite frightening, the Dowager Comtesse, I remembered her from her visits to Ancre, but I thought she was kind too. She used to smile sometimes like she knew I was there, and once she even used my name. I hoped she wouldn't mind too much when she found out the mysterious 'J' was really only me.

André never told her about the army either. He didn't lie, of course, but he did miss out rather a lot. After one messy action with a patrol he wrote something like 'It has been a lovely day, and J and I have spent much of it fencing in the fresh air.' I think he was worried she might order him back to Paris if she knew he was in danger, and he couldn't have borne that. He had a job to do here, and so did I.

It was a hard job too, we were working all the time. When we weren't on duty he was still giving me fencing lessons, and I was getting good now, I was learning all clever vaults and passes, I could do just about everything except hit bloody André. Sometimes Marcel joined us so we could practise two against one, but we still couldn't beat André, I began to think nobody could. But there was stuff I could teach him too, I was really pushing him with his riding, I was even teaching him to jump. I wished we'd had Tempête back for that, but Perle wasn't bad and I soon had him sailing over four-foot gates with ease. It didn't feel like work, though, it was just doing stuff together that we liked. Like I said, I was happy.

I still saw my friends in Dax, but André came with me now because he could pass as a peasant anywhere, he even spoke rougher than he used. I obviously saw Simone on my own, but we'd visit Colin together and sometimes Robert would join us, we'd sit round the fire talking and laughing about nothing, and it was just like it used to be, only better. I'd bring Mme Lefebvre vegetables from Ancre, so she'd be busy and happy at her cooking, and there'd maybe be cider going too, and Colin's dad hammering away in the Forge next door, and humming as he worked.

It's strange, when I think about it. That was the spring it all started, the spring d'Estrada went on leave. The Forge was right next to the barracks, there were four hundred soldiers just the thickness of a wall away, but somehow it never seemed to matter. It was the very last time, I suppose, the last time we were all the kids we used to be before the big things happened. When I think back to it now, the four of us laughing, and Colin's dad hammering away *tap-tap-tap* in the background, it's like that was the last of our childhood ticking away right there.

Anne du Pré

Extract from her diary, dated 14 May 1638

Capitán Martínez came today and announced grandly that he is in charge while Don Miguel is away. He has a very impressive beard, but it slopes inward at the bottom and I suspect there is not much chin underneath.

Colette asked about our exchange, but he says Papa seems of little account at court, and no one in the King's counsel seems interested in our return. He said 'Doubtless this will be because your father's title is of very recent acquisition,' which I thought was rather rude. Florian turned quite scarlet and pointed out Papa was so rich he owned the whole of Verdâme. The Capitán seemed very interested in this. He said his overlord, Don Francisco Mendéz, was considering requesting a pecuniary ransom rather than an exchange, and our information might do much to assist this idea.

We were all a little quiet after he had gone. I do not think Papa has the kind of money they will ask. Much of his fortune was sunk into this estate, and now of course he cannot even be living off its rents.

Colette is very depressed about it. She is to be sixteen next week and is convinced by the time we are free there will be no one left for her to be betrothed to of any quality at all.

Florian said she could always marry André de Roland, for he can hardly be betrothed while he remains in the Saillie, but Colette says he is unlikely to survive the Occupation the way he is going, and he is no good to her unless he lives to be Comte de Vallon. 'Besides,' she said, 'he is Anne's pet, and I would not fall out with my baby sister.' They are very mean, the way they tease me about André. It is only natural for me to be interested in what he is doing, Jeanette talks about him all the time. She says he is a real hero.

The soldiers are making a lot of noise in their mess tonight. I rather like it when they have the guitar, but tonight there are drums and I think they are singing marching songs. The floor seems almost to rumble with their voices.

I wonder how long Don Miguel is to be away.

Stefan Ravel

You know me, Abbé, a don's a don in my book, but there's no doubt things were different with d'Estrada gone. Martínez was weak as cat-spit, and we started to see what an Occupying Army can be like with no one to control them.

The looting started again, of course, food and livestock, the usual, but there was a lot more violence with it. We had one especially vicious couple of troopers in Verdâme those days, we called them Fat Pedro and Thin Pedro and made sure to keep out of their way. I saw them kick a dog to death in the street once, just because it failed to kill a mangy cat when they'd bet it would.

They did their women together too, and one day they went after the wife of our local saddler, Frédéric Truyart. I knew him, Abbé, a milder-mannered man you never met, but he came home to find those bastards at Christina, snatched up a knife and went for them. It was hopeless, of course, they beat him senseless then burnt the cottage down over his head, but it wasn't till they'd finished with Christina she was able to make anyone understand her baby was in the house as well. I tell you, Abbé, when the ashes cooled enough for the bodies to be brought out, there were maybe twenty Verdâmers watching, and the mood was nothing short of murderous.

Oh, we knew we'd got to get them, the army was in one mind on that. Young André was always touchy on the subject of rape for some reason, but Mercier was in a frenzy too, he was a friend of Truyart's sister Jeanette and desperate to see her family had justice. We'd have done it anyway. The baby wasn't even baptised yet, Abbé, and you know what that means. There was more fire in our bellies than you'd find in any man's Hell.

We'd have had them that first day, but the bastards had gone to ground and we set our reliable Arnould Rousseau to find out where. He did it too. Late that night there was a loud knock on my door, and in he strolled, our master spy of the saucepans. He didn't go much for discretion, Rousseau, he went where he liked when he liked, and no one ever questioned him. The dons had decided he was eccentric.

He sat down in my best chair, pulled his wig out of his pocket, shook it out over my floor, then perched it on top of his head to show he was off duty.

'Christ, this place stinks, Ravel,' he said amiably. 'What have you got in that lime pit of yours, a whale?'

'No,' I said. 'The body of the last man who came here and told me my house stank.'

He grinned evilly at me, and accepted beer.

'Those baby-killing bastards,' he began. I'd heard he'd had children of his own but lost them all to plague a few years back. 'Those bastards. They've got them hidden away for their own protection, I heard my lot talking. Seems they think we might be going after them.'

'Fancy that,' I said levelly. 'So where are they?'

'The Château,' he said casually, as if it weren't the most impregnable building in the Saillie. 'They seem to think they're safe enough there.'

'They're right,' I told him bluntly. 'We can't get within a hundred yards of it.'

'Defeatist, Ravel?' said Rousseau, fishing bits out of his beer. He was a picky bugger, that one, he always said he should have been born rich.

'Practical,' I said. 'It can't be done.'

Rousseau swivelled his beady eyes to Marcel. People always assumed he was the softer touch of the two, and they were perfectly right. 'But you'll do it, won't you, Dubois? Sod picking off the odd patrol, this is important.'

Marcel forked his hands through his hair and looked anguished. 'But the Château, Arnould, I don't think we're ready for something like that.'

Bless the lad, we were never going to be ready for it. I said soothingly 'It doesn't matter. They can't keep them there for ever, we'll get them when they come out.'

Rousseau shrugged. 'Well, if you want to be taken seriously you won't hang about.' He drained his beer, made a face at it, and stood. 'People need something to believe in, Ravel. You can at least give them that.'

I laughed. 'Who do you think we are? God?'

He turned his eyes back to me, and the face below that ridiculous wig might have been carved in stone. 'Someone needs to be,' he said. 'Baby-killing bastards.'

Anne du Pré

24 MAY

Poor Jeanette, her nephew was not above two months old. She says Christina has not said a single word since the bodies of her husband and baby were brought out, and they do not know if she will ever speak again. I could do little to comfort her but cry myself and talk of praying to our Saviour, but she only shook her head grimly and said 'Oh, I shall pray, Mademoiselle, I shall pray these men live to pay for what they have done in screaming agony, and I pray Christina lives to see it.'

I said 'André will avenge her, Jeanette, I know he will. You know his friends, can you not ask for his help?'

She gave a curious dry laugh, and scrunched my handkerchief in her hand. 'André de Roland is a great gentleman, Mademoiselle. What will he care for the wife of a saddler? What will anyone care?'

I said fiercely 'I care, and so will André once he knows.'

'He already does,' she said. 'My good M. Mercier promised to tell him, but there is nothing done. They say they cannot reach them here in the Château and so nothing is done.' She looked at me with little red eyes and such hopelessness behind them my heart seemed to burn in pain. She whispered 'There is no justice in this world for people like us, Mademoiselle. Sometimes I think there is nothing at all.'

25 MAY

It is done. I have only to wait for the barber, and I do hope he is quick. The blood is already coming through the bandage and there is a stinging sensation which makes me dizzy, but I think it was the only way.

The Owl took over duty from the Slug this afternoon, and I heard them talking about these two Pedros. The Owl is quite disgusted with them, for he is a good, kind man and has children of his own, but it seems others do not share his view. The Slug said Capitán Martínez is afraid of being unpopular if he punishes the men, so he is to send them to Arras for their fate to be decided there. Apparently the Snake is to be one of the escorts and says they are to go straight after the noon meal tomorrow. I knew this was information André must have at once, but could see no way of getting it to him, for Jeanette will not come until Monday and we have no other outside contact at all.

Then I remembered Pollet. We had him last year when poor Florian banged his head, and he seemed a nice man and told us such funny stories while he was dressing the wound. More importantly he is from Dax, and even if he does not know where to find André he must surely know someone who does.

I knew what I had to do, but am ashamed to admit how hard I found it. I managed to break the green vase without difficulty, but *could not* cut myself properly with it. Twice I dug the point into my arm and pulled, but somehow my hand seemed to resist and lift all by itself, so that all I had were little scratches and trembling fingers. In the end I went to the window, wrapped my handkerchief round my left wrist, knocked against the glass a couple of times, then finally closed my eyes and simply punched my whole arm through.

It was extraordinary. When I pulled my arm back through the jagged glass the blood seemed to appear quite suddenly, a bright scarlet rectangle above my wrist, then I saw the flap of white skin and really felt a little sick. Colette came running at the sound of the smash, but only screamed at the sight of my arm. She put her hand over her mouth and made strange sounds like 'Oh, oh, *oh!*' as if her stomach were behind them as well as her voice. My arm was shining and slippery with blood, and I was trying to say 'Colette, the surgeon, we must ask for a surgeon,' but still she only screamed. Florian was better, he ran and clasped his hand round the wound, but also yelled for the guard, and then the Owl came and it was all right.

He was wonderful. He took only one look, then simply ripped the sleeve from his own shirt and bound it furiously round my arm, making funny little tutting noises as if I were a little girl. I felt calmer at once, but had to pretend I did not, saying over and over again 'The Dax barber, Pollet, the Dax surgeon.' He said he would send for their own surgeon but I shook my head furiously and said again 'Pollet, the Dax barber, Pollet.' He seemed puzzled by my persistence, but perhaps he thought it modesty on my part to wish only for a surgeon I knew, for he bowed with great respect and stepped back as if he had been too familiar in touching me so closely, and said 'Yes, Mademoiselle, the Dax surgeon, I send now.'

I am almost ashamed for abusing his kindness. He walked out of our apartments with great dignity, even though one muscular arm was completely naked from the loss of his sleeve, and I thought to myself 'I must remember this. When everything seems black and terrible I must remember always that there are people like the Owl.'

Jacques Gilbert

He didn't mess about, M. Pollet. He sent a message to meet him that night at the Quatre Corbeaux and when Stefan heard it was about the Pedros he insisted on coming too.

I liked going to the Corbeaux, it was like things being normal before the Spaniards came. The whole of the left wall was covered in engravings of ladies from the big towns, while the right-hand wall had all holy pictures on it, and the dirty bit of cloth M. Moreau was convinced came from the headdress of a Saracen killed in the seventh crusade. People used to call the two sides of the room 'Sin' and 'Sacred', and the bit of wall by the kitchen was just called 'Hell Corner', because M. Moreau's ancient mother used to sit there, making a bowl of gruel last all night, and if you got too close she might wink and show you her legs.

M. Pollet was perched uneasily on a bench under the Saracen's headdress, raising his mug to Mme Moreau and looking like he wished he was at the seventh crusade himself. He seemed relieved to see us and poured out his information in a great lump, like a bomb he couldn't wait to get rid of. We were thrilled about it though, André was fidgeting with excitement. He was saying 'We'll get them on the way, won't we, Stefan, we'll get the bastards on the way.' Stefan just said 'Shut up and drink your cider,' but he was smiling when he said it, and the boy smiled back.

M. Pollet said quickly 'I don't need to know about that, Messieurs, I'm only passing on the information as she asked.'

'She?' said André. 'Have you got an informer?'

'Better than that, Sieur,' said M. Pollet, and actually winked. He'd probably been drinking a while before we got here. 'This was a lady, a real one, the younger Mlle du Pré herself.'

There were a bunch of men singing '*Il est bel et bon*' very badly over in Sin, I was suddenly very aware of them. Next to me the boy had gone very still.

He said 'They're still there?'

M. Pollet looked confused, but Stefan reached for the jug and started pouring cider.

'Politics, kid,' he said, like he knew anything about it. 'These things always take time. But they're all right where they are, aren't they, Pollet?'

M. Pollet seemed much happier talking about Mlle Anne than he was about the soldiers, he drank more cider and told us the whole story. André listened with eyes getting bigger and rounder like he was a child again, and said 'But that's so brave. To cut her own arm, that's so brave. Will she be all right?'

Stefan shifted on his seat next to me. 'Little scratch, that's all. She won't have been stupid enough to do real harm.'

M. Pollet sighed. 'I did the best I could, little tiny stitches, but there'll be a wee bit of a scar, I'm afraid. A terrible shame, and her so pretty. And brave too, Messieurs, never a squeak out of her while I worked.'

The boy looked at me with a kind of shy pride and said 'I told you, didn't I, Jacques, I said she wasn't like other girls.' I don't think he did actually, I think he just said she didn't giggle, but people do that, don't they, they make things bigger in their minds than they really were. Then I remembered the two of them sitting side by side in the sunken garden and wondered if there'd been more to it than he let on.

'You're right there, Sieur,' said M. Pollet, waggling his head wisely and knocking the Saracen's headdress askew. 'Very unusual lady. What it's like for them living up close with the Spaniards I can't imagine. Why, I'd say –'

Two things happened at once. I felt Stefan's foot lunging out under the table beside me, and M. Pollet stopped mid-sentence with an odd sort of grunt.

'What?' said the boy. 'What would you say?'

M. Pollet's eyes were fixed on Stefan. He said feebly 'Well, I don't really know, Sieur, I don't know anything about it.'

'We know we're lucky she's there,' said Stefan, pouring him more cider. 'Someone right up with the dons, having cosy chats with the officers, getting information, that's worth gold. It'll be a big loss to us when they're freed.'

'But will they be?' said André. 'I never thought it would take this long.'

'Oh, they'll be ransomed any day,' said Stefan firmly. 'Father's rich, isn't he? If the dons can't get anything else don't tell me they won't take money.'

André looked doubtful. 'I don't know, we shouldn't just leave them . . .'

M. Pollet's face suddenly cleared. He leant forward confidentially and said 'Now, don't you worry about them, Sieur. Snug as kittens in a box, that's what they are, nice rooms, every luxury, and going to be freed any day. You've no need to fret on their account, none at all. Now, shall I be getting us some more cider?'

I understood then, and actually I thought they were right. If André believed any girl was in trouble he'd go doing something stupid to save her, and this was his own friend, this was Mlle Anne, he'd probably try scaling the walls of the Château all on his own just to get her out. So we all agreed the hostages were really very comfortable and much better off where they were, then we thanked M. Pollet for his help and got the boy out quick.

He'd probably have still been wondering about it on the way home, but Stefan got the subject back on to the Pedros, then there wasn't room in our heads for anything else. We knew those two even in Dax, they used to stroll over from Verdâme when they got bored with bullying the people there, they'd beaten Mme Hébert because they said she was ugly, and threw Simon's brother Nicolas in the pond so they could see what a hunchback looked like swimming. The boy would have wanted to get them anyway, even before this terrible thing about killing the baby, he was determined to be involved.

He said it ought to be our unit did the action since it was us got the information, and Stefan didn't argue, he said yes, all right, he'd talk to Marcel.

Maybe he was just keen to take the boy's mind off Mlle Anne, I don't know. But that's all it takes, isn't it, for everything to change and go wrong. All it needs is for someone somewhere to say yes when they ought to have said no, never, fucking no.

Jean-Marie Mercier

I remember every detail of that day, as if it was now.

The action wasn't to be until the afternoon, so we waited together by the stream. It was summer, so the bluebells were over, but there were poppies blooming and foxgloves showing pink through the trees. I remember the sound of the stream trickling, and the bees humming close to the grass.

I was checking the muskets for the action, because I was a marksman now, I honestly was. The others were all relaxing. André was dozing on his back, Colin was playing dice, and Robert was rather ostentatiously trimming his new beard and asking how we thought he should style it. Jacques was carving a model of a wild boar, and finding it difficult making the bristles fine enough. Every time he nearly had one perfect it would break off, and he would say 'Bugger,' and shave another slice off its back so he could start again.

We were going to use what Marcel called the 'stones trick', which meant André had the principal role, because he looked the youngest. He was supposed to throw stones at the soldiers, you see, then pretend to trip as he turned to run, in order to lure one or more into dismounting and chasing him into our ambush. The others were bound to wait for their colleagues, and so far we'd always been able to get all of them. The difference this time was we hoped to take the two murderers alive, so we could hang them as they deserved.

It was a very important action, so Marcel joined us himself with some extra men. There were Philippe and Pinhead from Verdâme, as well as Bettremieu and Margot from Dax, which brought our strength up to ten. They seemed quite as relaxed as we were, and settled down perfectly happily to wait by the stream. I remember Robert saying casually 'Do you think I should keep the beard, Margot, or just have a moustache?' and Margot saying innocently 'Oh, are you growing a beard?' and everyone laughing while Robert looked cross.

I remember it all. I remember sitting in the sun working those muskets, with no idea then of what I would be made to do with them. I remember the guns themselves, the smooth feel of the stocks under my hand, the wood warmed by the sun, the smell of the gun oil and the sound solid click of a good action striking home. I remember Stefan next to me, those strong dye-stained hands deftly filling the bandoliers, and that oddly chemical smell you always associate with a tanner.

But most of all I remember André. He was flopped on his back, his hands tucked behind his head, and looking up at the sky. He was wearing that old white shirt with green grass stains down the front, and the neck open where the laces had torn. His sleeves were rolled up, and I can remember how the sun caught the fine dark hairs on his forearms, and the little grazes on his fair skin. I watched him lying there, enjoying the sun and the companionship, and the thought came into my head 'How very young he is.' I suppose it's quite ironic I should be thinking it then for the first time, when really it was the last time it was true.

Ten

Jacques Gilbert

It looked really safe.

Marcel placed us on the Verdâme side of the Flanders turn-off, with signallers in both directions and even one up as far as the first bend on the Flanders Road. We had Bettremieu as 'catcher' up in the tree to look out for the signals, and Stefan at the base as 'anchor man', relaying them and giving the orders.

The attack team was strong too. There was me and Marcel behind a thick tangle of brambles nearest the road, Robert and Philippe in a ditch behind us on one wing, Pinhead and Colin on the other, while Jean-Marie and Margot sat behind the signal tree with the guns in case we needed marksmen. The boy seemed quite happy with the back-up. I watched him checking over the ground, working out where he'd stage his fall, and measuring the distance to the clearing we'd picked for the killing site. Then he gave me his sword to look after, collected stones to throw, and sat down behind a clump of bracken to wait for Stefan's signal.

We waited. My neck started to ache with looking back at Stefan and I had to keep glancing away to rest it. Then I looked again and he was signalling. He pointed left to show it was a signal relayed from the Verdâme direction, so it wasn't urgent, Bettremieu couldn't see it himself yet. Then his fist banged his palm, which meant soldiers coming, then two fingers up, which told us how many. I was surprised there wasn't an escort, but wasn't about to complain.

André picked up his stones and went into a crouch, his eyes still on Stefan.

Stefan signalled again, hand flat, palm down, sweeping from side to side. Abort.

André settled again behind his bracken, and laid his stones back down.

I heard horses, then two soldiers came into view, trotting slowly past. It was only a regular patrol.

We went back to waiting. The boy seemed relaxed, but I noticed his right hand was moving, and knew he was squeezing that old tennis ball of his. I looked round at Marcel and saw he was biting his nails. I began to think I ought to be scratching my nose or something just to keep them company.

Stefan signalled again, a repeat from Verdâme. Soldiers coming. Four. That looked more like it. The boy put his ball down, caught up his stones and crouched.

Stefan repeated the signal. Soldiers coming. Four. He didn't point back, so Bettremieu could see them himself.

Then I heard them. André was on his feet and moving to the road, his head still turned back to Stefan, right to the last minute. The hoofbeats were louder, they were going faster than the patrol, they were nearly up to us. The boy turned to the road.

And Stefan signalled, he was signalling like mad, Abort, Abort, and a second later I could hear why, there were horsemen riding down the Flanders Road. The boy was facing the other way, so Marcel called urgently 'André, abort!' but he didn't hear, he just didn't seem to hear. Our targets were in sight, his arm was back, he was already throwing, and it was all too late.

Stefan Ravel

If I hadn't known better there are times I'd have said that kid was bloody deaf. He went right ahead as if we'd never said a word, he even yelled out 'Murderers!' and when they reined in to stop, he threw the rest of his stones right at the Pedros in the middle.

Marcel was still trying to signal him, I came half out of cover myself, but it was hopeless, Abbé, he'd done far too good a job for that. One of the escorts was off his horse in a second, and André made his turn, staging the best fall I'd ever seen him do. He scrambled up all right but he'd cut it bloody fine, the escort was nearly on him, and Fat Pedro pounding behind with a great shout of triumph. He'd no option now but dodge and run, run towards an ambush that was never going to happen.

Jacques Gilbert

He wasn't even running fast, he thought he wasn't meant to, he was just doggedly limping on, leading them right into the clearing we'd so cheerfully referred to as the killing site. I'd got to let him know he was on his own and must run to save himself.

I kept low and ran through the bracken to head him off. I knew I'd got to stay in cover, the troops were right round the corner, if they saw us now we were dead. The boy came panting round the trees, and I managed to wave to him, abort it, abort, and he saw me, I know he did, I saw him react just as I ducked back into the bracken. He tried to put a spurt on, but the soldiers were already in the clearing and the one in the lead leapt and brought him down.

Stefan Ravel

I'd have maybe risked it if it had only been a handful of troops, but it was a whole fucking column. The first few took the right turn for Dax, but the next glanced left and saw the horses and two of his colleagues waiting by the road, so of course the bastard stopped and all the others turned after him to investigate. That's soldiers for you, Abbé. Any excuse to take a break.

Thin Pedro and the other escort explained, but the struggle was pretty audible anyway, because of course André was putting up a fight. They'd got him down cleanly enough, but he was kicking and struggling and giving them no end of trouble. Fat Pedro had hold of his legs, but the kid smashed him in the face with his boot, then the escort wrapped an arm round his neck, but had to snatch his hand back fast because André actually bit him. I told you, that kid fought dirty.

He nearly got away then, he was half up and off the ground, but Fat Pedro tripped him, and the escort leapt on him while he was off balance. I couldn't see a great deal of what happened next, the kid was on the ground and the bracken tall and thick just there, but Fat Pedro's fist came up and clubbed viciously down, twice, maybe three times, then he and the escort got themselves up again, and there was André being pulled up between them, but his legs were hanging limp and he was dangling uselessly in their arms.

We turned to Stefan in panic, but he was just staring at André, as shocked as we were. I saw his lips moving. He said 'Christ.'

I reached for a musket, I couldn't think what else to do. Bettremieu slithered rapidly down the tree in a scattering of leaves, and Robert and Philippe started to climb out of the ditch, but Stefan seemed suddenly to realize what we were doing and hissed at us to stop.

'You bloody fools,' he said. 'You want to get us all killed?'

Robert protested 'It's André.'

Stefan turned on him, he was almost spitting in his face. 'And he'd be first. Don't you understand?'

Jacques Gilbert

Marcel was pressing my face down, I couldn't move, I could hardly even breathe. He was whispering desperately in my ear 'They'll beat him and let him go, that's all. He's just a kid throwing stones. But if they see even one of us they'll know it was an ambush and he's an enemy soldier, then they'll kill him and us too. We've just got to stay down.'

I knew he was right, I did understand, but I'm watching the boy being dragged towards a whole troop of enemy soldiers and I'm wondering if he does too. He's still struggling feebly, he's hurt and alone, he must know we're watching and doing nothing to help him, and I'm desperate to know he understands and doesn't think we've abandoned him or don't care. I'm half expecting him to call for me, and almost wondering why he doesn't, and if he does call I'll go, fuck what Marcel says, if he calls me, I'll go.

Stefan Ravel

There were more soldiers arriving all the time, a whole company from the look of it, fresh in from Flanders to reinforce our poor overworked conquerors.

When the first ones saw the battered state of Fat Pedro and his escort then realized the culprit was this fourteen-year-old boy, they fell about laughing, but they took the kid anyway and marched him on to the road to the others. There were lots now dismounted and standing on the road, some grabbing the chance to swig from their canteens, and others having a leisurely piss by the roadside. It looked as if I was right, and this troop had travelled a long way. They were just about ready for a spot of rest and entertainment, and André had turned up in perfect time to provide both.

Jacques Gilbert

I'm telling myself it'll be all right, I've trained him. Right since that first day I've shown him how to deal with some-thing like this.

And it's not too bad at first. They're smiling and laugh-ing, and their voices don't sound unfriendly, though of course I can't hear properly. They've got the boy on his feet, and they're taking it in turns to push him, quite gently really, like mock-fighting. He's got his wits about him, he's doing everything right, standing looking sulky, rocking when they shove him, keeping his head down, he's even got his hands in his pockets, and I'm really proud. Marcel's muttering next to me 'Good boy, André, keep it up.'

The escort with the bitten hand's protesting, like he doesn't think his injuries are being taken seriously. He barges in and starts yelling at the boy, shoving his hand in his face, showing it him and shouting. André mumbles something and looks down, but it's not enough, and the escort yells again and smacks him hard across the face.

For a second there's a tiny silence, except for the blow echoing in my head like the slam of a door. Then André wrenches his arm free and punches the escort right back.

A great yell goes up, and the soldiers are grabbing at him again, the escort's red with fury and trying to get at the boy's face, but he's struggling, tearing himself away and hitting out, he's trying to fight the whole bloody lot of them. It's hopeless, of course, they're all round him trying to pinion his arms, one's got his collar, the escort's cocking his fist, but André twists away and throws himself forward, he's actually leaping at the escort's throat. The man backs off, hands up to protect his face, but that's what André's been waiting for, he's reaching for the sword at the escort's hip, his hand's on the hilt, he's jerking it out, it's halfway out the scabbard before they even see what he's doing.

Then they're all going mad with panic and trying to get him off it, the soldier tries to snatch it back, but he's slicing into the palm of his own hand. Another grabs at the scabbard, but that's only pulling it further from the blade, and André's nearly got it, there are three trying to hold him, but his whole mind's set on getting the sword and nothing's going to stop him. Then one finally pulls himself together, rips a pistol from a saddle holster, and smashes the butt down hard on the back of the boy's neck.

For a second I think it hasn't done anything, then he goes

limp, drops the sword and sinks down on his knees. They're all round him, I can hardly see, there's just legs, and a great babble of voices as they're all laughing in relief or yelling at each other in recrimination, because it was a bloody close thing. Then I see something moving between them and know André's trying to get up. Marcel's whispering 'Stay *down* for God's sake,' but he won't, of course, it's that business with Stefan all over again. One of them knocks him down again, then someone else kicks him, and I can't see him at all now, there's just this great ring of men standing close together, and they're all kicking at something on the ground, and I can't see, but I know it's him, it's André, it's the boy. All I can hear is their laughter.

Stefan Ravel

No, it's never a nice thing having to watch one of your own men get done over, and this was maybe worse because André was so young. You don't have to be a gentleman to feel bad when nine strong men hide in the bushes and watch the shit kicked out of a kid of fourteen.

Marcel and Jacques didn't look happy. They'd got themselves back to their original position, and I could see them both clearly behind their brambles. Jacques had the back of his fist pressed against his mouth and I think the poor bugger was actually crying. I wouldn't have put it past him to do something stupid, and was just about to crawl up to them when there was a shout from the troop, and a group of riders came trotting up from the other end of the column.

The leader was a well-dressed officer on a smart bay with scarlet hangings, and the size of the escort told me at once who it had to be. It was that friend of the people Capitán d'Estrada himself, and I only hope the bastard enjoyed his holiday.

Jacques Gilbert

It was Tempête. I'd raised that horse from a colt, I'd been wretched when we lost him, but I couldn't feel any emotion at the sight of him now, I was all used up, like a rag that's been squeezed dry. I was just praying d'Estrada would do the decent thing and let the boy go.

He dismounted elegantly and strode straight up to the soldiers, snapping some kind of order. They sprang back at once and looked at the boy lying in the dirt like they couldn't work out how he'd got there. I could see him myself now, curled up on the ground with his arms wrapped round his head to ward off the blows. He looked very small lying like that, and d'Estrada said something pretty scathing to the one in charge. Someone got water and sat the boy up, and I saw he was alive but very groggy. He couldn't stand, and one of the soldiers had to kneel to support him while they gave him a drink and wiped the blood from his eyes.

D'Estrada folded his arms and watched them sarcastically. He was handsome actually, tall and lean, with black curly hair and his beard neatly trimmed to his jaw. I just hoped he was feeling kind as well.

Carlos Corvacho

Oh now, Señor, not to say a temper, he was just a little put about, and no wonder. Here he'd been to Madrid to beg and plead for a proper command again, but no, he'd got to stay here till the place was docile, and a new governor coming in over his head as well.

So he takes one look at this poor bedraggled creature our lads have been making game with, and gives Cabo Moya a right dressing-down, says he's made it clear there's to be no bullying of the locals, and this isn't the way to get them to co-operate. Then Moya says it's the child's own fault, he's been chucking stones at our troops, not to mention kicking their faces in and biting them, and my Capitán starts to look less sympathetic.

He says to the lad in French 'You would fight my soldiers?'

The lad mutters sullenly 'They deserved it, didn't they?'

My Capitán looks round us all with raised eyebrows, and naturally we laugh.

Then young Benito speaks up, that was his page, Señor, always a little inclined to push himself forward. 'Perhaps he's André de Roland, that would explain it.'

The men laugh again, which is understandable, Señor, since the Roland we're looking for would be firing muskets at us, not throwing stones, but my Capitán looks thoughtful, and I see him taking in the long black hair.

Moya says hesitantly 'He tried to take a sword to the men, Señor, tried to snatch one clean out of the scabbard.'

'Did he indeed?' says my gentleman. He looks the lad up and down, and he's thinking about it, he really is. 'Is your name de Roland?'

The lad looks blankly at him, sniffs, and wipes his nose against his sleeve.

My Capitán laughs shortly, and really it's too ridiculous. This lad had the most vulgar accent, while de Roland had an educated voice, beautifully clean of the patois. No, no, Señor, you misunderstand, or my French was at fault, I mean I remember it *now*. How could I remember at the time when I'd never heard it?

So now, bless me, Señor, if I haven't quite forgotten where we'd got to. Ah yes, *muchas gracias*, yes, my Capitán asks the lad to explain himself, and he does. He tells this whole story of rape and murder and baby-killing, and my Capitán's face growing darker with every word. He turns on the men who've been accused and says in his coldest voice 'Is this true?'

They shuffle their feet and say nothing. I knew them both, Señor, the big one was Pedro Jiménez, the other was Pedro Sánchez, very nasty pieces of work, not typical of our men at all. Another fellow speaks up and says it's all true, he was escorting them back to Artois, and he gives my gentleman a letter from Capitán Martínez which he was to hand to the commanding officer at Arras before returning home.

My Capitán reads the letter, then looks at Jiménez and Sánchez as if they're something nasty he's asked me to clean off his boot. He snaps his fingers for a pen, and starts to write on the end of the letter.

Moya says 'Do we let the lad go, Señor?'

My Capitán glances at the boy, opens his mouth, then shuts it again without speaking. It's the hair he's looking at, Señor, long and wavy, black as my own gentleman's, just like the hostages said. He says 'I haven't decided yet. I think I'd like him to meet Abanderado de Castilla first.'

I know what he's at, Señor, he's still convinced there's more went on at the Manor than de Castilla's letting on, and hoping he'd recognize de Roland if he saw him. It's naive of him perhaps, seeing as de Castilla's hardly likely to admit any such thing, but that was my gentleman, always inclined to think people more honourable than they really were.

Meanwhile Jiménez and Sánchez are still waiting, so he signs the letter, gives it back to the escort and tells him to get them out of his sight before he hangs them himself. The other escort, that was Galiano, Señor, he begs to be excused on account of an injury to his hand, so Moya details a replacement and we think that's the end of it, but suddenly our little captive goes wrenching himself away from the men supporting him and actually starts shouting at my Capitán.

He's yelling 'So that's it? You're just going to send them back to Flanders? You're going to let them get away with it? That's it?'

He's acting like a madman, yelling the same things over and over again, we think he's lost his mind. My Capitán tells him to calm down, but there's just no reasoning with him. Straight away he's off again, saying the Capitán has to hang them, he can't just let them go back to Flanders, he's yelling and yelling and no stopping him at all.

Jean-Marie Mercier

Stefan was already handing out muskets to the others. 'They're going by the Flanders Road, and they're going now. Cut through the woods, get them just beyond the bend. This lot will hear the shots, so get the hell out of it fast, run all the way back to base. Warn them André's taken and they need to prepare for evacuation.'

Robert said 'Jean-Marie's the best shot.'

Stefan snapped at him. 'I need him with me. Durand can use the bow, they're unarmoured, you've enough. Here, take this, that's five shots.'

He handed Bettremieu his own pistol. Bettremieu nodded and started to run, Colin, Robert and Philippe hard after him. Margot seized her own musket, but Stefan grabbed her arm and said 'Not you, *fifille*, you can't run in those skirts, start back to the Hermitage right now.'

Dear Margot. She hoiked her skirts up over her elbow, showing really quite a quantity of bare leg, said something very rude to Stefan and ran after Bettremieu.

Only Pinhead hesitated. 'There's no time, we can't get there in time.'

Stefan lost his temper. 'He's buying you time, you stupid bastard. He's buying you time with what might be his life, don't you dare fucking waste it.'

Pinhead took one look at his face, then turned and fled after the others.

Carlos Corvacho

Naturally I understand it now, Señor, but at the time you'll appreciate we found it rather irritating. When Jiménez made to mount his horse, the lad even took hold of the bridle to stop him riding away.

My Capitán had his limits, Señor, and finally raised his own voice to call for silence. The lad was quiet at last.

'Release the bridle,' said my Capitán.

The lad hung his head, but his hand remained firmly on the reins. The Capitán indicated with a jerk of his head I was to deal with the matter, so I'm afraid to say I cuffed him, just a little blow on the side of the head, Señor, perhaps a little box on the ear, just enough to show he must do what the Capitán said.

The lad reacted as if I'd really hurt him, which I'll swear I didn't. He jerked his head and cried out sharp, and if you'll excuse me, Señor, it's best I give you his exact words. He said 'Take your filthy Spanish hands off me.'

It wasn't just the expression, haughty as it was, but the way he said it. There was no mistaking it now, Señor, this was the voice of an aristocrat.

Jacques Gilbert

It's no good asking me, I don't know. To suddenly snap like that, after everything he'd taken already, it didn't make sense. Maybe it was because it was in front of another gentleman, I don't know. It didn't matter anyway, the fact is we were stuffed.

There was total silence, and some of the soldiers actually had their mouths open. D'Estrada flinched, then recovered himself, looked at the boy, and said what sounded like 'Ah.' I started wriggling closer to hear better.

André knew he'd screwed up, but there was no going back now. He shook off the servant, stood himself straight, and looked right in d'Estrada's face, ignoring everything I'd ever taught him. I found myself suddenly remembering his father.

D'Estrada just said 'A gentleman then.'

André half smiled. I don't know when I've seen an expression so insolent.

D'Estrada nodded, like he hadn't expected anything else. 'Well, are you?'

'Are you?' said André.

D'Estrada actually laughed. I noticed he'd shifted his position, like a mirror reflection of the boy's. They were facing each other very upright, legs apart, hands hovering near their hips as if to draw a sword. I was looking at them from the side, and that was odd, I even half thought it at the time, because I could see the boy's sword hand, but I could see d'Estrada's too. Then d'Estrada spoke again and everything else got shot out of my mind with shock.

'Are you André de Roland?'

My last bit of hope sort of fizzled and died.

André said nothing. He looked like d'Estrada hadn't even spoken.

D'Estrada sighed. He turned to the Pedros, told them to get the fuck out of it, watched them start to wind their way through the column towards the Flanders Road, then gave his attention to the boy.

'Then will you tell me your name?'

'Will you tell me yours?' said André.

D'Estrada smiled. 'I am not ashamed of *my* name, Monsieur. I am the Capitán Don Miguel d'Estrada of the Spanish Netherlands'.

André made a little bow. 'You are a long way from home, Señor.'

D'Estrada acknowledged the hit with a smile. 'Where is your home, Monsieur?'

André smiled back. 'Where I stand.'

'And your name?'

The boy was silent.

D'Estrada sighed. 'Monsieur, I say your father was Antoine, Chevalier de Roland. Will you give me the lie?'

The boy was finished. Nothing on earth would make him deny his father. He lifted his head higher and spoke in his clearest, most carrying voice.

'No. I am André de Roland, Sieur of Dax. And I say to you, Don Miguel d'Estrada of the Spanish Netherlands, that you are on my land, and I demand justice for the atrocities committed against my people. I demand it before God.'

And in the silence there came the crash of musket fire from the Flanders Road.

D'Estrada turned at once and ordered men to investigate, but they were in an almost superstitious panic, like the boy had called for justice from God and been granted it right away. They stumbled about, bumping into each other, and took ages setting off after the two Pedros. D'Estrada turned back to André with a stunned expression.

He said 'This is your doing.'

The smile on the boy's face was lovely.

'I, Señor? I have been with you the whole time.'

Jean-Marie Mercier

Marcel was already running back towards us, ducking in and out of cover, only just making it into the ditch before d'Estrada turned to face the woods. I think perhaps he suspected we'd been there, and wondered if we still were. His head turned slowly in a half-circle, scanning the whole area of woodland. Jacques had stayed near the road, but I saw him working his way carefully through the brambles until he'd disappeared right inside. Stefan motioned me to pick up my musket, and slung his own over his shoulder.

Marcel reached us safely behind the tree. 'They know who he is. And now, of course, they know he's army.'

Stefan closed his eyes for a second, then bent to pick up the last gun.

Marcel said urgently 'He mustn't talk.'

'I know,' said Stefan, and threw him the musket.

'Not here,' said Marcel. 'They'll get Jacques for certain,

he's almost on top of them. They were headed for Dax, I'll do it there.'

Stefan nodded. 'Take Mercier too. Make sure of it.'

I jumped. I was being terribly slow, but simply didn't know what they meant.

Marcel nodded, and turned to me. 'Come on. We'll have to run to get there first.'

I got up, still confused. 'Are we going to rescue André?'

They looked at me, and I was alarmed to see something almost sad in their expressions.

'We can't do that, Jean,' said Marcel gently.

'We'll save him this way,' said Stefan, and tapped my musket.

It was only then I understood what they were asking me to do.

Carlos Corvacho

My Capitán sent men to check the woods, but it was only a gesture, Señor, he knew the rebels had been and gone. All we found were a handful of abandoned bandoliers.

He looked even grimmer when Moya's team came back from the Flanders Road with the bodies of the escorts, and told us Jiménez and Sánchez had disappeared. My Capitán didn't like to lose men, Señor, he took it very personal. He turned to de Roland and said 'Where have they taken them?'

The Chevalier said only 'I'm afraid I cannot help you.'

He looked quite different now, Señor, really quite the gentleman, but he was still an enemy soldier, that latest escapade had proved it certain sure.

My Capitán said 'I will have an answer to that question, Chevalier.'

De Roland smiled, but this time he said nothing at all.

'Very well,' said the Capitán. 'We will resume this discussion at the barracks, when I'm afraid I shall have to insist.'

The Chevalier bowed correctly and seemed quite unmoved, but he wasn't really, Señor, nor was it likely. He took care to clasp his hands lightly behind his back, but not before I noticed they'd started to tremble. It was a shame of course, and him so young, but duty's duty, we all know that. He never shirked that, my Capitán, nor could he afford to, not with the Colonel Don Francisco on the way and likely to ask a few questions if we didn't get everything we could from our only rebel captive.

He still felt sorry for the lad, Señor, and said in view of his rank he would take him on his own horse. Young de Roland appreciated that, and went to the animal at once, stroking its nose and murmuring to it. I'd always found it a most bothersome beast, but the lad seemed quite at home with it. He looked less happy when my Capitán explained he'd have to be bound, but he understood it, Señor, he nodded silently, and when one of the men came with the rope he held out his hands in a detached way, as if they were servants waiting on him. He never even looked at them, but gazed firmly at the woodland as if they simply weren't there.

Jacques Gilbert

He was looking at me. He couldn't possibly see me, but he knew I was there somewhere. He'd seen the soldiers search the area and report it empty, but he still knew I'd never have left him.

A soldier lifted him on to Tempête's back, then another raised him so they could loop his bound hands round the

213

gelding's neck. Finally d'Estrada himself mounted behind him and signalled the troop to move ahead. They rode off towards Dax, then the road was empty and the boy was gone.

I fought my way out of the brambles, picked up his sword, and started the walk back. As I passed the bracken where the boy had hidden, something moved and rolled under my foot, the stupid ball he used for his exercises. I picked it up. It was the sun, of course, just the heat of the sun, but I thought I could feel the warmth of the boy's hand still in it.

I set off into the forest, and saw Stefan dropping out of a tree ahead of me. I half thought he might say something kind, but I didn't want it, I didn't want anybody to be kind.

He wasn't, anyway. He just said 'Come on, for fuck's sake, we've got to hurry. You'd better get your family safe, and warn the others at Ancre; it's only Gauthier, isn't it? I've got the Hermitage on standby, if we haven't heard in an hour I'll get them to evacuate and pass the word to Mercier's family.'

I didn't understand. 'Warn them?'

'If he talks,' said Stefan, impatiently. 'If he bloody talks. He doesn't know people in Verdâme except Mercier and me, but he knows just about all our people in Dax. Christ knows how we'll warn them all if we can't shut his mouth first.'

I was suddenly so angry I didn't know what to do with myself. I said 'He won't fucking talk, you know he won't, he'll die first.'

'I hope so,' said Stefan. 'Marcel's gone to make sure of it.'

It took me a second, then went right through me all at once. I know I cried out.

'It's the only way,' said Stefan, and he was suddenly gentle. 'Better for him too, a nice clean bullet.'

I think I was almost screaming at him. 'You can't. He can't be killed by his own people, it's wrong, we've got to stop them.'

'Calm down and think about it, you'll know it's best.'

'That's easy for you to say. You never bloody liked him anyway.'

He turned on me so suddenly I didn't see him coming, the next I knew my back was slamming into a tree so hard it smashed all the wind out of me. He had his hands on my collar, he was pressing me against the tree, and his breath was right in my face.

'Do you want him tortured? Is that what you want? You, you couldn't even stand seeing him get a kicking just now, what do you think they'll do to him in there, what the hell do you think they'll do?'

I couldn't think, he was banging my head against the tree, I said 'I don't know.'

He seemed quieter then. 'If you cared about him even half as much as you pretend, you'd do anything to save him from that.'

I couldn't make my mind work properly. I said 'Yes, I would, anything, just tell me what I can do.'

He slowly released me and stood back.

He said 'You can pray Marcel shoots straight.'

Eleven

Jean-Marie Mercier

Marcel ran so fast I was struggling to keep up. Perhaps that was good, because it stopped me thinking properly. I was watching his feet pounding into the ground in front of me and ducking my head to keep clear of branches, and all the time there was a voice in the back of my mind screaming that they wanted me to kill André.

We broke out of the woods into the graveyard behind St Sebastian's, and paused a moment to collect ourselves. Then we wedged our muskets under our arms, adjusted each other's cloaks to hide them as best we could, and walked across the graveyard towards the church. My heart was beating so hard I felt queasy.

There were a few people sitting inside, but it was gloomy after the daylight so I couldn't see if they were noticing us or not. I think honestly they must have, because the tips of our barrels were poking up like broomsticks, but perhaps people decided they didn't really want to know. We made it safely to the steps and up to the tower, and nobody said a word.

I went straight to the window. It was only a square hole in the stone, so I was able to look in both directions and see with relief there was no sign of the column. I expect they'd had to delay while they found out what happened at the Flanders Road, and of course we'd been able to take a much more direct route by travelling on foot.

I turned round and saw Marcel watching me.

He said 'It's all right, Jean, I'll take the first shot myself. Just remember it's what André would want. If he talks, half of Dax will lose a son, and he'd never want that.'

I knew that was true. It's why I loved him, you see.

Jacques Gilbert

I went to M. Gauthier's first, but he wasn't in. There wasn't even Dog barking, the cottage felt as empty as a house can be, and I remember thinking I knew how it felt.

Then I went home and broke the news to my parents. Father was good, actually, he was steaming angry, but he was much better in a crisis than Mother, who just walked about wringing her hands and getting in the way while we were trying to get bags together and lug everything over to the Home Farm.

M. Legros was very kind. He'd always agreed we could come if this happened, so he just stopped what he was doing and helped settle us in himself. We arranged all our stuff in the Third Barn, then built a wall out of hay bales to hide it, and it actually looked quite comfortable. It wouldn't be for long anyway. If the boy was killed, we could go straight home. If he wasn't, Marcel would get my family out of Dax by the *gabelle* road. I wondered when I'd know. That's all.

No, I'm sorry, but what do you want me to say? Look, it was André. I'd sat and watched those bastards beat and kick him till he couldn't stand, and now they were going to torture and kill him, and there was nothing I could do about any of it. Is that what you want to hear?

Jesus. Don't you *ever* stop writing?

There was a great cloud of dust approaching from the Ancre Road. Marcel took up position at the window, rested his barrel on the ledge and brought his hand ready to the trigger. There wasn't room for two, so I stood behind him, listening to the horses clattering on to the cobbles of the Square. There seemed an awful lot of them.

Marcel tensed his shoulders, and I knew he'd seen André. For a long moment I watched as he tracked with the barrel, then he flung back from the window and turned to me in frustration.

'It's no good, he's buried in them. Will you try? It needs a better shot than me.'

I took his place, and at once saw the difficulty. D'Estrada's scarlet saddle-cloth was clearly visible towards the back of the column, but André himself was mostly hidden by the horse's head.

'I can try,' I told him, 'but I might hit d'Estrada.'

'Don't do that, Jean,' said Marcel quickly.

None of us wanted to kill d'Estrada. Apart from the inevitable reprisals, André and Marcel always said he was the only decent Spaniard in Picardie.

I looked again. They were slowing as they approached the Square, and I noticed the bobbing motion of the horse bringing up André's body at a regular rhythm. If I aimed for the chest on the upbeat, then even if I mis-timed it I thought the ball could still take him in the head without touching d'Estrada. I watched him come up once, twice. I could see him quite clearly, down to the bruises on his face. He came up a third time, and I let him drop down. I couldn't do it. I absolutely understood it had to be done, but I simply couldn't do it.

'I'm sorry,' I said. 'D'Estrada's in the way.'

Marcel nodded, and resumed his position. 'All right. I'll wait till he's going past and we get a sideways shot.'

I went on looking over his shoulder. The horse came on towards the Square, heads turning to stare at every step. One by one people recognized André, and a dreadful silence fell. Word seemed to spread ahead of them, and little crowds started to form outside the Quatre Corbeaux, the Forge, the bakery, the alley to the mill. A rather podgy cabo lounging about by the barracks seemed suddenly to react and stand up straight. He took a hesitant pace forward, then stopped to await the Capitán's arrival.

We had only seconds left. D'Estrada was approaching the church. If we missed him here, he was only yards from the barracks, and the courtyard gate was already open to receive him.

Père Gérard Benoît

I watched the procession of soldiery with a heavy heart. However I had envisaged the return of André de Roland to his people, it had never been like this.

The only grain of hope lay in the presence of Don Miguel, for I knew him to be the kind of man who would never misuse a child, and had found him susceptible to pleading in the past. I accordingly removed my hat as he approached, and called deferentially for his attention.

Our Seigneur turned his head to me and smiled. Don Miguel checked his mount, paused, then urged the animal in my direction, signalling two of his men to follow.

Marcel swore under his breath. D'Estrada was trotting directly towards us and we'd lost the chance of the profile shot. If he came much closer I was afraid he'd be right below us and out of range completely.

Only he was slowing, and after a moment he brought his horse to a halt, as if to speak to the priest on the steps of the church below.

Marcel adjusted the barrel downwards. 'That's better. Now if only the priest can get d'Estrada to dismount, we'll get a clear shot.'

Père Gérard Benoît

As Don Miguel brought his horse to a halt I perceived for the first time the lamentable state of our Seigneur. There were clear marks of violence on his face and body, and his clothes were in shreds.

I demanded at once what the child had done to merit such mistreatment, but Don Miguel only smiled and shook his head.

'There is no more need for pretence, *mon père*,' said he. 'Your Chevalier has admitted his identity.'

I feared this might be a cunning trap to lure me into incautious speech, but André himself gave a little shrug and nodded sadly in concurrence.

Don Miguel looked between us a moment, then dismounted, passed the horse's reins to his servant, and walked across to join me.

It was still no good. D'Estrada and the page dismounted, but the man holding the Capitán's reins stayed in the saddle and planted himself square between André and ourselves. I think it was his servant, Corvacho, only he wore a helmet so I never had a clear view of his face.

He was the only one left. The rest of the troop had dismounted at the barracks, and were stretching and relieving themselves before wandering inside. If it hadn't been for Corvacho, André would have been the only person mounted in the whole Square and it would have been the easiest shot in the world.

The plump cabo I'd noticed before came wandering towards the church as if waiting to speak to d'Estrada. I suddenly wondered if he might have recognized André.

'Pray God he hasn't,' said Marcel, his eyes screwed up as he stared down his barrel. 'What if he's seen him with Jacques or his family?'

Père Gérard Benoît

Don Miguel remarked upon my lack of surprise at seeing our Seigneur in so humble a disguise, and enquired lightly if I had seen it before.

The principle of *Ad Maiorem Dei Gloriam* carried me onward, and I declared stoutly I had no idea of it until now.

Don Miguel sighed. '*Mon père*, I blame no man for loyalty to his liege lord, nor do I hold you accountable for the manner in which he has spent his time. For the Chevalier de Roland, however, matters are very different. Today arrives our new governor, the Don Francisco Mendéz of Seville, and the boy's capture is most untimely. There may have been a time his age might have spared him inquisition, but I fear that is now past.'

I was struck with horror, and he saw it.

'There is still hope,' said he. 'My Colonel could scarcely fail to extract the information he requires from one so young and unschooled, but if a good friend such as yourself were to supply it in his stead, there would be no necessity to try the experiment, and your Seigneur would be spared the torture.'

I said truthfully that I knew nothing of the Rebel Movement.

'But you know the Chevalier's friends,' said he. 'You know where he has been hiding and who has helped him. These are the people who will lead us to the rebels. Give me those names and I give you my word of honour to spare the child.'

I did not care for the office, for it felt like a betrayal of my beliefs, my community and my country. I said I could not help him.

'Then no one will,' said he. 'For you should know these same friends permitted him to be captured and beaten today without lifting a finger to save him. Of all Dax, yours is the only hand that has been raised to support him, yours the only voice that has spoken in his defence. You are his only friend. I would you were mine also.'

His voice was passionate, and I saw for the first time how genuinely distressed he was. There was a fine sheen of moisture on his upper lip and a vivid pain in his eyes. He said very quietly '*Mon père*, I have never yet participated in the torture of a child, and would not begin now. I beg you to help me.'

I saw the anguish he was suffering, and understood that any names I gave would be merely anticipating, as André would be compelled to yield them in any event. It also occurred to me that apart from the pain of the torture, a young man of the character of our Seigneur could never live content with the knowledge he had betrayed his friends. If somebody had to take upon himself the mantle of Judas, was not the truly Christian thing for me to do it myself and spare the boy? Might not dishonour itself be honour in such a cause?

I hesitated.

Jean-Marie Mercier

We honestly couldn't think what was going on. The Capitán's servant certainly seemed to imagine he was in for a long wait. He stretched, eased himself, then finally started to dismount.

Marcel had the stock tight against his cheek. André was now lying so low on the horse's back as to present only the smallest target, but we were above and looking down on him, and I didn't think Marcel could miss. His finger tightened on the trigger – but at that same instant André made his move.

The second Corvacho's feet struck the ground, André jerked the horse's head, and dug his heels hard into its flanks. The reins were simply wrenched out of the servant's hand, as the beast leapt forward and away. D'Estrada and the servant were left standing in amazement in a cloud of swirling dust.

Horse and rider simply streaked down the road to the Gate, right past the soldiers outside the barracks. There was shouting, but no one was mounted to go after him, and really it was chaos. Soldiers were running for horses or reaching for their guns, but crowds of spectators suddenly poured in among them, milling about between André and the pursuit. Our own Martin Gauthier was there, apparently chasing his dog, but always blocking the view or jogging the elbows of soldiers trying to raise guns. Some still managed to squeeze off a shot, but André was so low on the horse's back he was virtually no target at all. One soldier kept his head, but even as he lowered his musket to shoot the horse, Marcel fired and took him clean in the neck.

I quickly took his place at the window and levelled my own weapon. There were soldiers staring round below us, trying to work out where the shot had come from.

'Time to go,' said Marcel.

It took me a second to find the plump cabo in the mêlée, but he hadn't moved far. He was still standing alone and I didn't see how he could have yet told anyone whatever it was he knew. I fired, and watched him fall.

'Now, Jean!' said Marcel. 'Leave the guns, we'll have to mingle with the crowd.'

Père Gérard Benoît

The Chevalier was away before any man could lay hold of the bridle, and the speed with which he rode caused the soldiers to scatter before him. I was concerned he appeared to be heading towards the Gate, which was closed and heavily guarded, or that he might attempt the Dax-Verdâme Road on the left, out of which more Spanish horsemen were already debouching. Nor was I reassured when he turned instead to the right, galloping down the Market Street, which runs alongside the Wall to its west corner, for I could not see how he could hope to flee from this position. He must of necessity turn right again where the Wall lay in front of him, but this track led only to the Thibault farm, which was walled and offered no route of escape on the other side.

As I ran with the others, soldiers rode furiously past me and our Chevalier was trapped. Behind him were the soldiers, to left and in front was the Wall, to his right only the farm. I stood on the corner to watch the end. The pursuing soldiers dropped their pace and spread out, anxious to prevent their quarry doubling back and past them, which did not seem impossible for so fine a horseman.

Then I saw André was not slowing to achieve the right turn, but urging his horse to greater speed until its hooves flashed along the cobbles and scarcely appeared to touch the ground. As I realized what he was attempting I let out a cry, and so did others near me, but he would have been too far away to hear.

The great horse leapt, with the boy on its back. The silence was absolute, and I recall observing the event with extraordinary clarity, as if everything had slowed for this one instant of time. The horse was in the air, it was above the Wall, André rose from its back but kept his arms round its neck, and before the horse disappeared on the other side I saw him drop safely down on to its back.

He had jumped the Wall.

Jean-Marie Mercier

I know now it was his own horse. I knew he was tied on to it and couldn't fall. I saw the new fortifications hadn't extended this far and that he took off where the camber of the road was at its highest, so the jump was perhaps only five foot in height. None of that matters. He jumped the Wall.

I've never heard a silence like it. We all knew there was the moat on the other side, and I was terribly afraid the horse might break its leg coming down, so it was a huge relief to hear its hooves galloping safely into the distance. I remember Martin Gauthier behind me saying over and over again 'Oh, bravo, Sieur, oh, bravo.'

Then the laughter started. The soldiers chasing André had all balked at the Wall and were looking baffled and angry. One even threw his helmet on the ground in frustration. Perhaps that's what started the laughter, but once we began it was difficult to stop. I felt a curious emptiness inside because André was gone, but I know I laughed myself, and the relief of it was wonderful.

Père Gérard Benoît

Don Miguel's own face was expressionless, but he said only 'Well, *mon père*, it would appear your Chevalier has solved the dilemma for both of us.'

At that moment I became aware of the laughter dying away, and a sudden tightening about Don Miguel's mouth impelled me to follow his gaze to the Dax-Verdâme Road, where I perceived the new arrivals were greater in number and significance than I had first supposed. Gradually the crowd fell silent, as the first outriders stood aside and a group of finely dressed Spanish cavalry picked their way delicately among us.

In front of this troop rode a tall and most imposing figure, astride a magnificent warhorse with scarlet and gold hangings. Despite the fineness of the weather, a great cloak faced with dark fur was carefully arranged about his shoulders, and a scarlet sash was stretched across the expanse of his chest. He wore no helmet, only a hat of luxurious black velvet, which boasted a small red tassel depending above one ear. The face thus framed seemed larger than the average, but this was probably an illusion caused by the slenderness of the moustache and the tiny imperial which graced the tip of his ample chin. The brows, however, were full and black, which in turn made his eyes appear smaller than perhaps they were.

The figure drew to a halt opposite Don Miguel, who at once bared his head and dropped his knee.

'Ah, d'Estrada,' said the newcomer, with an air of apparent amiability. 'I appear to have come at a time of Carnival. Would you care to explain what the devil it is we are all celebrating?'

The Colonel Don Francisco Mendéz had finally arrived.

Jean-Marie Mercier

We should have gone sooner, but it was quite impossible now. The new cavalry were blocking the way back to the Square and we hardly liked to draw attention by trying to slip past.

As d'Estrada explained what had happened, the Colonel dismounted and gazed round at us all with the most chilling expression. I became very conscious we were the only strangers in the village, but a very pretty girl took hold of Marcel's arm and wrapped it firmly round her waist, while I felt a touch on my own hand, and looked down to see a little old woman regarding me with bright, determined eyes.

'By your leave, Monsieur,' she whispered confidentially,

drawing her arm safely through mine. 'Your name is now Hébert, and you are my grandson.'

I was astonished and warmed by the gesture, but perhaps I should have expected it. This was Dax, you see. They were André's people.

Père Gérard Benoît

This Don Francisco proved himself from the first a man of very different quality from our Don Miguel. His anger at what had occurred became immediately evident, the more so for being expressed in neither a raised voice nor an excessive gesture, but only through the medium of his eyes, the coldness of which was observed by many there.

He affected a lack of interest in the whole affair, announcing the escape of a child was of little moment, and perhaps the simplest way of cleansing his province of all remnant of the old regime. The manner of its achievement was unfortunate, but rendered a perfect opportunity to make an immediate example of all who had been involved in this escapade. With this last remark, he reached out a leisurely hand to his aide, and into it the man placed a pistol.

'Now,' said he. 'You tell me our men were hindered in their duty by villagers obstructing their line of fire. Who?'

There was a small silence, and then a hubbub of voices as many soldiers began to speak at once. Fortunately they had little information to offer, for these were troops newly arrived from Artois, and as yet unfamiliar with our local people. However, the presence of Martin Gauthier's dog, a devoted if insanitary animal which was snapping in a friendly manner among the soldiers' heels, drew attention to the ungainly figure of the gamekeeper himself, whose appearance was sufficiently distinctive for even these newcomers to remember him.

'This?' said Don Francisco, regarding Martin with distaste.

Two soldiers protested they were certain of it. Don Francisco nodded in a manner that seemed almost bored, aimed his pistol casually at Martin, and shot him in the face.

Jean-Marie Mercier

His face simply smashed open in front of me, spattering fragments on the clothes and faces of people beside him, his body flying back at the impact and crashing heavily down on to the stones. The little dog gave an agonized yelp, ran to the body and began to howl.

The grip on my arm tightened painfully. My old woman was speaking again. She said in a hard voice 'We don't cry, Monsieur. It is the Spaniards who will cry later when André hears.'

Only André was gone. I remembered the sound of the horse's hooves fading into the distance, and knew we were completely alone.

The Colonel reached for a second pistol, then raised his voice over the howling of the dog.

'Now,' he said pleasantly. 'Who will tell me the identity of the men who fired on my soldiers?'

Père Gérard Benoît

The people swore as one they had neither seen nor could guess from whence the shots had come. I had my own suspicions, for among the crowd I saw two foreign faces, in one of whom I recognized the Verdâme caporal, Marcel

Dubois, but his arm was about Mathieu Pagnié's daughter Suzanne, while his companion was supporting Béatrice Hébert, and I had hopes they might escape detection by the Spaniards.

The last voices faltered and died, and no name had been offered. The Colonel's response to this can only be described as monstrous. He fired his pistol randomly into the people gathered together, hitting the youngest Laroque boy full in the belly and driving him to the stones in agony. He then put the question again, and many now said they believed the shot to have come from my own church tower. The soldiers searched at once, and returned bearing two muskets, which they cast noisily down at our feet.

The Colonel turned his face towards me.

Don Miguel immediately explained I had had nothing to do with the assault, and that he had been in conversation with me himself up until the moment of the first shot. The Colonel nodded, but did not appear greatly interested, being still at the business of procuring yet another pistol from his escort.

'Very well,' he said. 'Then perhaps these people will tell me the name of the assassins who fired from his church.'

He began to raise the pistol, and a slight movement in the crowd showed me Dubois and his companion releasing their ladies in readiness to step forward. Their intended sacrifice was, however, forestalled by Jean-Baptiste Moreau, host of our little village tavern, Les Quatre Corbeaux, who barred their way and stood before the Colonel to plead.

'We do not know, Señor,' he said. 'No one could see faces at a window so high. If we knew, we would tell you, I swear it.'

I suspected this for an untruth, for not only had he deliberately interposed his own body between the Colonel and the strangers, I also knew him for a most loyal member of my congregation, whose eldest son Simon was rumoured among the rebels himself. It is possible the Colonel shared my doubts, for he merely responded 'Then tell me what you *do* know, Monsieur,' and aimed his pistol casually at the innkeeper's own stomach.

'I will, Señor,' said Jean-Baptiste immediately. 'I know the boy who just fled was André de Roland, who was previously our Seigneur. I know he has remained in the area since the Spanish liberated us from his rule, and has lived rough in the woods all that time. I believe he has formed a band of ruffians who threaten the peace of this district, and that his departure can mean only our good, for we wish nothing more than to live at peace with our new masters. In this, Señor, I believe I speak for us all.'

There was much murmuring of assent and nodding of heads within the crowd, although not one but knew the Seigneur had lodged this year past with the Gilbert family rather than in the woods. Their loyalty warmed my heart.

The Colonel appeared to find this response appropriately subservient, and of this our good Capitán hastened to take advantage, professing himself deeply impressed at the salutary effect his superior's demonstration had so speedily achieved.

He said 'Perhaps enough is done to teach the people of Dax they have now a new master to obey.'

'Perhaps,' said Don Francisco, with a sudden smile of extraordinary sweetness. 'We shall see.'

Jacques Gilbert

I couldn't stay there. Mother kept weeping, Blanche was fretting for her home, Little Pierre was grumbling and wanting to know how long it was for, and Father kept saying 'Ask Jacques,' like it was all my fault. In the end I just climbed out through the hay bales and left them.

I went back to M. Gauthier's. It wasn't just to warn him, I wanted to see him, he was the only person in the world who was going to understand. But the cottage was still dark and empty, he wasn't back from wherever he'd been, and I remember standing outside and stamping with frustration.

There was only one other place for me to go, and that was back to our own barn. There were no soldiers there, I'd known there wouldn't be, I'd said all along the boy wouldn't talk. Everything looked familiar inside. There was the chalk scribbling on the wall where André had drawn the fencing target with all the hitting positions marked. He'd written them out in full before I could even read them, low inside, *prime* with nails down, first position out of the scabbard. *Seconde*, *tierce*, I knew the shapes of those words before I even knew the bloody alphabet, *quarte*, *quinte*, there was a kind of magic in them like the runes of a spell.

I climbed to the upper level. My blanket lay as I'd left it that morning, I hadn't bothered collecting my own things when we left, and no one had thought to ask if I had. The boy's red blanket was still there, in the mess he usually left it. By now it sort of kept his shape, and I could almost imagine he was asleep underneath it and in a minute he'd stick his head out and ask where I'd been. There were all his other shabby little bits and pieces too. His books, his burnt wooden horse, his picture, and now his ball, his cloak, and of course his sword. I'd have to give that to Père Gérard to send back to the Comtesse, but I didn't think she'd want the rest. It wasn't much to show for his life, not really.

I sat on his blanket and watched as the light from the grain hole faded and a thick black line of darkness spread over the whole barn. I sat there a long time.

I wondered idly why Marcel hadn't sent to tell me anything, it was night, he must have known ages ago. Then I realized no one knew I was here. I'd been ordered to evacuate, any messenger would have gone to the Home Farm instead. It didn't matter, they'd have told my family, all I needed to do was go and ask.

Somehow I just stayed where I was. Here in the barn, with all his things round me, I could feel he was still with me a little bit longer. A part of me felt he really was.

Something stirred in the silence, a sharp scrape against stone, a hoof on the cobbles of our front yard. My heart went sort of *bonk*. I'd been warned, of course, but I hadn't bloody listened, I'd been so wrapped up in being miserable I'd never thought about being caught myself.

I was on my feet in a second, scooping up my blanket into a bundle and shoving the boy's things into it, listening out for more horses and someone banging on the cottage door, but everything seemed suddenly very quiet. Then a horse snorted and whinnied right outside the barn, and it was a horse I knew.

I didn't bother with the ladder, I dropped straight down to the lower level and peered through the crack in the door. There was Tempête on the cobbles, just Tempête, and a small figure still huddled shapelessly on his back. I flung open the door.

Tempête tossed his head at sight of me, and the boy stirred, trying to lift his head. I reached up to him, but his wrists were still tied round the horse's neck, and I couldn't lift him down. He managed to turn his face to look at me, but it seemed to take him a moment to work out who I was.

'It's all dark,' he said. 'I thought there was no one here.'

I led Tempête over so I could stand on the step, then rapped him on the nose to make him lower his head. I lifted the boy at the full stretch of my reach, passing the loop of his tied hands over Tempête's head, and brought him down safe into my arms.

I held him there a moment. I didn't dare hug him, I was scared his ribs might be broken, I just kind of folded my arms round to bring him close. What was left of his shirt was damp and cold in the night air, but I could feel the warmth of him through it, and his heart hammering against my chest like M. Lefebvre gone mad. I wasn't asking how he'd got here, why he wasn't dead or tortured, I wasn't even asking if anyone was after him, it's like none of it mattered. He was here, he was real and alive, and somehow in spite of everything he'd managed to come home.

Twelve

Jacques Gilbert

We dug out the boxes from the paddock, packed our things into sacks, and left the barn before first light. I remember glancing up at the fencing target as we went out. It felt like something I'd outgrown long ago.

We couldn't come back. The boy was known, and couldn't risk being seen here ever again. We daren't even stay till morning, because he'd seen that fat cabo who'd made us fix the wheel and thought he might have been recognized. My family was already in hiding, but we agreed I'd better go to Dax to find out about Colin.

We went to the Home Farm first to get supplies from M. Legros and say goodbye to my family. It wasn't quite dawn, but my parents were already up and dressed like they hadn't slept at all. Mother looked worried and dishevelled with straw in her hair, she didn't even smell the way I was used to. Father looked like someone who's had just about enough.

We spoke in whispers so as not to wake the children. André apologized for the inconvenience, and promised we'd let them know the moment it was safe for them to go home. He said we were going to live in the woods, but he'd speak to M. Legros and M. Gauthier to make sure they still got good food, and he'd send money regularly, so everything would be just the way it was before.

Then I kissed Blanche in her sleep, and actually I kissed Little Pierre too, he looked somehow young again, all curled up in the straw like a little animal, and I just kissed the top of his yellow head and hoped he wouldn't mind. I hugged Mother and she stroked my hair and reached up on tiptoe to kiss me, then I climbed out through the hay bales and left her.

The boy went ahead to collect our food baskets so I could be alone to say goodbye to Father, but it was awkward, I felt sort of shy. Father didn't look like he'd let me hug him, he was kind of leaning away from me, so I grasped his hand instead, and he said 'Go on looking after yourself, won't you, boy?' and let go. His hand was cold.

We were going to move into the Hermitage, of course, though we'd been careful not to let my family know that. It wasn't the most luxurious place to live, it was just another pile of straw like our own barn, but as I waved the boy off into the forest and set out for Dax in the pink dawn light I remember feeling oddly excited, like something was about to begin.

Jean-Marie Mercier

Quite a few of us had stayed that night at the Hermitage. There'd been the Pedros to deal with, you see, and then it was dark and there were soldiers questioning people in the street, so it really wasn't safe to go home. I'd liked to have gone, I'd liked to have told Jeanette her family had been avenged at last, only it honestly wasn't practical.

I remember being half wakened by a single thump on the roof from the sentry. I'm afraid I ignored it, because it only meant someone had crossed the second foresters' road and given the double wave to show they were one of us. I think I must have drifted back to sleep, because the next thing I remember was a really tremendous outbreak of banging on the roof, which certainly wasn't any signal I knew.

Stefan sat up and swore. 'That fucking Georges, I'll kill him.'

Dom never liked people being rude about his brother. He said reproachfully 'Easy now, no need for that,' and strolled calmly out of the door. I heard the murmur of voices as he spoke to Georges on the roof. Then he shouted.

'Oh, for Christ's sake!' yelled Stefan, and leapt furiously to his feet. Marcel and I followed him, because it really did sound terribly important.

It was André himself, walking rather wearily out of the woods towards us, leading the brown horse he'd escaped on and which was now laden with baggage. He stopped at the sight of so many of us crowding towards him, pushed his hair rather self-consciously out of his face and said tentatively 'Hullo.'

Stefan stopped dead and gave a great bellow of laughter, but the rest of us simply surged forward, all wanting to hug him, needing to be sure it really was André, he'd really come back. He seemed quite startled by our reaction, and said there was no mystery about his return, he'd simply ridden along the *gabelle* road and arrived last night. I don't think he quite understood we hadn't expected him to return at all.

He was clearly tired and in pain, so Marcel brought him straight into the Hermitage and sat him down in the soft straw. He looked terribly bruised, and I think he was feeling a lot of discomfort in his, you know, his behind part, but after a drink from Stefan's flask his colour returned and his eyes seemed as bright as ever. Marcel and I sat beside him, but Stefan stayed standing and only leant against a pillar, fingering his flask. There was something about his attitude that was almost defensive. He hadn't said a word since that first burst of laughter.

André himself was in the best of spirits. He didn't even seem to mind what Marcel and I had tried to do, he said Jacques had already explained, and we weren't to worry because it had been absolutely the right thing. When I told him about shooting the plump cabo he was so excited he actually kissed me and said I'd saved the whole of Jacques' family with that one shot. Then he gave us a wonderful account of his journey back, how he'd had to outride robbers outside Lucheux, bumping up and down on the horse's neck all the way. It was really terribly funny.

Marcel asked about his injuries, but he insisted he was fine. He said Jacques had already checked him over, and was convinced he must have broken ribs, which made us all laugh again. Jacques had broken his own ribs last year, you see, and now if anyone was injured he was always checking their ribs, it was the first thing he thought of.

Then André asked what had happened after he'd gone.

All the laughter dried up suddenly, because of course none of us wanted to tell him about poor Martin Gauthier.

'What is it?' said André. 'Jean-Marie?' He turned to Marcel. 'What is it? What's happened?' He even looked at Stefan, but Stefan just thrust his tongue in his cheek, hooked his hands in his belt and stared at his boots.

Marcel told him in the end, he was the only one brave enough. He did it as gently as he could, then said 'I'm sorry, André, I know you were fond of him.'

André looked ahead of him at nothing, and the bruises on his face seemed to stand out more clearly than before. Then he rose slowly to his feet as if he had to go somewhere but couldn't remember where. He said 'I'll kill that bastard don. I'll kill him.'

'It wasn't your fault, André,' said Marcel. 'You didn't ask him to help you.'

André shook his head quite violently. 'He couldn't have not helped me, not Martin. I killed him just by being there.'

Stefan pushed himself away from his pillar. 'That's right, André, you killed him, it's all about you.'

Marcel started to say 'Stefan, please . . .' but André struck out his hand as if he wanted quiet. He faced Stefan and said 'No, it's not, it's about Martin. I know you despised him, but he was good and kind and loyal, he was a far better man than I'll ever be, and he died to save me, how do you think that makes me feel?'

Stefan looked steadily at him, then took a swig from his flask. 'Gauthier was falling to pieces, he'd have been dead in a year anyway. Most of us get no choice in this world, but if he had, which do you think he'd have wanted? To moulder away slowly, growing more useless every day till he turned to pulp and died? Or be shot in an instant saving the life of someone he loved? Which would you choose?'

André made a curious little flinching movement, but his eyes never left Stefan's face.

Stefan nodded gently. 'You didn't kill him, André. You gave him something we'd all like. You gave him the choice.'

Jacques Gilbert

I was careful going to Dax. I knew if that cabo had talked I'd get scooped up on sight, so I walked through the woods to the graveyard and into the church by the north door. There were a load of people on their knees praying like mad, but no one looked up when I walked through. I slid cautiously out of the west door, pushed my hat lower over my eyes, and stood in the shadow of the porch to look over the Square.

Everything seemed normal at first, I couldn't understand why I felt it wasn't. There were more soldiers than usual clustered around the barracks, but I'd seen that before whenever there'd been a big changeover in the troops, it didn't have to mean anything. There were maybe fewer of our own people about, there wasn't such a big crowd outside the bakery, but it was still early, that didn't have to mean much either.

I walked gingerly down the steps and craned my neck to see the entrance to the Forge. It was right next to the barracks and I felt uncomfortable exposing myself that far, but there was hammering coming from inside, and when I looked further I could see Colin himself in the open-sided enclosure, fitting a shoe on a grey horse for a Spanish officer. He wouldn't have been doing that if that cabo had said anything, he'd have been in prison in the barracks. I risked a few more steps to bring me right on to the Square.

A bunch of soldiers came bustling importantly over, but they weren't interested in me, they walked straight past and went towards the little cottages by the Almshouses. I noticed the Laroque place still had its shutters closed, and somehow wasn't surprised when I saw that's where the soldiers were heading. They didn't mess about either, they just marched straight up to the house, pushed open the door and walked in. For a second I heard the terrible sound of a woman crying inside, great, tearing, wailing sobs, then the door shut behind them, cutting it off dead. There seemed to be a silence all over the Square.

That's what was wrong, it had been wrong from the start. Everything was so quiet. People weren't talking, there was no chatter or laughter, they were all sort of muted, like there was a soft blanket dropped over everything. I listened to the silence, and gradually became aware there was something in it after all, a little distant sound that had been there all the time, but so faint I hadn't really noticed it.

It was the desolate howling of a dog.

I made myself walk towards it, right across the Square, then down the main road as it sloped towards the Gate. My feet were kind of dragging, I think maybe I already guessed. As I got further down the slope I noticed a little knot of people ahead, then saw what it was they were gathered round and stopped dead.

Near the Gate, by the turn-off into the Dax-Verdâme Road, they'd put up a tall wooden post with a big crossbar which looked like a gallows. There was someone dangling from it, a tall, ungainly figure with white wispy hair, and I felt a cold lump in my stomach and something hard squeezing at my throat. Huddled at the foot of the gallows was Dog, and it was him who was howling. It wasn't very loud, even now I was closer. It was kind of hoarse like his voice was fading, and I had the feeling he'd been doing it a long time.

I walked up to the post. People parted to let me through, but I don't remember noticing them, I was looking at the body of my friend. I couldn't look at his face, I knew what a hanged man looked like, I couldn't bear to see M. Gauthier like that, with his tongue out and everything, I just stared blindly at his body, at that filthy old brown coat, those horrible baggy green breeches with all rips and stains in them, those strong hairy wrists hanging loosely out of his sleeves. Then that jolted me like a kind of boiling anger, because that's cruel, you can't hang a man without tying his hands. My eyes sort of lifted without meaning to, then I saw blood all over his chest, blood and bits of stuff, and I didn't understand because you don't bleed when you're hung, then I had to look up and saw his head. Not his face, because that wasn't there any more, only the hideous shapeless mess with white hair on top that was all that was left of it. Vomit rose sour in my throat. He hadn't been hung at all, they'd shot him, this wasn't a gallows, it was a bloody gibbet, and they'd hung him up on it after he was dead.

I backed away, retching. I was aware of more people arriving around me, but I couldn't face them, I couldn't close my eyes tight enough to shut it all out. Then there was a voice louder than the others, someone was saying 'Martin Gauthier' like he was a person, not that dreadful thing on the gibbet. I looked and there was the curé standing in front of d'Estrada and demanding the body of Martin Gauthier for Christian burial.

D'Estrada shook his head. 'I regret, M. le Curé, but the man was a troublemaker and a rebel. He obstructed my men in the execution of their duty, and is to remain here as an example.'

He made to turn away, but the curé took his sleeve. 'In the name of God, Señor, I demand you release this man's body to the Holy Church.'

He wasn't that big, Père Gérard, he had that mild, rather stupid face, and his grey hair was all fluffed up in agitation, but I thought there was something heroic about him all the same.

D'Estrada hesitated, but then his head turned sharply, and I heard it again, a woman crying and wailing, it was getting closer. Four more soldiers were coming down the slope, dragging a limp body in a blue shirt, but Mme Laroque was struggling with them and crying for help. Her elder son Yves was trying to support her, and then I recognized the shirt and knew the body was Pierre Laroque. He was one of us, he was in Jacob's unit. He was only about a year older than me.

The soldiers dragged him to the foot of the gibbet and began to fasten a rope round his neck. Yves was talking frantically to the curé, he was saying Pierre had died a few hours ago and the soldiers had just come and taken him. The curé seemed to grow taller with outrage. He shouted at d'Estrada, then shoved the soldiers aside, stood between them and the body, and held out his crucifix square in the air against them. He said 'In the name of Christ, you dare not touch this man. In peril of your immortal souls, you dare not.'

The soldiers started murmuring and one actually crossed himself, but then everyone went quiet and there was this big fat Spaniard striding towards us, dressed like a royal procession and looking like we were all dirt under his polished boots. This was Don Francisco, our new governor, but I didn't know that then, I only knew he was something very bad. He was even carrying a bloody great pistol on his belt, and I'd never seen anyone do that except Stefan.

D'Estrada started to explain, but Don Francisco waved him aside, like he could see what was happening for himself. He turned to the curé and said kindly 'Stand aside, Padre, and let my men do their duty.'

The curé didn't answer. He just stood with his eyes closed and his lips moving, but the hand that clutched the cross was as steady as the boy's with a sword. Everything was quiet, except for the buzzing of flies round M. Gauthier and the miserable, wavering howling of Dog.

Don Francisco sighed and stepped forward, ignoring the cross completely. He looked around at his own soldiers cringing away and the rest of us standing like frightened sheep, and he actually smiled. It's terrible, but in a funny way he reminded me of the old Seigneur, or even of the boy himself if he'd got grown up and fat and was evil instead of good.

There was a kind of fearless authority about him. Power was curling off him like steam from a cauldron.

He reached out his hand, touched the crucifix, and pushed it down.

There was a kind of sigh all round. I don't know what we expected, maybe a thunderbolt or something, but there was nothing, just this fat bastard holding Père Gérard's arm down and smiling into his face, and the priest was looking smaller again and nothing had happened at all.

'Do your duty,' said Don Francisco, pointing to Pierre, and the soldiers rushed forward to pick him up.

The Capitán saluted, and turned rather quickly away. Don Francisco gazed calmly round at the rest of us, then swung his cloak grandly about him ready to sweep off. The cloak actually struck M. Gauthier's legs and set them swinging.

Dog came feebly to life. He stopped that awful thin howling and jerked his poor old head to snap at Don Francisco's heel. I'd never liked that dog, no one did except M. Gauthier, but just for a moment I felt I loved it.

Don Francisco looked down at Dog with disgust, pointed his pistol and shot him. Dog gave one strangled yelp, then flopped on his side and lay still. Above him, M. Gauthier's feet half revolved slowly one last time, then came to a final stop.

Stefan Ravel

We'd hanged them the previous night. Marcel fussed about giving them a proper trial, but that was hardly practical, Abbé, our only magistrate being loose in France on a bolting horse, so we just said fuck it, and strung the murdering bastards up on the spot. They were riddled with gunshot wounds anyway, I doubt they'd have kept till morning. No, we didn't bother with a priest, why the hell should we? They hadn't given Truyart one, let alone that poor baby. It was Magdeburg Justice, Abbé, and that's all they deserved.

André didn't seem concerned. He watched the Pedros dangling for a moment, then simply nodded and said 'Good.'

I'd hoped for better. I'd hoped for a smile at least, but there didn't seem to be one in him any more.

I said 'You broke Fat Pedro's nose for him, you know.'

He turned away. 'Doesn't seem like much now, does it?'

He set off walking back towards the Hermitage, his shoulders hunched and the tatters of that revolting shirt trailing off him like the rags of his little victory. I wondered just how funny that journey of his had really been. Alone in the dark, battered and bruised, no means of defending himself except the horse's speed, while a faintly pungent smell suggested at least one thing he'd found difficult to do with his hands tied round a horse's neck. What concerned me most was that he didn't seem to care. All that bravado had shrivelled out of him as soon as he heard about Gauthier.

I said 'We'd better get you cleaned up and some fresh clothes on you. There'll be something in d'Estrada's baggage.'

He shrugged miserably. 'It doesn't matter.'

I grabbed his shoulder and swung him round so fast he nearly fell over.

'Don't you give me that, don't you fucking dare. You did a man's job yesterday, you took it for all of us, then stuck it to them in front of the whole village by jumping the Wall. Now you're back, and all right, it's not what you expected, the dons have been busy and a friend of yours is dead, but look at me and tell me you're going to just let it go. Look me in the eye and tell me you're giving up'.

He wrenched himself out of my grip. 'Get your hands off me.'

'All right,' I said, raising my hands in surrender. 'Whatever. But you can at least get yourself washed, can't you? I can smell you from here.'

He glared at me a moment, then a shadow of his old grin flickered over his face. 'You really are a bastard, aren't you?'

'Yes,' I said. 'But call me one again and I'll chuck you in that stream myself.'

'You could try,' he said, and smiled.

Jacques Gilbert

I don't really remember walking back to the Hermitage, I just remember arriving. I remember bursting through the door, and seeing André all clean and dressed in new clothes, and coming towards me saying 'What is it? Are you hurt?' I've planned it all out how to break it to him gently, but suddenly it's not like that and I can't speak at all.

Then his arms are round me and he's sitting me down, and I manage to say 'M. Gauthier,' and he looks sad and says 'I know,' and I say 'You don't, you don't know,' and then it all comes pouring out, the gibbet and the dog howling and Don Francisco and the green flies round M. Gauthier's head, I tell him about Mme Laroque sobbing, and the creaking of the ropes as they haul Pierre's body up on the gibbet till he's right off the ground and there's nothing left on the stones but a little pool of blood from his body, and then a great, disgusting, swollen fly goes and lands on that too.

'Drink this,' said Stefan. He shoved his flask against my teeth, and it was brandy, good and fiery, and some of the sickness went away. After a moment my head cleared and I started to take things in properly. There was d'Estrada's baggage strewn over the straw, stupid, irrelevant things like soap and handkerchiefs and a picture of a Spanish girl looking soulful. There was a dark shape in the corner that was Bernard waiting for sentry duty, and he was staring at me with open mouth and wide, dim eyes.

I said feebly 'I'm sorry.'

'No,' said André. 'But they will be.'

He gave my shoulders a little squeeze, then took his arm away and stood up. Stefan took back his flask and had a drink himself. He was watching the boy.

Marcel said doubtfully 'The Spaniards are Catholics too. Surely they'll . . .'

'You think?' said Stefan. 'They wouldn't take the bodies down for the priest.'

André was fastening his baldric over his new shirt. 'Then we'll do it ourselves.'

There was a little silence, broken only by a chuckle from Stefan.

'But can we?' said Marcel. 'Is the gibbet guarded?'

I said Don Francisco had only left three guards there, but it was right in front of the Gate, where there were always loads of them, six on the ground and two on the firing step.

'Ten, eleven, it's not so many,' said André. He started pacing backwards and forwards with his arms folded and his head down. 'Is it in sight of the barracks?'

I thought of the long, downhill slope to the Gate. 'No. But they could see it from the bottom end of the Square if they went down there.'

André nodded. 'Suppose we organized a demonstration of some kind, suppose we put a crowd in the way? They'd never see anything then.'

247

'They'd hear it,' said Stefan. 'They're not fucking deaf.'

The boy flushed. 'If we do it without guns. If we use the archers, or get close enough to use blades.'

Stefan sighed. 'This isn't an ambush in the forest, you're talking about the middle of Dax. One shout, one shot, and there's three, four hundred dons round our necks.'

The boy shook his head in irritation and went back to his pacing. Marcel watched him, and started biting his nails.

I said 'Can't we distract them?'

Stefan looked at me. 'Four hundred? How exactly?'

There was a kind of rumbling from the corner by the door, and I realized Bernard was actually saying something. He said 'We could blow up the barracks.'

Stefan snorted. 'Thanks for that, Rouet. Apart from the fact we haven't enough powder to breach those walls and the dons are rather likely to spot us setting a mine right next to them, that's really helpful.'

Bernard went scarlet, lowered his head again and cracked his knuckles. I began to see why he didn't speak much when Stefan was around.

André paused, thought a moment, then walked on. 'Bernard's right. That would do it, it's the only thing that would. Bernard's right.'

Bernard's head came cautiously up again, like he suspected a trap.

'If we didn't have to breach the walls,' said André, 'if we could actually set the mine inside, we've enough powder for a good bang, haven't we?'

'Oh yes,' said Stefan calmly. 'We've enough for that. What do you propose, my little general? You want Rousseau to smuggle it in under his apron?'

André had stopped again. He bent down suddenly, and picked up the rags of his old shirt. It was ripped down the back, it was filthy and worn, no good for anything except maybe cleaning the guns, but he looked at it like it was suddenly precious.

'Maybe there's another way,' he said.

Carlos Corvacho

We weren't having the best of days, Señor, no. The Colonel Don Francisco, he was what you might call a difficult man. A fine soldier, there's no denying it, wonderful reputation, but just a little . . . difficult.

Oh yes, he was sympathetic to my Capitán's position, especially as he wasn't happy to be exiled here himself. A little question of embezzlement in his case, or so I understood, but the end result was the same: no command in the army this year, and only the prospect of a long stay in what he called this pit of lost souls. He used to write poetry, Señor, did you know? A very refined gentleman, our Colonel. I helped his servant unpack his wagon, and there were wonderful ornaments in it, wonderful, he had a real fancy for anything in miniature. He even had toy soldiers, can you believe? Beautifully painted and all quite lifelike, they were really.

Oh no, he wasn't soft, I wouldn't want you to think that. We'd hoped he'd stay in the grand house we'd reserved for him, but he insisted on moving into the barracks itself. Quite commendable in its way, Señor, but not really convenient, with my gentleman forced to give up his quarters and move out to this chilly great lumber room, and me taking the whole day to make it nice for him. I did my best, Señor, I put up his tapestry with the hunting scenes and found some nice red poppies for his desk, because he did like flowers about the place, he said it made things cheerful. I showed him in the afternoon, and he put his hand on my shoulder and said 'You're a good fellow, Carlos. Take the evening off for a change, have some time for yourself.' That was just like him, Señor, there never was a more considerate gentleman. I said 'But what about your supper, you'll be wanting something brought in,' but he only shrugged and said he had no appetite.

I knew what that was about, it was that business with the gibbet. All morning he's been at the Colonel to reconsider, he says it's enough to drive the local people to rebellion, but the Colonel only laughs and says he thinks not. 'These are peasants, man,' he says. 'Without de Roland they're just sheep.'

My Capitán's not so sure. They were singing this new song in the alehouse last night, all about a bird being chased by soldiers, I expect you know it, don't you, Señor? Well, I don't know I'd care to repeat it, but the burden seems to be it defecating on the heads of the soldiers and escaping by flying over a wall. Seems a lot of nonsense to me, but my Capitán thinks it's important. The way he sees it, the Chevalier may have gone, but his reputation's all the higher for it, and that's dangerous with superstitious country folk. My gentleman's really quite fretting over it, he's pacing up and down so much he's making me dizzy.

I say 'If they do make a little demonstration, what does it matter? Ask yourself, Señor, what can they actually do?'

My Capitán stops pacing so suddenly he's got a leg stuck in mid-air. Then he puts it down and turns round to me, and bless me if he isn't smiling.

He says 'You're quite right, Carlos, of course you are. Now tell me, what would I do in their place?'

That's easy, Señor, I've known him long enough for that. I say 'You'd try to take the bodies down.'

He laughs. 'Of course I would. And so will they.'

We dug the graves at Ancre, in the burial ground for family retainers. The graveyard looked pretty in the evening sun, shaded by the beech trees but with that sea of forget-me-nots crowding all over it in a great froth of blue and white. I thought M. Gauthier would like it there. Georges even dug a little hole on the edge for the dog. I was glad he and Dom were with me, they'd been fond of M. Gauthier too. I remember our walking back to the Hermitage together, our spades over our shoulders. 'Still shovelling, little Brother,' said Dom peacefully. 'Still shovelling.'

As we approached the clearing I heard that grinding whirr getting higher and higher like a wasp getting closer, and knew the whetstone in the weapons outhouse was hard at work. Robert was walking purposefully towards the Hermitage with a great armful of bandoliers, while Jean-Marie sat cross-legged against the wall, stitching red Burgundy crosses on to a pile of dark coats to add to our stock of Spanish soldiers' dress. We'd collected a fair amount of Dax Company black and red by taking it off soldiers' bodies, but we were going to need more than that tonight.

The Hermitage itself was packed with men. I could hear them from outside, great loud voices and bursts of raucous laughter. There was something oddly intimidating about it, but this was my home now, so I climbed the steps and pushed open the door.

The place stank of sweat. There seemed to be naked torsos everywhere, as a whole bunch of men changed their clothes for Spanish dress. The first I saw was Bruno Baudet from the mill, and that was revolting, because he was the hairiest man in Dax, he didn't even look human. I walked past quickly, but now Giles was in my way, stripped to the waist, and swinging a Dax Company coat over his shoulder so violently it slapped me in the face. He turned and said 'Sorry, soldier,' and grinned at me with the kind of wildness you get on your second bottle of wine. The others seemed in the same kind of mood. Even Marcel wasn't his usual calm self. He was already dressed in his Spanish gear, and the black looked wonderful against his fair hair, it made him seem taller, stronger, more like a leader. He was giving instructions to Clement Ansel, who was in charge of the assault on the Gate Guards, he was speaking fast and decisively, his hand jerking his sword in and out his scabbard, *swish-click*, in and out, all the time he talked. Clement was a bit full of himself usually, but today he was listening attentively, he even started nodding. Behind them old Jacob started to slather black grease on Marcel's back hair, so the blond wouldn't show under the helmet.

Stefan was there too, but he didn't seem bothered with his own Spanish dress, he hadn't even buttoned the coat, it was just draped round his hairy chest like he was showing himself off. He was briefing the gibbet team, you'd have guessed that from the size of them, there was Colin and Bettremieu and Philippe and Vincent Poulain, there was Roger from the Pagnié farm, Jehan from the Thibault, and that git Pinhead from Verdâme. They were all big men, but somehow Stefan dominated the lot of them, he was the only man I ever knew who could swagger while standing still.

Watching them, listening to them, I suddenly understood what made it all intimidating. The building wasn't just full of men, it was full of soldiers. These weren't the farmhands and craftsmen I knew any more, they were soldiers and this was a bloody army. This was what we'd always wanted when we first started the whole thing, only somehow it never had been, it had always in the end been just us. Something had changed, something I didn't understand.

Then I stepped on to the platform, and saw André. He was sat by himself in the far corner, studying Arnould Rousseau's plan of the barracks. He didn't seem troubled by anything, and when there was an especially loud burst of laughter he only glanced up and smiled gently, like this was normal, this was what he'd wanted. When he lifted his head to reach for his pencil, I saw how calm his face was, and how it had a distant kind of glow. He was humming under his breath, and the tune was '*En passant par la Lorraine*'.

Thirteen

Jacques Gilbert

We gathered behind the mill shortly before nine. André brushed down my coat, straightened my helmet, then held out his hands. I tied them together in front of him, then suddenly he was a prisoner again, standing in the rags of his torn shirt and surrounded by a crowd of enemy soldiers.

The two half-Spaniards stood apart from the rest of us because of not really knowing anyone. Giulio wasn't actually in the army at all, he just translated dispatches from time to time. He was nearly fifty and rather timid with a club foot, but we'd dressed him up in a cabo's gear, and he looked really imposing, with a red sash and little rosettes at the top of his stockings. The younger one I didn't know at all, he was a friend of Giulio's from Verdâme and I think his name was Cristoval. He had a pointed black beard, and looked so Spanish I could hardly believe he was really on our side.

The Dax clock struck nine. Marcel nodded, and Giulio began to lead us round the mill and on to the Backs. That's that big cobbled area that runs behind the west side of the Square all the way to the Thibault farm, and it was a space I'd known all my life. It was the back way to Colin's, and we used to play here, him and me and Robert, we played boules and *saute-mouton*, we played soldiers. Now it was a stretch of grey stone to be crossed, with the rear entrance to the barracks right in front of us. They'd extended the back and stuck up a big iron gate, and there were four guards outside it who brought up their muskets as soon as they saw us.

Giulio was brilliant. His head went up, his shoulders straightened, and he walked towards the guards like they were the ones ought to be scared. The rest of us followed in a huddle.

'No entry this way,' said the senior guard. My Spanish wasn't good back then, but it helps a lot when you've already got an idea what people are going to say.

Giulio managed a laugh. 'I'm not risking this one in the Square.' He gestured behind him, and that was us, that was me jerking the rope to show the boy on the end like a horse on a halter.

The soldiers gaped, then burst out laughing as they recognized the boy. They all started jabbering, probably congratulating Giulio on his catch, I didn't really know, what mattered was their muskets were down, they were standing back for us, they weren't even asking for the password, because André was the only password we were going to need.

Bruno's men went forward first, they were right next to the soldiers, close enough to touch, then I glimpsed one flash of a knifeblade as Bruno's fist thrust forward, old Jacob slapped his hand round another's mouth as he stabbed hard into his neck, and the other two I didn't see at all, there were too many men between them and us. I heard it though, that hard squelch of a knife going in, like a punch into a damp mattress.

The bodies were dragged into cover behind the mill, and Bruno's team took their place. They looked all right if a soldier wanted to go in that way, and Bruno spoke enough Spanish to get by. It was hard to believe looking at him, all you'd expect to come out of that hairy mouth was a grunt, but he was actually the best in the army.

Marcel got us in order. He was leading with Giulio, then it was Stefan and me with the boy on the rope, then Giles with the sack of explosives, and Cristoval at the back. Marcel adjusted his helmet, tucked in a stray bit of fair hair, then turned and walked through the gate, with the rest of us following like a line of ducklings.

We were in.

Colin Lefebvre

Clock struck nine. Minute or two later there's the curé walking towards the barracks, leading the biggest congregation I've ever seen at a Compline. All carrying lighted candles, and the curé singing in Latin, all very innocent, but there was our own Edouard Poulain busy shepherding people down the south side of the Square, and Margot lining them up into a good thick screen. Curé looked a touch puzzled at that, wondering why they're not all in a lump behind him, but there, wasn't ever safe to tell him anything of that kind, he wasn't someone you ever told a secret. Crowd finished forming, screen complete, and we couldn't see the barracks any more. More to the point, they couldn't see us.

We were the gibbet team, all of us big chaps, lying in the woods behind Les Étoiles waiting for the bang. Oaf Pinhead said the barracks team ought to have gone in sooner, he said 'Dons won't let that crowd stay there for ever. What if they're gone by the time the bang comes?'

Durand the butcher, he said 'Don't be daft, Joe,' he said. All right sort of chap, Durand, for all he was a Verdâmer. 'Don't want them hanging about those barracks longer than they need, do you?'

Pinhead said 'More than their skins to think about here,

Durand, but maybe your precious Sieur doesn't care about that.'

Then wallop, out came Bettremieu Libert's great boot and there was Pinhead yelping and saying 'You're crushing my hand, you Flemish bastard.'

Libert looked tranquil as a nun at Mass. He said 'Pardon, Monsieur, my French is not so good. What was that you said about the Sieur of Dax?'

Jean-Marie Mercier

Our party were in the woods at the corner of the Dax-Verdâme Road, and our job was to dispose of the Gate Guards.

I think people were rather excited, because we'd never fought a cavalry action before. Robert was saying 'This is more like it, Jean-Marie, now we'll show the dons what we're made of.' Georges was actually bouncing in his saddle with eagerness.

I was less comfortable myself, because I'm not a very good rider and wasn't quite sure about the enormous horse they'd given me. It was one of the newly captured Spanish ones, and I had the feeling it didn't like me very much. Of course my job wasn't as important as the others'. They were proper light cavalry, but Simon Moreau, Luc Pagnié and I were what Marcel called 'carabins', because we carried muskets instead of swords, and could actually dismount to fight. Hopefully we wouldn't even have to do that, because there wasn't to be any shooting except in emergencies. Bernard and Marin were in the woods with crossbows to deal with the long-range work instead.

The Dax clock struck the quarter. Clement Ansel said 'Stand by, everybody. Any moment now.'

The leather of Georges' saddle gave one excited squeak and was silent.

I'd never been on an action without André and Jacques before. Never.

Jacques Gilbert

It was dark when we first went in. The new extension wasn't finished yet, and they obviously didn't bother lighting it after the masons went home. The floor sounded like stone under my boots, but I couldn't see it, I couldn't even see my own feet. I concentrated on the white of the boy's shirt ahead of me and stepped forward cautiously.

The dark began to get less black and more grey as we got nearer the inhabited bits. Gradually I made out a pattern on the floor, and saw it was the marble slabs they'd stolen from the hall at Ancre, those beautiful black and white squares like a giant chessboard. There were noises ahead now too, a deep murmur of voices, and a sudden burst of crude laughter.

We just kept walking. Arnould had given us a couple of choices of quiet places to set the mine, but even the nearest was the old lumber room of Le Soleil Splendide, and that was still a way to go. There was another rumble of laughter, then we passed an open door with candlelight spilling out on to the corridor, giving us tall, thin shadows that wobbled and stretched as we passed. I glimpsed beds inside the room, but only a few soldiers, and guessed the rest were on duty somewhere. One near the door glanced up as we passed, and I got my eyes down fast, like if I couldn't see him then he couldn't see me. It seemed to work all right, we just walked past with the boy hidden between us and the wall, and nobody said a word.

It was lighter now, there were sconces every few feet, and I saw for the first time how scruffy we looked and how crumpled our clothes were, and couldn't remember if real Spanish soldiers looked that way, I had this mad urge to go outside and check. Then we reached a plaster archway, the old boards of Le Soleil Splendide were creaking under my feet, and that was better, I knew this place. The lumber room was close, and I knew that even better, I'd had my first kiss in there.

We turned off the main corridor down a branch that led to the courtyard, and there was the lumber room on our left. Marcel stopped and whispered to Giles.

'Is it deep enough in? Can we do enough damage?'

Giles shrugged. 'Deeper's better if we want to draw guards from the front.'

Marcel hesitated. I was screaming at him in my head 'No, it's fine, let's just do it and get out,' but he looked back towards the main corridor and I knew he was thinking of going on to the pantry. Then the sound of tramping feet down the corridor decided him. He pushed open the lumber-room door and we all crowded in, anxious to get out of sight.

The room was bigger than I remembered, but everything else was different too. It was all clean and furnished, there was a bed in one corner and a tapestry and mirror on the wall, there was a bloody great desk off to one side, I remember staring stupidly at a vase of bright-red poppies. And behind it was a man, a man at the desk getting up at the sight of us, and it was bloody Capitán d'Estrada.

I've been happier to see someone. We outnumbered him seven to one, but we were in the middle of the fucking barracks, and all he'd got to do was shout. Still, there was no turning back now, so I jerked my head at Cristoval to join us inside, then closed the door.

He didn't seem suspicious. He snapped at Giulio, probably complaining we hadn't knocked, then spotted André and stopped dead in mid-sentence. He came slowly out from behind his desk as if he couldn't believe what he was seeing, and Giulio started talking fast. Don't ask me what he said, my Don-speak isn't what it might be, but I guessed it was the official story that we'd caught the kid climbing back in over the Wall. I wasn't really listening, I was more concerned with the fact the bastard wasn't coming any nearer. He was too far away to grab, and if we rushed him he'd still have time to shout.

André kept his head. D'Estrada motioned him to approach, but the kid stayed where he was, forcing d'Estrada to come a step closer. I edged nearer. Marcel did the same.

D'Estrada ignored us, and spoke quietly to André as if the two of them were quite alone.

He said 'Why did you come back?' He sounded rather sad about it.

'You know why,' said André.

'Yes,' said d'Estrada softly, 'I do. But I'm afraid you may have no army to come back to. I have taken steps to ensure it.'

I didn't like the sound of that, but I got another step closer while he was saying it. Unfortunately d'Estrada looked up, and made an irritated shooing gesture, so I had to stay where I was.

'What steps?' said André.

D'Estrada smiled. 'Would you like to talk to me? We don't need to see the Colonel yet, we can speak quietly, you and I.'

Smooth bastard. More to the point, he was costing us time. I looked urgently at André, and his eyes flickered.

'Well, Chevalier?' said d'Estrada.

André mumbled something. D'Estrada bent his head lower, and the kid spoke again, even quieter. D'Estrada brought his head right down, and that was it, Marcel was there in two strides, his musket crashing down hard on the back of the man's neck.

We got a gag on him fast while he was out, but he still posed something of a problem, since neither Marcel nor André wanted him hurt, and we'd been planning to set off a mine two feet away from where he was lying. Oh yes, we could have carried him to safety, but the dons might just have asked questions if they'd seen us lugging their officer about like a sack of turnips. No, there was only one thing for it, we'd have to set the mine in the pantry.

The clock was striking quarter past already, so Marcel hurried the others on while I stayed to tie d'Estrada to his chair. He came round while I was doing it, so I punched him in the face to quieten him and finished securing his arms round the back. Then I walked round and looked at him.

What you've got to remember, M. l'Abbé, is that for two years this man had been our main opposition. Oh, I knew why they didn't want him killed, I suppose he posed some defence against the worst excesses of Don Francisco, but he was still the enemy, and I found it hard to see why they made such a pet of him. It's always the same in this world, Abbé, punish the poor sod who actually does the job, but let the man who ordered it go free. So I looked at him tied to his own chair with Marcel's dirty handkerchief stuffed in his mouth, and yes, I'll admit it gave me a certain satisfaction.

But the bastard looked back at me, and I'd seen that look before. You get it on the faces of aristocrats if you dawdle in front of their carriages, you get it on the faces of their servants if they think your boots are going to muddy their floor or your breath offend the air their masters breathe. Oh, I've seen it, Abbé. I've seen it on the face of a sanctimonious officer sentencing a boy of eighteen to run the gauntlet that killed him, all for getting drunk after a day of hell in the trenches at La Mothe.

And here it was again, that old look, with enough moral superiority oozing out of it to paint the Vatican. This animal, he was thinking, this stinking, uncouth animal, who knows no better than to strike a helpless gentleman who's acting out of the finest dictates of honour. This animal with no feelings and no soul.

I took out my knife.

Jacques Gilbert

It was only a minute's walk to the pantry. We were getting nearer the big mess rooms and deeper into the heart of the barracks, we must have passed at least a dozen soldiers on the way, but no one stopped us, they just saw the boy and laughed, and some actually clapped Giulio on the back. No one seemed bothered by not recognizing us. I suppose the new arrivals didn't know many people yet, and the old lot just thought we were new.

The pantry was up a tiny dog-leg corridor and totally private. Marcel posted Giulio and Cristoval to stage a conversation outside the door, then the rest of us shot in and got on with it. The curé's demonstration could be broken up any minute, and we were running out of time.

It was very squashed inside, because the shelves took up so much space. They jutted out all round the walls, laden with bottles of fruit and vinegar, and jars of honey and shrivelled red berries, and there wasn't much room on the floor either, we had to pull out two flour barrels so Giles could set the mine against the outside wall to blast out into the courtyard. Marcel poured the gunpowder into two huge pickling jars to make a second explosion by the inner door, while I untied the boy's hands and gave him the cloak and helmet out of my pack to cover his clothes and hair. He'd been a password to get us in, but people were bound to ask questions if they saw us trying to take him out. He hadn't got a sword, of course, but we arranged the cloak to cover his hip and thought it would do. No one had looked closely at us so far, and I couldn't imagine why they would now.

We worked fast, and Giles was just trimming the second length of slow match when Stefan finally sidled in to join us. I wondered what had taken him so long, but he didn't say, he just smiled rather unpleasantly and asked if we were ready to get the fuck out.

Me and André were to leave first with the Spanish speakers while the others stayed to light the fuses. Marcel said seven men running were bound to attract attention, whereas three could just look like horseplay. It sort of made sense, but I guessed he was just making sure the boy got out safely, and maybe the Spanish speakers too. They weren't fighters, either of them, they were only helping us out, it wasn't right to put them in more danger than we could help.

We walked out of the dog-leg, back into the main corridor, past the turning to the lumber room, and ahead of us the corridor was greying into the darkness of the uninhabited part. I pictured the flambeaux outside the back entrance, and Bruno's team waiting to welcome us, then the horses just thirty seconds away behind the mill. The Dax clock struck half past.

We were coming up to that dormitory we'd passed on the way in, the last obstacle before the gate and freedom. I kept my eyes turned away, it had worked before and would work again now. Then there were footsteps ahead of us, and I looked up to see soldiers coming out, five of them, dressed for business and heading into the barracks like it was their turn for duty. It didn't matter, we'd passed loads already, we'd pass these too.

'Can't go out that way,' said a voice. 'You're new, aren't you? No way out that way.'

I looked up and my heart seemed to kick me in the chest. I knew him, I didn't need the bandage on his hand to recognize him, it was that sodding escort from yesterday, the one who caused all the trouble. Behind me Giulio said in his best cabo's voice 'There is for me, soldier,' and the escort's eyes lifted towards him, then he saw the boy.

It was so bloody unlucky. Loads of soldiers had seen André yesterday, they'd seen a boy with long black hair in a torn white shirt, but this one had seen him close up, he'd looked right in his face. His eyes widened at once, and I saw him reaching for his sword. I hadn't time to think, I punched him with my left hand and scrabbled out my sword with my right. I was the only swordsman, it was up to me, I threw myself at the next and lunged before he'd even had time to draw, I just stabbed him and yelled to the others 'Get out, get out!'

But they couldn't, could they, the bastard soldiers were between us and the way out. I pulled out fast, but that bloody escort was back up to me again, I hadn't hit hard enough, and the other three were pressing forward, drawing as they came, there were four of them, four, I couldn't hold. I fumbled my sword back into position and clashed it hard against the escort's, but he twisted his blade and threw mine aside. He shouldn't have been able to do that, he was a foot soldier, he was nobody, but he was big and strong and somehow knew how to use a sword, I only just recovered in time for the parry. The others were coming, there was a big gap to my right for them to push through, and behind it was the boy, unarmed and helpless, I think I screamed in rage. I was hitting out, *battement, battement*, get out of my face, you bastards, and then the gap beside me closed, there was another body there with a sword in his hand. It was Cristoval, the other Spanish speaker, he'd never fought in his life, but he'd drawn his sword and was standing beside me.

Just his being there steadied me. I feinted at the escort, turned and parried the next man, twist and flip his blade up, back to the escort, but he was lunging, I only just got the parry across in time. Behind me the boy was screaming at Giulio 'The sword, give me your sword!' and a fierce hope sprang up in me, André with a sword would see us all through. Cristoval was struggling, he was up against a big bastard, he couldn't do it, he'd never do it, and the fifth man was yelling for help, and someone was going to hear him, someone was going to hear and come at us from behind.

I wasn't good enough, I'd got to be better. I slashed out at the escort and engaged again with the other, but Cristoval was falling back beside me, he was giving ground, sword dropping, arms going up to ward off the blows, and then his man pushed him right behind me, I couldn't see him any more, there was only this awful grunt and the sound of his fall. His man was through, and I couldn't turn, I was still fighting two, I couldn't get a thrust in either of them, I was having to turn too quickly between them. There's a clash of blades behind me, and it's a good, decisive sound, *coup sec*, that's got to be the boy. Relief sluiced over me like sweat. I walloped the escort's sword down, nothing pretty, I just bashed it out of the way, ducked low in the spin and thrust my other man clean in the guts.

But for a second I'm vulnerable, I've not allowed time to pull out, the escort's thrusting, then there's a blade slicing in between us, and there's André, finished with Cristoval's man already and taking on the escort, I'm free to pull out and go for the fifth man. He was young and unbearded, he looked scared as shit, but he was the last one left and behind him the way out. I went straight at him, jump and lunge, but my right foot shot suddenly away from me, my whole weight pitched forward, there's blood on the marble and I'm slipping, stamping my left foot down hard to stop myself splitting in two. The soldier leaps at me, suddenly confident, but I'm falling as he lunges and he only scratches my shoulder, I'm on the floor, sick and dizzy, and he's coming at me again to finish the job. Then somehow, impossibly, André's there. He's still fencing the escort but he's spun out towards us, his blade flicking my man's up and away, he's got them both. A dark shape appears in the doorway they all came out of, someone's asking sleepily what the hell is going on, and I feel stupid, stupid, I can't think why I assumed there weren't more, but there are, there's a sixth man.

I'm aware of everything. The sixth man grabbing for his sword, the wall cold against my back as I slide myself up trying to clear my head, Giulio groping on the floor, to take a sword from one of the dead men, footsteps running towards us down the corridor. And André, fighting two of them and suddenly fighting three.

I'd seen him fence, but I knew now I'd never seen him

fight. His sword was whipping about like a streak of light in the dark corridor. He was scoring down the escort's face, turning and stabbing at my young soldier, twisting his body away from a thrust from the newcomer he can't have even seen, darting his blade under the incoming sword, thrust in, twist out, back to the young one and a good clean lunge in the chest, parry the escort, and now it's just the two of them, André and this man who slapped his face while others held his arms, and I know he isn't going to want any help killing this one, he'll stop me if I even try. I'm steady again, my sword's in my hand, I turn to face the men who've run down the corridor, but the one in the lead is Giles, and behind him are Stefan and Marcel.

There was still the ring of swords behind me, and I turned to see André finish the escort. I knew he was good, he was much bigger and stronger, and the boy already stiff with bruises, but I wasn't worried. The escort was using his weight to bear down hard on the boy's sword, driving him down on one knee, but André's left foot was already bending for leverage, and as the man disengaged and lunged down, the boy's left leg was kicking straight, propelling him forward and up straight in the lunge. The escort's sword thrust into empty air and there was suddenly a blade sticking out a foot the other side of his back. André pulled out and stood back while the body crashed heavily to the floor.

Nobody moved. Gradually I became aware of other things, Cristoval on his back, his dead eyes open, Giulio's ragged breathing growing softer and slower as he realized it was over, Giles's voice whispering 'Fucking hell.' Marcel was looking at the boy with glowing eyes. Stefan's face didn't seem to have changed expression, but his mouth was open all the same. They'd never seen this before. They'd seen the boy kill, but that was ambush, stab and run, they'd never seen him like this, fighting man to man and sword to sword, which is what he was trained for and maybe what he was even born for. No one had ever seen it except me.

Behind us in the barracks came an extraordinary deep whooshing noise, the darkness seemed to flash with pale light, then there was a tremendous rumbling boom. Stefan scooped up Cristoval, and we ran like bloody hell for the exit.

Colin Lefebvre

Couldn't see much myself, what with the crowd in the way, all I knew was this bloody great bang, then a huge cloud of grey smoke shooting up from behind the courtyard gate and coming down in a fog of choking dust. Looked to me like they'd blown right through the wall.

Couldn't complain about it as a signal, certainly no missing it, so we were up and out and legging it for the gibbet, that Pinhead all elbows through wanting to get there first. Horses coming too, down to my left, and there was the Gate team right on time, everything going as planned.

Jean-Marie Mercier

The Gate Guards hardly even turned to look at us. They were all staring up towards the barracks, and Robert brought his sabre down on the first one's neck while he was still facing the other way. The guards on the firing step both collapsed and fell in the same moment to crossbow bolts, and ahead of me I heard the foot party running for the gibbet.

I was trying to turn my horse to join them when there was

a sudden yellow flash ahead of me, and a shot cracked out from Market Street. Georges cried out and slumped in his saddle, then fell with a thud to the ground. More shots banged and whizzed around us, and now I could see movement in the dark. There were men hidden behind the Gate cannon shooting at us, my horse reared in panic and I started to slide off. I managed to fire my pistol, and I do think I got one, but I was slipping, and next moment I hit the ground hard and my horse was bolting away back to the Dax-Verdâme Road.

Soldiers were running towards us, and I turned to Robert, but his own horse screamed and fell, then Robert was down too. I tried to stand, but my legs were shaky, and I had to crawl to one of the fallen musketeers to take his gun. Robert was on his feet and coming to help me, but then he whirled round and fell to his knees, and I knew he'd been hit. The gibbet party were under attack too, I saw Colin slashing out wildly, with his back to the post. Bettremieu was supporting Vincent so he could cut down the bodies, but even as I looked, Vincent crumpled to a bullet and fell to the ground. We were meant to be covering them, but there were more and more soldiers coming at us, they weren't losing time on a reload, they were charging us with swords and pike, we were totally overwhelmed.

Jacques Gilbert

We weren't in any danger really, the explosion was never going to reach that far, but we didn't wait to see. We were back at the horses in less than a minute.

There were distant shouts and the crashing of booted feet pounding up the alley, but no one was coming near the mill, the soldiers were pouring into the barracks to help their comrades trapped inside. I was suddenly aware of another sound in the background, the distant barking of small-arms fire which seemed to be coming from the direction of the Gate.

'The gibbet,' said Marcel. 'D'Estrada.'

We should have known. He'd guessed we'd try for the gibbet, it's what any man of honour would have done, he'd gone and set an ambush. Col was at the gibbet, Jean-Marie was at the Gate, so was Robert, our friends were out there, all of them.

'Come on,' said André. He didn't wait for an order, he just turned Tempête and galloped straight round the mill, right past the soldiers and heading for the alley.

Stefan swore and wheeled after him. So did I, so did the others, we were all coming. It was mad, it was stupid, but there was so much chaos no one was noticing a bunch of their own horsemen, it's like we were invisible. Tonnerre was pounding under me, galloping towards the guns, the Seigneur's own warhorse, and me riding him into battle, and there was the boy ahead of us, his hand coming up with the sword in it, and he was crying out something, I don't know what, but the madness was catching, I found I was shouting myself.

Jean-Marie Mercier

I was trying to crouch behind Robert's dead horse to use it as a stand for the gun, but a man came round it with drawn sword so I pushed the barrel up high and fired. I think it must have been nearly touching him, because his whole stomach seemed to explode in front of me, and hot wet blood and flesh spattered over my face. I wanted to scream with the horror of it, but there was stuff over my mouth and I couldn't bear to open it, it was on my lips. The gun was useless now, I tried to turn it towards me to use the stock as a club, but there was blood in my eyes and my hair was sticking to it. I squinted up hopelessly towards the distant Square, and saw the crowd who'd acted as a screen starting to break up and disperse. There were riders coming through them, and they were Spanish cavalry, screaming as they came.

I groped over Robert's dead animal and found a pistol still in the holster, but it was only one shot. Dom was still up, but he was trying to pull Georges on to the horse with him, only Georges was wounded and Dom nearly out of the saddle trying to help him. A soldier was coming at them and I remember getting up on one knee and levelling the pistol on my arm, but then something slammed into my shoulder and the pistol went off in my hand. I could see hooves pounding towards us, and knew the cavalry was here and we were finished.

They wheeled off to the gibbet, but two came on towards me. I dropped the empty pistol and tried to swing the musket, but my shoulder wouldn't work properly and I was groping blind on hands and knees. The horsemen thudded past, then one slashed down at the soldier trying to pull Dom off his horse, and the sleeve reaching out from under the cloak was white.

Then a strong arm was reaching down to me, and a voice was saying 'Up you come,' and it was Stefan. He lifted me as if I were a child, and swung me safely up behind him, where I clung on desperately, hardly able to believe what was happening.

'Can you shoot?' he asked, passing me one of the saddle pistols.

My shoulder felt numb, but now I was seated safe I was

sure I could. He turned the horse back to the gibbet, where several of the ambushers were fighting with our men. At least two of our team were already wounded or killed, because Marcel was lifting one on to his horse, and there was another beast galloping to safety with two men on its back, but Giles was firing a pistol coolly into the mêlée, Jacques was riding down two pikemen, cutting at them as they ran, and in the middle of it all Bettremieu was still hanging off the cross-bar and working with the ropes as if nothing was happening around him at all. And André was there, his cloak fallen back and his tattered white shirt shining in the dark like a star, he was leaning halfway out of his saddle as he slashed fiercely around him, and the Spaniards were falling away from him as if he were making hay.

Père Gérard Benoît

The sound of gunfire intensified from below, while the press of people which had parted for the passage of our horsemen now moved swiftly to close the gap, almost as if to a pre-arranged plan. My heart leapt with hope as I guessed what this might be.

More soldiers proceeded from the barracks to force their way towards the Gate and we followed in their wake, but such battle as had been fought there appeared to be over, for I saw only a small group of horsemen retreating in the direction of the Dax-Verdâme Road. There were bodies left lying on the ground, particularly about the gibbet, and I confess to a sensation of disappointment when I saw that two figures still hung from it exactly as before.

Then a great shout went up from the first soldier to near the gibbet, echoed in a very different tone from those of our people closest to the front. As I was impelled forward by the motion of the crowd I realized the two hanging figures were not after all those of Pierre Laroque and Martin Gauthier, who had disappeared without trace. They were instead the bodies of two Spanish soldiers. They were the murderers from Verdâme.

The shout became a cheer. I looked up towards the Dax-Verdâme Road in time to see the last of the horsemen safely reaching the bend. Then I saw him. I saw André, Chevalier de Roland. He was last of all, and as he took the bend I saw him cast his sword high in the air, and reach up to catch it neatly by the hilt as it fell.

Fourteen

Jacques Gilbert

We caught up with the others in the trees behind St Sebastian's. Marcel was grabbing people to take the wounded back to the Hermitage, while Jacob shoved Dax men through the graveyard to get home under cover of the crowd. Stefan was smacking the rumps of the stragglers' horses, saying 'Go, go, quick as you can, they'll be searching the woods any second.' He turned as André reined up beside him and said savagely 'Bloody little show-off, what the hell did you think you were doing?'

The boy stared defiantly. 'I was out of range.'

Stefan said quietly 'I taught you better than that, André. I taught you for a soldier.' He turned back to Giles and said 'For Christ's sake, lead them, Leroux, they're drifting about like whores at a banquet. If they're not in the forest in ten minutes the dons will be on the Back Road to cut us off.'

Giles touched his hat and started urging the others onwards, back north towards the forest and safety. I looked at the boy, but his head was lowered away from me, a crimson flush down the side of his cheek.

'Move it!' snapped Stefan.

The boy hesitated, then dug in his heels and urged Tempête after Giles. I followed, confused and angry, the exhilaration beginning to ooze out of me like the sweat cooling on my face.

There was a kind of excited buzzing going on at the Hermitage when we got there, but I didn't feel in the mood any more, it was lots of people standing in groups saying 'Did you see?' and of course we saw, we were there. There was an undercurrent of something else too, like pockets of quietness in all the noise. As we walked towards the stables there were men carrying a body the other way, and the voices round us sort of hushed as they passed, then grew loud when they'd gone by. I caught a glimpse of red hair and a pale face hanging upside down, and recognized Vincent Poulain. Edouard would still be in Dax, keeping the civilian screen busy so our men could sneak home under its cover. I pictured him working till the very end, looking out for his brother, then realizing no one else was coming and he was alone in the empty Square.

They laid Vincent down by the side of the weapons outhouse, and I saw others lying there already, covered in blankets like they could feel the cold. There was a pair of smart bucket-topped boots sticking out from one of them, and I guessed it was Cristoval.

The crowd murmured. Giles was coming towards us, supporting a stumbling figure so saturated in blood it took me a minute to recognize Jean-Marie. André exclaimed in distress, but Giles shook his head.

'Don't worry,' he said. 'It's not his own.' He gave Jean-Marie's shoulders a little squeeze. 'Wearing someone else's guts tonight, aren't you, soldier?'

Jean-Marie looked at us with dazed eyes. He said 'They got Robert, did you know?'

Robert. Little pictures flashed up between me and the bloodied mess of Jean-Marie's face. Yesterday by the stream, and Robert trimming those weedy little bristles that would never get the chance to grow into a proper beard. The Lefebvre kitchen, and Robert saying 'I'm going to marry Suzanne Pagnié one day,' while Colin's dad hammered *bang-bang-bang* in the Forge next door.

'He was dead when we got here,' said Giles. 'Shame.'

We walked slower after that till André finally stopped altogether, like his legs had just forgotten how to move.

I said 'Look, I'll do the horses, you'd better get to bed. You're all in.'

'No,' he said, then jerked his head back towards the weapons outhouse. 'No, I need to see who else . . .' He gave an embarrassed shrug, hunched his shoulders and set off towards the row of bodies laid out on the grass.

I stabled the horses and went straight to the Hermitage, feeling if I could just unpack our stuff and make it like home then somehow things would be all right. I'd forgotten we were using it as a dressing station. Dom was coming out to empty a bucket of water as I arrived, and I saw it was bright red. I hurried past him up the steps, suddenly terrified of what I might find inside. It was cowardly, but if Georges was dead I didn't think I could bear to see Dom's face.

It was warm in the building, and all the candles lit, making little pools of magic pictures all over. To my relief the first person I saw was Georges, propped up in a corner with a bandage round his middle, but still grinning at the sight of me and saying proudly 'Look, I've been wounded.' There was Marcel, wrapping what looked like a whole sheet's worth of dressings round Bettremieu, who was bleeding from a score of gashes down his legs and arms but didn't seem bothered by any of them. There was Colin, thank God, alive and grumbling, hauling his breeches on over a huge bandage on his leg and looking critically at the lump it made. There was Stefan kneeling by Jean-Marie, with blood on his hands and speckling up his arms, caught in the hairs like tiny red dots. He glanced up when I came in, and said 'That shoulder of yours want seeing to?'

André had already dressed it on the way back. I said 'No, I'm fine, can I help?'

He grunted. 'You can get us a bloody drink.' He wiped his face with the back of his arm, leaving a bloody smear across his cheek, then turned back down to Jean-Marie.

Jean-Marie Mercier

I'm not sure I'm terribly reliable about this part. Jacques gave us all wine, then Dom made me drink some medicine made from poppies, which made me very dreamy. It came from Mme Hébert, who Stefan said was a kind of witch, but Dom was convinced it would do me good.

I do think it helped. Stefan had to dig the ball out of my shoulder, and while I felt every single thing he was doing, it was like the pain was happening to someone else. I did worry at first because Colin said we ought to be cauterizing the wound with hot iron, but Stefan said that was balls. He said he'd learned a lot from an army surgeon when he was wounded himself, and the man had been a very advanced type, a follower of someone called Paré. He told me I was getting the best possible treatment and if I died under it I'd have no one to blame but myself.

So I lay on my stomach while he operated, and drifted in and out of sleep. Stefan told me to look at Jacques, and I did find that soothing. Everything about us was so chaotic, but there was Jacques carefully unpacking his and André's things at the platform end, as if this were their home now and he wanted to make it nice.

I remember the door opening, then footsteps approaching, and Stefan's voice saying gruffly 'You're in my light.' The newcomer knelt beside me, and when I opened one eye I saw it was André.

He said quietly 'Can I help?'

'No,' said Stefan. 'It's nearly done.'

I felt the bullet come out and heard a tiny *clink* as he laid it on the floor. A dressing was clamped down hard over the hole in my back and I saw Stefan's other hand reaching out for the needle.

André's voice whispered 'I was a fool. I'm sorry.'

Stefan's hand paused, and I felt him turning round. Then he picked up the needle and began to stitch.

'It's natural,' he said. 'You had more cause than most.'

'I hadn't,' said André. 'It was my plan, and all these men died for it.'

Stefan didn't answer for a moment, and I felt him mopping away blood around the wound. Then he said 'Don't take it to heart, little general. War costs lives, everyone knew that, and they chose to do it all the same.'

'But so many,' said André. 'Robert, Jehan, Cristoval, Clement, Vincent.'

Stefan worked in silence for a moment, then said 'If you were a real general, André, you wouldn't even know their names.'

'But I do know them,' said André. 'I can't just not care, can I?'

'You can't do anything else.' He finished the last stitch, and I felt his breath warm on my shoulder as he bent to bite off the thread. He said 'Every single person you care about is just another hostage slung round your neck, another way to get hurt.'

There were footsteps near us, and a pair of black Spanish breeches came into view. Jacques' voice said 'Come on, André, I've unpacked our stuff.'

André's voice always sounded warmer when he spoke to Jacques. 'That's brilliant. You've made it look just like it did in the barn.'

'You ought to be in bed,' said Jacques.

Stefan made an odd little grunt as he reached for a bandage. 'I need your hands here, André. Hold this end firm.'

I felt André's hand cool against my skin as he held the dressing in place.

'Your wrists need looking at,' said Jacques obstinately. 'And I need to check your bruises.'

'They're all right,' said André. 'But I'm thirsty, I don't suppose we've got anything to drink?'

'Of course,' said Jacques, suddenly cheerful. 'I've got wine in the basket, I've got everything. You'll need food too, I'll get you something.'

He padded off purposefully. Stefan wrapped a length of bandage round my arm then lowered it gently back into the straw.

André said quietly. 'But you care. Look what you're doing. You care.'

'Not me,' said Stefan. 'Mercier's a good marksman, he's worth patching up. That's good husbandry.'

'Is it?' said André. 'You wanted to get Martin's body back as much as any of us, and where was the use in that?'

Stefan chuckled. 'They'll like you at the Sorbonne if you live that long. But Gauthier, it's the soldiers' bond, that's all.'

'It's still caring, isn't it?'

'Self-preservation. A soldier asks your help, you give it him, because next time it might be you.'

There was a long silence, then André slowly rose to his feet.

I felt Stefan lean back from me to look up at him. He said softly 'Don't go moping over it, all right?'

André's voice sounded light. 'I wouldn't dream of it.'

'Course not,' said Stefan. He turned to lay the blanket over my back.

Carlos Corvacho

Oh now, it could have been a lot worse. The fighting was all very scrappy, wild and in the dark, most of our men wounded rather than killed, and they'd put paid to a fair number of the rebels too. We'd have had them all if it hadn't been for their cavalry, but you don't expect a pack of peasants to have their own cavalry, no one could blame my Capitán for not predicting that. As for the explosion, we didn't lose many to that, it was mostly flash and noise.

No, it was the loss of face bothered the Colonel, that and what was done to my gentleman. He wanted reprisals, Señor, he was for burning the whole village, church and all. He'd quite a feeling about fire, our Colonel, said it was what he called 'cleansing'. Fortunately my Capitán got him to reconsider. He said if we destroyed the village we'd have to leave it, and where was the Cardinal Infante's new foothold in Picardie then? 'Very well, d'Estrada,' says the Colonel, all silky-like, 'then see you get on and destroy the rebels instead.'

My Capitán intended that, but it was a question of finding them first. We knew they'd a base somewhere in the forest, but they were being careful, they were sticking to the foresters' roads and riding up the streams, never so much as a hoofprint for us to start tracking. We still hadn't the men to search it end to end, nothing like, and I couldn't see how we'd ever find them.

'We won't,' says my gentleman. 'We'll get someone to

tell us where it is instead. All we need is to catch one alive, and I think I know how.'

It seemed he was sure one of them was a tanner, so we went after both local men right away. It seemed he was right about it too, the Verdâme man was away from home in the middle of the night, and guns and all manner of contraband hidden in his tannery. I thought the Capitán would be pleased at that, but no, he cursed himself something terrible. He said 'I should have waited, Carlos, I should have had more patience. The man must have stayed at the base, and now he knows I'm looking for a tanner he'll never come back.' And he was right, Señor, the tanner never did come home. I tried to say the man might not be important, but he wasn't having any of it. 'He was one of those in the barracks, Carlos,' he said. 'I saw his hands close enough. Filthy, stained hands and that animal smell, I shall never forget him.'

I understood him then, Señor. He never said a word about what happened that night, all I knew was we found him bound and gagged in his own office and a nasty deep cut right on his cheek, but he was most upset about that scar, he seemed to feel a shame in it he needed to wipe out. I don't know, Señor, I was only his servant, but it seemed to me the shame was theirs.

But my gentleman put his own feelings aside and set about catching one of the others instead. He said there'd been men speaking good Spanish on this raid, so next thing he'd got hold of the last tax lists and was reading all through them for names that sounded Spanish. There were a fair few, as you'd expect so near the border, but we narrowed it down fast enough, especially when Muños remembered one had a club foot. Muños was one of our inquisitors, Señor, the only man survived the fight in the corridor. He was slashed right across the belly, but played dead and lived through the whole thing. He identified this Giulio Romero from Verdâme, we whipped him into the Château where the rebels couldn't even think of rescuing him, and the Colonel had him put to the question without delay.

He was an elderly, rather bookish sort of fellow, so we went straight in with *bastinado*, which got us results in no time. It's no good with these peasant types, feet like old leather, you could be beating them for hours and they'd never even notice, but this one had nice delicate feet, he was jabbering away in no time. Not that it helped a great deal, as he turned out not to be part of the rebel army himself and had only been helping them this once. He didn't know much at all, not even when the Colonel tried him on the rack to make sure, but at least he gave us one thing before his heart gave out, and that was the rebel base.

He'd never been there himself but he'd heard it was the old hunting lodge in the Forest of Verdâme, and that was enough for my Capitán. He didn't know where it was, but he knew who would, and that was the Baron's children. They'd never been exchanged, you understand, the father being nobody to speak of, but the Colonel was after a ransom to buy his pardon, so there they still were, poor creatures, in the Château all this long while. We paid them a little visit, all very friendly and social, and my gentleman led them into a casual conversation about hunting in the old days, wondering where might be a good base to take a party for a boar hunt, oh, all very subtly done. The younger lady, that's your Mlle Anne, Señor, she seemed a touch suspicious, but her brother was a weak-minded, sickly kind of lad, and he told us where the lodge was right away.

The men must have been careless approaching because it was empty when they arrived, but they found guns and signs both men and horses had been there recently, so we knew we'd got the right place. The Capitán had it burnt down, and we all felt better for it. If the rebels stayed in the Saillie now they'd have to hide in the villages, where we'd a good chance of catching them. The Capitán had criers out and handbills up everywhere, offering three hundred livres for any man who'd taken part in the raid, and five for the Tanner of Verdâme. For your Chevalier we offered a thousand, and if we got him alive we'd make it two.

We knew he was the real leader, Señor, whatever Romero said. The villagers were always singing that dirty song of theirs, and the Colonel had to make it a punishable offence. They'd added a new verse about a soldier trying to catch the bird that was robbing its fruit trees and one morning he found his two finest plums had gone and the bird had hung his own testicles in their place. Very childish really, but that's the French for you, no sense of dignity, or so the Colonel used to say.

My Capitán had other reasons for wanting your Chevalier too. He was still after confronting him with de Castilla, Señor, he wasn't going to let that go, especially since there'd been trouble while we were away, something about raping a serving girl for not showing respect. But it was your gentleman's swordsmanship intrigued him most. Muños said he'd never seen anything like it, never, and the Chevalier not much more than a boy. It was only natural in a man of my gentleman's calibre to be interested, Señor. He'd have given a great deal for the chance to meet young de Roland blade to blade.

The Colonel didn't seem so fussed, not once we'd found the rebel base. He had us burn down a few cottages for the look of the thing, but seemed content to leave it at that. He was inclined to believe our finding the base meant the end of the Rebel Movement, and they were all fled into France with your

Chevalier. He said 'De Roland won't bother with a place like this now he's out of it, he's nobility, after all.'

'He came back last time,' said the Capitán grimly.

'And I should have anticipated it,' said the Colonel. 'You paraded him like a hunting trophy over its miserable streets, he had to make some gesture to save his face. But he'll be safe in Paris now, drinking chocolate in the salons, he won't risk himself further for the sake of a few wretched peasants. Relax, Miguel, I shall eat my own hat if he returns now.'

My Capitán bowed. 'If he does, he won't escape me again.'

'Well then,' said the Colonel, 'it seems to me that whatever happens we cannot lose.'

He still wasn't convinced, my gentleman, he kept us all looking and listening out for any sign of the Chevalier's return or the rebels still being about. He had Muños almost living in the Quatre Corbeaux watching out for faces he recognized, but there was nothing ever came of it. The months passed, and our patrols weren't attacked, our couriers weren't interfered with, there was no resistance when we took the harvest, it looked for all the world as if the Colonel was right and the rebels had given up or gone away.

Jacques Gilbert

We hadn't, of course, we were just lying low. Thanks to Giulio being so brave and sending them to the other base, the Spaniards thought they'd driven us out, and Marcel said we'd keep it that way till things calmed down.

So the boy and I had a quiet summer settling into the Hermitage and trying to make it feel like home. It would have been a lot easier with just the two of us, but then Marcel and bloody Stefan went and moved in with us too. It wasn't their fault really, I mean it wasn't safe for them to go home, there were soldiers watching the tannery day and night. Giulio had obviously said something about Stefan being a leader, because d'Estrada was offering more money for him than anyone except André.

I didn't actually mind Marcel living with us, he was nice and friendly and didn't smell. What really spoilt everything was Stefan. He went swaggering about the place, bringing in his women, eating all our food, calling the boy 'little general' like a private joke, and tousling his hair like he'd got any kind of right. This was André's own property we were in, he ought to have been grovelling with gratitude at being allowed to lay his smelly carcase down in it at all, but it got to the point we couldn't have a private conversation without him shoving his way into it like it was our food basket. I thought Marcel might have kept him in order, but he was always very tender with Stefan, it was one thing about him I couldn't understand. I think it even made Stefan uneasy, he sometimes looked at Marcel like he couldn't understand it either.

If it hadn't been for Stefan I'd have enjoyed living at the Hermitage. I liked having friends around and people to look after the horses, and not having to walk miles when it was our turn for duty. We still got fresh food too. Colin used to bring stuff from the Home Farm, Jean-Marie bought supplies from outside, we got meat from Philippe and game from Giles, and the streams were full of carp and eels. I worried about cooking because of the smoke, but some charcoal burners started up on the Artois side and after that we lit fires whenever we wanted. Simon Moreau made soups and stews, because he cooked for his dad at the Corbeaux, and Bettremieu used to do this Flemish thing with beef soaked in beer, he'd heat it in a pot then wrap it up in a box of warm straw and by evening it was wonderful. People started hanging about the Hermitage even when they weren't on duty, it was a place to eat and drink and see friends. I did miss Mother's cooking, though. I used to dream about her omelettes.

André was mostly all right. He was a bit more distant and moody these days, but he was just growing up, that's all. He turned fifteen that August, he was getting taller, his voice was breaking, no soldier would even think about chasing him now, they'd take one look and shoot him. They'd have been right too, he was still yearning to fight and getting more and more frustrated at the lack of action. He was haunted by what happened to Giulio and desperate to avenge the murder of M. Gauthier, but where a year ago he'd have been stamping and shouting 'We've got to *do* something!' now he just waited for Marcel to say it was right, fenced longer and harder every day, and gnawed himself to pieces inside.

What made it worse was him being cooped up at the Hermitage. He couldn't even go into Ancre, he was known by sight and had to stay mouldering in the woods like a hermit himself. He couldn't do much at all except listen to bloody Stefan giving his opinion on everything like someone who knew. He got more and more restless, and quicker to lash out with his fists, and that wasn't as funny as it used to be, he once nearly broke Marin's nose when he said Margot had a face like Bettremieu's arse and wouldn't take it back. There was one day Dom came running in to say he was fighting Pinhead, and he was, they were down by the stream simply hammering away at each other, I was terrified he'd get his ribs broken. Stefan practically threw Pinhead across the clearing and bawled at him to pick on people his own size, but Pinhead said 'Tell *him* that,' and sat wiping blood off his nose, looking all injured. I asked the boy afterwards what it had been about, and he said 'I don't really know,' and grinned.

I knew he couldn't last much longer, and he didn't. In October we heard there was going to be a thanksgiving service for our new Dauphin, and that was a huge thing for us, I mean we'd waited years for an heir to the throne. Everyone was going except Stefan, who didn't give a toss, and at last André said sod it, he was bloody well going too.

I didn't try to stop him. It was safe enough really, the soldiers never came to St Sebastian's, they had Mass in the barracks with their own priests. Besides, it was a chance for André to be the Seigneur again, and I thought it mightn't do people any harm to be reminded of that, like Pinhead and Stefan for a start.

So we did it all properly, and Jean-Marie bought fabric in Sus-St-Léger for his friend Jeanette to make new clothes. She'd do anything for André because he'd avenged her family by hanging the Pedros, but we had to keep her from actually seeing him, because she would keep banging on about the hostages, and we'd already agreed we didn't want him hearing any more about his Mlle Anne. Jean-Marie just took the measurements himself and delivered the clothes on the day.

It was the tenth of October. I even remember the date, almost like I'd known how important it was going to be, which obviously I didn't. At the time it was just exciting to be going and wearing our new clothes. André'd insisted I have them too because of being his aide, so we'd both got these white lawn shirts with huge sleeves and about a million pleats at the back, dark-blue sleeveless pourpoints to wear over them, and a falling lace collar at the front. I was boiling in mine, and my breeches were so full I could have carried a dozen dead rabbits down each leg, but Jean-Marie said it was very modest by today's fashions, so I supposed it was all right. Marcel even made us wear our hair loose and curling down our shoulders like proper nobility. When we'd finished André looked like someone too grand for me to even speak to, but then he showed me my reflection in the stream and I saw I did too.

We didn't risk the Square, we went through the Dax-Verdâme woods and into St Sebastian's by the graveyard gate. We stopped at the north door, and I reminded André to watch my signals and only come in at the last minute, then to stand quietly near the door so we could nip out fast if we had to. I remember looking at him in his smart clothes, the Chevalier de Roland going to church with his aide, and it was like getting a sudden picture of my future. Then I pushed open the door, and crashed right back into my past.

All the familiar things seemed to smack me in the face. There was that statue of the Madonna with lowered eyes, which Father said made her look like an Abbeville prostitute. There were the plaques for all the old sieurs of Dax, and the stained-glass window with the apostles on it, and St Peter pointing upwards with a finger so fat it looked like he was wearing a bandage. There were the choir stalls, and Colin at the front just as usual, then I looked over to the west door, and there were my family coming in like they did every Sunday, and me not with them, me nothing to do with them at all.

Mother still looked beautiful, even with her hair tucked into a scarf because of it being Sunday. Blanche looked older, and her blond hair was curling down her back. Little Pierre was a man now, a good-looking one at that, and there was something different about him I couldn't work out for a minute, then realized it was because he wasn't scowling. Last of all came my Father, and that was somehow the biggest shock of all, because he looked exactly the same. He had on his same Sunday clothes, with the grey coat too tight for his shoulders, making him look like a bull dressed up. He was strolling up the aisle with that same slight roll in his gait, his hat safe in his big fist, he looked easy and comfortable and indestructible.

Then he lifted his head, and our eyes met.

I don't know why it made me jump, I wasn't doing anything wrong. Then Mother turned and saw me, and it was like her whole face was swamped with a kind of disbelieving joy. It was only for a second, then she was just Mother again, and waving at me through the crowds as Father turned away and urged her into a seat. I didn't go to sit with them, of course, I couldn't leave the boy to stand on his own. It didn't look like they expected it anyway, Father put Little Pierre beside him like he was the eldest son now and I didn't even exist.

The bell was going into its final stage when it got faster and faster like an angry wasp, and the last people were sort of scurrying in looking embarrassed. I checked again for soldiers, then sidled back towards the north door and furtively waved my handkerchief to show it was all safe. André slipped inside just as the bell stopped and the west door was banged shut. I made space beside me like we'd agreed, but he said quietly 'Come on,' and began to walk openly down the transept towards the aisle.

I couldn't believe it. All the faces turned to follow him as he passed, and a murmur rustled all round the church, gradually fading away till there was nothing but the rap of his footsteps on the stone, and the confident jingling of the sword against his boots. I shambled furtively after him, wondering what the hell he was playing at, but of course I should have guessed. He turned down the aisle to the Roland stalls, stepped up and sat in his father's seat.

It was like everybody breathed out in the same moment. We had a Seigneur in Dax again, everything was back like it should be. It was a bit silly really, because he was still only fifteen, but when I looked at him I found I could remember really clearly what his father had looked like. I think other people were remembering too, some of the older ones looked like they were nearly in tears.

I shuffled quickly into the low seat beside André's and tried to be invisible. It felt strange seeing the church from a different angle, like looking through someone else's eyes. There was a bunch of rosemary tied to the rail in front of me, probably to cover the smell of the rest of us. I touched its prickly spikes with my finger, and it gave out a faint hint of scent in a crumbling dust. I looked up, and saw Father was watching me.

I don't remember much of the service. I remember the choir sang a *Te Deum* for Louis Dieudonné, and I heard Colin's powerful baritone, but not Robert's tenor, I'd never realized how beautiful it was till it wasn't there. I remember Père Gérard adding prayers in French at the end, thanking God Le Câtelet had returned to French hands, and praying this was a sign our own liberation might soon come. I remember the huge amen after it, which was the loudest I'd ever heard. I remember my Father's eyes on me, and the touch of André's sleeve as he sat by my side.

When it was over we nipped out quickly by the north door, but there was already a crowd gathering in the graveyard to pay their respects to the Seigneur. I stood back where I could see him and keep an eye on the Square at the same time, since this was the obvious moment for anyone who wanted a quick thousand livres to run and tell the Spaniards he was there, but then a hand fell on my shoulder, and when I looked round it was my Father.

He looked amused at my surprise, and took his hand away quickly, like he was embarrassed himself. I don't remember saying anything, I think I just stared.

'Don't do that, boy,' he said. 'You look like a sheep.'

I expect I went on looking like it.

He said 'You're a little dusty behind. Do you want me to . . . ?'

I shot my hand round to my arse, and he was right, there was all soft grit on the seat of my breeches, I suppose it had been years since anyone bothered to dust the Roland stalls. I brushed it off furiously, feeling stupid, but when I looked up at Father he just nodded and actually gave me a smile.

'Looking good, boy. I understand why you couldn't sit with us.'

I stared at him. 'I thought . . .'

'What?' he said, and tipped his head to one side. 'What?'

I'd thought he didn't want me.

'So when are you coming to see us?'

My heart jumped. Maybe he was trying to make things up between us. Maybe it was really possible we could somehow put things back the way they used to be.

'Think about it,' said Father, gazing vaguely over the crowd, looking at everything and anything that wasn't me. 'Your mother misses you. Give us a bit of notice though, she'll want to kill the fatted calf.'

He patted my elbow and wandered off to join Mother, who was smiling and waving goodbye from the road. Blanche waved too, but Little Pierre stuck his hands in his pockets and scowled, like he always did when he wasn't coming first. I began to realize Father was serious, and when he said Mother missed me, what he really meant was he did too. I felt happiness floating up inside me like wine.

The feeling lasted all the way back to the Hermitage, and it's like it had sort of come on ahead of us, because there were loads of people there already, just having a drink to celebrate. Jacob wedged the door open so the sunshine could pour in, and the Hermitage looked quite different. People were dressed nice from going to church, there were bright colours everywhere, blues and reds and yellows, and people talking in happy voices, with little threads of laughter weaving through the babble. It's like the service had had the same effect on everyone, we'd got a new Dauphin, things were going our way, and everything felt full of hope.

Marcel obviously felt it too. He stood up at the platform end and said we'd lain low long enough, it was time to get active again as soon as we could think of a worthwhile target. Everyone started shouting out at once, some wanted to raid the Spaniards' stores, others wanted to get back at the looters, one or two really drunk ones suggested the Château but shut up fast when they saw Stefan's face. Then Giles said 'What does André think?' and others started calling it too, everyone turned to look at the boy.

He was leaning against a pillar with his head down and hadn't said a word, like it all meant too much to him for that. Now he lifted his head and said 'We want to hit back, don't we? We want to make them pay for Giulio, and Martin and Pierre and Robert and Vincent and Clement and Jehan and Cristoval?'

Everyone went very quiet.

'Well then,' said André. 'We don't waste time on the petty things or the soldiers following orders. I say we go for Don Francisco himself.'

There was a few seconds' silence, then suddenly this great roar that was even louder than the amen in church. Marcel was smiling and nodding, everyone was shouting 'Don Francisco!', it would have scared the fat bastard to death if he'd heard it. Then I noticed a still patch in all the movement, and there was Stefan, standing by himself in his shabby brown coat, holding a wooden mug of cider and watching the boy in silence. When André glanced round at him he lifted his mug a few inches, and bobbed his head in something oddly like a salute.

Carlos Corvacho

I can't think what possessed him, Señor, coming to Sunday Mass in the very place he was an outlaw. Naturally we found out, Muños still had his ears open at the Corbeaux and we had the full story within a week. He'd not only been in Dax, he'd sat in his father's seat, and he'd done it in full daylight while wearing a sword.

I thought the Colonel would have a fit when we told him, but he was surprisingly composed. He sent for the chef, laid his hat on the table in front of him, and said 'There you go, fellow. Can you cook that?'

Rousseau was a funny-looking chap, but a genius at cooking, he used to make this *pâté de canard en croûte* I still dream about. He doesn't flicker so much as an eyelid, he just looks the Colonel in the eye and says superbly 'Entrée or dessert?'

'Entrée,' says the Colonel, smiling with all his teeth. 'The Capitán d'Estrada will provide dessert.'

So Rousseau takes away the hat and serves it to the Colonel at dinner that night. He minced it into pieces with pork, Señor, and simmered it with onions in cider to soften it, then he served it in a pastry case shaped the way the hat used to be, and on the top was the plume, each little strand coated and cooked brittle in sugar. It was very pretty, but I couldn't say how it tasted, the Colonel insisted on eating every mouthful himself.

When he'd finished, he raised his glass to the Capitán and said 'My word is now honoured, d'Estrada. May I ask if you hope to honour yours?'

It wasn't really fair, Señor, my Capitán never passed his word of honour, not strictly speaking, neither of them did, but there's only one answer for a gentleman, so he drew himself up and said 'I shall honour it or die.'

'Oh good,' said the Colonel, picking pieces of hat from his teeth. 'But I do hope it's the former, d'Estrada, I should hate to have to spend evenings with that boor Martínez for company. The man can't even play chess.'

My gentleman was rather broody after that, but he never liked a fuss, so I pretended everything was just as usual and went to get our horses for his evening ride, and that's when it happened, Señor, almost like a miracle.

Not that it looked much like it at first, only one of the grooms saying he wanted to see my Capitán. Naturally I told him no, I didn't let people like that near my gentleman, least of all the French ones who worked here as a labour tax, but he only said 'Oh well, if your officer isn't interested in laying hands on André de Roland, then that's his affair, isn't it?' and turned to walk away.

My Capitán didn't like informers as a rule, but he was a practical man who understood soldiering. 'Carlos,' he'd say, 'you have to touch pitch sometimes, and count the being defiled as an occupational hazard.' This groom now, he was what you'd call pitch in any language, but there's no denying my Capitán was in a very delicate situation, so I said 'All right, but you'll catch it hot if you're wasting his time.'

He smiled at me, insolent as you please, and sauntered after me to the barracks, whistling as he went. He was forever whistling while he worked, and quite catchy little tunes they were too. There's this one, goes like this, do you know it? I think he called it 'La Pernette'.

That's right, Señor, that's the fellow. Gilbert, they called him. Pierre Gilbert.

Fifteen

Jean-Marie Mercier

It was the most wonderful October, with blue skies and sunshine, and everything full of promise. The apples were being harvested all over the Saillie, the wine presses were busy, the farmers were grazing their pigs in the forest, and the soil looked rich and brown for the sowing of the winter corn. The Spaniards had taken a lot of this year's harvest, but everyone felt next year's would be ours.

We had a purpose of our own too, and all over Dax-Verdâme our people were looking out for Don Francisco. Unfortunately he was very difficult to target, because he lived in the barracks and never came out without an enormous escort. When he did travel anywhere, he went in a closed carriage with no escort, so we could never be sure whether he was really in it or whether we'd be giving away our intentions by attacking it and finding some innocent person inside. We knew our best hope was to learn his movements in advance, but that was proving quite impossible. Arnould Rousseau listened out for rumours in the barracks, but while he was able to repeat some splendidly scurrilous stories, there wasn't really anything we could use.

Then two weeks after the thanksgiving service I bumped into Jeanette Truyart after Mass and we finally had our breakthrough. We might have had it earlier, but I'm afraid I rather avoided Jeanette in those days, because of the embarrassment of the hostages. I know I ought to have been able to prevent her directing the conversation on to the subject, but she was really very persistent. I was quite sure she wanted me to repeat what she told me to André, and was afraid she must think me terribly obtuse for not taking her hints.

Only I simply had to talk to her this time, because André had insisted I thank her for the clothes she'd made, which were honestly quite marvellous. Jeanette was a wonderful dressmaker, which was all the more astonishing because her own taste was quite extraordinary. I think perhaps she made her clothes from offcuts she saved from those she made for others, because there were often patches of different fabrics incorporated into the patterns and she particularly seemed to favour stripes. Today there were inserts of lemon muslin in the fall of her skirt, and a square of vivid cerise implanted in her bodice.

She was delighted with André's message, and blushed really quite becomingly. 'Oh, M. Mercier, as if it wasn't the greatest pleasure to do the smallest little thing for him. He is in my prayers every night, and in Mlle Anne's too, she told me so herself.'

I said hastily 'Well, they really were very fine clothes, and we're extremely grateful.'

'It was no trouble at all, M. Mercier, none at all. Your M. Gilbert is much of a size with my poor M. Florian, I beg your pardon, M. du Pré I should say, only rather broader, because of course my poor children don't get the food and exercise they should, nothing like, not with only three rooms to live in these two years past. It's small wonder they're so excited at the prospect of coming out for a few hours, even if it is for a dinner with that Don Francisco.'

I had been about to pretend I had another engagement, but these last words arrested me at once. I said carefully 'With Don Francisco?'

'I know, Monsieur,' she said at once. 'A terrible thing for a fine French family to stoop to, but they can hardly pass up the chance of a proper meal, the food they're given you wouldn't believe, soup like the common soldiers get, and them brought up like gentlefolk . . .'

I asked casually 'And when is it, this meal?'

'Oh bless you for your interest, Monsieur, I'll tell them if I may, it's so good for them to know they're not forgotten. But it's a week from today, as if it weren't irreligious enough without having it on the Lord's Day and a Vigil at that, only it's his fête day, Monsieur, so he's to be given a banquet at the Château to celebrate. My M. and Mlle du Pré, they're that excited you wouldn't believe, it's only my young Mlle Anne not so keen. She says to me right out she's no wish to make the fat oaf's birthday any nicer, oh, quite a way of talking she has, my Mlle Anne, not exactly fitting for a lady but then what education is she getting, and no one can accuse her of want of spirit.'

She drew breath at last, so I quickly made my excuses and hastened to the Hermitage to give them the news.

I feel terrible about it now, of course, but I couldn't possibly have known. At the time it honestly felt quite perfect.

Jacques Gilbert

It might have been awkward when Jean-Marie said the information came from the hostages, but Stefan just said it proved how comfortable they were in the Château, and André had to agree.

We worked out a plan right away. It was obviously impossible to get the bastard in the Château, we'd got to do it on the way. Whichever route he took he'd still have to pass that last section between the Back Road and the Château gates, and that's where we'd nail him. He'd be in that closed carriage, of course, but it didn't matter if he rode in a hay cart now, we'd still know it was him, and the lack of an escort would only make things easier. The only worry was doing it quietly enough, with three hundred troops at the Château just round the corner, but Marcel said we'd put up ropes to stop the horses, use archers to kill the driver, then turn the whole carriage with Don Francisco still inside and drive it back to the Flanders Road so we could do what we needed undisturbed. It all felt perfect and like nothing could possibly go wrong.

That evening the boy suggested casually we might stroll into Ancre, and I understood why. We hadn't been back since the funerals, but it felt different now we were going to put things right. All our men were buried there, it hadn't been safe at St Sebastian's with d'Estrada's men watching it all the time, but I could see from the flowers that the families visited regularly just the same. The only grave a bit bare was M. Gauthier's, because he didn't have any family, but the boy said 'Yes he does, he's got us,' and we went scouting round the gardens for late roses and scattered them all over. The earth had only just settled, there wasn't grass on it or anything, but I didn't mind, it felt more like M. Gauthier was still there. Sitting beside it with the boy, I felt more peaceful than I had in ages, and there was this strange feeling stealing over me of everything coming right.

'Why don't you visit your family?' said André softly. 'They're just across the drive.'

It seemed like a good idea. I was desperate to find out if Father had meant what he said, I'd been wondering about it for days, but hadn't had the courage to test it out. Now I thought I had.

André settled comfortably to wait by M. Gauthier, and I crossed the drive. I told myself I wouldn't have lost anything if Father was in a different mood today, it would just be like it was before. In fact it wasn't, it was the best things had ever been. Father sat me down by the fire, and let me fill his pipe for him even though Little Pierre was reaching for it at the same time. Mother was so pleased she cooked an omelette specially, even though it was Sunday and she shouldn't have. Blanche played with my hair, said it was 'as long as Dré's now' and wanted to know why I wasn't wearing my nice clothes. Everything felt warm and like home.

Little Pierre was the only grumpy one. He wasn't impressed by anything, not even when I told them about our plan to kill Don Francisco. I obviously didn't say anything about the army, I only said it was me and André, but he still went sort of 'Huh,' like it was nothing. Father seemed to approve though, he gave a kind of slow nod of acknowledgement, and I knew he was proud. When I was leaving he said again about giving them notice so they could get special food in, and even asked if I'd join them for Christmas. I didn't hesitate this time, I said of course I would, and meant it.

It was dark when I left, but the boy had waited, and we walked back together through the back meadow, like we'd done that very first day. I can still remember the smell of roses drifting soft in the evening air.

Colin Lefebvre

Good action to be part of, everyone wanted to be in on this one. Team were hand-picked, all of us skilled and burning to be in at the kill.

Started off right and tight in the morning, hid the horses by the main foresters' road, then went on foot to the site itself. Got there good and early, plenty of time to sort our positions and load the guns.

I was on the fringes of the Dumont farm, holding the ropes on the east side of the road with Margot. Didn't seem right putting a woman on a job like that, only there on account of being a marksman, no call to go asking her to take the weight of carriage horses as well, but I told her not to worry, if the strain was too much I'd help her. Funny woman. Said to me straight-faced 'And if you're in trouble I'll help *you*.'

Jacques was with us as swordsman, along with Dubois himself. No one else on our side, cover being rather thin, they were all tucked away across the road in the Forest of Verdâme. Luckily we'd a runner to nip between us, Pepin or some such name, only about twelve, but Leroux said he was the best little poacher in Picardie, said if he was half as good with a musket as he was with a sling he'd soon be rivalling Mercier. Wasn't sure I liked the idea of giving him a musket, truth be told. Dark skin, dark eyes, shifty look, I'd have said he was more than half gypsy. Still, I sent him for more powder from the other team, and off he went, happy as a little dog.

So there I was, right, waiting for him to come back, when there's movement over the other side, flash of something tan-coloured dropping through the leaves. Leroux coming down off the tree, and I realize something's up. Take a step towards the road, but there's Dubois beside me, pushing me back against the wall of the barn.

'Soldiers,' he said. 'Coming out the Château gates.'

So they were, maybe two dozen of them. Lined up across the road in three whole ranks, muskets on the stands like they meant business. Looked to me for all the world like a firing squad, only with no one to shoot at.

'Georges is signalling,' said Margot, and we all looked down the Kingsway to see this white handkerchief waving from a tree in the distance. Soldiers coming from that way too.

Jean-Marie Mercier

Giles said there were men in the woods behind us.

'How far?' said Stefan.

'Six, seven hundred yards. Going slowly, keeping hidden, checking no one's getting past them.'

'Do they know we're here?'

Giles shrugged.

A muscle twitched high up on Stefan's cheek, but that was the only sign he made. He turned to us, said 'Abort,' and began to jog towards the road to warn the others, but Marcel was already signalling frantically to urge him back, and pointing towards the Château. Stefan halted on the edge of the woods, and they stood whispering and miming to each other across the road.

Philippe adjusted the quiver on his back and reached for his bow. Bernard settled his crossbow under his arm, and pulled down his woollen hat with trembling fingers. Young Pepin started dumbly gathering up the bandoliers. I had my first musket already slung round my shoulders, but when I reached for the second Giles stopped me.

'You can't run like that, soldier,' he said. 'Leave it. Leave them all.'

It went against everything we'd ever been taught to leave the guns, and I think it was that more than anything that made me realize how serious the situation was. It was so quiet, you see. I couldn't hear anything wrong, I couldn't see anything that looked different from a moment before, but suddenly there was danger screaming all round. I watched in a kind of trance as Giles calmly shouldered his own musket and stood tapping his fingers on the butt as we waited for Stefan to get back. Bettremieu was reeling in the ropes under the dead leaves like a fisherman with a line, while André lingered by the road, with Jacques staring desperately at him from the other side.

'Musketeers,' said Stefan, picking up his own gun. 'Both directions. The road's blocked. Can we get through them in the woods, Leroux?'

Giles bared his teeth in a fox-like smile. 'Can try,' he said, and turned to lead the way.

Jacques Gilbert

I couldn't get to him. The musketeers outside the Château weren't moving, there were more setting up position down the Kingsway, one step on that road would get us blown to pieces in a second. The boy was only yards away, but I couldn't get to him, and he couldn't get to me.

Colin said 'They'll be all right, they've got Leroux. Verdâme verderer, isn't he? He'll get them through.'

Stefan was moving the team after Giles. The boy trotted after them, then gave me a grin and a wave before he turned and the forest swallowed him.

'Come on,' said Marcel urgently. 'They'll be after us too, if they're not already. Back to the horses, then we'll try and support the others.'

Our own escape was easy, we'd only got to make our way down the farm till we were behind the musketeers on the Kingsway, then nip over into the Dax-Verdâme woods and run like hell up to the Back Road. We never saw any soldiers after us, I suppose the farm was too open to look a good site for an ambush.

The horses were just where we'd left them, grazing contentedly near the Flanders Road with Pinhead keeping guard. We'd expected to be coming back here with a carriage and Don Francisco, I'd seen us in my head all whooping and laughing with excitement, and here we were running in grim silence with a million questions in our heads and a sick sense of fear in our stomachs.

Marcel seemed as desperate as I was. He shoved us towards the horses and said 'We'll go north of the site and work back down towards it. Lead as many horses as you can. If they break through, there may be pursuit close behind and we'll need to get them out fast. If they don't, maybe we can at least give them cover to help them disperse.'

It sounded good, it sounded like something. But Tonnerre was snorting uneasily as I mounted him, and as I grabbed his reins Tempête was doing the same.

Beside me Colin stiffened and said 'Smoke.'

There was something tingling at my own nose too. I turned east to stare into the forest back towards the ambush site. It seemed quiet and peaceful in there, we still hadn't heard so much as a gunshot, but away in the distance something was obscuring my view of the trees, blurring them over with the faintest bluish haze.

Colin was right. Smoke.

Jean-Marie Mercier

'Smoke,' said Philippe. 'From the west.'

I don't think I'd ever seen Philippe when he wasn't smiling. He was always jolly, you see, always flashing that great gap-toothed grin, but now there was just the face of a man I didn't know and his lips forming the word 'Smoke.'

Stefan swore. 'Trying to drive us to the gorge and trap us there.'

There was a sudden rustle of leaves, then a weasel broke cover right in front of us. We watched uneasily as it darted away noisily through the bracken.

Giles' voice seemed quite without expression. 'I'll have to turn us north-east, no choice about it. Maybe we can break through their line before we reach the gorge.'

I heard a tiny rasping sound behind me and saw André drawing his sword. He caught my eye and smiled. 'There's eight of us, Jean-Marie. I don't think we'll have any trouble breaking through.' He started slithering his way past me through the undergrowth. 'Can I come to the front, Giles?'

Giles turned to face ahead, but not before I saw a tiny smile crinkling the corners of his eyes. I heard Stefan muttering 'Bloody little hero,' as he came worming after André, and saw to my surprise he was grinning too. For a second I caught sight of Philippe's old smile as he bent to start crawling again, while Bettremieu was actually rumbling an odd little tune under his breath as he followed. I looked round at the new volunteer, who was crawling at the back with Bernard, and said 'It's all right, Pepin, we'll get through.' He beamed at me and continued wriggling along, happy as an eel in sand.

The smoke seemed to have grown thicker as we talked. I felt it tickling my throat, and was afraid I might cough. I tried to suck in a breath, but my lungs constricted and panic tightened my throat. 'Heads down, lads,' Stefan was intoning ahead of us. 'Faces down, it'll clear in a minute.' Behind me Bettremieu was making a noise like 'Pom, pom, ti-pom-pom,' and Stefan's voice drifted back 'Stop that Flemish grunting, Libert, or I'll kill you.'

As Giles led us slowly eastwards, the smoke gradually thinned again and my hopes began to rise. The maquis grew more sparsely now so I knew we must be getting nearer the gorge, but we were progressing northwards too and I began to wonder if we mightn't have passed the Spanish line after all.

Giles looked back and put his finger to his lips, and after a moment he held up his hand to stop us altogether.

'Can't get past that,' he whispered. 'Let them come to us, then we'll break through.'

We crawled into a dense area of tall bracken and waited. Now we'd stopped moving, I found I could hear the enemy for myself. I heard swords jingling, the rustle of leather against steel, the faint clinking of the little flasks on the bandoliers, all the usual noises of an army on the move, but almost eerie because of the total absence of voices. There was a swishing sound as well, and I guessed they were beating the bushes. Stefan drew his knife. André coiled himself into position, knees bent, sword poised, his other hand resting lightly on the ground to give purchase to the spring, long fingers spread in an arc in the dirt.

Giles was whispering again. 'When it goes off, we all run like bloody hell, right? Follow Ravel and head for the gorge.'

He'd hardly finished when the bracken parted ahead of us and a pair of dark breeches suddenly appeared. André thrust forward at once and the breeches went down, but another man behind let out a yell, and I knew we were finished.

'That's it, boys,' said Giles, not even whispering any more, and crashed forward through the bracken. Stefan overtook him, and we all followed, running as fast as we could, not looking at anything or anyone but Stefan running ahead of us.

There were shouts all around, and the crack of a musket as someone recovered enough to take a shot at us, but it came from behind, and I realized we were through the line and past them, we had only to keep running to reach safety. But Stefan was still going east, he was heading for the gorge, and after a moment I realized why. There was movement far ahead of us in the trees, someone was shouting, and I knew there were more soldiers coming down at us from the north. It felt as if the whole Verdâme garrison must be loose in that forest, they were hunting us like animals, and nowhere to run but the gorge.

Stefan Ravel

No choice, Abbé, we'd got to cross the bloody thing or die. There were a couple of hundred dons out there, and even with the fearsome André de Roland on our side those were odds I didn't fancy at all.

I got them to the edge of the gorge and started leading them north along its bank. The dons had lost sight of us for a while, but I guessed we wouldn't get far before hitting the next cordon. At last I saw what I wanted, a good sturdy tree with high branches sited near the edge on the far side. I halted them and asked Libert for the ropes. It took him long enough unwinding them, he was carrying so many muskets he looked like a giant hedgehog, but he got them in the end, Leroux knotted them together, and I ripped off a branch to make an anchor. I looked round for a volunteer as I worked, and saw the perfect one right away.

'Now then, young Pepin,' I said in my most fatherly tone. 'How'd you like to be a hero?'

Stefan and Bettremieu swung Pepin between them and simply threw him over the gap. He landed quite easily on a large patch of heather and seemed almost to bounce to his feet as if this were all a great game. Then he took his end of the rope, scrambled up a big tree and secured it above a high branch, while Stefan reeled in the other end, and we had a crossing.

Unfortunately only one man could cross at a time, and the Spaniards were bound to search this section of the gorge any minute. Stefan was clearly aware of it too. While Pepin was still tying the rope he glared at the rest of us and said 'No argument about this, you'll go when I say. André first, then Mercier –'

'No,' said André. 'I can't give cover, you know I can't. Marksmen first.'

Stefan's head jerked towards him, then he hesitated and dropped his eyes. 'All right. Mercier, you first, then Rouet, then Durand, then Leroux. Don't hang about when you get there, we'll need all the covering fire we can get if we're all to cross. If we're in trouble, Libert, throw André over before crossing yourself.'

'If we're in trouble,' said André, 'you'll need a swordsman to cover your back.'

Stefan said calmly 'I'll need soldiers who'll do what they're fucking told. Now keep your voices down or we'll draw the dons.'

The rope was ready and people were pushing me towards it, then Bettremieu was slinging two more guns round me, and there wasn't time to think about anything else. I clutched the rope tight and closed my eyes as I stepped off the edge.

It was only when I was in the air that I thought with sudden panic I might simply crash straight into the opposite wall of the gorge, but of course Pepin had secured the rope very high, and my feet no more than skimmed the grass of the far bank. Stefan started reeling it back as soon as I let go, then I quickly found cover and positioned my first musket. I'd hardly laid out the others when Bernard was dropping beside me, and on the far bank Stefan was hauling the rope back for Philippe. We might do it yet. I pulled off my bandolier so I could reach the flasks quickly. There were twelve reloads, Stefan used to call them the 'Twelve Apostles'. Twelve shots, but it could take twenty minutes to load them all.

'I can load, M'sieur,' said Pepin, sitting behind me with crossed legs. 'Pass me your guns as you finish and I will load.'

Beside me, Bernard finished ratcheting up his string, locked the bolt in place, sat back and cracked his knuckles.

Jacques Gilbert

We were belting through the forest as fast as the horses could go. The sight of Tempête galloping beside me gave me an odd kind of superstitious hope. He'd saved the boy's life once, a bit of my brain thought he could do it again.

We stopped on the *gabelle* road to take stock of our position. The smoke was well south of us, the Spaniards had only fired the bit between the last two foresters' roads, but it was enough to drive anyone more than a mile south of us east and to the gorge. We were about to ride down and follow it, when there came muffled reports off to the east, gunfire reaching us through the smoke.

'Bloody hell,' said Margot. 'It's on the other side of the gorge.'

That was impossible. The bit north of the Château between the gorge and the Wall was just called the 'dead land' because no one could get to it, except of course by crossing the gorge at the *gabelle* road and riding down, which it had never been worth our while to do.

'It is now,' said Marcel. 'Come on.'

Jean-Marie Mercier

Two soldiers appeared further down the gorge, looking up and down the bank, trying to see where we'd got to. Our men were hidden by the trees that grew right up to the edge, but just then Philippe came sailing over on the rope, it was too late to signal him to wait, and they saw him at once.

I fired immediately, and Bernard loosed his bolt, but we'd had no time to consult, and both fired at the same target. Philippe landed safely, but the second soldier was firing even as he touched down, and suddenly he was falling backwards and away from us, his mouth open in a kind of terrible surprise, his hands open and releasing the rope, his body dropping out of sight, thudding terribly against the side of the gorge as it fell.

Pepin was pulling the musket out of my hands, I grabbed the next and shot the second man. There was still one loaded musket left, but no one yet to fire at. André, Stefan, Giles and Bettremieu were alone in the clearing, and Stefan was reeling back the rope. Unfortunately the sound of our shots was having its effect, and I could hear distant shouting as the pursuing Spaniards began to realize our direction. I said to Bernard 'You take right, I'll take left,' and he nodded dumbly even as he was screeching back the string for his next bolt. Another man appeared higher up the bank, I shot him quickly, then Giles was swinging over towards our side.

Pepin was loading frantically, but there were soldiers nearly up to our men, I could see movement in the trees behind the clearing. Giles skidded to a halt on our bank, his heels scoring up two great furrows in the dirt, and I stood to snatch the musket out of his hands as two dark figures rushed into the clearing on the other side.

I fired half-blind, but even as I jerked to the recoil I heard Bernard call out, and turned to see horses pounding towards us from the north. I jumped back into cover, but the rider in front was blond, he was blond, and I realized with shattering relief that it was Marcel.

Stefan Ravel

Someone shot straight, I'm glad to say, and André had the other, stabbing straight into his belly before he'd even taken in the sight of us.

Me, I just kept hauling in the rope and said 'André next.' The kid went on facing the trees, sword in hand, but I'd known he'd be trouble, I was ready for it. I jerked my thumb at Libert and said 'Get him.'

The big Flamand moved fast enough when he needed to. He was scooping up his young Sieur under one arm and back to me before I'd finished reeling in the rope. I left them to it, drew my own sword, and turned to the trees where three of the buggers were bursting through at once. I slashed one, saw the furthest fall to a bolt, and punched the third hard in the jaw, but the bastard had a pistol which flamed out as he fell. Libert cried out and clutched his arm, then another shot cracked out, and he collapsed on his knees. Then for the first time there was something like a real volley of answering fire over the gorge, and we were covered.

I legged it back to André, who was wrapping the rope under Libert's armpits. The poor brute was protesting feebly, but André was saying 'They need your guns, Bettremieu, I'm ordering you over,' and the Flamand was too dazed and sick to resist. I didn't bother either, we couldn't waste another second on argument, and the man would never get over alone. He managed to get one hand on the rope, and between us André and I launched him across the gap. To my surprise, the men who emerged to catch him on the other side were Lefebvre and Pinhead, and I gathered we'd somehow acquired reinforcements.

Jacques Gilbert

I couldn't believe it. They'd got themselves over and left the boy behind.

Marcel was frantic. He was snatching pistols from the saddle holsters and throwing them to Jean-Marie and Giles, while Colin and Pinhead pulled Bettremieu in cover and grabbed the muskets still slung round his body. It was all about fire-power now, there was nothing else going to save the boy, not with half the Spanish army thundering towards him through those trees.

'Pin them down,' Marcel was shouting. 'Keep them out of the clearing while our men cross. For God's sake, pin them down!'

Stefan finished reeling in the rope, and his arm went out for André so they could cross together. Shadows shifted in the trees behind them, Margot blasted away at the movement, but there was an answering orange flash in the darkness. Marcel fired at the gunsmoke, but something was wrong, Stefan was jerking back from the rope, he was spinning on his heel, then his whole body crashed heavily to the ground.

Jean-Marie Mercier

Marcel cried out behind me, and I think I did too. It seemed impossible that Stefan could be down, but he was, and even from this distance I could see the bright redness of blood running down his face and soaking into the earth. André dropped to his knees beside him.

More soldiers were charging through, but Colin, Giles and Jacques all fired at once. The smoke faded, and for a moment the clearing was empty except for André, kneeling all alone, looking bewildered and shocked. I turned desperately to Marcel, but he was staring over in disbelief at Stefan's body, and for the first time since I'd known him he seemed at a loss.

'The rope!' yelled Jacques, scrambling to his feet. 'André, the rope!'

André turned jerkily round towards us as if he didn't know who we were.

'The rope!' I shouted.

He understood all at once, and picked up the rope where it lay limply across Stefan's open palm. His movements were very slow, he seemed dazed and confused. Only there wasn't time to delay, the woods behind him were simply bristling with movement.

'André!' called Jacques in anguish.

André's head came up and he seemed to pull himself together. He climbed to his feet and came towards the edge

312

just as more soldiers appeared through the trees. I seized the last gun from Pepin and fired at the first, and just for a second André glanced behind him.

And Stefan moved. His arm stretched and clenched, he seemed to be trying to roll over.

A soldier sprang forward, sword raised to hack down at Stefan, but André leapt at him, parrying and thrusting him back, then turning fast to face the others. The rope slipped unregarded through his fingers, and flopped uselessly to the ground.

Jacques Gilbert

He went back. The stupid little bugger, he went back. There were three, now four of them breaking through, but still he went back.

My bloody gun was empty, we were all reloading like mad, there were ramrods waving all about me like a forest. Only Bernard was ready, and he loosed a bolt into one of the bastards, but there were three still up. The boy was pulling out of the first, but they were too close, he was having to jump back, he was off balance. One of them lunged down, the boy was twisting away, helpless, his left arm coming up uselessly to ward off the blades, I think I was sobbing as I tried to load, and the bloody, bloody ball slipped out of my hand and rolled into the grass.

Pepin had a musket ready, but it would take seconds to pass it on, he levelled and fired it himself. He'd never been in action before, but it was a great shot, it took the nearest man clean, and gave André the seconds he needed to get himself upright, then step forward to engage the next man. Another was coming through now, but the boy was back in control, and behind him Stefan started heaving himself on to his hands and knees. I felt my breathing subsiding as I retrieved my ball.

Marcel seemed to have got a grip of himself. 'Marksmen only!' he was shouting. 'Everyone else, load. Pass your guns to Mercier, Leroux or Margot as they're charged. Marksmen only, make every shot count!'

André was keeping both his swordsmen in play, working them in front of him like a screen, so their comrades couldn't touch him. Behind him, Stefan knelt himself upright and mopped the blood from his face.

I finished loading and passed my gun to Margot, starting to feel more confident. Then a bullet whined and pinged into a tree behind my head, and a second later Bernard gave a yelp and dropped in a huddle over his crossbow. Cover or not, we'd got two dozen Spaniards shooting in our direction and couldn't keep it up for ever.

'Come on, Stefan!' shouted Marcel. 'For God's sake, man, move!'

Stefan Ravel

Oh don't ask me, Abbé, I was out of it. I'd had a fucking musket ball graze my skull and my brain wasn't quite working as it should.

The first I knew was lifting my head with a mouthful of earth and seeing a pair of feet leaping about in front of me. It took me a second to realize it was André, and he seemed to be fighting the entire Spanish army a foot away from my nose. I hauled myself up on to my knees.

'Take your time,' said André, fencing furiously and stepping neatly to one side to avoid a lunge.

I shoved my hair out of my eyes and squinted up at him. 'Fuck you,' I said.

He laughed. 'Just get the bloody rope.'

I was already reaching for it. I stood slowly, gave it a couple of good turns round my waist, and wedged the anchor under my arm.

'Ready when you are,' I said.

He leapt forward at once and thrust the nearest swordsman right in the guts. He'd probably have had the other too, but I was nearer so I simply whacked him down with the anchor. There was no one behind him. Gunfire was cracking merrily all round us, but for the moment the clearing was free.

I adjusted my grip on the rope and reached out towards André, but he spun round to me so suddenly the force knocked me back towards the edge, so I just grabbed him up in my left arm and launched us both into space.

The sudden pull startled me. He wasn't carrying himself at all, I was taking his full weight. I grappled him closer, but a glance showed me his head flopping loosely back to expose his throat, while his eyes were fast closed in a face that was suddenly white. As my feet touched the ground on the other side, I felt a warm wetness soaking my arm, and it was only then I understood.

Jean-Marie Mercier

I don't think any of us knew. As Stefan landed safely, men all about me started to cheer. I thought I could hear a cheer from the other side as well, but it didn't make sense, and I ignored it. Marcel was shouting at us all to pull back, pull back, retreat to the horses, then he was darting out of cover to haul in the remnants of the rope so the Spaniards couldn't reel it back to the other side. Stefan headed straight for the trees, but André's feet were dragging as Stefan supported him, and I remember thinking 'Why, he's hurt, he must be hurt.'

We struggled back through the trees to the horses. Pinhead and Giles were propping up Bettremieu, who incredibly seemed to be still alive, while Pepin and Margot were helping Bernard, and I was thinking 'It's only one, we've only lost Philippe, honestly it's a miracle.'

Then I saw Stefan wasn't supporting André any more, he was carrying him in his arms, and Colin was making the great warhorse bend his knees so Stefan could lift André on with him. Jacques came skidding up to them, anxiety distorting his face, he was stretching out his hands insistently towards André and saying something I couldn't catch, he was almost babbling. Marcel came and put an arm round him, and I heard him say gently 'Let Stefan take him, Jacques, it's best if Stefan takes him now.'

Jacques stared at him in terrified comprehension, and said 'No.' Marcel only looked sadly at him, and Stefan started to mount the horse, laying André carefully over his lap. Jacques looked wildly round at us, and I became aware the sounds of gunfire had stopped. There was nothing but silence, and Jacques looking desperately from face to face as if appealing a terrible decision. Giles was gazing at him in a kind of dreadful pity, and I felt the tears starting in my eyes.

Suddenly, shockingly, Jacques screamed at us all 'No!'

And in the silence I heard it again: a distant cheer from the far bank, and the derisive sound of men's laughter.

Sixteen

Anne du Pré

Extract from her diary, dated 17 October 1638

I can't remember André's face. I try so hard, but it keeps slipping away, and all I remember is how I felt when he found that stupid snake and looked properly at me for the first time. I wish I could see him still. I am very lucky to have known someone who has been such a great hero, even if we were only children at the time.

I know I disgraced myself at the banquet, but I really could not help it. I knew something was wrong from the first, when Don Francisco arrived so late and then all those soldiers kept coming in to whisper reports, but I could not guess what the final horror would be. The smell of partridge will always bring it back to me now, the sickly sound of the guitars playing '*Triste España*', the sentimental tears on the face of Don Francisco, then the dreadful outburst of clapping and cheering at the news they had murdered a fifteen-year-old boy.

Colette managed much better than I, she behaved as if it were nothing to her at all, and continued to giggle with that good-looking enseigne with the boyish smile, the one she now calls Pablo. Even Florian covered his feelings better than I did, although I noticed he drank a great quantity of wine, which he is suffering for now. It was only I who was weak enough to beg to leave the table. Don Miguel was very kind, and told Don Francisco it was understandable I should be upset since I had known André personally, but he only peered at me as if I were a doll and said 'She is, d'Estrada, she really is, look, she's crying.'

Don Miguel offered to have me escorted back to our room, but I did not like the idea of being alone with the Slug, so he had Carlos take me to sit in a quiet corner by myself and fetch me a glass of water. I was not really unwell, I only wished to be alone, but Carlos stayed by me to make sure I was not molested, and I did not like to ask him to go away. I could only sit pretending to be quite composed, and listening while he spoke with that enseigne with the shiny hair who brought the news.

It was an extraordinary conversation, and I think they would not have held it so near me if they knew I spoke Spanish. The more I think about it, the stranger it seems, but I did not concentrate very well at the time so perhaps I misunderstood.

Carlos said 'You'll feel better now, I warrant, Señor de Castilla?' He always seems so jolly when he is with Don Miguel, but I thought today he sounded rather sly. He said 'If they'd taken him alive, who knows what he might have said?'

The enseigne said something that sounded like swearing. He said 'If he recognized me, he'd have known you too.'

'Not me, Señor,' said Carlos. 'I'd my helmet on, remember? It was only you in your pretty hat.'

The enseigne said bluntly 'Drop it, Corvacho. He's dead, now forget it.'

'Ah,' said Carlos, 'but you haven't got the body, have you?'

I felt a sudden fierce hope springing up inside me, but the enseigne only laughed and said 'We don't need it, man. He took a ball in the spine, he won't walk away from that.'

'Are you sure?' said Carlos, and there really was something

318

most insidious about the way he spoke. 'Did you see it your-self?'

'See it?' said the enseigne. Perhaps it is because his complexion is so swarthy, but I thought his teeth looked very white. He said 'I pulled the trigger myself.'

My last little quiver of hope died then, and I could not listen any more.

And now I think I really have to be honest with myself. This is my diary and I can speak the truth. My feelings are more selfish than I have ever dared admit, because I have always nurtured this secret hope that one day André would come and rescue us. I have this foolish dream when he appears at our door looking handsome and splendid and holding out his hand to me, saying 'Mademoiselle, I have come to take you home.' It was stupid, *stupid*, and I know I have to grow up as Colette says.

Only I do so wish I could remember his face.

Colin Lefebvre

News had gone ahead with the signal team, men rushing out all over when we got back, eager to see who'd made it and who hadn't. They fell back smart enough when they saw the look on Jacques' face, then Ravel coming up slowly at the rear with our Seigneur in his arms. Knew what was up then all right, and the silence we rode into was thick as fog. Men took off their hats in respect.

That set old Jacques off again straightaway. 'He's not dead,' he said, 'he's only wounded, isn't he, Stefan?' True enough in its way, Seigneur was stirring as they lifted him down, but Ravel said 'He's shot in the back, what do you think I can do?' Then Jacques shouted. 'I don't know,' he was shouting. 'Whatever it is, just bloody do it.'

Poor old Jacques. I tried to explain to people they'd got to make allowances, right, it was the whole of his future he was looking at losing, his whole life wrapped up in that bundle Ravel was carrying into the Hermitage, small wonder he was upset. Leroux gave me a nasty look at that, but then he'd no sensitivity, Leroux. Man's got to defend his friends, and me and Jacques went back a long way.

Other things on people's minds too, and as evening drew on a few of us took cider into the outhouse to talk things through. Fact is, look at it how you like, the dons were lying in wait. They knew we were coming, and what we wanted to know was how. Seemed to me we'd got a traitor somewhere, and not far to look for him neither, not with young Pepin out on his first ever action, not to mention him being dark and swarthy as he was, might be gypsy, might be Spaniard for all we knew, and no one with the smallest idea where he'd sprung from.

Leroux flushed right up at that. Said there was no way the kid informed, he saved the lot of them, not to mention being in danger himself throughout. Said if we'd got a traitor at all it was more likely someone safe on the other side of the road, maybe someone doing business with the dons on their own account. Now I wasn't having that, not taking that from anyone, and things were looking to get nasty when suddenly there's a shadow at the door, and Ravel himself standing watching us. Didn't say a word, just stood in silence and took out his smelly old pipe. Made everyone very tense.

'Well?' said Leroux.

Ravel fumbled out his tinder box. 'Libert's all right. Two balls I've taken out of him, and he's sitting up drinking soup, man's not human. Rouet's fine, chipped ribs, that's all.'

'And André?' said Leroux bluntly. 'Is he dead?'

'Not yet,' said Ravel bitterly. He lit his box, sending a great shower of sparks flying off into the dark. 'Not yet.'

We all felt more subdued after that. Leroux said wearily 'There is no traitor, Lefebvre, not a man among us would risk André. If there were, they could have blabbed on the Hermitage and scooped the reward long since. There's no traitor, only a bunch of careless bloody fools, any one of whom might have opened his mouth in the wrong alehouse.'

Not sure that would have convinced everyone, but then Simon Moreau spoke up, him whose dad ran the Corbeaux, he said there was this big Spaniard used to come in of an evening, sit by himself in Hell Corner drinking cider, Moreau was certain sure he was listening in to people's conversations. Dressed like a regular chap, not a soldier at all, but Moreau was pretty sure he was a Spaniard, guessed it by the accent.

'All very well telling us now,' I said. 'Might have warned us a bit sooner.'

Couldn't take criticism, Moreau, touchy sort of chap. Said 'How was I to know people were going to come blabbing military secrets in the middle of the alehouse, eh? Can't go blaming me if someone's been stupid.'

No call for that, and I'd have maybe took him up on it, only it didn't seem respectful, brawling over nothing with the Seigneur dying next door. Leroux felt the same. He told Moreau to leave it, said it was done now, and all of us taught a lesson for the future. Turned to Ravel and said 'Anything we can do? Drugs need fetching, anything like that?'

Ravel shook his head. 'All done. We need all the clean linen we can get, but that's all. Or you could pray, if you believe in that sort of thing.'

Leroux paused in the doorway and looked in his face. 'I'll see about that linen,' he said, and walked out.

There was nothing to be done but wait.

Stefan took out the ball, and that was awful, André woke up while it was still happening. We had to give him poppy medicine to ease the pain, but we couldn't wait for it to take effect, his back was already cut open and Stefan hacking about inside. Jean-Marie brought him his tennis ball to squeeze, and afterwards I found his fingers had dug right through the outer skin and the cloth inside had started to unravel.

Even then Stefan didn't think he'd got it all. He was afraid there were fragments left inside the wound along with bits of fabric from the boy's clothes, but didn't dare probe deeper because of being so close to the spine. He said all we could do was get fresh linen from somewhere, keep the wound clean, and pray to God it didn't get infected. It didn't sound much.

Georges went for more medicine from Mme Hébert, Dom rigged a screen of sacking over our corner to give the boy privacy, then I washed and bandaged him, and at last the poppy medicine made him sleep. I lay beside him and listened to his shallow breathing, and he looked young again, like he did in the beginning, before all these other people came along, when it was just him and me.

I knew he wouldn't die. There were so many things we were going to do together when the Occupation was over, there was his whole life to come. I found my mind stewing away all the same, and deep inside was a kind of anger that the boy could just get broken and maybe not put right, and all because someone had been showing off and talked somewhere and the Spaniards had heard. I wondered if I'd ever find out who it was, and what I'd say and do to them if I did.

I must have slept in the end, because I know I dreamed. I dreamed of being back at the gorge, and this time Stefan didn't move so André didn't go back, he just looked round once, sad and regretful, but he didn't go back, he came swinging across on that rope, and I stood to catch him, alive and strong and laughing, his skin warm and whole, unbroken.

When I woke, the sun was oozing between the slats, and there was the boy lying beside me, his eyes awake and red with pain, his face yellow-grey, a kind of blueness round his mouth, and his fists clenched tight by his sides. He wouldn't move, he whispered 'I'm all right now, I've found a position it's not so bad, if I just lie like this and don't move it's not so bad.' I ran for Stefan.

Stefan Ravel

Nothing to be done, Abbé. I'd have bled him if I could, but he was losing too much as it was, he hadn't a dropful to spare for a leech. I tried cupping, but I'd had to widen the wound too much for that, and couldn't do much more than tackle the edges, bring up some strong, good blood to drive out the shit. It wasn't enough, nothing was, the dressing was getting yellower every time I looked.

Georges reported back from his witch, and by that stage I was prepared to try anything. I'm not sentimental, Abbé, but I don't like losing men at the best of times, and it wasn't going to do a damn thing for morale if we lost this one. Besides, some of these old women know a thing or two. Oh, you wouldn't believe the superstitious crap they'll sometimes try and hand you out, but Dom and Georges swore by this one and we'd got bugger all left to lose.

She'd sent us more of the poppy tincture, but she also

gave us some vile-looking physic she claimed was made from spiders, and I'm not ashamed to say we gave him that too. Her suggestion for the wound itself was probably the stupidest I'd ever heard, mind you, but it wasn't for me to protest, so off they went hunting round the outhouses for cobwebs and mould, and when they brought back an old saddle sprouting Christ knows what, I did my best to scrape off the blue mould and spread it on the dressing.

It didn't look good. The kid was starting to writhe by now, complaining of itching. I said 'Hardly surprising, little general, you should see what I'm putting on your back,' but he shook his head vaguely and said the prickling was deep inside and he needed to dig it out. I laid my fingers gently on his skin and took them off again fast. He was burning up with fever.

By noon he was tossing and turning, and muttering fitfully. Dom said we should send for a priest, but Jacques was having none of it. He said 'If André sees a priest, he'll give up, if we bring him a priest he'll think he's dying.'

Dom was a gentle, rather fey sort of lad, but he was braver in his way than we were. He said 'Yes, little Brother. Yes.'

Jean-Marie Mercier

I walked slowly to the Hermitage that evening, I think I was afraid of being told André had died. Only I had to go, because I'd brought food and some linen Jeanette had sent, which looked beautifully clean and fresh and had been given her by the hostages themselves. I'd have hesitated about taking it once, because of having to tell André where it came from, but nothing like that seemed to matter any more, it was hard to believe it ever had.

I heard raised voices as soon as I opened the door, but the only people I could see were Bettremieu, who hadn't been well enough to go home last night, and Dom, who was changing his dressing. The others were behind the sacking screen, and I'm afraid we could hear them. There was something thrashing about in the straw, and Marcel saying 'I can't hold him,' and Stefan swearing as I'd never heard him, a great upheaval of rustling and a sound like a muffled slap, then nothing but this one little whimper, and then silence.

I looked away quickly and just for a moment I caught Dom's eye. He was talking quietly to Bettremieu, but his face was tense and his eyes white and scared. Bettremieu seemed little better. He had a great bandage round his chest and another round his arm, but the misery on his broad face had nothing to do with either of them. He whispered to me 'M. André is very sick, and it is all my fault.'

I said 'You were wounded, Bettremieu.'

He looked at his bandages as if surprised to see them, then waved them away. 'He ordered me, but I should not have left him. If I were stronger, I should have just held him, so.' He placed his two great hands a slim distance apart and I could almost see André standing between them. 'I should not have left him,' he said.

Stefan came out from the screen and honestly seemed pleased with the linen, he said it was the best they'd had. He tore up the first sheet at once, and took me with him behind the sacking to help redress the wound. André lay on his side, his eyes closed, and his head resting on Jacques' lap. He seemed to be asleep, but his breathing was rattling and shallow, and the hand that lay limply beside him in the straw was curled like a dead leaf.

Jacques tried to smile at me as Stefan applied the dressing.

'He's better now,' he whispered. 'He's had his medicine and he's better now. Look, he's asleep.'

Stefan finished bandaging, sat quite still a moment, then lifted his head to look at Jacques. 'Listen, lad, you have to understand I can't save him. The witch's stuff is helping, but while there's crap still inside the wound, it's just going to go on churning out muck till it rots the spine, and then it's over.'

'Then we've got to get the bits out,' said Jacques.

'The spine's too close,' said Stefan. 'I'd cripple him.'

'Better than being dead,' said Jacques.

'Is it?' said Stefan. 'André de Roland? Are you sure?'

Jacques was silent, and I think we all felt the horror of his decision. He said 'Isn't there anyone could do it? M. Pollet –'

'Is a barber,' said Stefan. 'The surgeon in Lucheux's no better, nor the one in Abbeville, they're neither of them experienced with gunshot wounds. Our only chance is a proper military surgeon, and anyone like that's already with the army.'

'What about Doullens?' said Jacques. 'The citadel, they're bound to have someone there.'

'Yes, of course,' said Marcel, 'but they won't deprive a whole garrison of a surgeon for one sick boy.'

'He's André de Roland.'

'He's no one,' said Stefan roughly. 'Not outside Dax. He's not powerful enough for the army to care about.'

None of us said anything for a long while.

Jacques sat looking down at André's face as if he wanted to memorize every tiny detail. Then he ran his hand down his own fingers and held something out to Marcel.

'Give them this,' he said. 'Maybe they'll care enough if we give them this.'

It was his diamond ring.

Marcel stared at it, then up at Jacques. 'You can't. If André dies, you'll have nothing else.'

Jacques said 'If he dies, I don't want it.'

Stefan made an oddly abrupt noise and turned away. But Marcel leant forward, kissed the top of Jacques' head, and took the ring. He said 'I'll go myself.'

Jacques looked up at him with sudden hope. 'Take Tempête,' he said. 'He's fastest, he's . . . Take Tempête.'

Marcel smiled. He backed away through the sacking, and a moment later I heard the door of the Hermitage close.

I stayed with them all night. Marcel couldn't possibly be back in less than a day, and Stefan and Jacques couldn't manage André alone. It was quite all right while the poppy medicine made him sleep, but we couldn't give it to him all the time, Dom said that was dangerous, and when he was awake I'm afraid it was really quite dreadful. He kept trying to rip off his dressing, you see, he was writhing and thrashing about, tearing at his own body.

It was taking a terrible toll on Jacques. He desperately needed rest, but absolutely refused to leave André. I sent a little message to Colin's sister, Simone, because I knew she and Jacques were courting and thought perhaps she might help, but Colin said she was busy and wouldn't quite meet my eyes when he said it.

'What did you expect?' said Stefan to me afterwards. 'Jacques isn't the catch he used to be, not now. You'll find you're the same.'

I already had. People like Jeanette honestly couldn't do enough for us, but there were others definitely less friendly now I was no longer in a position to obtain favours from André. I think what depressed me most was their assumption he was already dead. The soldiers certainly thought so. I'd heard them singing a song of their own, set to the tune of

327

'*Le Petit Oiseau*', about a little bird who tried to fly over a gorge but was shot in mid-air and ended on a soldier's gibbet. It was quite beastly.

It was Margot who helped in the end. She wasn't on duty, she just came and shoved straight past the sacking, said 'Bugger off, Jacques, it needs a woman here,' then took André's head on her lap, and soothed him back into sleep. There was something very calming about Margot. She stroked André's forehead and said 'Poor little bugger, it doesn't seem right at his age. Never even been kissed, I'd guess, not so much as one little kiss.'

Jacques made a choking sound, and I think Margot understood, because she laid André gently back down then went and put a firm arm round Jacques instead. She said 'As for you, young man, he's going to need you in the morning so you'd better be ready, hadn't you?' She led him out of the enclosure and made him lie down, and he did it because Margot told him. She even made Stefan rest.

She left at first light to work at the bakery, but I didn't want to wake the others just yet, not after so little sleep. I sat alone and watched André as the dawn pink began to glimmer through the slats and make patterns on the inside of the sacking. I knew he would die today. His skin had that extraordinary translucent quality, and every feature was standing out as if someone had painted him for posterity. His lips were cut in that delicate sculpture you never see after twenty. The scrollwork of his ears was like the inside of seashells, fragile and perfect. Every single eyelash was a fine, black curve. His eyes were open, and he was looking at me.

He whispered 'Where's Jacques?'

I hesitated.

'My father will know,' he said confidentially. 'He says you can always tell where Jacques is.'

I was beginning to be frightened. I said 'How?'

'Because Jacques is always where he's meant to be.'

I wondered if I ought to fetch someone, but he seemed quite calm.

He said 'I wasn't, was I? My father says so. He says Pierre Gilbert was lucky to have a son like Jacques, someone he could always rely on. He says I could learn from Jacques.'

He sounded quite natural, only very, very quiet. His eyes were wide and dark, and I thought I'd never seen pupils so large.

I said 'Your father loved you, André, I know he did.'

His lips smiled. 'You talk as if he's dead.'

'André,' I said.

His eyes creased in confusion, and he tried to speak. I bent forward to catch what he was saying and his eyes looked directly into mine.

'Where's Jacques?'

I stumbled out through the sacking to fetch him. He was up in a second, and Stefan behind him. In the moment I'd been gone André had deteriorated, and he was writhing again, only his movements were brittler and feebler than they'd been before and he was making a kind of clicking noise with his tongue.

'That's it,' said Stefan, looking down at him. 'This is it. Dom, get me the coldest water you can get from that stream. Keep it coming.'

Dom was behind us, his usual serenity quite shattered. 'A priest, I'll send Georges . . .'

'Too late,' said Stefan. 'Just the water, nothing else.'

I half thought Jacques would protest, but he didn't. He sat down by André's side, quiet but determined, and I knew the time for arguing was over.

Everything happened very fast. Dom brought water, and

Stefan threw it over André, dousing him over and over again. André was shivering and trying to shrink away, but Jacques wouldn't let him, he pinned his wrists down in the straw. Stefan worked like a demon, throwing the water, checking his palm against André's skin, yelling 'Come on, come on!', calling for more water, taking André's face in his hands, turning him, talking to him, sometimes shouting, once slapping his cheek and shouting 'Don't you fucking dare!' Once André managed to look at him and say weakly 'Stop it, you bastard,' and Stefan was elated, he hissed 'Good, good, fight it, go on and fight it,' and for a moment Jacques' eyes fixed on him in fearful hope.

I honestly don't know how long it went on. There were just the four of us trapped in that little corner, all of us soaked, but Stefan's face dripping with sweat and his eyes red and savage, his naked chest glistening damp, the scarlet gash down the side of his head shining like an open mouth, his hands working endlessly, lifting André's arms and l egs, swearing, swearing, awful words that after a while lost any kind of meaning and began to sound like a familiar prayer.

Dom brought more water, but Stefan didn't throw it, he asked for a cup instead. I filled it myself, and Stefan poured it into André's mouth, holding his jaw to make him drink. André spluttered and dribbled, but some of it stayed in and after a moment Stefan released him. At once André shuddered and tried to curl into a ball, and Stefan took him by the shoulders and almost shook him. André's head lolled weakly but he stayed conscious, and after a while he managed to hold his head up and turn in desperate appeal to Jacques. Stefan gave an exclamation, said urgently 'Take him, for God's sake,' and Jacques opened his arms and rested André's head on his chest. For a moment everything was still.

'His skin's cooling,' said Jacques, stroking André's forehead.

Stefan sat back on his heels and breathed out heavily. 'Talk to him.'

And Jacques did. No, I'm really sorry, it wouldn't be right for me to tell you, I think that's rather private. He talked, that's all. Stefan and I went in and out, fetching linen, removing the wet blanket, bringing brandy, and still Jacques talked, gently and evenly on and on, until at last André's head drooped again. Stefan laid his fingers against the side of his neck and gave a little nod.

'Steady enough,' he said. 'Move fast now.'

We laid André back down on a dry blanket, and Stefan removed the sodden dressing. I brought more of the Château linen, but he didn't reach out to take it, he seemed quite transfixed by the sight of the wound. I looked myself, and saw to my astonishment the edges were pinker and cleaner, and although there was still a very nasty area where the skin looked yellow and swollen like an overripe pear, it seemed definitely smaller than it had been.

'More mould,' said Stefan suddenly. 'More of that mould. Cobwebs, anything, whatever the old bag said. It's fucking working. Whatever it was, get me more of it'

The saddle was nearly finished, but I found more blue mould under some old leather bandoliers and a great swathe of cobwebs from the stables outhouse. Stefan took it all without comment, spread it on the Château linen and laid it gently over the great hole in André's back.

André spoke quite distinctly. 'That's nice,' he said. 'Cool.'

A moment later he was fast asleep.

He slept most of the day, and in the evening Marcel arrived back with a wrinkly little man he said was the chief military surgeon from Doullens. The surgeon seemed quite grand for someone who was only a jumped-up version of M. Pollet, and came in all grumpy like he was already convinced we were wasting his time. When we told him André was alive and seemed better, he just raised his eyebrows, exchanged a funny look with his miserable assistant, and said 'Well then, let's get on with it, shall we?'

The boy had just had another belt of his poppy medicine and was deep asleep, so the surgeon rolled up his sleeves, drank off a huge mug of cider, sat down in the straw and got started right away. He had big fat candles that gave him loads of light, and he got us to stick them in shallow pans of water, which made the light reflect even further. He peeled off the dressing, made a face at it, and chucked it to his assistant, saying 'Filthy, of course,' like we were all deaf and couldn't hear, then looked more closely at the wound and said 'Hmm.' He sat back on his heels a moment, looked round suspiciously, and said 'Hmm' again. We all looked at him blankly, and I noticed Jean-Marie had casually sat himself down in front of the mouldy saddle to hide it from view.

'Nice job,' said the surgeon at last. 'There's a chance here.' He attached a strange pair of eyeglasses to his nose to make everything look bigger, then started picking in the boy's back with long tweezers, like a chicken finding grain in a heap of sand. He got a shred of cloth and some little black specks of powder out of the wound, swabbed it clean, then stitched the whole thing up again. It only took about ten minutes. Then he stood up and held out his mug for more cider.

'Remarkable,' he said, sounding almost human for the first time. 'Anything can happen, of course, you'll need to take care with the dressing, but he's a good, strong boy, no reason why he shouldn't make a complete recovery.'

It's funny, but it was only then I felt my knees start wobbling, and had to sit down. Things felt even odder on the ground, because it was all going on above me. I remember sitting there, my palms pressed hard against the spikiness of the straw, and looking up at the surgeon's fashionable mauve breeches as he talked to Marcel like he was the only person there. It felt like something I was dreaming.

Then I saw Stefan. He was standing back apart from everyone else, leaning against a pillar with one great booted leg thrust out in front of him like he didn't care who tripped over it. As I watched, he pulled out a flask from an inside pocket, flipped the stopper off with one dirty finger and put it to his lips. He watched the surgeon over the rim as he drank, and there was no expression in his eyes at all. Maybe he sensed me looking, but his eyes suddenly flicked to mine, and for a second he felt more real than anything else in that whole room.

Marcel said something to the surgeon, then led me over, and we looked down at André together. He was breathing softly and evenly, there was a faint pink tinge in his cheeks, and his lips were red. I didn't cry, I didn't even want to, I felt the way you do after Confession, that clean feeling sort of whooshing through you like you've been forgiven and given a fresh start. I wanted to share it with someone who understood, but when I looked round, the door was swinging open and Stefan was gone.

I escorted the visitors back to the *gabelle* road, because they preferred to stay the night at Lucheux rather than with us.

Everything looked peaceful at the Hermitage when I got back. Pepin waved happily to me from the roof, and I knew that inside there would be light and warmth and everyone celebrating because André was going to be all right. I stabled the horse in the outhouse, brushed myself down and walked towards the door, but as I reached it I jumped back suddenly in fright. There was a huge dark shape huddled against the wall. In the gloom I could just make out a shaggy head and two glinting eyes, and then I saw it was Stefan.

I came closer. He had his flask of brandy in his hand, and there was quite a strong smell of it about him too. He took another swig as he looked at me, and a little dribble came trickling down his chin. He didn't even bother to wipe it.

I didn't quite like to walk past, not while he was looking at me. I thought perhaps I ought to say something, but he was very drunk, and I wasn't sure how he'd react.

He stretched up his arm and offered me the flask. 'Drink?'.

I could see he thought I wouldn't, and perhaps that's why I took it. I actually took quite a large gulp, and it scalded all the way down my throat, but it warmed my stomach and I felt better for it.

'That's right,' he said, taking it back. 'It's good stuff. André's, of course, it's all André's. Couldn't afford it myself, not a humble tanner like me.'

I moved past to the door, but as I opened it I heard his voice again behind me.

'What made him do a thing like that anyway?' he said. 'Do you know?'

I looked back at him, but I'm afraid I didn't understand. 'The brandy?'

He looked blankly at me, than gave an odd short laugh like a bark.

'No,' he said. 'No, no, no.' He knocked the back of his hand gently against the wall. 'No. I mean back there.' He gave a little jerk of his head, and I suddenly understood.

'He wanted to save you.'

His hand stopped moving. His eyes seemed to be trying to pierce through the darkness at me.

'Do you know,' he said, 'I'd worked that out all by myself.'

'It was his choice.'

He took another swig from his flask, and looked carefully at the ceiling. 'Saw it, did you?' he said. 'From your little nest in the heather?'

He didn't ask even now, but I saw he wanted to know, so I described everything I'd seen, and how André had stood in front of his body and defended him against them all.

Stefan never looked at me once while I was talking, he never moved at all. When I'd finished, there was a little silence, and then his lips moved, and he started cursing quietly, almost under his breath.

I said 'You know the rest of it.'

His face turned slightly, his eyes glistening in the moonlight.

'Oh yes,' he said. 'I know.'

He started to clamber to his feet, but was rather unsteady, and had to grasp my shoulder to haul himself up.

'Stupid little bastard,' he said. 'I trained him better than that. You know I did, Mercier, I did everything I could.'

I picked up his flask, which had fallen in the straw, and handed it back. He looked at it incuriously, flipped it open, drank, then passed it back as if it were mine.

'Do you know,' he said, 'I never asked for anything in my whole fucking life?'

I took another sip of the brandy, and perhaps it made me braver than usual. I said 'Well, perhaps you should.'

He stared at me incredulously for a moment, then gave a short, huffing laugh.

'Blessed are the meek,' he said. 'Is that right, you fucking little oddity?'

He reached out suddenly, seized my head and crushed it against his chest, and I realized he was actually embracing me. He released me just as suddenly, flapped a hand at me and reached for his flask.

'That's mine,' he said, and heaved himself into the doorway. He looked back for a moment, but I don't think he was really seeing me, I think he was too far gone.

'Blessed are the meek,' he said again, then laughed. He swung himself out through the door and into the darkness, his laughter seeming to grow louder as he wandered away into the trees.

Seventeen

Jacques Gilbert

He got better every day. One moment he was this pathetic creature meekly taking everything we gave him, the next he was spotting me mixing spider medicine with his wine and saying if I tried it again he'd break my arm. He was out of bed in a week, walking about in two, and a few days after that I caught him trying to fence.

Stefan got all the credit, of course, he went swaggering about like a King's Physician and wouldn't let anyone else touch the boy without his say so. I didn't mind at first, I thought it was fair enough. I never forgot what he did when things were so desperate, or those hours in the dawn behind that cold wet sacking when it looked like Stefan was our only hope.

People thought André's recovery was a kind of miracle. The army got almost superstitious about him, and went singing that '*Petit Oiseau*' till we were sick of the sound of it. I can't remember what the new verse was this time, something about a bird flying over a cliff on the back of an eagle, but they probably had it crapping on something on the way, it seemed to be always doing that, you'd think it had diarrhoea. But they sang it in the villages too, and the Spaniards didn't like that at all. They still went round saying André was dead, they talked like we were just making it up to save our faces, but they put up big posters offering two hundred livres for his body, so I knew they wanted to be sure. Don Francisco was probably having a few sleepless nights over it, and serve the bastard bloody well right.

The odd thing was I didn't much care any more, it was like a lot of the hatred had burnt itself out. They'd trapped us and made us run for our lives, they'd murdered Philippe and nearly crippled André, it was like the worst defeat ever, but somehow the boy surviving made it like we'd won after all. Nothing else mattered. D'Ambleville at Doullens actually sent me back my ring, he said loyalty like that was worth more than the diamond, but even that didn't seem important. André was going to be all right, and all I remember clearly is him putting it back on my finger himself.

The next day I went to see my family. It was a bright, cold morning, with the ground making crunching noises when you walked on it, but I felt warm inside, like a kind of hero returning home. I'd got tobacco for my Father too, and I knew he'd be pleased about that. M. Merien couldn't get it any more, but Stefan used the couriers to buy it from the apothecary in Lucheux and André paid for us to have some too.

By the time I got to Ancre my nose and ears were so cold I had to keep pinching them. I remember opening the cottage door and the warmth rushing out at me with a burst of laughter from Blanche. I shut it quickly behind me to keep the draught out, and turned to look at my family.

They were all sat round the table with steaming bowls of soup in front of them. Their faces looked orange in the firelight, their hair all shining yellow and Mother's bright gold. Blanche was on Father's lap, his big hands clasped round her back, and the faces they all turned to me were still smiling from whatever they'd been laughing about. For a moment I felt sort of awkward.

Then Mother was up and scrambling round Little Pierre

to get to me, hugging me so tightly I felt her warmth like a shock. Father looked shaken too, Blanche sliding slowly off his lap as he stood.

I said quickly 'I'm all right.' I could see he'd been worried, and that was warming me even more than the fire.

'Oh my darling,' said Mother. 'We've heard so many stories, we didn't know what to believe.' She dragged me to the table and poured another bowl of soup. It was turnip, of course, but thick and sludgy and with chunks of pink bacon, so I knew M. Legros was looking after them all right.

Father still seemed shaky, like he couldn't really take it in. He said 'Lefebvre's been saying all kinds of things, a big battle and God knows what. I thought it was just you and André.'

I felt a bit bad about that actually. It's true I'd implied it was just us, I think I'd wanted to impress them, but they were impressed enough now, they wanted the whole story, and even Little Pierre listened with his mouth open and forgot to look grumpy. Father actually seemed upset, he made a mess lighting his pipe and bits of tinder went fluttering all over the floor. When I told about Philippe being killed, he made an exclamation and pushed right back from the table.

'Oh poor Philippe,' said Mother. 'He went with you to the livestock markets, didn't he, Pierre?'

Father grunted. 'Every year.' He pulled out his old red handkerchief and mopped the back of his neck. 'They were good times. The ones at Abbeville were the best, we'd stay up the whole four days.'

'It sounds like a lot of drinking,' said Mother, but she said it nicely, and stroked his hand.

He looked at her fingers, patted them idly, then turned and stared into the fire. 'We used to share a room with Gauthier,

Ravel and Leroux, we'd split the money we saved and buy spiced apples. Yes, Nell, we'd have a drink or two, we were on holiday, all of us.' He touched the tips of Mother's fingers to his lips, and smiled.

It was lovely seeing them tender with each other. I said 'I'm sorry about Philippe.'

Mother reached out her other hand to me, all warm from the fire. 'It's not your fault, my darling, we're just glad you're all right. And André too, we heard terrible things, people saying he was crippled and M. Ravel having to operate to save him. I've been so worried.'

Father sat back suddenly and let go Mother's hand.

I said 'It wasn't Stefan, it was me. I got him a surgeon all the way from Doullens, and he's walking already, he's going to be good as new.'

'Is he?' said Father. 'There you go, Nell, you can stop worrying now.' His voice was still soft, but he didn't take Mother's hand again, he just went on staring into the fire and hardly said another word.

Anne du Pré

Extracts from her diary, dated 8–9 November 1638

8 NOVEMBER

I am so happy. Jeanette says André is expected to make a full recovery. Her friend Mercier told her our linen was the best of anyone's and it is all they use for his dressing now. I feel quite strange about that. I took it from the press with my own hands, and it feels so odd to think of it now being wrapped round André's body.

Jeanette said 'Who knows, Mademoiselle, perhaps once he is stronger he may think of coming to rescue you to express his gratitude.'

It is a very salutary experience hearing one's own fantasies spoken aloud. I managed to laugh and say 'For a little linen, Jeanette?'

'Ah, but this was very special linen,' said Jeanette, and there was something coy in her manner I could not explain. 'M. de Roland is a gentleman and will doubtless soon work it out for himself.'

We had a visitor today, and it was that loathsome Pablo Colette liked so much at the dinner. I could not understand how it was permitted, but it was the Slug who let him in and I should not be surprised if he took bribes. Florian made no objection, but I think that was because Pablo brought us a cake. Poor Florian, he is getting so thin, and the soup has been very watery this week. Last night I dreamed of cheese.

Pablo pretended his was merely a visit of courtesy, but since he sat next to Colette and spoke to her the entire time his real purpose was clear to us all. What is most distressing is that Colette did not seem to mind. She fluffed up her hair and stuck out her chest and giggled, so that I was really quite ashamed. She seems quite to forget that Pablo is Spanish and our enemy.

He seems to forget it too, and speaks as if we were all on the same side. He even expected us to commiserate with him that there was still no sign of André's body when Don Francisco wanted to put it on a gibbet. I had difficulty remaining silent when he said that, and jabbed the needle so hard into my embroidery I pricked my thumb. I would have left the room, but then he said casually 'Some people think we shall never find it. Don Miguel's informant says de Roland is still alive.'

The thought of anyone being so disloyal made me burn with anger. I listened intently in hope he would say more about the informer, but naturally he did nothing so useful. He only sighed and said 'It is very hard on poor Don Luiz. There was a bonus promised for whoever killed de Roland, but it won't be paid now.'

'Don Luiz?' said Colette, her eyes wide open, as if everything Pablo said had to be interesting.

'Oh, he is a splendid fellow, Mademoiselle,' said Pablo. 'He comes from a very old family, one of the greatest in Spain. You will meet him yourself soon, for he is to be transferred from Dax to replace poor Santos, who was killed at the gorge.'

I know who he means by Don Luiz, it is that man at the dinner who told Carlos he killed André. I am not looking forward to seeing him again, I don't see why these officers must visit at all. I told Colette so this evening, but she said I was only in a bad mood because I will bleed again soon. She says it is always like that, and I must accept it as part of being a woman.

I do not see why being a woman means one must be nice to people who have tried to kill our friends. I may be very stupid, as Colette says, but I do not see it *at all*.

Jacques Gilbert

By mid-November he was out trying to fence again and this time there was no stopping him. He'd have healed much faster if he hadn't tried to do stuff so quickly, but that was André, he wanted to be back to strength right now and no one was going to tell him not. Stefan said it wouldn't do him any harm, I'd got to let him go at his own pace, but it wasn't anything to do with Stefan, it wasn't his job to look after André, it was mine.

He didn't need Stefan's encouragement anyway, he was just pushing and pushing himself so I could hardly bear to watch. Those fencing exercises were the worst, he'd be doing that crouching down and springing up thing over and over again, his breath coming in gasps and sweat breaking out on his forehead, and I'd say 'You can't, André, you can't, you're going to tear yourself open.' Then one day he put his hands on my shoulders and said 'Jacques, I'll have to wear this sword all my life, do you really want it to be just an ornament?'

I understood then. He was *noblesse d'épée*, and that was something M. Gauthier said, he'd said the boy needed honour, courage, and the use of the sword. So I made myself bear it, I stood back and watched him rip himself open time and time again. The next week I even let him fence me, I let him keep at it, stabbing and thrusting, stamping and lunging, smashing and scraping his blade against mine till there were blue sparks from the force of it, I let him fight till he could beat me again, and only then did he collapse.

That's what started it all, I suppose, him collapsing and needing more stitches. Stefan grumbled like it was my fault, so I said it was him told me to let André go at his own pace, but he only looked at the boy lying flat on his belly and said 'And what pace is he going at now exactly?' He wouldn't even let me help with the dressings at first, but I spoke to Marcel, I said it was me was André's aide, and he agreed it was my job to look after him. Stefan just shrugged and said 'Well, if you want to get possessive about pus, that's up to you.'

So it was me changing the boy's dressing that day in December, and maybe that's why things happened how they did. I was rubbing in ointment while the boy lay on his stomach idly looking at the old bandage, which I know is disgusting but everyone does it, when suddenly he froze quite still, and his back went tense under my hands.

'What is it?' I said. 'There's nothing yellow, is there?'

He twisted his head round to look at me. 'This linen, it's from the Château at Verdâme, how on earth did we get it?'

It was our very best linen, white and new and so fine it was almost shiny, but the boy was right, it was from the hostages. Stefan was always careful not to let him see it.

I said lightly 'Oh, I think a maid who works there gave it to Jean-Marie.'

'Well, she shouldn't have,' he said. 'Look what it is, Jacques, this is Mlle Anne's own linen.' He showed me the monogram embroidered on a corner in fine white silk. 'It's her dowry linen, it's just like my mother's. They'd no right taking that. Is there much left?'

I riffled through the bale and saw there was a little lump in the middle. I peeled off the sheet above it, and there it was, a crushed rose, dried and falling to pieces, but still dark red and smelling beautiful.

'What's that?' said the boy before I could hide it.

I showed him. 'It's just a flower, to keep it fresh.'

He reached out and took it. I watched him apprehensively as he turned it over in his hands then smelt it.

'It's not,' he said decisively. 'It's too new for that. It's this year's.'

I quickly slapped the new dressing on his back. 'You think Mlle Anne is sending you flowers?'

'Of course not,' he said, reddening. 'That's silly.' He laid his face back down in the blanket.

I stared down at the back of his head. I'd always known he liked Mlle Anne, he liked her even more after what she'd done about the Pedros, but this was the first time the thought of her made him blush. Something inside my chest gave a single soft thump.

I should have seen it coming. He was fifteen, his body had changed, of course he was going to be thinking about women. There hadn't been any obvious signs of it, he never talked about them or anything, but then I suppose he wouldn't, he'd think it dishonourable. He'd always been romantic that way. He wasn't interested in Stefan going on about all the women he'd had, he liked books like *Amadis de Gaul* about knights being faithful and saving ladies in distress.

And now here was a girl imprisoned in a sort of castle actually smuggling him out a rose. It was bound to appeal to him whoever she was, and this was Mlle Anne, the only girl of his own kind he'd ever known. I tried telling myself she was only like a childhood sweetheart, then I remembered that so was the heroine of bloody *Amadis de Gaul* and I could have groaned aloud. She was so obviously perfect for him, perfect in every way, except that she was locked up in the Château and he'd only go trying to rescue her and getting himself killed.

I forced myself to go on with the dressing. I said 'You'd better not tear this any more, André, you'll end up with more scar than back.'

'Mm,' he said into the blanket. He reached out for some bits of straw and began twisting them in his fingers. 'I wonder how old she is now. She wasn't much younger than me, she must be at least fourteen. What do you think? Did you ever see her?'

I had a sudden memory of the two of them sitting side by side on the wall of the sunken garden, their heads close together as they talked.

I said 'She's still a little girl. Lift up a bit, I need to get the bandage round you.'

345

He hoisted himself a few inches off the straw. 'Girls can marry at twelve.'

I pulled the bandage as tight as I dared. 'Not when they're stuck in the Château Petit Arx.'

That was a mistake, I knew it as soon as it fell out of my mouth. The boy sucked in his breath and said 'You're right, it's cruel leaving them there. At her age, it's just cruel.'

Panic prickled me all over like pins and needles. I said 'Their father doesn't seem to mind, he could ransom them if he wanted, but he knows they're all right there. They're probably safer than anyone in Picardie.'

He sank slowly back down. 'That's what Stefan says too.'

I finished the dressing and gave it a little pat. 'All done. We could fence now if you like, as long as you're careful.'

He didn't get up for a minute, he kept his head down and started making the straws into plaits. 'I wonder what she looks like now.'

'Probably fat,' I said quickly. 'They're being looked after with the officers, aren't they, I'll bet they eat a lot better than we do.'

He rolled on to his side so he could look at me. 'She had beautiful hair,' he said. 'It was brown, but there was gold in it and flashes of red like little flames. There was so much of it, Jacques. It was thick, and looked soft and heavy, like silk. I wanted to play with it, but she wouldn't let me.'

I said primly 'You were only children.'

'Not any more,' said André, and suddenly there was a flash of his old grin, only with something in it I'd never seen before. 'Not any more.'

This was bad. If he was just romantic about Mlle Anne that could still be harmless, it could be a nice little dream, he could even go singing slushy songs outside her window if he wanted, but if he was thinking about her with that look in his eye he wasn't going to be content to adore her through three feet of solid wall, he was going to want her out and in his arms and in his bed.

I knew I'd got to do something, but couldn't think what. The obvious answer was to distract him with another woman, but I wasn't very hopeful about that. I'd watched him help Giles train the loaders while he was convalescing, and he'd never shown the slightest interest in the women, not even Simone. She and I had sort of fallen out when the boy was ill and I never felt the same about her afterwards, but she was still a beautiful girl, and she really tried hard for André, she wanted a go at a real live Seigneur. She'd leave her blouse unlaced and sit there sort of panting, pumping the ramrod in and out the muzzle, her eyes full on the boy's face, but he never responded, he just went pink and looked away. Stefan said 'What's the matter with him? She's practically begging for it,' but Marcel just sniffed and said 'I think André's looking for something more meaningful than a roll in the grass with Simone Lefebvre.'

That was the problem. The boy was too chivalrous to go pouncing on people, he wanted love and romance, that's why he got so excited about Mlle Anne and her bloody rose. I tried to think of anyone I could push him into falling in love with instead, but the only girl he had any kind of feelings for was Margot, and that wouldn't do, I mean Margot was Margot, even Giles hadn't tried. The one thing beautiful about her was this lovely soft skin, but when I said that to her once she laughed and said it came from working up to her neck in flour, which I wished she hadn't actually, it kept me awake nights wondering what she'd taste like. But André never thought of her that way, he liked her because she used to gob in the pies she made for the soldiers. He wasn't going to go falling in love with Margot.

347

I think the truth is he'd already decided to fall in love with Mlle Anne and there was nothing I could do to stop him. I did my best to keep him busy with fencing and stuff and changed the subject every time it looked like he might mention her, but none of it was any good. That evening he said casually 'When does Jean-Marie next come on duty?' and looked hard at the wall like he wasn't in the least interested in the answer. I said 'Oh, not for a couple of days. Why?' He looked at the floor instead and said 'Oh, just wondering.'

Jean-Marie Mercier

I enjoyed guard duty at the Hermitage, it was always very sociable. I was particularly looking forward to today because Jacques was spending time with his family for Christmas, so André would be especially glad of my company. I thought we might play boules.

Only I hadn't even reached the steps when Jacques himself came hurrying towards me, and began steering me forcefully away and down the track to the stream. I said 'What's happened? Is anything wrong with André?' but he only pushed me along more urgently and said grimly 'Not yet. But he's going to ask you about that linen from the Château, he's going to ask you about Jeanette.'

I saw at once what he was afraid of. Stefan had already said quite unequivocally that if I allowed Jeanette within a mile of André he would personally do something very nasty. I sat down rather abruptly and said 'What shall I do?'

'Lie,' said Jacques, really quite bluntly. 'Tell him she's dead or left the Saillie, tell him what you like, but don't let him think he can see her or talk to her.'

I knew what was at stake, but I'm honestly not very good at lying. I said 'He might find out.'

'He won't,' said Jacques. He sat beside me on the bank and patted my arm reassuringly. 'He can't move from the Hermitage, you and me are his eyes and ears, he won't know anything we don't tell him.'

I think perhaps I was a little agitated. I said 'I'll try, Jacques, honestly I will, but I really don't know if I can lie to André. He's been so good to me, I don't —'

There was movement behind him, and I looked up to see André stepping out from the trees. I realized how loudly I'd been talking, and my tongue seemed to shrivel in my mouth.

He stood and looked down at us, tall, relaxed, his left hip leaning slightly outward to point his sword hilt towards his hand.

'Hullo,' he said lightly. His eyes flicked from one to the other of us, and there was a strange little half-smile on his face. For a moment I glimpsed what he might look like to someone who didn't know him, and it was really rather frightening. 'Hullo, Jean-Marie. What is it you don't want to lie to me about?'

I simply couldn't speak. Jacques scrambled to his feet and said 'It's nothing, André, it's just . . .'

André didn't even look at him. He said 'I was speaking to Jean-Marie.'

The hurt on Jacques' face was quite terrible. I said quickly 'It's nothing, it's only we don't know what's best for you.'

André said 'Why don't you let me decide?'

I felt dreadful. I couldn't look up at him, I could only see his legs stretching above me, but I didn't dare stand and face him as Jacques had done. Then his legs seemed to foreshorten in front of me, he was crouching down to my level and looking in my face, and it was still André whom I loved.

He said 'It's all right, Jean-Marie, don't be upset. Just tell me and everything will be fine.'

I said miserably 'But you want to know about the linen and Jeanette.'

'Jeanette?' he said. 'Is she the maid who gave it to you?'

I explained. She wasn't really a maid, you see, she was an independent dressmaker who used to make clothes for the ladies at the Château, only they couldn't afford dresses now, so she pretended to be a lady's maid just to go on seeing them.

André's eyes seemed to widen as I talked. 'What a splendid lady. Could you arrange for me to meet her, do you think?'

I knew this was the moment I was meant to lie, but I honestly couldn't do it, I felt my face quite throbbing with heat. I turned in distress to Jacques, and he took a deep breath and said 'It's not Jean-Marie's fault. It's Stefan's.'

'Stefan?' said André.

Jacques nodded firmly. 'He said no one was to talk to you about the Château.'

'He did what?'

Jacques explained Stefan had only meant it for André's own good because he didn't want him upset, but André didn't seem to take it very well. He stared hard at the ground and his breath came out in snorts like a little bull.

At last he said 'All right, I understand. Stefan thinks I'm so stupid I'll go trying to rescue people who don't need rescuing. But you don't think that, do you?'

'Of course not,' said Jacques quickly.

'Then you won't mind my meeting Jeanette, will you?'

Poor Jacques. He swallowed and said 'No, not at all. We'll set it up right away.'

There's a little glade in the Dax-Verdâme woods with a fallen tree in the middle, and we arranged to meet Jeanette there on New Year's Eve. I remember waiting in the December sunshine and feeling sort of nervous, like I was going into a fencing bout with someone I'd never met. I watched Jeanette walking towards us in a yellow and black dress that made her look like a giant wasp, and had this awful urge just to scoop up the boy and run.

She looked harmless enough when she got closer, she had frizzy blonde hair, bright pink cheeks, and a pointed chin so tiny her smile had to wrap round the corners, but her eyes were bright and sharp like she saw more than you'd think, and I guessed from the first she wasn't going to be easy.

I was right. She began a bit timidly, and was obviously hugely in awe of the boy, but the minute she started talking about the hostages she warmed up till there was no stopping her.

There were three of them. There was Florian, who was seventeen, Colette, who was sixteen, and Anne, who'd turned fifteen last week. They were all cooped up together in the Château, and that's where they'd been living ever since the soldiers came, more than two years ago.

'But why?' said André. 'What can the Spaniards possibly want with them all this time?'

'Well may you ask, Sieur,' said Jeanette. 'Mlle Anne says her father would pay the ransom if he could, but he's clearly not a penny to spare.'

I don't think Jeanette believed that actually, and neither did I. Everyone said the Baron was mean.

'Then surely in humanity they must let them go,' said André. 'If they're no use, why hold on to them?'

351

Jeanette seemed to realize for the first time how young he really was. She said gently 'Well, Don Francisco says it's a matter of principle. He says if hostages are let go every time people refuse to pay, why would anyone ever pay at all?'

There was no answer to that, and even André knew it. After a moment he said 'But they're looked after all right? They're comfortable?'

I said quickly 'M. Pollet says they're very comfortable, he says they're in their own apartments.' I stared really hard at Jeanette as I said it, I tried to make her understand.

But Jeanette wasn't M. Pollet, she didn't even flinch. She held my gaze and said levelly 'That's right, Monsieur, they're in their poor dead mother's rooms. My ladies share their mother's bed, M. du Pré sleeps in the dressing room, and they live the rest of their lives in the little parlour.'

'They can't go out at all?' said André. His head was down, like he felt ashamed to look at the trees and the sunshine that was clear and bright around us.

'Oh no, Sieur,' said Jeanette. 'But she keeps herself occupied, my Mlle Anne, she sews and she writes, oh, page after page in tiny little writing to save the paper. She used to play the harp too, but the soldiers took that last year.'

I couldn't believe Jeanette was so stupid, she ought to have seen that was bound to upset the boy, and of course it did, he looked up at once. 'The soldiers are robbing them? They've got as little as that, and the soldiers are robbing them?'

'Well, not to say robbing, exactly,' said Jeanette. 'Don Miguel said there was to be no looting, and strictly speaking there hasn't been, but of course there are other ways.'

'What other ways?' said André bleakly.

'Well, the food, Sieur. In the beginning it came out of the Château kitchens, same as the officers had, and no questions asked. Then the guards said they could only have the soup the servants had, though they were welcome to exchange goods for extra if they wanted. And so of course they do, Sieur, not that they get value for it, nothing like. There was Madame's lavender bowl from her dressing table, a very beautiful thing, cut glass and solid silver, and very precious to the girls because it had been their mother's, but they only got three meat meals for that, then it was back to the soup and having to sell something else if they wanted more. They've precious little left now, Sieur.'

He leant against a tree, and I wondered if his back was hurting him. 'The linen. They could have sold that.'

'Oh no, Sieur, that was my Mlle Anne's wedding linen, they'd have kept that as long as they could. But she was happy to part with it for you, Sieur, it was quite her own suggestion.'

I began to realize Jeanette wasn't being stupid at all, she knew exactly what she was doing and she was bloody good at it too.

The boy shifted against his tree. 'But they're being robbed, surely they can report it to the officers.'

'The officers,' said Jeanette. Her mouth sort of squirmed a second and I knew she'd only just not spat. 'Oh, the senior ones are all right, Sieur, but what do they know what goes on when they're not there? It's the regular soldiers have the keeping of them, and not likely to take kindly to reports behind their backs. As for the junior officers, well, they're trouble of a different kind.'

André had his arms folded, but I noticed how tightly his hands were gripping them. 'What kind of trouble?'

Jeanette's hands were starting to twist in her dress, and she seemed uneasy.

'Well, it was that dinner for old Don Francisco, Sieur, the young officers were very taken with Mlle Colette, and now they're in and out all the time, sniffing round her like tom-cats. There's been nothing worse yet, Don Miguel having given strict instructions they're not to be harmed, but he spends all his time in Dax since the governor came, so who's to protect my ladies I don't know.'

The boy had gone very white. 'The guards . . .'

'Them,' said Jeanette scornfully. 'They're no better. There's one Mlle Anne calls the "Slug", and she doesn't know it, Sieur, but he watches her, I've seen him at it. I've known him stand and watch her in the mirror while I'm brushing her hair.'

André nodded like he was deep in thought, and slowly swivelled his body round to face me. He said under his breath 'We have to get them out.'

I'd known all along he'd say that, so had Stefan, that's why we'd tried to stop him ever hearing this story. It couldn't be done, the Château was impregnable, but he couldn't be André and not want to try all the same. I thought I could still limit the damage, there was nothing wrong with saying we'd try, then quietly giving up when he saw it was impossible. I tried to look keen and said 'Of course, but don't promise, you mustn't promise, you know how hard it could be.'

He nodded gravely and turned back to Jeanette. She was gazing up at him expectantly, and I bet she'd heard every word.

He said 'Well, we must try to help them, mustn't we, Made-moiselle?'

She didn't so much as blink, but then she wouldn't, it's what she'd been after all along. She said simply 'I knew you would, Sieur. My Mlle Anne always said so.'

He couldn't resist it. 'She's mentioned me?'

'Oh, bless you, Sieur, a score of times. She was that distressed to hear you were hurt, she cried, poor lady. She prays for you every night.'

The boy's head was down, he couldn't say another word.

I thought I'd better do it for him. 'We can't make any promises, it could take ages, and of course the Chevalier's not properly recovered yet, it could be months.'

She turned towards me, and I felt those shrewd little eyes on my face. Then she smiled, and I knew she recognized me in just the same way I recognized her.

'Of course, Monsieur,' she said. 'But it's having that little bit of hope to give her, do you see? She's had precious little of that all this time, my Mlle Anne.' Her eyes seemed to become brighter, then suddenly there were tears spilling out and running down her face, washing pale little tracks in the paint.

I felt ashamed suddenly. I'd been making sure the boy could back out, I'd never thought about giving the hostages hope that was bound to be disappointed. I couldn't blame Jeanette for it either, she was just fighting for that girl the same way I was fighting for André.

She was also better at it. The boy saw her tears, and his whole face froze up with shock, his jaw went all tight. I knew what he was going to do, I felt it coming, I wanted to clamp my hand over his mouth to stop the words coming out, anything to stop him saying what would either break his heart or get him killed.

'She has now, Mademoiselle,' he said firmly. 'We'll get her out for you. I give you my word.'

Stefan Ravel

Of all the stupid, insane, irresponsible things.

I hoped Marcel might talk them out of it, but no, he'd always been desperate to atone for his failure to protect those children, and his eyes were positively glowing with heroic ardour. I tried to appeal to his professionalism, I reminded him he'd said himself we couldn't tackle the Château, but he only said 'We're much stronger now, Stefan, surely we can at least try?' Honour doesn't just kill people, Abbé, it rots their brains as well.

But I didn't give up, I tend not to when it's my skin at stake. It was New Year's Eve, so when the others were rounding up wine and cider for the celebrations I stayed behind in the Hermitage for a friendly little chat with André. He used to listen to me in those days, strange as it may seem, and I thought I might get him to see sense.

He didn't seem very receptive. As soon as the door closed behind the others he started bundling away the blankets and scraping out the candle-holders, making things nice for the party, bustling about all round me as if I wasn't there at all.

I said 'Hold on a minute, little general, don't you think we ought to talk about this?'

'Don't call me that,' he said, grabbing an armful of fresh candles from the basket.

It wasn't the most promising of starts. I said 'No real general would even consider what you're doing, you know that, don't you?'

'I'm not considering it, I'm going to do it. I've given my word.'

This was more serious than I'd thought. I said 'You'd no fucking business doing that, you've no right to commit the army.'

'And you've no fucking business treating me like a child.'

That seemed rather excessive. I said 'I'm only trying to help you make a proper decision.'

'Yes, now you are,' he retorted. 'But what about the last two years? Jacques told me you've kept everything about the hostages away from me.'

That was a nice little hypocrisy I hadn't anticipated. I said pleasantly 'Did he now?'

'Yes he bloody did,' he said. 'Those are friends of mine, Stefan, they've been living like convicts all this time and I never knew. I've been free and doing what I like while they haven't even got enough to eat. What the *hell* must they have thought of me?'

'Vanity, little general,' I said. 'You want to watch that.'

That was possibly a mistake. He threw the candles down so hard they bounced and rolled all over the straw. 'Don't you dare judge me, you've got no right. I know how selfish I am, all this time I've only thought about me, and she, she's been *crying* for me, Stefan, can't you see how that makes me feel?'

I said 'You can't help them, you'll only get yourself killed, what was the point in letting you suffer?'

'Because it's my choice!'

The sound of raucous singing outside suggested Pinhead had found the barrels in the outhouse and the party was starting already. I was running out of time.

'This isn't a choice,' I said brutally. 'You haven't thought about it, you haven't even looked at the problems, you've just started chucking promises around without the smallest idea how you're going to honour them. I'm ashamed of you.'

He sucked in his breath. 'And what makes you think I need your approval?'

I said evenly 'Take that tone with me again and I'll show you.'

He glared at me in fury, then turned hard for the door. I grabbed his arm and jerked him back. 'Oh, come on, André . . .'

He shook me off like something filthy. 'Don't you *dare* touch me.'

I stared at him. He was suddenly a little nobleman again, prickling all over with outraged dignity. He brushed down his shirt, then jerked his chin up at me, and there it was, Abbé, that look again, I might have been back in the mud of La Mothe watching an officer looking down at a poor drunken devil of a private soldier.

I stepped back as if he had plague.

He said calmly 'I'm sorry, Stefan, I understand you meant well, but please don't ever tell me how to live my life again.'

He gave a curt little nod and walked out.

Oh, it was my own fault, Abbé, I'd been a fool to expect otherwise. I thought he was a soldier, I'd maybe even allowed myself to feel a little affection for him, but there, even I make mistakes sometimes. I should have known he'd revert to type.

They were his own kind, you see. There are people starving in this world, and others risking their lives for the sake of a flag that's never put a crumb of bread in their bellies, but André de Roland was in a chivalrous frenzy because three children of the nobility were living in rooms bigger than my whole house and eating food some of us would probably kill for. Oh, I'll admit they were prisoners and that's all very sad, but really, think about it, Abbé. What could be safer than that?

Anne du Pré

Extract from her diary, dated 1 January 1639

I wished to begin the New Year by behaving better, but I'm afraid I have not done very well. The Weasel allowed loathsome Pablo to visit, which was enough to annoy me in any case, but he also brought with him the officer who shot André, whom he says is transferred here to stay.

I could not have liked him under any circumstances. He clearly considers us lowly *parvenus* compared to his noble self, and talked incessantly about his ancestors and their great achievements in Spanish history. He is older than Pablo and strikingly plain, but with very shiny hair which he appears to admire very much, judging by the time he spends running his hands through it. He told us we could call him 'Luiz', but I worked sedulously at my embroidery and paid him no attention at all. I am doing the collar about the pheasant's neck, and only hope I have enough white silk.

Pablo seemed even more determined to show off than usual, perhaps to impress his new friend. Today he demonstrated his ability to extinguish a candle by parting the wick from the flame with one swipe of his sword. Colette clapped her hands with pleasure and said she thought Pablo must be as good a swordsman as Don Miguel. She makes her voice very breathy when she speaks to loathsome Pablo, and I do wish she wouldn't.

Pablo smiled modestly and said 'No one is as good as Don Miguel, Mademoiselle. He is the finest swordsman in Europe.'

I had had quite enough. I said 'As good as André de Roland?'

They all turned to me, and I stared hard at my embroidery.

'Hullo, little Mademoiselle,' said Pablo affably, with that appalling boyish smile Colette likes so much. 'You're with us, are you? What do you know about André de Roland?'

Luiz spoke in my direction for the first time. His voice is deeper than Pablo's, and I do not like the way he stares. He said 'You remember, Vasquéz, this is his little sweetheart, who was so distressed to hear we had shot him.'

Pablo laughed, and I quickly reapplied myself to my embroidery.

This evening Colette took me to task for my behaviour. She said I must be more polite to the officers, because they could make life much better for us if they chose. I said I considered she gave them quite enough politeness for all of us, but she only sniffed and told me not to be childish. I feel rather bad about it now. Poor Colette, she only does what she does for our sake, and because it is hard for her to be growing up so pretty with no one to notice.

But I do not like that Don Luiz and cannot pretend I do. Perhaps it is because Pablo's gallantries seem even more insufferable now he is here, as if he is pretending an intimacy with Colette he does not have. Perhaps it is to do with that strange conversation he had with Carlos, in which they talked about being recognized. There was something very furtive about it that makes me feel most uneasy.

I wish he had not come.

Carlos Corvacho

Oh now, forgive me, Señor, but you'll admit it's all too funny. So she spoke Spanish all the time, that little girl?

Oh, the joke's on me this time, no denying that.

But really, Señor, being fair now, I can't see why it's so very important. This was all back in 1636, what happened at Ancre, all over and done with long ago, I'm not sure why you want to talk about it now. Oh no, I don't mind telling you, I've nothing to hide. Yes, certainly I should have told you from the first, but you'll understand I was a little concerned how M. Jacques would react. You won't tell him, will you, Señor? You and me, we're men of the world, but M. Jacques . . . You understand.

It was no more than an accident really, no harm intended to anyone. The Chevalier Antoine, that was quite a fight he put up, he killed five of us at the doorway, five. You know how it is, a man needs to be *apasionado*, yes, he must be hot-blooded to kill, and we did kill him in the end and burst through that door, ready to go on killing again and again, everything that was his. And there she was, Señor, Madame de Roland, dressed in nothing but a shift. Even then the abanderado was honourable, he merely dashed the knife from her hand and grabbed her shoulders, telling her there was no need to be afraid, she was a prisoner. She wouldn't have it, Señor, she struggled and fought him, she called him *canaille* and spat in his face.

Now that's going to be too much for any gentleman, especially this one. I've told you about de Castilla, Señor, very noble family but no money, had to sell their estate to *nuevo rico* and resenting them all the while. There's a man like this being spat at by a woman who's nobody, Señor, only a rich girl who married a man with a title, well, it was too much for him to take, that's all. He said 'You don't know who you're dealing with, Madame,' and when she went to claw his face he straight and ripped down her shift, tore it right down the front, and pushed her back on the bed while he showed her.

Well, it was funny, Señor, I'm sure you can see that. One moment she's giving it haughty French aristocrat, the next she's on her back with her legs open and our officer giving it her hot and strong where she needs it. You'll understand why we laughed, Señor, you'd have laughed yourself. Yes, maybe it got a little out of hand, though I took no part in it myself, you understand, never laid a finger on her, but it's still harmless enough. There's not a lady in the world going to tell about something like that, no, not even a French one, it's all safe enough until the child comes in.

That's what turned things bad, Señor, the child. Rushing in, hurling insults, slashing poor Bárba's face, killing young Serrano stone dead, if you'll believe me, then fighting the lot of us while Madame suicides herself, and that's a terrible thing, Señor, that's a mortal sin. Then it's all very different, it's something the Capitán mustn't ever hear about, or de Castilla's in real trouble. Not us, Señor, we were only obeying orders, but the officer's another matter, and more than our lives are worth to go against him.

So you'll understand why I kept it from my Capitán, won't you, Señor? It's not as if he was dangerous. No, not the nicest of men, and that's why my gentleman had him transferred to the Château, but he only did what he did under those circumstances and because of the lady acting so foolish. It wasn't as if he was likely to do it again.

Oh, didn't I tell you, Señor? It was Luiz, I think. That's right, the Don Luiz de Castilla.

Why?

PART III
The Chevalier

Eighteen

Anne du Pré

Extract from her diary, dated 3 January 1639

I knew as soon as Jeanette arrived she had something important to say, but it seemed the Slug was hanging about on
purpose to prevent us. He always comes in now when Jeanette is here, he leans against the wall by Florian's door, and
simply watches. There is a dark smear coming on the wall
from the grease he puts on his hair. Today he seemed to
be lurking even closer than usual, but at last Françoise
finished cleaning the bedroom, so I retreated inside and
Jeanette followed.

She said she had seen and spoken to André himself, and
he was willing to help us. I sat down rather hard on the bed,
and Jeanette patted my hands and said 'There now, Mademoiselle, I always said so, didn't I say so?', then Françoise came
back with the empty chamber pots and we had to sit in
awkward silence until she went away.

There were a hundred questions I wanted to ask, but Jeanette glanced at the open door, produced a slip of paper she
had concealed inside her chignon, and pressed it into my
hand.

André de Roland

My dearest Mademoiselle,

I hope you will forgive this liberty, but beg you will allow me at least to thank you for the generous gift of your linen.

Your other gift touched me even more profoundly, and I keep it always by me. I am fearful of construing too much from your kindness, but its scent is all about me as I write, and I cannot help but stroke the petals and dream. At the least I hope I may take it to mean you remember the day of our first meeting, and can perhaps forgive my boorish behaviour on that occasion. Certainly this is a far lovelier present than your first, although I fear it is *less well deserved*.

But *it will be*, as our mutual friend will explain, and when that time finally comes, I shall send the finest rose at Ancre as both a token of our intentions, and a reminder of the most beautiful gift that ever a man received.

Until then, dear Mademoiselle, I beg to remain your most devoted servant,

A de R

P.S. I'm sorry this is such a poor letter, but my education has been a little disrupted. I wish there were a proper way of saying I am thinking of you all the time, because that is what I really mean.

Anne du Pré

Extract from her diary, dated 3 January 1639

I am ashamed to write that for a moment this did not seem to me an odd letter. It was almost as if he had shared the same dreams as I. Then I recollected that in reality we have not seen each other for quite three years, and truly it made no sense at all. I could do nothing but pass it to Jeanette, and hope she could explain.

She coloured a little, then confessed that when we sent the linen she had slipped a rose into the bale in the hope he would believe it came from me.

I said 'Jeanette, O Jeanette, whatever will he think of me?' and hid my face in my hands, almost as if André could see it himself.

'Now don't take on, Mademoiselle,' said Jeanette. 'Look at the letter, and you will see exactly what he thinks of you.'

I looked at it again, and truly it did seem kind.

'Oh it's ever so much better than that comes to, Mademoiselle. He was such a nice young gentleman, your M. de Roland, very sympathetic and most upset when I told him how you've been treated. He says he won't rest until he's found a way to get you all out of this horrid place and you know what that means, Mademoiselle, you know what it means when a Roland gives his word.'

I do know. When I thought of it, it was almost as if someone had knocked a window into our bedroom and daylight came flooding in. I couldn't allow myself to think of it properly, it was almost too frightening.

I said 'But it isn't fair in us, Jeanette, it's not right to make M. de Roland think something that isn't true.'

'Who says it's not true, Mademoiselle?' said Jeanette, and her eyes were twinkling. 'Yes, M. de Roland may imagine you have been thinking of him, I dare say he may even think you've harboured a romantic notion or two, but now I ask you, Mademoiselle, who says that's not true?'

Stefan Ravel

Let's be clear about this, Abbé. The Château Petit Arx is built like a fort. It's a big stone block with three storeys, a crenellated roof, turrets at each corner, and a vast courtyard enclosed with iron gates. There's a paved terrace surrounded by open lawns and square flower beds, and round the whole lot there's a bloody great perimeter wall. Soldier that I am, I thought to myself 'Fuck that.' But, well, they were set on it. I was tempted to let André de Roland discover the painful consequences of his own actions, but there were good men might be dragged down with him, so I gave the poor sods the benefit of my experience, and I hope you're impressed by my magnanimity.

Being rather short of the cannon and two regiments a frontal assault required, it didn't take long to decide our best option was stealth. But the Château wasn't like the barracks, Abbé, we couldn't simply stroll up and touch it, we had to start by finding a way over that wall. On the east side it was the Dax-Verdâme Wall itself, complete with moat. On the west side we had the heavily guarded entrance, with a lodge so full of men it was a miniature barracks in itself. The north backed on to the dead land between gorge and Wall, but if the dons caught us using it with horses, they'd realize we'd a way in they didn't know about, and that, dear Abbé, would have meant the end of the *gabelle* road and our whole communication with the outside world. The south wall was our only option. It bordered the orchard at the north of the Dumont farm, which at least provided the rudiments of cover, so the four of us rode to Verdâme to have a look over the top.

At first sight it was promising. The west entrance faced square on to the Château down a long straight drive lined with trees, so while the guards at the lodge could see right up it to the guards at the courtyard gates, neither could see down to the south side itself. Provided we stayed clear of the corner, we could hop over the south perimeter, run across the lawn, and make it to the wall of the Château itself without guards at either gate or lodge seeing us at all.

There was just one snag. A guard in the middle of the terrace seemed to be staring right across the lawns at us, and though we watched for half an hour he never moved from that one spot. We had a nasty suspicion he was a permanent fixture, and when we went down to the far corner and peered over to the east side we saw there was one there too. They'd got permanent wall guards on all sides, each in full armour. They were too far away for a bolt to penetrate the plate, and though we could pick them off easily enough with a musket, the noise would fetch three hundred inquisitive dons in seconds.

'Just one man,' said André in frustration. 'Just one man.'

But it wasn't. There were four patrollers walking round the Château, one after the other in constant rotation, and though they might be near enough for a crossbow, the wall guard was rather likely to notice if a patroller dropped dead in front of him. The guards on the other sides would know too, they'd spot the gap between patrollers. I had to admire the thinking behind it, Abbé, it was a very effective way of guarding a large area with minimal manpower, but that didn't make it any easier to beat.

'But we will,' said André fiercely. 'We'll do it somehow. Won't we, Marcel?'

Poor Marcel. He stopped chewing his nails, stared seriously at those grey stone walls, then turned to meet André's expectant gaze.

He said gently 'We'll try.'

Jacques Gilbert

André was fully recovered by mid-March, but nothing else was ready. Marcel did a detailed plan of what he remembered inside the Château, and Jeanette told us some of the places the guards were now, but none of it brought us any closer to getting in. We wanted a way to distract the wall guards while we killed a patroller and climbed over the wall, but nothing seemed to work. We even set off a small mine in the woods one day, but while soldiers came piling out of the lodge and courtyard, the wall guards stayed exactly where they were, and the patrollers kept going round and round without so much as breaking step. There was something inhuman about them, like a kind of mill wheel nothing could stop.

Stefan was no use, of course, his idea of helping was to come up with objections to everything we thought of. It was Stefan ruled out the north wall because of giving away the *gabelle* road if we escaped over it, but the boy and I started to wonder if it mightn't at least get us in. Next day the two of us got up before first light, sneaked out while Stefan was still snoring, and rode all the way down into the dead land to take a look. The forest grew right up to the wall, so we picked the biggest tree, scrambled up and peered over.

We were looking into an orchard. They were apple and plum trees, and a bit spindly now, but in summer they'd be thick and bushy, and if we were careful we could climb over the wall into them without anyone noticing. The trees came only about a hundred yards short of the terrace, which meant for the first time the wall guard would be in armour-piercing range of a crossbow. We'd have to get the patroller too or he'd see us doing it, but it was possible with two good bowmen, and we had them, we had Bernard and Marin. Actually, when we thought about it, we had a way of dealing with all four patrollers and the wall guards too. We looked at each other and grinned.

Now all we needed was a way into the Château. We peered through the trees at the windows, but the upper ones were no good, we weren't going to go lugging bloody great ladders about, and there wasn't anything for a grapnel iron to grip on to. There were several ground-floor windows, but the only one that wasn't barred was so big it obviously led somewhere public, it would probably land us in the middle of a hundred sleeping soldiers.

'We need Marcel's plan,' I said. 'Let's get some breakfast and talk about it.'

André shifted position to start down, but suddenly jerked to a stop and stared. I followed his look across to the Château, and he was right, there was movement at a first-floor window, a flash of something white. Then the top half of the window actually opened, and someone leant out.

We ducked so quickly I clunked my head against the tree trunk, which was stupid really, they were miles away, they couldn't possibly have seen us against all those trees. So we cautiously raised our heads again, then both stopped at the same moment, and I heard André catch his breath. The person at the window was a girl.

It wasn't much of a window. The bottom half had crude bars nailed over it so it wouldn't open, and the girl could only lean her head and shoulders over the top. She reached her hands over the barrier to scatter something on the sill, then straightened again, rested her arms on the top bar, and lifted her head.

It was the hair you noticed first. The early-morning sunlight was catching it, and it seemed to gleam and burn in hundreds of different colours, red and yellow and brown and gold. It was like sun on the woods in the middle of autumn.

'It's her,' said the boy beside me. 'It's Anne.'

She was quite small and slender, but we couldn't see her face from that distance, only that it was pale. I wondered if she'd turn out to have a big nose or something, just to even things up because of that hair.

André whispered 'She's feeding the birds, look.'

There were little dots on the window sill, and the boy was right, they were birds. They were moving about quite happily, but I suppose there was the window between them and she was standing very still. You don't often see a woman doing that. Only her hair moved when the wind brushed it, and once she tilted her head to feel the breeze on her face. Her throat was very white.

There was a sudden flapping on the sill as the birds rose together and flew away. The girl turned sharply back into the room, but the figure appearing behind her was in nightclothes, and we guessed it was her brother. A moment later he moved away, and the girl closed the window. André let out his breath in a little sigh.

He was still sort of dazed all the walk back. He kept talking about what they'd do when we got her out, and I tried not to think what he'd do if he found we couldn't. I knew it was only a harmless childish fantasy, but when I looked at his face I found myself wishing she'd been a bit plainer. To be honest, I wished he'd never seen her at all.

Anne du Pré

16 APRIL

Florian caught me feeding the birds and lectured me about wasting food. It was only my own bread, but he says if I am not hungry then I should consider Colette or himself. I have fed the birds so long I could not bear them to be disappointed now, but I will ask the Owl for more scraps instead.

At least Colette is in a good mood. Pablo has invited her to a party while the senior officers are at the monthly dinner in Dax, so she is to leave the apartment for the first time since October. I fear Don Miguel may be annoyed if he finds out, but Colette laughs and says I am only jealous. Perhaps I am. It would be a chance to look at different surroundings and listen to music. It will be quite wasted on Colette, who only goes to wear Mama's gold dress and flirt with loathsome Pablo.

At least she will be able to observe how the house is guarded at night, but I'm not sure she takes it very seriously. She says 'If your boy lover were really intending to rescue us, surely he'd have done something by now?' I have explained he was wounded and such things take a lot of planning, but she never listens. I think Florian would like to believe me, but he is not capable of arguing with Colette any more. He has taken to sitting and rocking himself in Mama's chair all day, and sometimes he hums as well. Poor Florian, I was wrong to anger him over the birds. I keep forgetting how much worse this captivity must be for a man.

I did my best to cheer him this evening when Colette had gone. We listened to the music together through the floor, and it was quite enchanting, someone played '*Guárdame las vacas*' on the guitar. I sang it for him, but it only seemed to make him sad, so in the end we just sat together in the dark and I held his hand.

It is all quiet downstairs now, and Florian has gone to bed. I shall sit up a little longer until Colette returns. She will have so much to talk about, it would be awful for her to come back and have no one to share it with.

Only the clock has just struck two and still she has not come.

17 APRIL

I was asleep when Colette finally returned, and only woke because she was blundering about the room and knocking things over in the dark. She wouldn't let me light the candle, she wouldn't even talk to me, she kept telling me to go back to sleep, and was obviously very upset. When she came to bed at last she was so cold it gave me a shock to touch her. I cuddled up and tried to warm her, but she didn't seem to want me close. She was shivering, and when she thought I was asleep I heard her start to cry.

Now I understand it. This morning I found the gold dress at the back of the clothes press, and now I know. My poor, poor, darling sister. When I escape, I will find a way of coming back and *killing* those men.

I have not told her, she could not bear me to know. I cannot tell *anyone*, because she left the apartment against Don Miguel's orders, so it will be seen as quite her own fault. No one must ever know what has happened here. *No one.*

Anne du Pré

Letter to André de Roland, dated 18 April 1639

My dear M. de Roland,

I hope you will not mind my sending you this, but it is a plan of how the guards are placed upstairs at night when the senior officers are away. I know there may not always be so few, but these dinners occur on the third Saturday each month, alternating between the Dax barracks and our own house, so the same situation should arise in June. I don't mean to suggest this would be a particularly good time, I wouldn't dream of hurrying you in any way. We are managing perfectly well here, and it is very kind of you to think of us at all. We are all more grateful than you can possibly imagine.

I hope the information is helpful. My brave sister managed to find it out herself, and I am very proud of her.

M. and Mlle du Pré send their most respectful good wishes, and I hope you know you always have mine.

A du P

Jacques Gilbert

André was overwhelmed. We didn't send written messages after that first one, it was too dangerous for Jeanette to carry them through the searches, but Jean-Marie said she'd take any kind of risk for Mlle Anne, and I think he was right.

André took the letter like it was precious silk, opened it carefully on to his blanket so as not to get straw on it, then sat with his shoulder slightly turned away from us to read it. He seemed to take a long time for something so short, but at last he lifted his head and said 'Something's wrong.'

I looked myself but couldn't see it. The writing was maybe a bit trembly, but that didn't mean anything, André's was atrocious.

He shook his head obstinately. 'I can't explain, but there's something. What did Jeanette say, Jean-Marie?'

Jean-Marie hesitated. 'She said Mlle Anne seemed a little upset.'

André stared back down at the letter. He stroked it gently with the tip of one finger, said 'I knew it,' got up and walked away.

I thought it was good news myself, and so did Marcel. She'd got us a date when the Château was going to be seriously underguarded, and it was the right date for us too, it was summer, and the trees would be thick enough to give proper cover. It was perfect in every way except one, which was that we still weren't ready.

We'd come a long way, we'd got a really good plan, but we still couldn't get in the building itself. Marcel had identified windows which led to what used to be quiet places, but of course they were all barred and we wouldn't have time to file them. André suggested just smashing any unbarred window and forcing our way in, but even I could see that wouldn't work. We needed to get the hostages clear before the alarm was even raised.

We'd got one last hope, and that was Arnould Rousseau. He was doing the cooking for the officers' dinner in May, and Mlle Anne was right, this one was going to be at the Château. Marcel spent ages briefing him what to look for, then we just sat back and waited. It would leave us only four weeks till the raid itself, but we simply couldn't think of anything else.

It was awful, just waiting. André was getting almost feverish, he wasn't eating, and he didn't sleep much either. He got great black circles under his eyes and his face looked white and sort of stretched. Marcel worried about him, but Stefan just grinned and said 'Maybe next time he'll think twice before making promises he can't keep.'

I thought of M. Gauthier, and knew it mustn't come to that. I'd got to find a way out of it without André breaking his word.

Anne du Pré

Extracts from her diary, dated 25–28 April 1639

25 APRIL

We had meat again for dinner, which makes twice in a week. The Owl seemed pleased, and said in his awful French 'This is more like it, Mademoiselle.' I think he worries about us.

Then the Slug took over duty, so of course Pablo came. I cannot call him 'loathsome Pablo' now, he can never be any kind of joke to me again. I would never, *never* have thought he could turn out so evil, and cannot help wondering how much Luiz is responsible for the change in him. When he came in today, he even walked like Luiz, he simply swaggered in without any greeting and asked if Colette would see him. I said I was sure she would never see him again, but he only smiled and asked if we had enjoyed our dinner.

A terrible suspicion occurred to me, and I found to my shame I could not meet his eyes. He laughed, and said 'No matter, but I would be disappointed if the mutton were not as good as I was promised. Perhaps there may be more next week if Mlle Colette is feeling better.'

377

Florian asked me afterwards what it was Pablo had wanted. I told him 'Nothing.'

O thank God, Colette is ill.

I think she's guessed I know. I saw her sitting on the bed tearing up the rags, and I couldn't stop myself, I asked 'Is it your time?' She said 'Yes,' then looked up and asked 'Why?' and I think she saw in my eyes I knew. She didn't ask again, she only looked back down at the rags, and went on tearing them without saying anything. I left her alone and sat with Florian, but I could still hear the sound of her tearing. It seemed to go on for hours.

Pablo came again this evening. This time Colette remained in the room, and he sat whispering to her for ages, though I was glad to see she kept her head lowered and would not answer him. He gave us some white bread to have with our soup, but Florian said it would be better if we could have more meat. Pablo said 'I don't know, what do you think about some meat, Mlle Colette?' Colette didn't look up, but he waited courteously and after a moment she nodded.

He must have been very prompt, because there were stewed pullets this evening. I ate as much as I could of the vegetables, but divided my chicken between the others, saying I was not hungry. Florian insisted I at least eat my bread, until at last I was compelled to tell him I would rather starve. They said nothing, but both stared at their plates for some time. I offered Florian my bread, but after a little silence he said 'Give it to the birds.'

The May dinner came and went, and we still hadn't got a way in. Arnould had poked and pried as much as he could, but hadn't found see any way without going through the courtyard gate. He was sure there was one, though. The Château wasn't like the Dax barracks, there were no whores allowed, but he was certain he'd heard some in the soldiers' mess.

He said 'They're getting them in somehow, I'd stake my life on it. All you have to do is find out how.'

So we tried. We tried all we knew. We watched the Château day and night, hoping to spot someone sneaking in, but we never saw a thing. We went out into France, got siege ladders over the moat, and tried watching from the west side, but there was nothing happening there either. Stefan said maybe someone got caught the night of the dinner and they'd decided not to risk it for a bit. Marcel tried asking Verdâme prostitutes, but they said local girls weren't allowed in the Château because of security, it was all women brought in from Artois.

Nothing worked, and after a week we sat down and confronted the fact we were no nearer getting in than we'd been in April.

'We can still go ahead, can't we?' said André. 'Once we're at the Château walls we can try every window for ourselves.'

'No time,' said Stefan. 'We've got to complete the whole thing before they change patrollers. It can't be done.'

We were sitting at the platform end, huddled over Marcel's map like we hadn't studied it a hundred times before. There were all blobs of candle wax on it from nights just like this one, going over and over it, looking for an answer that wasn't there.

Marcel sighed and sat back. 'It's no good, André, we'll just have to forget June. Maybe we'll come up with something by August.'

'I've a better idea,' said Stefan. He stretched, leant back against the wall, and took out his flask. 'Let's forget the Château altogether.'

André didn't even look up from the map. 'We're just tired, that's all. There'll be a way, we'll find it.'

'We won't,' said Stefan. 'It's time to stop messing about and call a halt.'

André stared at him, but Stefan just stared back. The boy turned quickly to Marcel, but Marcel only lowered his head. Then he looked at me.

I felt like every kind of shit, but there wasn't any point lying. I said 'It's not breaking your word, André, we only promised we'd try.'

He didn't move. He just went on looking at me.

I said desperately 'We've tried, haven't we? There's no shame in it, we've tried.'

He said 'No, we haven't. Four of us here, four soldiers, how can we sit without so much as a scratch between us and say we tried?'

Stefan started to roll up the map. 'I suppose you'd rather we all died first.'

'I don't want anyone to die,' said the boy. 'I just want to get the hostages out.'

I said 'But we can't . . .'

He rounded on me, and for a second it was the old André. 'Don't you dare tell me I can't. I must, that's all there is. I must.'

No one said anything. The boy climbed slowly to his feet and I felt him looking down at us. Then I heard him step off the decking and head for the door.

I scrambled up but Marcel was quicker. He laid his hand on my arm, said 'I'll do it,' and went after the boy. I stood miserably listening to his footsteps and the banging of the door.

The decking creaked as Stefan stood. I heard him brush the straw off his breeches, then walk up behind me and stop. I felt his breath on the back of my neck.

I said 'If you start gloating over him now . . .'

'Oh, grow up,' he said. He stepped past and down off the platform, looking thoughtfully at the open door. 'There's more to this than a nobleman giving his word, isn't there? There's something else driving him.'

I said bitterly 'You've never understood him, never, you couldn't begin.'

His head screwed round to me for a moment, then he looked back at the door. 'Thanks for the enlightenment,' he said, and walked after the others.

Anne du Pré

Extract from her diary, dated 30 May 1639

I had looked forward so much to Jeanette coming, but now everything is spoilt.

Pablo and Luiz visited during the Slug's duty, and again Colette allowed it. She remained on the *lit de repos,* but Pablo sat with his arm along her headrest and whispered down at her, and she did not turn away. Luiz leant against the wall and watched them with a proprietorial smile on his face. I hate him so much it hurts.

Florian was no help, he merely yawned as if he were tired, and strolled into his bedroom so he didn't have to see. I knew perfectly well they wanted me to leave too, but I wouldn't. I worked on the red of the pheasant's face, and listened as hard as I could to Pablo.

He had the effrontery to ask Colette if she would attend their party when the senior officers dined again in Dax, and simply would not accept her refusals. He was speaking very softly, but I think he said something about it all being very different. He said the wine and her beauty were enough to go to any man's head, but this time she would be treated like a queen.

Then the Slug brought in Jeanette, so I stood at once and said 'You will have to leave now, gentlemen, our maid is come.'

Luiz looked at me quite impertinently and said 'Oh-ho, little Mademoiselle, that is for your sister to say. Do you wish us to leave, Mlle Colette?'

Poor Colette. She dare not tell them to leave because she is afraid the meat will stop. She said timidly 'No.'

Pablo smiled at me and said 'You needn't trouble to stay, Mademoiselle, if you need time with your maid. We shan't be offended if you go to the bedroom.'

Luiz laughed, and I sat down again at once. I would not leave my sister alone with them, I *would not*.

Jeanette was disconcerted, for she had never seen behaviour like this before, and seemed unsure what to do for the best. At last she said 'I will see to your clothes then, Mademoiselle,' and I just said 'Yes.'

I cannot believe I was such a fool. It was not until I heard her opening the clothes press that I realized the danger and ran to the bedroom, but I was too late. She was on her knees in front of the press, the gold dress in her hands, and the face she turned to me was quite immobile with horror. She clearly understood the significance of what she had found, and indeed how could she not? The rips might be explained another way, but the stains are quite unmistakable.

'Mademoiselle,' she whispered to me. 'Oh, Mademoiselle, why didn't you tell me?'

I had to explain, for fear she would think it was me. In a way I was glad to, for she put her arms round me and gave me a hug such as I have not had in years, not since Mama died. I'm afraid I think I cried a little too. That is very weak of me, I know, but I have been so lonely.

Perhaps it was not so very dreadful. At least I know the secret is safe with Jeanette. She has promised not to tell anybody, she swore it by the Blessed Saints.

Jacques Gilbert

Jean-Marie broke every rule we'd got by bringing her to the Hermitage but I didn't give a stuff when I heard what she'd got to say, I was just worried about the boy. He said he was all right, he just wanted to be by himself, but when I heard him galloping off on Tempête, I knew we were in for trouble. This was his own private nightmare come back, and I knew he couldn't bear it a second time. I threw a saddle on Tonnerre and went straight after him.

He was up the tree overlooking the Château grounds, his eyes fixed on that first-floor window like he could see straight into it. He didn't even turn when I climbed up, he waited till I was right behind him, then just glanced round briefly before going back to staring at the window. It was dark by then, and all we could see was the faint flickering light that meant candles lit inside.

He said 'She's in there. She's in there going through God knows what, and I can't get to her.'

I reached out and touched his shoulder. 'Let's go back and talk about it. We're not doing any good out here.'

He shook his head. 'If there's trouble, I'm going in.'

'The patroller will have you as soon as you clear the trees.'

He smiled grimly. 'He won't.'

'You can't get in.'

'I'll force a window.'

'The guards will hear, you'll be killed. Who's going to help, her then?'

He stared at me, but then there was a loud clatter, and we saw the big window on the ground floor had been thrown open. A great gust of male laughter drifted out, and somewhere in the middle was a girl's voice, raised in a kind of squeal.

The boy moved in the same second, hurling himself forward on the branch to leap over the wall. I grabbed his leg and pulled back hard, but he smashed his boot right at me and I had to let go and snatch his belt instead. He was struggling and kicking, there were leaves scattering everywhere, but I dragged him near enough to get hold of his arms and thrust him down the tree on our side. I jumped down after him, but he was already scrambling to his feet, and I had to grip him by the shoulders and shove him hard against the trunk; it was all I could do.

We heard the men laughing again, and then the girl's voice sounded in another squeal, but this time very high-pitched, and ended in gurgling laughter.

I said 'It's not her. For Christ's sake, André, it's not her.'

He struggled weakly for a second, then went still and listened. The girl laughed again, and this time I knew he heard it. I stepped back and let go of him, but he didn't move, he just stayed stuck up against that tree and staring at me.

'All right,' he said at last. 'You're bigger than me and you've stopped me. What are you going to do next time? Go all the way?' His hand patted his sword.

'Never,' I said in disbelief. 'Never, you know that.'

'Do I?' he said tiredly. 'If you don't, you won't stop me.'

He looked so wretched I wanted just to scrape him off that tree and hug him, but he wasn't a little boy any more and he meant every word he said. We stared at each other with two feet of space between us that was suddenly like a mile.

The girl's laughter rang out again, nearer and shockingly loud in the night air. It sounded mocking and horrible. Then there came a single man's laugh, low and intimate, and suddenly my brain cleared.

I said 'André, it's a prostitute.'

'I know,' he said dismissively. 'But next time . . .'

I was already reaching for the first branch of the tree. I said 'That's the men's mess, they've got a whore in there. How?'

I was swinging myself up, and he was only a second behind me. We wriggled up so fast it's a miracle the patroller didn't hear the rustling. Then we were back in position and looking over, and we were only just in time.

There was a girl in a light-coloured dress standing on the terrace holding her shoes, and a soldier climbing out of a window behind her. It was the little window on the corner of the north and west walls, the one Arnould said was a store-room, but it was barred, I knew it was, we'd looked at it a hundred times.

The soldier straightened up, waved cheerfully at the passing patroller, then turned back to the window and carefully screwed the bar back in place. The girl took his arm and they set off towards the trees together, swinging their shoes as they went.

Anne du Pré

Extract from her diary, dated 6 June 1639

My hand is shaking so much it is difficult to write.

Pablo and Luiz came again, doubtless hoping Jeanette's visit would draw me away as before. I know they blame my presence for Colette's refusal to go to their hateful party, for they continually speak in whispers, looking round in the most irritated way.

Today, however, Luiz came to speak to me. I am sure he only wished to distract me, but he really was quite unbearable. He sat on my footstool and told me stories about his father at the siege of Breda. I displayed no interest in his remarks, but he would not leave me alone, and when I went to fetch green silk from my box to do the patch by the eye, he followed and leant over my shoulder to admire the colours. I turned at last and begged him to go away and let me attend to my embroidery.

He appeared oddly disconcerted, and said sulkily 'Why must you always be so unfriendly, Mademoiselle? Your family is nothing special, I think. There are ladies at home who would go on their knees to have me pay them this much attention.'

I said politely 'Then the remedy is in your own hands, Señor.'

He laughed. 'Ah, but we are stuck in this wretched dungheap, Mademoiselle, we must take such company as we can find.'

He stood smiling at me, his dark eyes gleaming, this man who connived at what was done to my sister. I said in desperation 'You have women of your own here, I have heard them downstairs. Why must you bother my sister?'

He said 'Really, Mademoiselle, such a question. Your sister

is the daughter of a Baron, how can you speak of her in such a connection?'

'How can you *think* of her in such a connection?'

He regarded me in silence for a moment, and I think he saw the need for pretence was over. He sighed, reached out to the dressing table and picked up my handkerchief. 'It thinks itself very fine, does it not?' he said, admiring the lace edging and embroidered crest. 'But it is still a handkerchief, and has exactly the same purpose as my own. And when I need to blow my nose, I derive much greater pleasure from doing it on this one.' He actually blew his nose into my handkerchief, right before my face. 'A gentleman can develop a taste for such things, Mademoiselle. Do you understand?'

He was grinning at me, a terrible, knowing leer, and I could not bear it a moment longer, I struck out and slapped him with all my might.

Colette gave a little cry, but Pablo only threw back his head and laughed. 'Poor de Castilla!' he said. 'I take it that's another "no"?'

Luiz's face was darkening red, and he turned on me so savagely I was forced to back away. He planted his hand against the wall and leant forward over me, pushing his face close to mine, and I couldn't move any further away, the dressing table was hurting my back. I was aware of the door opening and people coming in, but could not take my eyes from Luiz, he was frightening me. He said 'You don't know who you're dealing with, Mademoiselle,' and I tried to turn my head away, but then a voice cried 'Leave her alone!' and there was Jeanette seizing hold of Luiz's arm and trying to pull him away.

Luiz turned and struck her so hard across the face she fell against the wall. Colette was screaming, the Slug was shouting, Pablo was laughing, Florian was storming out of his bedroom, then I heard a new voice in the hubbub, there was another

387

soldier in the room, and I saw with relief it was the Owl. Perhaps he was due to take over duty from the Slug, or perhaps he just heard the shouting, it didn't matter, he was *there*, and at sight of him everything went quiet. Luiz stepped casually away from Jeanette, as if he had never touched her.

The Owl looked quite red with anger at seeing two junior officers in our apartment, and one of them assaulting our servant. He assisted Jeanette to her feet, then turned sharply on Pablo and Luiz, firing questions in rapid Spanish. It was too fast for me to follow, but I think Pablo tried to dismiss him, and the Owl stood his ground. He was only a common soldier and they were both enseignes, but he stood his ground, our good, kind Owl. I heard him say several times the words 'Capitán d'Estrada', and finally 'Don Alonso', who is chief of police, at which both Pablo and Luiz began to look like sulky children, and the Slug seemed quite terrified. Beside me Colette was muttering 'Oh God, Anne, what have you done? Everything's ruined, what have you done?'

The Owl finished speaking. After a moment, Luiz turned to us, but he wouldn't look at me, he spoke only to Colette. He said 'I'm sorry, Mademoiselle, but it seems we are no longer welcome here.' My heart leapt with joy, and perhaps he sensed it, for he turned next to my gallant Jeanette and said contemptuously 'And neither is this woman. If she sets foot in the Château again I'll have her arrested.'

I protested at once that Don Miguel himself had said she could come, but he only slid his eyes round to me, and the look in them was so cold I wanted to shiver. He said 'She is no hostage, she is an ordinary civilian who has attacked a Spanish officer, and can count herself lucky she's not hanged.'

There was a dead silence. The Slug stepped forward and seized Jeanette by the arm, but she insisted she had clothes to return to us, things to sort out, she could not just leave. I think the Slug would have dragged her out anyway, but the Owl spoke shortly to him, and he grudgingly accompanied her to the bedroom. I tried to follow, but the Slug ordered me back. We were not even to have a chance to speak.

I could not bear to lose Jeanette. She is our only link to the outside world, and our only means of communication with André. Sometimes I feel she is my only friend. I whispered to Colette 'I will not accept it, I will appeal to Don Miguel.'

'And how will you explain it?' said my sister. There was no sympathy on her face, only a kind of miserable anger. 'For God's sake, Anne, haven't you done enough damage?'

I felt as if she had struck me. I looked wretchedly round the room, but the Owl was helpless and Florian only looked away. Luiz regarded me with satisfaction, and nodded his head as if pleased with what he had accomplished. He said to Pablo 'Come on, Vasquéz, we're finished here,' and strolled complacently out.

Pablo looked at Colette, shrugged, and said 'Well, goodbye, Mademoiselle.' Colette looked up at him, her face both anxious and strangely hard. Her voice was very low, but I heard her say 'You can always come back.'

Pablo hesitated, then said 'I'm sorry, but de Castilla's right. There's nothing for me here.' He started after Luiz, then paused and looked back at her, and for a moment the old boyish smile flitted back on to his face. He said lightly 'Unless, of course, you've changed your mind?'

They looked at each other, and I think I held my breath. Colette was very still.

'Will you?' said Pablo softly. The Owl was watching uneasily, uncertain what was being discussed. His French is still poor.

Colette took a deep breath and said 'Yes.'

Pablo smiled in triumph, bowed and went out. The sound of the door closing behind him felt like the end of my whole world. Jeanette was lost to us, André was beyond reach, and what would become of my sister I knew only too well. Almost worse than anything was the terrible truth that Colette was right, it was all my own fault. I think for a moment I wanted to die.

Jeanette came out of the bedroom with the Slug close at her elbow, hustling her to the door. She paused in front of me, managed a little smile, then took out the rose from her corsage and laid it gently in my hand. It was small and tightly furled still, but it was salmon-pink and smelt of summer in the garden, and I thought it beautiful. The Slug looked at it suspiciously, as if it might be some kind of weapon, but Jeanette ignored him and spoke directly to me.

'It's not much, Mademoiselle,' she said. 'It's only from the garden of a friend, and he's afraid it won't keep above a fortnight.' Her eyes found mine and held them.

I managed to say 'A fortnight?'

'Not even that,' she said. 'If you keep it in water it might last twelve days, but my friend is certain it will be no longer.'

I felt my knees trembling beneath my dress, and could not say a word. There was no opportunity anyway, for the Slug was hurrying Jeanette out again and we could do no more than exchange one last look before the door was shut.

Our darling Jeanette. After all she was threatened with, she still braved everything to give me this message and the hope it brings with it. André is coming. He is coming when I asked it, on 18 June. He is coming to rescue us.

Oh God. *Oh God.* He is coming at last.

Nineteen

Jacques Gilbert

18 June 1639. That's the day my world ended.

I remember waking up that morning. You know what it's like when there's something scary ahead of you, it's like your body has a better memory than your brain. You wake up with that kind of distant sick feeling in your belly, and you say to yourself 'What's this?' and then your brain catches up and you remember. That's what it was like when I woke that morning, and remembered it was Saturday 18 June, and it was today.

I sat up and looked around me. Stefan was flat on his back snoring as usual but Marcel was sitting hugging his knees and biting his nails, and we exchanged a look that said he was feeling as sick as me.

The door banged open, and sunlight smashed into the Hermitage as André strode in. His breeches and boots were all muddy, his jerkin was over his arm and his shirt unlaced, he was glowing with sweat and reeked of outdoor energy.

'Sod off, André,' said Stefan, burying his face in the straw.

André chucked his jerkin at him, came briskly up to the platform end and started rustling about in our food basket.

'Did you see her?' I asked blearily. He rode to the Château every morning these days, just to see Mlle Anne feed the birds. It was his way of assuring himself she was still all right.

He nodded. 'I was only just in time, she'd nearly finished.'

He picked the least slimy bit of cheese, broke it in two and handed me half. Then he grinned sheepishly and said 'Maybe she couldn't sleep either.'

Everyone was feeling the same. When I went outside there were people arriving already for last-minute preparation, and somewhere in the trees I could hear the tell-tale *thunk* that was bloody Bernard practising his crossbow again. He was always at it, Bernard, he knew everything was depending on him, and the trees round the Hermitage were starting to look like giant woodpeckers had been at them.

We were all taking this seriously. Marcel had made sure of it, he didn't want a repeat of what happened at the gorge. He'd told everyone over and over again about the importance of secrecy with the whole army at stake. We'd been careful anyway, nobody knew the whole plan but the four of us, but the thought of what could happen still scared me. If anything went wrong, the boy would be trapped in the Château, and me not with him to protect him and get him out.

That's what was really bothering me. It was only Marcel, Stefan and André going in the Château, and for the first time ever I wouldn't be with him. I knew it made sense, they couldn't have more than three for the inside team, not with all that furtive shuffling down corridors and hiding round corners, but that didn't make me feel any better. Stefan couldn't look after the boy like I would, he didn't care about any of it as much as we did, all he said when we found that window was 'I suppose that means we'll have to do it.' A bit of me thought André might have insisted on me going in instead, but he didn't, he knew Stefan was stronger and was only thinking about the best way of getting to Mlle Anne. I understood that, obviously I did, I just couldn't help wishing we were together, that's all.

I went back inside, but the boy was poring over the map

of the Château with Stefan and Marcel, so I just grabbed my cloak and went to see my family. Lots of people did that before an action, and somehow I was just in the mood. I felt a bit guilty about them actually, because I'd let them down over Christmas and Father had been very disappointed.

It was a good thing to do. Father went on again about giving them notice, and even offered to go to the farm to get something special, but all I really wanted was one of Mother's omelettes and she'd got eggs enough for that. I used to spend a lot of time thinking about my Mother's omelettes, especially the ones with cheese in. Simon Moreau was the best cook at the Hermitage, but he couldn't make omelettes, they came out like sponge.

She made one for me now, and just the smell was calming, but Father still noticed I was jumpy. He said 'All right, boy, spit it out. What are you up to this time?'

I told him. There wasn't anything wrong with that, he'd guessed anyway, and this was family, they weren't going to tell anyone. Besides, it was important what I was doing, Marcel had put me in charge of the whole outside team, I was one of the leaders myself.

Father looked thoughtfully at me. 'A big operation, then. A lot of men could be killed.'

I mopped up the last bits of omelette with my bread. 'Someone from just about every family in the Saillie.'

He nodded. Little Pierre wanted more detail, but Father said 'No more questions, lad, we've got to think of security,' and asked after the horses instead.

I was a bit pissed off actually, I'd have liked him to be more interested, but I knew he meant it for the best. When I was going, he came out after me and said 'Look, boy, you've got to understand this is all very worrying for your Mother.'

I felt bad then, and said I was sorry.

'It's done now,' he said. 'She'll be up all night fretting. Isn't there any way you can let her know you're safe?' He talked like it was only Mother who worried, but I noticed he was the one who asked.

I said 'It'll be late, you'll be in bed.'

'We'll be awake,' he said.

He said 'we'. That meant he was worrying too.

So I said 'All right,' and he patted my arm, and I set off for home. I turned back at the stable track, and he was still standing looking after me, my Father, so I waved and he lifted his hand in reply, then I walked on a bit, and when I next turned round he was gone.

Anne du Pré

Extract from her diary dated 18 June 1639

We have had a dreadful scene with Pablo. I do wish we could have told him sooner, but both Florian and Colette were adamant the good food should continue as long as possible and nothing be done to rouse his suspicions.

We did our best. Colette hid in the bedroom, and when Pablo came strolling in with wine to 'get her in the mood' for tonight, Florian told him firmly she had a headache and could not come after all.

Pablo was furious. He said she was expected, people would be disappointed, she was going to make him look a fool. I think he is afraid of what Luiz will say. He went to the bedroom door and tried to call Colette, but Florian told him she mustn't be disturbed.

Pablo looked him up and down in the most despising way, and said 'Hullo, you've woken up at last, have you?'

Florian flushed, but held his ground. 'My sister is unwell, that is an end to it.'

'Is it indeed?' said Pablo. 'It will take more than you to stop it, *hijito*.'

Poor Florian. He tried to speak but failed, and in the presence of such insolence I am not surprised. Finally he said only 'This conversation is concluded. Please leave us,' and retired to his room.

Pablo looked at his closed door, then at Colette's, then last at me. He said 'Do you know, *niña*, I have the strangest suspicion this is somehow your doing.'

I said 'I can't give my sister a headache.'

He laughed and said 'I think you could give anyone a headache.'

I couldn't think of a single thing to say, so I picked up the jug of wine and offered it back.

'Keep it,' he said. 'You'll need it.' Then he walked out without another word.

Colette was very worried afterwards. She said 'He sounded very angry, Anne. He could make a lot of trouble for us.'

I told her he couldn't, because tomorrow we will be gone. There is nothing any of them can do to us now.

Jacques Gilbert

As dusk fell we went over the wall and into the cover of the orchard. We went one at a time so the patrollers wouldn't hear the rustling, but it was odd how exposed we felt. We were still hidden in thick trees, but they were trees on the other side of the wall, and suddenly we weren't peering down at the guards, we were all on the same level. It made them look bigger.

The first signs were good. The trees were soughing in the wind, which was useful cover for any rustling or whispering. There was a flickering light in the upstairs window, which meant the hostages were there and awake. Best of all, the big room downstairs was blazing with light and laughter, like every soldier in the place was in there getting pissed, instead of prowling round looking for people like us.

A bored-looking soldier came and lit the flambeaux, then wandered back towards the west entrance. The flambeaux on the north side were a bit puny really, they only lit like this little puddle in the middle of the terrace, but that was perfect, we needed those dark shadows to hide in. As I looked, I saw they really were dark now, and so were the grounds. A double owl hoot from the south wall told us the musket teams were in position and ready. It was time.

Marcel signalled, and Bernard and Marin brought up their crossbows. Colin's boots creaked as he eased his position, ready to run at my word. He was the first of our substitute patrollers and I'd have thought he'd be really nervous, but he wasn't, his face looked its usual blank. He'd spent the whole ride here talking about the new gates he and his dad had made for the back entrance to the barracks, like it was the most important thing on his mind.

The next patroller came round the corner and started on the straight. There was a pink bush about a third of the way across I'd picked for the target area, far enough from the west side for the sound not to reach them but still leaving us time to make the changeover before the east-wall guard noticed the patroller hadn't come round.

He was two steps from the bush, Marcel's hand was up, then there came the sudden crack of a musket from the south side.

It was the most terrible bad luck. Somebody in Giles' team must have shifted position, and the barrel caught in the branches, jerking the trigger. I guessed afterwards it was poor Pepin, who was on his first official action. He must have felt dreadful.

It alerted the enemy at once. I was on the near corner of the south wall, and was one of the few who could see up the west side as well as our own. The nearest patroller yelled, while the guards at the *porte-cochère* furiously brought up their muskets to the stands. Soldiers at the lodge ran down the drive towards the Château, while others charged out of the gates to come round and take us from behind. I simply didn't know what to do.

But Giles did. He came hurtling down from his tree, the spent musket in one hand, and his own in the other. He ran straight for the big middle gap between our teams, and started yelling at the top of his voice in very bad Spanish, calling the soldiers appalling names, and doing his best to sound extremely drunk. He hauled himself halfway up a tree, called the soldiers sons of whores, fired his musket over their heads, gave a great drunken laugh, then dropped and ran, leaving Pepin's empty musket on the ground behind him.

There was yelling on the Château side of the wall, and the crash of at least two muskets returning fire, but I simply daren't look. The soldiers were coming up fast from the west gate, and running right by the trees, I could almost have reached out and touched the helmets of the closest. Georges, who was loading for me, had managed to squeeze himself between the trunk of my tree and the perimeter wall, but I was afraid not everyone would find such good cover. If they saw the loaders we would be forced to shoot, and that would be the end of the mission.

They stopped at the sight of the spent musket, and began talking and laughing. A couple did glance up at the trees, but of course there was nobody there. We'd left a gap between the teams, you see, to accommodate the horses and ladders later.

A soldier shouted 'There he is!' and one fired over the fields in the direction Giles had run. Two more raced after him, but the others seemed more amused than anything. None of them seemed concerned with making a proper search, which was quite understandable. They couldn't possibly know the entire musket section of the French Occupied Army was clinging for cover in the trees all around them.

The soldiers came back laughing and shaking their heads, which I hoped meant Giles had escaped them, then picked up Pepin's dead musket and ambled back towards the gate. We listened as their voices slowly died away.

Anne du Pré

The shots sounded muffled, and we guessed they came from the other side of the building, but that was all we could tell. We pressed our heads to the floor to listen downstairs, but could only hear doors banging, and booted feet running in the hall.

Florian was sure it must be our rescuers, and it had started at last. He put on his cloak, and wished Colette and me to do the same with our wraps, but I argued against it, in case the soldiers visited and wondered why we wore outdoor garments over our nightclothes. It didn't matter so much with Florian, who had obstinately remained dressed throughout, because

398

the soldiers knew him to be eccentric, and would have thought little of anything he did.

Florian poured us all wine to keep up our spirits. It felt strangely exciting sitting round the parlour table in the middle of the night, with Colette and me both in nightclothes and Florian dressed for a hunt. However, the noises from downstairs grew quieter, music came again from the drawing room, and it seemed clear that if the Château had indeed been attacked, then the raiders had been driven off and everything was back to normal.

We were silent a while, hoping to hear other noises. Florian poured more wine. Then Colette burst out at last. She said she should never have trusted me, she had known this would happen all along. Our rescuers had been beaten off, and now we were stuck here to face the anger of the officers on our own. She said she ought to have gone with Pablo after all, and now what would become of us? Florian was quite stern with her, and said he was sure our rescuers would still come. I was cheered by that, but when Colette asked the reason for his confidence he turned to me and said 'Because you said so, didn't you, Anne?'

I felt terrible. I did still hope André's men would come, but was dreadfully afraid they might not. They might have been hurt or even killed in the fighting, and be unable to continue the attack tonight. However, I feared a further disappointment would totally disorder Florian's wits, so I said yes of course they would come, and what we had heard was probably a diversion. Florian nodded a great deal when I said this. He explained to Colette the military importance of diversionary tactics, although she could scarcely bear to listen. At last she broke away and ran into the bedroom, where she flung herself on the bed in despair.

Florian refilled his glass. I wasn't sure that was wise, and suggested we should rest instead, but he only said 'Last night I swore I would never sleep in that bed again, and I *never will*.' So I left him sitting alone and joined Colette, but she lay with her head turned away and wouldn't speak.

I couldn't sleep. I was straining to listen for sounds outside, hoping desperately for more gunfire, or any sign at all to let us know we weren't alone.

Jacques Gilbert

Everything was quiet. In the distance the Verdâme clock struck ten.

Marcel waited for the next patroller to get almost to the bush, then signalled Bernard and Marin. The two bolts flew at once, both good shots, face and throat, they didn't even need to pierce the armour. Both wall guard and patroller crumpled and fell in total silence.

Then I was pelting through the trees with Colin and Bruno beside me and the inside team behind, all pounding across the grass towards the Château. It felt strange after looking at it all these months, like having a painting you know really well then finding yourself actually inside it. Stefan and I lugged the patroller into the darkest corner of the terrace, while Marcel and André bundled the wall guard out of sight. Bruno stood in his place with his face in shadow, and Colin took up position near the corner, brushing the leaves off his Spanish dress. I signalled him '*Now*,' and he nodded and walked round the corner to the east side as easily as crossing the Square in Dax. Just as he disappeared, the second patroller came round the west corner, and we were off.

This one was easy. We were close enough and well hidden in the shadows, it didn't take a second for Stefan to grab a hand over his mouth, and me to stab him in the neck, the only sound was a wet gurgle. Roger was through the trees and in position, but I waited a second so he wouldn't be too soon on his beat, then signalled him 'Go,' and he went, just as easily as Colin.

The third patroller trudged round the west corner and was nearly up to us when there was a great rustling from the orchard, which must have been bloody Pinhead shoving through too eagerly. The guard veered sharply out from the terrace and peered cautiously into the dark. He was too far away for us to leap on him, but the bowmen couldn't get him either, if they'd stepped out for a shot he'd have seen them instantly. One shout was all we needed to screw the whole operation, we'd been banging that into everyone for days. One shout.

He stood listening to the trees swishing in the wind, then looked back towards the terrace to see if the wall guard had heard anything. The instant his back was to the trees I heard the whizz of a crossbow and he dropped where he stood. Stefan and André were nearest, they just belted on to the grass to pull the body back into cover. Pinhead dashed out from the trees and I signalled him round the east corner, but there were footsteps behind me, someone was coming from the west, we'd been too slow and the fourth patroller had caught up. In a second he'd see Stefan and André, he'd yell, we'd be finished.

I was running even as I was thinking it, but Marcel was nearer, he just hurled himself at the man and smacked a hand round his mouth, elbow jutting back for the thrust. But this was a big bugger and more awake than the others, he grasped Marcel's knife-hand and they were swaying and grappling as I reached them. I couldn't see clear to stick the knife in, but then the man punched out wildly at Marcel, slamming him back hard on the terrace, and I was up and on him, slashing at his throat before he could take breath to shout.

Stefan and André were back with the other body, I was sending Bruno round after Pinhead, but it all felt hasty and panicky, Marcel was lying still on his back, and there was hot blood gushing out over my hands. There were more footsteps at the corner and I jumped at the sight of the next patroller, but he came within light of the flambeaux and of course it was Colin. We'd done it, we'd got all four of them, it was over. Colin plodded past without giving us so much as a glance. I expect he was thinking about wrought iron.

Anne du Pré

It seemed hours before I finally heard movement outside our door, then the discreet rattle of a key in the lock. I leapt from the bed, seized my wrap, and ran out into the parlour. Our door was opening, but to my dismay the person appearing round it was the Slug, and behind him were Pablo and Luiz.

I shut the bedroom door and quietly turned the key behind me. They didn't see me do it, they were too busy laughing at the sight of Florian sitting fully dressed and drinking his wine.

'Having a party of your own, *hijito*?' said Pablo.

I think Florian had a little difficulty adjusting to the sight of them. He had probably thought as I did, that here were our rescuers at last.

He said 'No one invited you in. Please go away.'

'That's not very nice,' said Luiz, picking up the empty jug. His hands seemed unsteady, and I guessed he must be drunk. 'I see you're enjoying our hospitality, you can scarcely object to our extending it to your sister as well.'

I kept the key behind my back and edged away from the bedroom. I felt the little table behind me, groped blindly for the vase and slid the key gently inside. As I withdrew my fingers, they brushed against the petals of the faded rose.

'I've told you once,' said Florian, and his voice sounded almost as strong as it used. 'My sister is not well. Now please leave.'

'No need to shout,' said Pablo, almost pleasantly. He crossed the room to the window, looked down at the patrolling guards, then firmly pulled the casement shut.

I felt suddenly very afraid.

Jacques Gilbert

Stefan and André attended to Marcel while I signalled the bowmen out of the trees and gave the patrollers the go-ahead to take out the wall guards on their next round. Pinhead was to deal with the guard on the east, and Bruno the one on the south, then we'd have control of three of the four walls. We couldn't touch the west guard, not in full sight of the soldiers at the *porte-cochère,* but we didn't think it mattered. We'd got the east wall to get us safely round to the south side, we didn't need to go near the west at all. As long as they saw four patrollers going constantly past they weren't going to worry about anything else.

I was, though, my brain was fuzzy with panic because of Marcel. If he was seriously hurt we were stuffed, there was no one else could go inside with Stefan and André. He was sitting up when I joined them, but he'd cracked his head on the flags when he fell, and still looked sort of dizzy and unfocused. There was dark blood gleaming in his fair hair.

'He'll be all right,' said Stefan, checking Marcel's eyes. 'He'll be fine, he just needs a few minutes.'

I unscrewed the bar in the store-room window, then stood back and waited, listening to the music and laughter seeping out of that big mess room. It was unnerving thinking of all the soldiers milling about on the other side of that glass, the light from the window making a great square patch on the lawn. I knew perfectly well they couldn't see us, we were in the dark and they were in a room with about a million candles, but it somehow didn't feel like it at the time.

Something changed on the fringes of the square of light, something was shadowing it in a far corner, and I peered up to see a dark shape leaning out of the hostage's window. I caught a quick glimpse of a black sleeve and a bearded face before the window was pulled shut, but that was enough to see it was a Spanish soldier. For a moment I just stared, with the same sick feeling as that night at Ancre when I saw the soldier in the Seigneur's apartments. Only this was even worse, because it was Mlle Anne's window, and she was in there with him.

A tiny intake of breath beside me told me the boy had seen it too. He whispered sharply to Stefan 'How long?'

Marcel was trying to stand, but it was no good, his knees were buckling. Stefan said irritably 'I told you, just give us a minute.'

André looked up at the window, then back at Stefan. 'No,' he said calmly. 'We're going in now.'

He turned to Bernard and Marin, who were watching us nervously, and said 'Take Marcel to Dom at the south wall for dressing. Then go over the wall yourselves and join the musket teams, all right?' There was an authority in his voice I'd never heard before, and Marin actually saluted.

But it was still madness, we'd always said it needed three,

404

they couldn't not wait for Marcel. I turned quickly to Stefan, but André didn't wait to be argued with, he just turned and headed for the window. I ran after him but he stuck his palm against my chest and said 'It'll be all right, you know I have to.'

'Then I'm coming with . . .'

'No,' he said simply. 'If there's no one to follow the plan out here then it's all for nothing.'

It was the bloody Manor all over again, only this time I couldn't stop him, I couldn't knock him out, I couldn't do anything but watch helplessly as he started climbing over the sill. 'Come on,' he said over his shoulder to Stefan. 'We can do it with just two, come on.'

Stefan grabbed his shirt and yanked him back. 'Wait, you stupid bugger, *wait.*'

André didn't struggle, he just gently detached his collar from Stefan's hands and looked up into his face. I heard him say 'Please, Stefan. Please.'

I could only see Stefan's back, but it had gone sort of rigid. Then André smiled at him, turned and disappeared inside.

Stefan said 'Oh, fuck it,' and went through the window after him.

Anne du Pré

Now I know what courage is. Pablo went towards our bedroom, but my brave Florian simply threw himself at him, trying to force him away from the door. He didn't know it was locked, he thought this was the only way to protect Colette, but Luiz joined them immediately and Florian was no match for two. They overcame him in seconds, and dragged him back towards his own room.

'Come on now,' said Luiz. 'If you can't behave yourself we'll have to send you to bed.'

I tried to go to my brother, but the Slug caught my arm and held me back. Florian looked desperately at me, and his face was wretched. 'Where are they, Anne?' he whispered. 'Where are they?' His eyes were fixed on my face, as if he believed I had the answer.

'He gets madder every day,' said Luiz. They pushed him inside his room and locked the door.

Then they turned to me.

Stefan Ravel

Two men against two hundred. They weren't quite the odds I'd have chosen for myself, Abbé, but I could hardly let the kid go in on his own. He knew it too, which I thought was interesting. Sod his nobility, when it came to it he just called me as soldier to soldier, so of course I came. He never even turned to see if I was following, he was already at the store-room door and flapping a hand behind him to warn me there was someone outside.

I stood behind him and picked the leaves off his smart black cloak. It was important, Abbé. Of the two of us, André was the only one who could pass for an officer, with all the freedom of movement that entailed. Apart from the nice clothes and fancy rapier, he'd got the hair for it. A lot of working men don't bother growing it below their shoulders, and if you've ever caught a hank of hair under your knife when scraping and graining a hide you'll know why. But André had gentleman's hair, long and well kept, and what's more he'd got the look, that 'don't fuck with me' arrogance that distinguishes the officer. All right, he was beardless, but

406

they'd got young ones in the Spanish army too, I'd seen them strutting around in charge of experienced men, fresh off Daddy's *hacienda* and thinking themselves heroes. André would fit in a treat.

He stepped back, held up a finger to tell me 'one', picked up a handful of cherries from a basket, and strolled into the corridor, casually popping one into his mouth. I watched through the crack in the door.

There was a single officer wandering about the passage, looking confused and more than a little pissed. André leant against the wall opposite and ate his cherries, looking the man in the eye the whole time.

The officer said something, and I'd love to tell you what, Abbé, but my Spanish isn't all it might be. The tone gave me the impression he was telling André he ought not to have been in that room, let alone eating the food out of it.

André went right on looking at him, and spat out a cherry stone. That got his man moving all right, he came charging up in a flurry of outrage to snatch the cherries out of André's hand. His back was towards me, but over his shoulder I saw André smile, then the man sagged down, and there was André standing alone, the cherries in one hand and his bloodied knife in the other. Nice job. It would be, of course. I taught him myself, remember?

We dragged the body into the store-room, concealed it tastefully behind some cheeses, then started off down the passage to the back stairs, though it took us rather longer than it should have done without Marcel to lead the way. For one thing, his description led us to expect a grand north entrance hall with rock-crystal chandeliers, enormous tapestries, paintings and gold-framed mirrors, and we had to walk through twice before realizing we were actually in it. The floors were black with grime, the walls bare and stained with smoke from the chandeliers, the one mirror had a crack right across it and a surface so grimy with handprints and dust you couldn't see a candle in it, let alone your own face. It was a relief to reach the more normal squalor of the nether regions where we found the back stairs.

There was a miserable-looking guard there, just as Jeanette said there would be. He was probably pissed off at missing the party, but we soon sorted that for him, I parted his windpipe in the first blow. We stuffed the corpse under the stairs to stop a passing don tripping over it and giving the alarm, then mopped up the blood trail with his own shirt. André was muttering under his breath at the delay, but it was his own fault for leaving Marcel behind. We had to clear up after ourselves, but there were too many guards to tackle alone. I said 'Come on, little general, the hostages have been here three years. What difference can ten more minutes make?'

Anne du Pré

Pablo smiled almost reassuringly, then went to try the bedroom door.

'It's locked,' he said petulantly. He rapped sharply on the door and called to Colette 'Open up, sweetheart, it's me, I've come to take you down.'

We could hear her rustling inside, and I pictured how scared and undecided she must be. I called out 'Don't, Colette. Stay there.'

Luiz swung round and told me to shut my mouth. He'd never spoken so before, he'd never dared, and it frightened me he did now, it made me feel our last protection was gone.

'Come on, Colette,' said Pablo, impatiently. 'You'll regret it if you don't.'

I heard her try the door handle, then rattle it again. Her voice came thinly through the door as she said 'I can't. It's locked on the outside.'

Pablo stared at the door as if he couldn't understand it, then kicked it with temper. The Slug jumped nervously. I think he was afraid Pablo would force the door, which was something he could never have explained away.

Luiz laughed, then turned back to me. 'Come on, where is it?'

Pablo looked round, then seemed to understand. 'The key,' he said to me. 'Where is it?'

I said nothing. They began to hunt around, while I backed myself up against Florian's door and stayed out of their way. Pablo went right by the table with my rose on it, and after a moment he lifted the vase to see if the key was underneath. I quickly pushed away from the door to draw their attention.

Luiz looked at me, then again more closely. 'She's got it on her,' he said. 'It's in her hand.'

I kept my hands behind my back, but curled them into fists. Pablo came briskly up and actually took hold of my arms. He said 'Come on, hand it over.'

He took my hands and tried to force them open. I couldn't believe he dared. I twisted my wrists away, but he held me quite firmly, and pressed me against the wall to give himself freer play. He was laughing and saying 'Come on now' in almost a friendly way, as if this were a game and at any moment he would start to tickle me instead. He was obviously as drunk as Luiz.

The Slug said nervously 'Keep the noise down, will you?'

Pablo threw him an irritated look, then addressed himself again to my hands. He took the right one first, held it in one hand, and forced it open with his fingers. When he saw it was empty, he did the same with the left, then threw it down in disgust.

'She's got it on her somewhere,' said Luiz. He was leaning back against the mantelpiece, and watching us with real amusement.

'Have you?' said Pablo to me. He felt my sleeves, then began to run his hands down my chemise, as if I could possibly have hidden something in there. Then he said 'I don't suppose . . . ?' and actually slipped his hand inside. I understood what he meant, I've seen Colette put things in there, but she is bigger than me, and you need a proper dress to do it. I think Pablo realized that at once, but he didn't withdraw his hand. He slid it over me, actually over my skin, until his palm brushed my breast. Then his hand curled round and held it.

I wrenched away from him so violently the ruff of my chemise tightened against my neck. Pablo only laughed, but he did withdraw his hand.

He said 'I'm sorry, de Castilla, I don't think she's got it.'

The smile seemed to grow tighter on Luiz's face. He said 'If you imagine I'm going to be made a fool of by a couple of—' and then a word I didn't understand.

I think Pablo was nervous of Luiz's tone. He looked at me irresolutely a moment, then said 'There's always an alternative.' His hand cupped my breast again, he was pushing it up in his palm. He said 'This one's—' and then something like 'madura'.

Luiz looked at me, and shifted position against the wall. He said 'You'd never get her downstairs unnoticed in that nightdress.'

'No need,' said Pablo. 'We can stay here. Rivera will say she invited us in, won't you, Rivera?'

There was something funny about the Slug's face. It was always sweaty, but now it almost seemed to gleam. His mouth looked wet.

Luiz smiled and held out his arms towards me. Pablo didn't move, but Luiz made an impatient noise between his teeth and clicked his fingers, then Pablo shoved me in the back so that I stumbled across the room, and Luiz caught me in his arms. His shirt was unlaced at the top, my cheek was pressed against the sweat of his naked chest.

He lowered his face to mine, and I could smell the wine on his breath.

He said 'It's your choice, Mademoiselle. Would you like to entertain a couple of gentlemen of Spain?'

I jerked back my head and spat in his face.

Stefan Ravel

We were going too fast and too loudly, the guard at the top of the stairs had plenty of time to turn and see us before we reached him.

He drew his sword, poor sod, but that's about all he did. I suppose what he saw was one of their own officers (which was André) being pursued by a great disreputable brute (which was me) so when the kid reached him he only stepped politely aside to deal with me, and André thrust him in the guts before I even got there. He was still alive, mind, I had to shut his mouth and wrestle him down, though André's knife was still in him, buried so deep I could hardly see the handle. I was still at it when we heard a woman's cry across the landing, abruptly cut off as if someone had slammed a door.

André was scrambling up, soft shoes slithering on the

boards. I grabbed his arm and hissed 'Wait!' but he tore himself away and was off and running across the Gallery, drawing his sword as he went. I bundled the corpse behind a filthy velvet curtain so I could go after him, but there were footsteps on the stairs, another of the bastards on his way up. A guard missing at the bottom mightn't have bothered him, but I'd have to chop him before he found one missing at the top as well. The kid was on his own.

Anne du Pré

I cried out for Florian, which was foolish because he was quite unable to help, but Luiz was like a madman, he smacked his hand over my mouth so tight I couldn't even bite, his palm was squashing my lips and his fingers locked round my chin. I could hear Florian calling 'Anne, *Anne!*', his voice muffled through the bedroom door.

Luiz was tearing at my chemise. The Slug turned to close the door, but it opened hard against him, and a young officer I'd never seen before came bursting into the room. The Slug recoiled backwards, then slumped and seemed to fold on to the floor.

Luiz half released me, and said 'What the hell?'

I thought the Slug had been knocked down by the door, but then the new officer stepped over him, and in his hand he carried a bloodied sword.

Luiz reacted quicker than I. He dragged me between his body and the officer's blade, and spoke furiously in Spanish, his voice close to panic. The new officer paid no attention, he looked quite pale with fury as he advanced, and then a startled look leapt into his eyes and he stopped abruptly, staring at Luiz's face.

Luiz's voice trailed away, and his fingers dug suddenly into my arms. He muttered only one word, but it sounded like '¡*Diablo!*'

The officer hurled himself forward, sword thrusting over my shoulder full at Luiz's face. Luiz stumbled back against the *chaise-longue,* pulling me against him with one hand while the other groped for his sword. I tried to twist round and away, but Luiz stuck out his leg as we turned, tripping the officer so he fell backwards over the Slug. Brave Pablo, who had stayed quietly hidden behind the door, at once came rushing out with his own sword drawn, and charged straight at the officer while he was still on his knees. Luiz started forward with a grunt of triumph, but I seized his arm and pulled him back, just as Pablo thrust violently downwards. The officer flung himself hard to one side, and Pablo's sword plunged right into the Slug behind him, hitting the floor with a *thunk* on the other side.

The officer scrambled to his feet, but Luiz was on him at once, shoving me away with such force I crashed into the dressing table and fell down hard by the Slug. Something struck my head and glanced off, and it was my silk box, jarred from the table by the impact, scattering its contents and rolling away under the green chair.

The officer and Luiz were wrestling each other, too close to use their swords, and I could hear the panting of their breathing as they fought. The officer was saying words too, he was almost sobbing them, I heard him say 'Bastard' over and over again. Pablo would have intervened, but Luiz's back was towards him, and there was no opening for his sword. Then the officer managed to free his elbow, wrenched back his arm, and smashed the guard of his sword into Luiz's jaw with such force he broke his teeth. I heard them crack.

Luiz fell on his knees, making a bubbling, moaning sound,

and I turned away, dazed and sick, to find myself looking directly into the face of the Slug. There was a skein of bright-blue silk hanging absurdly in his hair. He was making a curious grunting noise, and there was thick, dark blood oozing out of his mouth. Then his face seemed to freeze, and I think he died there and then. There was tinkly music coming up through the floor beneath my head, and I was looking in a dead man's eyes.

I heard the ring of swords above me as Pablo and the new officer locked blades in earnest, fencing fast and savagely. I was afraid for my officer, because Pablo was the best swords-man in the Château and the newcomer looked really very young. Pablo's face was stretched wide in a grin of anticipa-tion.

I struggled to pull the Slug's sword out of his belt, but it was cumbersome, and my hands were shaking for fear I would be too late. I had it at last and turned back to the fight, just in time to see Pablo dart his rapier straight at the offic-er's chest. The officer swivelled sideways, then swept Pablo's sword aside with his own, and thrust the blade hard into Pablo's body. Pablo made a terrible noise like a kind of whoop, his eyes bulged, then his hands began twitching and groping at his belly. The officer tried to withdraw his sword, but Pablo's hands clutched desperately at the blade, trying to keep it in, trying to hold his insides together.

Luiz was on his feet again, blood over his face but his sword in his hand. He was coming at my officer from behind, but the officer did not seem to hear, he was struggling with Pablo to retrieve his sword.

I cried 'Look out!' as Luiz lunged forward, and my officer twisted to one side, but his blade was still stuck in Pablo and he was helpless. I thrust the Slug's sword up at Luiz with all my strength, but I was on the floor, and it only stabbed in the lowest part of his body, just between his legs. Luiz pulled away, making a dreadful noise like a cow in pain, but my officer wrenched his own sword free and turned on him, slashing the blade across his face like a whip, once, twice, before pulling back and thrusting him full in the throat.

Luiz was falling, and there was blood running down the Slug's sword on to my hand. I turned away in panic, and jumped at the sight of a huge man standing in the doorway. He wore a military buff jacket, but his brown beard was ragged, his whole appearance unkempt, and in his hand he carried a bloodied knife. I realized with an almost over-whelming sense of relief he must be one of André's men, and our rescuers come at last. Everything was suddenly very quiet, and I became aware of Florian beating his palms more and more weakly against his bedroom door, and the sound of his muffled sobs.

The big man stepped forward, and I was afraid for my gallant young officer, who was staring down at Luiz's body and seemed quite unaware of anything else. I said 'Wait!' as fiercely as I could, and they both turned to me on the instant. I was suddenly acutely aware of the appearance I presented, crouched on the floor with my chemise torn open and the Slug's bloody sword in my hand.

Then the big man spoke. He said 'For Christ's sake, André, get it off her before she sticks it in anyone else.'

It was only then I realized who he was.

Twenty

Stefan Ravel

Right in the balls, and no mistake. You've got to hand it to that girl, she knew how to hurt a man, and wasn't scared to do it either. It made my eyes water just to watch.

Oh, don't get me wrong, I've a lot of time for your Mlle Anne, but she was a strange sight all the same, first time I clapped eyes on her. There was that hair, of course, you know all about that, but the first thing that struck me was how pale she was. I'd never seen a living person that white. They'd been in that room three years without seeing the sun, and she certainly looked it. Her face was thin too, which gives you some idea how the dons had been feeding them; there seemed to be nothing of it but these big, dark eyes. I'm not generally attracted to ladies of the nobility, M. l'Abbé, but I'll admit I quite took to this one.

For one thing, she didn't waste time. There was no bleating for explanations, she was on her feet in a moment and unlocking a door to release her brother. He was a thin, wretched spectacle of a youth with trembling hands and red eyes, and the only thing that made him even lift his head was when André bowed and called him 'Seigneur'. Nobility and titles, Abbé. Most wouldn't even need torturing, just call them rude names, and they'd break in a week. This one was broken, and in my opinion fatally. He said only 'Thank you, Monsieur,' in a ghostly voice, then turned towards his little sister as if waiting for her orders.

What came out of the second door was even worse. It was blond, with a shy, fluttery expression on its face that would have worked better without the acres of heaving bosom beneath it, and wore the kind of nightdress that was never intended to keep anyone warm. If it had been up to me I'd have shoved her and the lad back in their bedrooms and let the dons keep them. The only one with her mind on the job was Mlle Anne.

Anne du Pré

I feel such a fool for not recognizing him at once. I think it's because when I've dreamed of this moment he used to come sweeping superbly into the room wearing a pourpoint of bright turquoise with a white sash. I don't even know why turquoise, except I like it. Of course it was silly to think that way, because he can hardly dress like a proper gentleman in the life he is living now, it wouldn't be practical. In fact, I'm glad he wasn't. He looked very fine as he was.

And once the big one said his name, I knew him immediately. The hair is as black as I remember, and the face as attractive, but perhaps a little slimmer and finer and harder than it was. He is almost as tall as Florian, but then I always thought he would be by now. Of course we were only children when we met before.

I am not a child now.

He saw me tip the rose out from the vase to retrieve the bedroom key, and when we were releasing Colette he reached out and picked it up.

I said 'My rose, Monsieur,' and held out my hand. I knew we couldn't bring luggage, but didn't think he would grudge me that.

He said 'It was always your rose from the moment I picked it.'

I was so surprised I looked up at him, and for a second our eyes met. I turned away *at once*, but my heart was hammering against my nightgown, I felt as if everyone in the room must see it.

The big one started uncoiling a rope from around his waist and left the room, saying to André 'I'll do the window, get them there as soon as you can.'

Colette asked if we had time to dress, because she was wearing one of Mama's more revealing nightdresses and seemed to have lost her wrap, but André shook his head and regretted not, so I took off my shawl and draped it round her. André made a little noise of protest, took off his own cloak and wrapped it round me instead. He was very gentle, and his hands only just brushed my shoulders when he did it. He clasped the cloak round my neck so it shouldn't get in my way, and I felt him looking down into my face. I couldn't meet his eyes after what I'd seen there before, so I looked at his throat, his chest, his hands as they fastened the clasp. I turned as soon as I could and picked up my diary, but he took it from me, saying I would need my hands free, and put it into his breeches pocket.

He hurried us out into the Gallery, and it felt very strange just stepping out of the room, as if the barrier had only ever been inside my head. The feel of the boards under my bare feet transported me right back to that first night when they brought us into Mama's rooms and it all began, but the floor felt rough and sticky, much of the balustrade is broken, and the portraits are all gone from the walls. I almost wish I hadn't seen it, for now when I picture our Gallery that is how I will remember it. Yet I will also see

André's back as he walked in front of me, sword in hand, tense, strong, ready to die for us if he had to.

We walked quietly round the Gallery towards the main staircase. Colette whispered anxiously there would be a guard at the top, but André turned and gave her a reassuring smile. 'Not now there won't be, Mademoiselle,' he said. 'Stefan has come ahead of us.' His confidence in this one man is extraordinary, but also clearly justified, for there was no one there, only the great sweep of empty marble. The sound of music and the rumble of men's voices floated up towards us from the hall below, but André ushered us swiftly past, and I saw with relief we were not to take that way. Instead we walked along the east landing to the musician's gallery on the south side, and there was the big man standing by the arched window, indicating a rope tied round a stanchion which was to be our way out.

There was no time to think or be afraid. The big man showed Colette how to stand so he could stoop and hoist her over his shoulder, then at once stepped on to the sill and seized the rope. My poor sister was clearly shocked at the indignity, but had no time for more than a faint squeak before the man began to descend and she disappeared from sight. André signalled Florian to follow, but my poor brother looked at the great drop of the rope and said he could not do it.

I said 'You can, Florian. It's the way out.'

I guided him on to the sill, André placed his hands round the rope, and together we helped him start down. But his head had hardly dropped below us before his voice came weakly up to say he could go no further. I peered down into the dark and saw his hands still clutching the rope, but his eyes were closed and he seemed unable to move. The big one was trying to climb up again for me, but could not get past.

André leant out of the window and said quietly 'Help him, Stefan, I'll bring Mademoiselle.' Then he turned to me and held out his arms as the man called Stefan had done. I hesitated a little, for he was not of as substantial a build as his companion, and indeed he is older than me by only a few months.

He smiled and said 'Oh, I think I can manage you, Mademoiselle.'

I stood to face him and he lifted me easily. His hands were warm and firm through my chemise, and it was quite different from what Luiz or Pablo had done. I grasped his belt behind his back so he wouldn't need to keep his arm across me while he climbed, and he said 'That's good, stay like that,' then turned sideways to the sill to hoist himself up.

There were footsteps on the little gallery staircase, and the sound of voices and laughter. I twisted behind André's back to see two soldiers walking cheerfully round the bend of the stairs.

Jean-Marie Mercier

Jacques was wonderfully calm. As soon as his patrollers had killed the wall guards he came strolling round to the south side, showed Edouard where to put the ladders, signalled Dom to start bringing up the horses, then called Bettremieu over and showed him a window directly facing us where he said the hostages would come down. Marcel was much better by this time and insisted on going back over to help.

We all stared intently up at the window. I was still telling myself it would be a long time yet, when suddenly it opened and there was Stefan leaning out and throwing down the rope to Bettremieu. Jacques turned to the patroller going past and signalled him to be ready to break and run when Dom gave the call. Colin nodded and walked on. A moment later Roger came round, and again Jacques signalled.

Margot reached out from her tree to nudge me, and said 'Look!'

A nudge from Margot was rather like a punch from anyone else, but I recovered enough to see Stefan starting down the rope with a girl in a nightdress over his shoulder.

'I wouldn't mind Bettremieu's view of that,' said Marin, which I thought was rather coarse.

'Closest you've ever come, is it, Marin?' asked Margot, with interest.

Marin reddened and went on setting up his crossbow.

A minute or two later a young man followed. He seemed to be in difficulties, but Stefan climbed underneath to take his weight, and brought him safely to the ground.

'Where's André?' said Margot. 'What's happened to André?'

Anne du Pré

André released me immediately and drew his sword.

The soldiers dropped the platters they were carrying and ran straight for us, shouting an alarm. The clatter of the pewter as it bounced down the stairs was even louder than the shout, and I heard voices responding below.

'Climb down,' said André, stepping in front to shield me.

I was reluctant to leave him, but he turned and repeated 'Climb down!' so sharply that I swung myself on to the sill at once. I could not see how to back down on to the rope, but the one called Stefan was coming up again below me, and he said 'Just let yourself go now,' and pulled me backwards into the air. He must be immensely strong. He simply clapped me one-handed over his shoulder, winding me completely, and started back down. I heard the clash of swords above us and more shouting, and knew André must be overwhelmed.

Stefan struggled down another two steps, then let me drop into the crook of his arm so he could lower me. A voice with a Flemish accent said 'Is all right, I have you,' and there was an even larger man taking my weight from behind, and bringing me safely to the ground. I straightened up to find myself looking directly into the face of a third man, illuminated in the glow of the flambeau. He had bright-blue eyes and very black hair, and I'm sure I'd never seen him before, but he looked familiar in a way I can't explain.

Everything seemed very unreal. The stones of the terrace were cold under my feet, and there were weeds growing through them that felt like rough grass. The smell of the flambeau was overpowering, and its light shimmered and made rippling shadows over all of us. Florian looked lost and confused as the glare of the flames made dark caverns of his eyes. Across the lawn I saw the white of Colette's chemise as she was helped over the wall, while a man with a bandage on his head walked quickly towards us, coming nearer the light and suddenly turning into Marcel Dubois, our Caporal Dubois, who I thought was killed the night the Château was taken. There was a Spanish soldier actually walking past, but even he only smiled vaguely at us and kept walking, as if we were no more than figures in a dream.

Stefan was already on his way back up the rope, and the blue-eyed man hard after him. I didn't want to leave until I knew André was safe, but the huge Flamand said 'I'm sorry, Mademoiselle,' lifted me in his arms as if I weighed no more than a kitten, and began to run towards the wall. Florian came pattering quickly after us. As we went, I heard the insistent hooting of an owl, and became aware of other men running across the grass to join us. They seemed to be Spaniards too, but made no attempt to hinder us, and only ran just as we did. I thought I really must be dreaming, and tonight was still to come.

Stefan Ravel

He had his back to the window and was close enough to touch, but I didn't think he ought to be distracted just then, Abbé was fighting three of them all by himself.

He couldn't keep it up much longer. He was parrying well, but couldn't reduce the odds; if he stuck one, the others would have him while his sword was engaged. He was weakening too, his movements jerkier, they'd get in a lucky thrust any second. I took my weight on the stanchion, drew my pistol, and fired the thing one-handed into the throng.

It stopped them dead for a moment, and one quite permanently. It stopped André too, which gave me the second I needed to drop the pistol out of the window then grab him from behind. I'd no hand free to climb with, I could only drag him over the sill and lower him, but Jacques was close behind me and reached out to take André's weight while he jumped the last feet to the ground.

Then we slid down the rope ourselves, and only just in time, because some bastard had set about cutting it at the top, and it fell in a heap just as I hit the ground. We were out, we were down, and time to get the fucking hell out.

It was extraordinary to see the hostages being helped over the wall. We had talked and thought about them so long, it felt honestly unreal for them to be actually among us. All three were pale as linen, which made them look unearthly and strange in our midst. The ladies were barefoot and in their nightclothes, while the young lord was dressed in elegant but old-fashioned hunting dress.

A ripple of murmuring ran all along our line, the men were saying 'André', 'André's out.' The last hostage, the younger lady, turned back quickly as if she could see through the wall, and her face seemed to glow in the moonlight. I looked over myself, and saw Pinhead running round from the east wall, and Bruno almost at the ladders, with Roger just behind him. André, Stefan and Jacques all seemed to be safe at the bottom of the rope, and were starting back towards us with Colin and Marcel, but to my left I saw soldiers beginning to pour out of the courtyard gate, and knew our turn had come at last.

I fired. While I passed my gun down to Georges, I heard Margot fire, then Simon, then the next, one after the other as we'd planned it. We'd never been able to keep up such a disciplined line of fire, and the effect on the soldiers was dramatic. The one in front was always being shot, so they began to fan out, but now they were nearly in the middle of the wall, so Giles' and Jacob's teams could bring their pieces to bear as well. Caught from both sides, the Spaniards simply broke and ran. Perhaps it was because they had no senior officers, but the fact is they *ran*. There were others starting down the drive from the west gate and one or two loosed off shots at us, but Georges had passed me my second musket, and I took the first, Margot the second, our men kept firing all along the line, and they turned and ran like the others.

I'd never, never seen anything like that before. This was the enemy, and they were frightened of *us*. I wanted to keep firing and firing even when they were all back inside.

Anne du Pré

There were men all about us, the trees above our heads were alive with them. I think I'd expected André's men to be something like a group of bandits, but this felt like a whole army. The gunfire seemed to crash out over and over again as if it would never stop. There were horses near us, and we took care to keep clear because the firing disturbed them, and they stamped and reared in the dark so the men could hardly hold them. We clung together and waited for the shooting to stop.

A man came limping towards us from the fields, and said 'Don't you worry, ladies, we'll have you out of this in a second. We're just waiting for the captains, then we'll get you up.' It was Giles, dear Giles Leroux, who used to be our gamekeeper. He beamed at us, and I saw his face was scratched and bleeding while his clothes were desperately ragged and torn, and I was afraid he must have been living hard all this long while. But he only laughed kindly and said he'd been playing a little game of hide-and-seek with the soldiers, otherwise he'd have presented a more respectable appearance.

There was a stirring near the wall, and here came our own rescuers safely out of the grounds. Men were crowding round and clapping them on the back, and there seemed a great deal of talk and laughter. Giles stood beside us to keep us safe in the press, he kept saying 'Mind yourselves there, keep those bloody horses back!' and the familiarity made me want to laugh and cry at the same time. Then a man helped Florian on to a horse with Stefan, the large Flemish one passed Colette up to Marcel, then Giles said 'By your leave, Mademoiselle,' and lifted me so André could take me in his arms and rest me on the horse in front of him. I would perhaps have been more secure if I had straddled the animal, but André slid me right across its back so I was safe in the crook of his arm, then wrapped the other round to hold me firmly into his body.

'Comfortable?' he said. Our heads were now so close together his eyes seemed almost to blur into one.

I said 'Yes,' but nothing else, because I felt a little embarrassed, although I was well wrapped in his cloak and was quite decent.

He said 'Good,' and began to turn the horse to ride us away. As we went round, I saw the man with the blue eyes standing on the ground looking after him. There was still something haunting about his face.

We came clear of the crowd, I saw the others riding ahead of us, and beyond them lay the open fields. There was still occasional firing, but it seemed far away and nothing to do with us, because we were still in my dream. The fields simply fell away beside us as we picked up speed. My hair was working loose in the wind, but my only fear was it might blow in André's face and distract him while he was riding. Then the sound of the hooves changed from a thump to a clatter as we galloped across the Kingsway, and our pace slowed as the horse carried us on into the darkness of the forest. It was colder in there and quieter, and the stillness of it seemed to clear my head.

I was riding through the woods in the middle of the night with André de Roland's arm about my waist, and my head against his shoulder.

We got the marksmen peeled off the trees in the end, and the ground started to clear. Jean-Marie was riding with me, and he bounced with excitement all the way back. He couldn't get over what we'd done, and the fact we hadn't lost a single man doing it. He kept saying 'Not a single man, Jacques, isn't that wonderful?' He was starting to get on my nerves. Nobody seemed to realize just how close we'd come to losing the boy, how easily he could have been killed. I knew Stefan had got him out, but if it had been me I'd never have left him in the first place, never.

I dropped Jean-Marie just south of the Hermitage, telling him casually I'd promised to see my Mother about something, then belted down to Ancre as quickly as I could. It was a bit of a nuisance really, but in another way I was looking forward to it. The news of the raid was going to be all over the Sail-lie tomorrow, it was like the biggest thing ever, and I was going to tell my family I'd really been part of it.

Anne du Pré

I might have been cold in the forest, but André's arm was warm around me and I was sheltered by his body. I felt very safe.

The trees became gradually denser, and the horses needed to slow almost to a walk. I missed the exhilaration of the speed, and became much more aware of the silence between us. At last I gathered my courage to ask where we were going, but to my surprise he did not answer. I wondered if perhaps he didn't like to be distracted by conversation while he was riding, but a moment later he turned his head round to me and said 'Are you still all right there?'

I said yes, then added a little timidly that I was wondering where we were going.

He answered without hesitation, and I realized he simply could not have heard me the first time. He explained we would have to ride almost as far as Artois to get past the Wall, but I need not worry, we would not be going near any Spanish-occupied roads or villages. He said there was a single-track road which enabled us to cross the gorge and come out in the woods of France.

I said 'Do you mean the *gabelle* road?'

He smiled. 'Yes, Mademoiselle, I mean the *gabelle* road.'

He stayed looking at me, which concerned me a little, although the horse seemed to be following Stefan's quite happily without any help from its riders. I started to say 'Thank you,' but noticed his eyes went at once to my lips as I spoke. That made me feel strangely self-conscious, but suddenly I remembered how Papa's mother used to look at us when we were talking, and then of course I understood. I should have guessed it before, when André failed to hear Luiz coming up behind him, but perhaps it is only in the one ear, for there had been no other sign until now.

He said 'Something is troubling you.'

I said quickly 'No indeed, Monsieur, I am very happy.'

He was silent a moment. I thought he was going to say something, but when I looked back at him, he was frowning fiercely at the horse's neck. At length he cleared his throat, and this time he did speak, but he was still looking at the horse.

He said 'That man, the one who was holding you when I came in. Did he touch you?' He turned to see my reply.

I knew what he meant. I remembered Luiz's hands on my

chemise and the sudden hardness of his body as he pressed against me. I said quickly 'No. I think he would have, but you came in time.'

His face relaxed, and his arm seemed to tighten about me. I remembered the way he and Luiz had stared at each other, and the expression on André's face as he looked at the body. Something else caught in my mind, and I remembered that strange conversation between Luiz and Carlos, when they talked about being recognized.

I said hesitantly 'You knew him, didn't you?'

He did not answer immediately, and I thought he had not heard, but then he said quietly 'Had I known he was with you at the Château I think it would have driven me mad.'

The horse was slowing again, and we were approaching an opening in the forest, dominated by a rocky outcrop with sides like cliffs. There were people in the clearing and to my amazement one was my dear Jeanette, waving her handkerchief and smiling so widely I thought her face would split.

'This is where the first stage ends,' said André. 'You will need to change your clothes before you proceed, then our guides will take you on to Lucheux. You will have to wait there a day, I'm afraid, but on Monday there will be a coach to Paris, and you will soon be home.'

I was so startled I started to fall forward, and he had to catch me back with his arm.

I said 'Don't you come with us?'

He reined the horse to a stop. 'Your brave Jeanette is to accompany you, if you will allow it, but you will be safe with our guides.' He lowered me carefully to the ground, and dismounted himself.

I said 'I do not doubt it.' They were strangers and all men, but they were André's men, and I would have trusted myself to them anywhere.

He said 'Then don't worry, Mademoiselle. Any of these men would give their lives to protect you. There is nothing to fear.'

I spoke quite fiercely. 'Do you think I am afraid?'

He regarded me seriously, then took a little step towards me. 'No.'

I turned away quickly and began to pat the horse.

After a moment he said 'I would like to come with you. I really wish I could. But I have responsibilities here I can't abandon. I have friends I can't leave.'

I remembered what I'd seen as we rode away from the Château. 'The man with the black hair and blue eyes.'

His own eyes seemed to widen. 'Yes. That's Jacques. How did you know?'

I couldn't answer because I didn't know. I began hurriedly to pet the horse again, but he came and stood beside me to stroke him too.

He said 'I will come as soon as Dax is free. Will you speak for us in Paris, Mademoiselle? Will you tell them we have been fighting a long time and need some sign we are not forgotten?'

I said 'I will tell everyone who will listen. For myself, I will never forget.'

I heard him catch his breath a little, but he went on stroking the horse. His little finger just brushed against mine as he did it, so I moved my hand at once, but then he gave an exclamation and reached up to where my other arm rested on the horse's flank. My sleeve had fallen back, and he was looking at my scar.

I moved to cover it, but he caught my hand to stop me. He said 'Do you really not know how beautiful that is?'

He cannot really think so, it is a little patch of foreign white skin and I hate it.

I heard him say 'Anne . . .'

Colette called 'Anne!' I turned and saw a blanket rigged between two trees to make a screen, and Colette's head sticking out of the top as she changed her clothes. Jeanette was beside her, waving me to join them.

I turned quickly to go to her, but then realized Marcel and the one called Stefan were standing by their horses, and clearly ready to leave. I could not possibly allow them to go unthanked, and poor Florian was in no condition to do anything, so it would have to be me.

I went first to Marcel, and said 'M. Dubois, I am so glad you survived,' which was an *unbelievably* stupid thing to say, because I would hardly have been glad to find he was dead, but he smiled at me so nicely I knew he understood. I reached up as I used to as a little girl and kissed him on both cheeks, and he gave me a respectful little bow.

Then I turned to the big one called Stefan, and it would have looked rude not to embrace him as well. I hesitated, and he regarded me with his eyebrow raised as if to say 'Now kiss *me*, Mademoiselle, if you dare.' Well I do dare, I won't have that kind of challenge from anyone. So I reached up to kiss his cheek, and he suffered me with a good grace. His face was rather rough and bristly.

Then it was André, and I know I should have kissed him too, but somehow at the last minute I couldn't do it. So I curtsied and gave him my hand, and he kissed it. His lips felt warm on my skin, but I expect my hand was cold after the ride. He said he had to thank me also for saving his life, but that was only politeness, for I know he would have killed his man without me. I said I was sure Papa would write to express his own gratitude, then returned him his cloak and went quickly to join Colette.

There was a pretty riding habit in dark green laid out ready for me, but as I was about to change I suddenly remembered this diary was still in André's pocket, and rushed out behind the screen to find the men already mounting up to leave. André's boot was in the stirrup, but when he saw me he stepped down and waited.

I asked for my book, because I didn't want him to know what it was he carried. He exclaimed as he remembered it, and quickly returned it, the cover still warm from having been pressed so close against his body. He did not immediately turn again to his horse, and for the first time since he came into our apartments I thought him ill at ease. Finally he jerked his head up quite abruptly and said 'Tell me, Mademoiselle, why you would not kiss me as you did my friends?'

I began 'Because . . .' but could not think how to finish. Perhaps my face told the story for me, for he suddenly took a step towards me, put the palm of his hand up to the side of my face to turn it towards him, and kissed me. It was a gentle and respectful kiss, a very little one, but it was on my lips. Then he stepped back and bowed, and looked at me a little nervously. He probably expected me to slap his face, and of course I should have, but I didn't, I just stood like a complete *idiot*, and did nothing at all.

His expression changed. He glanced round to make sure no one was watching, then stepped up to me again, and took me in his arms as if he meant it. I don't think it was so very wrong, because really we were no closer than we had been on the horse, but I stared very hard at his shirt all the same. Then he said 'Anne,' again, and it's strange, because his arms about me felt so strong and confident, but his voice was humble, it was almost trembling. I looked up at him in wonder, and it was there again in his eyes, what I had seen the first time, and then his face was moving closer, and then he really did kiss me.

It is nothing like as difficult as I thought. You tilt your face one way, and he tilts his the other, and then it is easy. He opened his lips a little, so I had to open mine to stay with him, and then of course I found I was kissing him too. I was so ashamed I pulled right back, and he opened his eyes to look at me, and there was something almost startled in his gaze. He was breathing rather quickly, then I felt the pressure of his hand on my back to draw me to him again, but I heard Jeanette calling me from behind the screen and knew I was behaving quite dreadfully, so I turned and fled, and never once looked back. While I dressed, I heard them riding away.

I know what will happen. We will go to Paris and it will be years before I see him again, and then he will not remember, or if he does, he will not care. But I am writing this at the Poulet Noir at Lucheux, it is a day since I have seen him, and I still have butterflies in my stomach and a dreadful emptiness in my heart.

Jacques Gilbert

I didn't risk the back meadow, I was being very careful. I stayed in the forest all the way down to the orchard, then cut across through the Home Farm. Tonnerre's hooves seemed very loud in the dark, so I dismounted and led him round the big barns to keep him on the grass all the way to the paddock, then hid him in a little patch of trees with his muzzle on in case of a passing patrol. I was being so careful you wouldn't believe.

I walked the last bit along the edge of the drive. I remember I was thinking about Anne. I'd not seen much of her, I'd been too worried about the boy, but there was just one moment when we were both under the flambeau and I saw her face really clearly. There was still that hair, of course, and under the flickering light it blazed like a bonfire all its own, but it was the first time I'd really seen her face. She didn't have a big nose, she wasn't ugly, she wasn't even plain, she was just beautiful. If André got a good look at her in any kind of light he was going to be in real trouble.

As I passed the last bushes, they seemed to come alive and rush at me. I made to run, but my legs got tangled, something tripped me, and I fell forward heavily, losing my hat and knocking my head on the ground as a great weight landed on my back and pressed me down into the gravel. I heaved backwards to push it off, but there were men all round me, and someone was kneeling on my back and grinding my face down into the dirt. I was dizzy from the blow on the head, and could hardly breathe from the weight on my lungs. I felt gravel in my mouth.

'All right,' said a voice in Spanish. 'Turn him over.'

The man holding my right arm released the pressure and bent it back the other way, and the one on my back got up. I tried to jerk myself upwards as they turned me, but they had my arms fast and someone else was holding my legs, and I could only flop about like a fish on a hook. They got me on my back, and someone put a knee on my chest to keep me down. Someone else was unbuckling my scabbard.

'Let's have a look at him,' said the first voice, and a man's face appeared close in front of mine. I had this terrible urge to spit at him, but you can't spit upwards when you're lying on your back, it would have just flobbed back in my own face.

'Is it?' asked one of the others.

'Description's right,' he said, studying my face like it was satisfactory. 'Get him up, and we'll find out for sure.'

They pulled me to my feet, then tied my hands together behind my back. I'd thought it was bad enough when I watched the boy's hands being tied, but it's worse when they do it behind your back, it puts you off balance, and you feel exposed to anything in front. I felt dazed and sick, and wanted to wipe the gravel off my face, but I couldn't reach it, even with my shoulder.

They started to walk me between them, heading towards my own cottage. As we reached the cobbles, the door opened and Father came out. My heart leapt for a second, then sank back again as he just stood and watched us come nearer.

'Is this him?' asked the leader.

My Father looked at me as if I were a chair, a table, a piece of wood. He nodded without a word.

'All right,' said the leader. He gestured his men, and they started to pull me away back on to the drive. I twisted my head round away from them, and watched helplessly as Father went back into the cottage and closed the door.

Twenty-One

Jean-Marie Mercier

It felt rather jolly in the Hermitage. Many of us hadn't been able to go home, and it really felt like being part of something. Giles came and settled next to me, and even offered to share his blanket because I hadn't thought to bring my own.

There was a lot of chatter and laughter as we went over the raid. Bettremieu had managed to get himself wounded for the fourth time, even though we calculated the Spaniards had only fired five shots the whole night. Georges said a man could fire a shot into the sky and it would still somehow find its way into Bettremieu. It was really very silly, but Bettremieu was laughing as much as anyone, his great bare shoulders shaking up and down all the time Dom was trying to bandage him.

Colin wanted to know whose musket had gone off, but Giles said sternly it didn't matter, it could have happened to anyone. I noticed Pepin sitting apart with a bright-red face, so asked quickly what Giles himself had been up to for so long during the action. Margot laughed and said 'Found a woman in the fields, I expect. Your sister lives down that way, doesn't she, Joe?' Pinhead bristled a little, but Giles only looked consideringly at Margot and stroked his moustache. He told us he'd squeezed between a barn and the Wall to hide from the soldiers, but found himself trapped in the brambles and was forced to wade through a mound of cow dung in order to get out.

Gradually people finished talking and drinking, as one by one they drifted off to sleep. I stayed up a while, wondering what was keeping Jacques, but at last I gave up waiting and settled down to sleep with my cloak for a blanket, because I didn't quite like to share with Giles after what he'd said about the cow dung.

I think I'd hardly more than dozed off when the door banged open and André came in with Marcel and Stefan. They were laughing and joking together, so I knew their end of things must have gone well. André in particular seemed to stand rather taller, and there was something almost self-conscious about him as he took off his cloak. He started towards the platform, gazing round at the men sleeping all about us, then slowed, stopped, and looked again. I sat up, and his eyes fell on me at once.

He said casually 'Where's Jacques?'

Stefan Ravel

Someone had to go with him, Abbé, it wasn't safe for anyone wandering about alone that night with the dons swarming out like maddened bees. Marcel needed to rest after that nasty crack on the head, so good old reliable Stefan volunteered for the job, with Mercier along as marksman for emergencies. Mind you, if all we found at Ancre was Jacques Gilbert throwing back wine with his pisshead of a father I was going to kill the little bastard myself.

We found his horse all right, tethered in an overgrown paddock near the Roland farm, and when we peered through the bushes we saw candlelight glowing through the cottage windows. Everything looked nice and quiet, and it stank like hell.

'He wouldn't have left Tonnerre if he was planning to stay this long,' whispered André. 'He'd have rubbed him down and stabled him in the barn.'

I took out my knife. André had left his own in the guts of that don on the Château stairs, so I gave him my sleeve-knife, then crept cautiously towards the shrubs that lined the drive. When we got within a couple of feet we stopped and crouched together, listening. Bushes are wonderful things to hide in, Abbé, but they do have a habit of rustling.

But it was something even louder we heard first. I wriggled quietly forward, and there was an elderly soldier nestled comfortably in a thick patch of broom, snoring like a sick pig. His companion didn't look much brighter, and the empty jug beside him told its own story. We crawled along a bit further to see if there were any more.

The place was bristling with them. There were three in the next clump of bushes, and a whole lot more beyond them, judging by the rustling and murmur of voices. I have to say it, Abbé, as an ambush they were a shambles. I suppose they'd given up expecting anything to happen this late, but that's no excuse for bad soldiering.

As I carefully turned myself round, I put my hand on something soft on the grass and saw it was Jacques' hat. André snatched it from me at once and crushed it tightly, but there was no hope in it, Abbé, the thing was cold and damp in the night air, it had been there for hours and already felt like a piece of history. André knew it too, his face was bleak in the moonlight.

I whispered 'Come on, little general. We can't help him here, he's long gone.'

A loud creak ahead of us brought our heads sharp round as the cottage door opened. A man was coming out, a short thickset man I knew through many a tedious afternoon in his company at the markets. It was Pierre Gilbert himself, and he was carrying a jug.

We watched in disbelief as he strolled to the bushes ahead of us and passed it to someone inside. There was a certain amount of chat we couldn't hear, then Gilbert said cheerfully 'Ah well, if he doesn't come tonight, you'll make sure of him tomorrow,' then turned and sauntered back to the cottage.

We returned to the horses in total silence.

Jacques Gilbert

I don't want to talk about how I felt. How do you think I felt? It was my Father.

I don't remember much of the journey. They slung me over a horse's back like a sack of corn, but it didn't matter. They rode straight into Dax, right up to the barracks, and through their gate into the courtyard. The last time I'd seen it properly it had little tables and people eating and drinking outside in the sunshine. Now it was dark and cold, and there were horses snorting and men shouting and soldiers everywhere you looked. They hauled me inside through a side door, and my mind was trying to tell me I should notice everything and remember it because it might come in useful, but I knew nothing was ever going to be useful again, and that didn't matter either.

As we went down the corridor other soldiers came and stared, and one kicked me as I went past. The man in charge told him to stop it, I wasn't to be marked, but the soldier said something bitter I couldn't catch, then spat at me instead. We passed others who looked like they felt the same. I guessed they'd got news of the Château already, and maybe some had

439

lost friends. They looked at me with hatred in their eyes. At least it was an emotion.

They took me up two flights of stairs, then into a little corridor. They searched me and took my knife, but nothing else, not even my ring, then untied my hands and led me into a cell. It was one of the inn's old bedrooms and still had a straw-filled bed in it, but that was about all. They slung me on top of it then just left me. I lay with my mouth in the pillow, and the gravel still gritty on my lips. I lay there a long time.

Stefan Ravel

I've never seen fourteen men wake up so fast.

We'd made contingency plans, we'd done those long ago. Those the captured man didn't know well enough to pinpoint would go home and warn the others. Everyone else would stay in the Hermitage and go on stand-by for attack, with outguards stuck at the main approaches to give the roof-guard early warning.

We sent Moreau off with a team to get the horses fed and saddled for a quick escape, and Leroux with another to pack up the guns. As a Verdâme man Leroux had no need to stay, but under the circumstances I thought I'd be glad of his cool head with the men. Dawn was on the way, and for all we knew the dons were too.

Someone else I'd have been glad of was André. The men responded to him, I'd seen it before, just the sight of that cocky little figure strutting about was enough to reassure the jumpiest of them. But he was out of it now and I'll admit I was concerned. The trouble with old-fashioned nobility, Abbé, is they're modelled on the old Roman types and keep their emotions well underground. Oh, it's different now, these days nobility compete with each other to see who can sob loudest at the theatre, but André de Roland wasn't that kind, and whatever was going on there was all on the inside. I was afraid he'd do something stupid.

He knew what it was about well enough. He understood Jacques' real value to the enemy, and that the ambush we'd nearly walked into was for himself. He knew any attempt at rescue would just be sending men to die in a trap. He knew giving himself up would only sign the warrant for Jacques' execution. He knew there was nothing to be done at all. And that's just what the Andrés of this world can't handle, Abbé, their answer to anything that hurts is to get angry and fight it. Well, we all have to learn sometime. There are things you can fight, and there are things that just hurt and hurt and there's nothing you can do about them at all.

I knew where to find him. There's just one spot at the Hermitage that's out of sight of the roof guard, and that's close behind the back wall of the weapons outhouse. I'd found it handy myself from time to time when I fancied a little privacy with a woman, and Leroux practically lived there. But it was a good place to be alone too, and that's what I guessed would attract a lonely nobleman whose world had just caved in.

He was there. He was leaning his head against the wall, and punching the side of his fist on the wood. Nothing wild about it, he just stood there, thumped the wall once, let the heel of his hand slide slowly down off the wood, then thumped it again.

I said 'Pack it in, André, you'll unsettle the men.'

He turned round slowly. The pain in his face shocked me, but the discipline held. He muttered 'I'm sorry,' and let his hand drop back to his side.

I said 'Leroux has a team inside packing up the guns for evacuation. God knows what they'll think with you pissing about.'

He still didn't get angry. 'You don't understand. What's happened is my fault.'

'On your account perhaps, but not your fault.'

'No,' he said. 'My fault. It was me who turned Jacques' father against him. He'd never have done this but for me.'

I said 'I don't give a fuck whose fault it is, and you shouldn't either. You're soldiers. He could have been killed in action tonight, so could you. Just think of it like that.'

'Give up on him? Is that what you're saying?'

'I'm saying you can't go tearing yourself in pieces every time someone gets hurt.'

He stared in outrage. 'But this is Jacques!'

'So? You've lost friends before.'

He shook his head. 'He's my family. If you knew how he's looked after me . . .'

'Oh we all know that,' I said. 'He told us often enough. But be honest, you don't need him any more, you haven't for months. He knew it himself. He knew you were outgrowing him. Why do you think he went to see his dad in the first place? He was pissed off you didn't need him in the Château, he needed to feel better about himself, to brag about what a big man he was . . .'

He turned on me with such passion I had to take a step backwards.

'Why do you hate him?' he said. 'Why can't you leave him alone?'

I said patiently 'I don't hate him. I'm very sorry for him, he's had a fucking horrible life, you're the only good thing that ever happened to him and he knew he was losing you. But it happens, little general. The man had food in his belly, his future was secure, he was better off than most. Most of us are alone in this life, that's just the way it is.'

He said 'You don't have a brother, do you?'

I kept my eyes steady and my voice level. I said 'No, I don't have a brother.'

'You don't know what it's like to lose someone you love.'

That was harder, I'll admit. I said 'Maybe I don't. Maybe I think it's more important to get on with my own survival rather than wallowing in self-pity.'

He stared at me, half turned away, then spun back. 'You,' he said, 'you think you're wiser than anybody, but you're the biggest fool of the lot. Why do you pretend feelings don't matter? Why do you pretend you haven't got any, and despise anyone who has?'

I laughed. 'Feelings, André? If you didn't love Jacques, they wouldn't have taken him. That's your real crime. By caring about the poor sod you've driven him to torture and death.'

He jerked back, eyes blazing, then his fist shot out and cracked hard into my face, catching me smack in the mouth.

I rocked backwards, but stamped down and managed to keep my footing.

He stepped back, and faced me warily.

I touched the back of my hand gingerly to my lip and it came away bloody. I looked at him reproachfully.

He said 'Fight me. For God's sake, fight me.' His breathing was ragged, his eyes desperate, and his hands clenched tight into fists.

There was only one possible answer, and I gave it.

I opened my arms.

We hadn't told anyone what really happened. Marcel said the Spaniards might use Jacques' father to set a trap for André, and they mustn't have the smallest suspicion that we knew. I don't think I'd have said anything anyway. It felt like something very private to Jacques.

Everyone was quite upset enough as it was. Jacques was popular, you see, and all the Dax men were very subdued. I think Dom was almost in tears. He told us what Jacques had been like as a child, how lonely and unhappy, and how he used to try and cheer him up when they worked together with the manure. Then Colin said he'd known Jacques since they were both two years old, so he was obviously more distressed than anyone.

It was André I was most worried about, and so was Marcel. There were refugees beginning to arrive from Dax, Edouard, Bruno, people Jacques could identify from either full names or profession, but there was no sign of André anywhere. Then Giles told us he thought he'd heard him behind the weapons outhouse, so we went to look.

Stefan was there already, and he had André in his arms. André's head was buried deep in his great chest and his arms tight round his body, and Stefan was holding him close. He saw us, of course, but didn't move for fear of disturbing André, he only looked at us over the top of his head and smiled with gentle pride.

I whispered to Marcel 'He'll be all right now, won't he? Stefan's looking after him.'

Marcel didn't speak for a moment, and I thought he seemed quite tense. He said 'Yes. Yes, he'll be all right now,' but he didn't sound quite himself. He didn't seem to want to move either, so I slipped back to the Hermitage by myself.

I found Jacques' blue blanket on the platform, folded up neatly as he'd left it. I picked up his hat, and placed it carefully on top of it, but then I absolutely had to take it off again. There was something strange about seeing his things piled up in a collection like that. It made me think he was dead.

Jacques Gilbert

D'Estrada came to see me after a while, and I saw it was morning.

'So you're Jacques Gilbert.'

I didn't say anything. He knew who I was, he knew it better than me.

He said 'We've been wanting to meet you for some time. You disappointed us rather badly at Christmas.'

I understood that, I just didn't want to think about it. I lay on the bed and looked at him instead. I felt I was in a dream, or on that poppy medicine the boy used to take, I could look at him like he was a picture and couldn't see me back. I noticed what dark-brown eyes he had, as dark as Tonnerre's. I noticed the tiny black dots fringing the sides of his face, and knew his beard was only so neat because he shaved it that way. I noticed a ragged little scar on his face, then the cheek seemed to redden around it, and I knew he didn't like me noticing it, it's like he was ashamed.

I said 'Did we do that?'

His eyes seemed to get thinner. 'How do you mean?'

'In the explosion. We thought we'd left you far enough away.'

He looked at me intently, like I was a book and he was trying to read me. Then he sat back in his chair, and ran his fingers over his beard. It made a faint scraping noise.

'It wasn't the explosion,' he said.

I said 'Oh.' I couldn't think of anything else to say.

He said 'I'm sorry about your father. Sometimes one has to employ methods one might normally deplore.'

His French was very good. It was better than my Spanish. It was better than my French, come to that.

He said 'Let's talk about André de Roland.'

I looked away and studied the wall. There were grey cracks in the plaster like someone had drawn lines with a pencil.

D'Estrada sighed and said 'You might as well. Nothing you say can save him now.'

'Why not?'

He made an impatient gesture. 'It's done now, there's nothing we can do. But we can give him a quick death. I think you know I would prefer that.'

'What do you mean "It's done"?'

'I am sure I can get the Colonel to agree to a quick death if you tell me some things I really want to know. For instance, why don't you tell me where I can find the tanner of Verdâme?'

I said 'What do you mean "It's done"?'

Colin Lefebvre

I brought the letter myself.

No one else, was there? Soldiers turned up at Mass that morning, said they'd a letter for the Seigneur, left it by the font and buggered off again, just like that. Not many of us there, as it happened, lot of people too scared to show their

446

faces. Dubois said I ought to stay at the Hermitage myself, matter of fact, but I'd a business to work, wasn't going to go living in a pile of straw in the woods, not for any number of Spanish soldiers. Wasn't going to miss Mass that morning either, not at a time like that. Say a prayer for old Jacques, you know, seeing he was such a friend of mine. Lot of people forgot that. Everyone fussing round the Seigneur, they forgot Jacques and me were close years before he came along.

So I checked the soldiers weren't searching people outside, swiped the letter on the quiet, and ran straight round the base to give it the Seigneur in person. Maybe I'd have thought twice if I'd known what was in it, but I'm a plain man, it had the Seigneur's name on the front, that was good enough for me.

He wasn't in the Hermitage, and can't say I blamed him. Place packed solid with refugees, stuffed in like so many herrings and stinking like them too. I backed out again fast and headed down for the stream. Few chaps out and about changing the guard duty, Ravel laying turfs on a fire, controlling the smoke, you know, and there was the Seigneur himself washing his face in the stream. Looked a touch peaky to me, but there, he was fond of old Jacques, never said he wasn't.

I got him moving all right. Gave him the letter, and he read it right away, then he was up on his feet and saying 'Col,' he said, 'Col, this is the best news you could possibly have brought me.' Slapped me on the back and set off to the Hermitage at a run.

Miguel d'Estrada

Letter to André de Roland, dated 19 June 1639

Chevalier,

This is to inform you we have in our custody a certain Jacques Gilbert. He has been condemned to death for the crimes of murder and sabotage, and his execution is to be by public hanging two days from now.

However, the Colonel Don Francisco Mendéz and I are prepared to show him clemency on the grounds that the crimes of the servant are the responsibility of the master. Should the Chevalier André de Roland surrender his own person that justice might be executed upon him, we would immediately release the said Gilbert and grant him amnesty for a period of twenty-four hours to enable him to leave Spanish territory. He is at present unharmed and as captured, and it is in that same condition he would be released. That this is a true offer I give my word both as a gentleman, and as an officer of Spain, and it remains open until midnight tonight.

I have the honour to sign myself

Miguel d'Estrada

Jean-Marie Mercier

The door banged open, and André strode in. He looked determined and somehow happier, there seemed even a spring back in his step. Marcel rose to meet him, but André only gave him a brief smile, then carried on up to the platform where his blanket lay. He shot me a meaningful look as he passed, so I waited a moment then followed him.

He'd unearthed the latest clothes Jeanette had made for him and was calmly changing his shirt. I was puzzled. It was a beautiful shirt, very full and pleated, really far too good for everyday wear. He laced it at the neck, shook his long, black hair down over it, then said under his breath 'Will you lend me your sword?'

My sword was honestly very ordinary and nothing like as good as his own, but he nodded insistently, so of course I gave it to him and he put it in his belt. He laid his own sword and scabbard on the blanket and said 'If anything should happen to me, you'll know to give these to Jacques, won't you?'

I said carefully 'Jacques has been captured.'

'I know. I'm just saying, that's all.' He reached for his cloak.

The door was thrown open and Stefan came bursting in with Colin. He made straight for André and demanded rudely 'What the fuck was that letter?'

André straightened, but seemed to avoid looking Stefan in the eye. He fumbled on his cloak, said 'It's all right, I'm just going out for a bit,' and stepped off the decking, but now Marcel came up too, asking 'What is it? What letter?' and they were both in front of him, blocking his way to the door.

André stopped and looked at them. Then he sighed and produced a paper from his breeches pocket. 'I have d'Estrada's word that if I give myself up they'll let Jacques go.' He handed Marcel the paper.

'And you believe him?' said Stefan.

'He is a gentleman,' said André.

Stefan laughed bitterly, but Marcel didn't. He read the letter carefully, then handed it back without a word.

449

Stefan glared at him. 'Well, go on, tell him he can't do it. Tell him it's mad. Doesn't he know they'll kill him?'

'He knows,' said Marcel wearily. 'D'Estrada is quite explicit.'

Stefan swore violently and really shockingly, I'm sorry but I honestly couldn't repeat it. He turned on André and said savagely 'You don't know. You think you do. You think this is going to be a nice honourable thing to do, lay down your life for your friend, go out in a blaze of glory. Don't you know they'll torture you? Have you thought of that?'

'Yes. It's all right, Stefan, it's what I want.' He laid a tentative hand on Stefan's arm, but Stefan absolutely shrugged it aside.

'No, it isn't. Christ knows what kind of nice, clean, dignified picture you've got in your mind, but it's not going to be like that. They won't spare you anything.'

'I know,' said André. 'They didn't spare Giulio.'

'You think doing this makes up for Giulio?'

'No, I think it'll save Jacques.' He turned to Marcel. 'At least I don't know as much as he does. The Verdâme men, I know Christian names but that's all. I know the Hermitage, of course, but maybe I can confuse them a little.'

We were all staring, and he seemed suddenly almost embarrassed. He said in a small voice 'Well, I'll do my best anyway,' put his head down, and started again towards the door.

Marcel hesitated, then stepped back to leave him a clear path.

'Stop him,' said Stefan, his voice curiously high. 'What's the matter with you? Stop him.'

'I can't,' said Marcel. 'I've got no right.'

Stefan didn't even pause, he ran ahead of André and pushed him back, making him stumble against a pillar.

'You don't go until we've talked about this.'

'We have talked about it,' said André. He stepped back and drew his sword.

There was absolute silence. Nobody moved. We hadn't the right, you see. Stefan was a leader in the army, but André was Sieur of Dax, and no one could possibly take sides.

'Come on now,' said Stefan. He took another step towards André, speaking softly. 'There's no need for this.'

André brought his sword up fast, and levelled it at Stefan.

Stefan gave a short laugh. 'Have it your own way. But you won't kill me, not for trying to save your life.'

He reached out to take hold of the sword. André feinted to drive him back, but Stefan ducked away from the blade and reached to grab his other arm. The sword came whipping round, Marcel gave a cry of protest, and there was Stefan standing back, his left hand wrapped round his right arm, and blood trickling down between his fingers. Marcel stepped quickly to his side.

I didn't think Stefan could be badly wounded, but he raised his eyes to André, and the hurt in his face was shocking. Then he stepped forward.

André cried out 'Don't!'

His voice cracked a little, and people shifted in the room. Stefan sensed the change. He gave a little smile and moved forward again, bringing his body right up against the point of André's sword.

'Get back,' said André desperately.

Stefan moved forward, pressing his own chest against the sword. André jerked the blade back fast, and at once Marcel seized his sword arm from behind. André struggled to wrench it free, he twisted his head round and cried out 'Jean-Marie!'

It was like waking from a dream. I started forward at once and jumped from the decking, but of course I was too late.

Stefan's fist flicked out and caught André deftly under the chin, and Marcel caught him as he fell.

Jacques Gilbert

I knew he'd come. I tried telling myself he'd have too much sense, but I knew he'd come. He was never going to stand by and see me executed, he just couldn't do it.

But I didn't want him using my life to make things right with his honour, I didn't want my life at all. There was only one thing I wanted to stay alive for, and even then I'd have to kill myself afterwards. I knew that was wrong, but thought God would understand. I thought the boy would too. I dreamed I'd find him on the other side, and he'd be missing and needing me again, the way he used to before Stefan and Anne got in the way. Maybe it was stupid to think like that, but you've got to grab something to hold on to when everything else is dark.

Then I opened my eyes and saw it wasn't all in my mind. The chair across the room was in shadow, I couldn't make out the cracks in the opposite wall. I turned my head towards the window, and saw the sky was a deepening grey and the clouds had turned black. It was getting dark, and André hadn't come.

Twenty-Two

Jean-Marie Mercier

People were frightened. All round the base they were murmuring in little groups, trying to decide what they'd do if they had to flee the Saillie. People like Bettremieu could just walk anywhere in France and be sure of finding work, but the weaker ones or those with businesses were afraid they might be destitute. Marin and Bruno were worrying how their fathers would cope at the bakery and mill, and Simon was the same about the Corbeaux. Those places were their whole lives, you see. Since they were small they'd known they'd grow up to inherit them, and now it might all be taken away.

It wasn't honestly so bad for me. My own family had lost their business ages ago, and we'd really only been surviving because of André. He used to call me his 'agent' and pay me for doing little errands, like fetching supplies or selling jewellery in Lucheux. I don't think he needed to, lots of people would have done it for nothing, but he knew my family were struggling and wanted to help. He was like that, you see.

Only now he needed our help, and we were none of us giving it. Even with our own problems, we were all terribly conscious of André suffering, and it cast a miserable shadow over everything. Stefan had locked him in the stable outhouse, and we could hear him shouting and banging at the door for what seemed like hours. After a while he stopped sounding angry and that was even worse. He was calling 'Please,

Stefan, please, Marcel, you have to let me out, *please*!' I simply couldn't bear it.

Neither could the guards. Stefan caught Simon trying to release him, and poor Simon could only say 'It's André, I have to, he's the Seigneur.' I think Stefan did understand really. He had a plank nailed over the door, refused to allow any more Dax men to stand guard, and told André if he gave any further trouble he would have him tied up and gagged. It was very quiet after that, but somehow it made us even more aware of him than before. People felt uncomfortable simply walking past the building.

I knew I'd let him down. Of all the men in the Hermitage that morning, it was me André had called. Not Colin, not the Dax men, but me. I knew he needed my help, but simply couldn't see what to do for the best. It's hard when someone you love wants you to help them die.

The best answer for everyone would be to rescue Jacques, but the reports from Dax showed it was hopeless. There was a cordon of extra guards all round the barracks, and Colin even had difficulty getting home because he lived right next door. Nobody was being allowed inside, not even the civilians who worked there regularly. There was no hope for Jacques at all unless André gave himself up, and that was the real difficulty for me. I loved them both, you see, and couldn't bear to have to choose.

Only in the end it was André, and if he wanted to do it, I knew it had to be right. I thought he might even have a plan to escape, and then we'd have them both back and every-thing would be wonderful. We'd thought he was lost before, but he always came back, and I simply couldn't believe he wouldn't this time. I think that's what finally made me realize what I had to do.

I had one hope. Bernard and I were the only Verdâmers

Jacques knew well enough to be in hiding, so I knew I must get my chance to guard him in the end. But Bernard was replaced with Stefan himself, and then by Giles, who really shouldn't have been there at all, and it wasn't until Stefan went on outguard duty that Marcel sent me out to take my turn. By then it was dark.

Giles was quite happy to be relieved. He only said 'Keep your wits about you, soldier, he's up to something. There hasn't been a sound out of him for over an hour.' We laughed together, then I watched him out of sight.

It took me a little while to unpick the nails with my knife, especially as Bruno was on roof guard and I was afraid he'd see, but I did it at last, slid the plank down on one side, then unbolted the door and opened it. It was quite black inside, and at first I saw only the horses, their eyes gleaming white in the dark. Then I heard rustling at the far end, and there was André sitting with his back to the wall, looking innocent.

'Oh, hullo, Jean-Marie,' he said.

I said 'I've come to get you out. Look, here's my sword. There's still time.'

His smile was just beautiful. He stood at once to embrace me, and I saw what he'd been hiding. There was a deep trench gouged out of the earth, and a gap of almost a foot under the wall. Goodness knows how he'd managed it with only his hands and a sleeve-knife, but I should have known André would never simply sit still and wait to be rescued.

He brushed himself down, wedged the knife in the lining of his boot, then straightened and said 'Ready for anything.'

I couldn't answer. I knew it might be the last time I ever saw him, but I couldn't speak at all.

He grinned and said 'It'll be all right, Jean-Marie, I'll be a really horrible prisoner, they'll wish they'd stuck with Jacques.' He went to choose a horse, and said casually 'You won't need to worry about anything when I'm gone. I've still got money, Jacques knows where it is, you'll be looked after.'

I managed to say 'It's not that . . .'

I think my voice may have choked a little, because he turned and put his hands on my shoulders.

He said 'Do you remember what Stefan said about Martin Gauthier? Because that's what you're doing, Jean-Marie. You're giving me the choice.'

He patted my shoulder, and turned to lead a horse from the wall. It was quite a scruffy-looking beast, and I knew he'd only chosen it because there was a good chance we wouldn't get it back.

The movement of hooves must have covered the approaching footsteps, but the door gave a sudden creak, and when I turned in panic there was someone coming in, the moonlight gleamed on blond hair and I saw it was Marcel.

André's hand flew at once to his sword.

Marcel said mildly 'I'm unarmed.'

He was. He wore no belt, no sword, just ordinary shirt and breeches, and really looked astonishingly relaxed. He took a step forward and said 'Bruno reported no guard on duty.'

André's hand never left his hilt. 'Don't blame Jean-Marie. He knows I have to do this.'

Marcel only nodded, as if the debate didn't interest him. He reached out to pat André's horse and said lightly 'It will break Stefan's heart if you go.'

André's eyes seemed to be searching him in the dark. 'He'll understand. I'd do the same thing for him.'

'Would you?' said Marcel. The horse was blocking the moonlight, his face was in shadow. 'So would I.'

He gave the horse a last pat, then stood aside to leave the doorway clear. He said 'You'll need to be quick. Bruno's alert, he'll give the alarm immediately.'

'I'll be quick,' said André. He touched his hair in salute, gave me a last little smile, then led the horse out into the night.

Père Gérard Benoît

Compline was poorly attended that evening. Many of my regular congregation seemed unaccountably to have disappeared, while others may have been deterred by the cordon of soldiery stationed about the barracks to a distance of some thirty feet. As I stood on the steps to bid the remnant goodnight, there came a horse fast approaching from the north, and as the rider entered the Square we beheld with amazement the figure of our Seigneur himself.

I could not imagine what had impelled him to such a foolhardy course of action and stepped down quickly to remonstrate with him, but he did not check his horse until he had reached the cordon, which parted to let him through as if he were expected.

I stood helplessly beyond the soldiers and watched as he dismounted. Although regrettably hatless, he yet presented a splendid figure and seemed altogether in the greatest of spirits, as if on the edge of some particularly stirring adventure. He gave me a wave, then turned and cheerfully announced himself to the guards as André de Roland, Sieur of Dax, come to call upon the Don Miguel d'Estrada as arranged. The soldiers seemed inclined to be merry with him, but his look silenced them, and one at least of their number had the grace to bow and run ahead to take his message. As the others escorted him politely through the entrance he turned for a moment, said 'Goodbye, Father,' then walked into the courtyard, and the gate was shut behind him.

I knew he was there before they told me. My window over-looked the courtyard, and there were shouts of excitement and sounds of people running, then this tremendous outbreak of laughter and cheering. I peered out and could actually see him. He was walking by himself, nobody was touching him, he walked like he was in charge and they were his servants. The church clock was just striking eleven.

I squeezed as much of my head as I could out of the window, which wasn't much because they'd stuck a bar in the middle, and yelled 'André!'

He looked up, and I saw his face quite clearly in the torchlight. I don't know how it's possible to look into someone's eyes from that distance, I only know he did it. Then he waved.

I yelled 'Go back!' but he was already disappearing below me, then the gate was shut and it was too late. I smacked my fist into the bar, and it actually gave a little, which pissed me off because if I'd known it was that feeble I could have knocked it out and thrown myself after it, then none of this would be happening. I ought to have known it wouldn't be that strong, it wasn't likely to be part of the building itself, I mean I couldn't see Le Soleil Splendide sticking bars in its guest rooms just to stop people sneaking out without paying. But of course I didn't think of that before, I never thought of anything till it was far too late.

They came for me a few minutes later, and took me all the way down to d'Estrada's office. There were soldiers sort of bulging round the doorway in order to see inside, but they parted to let me through, the guards shoved me in, and there was d'Estrada with André beside him. They both turned to look at me, and the boy actually smiled. I tried to smile back, but couldn't.

'Are you satisfied, Chevalier?' asked d'Estrada.

'Quite, thank you,' said André, and bowed. I felt like they were gentlemen playing a card game, and I was the thing they'd wagered. Everything about what was happening felt unreal. The candles were twinkling in bright, shiny candlesticks, and d'Estrada's desk even had a vase with red and blue flowers in it like we were in someone's drawing room. The guards lining the walls looked sort of out of place against the tapestries, and there was a bottle of wine with glasses on an oak chest, like we were all going to be offered a drink.

We weren't, of course, because now it was André's turn to pay. He stepped back from the desk, drew his sword, and broke it formally over his knee. I saw at once it wasn't his own sword, and felt stupidly glad. He dropped the pieces on the floor, let his hands fall to his sides, and stood in front of them unarmed.

D'Estrada made a gesture, and two men stepped forward to search him. They were just finishing when there was a stir at the door, and in swept that fat bastard Don Francisco. He'd never bothered to visit me, but obviously couldn't wait to see the boy. He'd got one of his magnificent cloaks on, but underneath he was wearing a huge white nightshirt that looked like a ship's sail.

'Ah, Chevalier,' he said politely. 'How nice to make your acquaintance at last.'

André bowed stiffly and said something about it being an honour, which was a flat lie, but I suppose it doesn't count if it's manners. Don Francisco inspected him carefully, and I noticed for the first time the boy had dressed himself up. They were the same smart breeches from last night, but he'd gone and put his new shirt on, a really fancy one Jeanette had made for when we went to Paris.

'I see you've made an effort for our benefit, Chevalier,' said Don Francisco. 'You will make a very creditable appearance on our gibbet.'

'One tries,' said André. He didn't seem to be scared at all, but maybe people aren't when they're doing something for honour.

Don Francisco smiled. 'Quite right. Do you know, I have given a little thought to the subject myself?'

He said something I didn't catch to one of the soldiers, who bowed and left the room. André's face tightened and he made a quick movement, but the men who'd been searching him grabbed his arms to restrain him. He didn't struggle, he could see it was hopeless, he just stood still and very dignified, and I wondered desperately what it was I'd missed.

'Is this really necessary, Señor?' asked d'Estrada with some distaste.

Don Francisco nodded absent-mindedly, and continued studying the boy's face. He said 'We must be careful not to give the wrong impression. This is not a hero dying for France, but a citizen of Artois rebelling against his lawful masters. People need to see him as a common felon.'

He spoke like the boy wasn't standing there in front of him, and I suddenly understood something of what made him so powerful. I don't think other people were actually real to him, it's like he didn't believe we existed.

The soldier came back in with a pair of shears, went behind André, took a handful of his hair, looked questioningly at Don Francisco, then lopped it right off. I nearly cried out with the shock of it. They were cutting his hair, that long black hair that was just like his father's, nobleman's hair, they were making him look like nobody. The soldier brought the shears right up to the boy's neck, and just went on chopping, hacking the whole length of it off. I couldn't bear to watch. I listened to each cut, that long tearing sound ending in the clack of the shears, I stared at the floor as the hair fluttered down, great soft waves of it, the soldier's boot trampling it as he moved along to reach the other side. Someone in the room sniggered, some bastard laughed, and d'Estrada snapped an order for silence. The hair stopped falling, the shears went silent, then I had to look up, and it was awful, I could almost have cried. His hair didn't even reach his shoulders any more, I could actually see the back of his neck, all white and naked where the sun had never been. His head looked smaller, he didn't look noble any more, how could he, you never see a nobleman with short hair. I couldn't look at his face.

Carlos Corvacho

Your M. Gilbert was most upset, and I can't say I wonder at it. It was a shocking thing to do to a gentleman, and in front of the men too.

When it was over the Colonel had himself a look at the final result. He took the Chevalier's chin in his hand and turned his face to inspect it, which was a terrible indignity, terrible, then said 'I think that will do, d'Estrada, what do you think? A little more?'

My Capitán was a kindly gentleman, and he says 'I think that's quite sufficient.' Then he looks at poor M. Gilbert who's straining at Muños' arm like a wild dog, and says 'I think we might let this man go now, Colonel.' The Colonel only turns to him and says 'Really, d'Estrada? I don't.'

It takes a minute, Señor, even for me. My Capitán, it takes him even longer. He thinks it's just the Colonel not quite

461

understanding, so he says 'I did promise the release would be immediate, Señor.'

'And I,' says the Colonel, 'made no promises at all. This man is far too valuable to let go, I am sure you can see that.'

My Capitán goes quite pale with shock, but the Chevalier, he's even madder. He turns to my gentleman and says 'You gave me your word. Am I to understand you intend to dishonour it?' His eyes are proper blazing, Señor, burn a hole just to look at you.

My Capitán pleads with the Colonel, he says 'I have engaged my word of honour, Señor, you cannot ask me to break it.'

'And I don't, d'Estrada,' says the Colonel, all smiles. 'I am ordering you. You have given your word, you have done all in your power to keep it, but as senior officer I have overruled you. It's quite simple.'

'Señor,' says my Capitán, and there's a line of sweat breaking out on his brow, which was most unlike him, Señor, he was calm at all times. 'Señor, you authorized me to go ahead with my plan. You permitted me to make this promise, you must allow me to keep it.'

Now 'must' isn't a good word to use to a senior officer, and the Colonel doesn't like it at all. He says 'I authorized your plan, but I did not promise. I have not given *my* word, and am not required to do anything.'

My Capitán still doesn't give up. He says 'How can I possibly obtain information on the rebel army if the people cannot trust us to keep our promises?'

'My dear d'Estrada,' says the Colonel, yawning. 'Do you really imagine that in twenty-four hours there will even *be* a rebel army? M. de Roland will tell us all we need to destroy the old one, and the example of his execution should deter anyone from starting another.'

'I won't tell you anything,' says the Chevalier, outraged.

The Colonel turns round with an air of exaggerated patience. 'I think you will, Chevalier. You will tell me whatever I want to know the moment we begin to interrogate your friend.'

I can't say I liked the Colonel very much, Señor, he wasn't the kind of officer a man could warm to, but I'd have to credit him with intelligence. There wasn't any doubt in that room where the Chevalier's weak point lay, his very presence here told us that.

M. de Roland stares at him, breathing heavily, then with no warning at all he goes right for him, throws himself full at the Colonel and tries to get his hands on his throat. The Colonel steps back nimbly while our men grab de Roland from behind, but it takes two of them to hold him, Señor, he's struggling that wild. M. Gilbert's trying to spring across the room to help him, and my Capitán has to signal his guards to hold him too. He's still fighting, though, I'm worried he's going to have my wine glasses over, so I move the tray safely on to the desk.

The Colonel adjusts himself, and looks at the Chevalier with disdain. Your M. de Roland, he looks right back at him and says 'You bastard.'

I'm not saying there weren't some of us would like to have said that about the Colonel a few times, I'd thought it myself on occasion, but it's no way to speak to an officer, let alone one of the rank and status of our Don Francisco. For a moment I thought the Colonel was going to forget his position and give the Chevalier a good slap. But he was a gentleman, Señor, whatever else he may have been, and he keeps his control. He simply gives an order, and Muños goes and smacks your M. Gilbert across the face, good and hard too, sound like a musket shot.

The Chevalier flinches as if he's been hit himself, and our Colonel, he just smiles. He says 'Now then, Chevalier, what was that you just said? I don't think I quite heard you.'

I felt quite sorry for the lad, your M. de Roland, I mean. He just stared at the Colonel, but daren't say another word. M. Gilbert, he was game all right, he called out 'Tell him, André!' And with that, there's a flicker of the old spirit across the Chevalier's face, he sticks his head up and says 'I called you a bastard. A filthy, stinking, evil, rotten, cowardly bastard.'

The Colonel's smile broadens over his teeth, which was always a bad sign with him, Señor, very bad indeed. He sighs, indicates the Gilbert boy, and says to Muños 'Beat him.'

Muños is only too happy to oblige, as he tells me afterwards it was the lad himself gave him that sword slash when they were here before. So Hernandez shoves young Gilbert against the wall, and tears his shirt down, and we're all a little shocked at that, as the lad's back is that scarred already it's hard to see much point in giving him any more. We don't do so much of that in Spain, Señor, we treat our peasantry a little better than that. Still, Muños gets his whip and lashes down hard on the lad's back, and poor M. de Roland closes his eyes. Don Francisco raises his hand to tell Muños to stop.

'Well, Chevalier?' he says, and it's that silky voice of his again. 'Have you anything else you wish to say to me?'

The Chevalier opens his eyes and looks at him, and there's no more calm in it, Señor, no more dignity, no pride, no honour, there's nothing there but hate. But M. Gilbert, he's not finished yet. He turns round against the wall and manages to say 'Go on, André!' It comes out a little thickly, Señor, because of the breath being beaten out of him and blood in his mouth from that first blow, but it's clear enough, and the Chevalier ups with his chin again and young Gilbert looks back, and there's something passes between them that's like a shot of Madeira wine. The Chevalier's face is lit up with pride in him, and I can understand that, Señor, because this is only a peasant when all's said and done, but he's showing like a gentleman.

So de Roland turns back to Don Francisco, and he's looking relaxed now, insolent as you like, and he says – well, I can't really repeat what he says, Señor, it's not really fitting, but the sense of it is a little like telling the Colonel to get stuffed, if you understand me. M. Gilbert gives a snort of laughter, and I think there's a moment my Capitán nearly does the same.

But the Colonel's proper raging, and with him that means he goes very cold. He orders Muños again, and the beating goes on. Nasty business, Señor, I've never cared for flogging, and I'm worried the blood's going to splash on our forest tapestry. The Chevalier doesn't like it either, he starts struggling again, trying to get to his friend, and the Colonel watches with a little smile on his face.

He says 'Would you like me to stop the beating, Chevalier?'

Young de Roland stops struggling and drags his eyes back to the Colonel, who's affecting total unconcern, Señor, he's even managing to look bored. Muños flexes his little whip and grins.

'Yes,' says the Chevalier. 'Stop it. Now.'

The Don's examining his fingernails, which was just an affectation of his, Señor, his nails were always perfectly groomed. He says 'Ask me nicely.'

The Chevalier stops dead and his mouth tightens shut. He knows what he's being asked now, Señor, and this is his honour on the line. He doesn't say a word, and quite right too. M. Gilbert's with him on that, Señor, he turns his head against

465

the wall and says 'No!' but Muños already has his arm back for the stroke, and now it cracks right across M. Gilbert's face. The lad can't help a little cry, Señor, and his hand's up to his face, but there's blood trickling down behind it and there's no doubt there's a bad cut there.

De Roland's head twitches in anguish, I think he's about to speak, but he can't, of course, and forces himself to silence.

The Colonel says 'All right, Muños, break his arm.'

And the Chevalier says 'No.'

We all look at him. He's scarlet with the shame of it, and well he might be, but there's pain on my Capitán's face too. He doesn't approve of this, not one bit. If it's for military information that's one thing, Señor, that's war, we all understand that, but this was being done to save the Colonel's face, and that's another matter.

The Colonel waits courteously a moment, then turns to Muños again and opens his mouth to speak, but the Chevalier's there first. He says quickly 'No, stop.'

He takes a deep breath, and it was that ragged we all heard it, I could feel it in my own throat.

He says 'Stop. Please.'

Jacques Gilbert

I heard it. André de Roland saying 'please' to that bastard Don Francisco, the man who'd murdered M. Gauthier and tortured poor Giulio till he died. André. My mind couldn't accept it.

Because it wasn't his fault, any of it, and I knew that now. I'd thought he was here because of his honour, but he wasn't, he'd just proved that, he was here because he cared about

466

me. He was letting them break his spirit and piss on his honour, and no one in the world could have made him do that but me. All this time I'd wanted nothing more than to protect him and keep him safe, but it was me who'd brought him here, me who'd made him weak, me who'd brought him to this.

They were helping me up, someone was even wiping my face, but I didn't care, I just wanted them all away from me so I could get to the boy. I could see him, he was standing with his head down like he wanted to die, and that bastard Don Francisco reached out and patted his cheek.

'You see how simple, d'Estrada? I think we shall have a profitable morning.'

He swiped a candle off someone, smiled round graciously, and swept off back to bed. I wanted to go after him, I had this picture in my head of running after him, grabbing him in the corridor and smashing his head against the wall, smashing it over and over again till his eyes popped and blood came out of his mouth. But he'd gone, I heard his footsteps padding away, and we were all just left there, with even the soldiers looking embarrassed.

André wrenched himself away from the men holding him, he just tugged his wrists free and shook them off, but he didn't go anywhere, he just stood looking at the floor, his ragged hair in his face, his shoulders bowed and defeated, his fists clenching and unclenching and no one to hit. I pulled away from my own guards, I felt them reaching for me again, but d'Estrada said 'Let him go, for God's sake,' and I crossed the room and no one stopped me, I reached him, and he turned round but couldn't speak or look at me, he just stood like something broken and whispered 'I'm sorry.' I looked down at the top of his head, and knew this was it, this was what M. Gauthier had been trying to say to me all those years ago, this was it, and he was right, there was nothing in the world worse than this, this was shame.

Carlos Corvacho

My Capitán was as angry as he'd ever been in his life, and quite right too, because the Colonel had done a shocking thing, dishonouring him in front of his own men, to say nothing of enemy prisoners. There's no question but M. Gilbert's going to be useful to us, not now we've seen he's the way to break the Chevalier, but that doesn't alter the fact he shouldn't be here in the first place. My gentleman's quite flushed with the shame of it and determined to do what he can to put things right.

First he gets the surgeon to see to the cut on M. Gilbert's face, not that it was any good, Señor, anyone could see it was going to scar, but we couldn't have him bleed to death on us, the Colonel would have had a thing or two to say if we allowed that. Then he takes the Chevalier aside and actually apologizes, he says 'On my honour, I had no idea, I swear I had no part in this.' The Chevalier says he never doubted it and still trusts my Capitán to do what he can to see his word honoured. We both know there's no chance of that, Señor, but my poor gentleman says he'll help them in any way he can.

So we escort them up to the cells personally, and we're letting M. Gilbert back in his room, but he says 'Please let me stay with André,' and my Capitán looks at the two of them, both gazing up at him with the exact same expression, it's almost like seeing double. So he says 'Yes, of course,' because he won't deny them anything now, so we put them in the same room and tell the guards they're to have wine,

468

food, more blankets, anything they want, then we go back down to his office, and shut ourselves in.

The Capitán pours himself a glass of wine, and another for me. We'd planned on a little celebration, Señor, not that we feel much like it now.

'God rot him,' says my Capitán, throwing his drink back in one gulp. 'God rot that stinking bastard to hell.' He smashes his glass on the floor, sits down heavily at his desk, and buries his head in his hands.

Jacques Gilbert

We heard the keys rattling in the lock, then the sound of them marching away. We looked at each other in miserable silence.

I started to say 'André . . .' but he just said 'Please don't,' and sounded like he meant it, so I stopped, and there we were looking at each other again, and not a word to say between us.

He gave me his handkerchief, and I wiped the blood that had oozed under the dressing on my cheek. I went to give it back, but it was bloody and disgusting and I didn't like to, I just showed him and shrugged and said 'Sorry.'

He made an odd little noise of distress. Then he took a step forward and opened his arms sort of shyly, like he thought I might ignore him, he stood with his arms out, and I met him, I grabbed and hugged him as tight as I could, and we just stood there holding each other, and in the end we didn't say anything at all.

Twenty-Three

Père Gérard Benoît

A great crowd was by this time gathered, waiting in silence for the release of Jacques or the restoration of our Seigneur. One woman stood apart from the others, and beneath the hood I discerned the anguished face of Hélène Gilbert herself. I wondered that her husband should leave her alone at such a time, but Jean-Baptiste informed me he was to be found in the Quatre Corbeaux, at which I understood him to be seeking solace in his own way.

At last the gate opened, but there issued forth only a soldier with a sheaf of papers under his arm and a leather pouch slung over his shoulder. He smiled at sight of me, and asked if I would save him a journey by fastening one of his sheets to the wall at St Sebastian's. His tone informed me this was by way of an unpleasant jest, so I read the document immediately as he seemed to wish.

It was in the manner of a handbill, and advertised the execution by hanging of André de Roland for eight in the morning of the coming 21 June. A second paper had been pasted over the bottom of the first, announcing that one Jacques Gilbert was to be hanged beside him.

Murmurs of dismay arose as this paper passed from hand to hand, at which the soldier appeared mightily amused. He announced that all in the Saillie were invited to attend, and that furthermore his Colonel thought they might like a little souvenir by which to remember the occasion. He cast the

470

contents of his satchel on to the ground, and we saw with horror a quantity of fine black hair strewn over the stones.

The soldier laughed at our stricken expressions. 'There's your precious Seigneur,' said he. 'You'll get what's left on Tuesday.'

He turned jauntily away, but at that moment the words '*Il y avait un petit oiseau . . .*' rose softly but distinctly from the crowd behind me. Another voice joined the first, then yet another. In seconds the murmur of the song was everywhere.

The guards at the courtyard gate started forward at once, for the singing of this air was a punishable offence, yet there beside me stood Michel Poulain, singing now both openly and lustily, and as a soldier swung his musket at him, Jean-Baptiste Moreau immediately took up the strain.

> '*Les soldats le chassaient,*
> *Il avait l'aile cassée . . .*'

There were now scores of voices singing. Henri and Colin Lefebvre were among them, Marc Pollet, Daniel Merien, and our largest tenant farmer, Mathieu Pagnié himself.

> '. . .*"Rentre au nid!" un soldat fit . . .*'

The sergeant at the gate called loudly for silence, threatening to fire unless we desisted, but still the singing continued.

> '*"Je ne suis pas aussi bête,"*
> *Et il chia sur leurs têtes . . .*'

The words of this ditty were not edifying, but I ask my readers to forgive their inclusion, for on this one night they seemed as uplifting as an anthem. There were women singing too, fearless of the consequences. I remarked among them Mme Laroque, our own Beatrice Hébert, and the indefatigable Mlle Tissot, who was reputed to be eighty years of age. Hélène Gilbert joined them, the tears trickling down her face.

'*Et l'oiseau s'envola,*
Dessus le mur il passa!'

The sergeant called more men from the courtyard, who fired a great volley over our heads. The song continued, but as the sergeant issued another command and the guns now aimed within the body of the crowd itself, at last and with great reluctance the people began to disperse. As the crowd thinned, I looked again at the ground, and perceived with a start that not a strand of the hair remained. As I looked up at those departing, I noted that many were concealing hands beneath their coats or in their pockets, while faint in the distance a last brave voice could be heard to sing '*Il passa, il passa, il passa, il passa, Dessus le mur il passa!*'

Where there was so much courage and defiance I believed there was also still hope. If I could channel this resolve into prayer as well as song, it seemed to me we had but to keep our faith in Almighty God, and trust to the indomitable spirit of our two young heroes to bring themselves safe home.

Jacques Gilbert

I was all right actually, in a way I was almost happy. If I'd been let go, I'd got nothing to go back to, I'd have no family and no friends, I'd always be the man who got André de

472

Roland killed. This way we were together, I could look after and comfort him right to the end.

Of course he saw things differently. They'd cut his hair and humiliated him but he was still André. He pulled away from me at last, rubbed his sleeve over his eyes, and said 'I think we'd better get out of here, don't you?'

He just couldn't accept reality at all. It made me sad to watch him prowling round that tiny room looking for ways of escape when there weren't any, it's like he couldn't understand that hope hurts. I begged him to stop and sit down, but he said 'You're just tired and hungry, we'll soon get you right.' He banged on the door, and when a guard peered through the hole he said we wanted everything d'Estrada had promised, food and water and wine and more blankets, and if he thought of anything else he'd call again.

The guard looked at him sourly and said 'You enjoy it while you can, little prince, you'll be singing a different tune in the morning.'

André said 'Ah, but we'll have a much better night than you will, *cabrón*,' and his voice didn't sound like he'd ever said 'please' to anyone, least of all Don Francisco.

I drank the wine when it came, but it only made me want to curl up and go to sleep, and I couldn't face the food at all. André said it didn't matter, we'd got a jug and a bottle, and they were good weapons if we wanted to hit. He said he'd got something else too, and proudly produced this little sleeve-knife he'd hidden in his boot. The blade was about an inch and a half long and covered in earth like he'd been gardening with it, but he said 'It's still something we've got they don't know about,' like that was a kind of triumph all its own.

He just didn't know how to give up. He discovered the wonky bar in the window much quicker than I had, and got very excited till I pointed out we were on the top floor and the only way out was by breaking our necks. Then he said we could make a rope from the blankets to let ourselves down, but I made him look at what we'd be lowering ourselves into, and he went very quiet. The courtyard was still part of the barracks, it had soldiers everywhere, guards by the stables and all the doors, and a dozen to protect the gate. They weren't bothered with us at the moment, none of them ever looked up, but if we came clambering down the wall they were sort of bound to notice, and I didn't see a feeble little sleeve-knife and a broken bottle being enough to fight our way past them all.

He kept trying, he looked at the cracked plaster and suggested breaking through into the next cell, but I pointed out there were guards in the corridor who weren't going to let us just walk past them, even if they didn't hear us crashing our way through the wall, which they would. At last I just said 'Please stop it, André, you're making it worse,' and he said 'I'm sorry,' and came and sat beside me on the bed. Even then he didn't sit heavily, he just perched on the edge, like he wasn't going to do anything that even smelt of defeat. He said 'We can't afford to give up, Jacques. It's not just us, we've got to think of everyone else.'

I said fiercely 'We won't talk.'

He looked at me sadly and said 'But I might.'

All at once I understood. I tried to tell myself I'd be strong enough, but knew I wouldn't. There's this thing called *garrucha*, when they tie your hands behind your back then hoist you up by your wrists. Colin and Robert and me had a go at it once when we were playing at the Inquisition, and I remember after a second I was begging them to stop. I tried to imagine going through five whole minutes of it, and I couldn't, I'd be screaming and crying in no time, then the boy would talk, he couldn't help it. Left to himself he wouldn't, he'd never, but he couldn't bear me to be hurt, it was me who'd make him do it. Just by being here and alive I was destroying him and everyone in the whole army. I should have died before I let this happen, I should have bloody died.

Then I remembered the knife. The boy was still playing with it, flipping it round, tossing and catching it. It was only a small blade, but looked suddenly very white. There wasn't any light in the room to be reflecting off it, it's like it was making it all by itself.

I heard my voice say 'André, there's another way.'

He turned and saw my face.

At first I said just me, but he wouldn't have it, he said 'And leave me on my own to face Don Francisco?' and I understood. So then I said 'Why not both of us?' I told him it would be a wonderful way of stuffing Don Francisco. I said we wouldn't go to hell because we'd be doing it for other people, we'd be doing something heroic like the people in his books, it would be the most honourable thing ever.

The thought of it was starting to make me light-headed. I remember hearing distant singing, and a bit of my brain thinking it was like a heavenly choir of angels, but it wasn't, of course, it was real, and not all the singers had good voices, some sounded more like frogs. We went to the window and heard it floating over the wall towards us, and it was '*Le Petit Oiseau*' again, the courtyard soldiers were looking very fed up about it. There was a distant volley of gunfire, but the singing went on, it just gradually sort of faded away, with a faint sound of laughter as it went. I felt like the laughter was inside me too.

I said 'That's what we'd be doing, we'd be escaping. We'd be flying away.'

'Yes,' he said. 'Yes.' He looked at me with an excitement

in his face that made my heart beat faster. 'We're going to fly all right. We're not going through that wall, we're going over it.'

I looked at him blankly, but he was concentrating on the window again, holding the bar in his fist and twisting his head upward.

'What? André, what?'

He turned back to look at me, his eyes shining in the gloom. 'Not down into the bloody courtyard. We're going up on the roof.'

Colin Lefebvre

Shocking state of things at the Hermitage. No one talking to poor Mercier, and not much better with Dubois, seeing it's him authorized it. Ravel shouting and cursing, calling the pair of them murderers and God knows what else. Dubois tried to explain he did it for the best, said it was Seigneur's right, said he really believed they'd let Jacques go, but Ravel just turned on him and said 'Don't give me that shit. You know exactly what you've done, and I know exactly why you did it.'

However you looked at it, fact was we'd lost both of them. There was a fair few panicking, since d'Estrada's promise was over and for all we knew our men being interrogated right now. Some said Seigneur wouldn't talk whatever was done to him, Dom said Jacques wouldn't either, but Leroux said 'Face it, boys, the dons have got double the chance now,' and no one could argue with that.

Looked like time to get out. Not me, of course, we're loyal, the Lefebvres, and I had the Forge to think about. Spaniards knew me well enough, I'd a name as a good, reliable man, seemed to me I could bluff out anything said under torture. But others feeling different, men with maybe not so much to lose or not the guts to risk it, and the bulk of the Dax men were for getting out right then.

Dubois quite frantic. Said there was no need for that, they could stay at the Hermitage till we knew the worst, but Bruno Baudet said that may be too late. 'What if André tells about the *gabelle* road?' he said. 'We could find ourselves trapped.' People were all for packing up their families right this minute so they could get out soon as it was light.

Dubois started shouting, saying there's a chance the Sieur won't talk, saying if they run now that's the end of the army. Marin Aubert yelled back 'What army? Without André there is no army,' and others saying the same thing. Edouard Poulain said Dubois had forfeited the right to lead us anyway, said this was André's army and no one else's.

Then poor old Mercier tried to speak. He said 'If this is André's army then we can't run away now, we have to be here for him to come back to.'

Fair bit of jeering at that. Georges shouted it was Mercier's own fault Seigneur was gone in the first place, and Baudet gave him a real hard shove and told him to sit down. Mood started to turn ugly, but that Margot stuck her elbows in and shoved people back. 'Let the man speak!' she was bawling. 'André's friend, isn't he? Best marksman we've got, saved the lives of most of you one time or another. Let the man bloody speak!' She was something, that Margot, voice like a heron, tits like cannonballs, you didn't want to come up against her in a crush, straight up you didn't. Leroux backed her up and all, said 'Calm down, lads, lady's right.' Turned to Mercier, said 'You go right ahead, soldier, say what's on your mind. You'll get a hearing, or I'll know why.'

So Mercier tried, right, he said 'André'll come back, he'll

477

have some kind of plan. Even when you locked him in the stables he dug himself a tunnel. If there's a way out he'll find it, and we've got to be here to help him, we can't let him down now.'

Bit of murmuring at that, but no one that convinced. Mercier turned in desperation to Ravel, who was sitting hunched in a corner turning a bit of the Seigneur's hair over in his hands. Mercier said 'You know I'm right, Stefan, why don't you say something? You care about him, don't you?'

Ravel lifted his head and said 'I care enough not to see him hanged. And he won't be, Mercier, not as long as you and I can hold a musket. That's all we can do.'

Dubois said urgently 'But the army, Stefan, the army, we have to keep it going.'

'Do we?' said Ravel. Stood up, shoved the hair in his coat, and started pinching out the candles at the platform end. 'You do what you like with the pieces, Marcel, you've broken everything that mattered.'

Jacques Gilbert

We started with that bar.

It wobbled so much you'd have thought it would just take a couple of bangs and a tweak, but it seemed like it was only loose where the top hadn't been set properly, and after an inch it just went clang against solid mortar and wouldn't budge. In the end we scraped out the mortar round it, and it felt like we did it grain by grain. At least we'd got the knife, but we still couldn't really saw properly because of the noise. It must have been close on two o'clock when we finally prised it out.

Then there was the rope. We'd got that extra blanket, but

it was too thick to tie properly, it just made this kind of bulgy knot that slid apart the second you put any weight on it. It worked better when we cut it into thin strips and soaked them in the water jug, but it still felt like more knot than rope, and we had to cut up our cloaks as well. Even then I wasn't sure it was long enough for three whole floors, but the boy said if we had to jump and break an ankle that was still better than staying here, and I've got to say I agreed.

I'd have agreed to anything. The thing about despair is you've nothing to lose, whereas now we had, we'd got hope. My hands were shaking, and every time I heard the guards near our door I jumped in panic in case they looked in. We didn't even know how long we'd got, whether they'd really leave us till morning or take us by surprise. I had this awful picture in my mind of us being just about to go, then the door opening and Don Francisco being there laughing and us being taken down to the cellar to be tortured after all. I think maybe André had the same picture, because he suddenly stopped testing the rope round the bed and said 'I think it's time to go.'

There were still soldiers in the courtyard, but no one was looking up, and we thought we'd be safe as long as we were quiet. We fastened one end of the rope round the bed and the other round André's waist, then he sat backwards on the ledge and leant out. He gave me a little nod, pressed his hands into the wall above the window then slowly started to stand up.

I took the strain. It relaxed after a moment and I knew he'd got a handhold. Then one of his legs started to lift off the ledge, and a moment later the other followed. There was a faint scrabbling sound above me, then one of his feet came flying back in, flailing about for something to rest on, so I twisted quickly and shoved my shoulder under it. After a second he steadied, then dug in hard and sprung up again. I stared out at that black hole of window and waited.

The rope pulled gently in my hands, and I let it pay through slowly. A minute passed, then another. I had to resist the urge to lean out of the window and look up, I just concentrated on staring at the rope and praying it stayed slack. My hands were biting into it so hard the blanket felt like iron. Then it jerked three times, and I let out my breath for what felt like the first time since he'd gone.

I untied the rope from the bed and secured it round my waist. It felt thick and lumpy. Then I went to the window and gave three quick tugs. Slowly the slack started to unwind and disappear till I gave the one jerk for 'stop.' Another minute passed, and I pictured the boy tying the rope to something, I was almost doing it with him in my head, making sure he was giving it enough turns, making it really solid. He'd never be able to take my weight on his own, not if I fell suddenly and pulled on it, he needed a secure anchor. I wondered what he'd found.

Three more jerks, and it was my turn. I looked down into the courtyard, and it was still all clear. I backed on to the sill, held the rope firmly and stood up.

It should have been easy. It was only a few feet, the rope was firm, and all those knots just made it more like a ladder, but my back was stiff and painful and I just wasn't sure I could trust the rope. I kept trying to press my feet into the wall like I was trying to climb up it, but that was pushing my body away from it in a kind of bow, and I felt the great drop swirling below me like a cold draught. Then I saw the roof parapet just above my head, and over it was stretching André's hand.

'If the rope starts to go, just grab my hand.'

'I'll pull you over.'

'It's all right,' he said dismissively. 'I'm tied to a lion.'

My mind couldn't make sense of that. I gripped the rope more firmly, yanked myself up the last bit, whacked one hand over the parapet, then the other, and hauled myself over.

'What lion?'

He grinned smugly. I looked at the great stone lion he'd wrapped the rope round, then back at the boy, and all at once I took it in. We were standing with solid ground under our feet. I'd made it, we both had, we were safe and out in the open air. I know we were still sort of in the barracks, but it didn't feel like it, it felt like we were free. All we'd got to do was find a way down.

I ought to explain about that barracks. It was the original Roland home, and really big and impressive. It was stone built with three wings round a courtyard, like a letter E on its side with the middle prong missing. It looked a bit ridiculous in a village, but I guess it was built before the village was, it was certainly old-fashioned enough. The roof was mainly flat but had odd little turrety bits sticking up like a cheap version of the Château de Chambord, and stone carvings all round the parapet. I'd never liked the look of it much, but I just loved it now. It was flat enough to walk on, but with decorative little towers for cover, it was absolutely bloody perfect.

We still didn't want to stay on it longer than we could help. Anyone who went in our cell was bound to see where we'd gone, I mean the bar was missing from the window and no rope hanging down to the courtyard, even the dimmest guard was going to work it out and send someone after us. We untied the rope, kept to the outside edge away from the courtyard, and set off to look for a way down.

We were on the north wing, the one that used to be Le Soleil Splendide. We looked down into the Square but there was no chance that way, not with the guards at the entrance, let alone the bloody great cordon they'd got across it like we were boar at a hunt. There were people moving about down there all the same, I saw the Pagniés coming out of church and the Auberts going in, clutching candles big as my arm.

'That'll be for us,' whispered André. 'I'll bet Père Gérard's having another prayer vigil.'

I remembered the last one, for M. Gauthier and Pierre Laroque, and how we'd given it a happy ending by taking down the bodies ourselves.

'We're going to do it again,' said André. 'At this rate they'll have to make Père Gérard a saint.'

We went to find a less public way down. The obvious place was over the side into the little alley that runs from the mill, but there were guards at each mouth, we could see the moonlight gleaming off the top of their helmets. André said 'Well, maybe not this way.'

We crept along to the back wing, the long bit of the 'E' where a lot of Ancre staff and pensioners used to live. It overlooked the Backs and we hoped we could nip down and escape over the bridge behind the mill. But we couldn't. There were soldiers all over it, and at their new back gate they were standing two deep. I felt the fear coming back.

We'd hoped to avoid the south wing, because right in the middle was this watchtower the Spaniards had put up, which was supposed to be always manned. André said 'It'll be all right, they're watching for French troops, they'll be looking over the Wall and outside,' but I wasn't so sure. If the guards everywhere else were worrying about us being rescued I bet the men in the watchtower were doing the same.

We stayed near the corner as long as we could, but there was no way down. There were more of those stone lions that would have been perfect for fastening the rope, but the

Backs sort of curve round with the buildings, and the patrolling guards couldn't miss us climbing down. We kept being forced further towards the front, nearer and nearer the watchtower.

It didn't look that frightening in itself. It was a crap building actually, planks of wood just nailed together and sunk into a kind of cement, you'd think the smallest wind would blow it over. At its base was a wooden passageway like a tunnel and we guessed the entrance must be inside the barracks to stop the soldiers getting wet when it rained. There was a door at the base of the tower too, a widening dark line all round it, then a sudden loud creak made us jump in alarm as we realized it was opening.

We dropped behind the last turret, my mind blanking out in panic, I didn't dare even look. There were footsteps hard on the stone, but it sounded like only one man, and a few seconds later I heard a familiar gushing sound, then a long sigh. There was a rustle of clothing, the footsteps walked away from us, then the door shut with a loud bang.

The roof was empty again, but the panic didn't leave me. I'd felt stupidly safe up here until now, but that door changed everything. Any moment it could open again and a whole load of soldiers just stream out on to the roof and us with nowhere to run. We took our boots off and actually tiptoed past that watchtower; we went so slowly I almost fell over.

But we made it past and no one shouted, and the door didn't open, and we were still free. We kept going until we were nearly at the front of the barracks, then it felt safe to breathe again. We put on our boots, crept to the edge of the parapet and peered over.

The Backs had finished by now, we were into the row of buildings that fronted the Square. We were looking down on something that looked oddly familiar, an enclosed yard and a stone building with a flat roof and huge chimney, and then my mind swam back into some kind of sense and I pictured exactly what I'd be looking at if I were standing in the Square like a normal person, not creeping around roofs like a bird.

We were looking down on the roof of the Forge.

Colin Lefebvre

First I knew was a soft thump on the roof. I said to my dad 'What's that?', then a few seconds later there's another. This is, what, coming up three in the morning, a man's bound to think the worst. I said to my dad 'There's someone on the roof.'

I was out of bed and into the back yard, my dad fast behind me, and there's a man by our back door, and another sliding off our roof right in front of me. I grabbed the first, whirled him round to give him a good smack, then he said 'Hullo, Col,' just like that, 'Hullo Col,' and it was old Jacques himself, wasn't in prison being tortured at all, he was standing in front of me in our own back yard. Then the other straightened up and it was the Seigneur. Took me a second, since you ask, hair all lopped off, looked like something off the street in Abbeville, but it was him all right, and when he said 'Hello, Colin, sorry to trouble you,' well, there was no mistaking it.

He was quick, my dad, knew there were soldiers about, Backs were heaving with them. Seized them both by the shoulders, Seigneur or not, bustled them inside, and shut the door. Simone and my mum started squeaking in panic, but my dad told them to shut their noise, then lit a candle, and there we all were, gawping at each other like village idiots in a play.

Seigneur seemed unhurt apart from the hair, but poor Jacques looked in a right old state, dressing on his face, shirt ripped and bloody, hands torn and scratched. Something wrong in his face too, something missing. Looked like the same old Jacques, sounded like him too, but I caught myself wondering if he'd really died in that barracks and what we'd got here was his ghost. You hear stories about things like that, don't you? You hear things.

My mum was worried too. All for getting them in bed right away, she was saying 'You're safe now, you can stay here, you're safe.' But no, Seigneur said they weren't, on account of there being a ruddy great rope hanging down from the barracks right on to our roof, be a bit of a giveaway in daylight. He said to report it ourselves just before dawn so the Spaniards didn't go suspecting us, but him and Jacques, they'd got to go on.

Easier said than done, in my opinion, on account of them soldiers in the Square. Man might stroll through in a crowd in daylight, but this time of the morning was another matter.

My dad laughed suddenly. 'No, Col,' he said, 'not this night. This night the curé's given us the perfect excuse.'

He turned to Simone and said 'Here, girl, get your frock on. We're going to church.'

Jacques Gilbert

Colin lent me his coat, we squashed my hair up under his hat, and M. Lefebvre thought I'd pass. Colin was bulkier than me, but if I kept my head down and stuck my chest out I'd look vaguely right, and it'd be dark after all. It was harder with André, but M. Lefebvre sneaked next door to borrow the youngest Poulain's red coat, and with a hat over his hair he looked fine. It was the coat was the thing. If I'd seen that red shape anywhere I'd have said to myself 'There's Edouard's brother,' and thought no more about it. I guessed the Spaniards would think even less. So we scavenged round the house for candles, brandished them sort of ostentatiously in our hands, said goodbye to Colin, and stepped out into the Square. Simone was on one side of us, Madame on the other, and M. Lefebvre in front.

I kept my head well down, so I didn't see much except cobbles, but I sort of sensed the soldiers off to our left by the barracks doors, they were murmuring and laughing together in a kind of low growl. I was startled when a voice came from in front of us, but then guessed that was the cordon we'd seen, the soldiers blocking the Square.

'Not like you, Lefebvre,' said the voice. 'Praying for the little Sieur?'

M. Lefebvre sounded a bit embarrassed. He muttered something about it being good for business to be seen at the vigil. 'Good will of the community, you know, important in a village.'

The soldier laughed. I could see his legs ahead of me, and the gleam of a musket butt on the cobbles. 'Don't forget the good will of the Colonel.'

'Not likely,' said M. Lefebvre, laughing in a forced kind of way. He walked on quickly, me right behind him and the boy tense beside me. St Sebastian's was clear ahead of us, I'd have given anything just to run, but we had to keep walking sedately in case the soldiers were watching.

The church clock was striking three as we walked through the west door. The smell of the incense took me back to the last time I'd been here, the sound of the *Te Deum*, and my Father watching me with that almost kind look on his face. Everything else was different. The church was full of candles, little yellow pools of light in the darkness. I could hear people rustling and creaking in their seats, and someone

486

was coughing on the other side. Père Gérard was praying at the altar in his soothing monotone, then the words jumped out at me as he said '*André de Roland et Jacques Gilbert, salva eos, Domine*' and I really took it in who it was they were all praying for. I wondered if they'd been doing it when we climbed out that window, and if it had made a difference.

There was a wicked gleam in André's eye, and I knew he was tempted just to tap Père Gérard's arm and say 'Here we are,' but the curé would only have gone ringing joybells or something, then we'd have been stuffed and the Lefebvres along with us. So we shuffled towards the north end and let the Lefebvres get seated, then we thanked them in whispers and legged it for the door. We were out into the graveyard and running for the back gate, then we were through it and in the woods and we'd done it, we were really free. We looked at each other, then he said 'Bloody hell, Jacques, I don't think I've ever been that scared in my life.'

We stopped at the Home Farm to borrow horses and got back to base before dawn. André warned me we'd find half Dax there because of not knowing if we'd talk, but actually it seemed practically empty. Pepin was on the roof, but he didn't even look at us, he was too busy staring out into the dark for the outguards' signals saying the Spaniards were coming. It all felt a bit unwelcoming.

We went in. It was dark with only a couple of candles lit, but we could see at once there wasn't much happening. Bettremieu was sleeping in a huge mound near the door, Bernard was lurking in a corner looking miserable, Dom was playing dice with himself, and Jean-Marie was curled up by our food basket like a protective dog. Marcel was asleep up the platform end, but Stefan was sat up playing with his knife, balancing it on its tip and catching it as it fell. It felt like he'd been doing it a long time.

Then he looked up and saw us.

His hand stilled on the knife, and it poised for a second before dropping to the floor with a clatter. There was a sudden squawk from Bernard, and all at once a great rustle of straw as everyone sat up and stared. I think I'd expected them to come rushing up and hugging us, but they didn't, they stood very slowly without taking their eyes off us, like we were something in a dream. Jean-Marie said in a hushed voice 'I told you so, I said they'd come back,' like we weren't even there to hear him.

The boards creaked as Stefan stepped off the platform and walked towards us, that slow smile growing as he came. I thought he'd embrace André, but he didn't, he turned to me first and laid his hand gently round my arm. He said 'All right?' and when I nodded dumbly he squeezed my arm and let it go. Then he turned to the boy.

'You, you little bastard,' he said. 'You.'

André smiled at him and dug something out of his pocket. 'I've brought back your sleeve-knife.'

'Have you?' Stefan's smile finally made it into a great grin, and he grabbed the boy and squashed him flat against his chest. Then they were all at it, just the way I'd thought, they were piling on top of us and embracing every bit they could get hold of, even Bernard was patting us in a timid kind of way, and it was all right, it was all right, we were home.

Stefan Ravel

It was André all right, talking and laughing as if his being here alive and free was only what anyone would expect, and no kind of miracle at all. He even seemed mildly surprised when we sent Dom galloping into Dax to stop the evacuation, as if we ought to have had faith in him all along. Well, I don't know, Abbé, maybe I should have, but I watched him drinking back a whole mug of cider in one breath, and saw the way his hand trembled when he put it down, and I wasn't so sure he'd had all that much faith himself. Poor kid. It's one of the few things you can't mistake in this world, the look of a man who's been tortured.

Jacques looked in even worse case. His back was half shredded, and he'd an impressive little scar coming under his bandage, but I was more worried about the damage done inside. He'd a dead look about him I didn't like at all, and I wondered if André had told him about his father. He insisted he hadn't, he said Jacques wasn't in any state to hear the truth just yet, and I'm bound to say I agreed. It wasn't going to be nice hearing for anyone, especially if he started to think through the implications of who might have betrayed us last winter. So I slapped ointment on the visible injuries, packed the pair of them off to bed like children, and decided we'd keep our secret a little longer.

Oh, be reasonable. How could I have known the stable boy was keeping a secret or two of his own?

Jacques Gilbert

I had to wait till André was asleep.

He went on talking a while, telling me all the stuff there hadn't been time for, like what happened at the Château, and what he'd said to Anne on the *gabelle* road, and what she'd said to him, and what a fool he'd made of himself. I asked if he'd kissed her, and he got all huffy and dignified so I knew he had.

Then he rolled over to face me and said 'There's something else.' He sounded suddenly very serious.

I looked at him warily. He'd never asked how I'd got caught, and I didn't want him to, I didn't want him knowing anything about that. But he only screwed up his face and said 'That night the Spaniards came. That man, the officer, you remember?'

I wrenched my mind back, and did. The enseigne who'd made him watch.

He said 'I killed him last night.'

I couldn't take that in, it was too big. I said stupidly 'What?'

He nodded. 'I didn't think I'd recognize him. I've never been able to picture his face, not even in my dreams, there was just the dark and the hat, and the whiteness of his teeth as he laughed. Then last night I saw him, and it could never have been anyone else. I was remembering the Manor anyway, and then to see him with Anne . . .'

I must have made some sort of movement, because he grasped my arm and said 'It's all right, we were in time. But another five minutes and . . .'

If he'd listened to me and waited for Marcel. I didn't want to take that in either, I was beginning to think I'd been wrong about just about everything in my whole life. I said feebly 'But she's all right?'

'Oh yes,' he said. 'She killed him herself really, I only finished it. You never saw anything so brave as that girl, Jacques, you never did.'

I dragged him back from thinking about Anne. 'But don't you mind? Didn't you want to kill him yourself?'

He shrugged. 'He recognized me. He saw my face, it's the last thing he saw before he died. That's good enough for me.'

I saw how relaxed he was and knew it was true. After a while his eyes closed, and he settled deeper into his blanket with a little sigh. I'm ashamed now, I knew more than anyone what this meant to him, I ought to have been sort of bubbling with joy, but I watched him drifting peacefully into sleep, and all I really felt was envy.

I leant back against the wall, looking at the knots in the rafters and listening to his breathing. Everyone else was already asleep, and I was completely on my own. After a moment I sat up cautiously and put on my boots. I needed a sword too, so I reached out quietly and took Marcel's. The touch of the metal felt cold and hard and final in my hands.

I stood up. André stirred in his sleep, disturbed by the movement. I could see him more clearly now, there was a faint, pale light creeping in through the slats. It touched his hand outside the blanket curled into a little fist against the straw. It crossed his arm, then his shoulder, and found his face. The hair fallen over his cheek ended abruptly in a jagged line.

I rammed the sword in my belt and went out.

Georges was riding back from courier duty as I led Tonnerre out, and nearly fell off his horse at the sight of me. I told him I couldn't stop, I'd got to see my family, and he nodded seriously and said he understood. Of course he did, it's what anyone would do if their execution had been announced, I mean they'd want to let their family know they were all right.

I was certainly looking forward to telling mine.

Twenty-Four

Stefan Ravel

We were woken by that bloody Georges crashing in with the dawn light shouting 'Isn't it wonderful? Where's André?' I told him to fuck off.

It was too late, everyone was waking, and when André heard Georges had been to Lucheux he was struggling out of his blanket and wanting to know if he'd seen the hostages. Tortured or not, he was still firmly in the grip of his little romantic fantasy.

Georges said cheerfully 'I saw the younger lady, she was up getting ready for the coach. She wanted me to give you a letter, only of course I couldn't take it.'

André looked at him blankly, and Georges actually seemed abashed. 'Well, we all thought, I mean it looked as if . . .' He ran out of words, dug a poster out of his pocket, and handed it miserably to André.

The kid studied it in a grim silence. 'Is she all right? Was she upset?'

Poor Georges was going an interesting shade of pink. 'I think she was a bit faint.'

André scrambled up and was all for dashing to Lucheux right away until Marcel pointed out it was far too late. The coach left at dawn, and his lady love would be on her way to Paris by now, carrying the news with her.

That horrified him even more. He said 'I'll have to write. I'll write to my grandmother, she'll be worried too.' He turned to grope for paper, and for the first time noticed the blanket next to his own was empty. He stared at it uncomprehendingly for a moment, then turned slowly back to us. 'Where's Jacques?'

I had the sickening feeling of having been here before.

Jacques Gilbert

I didn't have much time. Colin would have reported the rope at first light, and once the panic was over there was a good chance d'Estrada would guess exactly what I'd do, and send soldiers round to pick me up. I galloped Tonnerre fast as I could through the forest and arrived at Ancre only shortly after sunrise.

I didn't think the Spaniards could be here just yet, but I was careful all the same. I went round by the Home Farm, took Tonnerre to the paddock and left him out of sight, just as I'd done before. Somewhere in my brain I felt like none of this had happened, and I was being given a chance to live the same day again, and this time my family would be pleased to see me and none of the rest of it would happen at all.

But of course it wasn't like that, and this was one place I was never going to be welcome again. I didn't even go straight in, I went behind the barn into the yard and listened at the back door. I could hear Mother's voice raised in distress, and then the rumble of Father's, which gave me a strange feeling like a thump in the pit of my stomach. I couldn't believe they'd be talking like that in front of a load of soldiers, so I decided to risk it. I drew my sword, quietly pushed open the back door, and went in.

Blanche was curled up on the bed, probably hiding from my parents arguing. She was about to squeal when she saw me, so I put my finger to my lips and made a face like we were playing a game, and she gave a tiny giggle and hugged her knees and grinned. I felt a bit bad about that actually, even at the time. I feel bloody terrible about it now.

I tiptoed across the room in an exaggerated way to keep up the idea of a game, then peered round the doorway into the main room. Father was sat in his usual chair, and looked exactly the same as he always did. I don't know what I'd expected, but it seemed all wrong he hadn't changed, it made me feel I'd made a mistake. Mother was wandering about the room, her hands picking restlessly at her apron. Her face was pink, her eyes puffy from crying, and there was a grey bruise all down one cheek. There was no sign of Little Pierre.

I pushed the door fully open and walked in.

Mother cried out in shock, then her face opened up with a kind of frantic happiness, but it was how Father looked that pleased me most. He leapt up, pushing his chair back so fast he knocked it over, and just stared at me in disbelief. I'd wondered sometimes what it would take to scare my Father, but never thought it would turn out to be me.

Mother took a step towards me with her arms out, then stopped in confusion as I moved past. Father said nothing, but his eyes followed me as I walked up to the table, the sword in my hand.

'I'm back,' I said.

'Oh darling, we thought . . .' began Mother.

'I know what you thought.'

She stared at me. 'But it's not true. Oh my darling, they let you out after all.'

'We broke out,' I said. 'I had something to discuss with Father.'

I levelled my sword at his face. He looked at it impassively, but Mother started with panic.

'Jacques, don't . . .'

'You know what he did,' I said, and it came out rougher than I'd meant. 'You fucking know.'

I heard Blanche squeal at the door to the other room, then Mother saying 'It's all right, darling, come in, look, it's Jacques.' I said 'Not just now, sweetheart,' and mouthed to Mother 'Get her out.' Mother looked at my face, then took Blanche's hand, said 'Don't worry, darling, it's only a game the grown-ups are playing,' and led her away into the back room. I never took my eyes off Father the entire time, and he never took his off me.

He said 'What have you done to your face?'

'Would you like me to show you?' I touched his cheek with the point of the sword.

I heard Mother gasp, and saw she was back in the doorway. Her eyes were huge with fear, but I wasn't sure who for. It could have been any of us.

Father said 'You're upsetting your Mother.'

'All right,' I said. 'Then we'll go for a little walk. Somewhere your friends the Spaniards won't come interrupting us.'

He didn't move.

I said 'You think I won't do it in here?' I scratched the sword point lightly down his face and watched as the skin opened behind the blade. It was an interesting effect until the blood trickled over and spoilt it. He jerked his head away, and the fear was back in his eyes.

Mother was talking desperately behind me. 'Please, Jacques, please, darling, we have to talk, I need to explain . . .'

I ignored her. It was hard, but I did. I said to Father 'You want me to do it in front of her?'

He looked at me without expression, then indicated his coat with his head. I nodded, and he stepped to the table to pick it up. The alarm in Mother's eyes would have warned me even without the metallic noise as the coat slid over the table. I clamped my left hand quickly over Father's wrist, prodded him back with the sword, then jerked back the coat. Underneath it was a pistol.

I picked it up in my left hand and gestured towards the door. This time he moved immediately, but I kept my sword in his back all the way. Mother stood watching wretchedly, her hands knotting in her apron, but I forced myself to ignore her, pushed Father out on to the cobbles and shut the door firmly behind us.

I herded him along the drive and up the track to the stables. It seemed to be the right place. We used to work there together side by side. When I was little I used to watch him working on his own, I'd stand in the doorway and he'd talk about what he was doing, and tell me one day I could do it with him.

The sun was properly up now, it was actually a nice day. The sky was pale blue, and there was a cuckoo calling somewhere, it made me remember summers when I was small. Father seemed more like himself out here too. As we walked up the track he put his hands in his pockets and actually whistled, like we were just going to work together on an ordinary day. I ignored it and concentrated on watching his back. He moved easily and confidently, and the muscles beneath his shirt were as strong as ever. The back of his neck was thick and red with sunburn, but I noticed with a pang that the little hairs there were white now, like the soft fuzz of a baby's hair. He was getting old.

We reached the stables and I told him to stop.

'Getting used to giving orders now, are you, boy? What are you in that army of yours, a general?'

It was good to hear that mocking tone back in his voice, it made him easier to hate. I told him to sit down, then turn and face me. He did it with almost exaggerated obedience. I didn't know anybody could sneer with their body, but they can.

'Stones aren't very comfortable,' he remarked. 'Can't we go inside on the straw?'

'There won't be any straw now.'

I didn't want to go in there. The ghost of what he used to be to me would be hanging in the dark like a giant cobweb, floating like dust in the very smell of the place. I sat in front of him, laid the gun close by my left hand, but kept the sword in my right with the point towards him.

I said 'Well?'

He looked quizzically at me like he didn't know what I meant. I felt the coldness inside me beginning to break up, and found I was getting angry instead. I needed him at least to try to explain. It didn't have to be an excuse, I just needed him to give me something I could make sense of, something I could believe.

I moved my sword back up to his cheek. 'Haven't you anything to say at all?'

'Can't talk with that thing in my face,' he said, and pushed the blade away. I tried to return it, but he blocked it mildly with the side of his hand. I retracted to get the point to him again.

'I'll do it.'

'No, you won't,' he said kindly. 'You're not a murderer.' He reached out to take hold of the *faible*, but the sword was edged, his hand sprang back.

I said 'They were going to hang me. They were going to have me tortured.'

'Don't get yourself in a state, lad, you'll do someone an injury.'

He was reaching for the sword again, so I pulled back and

whipped at his face with it, and the blade slipped down and scratched his chest.

He looked at the thin line of blood trickling down onto his shirt. 'Now look what you've done.'

'You sold me,' I said. 'You betrayed me to the soldiers.'

'True.'

'You lied to me. You pretended you wanted me back, you made me trust you just so you could do this. They were going to kill me and you didn't care, I know you didn't, I saw your face.'

'I don't suppose you've got a handkerchief,' he said.

'You can bleed to death for all I care.'

'Not me, lad, you,' he said patiently.

He took out his big red handkerchief and offered it to me. I took it without thinking. He was right, there were tears running all down my face, I could taste them on my mouth. I wiped them, and clenched the handkerchief in my hand. He'd had that same handkerchief for as long as I could remember. He wiped his brow with it when he sweated, or cleaned his hands on it when we were mucking out. Once when I cut myself on a broken harness he bound my arm with it. He was very gentle.

'You've got to tell me why,' I said. 'You've got to.'

He reached out for the handkerchief and I gave it to him.

'It won't help,' he said. 'It never does. Don't you know that by now?'

'Was it the money?'

'Perhaps.'

'I'd have got you money, I could have got it from André.'

For the first time his face changed. It darkened down the sides of his nose and round his mouth. His eyes seemed deeper.

'I wouldn't have touched his money.'

'But you took it from the soldiers?'

'A thousand's a lot of money. Thirteen hundred if they counted you in, but I wasn't bothered about that. After all, we were supposed to be getting you back.'

'Is that what they told you?'

'Of course. You didn't think I'd want you hurt, did you, boy?'

That was too much. 'You didn't want me *hurt*?'

'Oh, come on, what's that, a little scratch on your face? You look all right to me.'

'I'm not talking about that.'

'Ah,' he said. 'Feelings. Is that what you want to talk about?'

I didn't say anything. I don't think I could.

'You don't know anything about feelings,' he said. His whole face was darker now, and his voice deeper. 'There isn't any pain at your age. Who are you fucking these days, I wonder? I hear you dropped Lefebvre's girl.'

'I can still have feelings, can't I?'

'I don't know,' he said. 'Can you?'

'How can you say that?' I said, and I could hear my own voice trembling, because this was it, really, this was what I needed to know. 'You're the one with no feelings, you don't love me, you never have.'

'True,' he said again. 'True.'

I reached blindly for the handkerchief again. 'You can't just sit there and say that like it doesn't matter. You're supposed to love me, you have to love me, I'm your son.'

'No,' he said tiredly. 'You're not.'

It had to be just the four of us. No one else knew it wasn't exactly a good idea for Jacques to go home, and it wasn't something we thought he'd want spread around

We found his horse where it was last time, and left ours beside it. We checked the bushes, then André crept to the front of the cottage, peered through the window, then drew his sword and motioned me to open the door. I kicked it open, actually, I wasn't in the mood for pissing about. This whole house and everything in it made me sick.

There was just Gilbert's wife there with a little girl. She looked terrified when I burst in but then saw André and rushed up calling his name. He checked her politely, and I saw he wasn't in the mood for any flannel either.

'It's all right, Nelly,' he said. 'Just tell me where he is.'

She dug her hands in his shirt. 'I think, I'm afraid, oh, I think he's going to kill his father.'

So he knew after all, poor bugger. No wonder he'd looked so bloody awful.

'Where did they go?' asked André.

'He didn't say. André, please, you must stop him. There are things Jacques doesn't know, things I ought to have told him, if he kills his father it will all be my fault.'

Typical woman. Every second counted, so she had to talk about blame instead of giving us what we needed to know.

André tried again. 'How long ago did they leave?'

She made an effort at last. 'Only a few minutes. They're not in the barn, I looked. Jacques wanted to talk privately but I don't know where.'

'All right,' said André. 'I can guess.'

He turned to leave, but from the doorway Mercier said 'Horses on the Ancre road.'

André jerked his head towards the back room, and we all piled in to find a door out to a little yard with a well in it. There was a track running behind the barn back to the paddock, and Marcel and Mercier started down it right away. André hesitated, then said to the woman 'Nelly, you are going to tell the soldiers your husband has gone to the village and you have never seen Jacques at all. Do you understand?'

She was useless as soft string. 'Oh, André, I can't.'

Me, I'd have smacked her one, but André merely pressed her hands together and leant down to speak directly into her face. 'You can. You'll be quite safe. They won't hurt you, your husband is too important. You can do this, and it will buy me the time I need to save your son.'

She seemed quite fascinated by him. She nodded like someone in a trance.

He said 'Good girl,' kissed her quickly, then turned and ran to join us on the track. Behind him I heard horses pounding up the Ancre drive.

Jacques Gilbert

I know it was obvious, I've been seeing it all the time I've been telling you, but it's different for you, you're only getting the important bits, then it's easy to see where it's all going. It's not so easy when it's your own life, and you don't know beforehand what the important bits are, and you've got a habit of believing the things you've believed since you were too tiny ever to question them.

As soon as he said it I knew it explained everything. I didn't even need to ask who my real father was. There'd been too many signs for me to have missed them all. The way my Father hated him, the way he hated André who looked so like him, the way he talked like Mother loved him.

'The Seigneur,' I said.

He nodded, pleased, a grown-up approving a child's intelligence. 'Of course the Seigneur.'

I think there was a part of him actually glad to tell me. He'd almost told the truth lots of times, it's like he'd been finding it harder and harder to keep it in. He'd called me a bastard to my face.

He started to reach in his pocket, then stopped and raised his eyebrows in a kind of exaggerated way of asking permission. I felt embarrassed, it was all wrong him asking me, I just nodded, yes, yes. He took out his pipe and box, and lit up.

He said 'I fell in love with your Mother when she was thirteen years old. Everyone did, she was the most beautiful thing you ever saw.' He looked oddly young when he said that, he had a look in his face that reminded me of Little Pierre. 'I'd nothing then. I was stable boy, same as you, but my dad worked the Pagnié farm, he was nothing. Not that Nell was much more, she worked as maid up at the Manor, but I courted her like a lady all the same. Never laid a finger on her, never so much as kissed her, I did it properly and by the Church, because that's what she deserved.'

He took his pipe out of his mouth and spat.

'Then he took her. Your father. He came across her one day in one of the bedrooms, fancied a bit of it, and took her just like that. That's how you were made, boy. *Droit de seigneur.*'

I said 'I don't believe it. She liked him, she'd never have felt like that if it was how you said. I think he loved her.'

'Oh call it what you like, boy,' said Father, waving it away with his pipe. 'Your Mother deluded herself long enough, why shouldn't you? What does it matter anyway? There she was at fifteen with a baby on the way. Your father couldn't help even if he'd wanted to. He was sixteen back then, old enough to marry, but old Michel got himself killed, Hugo was off to Paris as Comte de Vallon, so Antoine was our new Seigneur, and his mother betrothed him to a rich woman in Paris.

'And there was the snag. In the normal run of things a bastard or two wouldn't bother the Rolands, Hugo had plenty in Paris, but the Delacroix girl came from different stock. Nothing noble about them, only rich and religious, and if they'd found out about Nell there might have been no wedding, and no money to pay Hugo's debts.

'The old Comtesse came down herself to make me a pro-posal. I married Nell and brought up the child as my own, and in return I got the job of stable-master for the whole Ancre estate. The fools. They were offering me everything I'd ever dreamed of, and the only price I had to pay was your Mother coming to me second hand with another man's child in her belly. So I married her, God help me, the Seigneur married his rich girl, the Comtesse went back to Paris with no one the wiser, and there we all were.

'Then you came. You had that dark hair right from the start, like an animal, a devil, nothing to do with us. When Nell suckled you it was like seeing another man at her breast. I used to dream of smothering you. I'd watch you sleeping and think about pressing your face into the crib until you died.'

'Why didn't you?' I couldn't look at him, I didn't want him seeing my face.

'I don't know,' he said thoughtfully. 'It's hard to kill a baby. But there was never any doubt whose son you were, not from the start. You liked the horses, but you didn't want to groom them, you wanted to use them. You wanted to play with swords, you wanted to go for a soldier. You used to sneak off and watch the Seigneur fencing, I saw you, more than once. You started carving little animals, and God knows how you picked that up, it was something he did too. Maybe you watched him. Maybe you and your mother spent time with him I never even knew about. I used to wonder.

'Then we had my Pierre, and things could have been so perfect, but she went as nurse to the Seigneur's brat instead. I met you once, the four of you. Her carrying that mewling brat in her arms, the Seigneur walking beside her like her husband, and you running along behind, with him sometimes reaching out to ruffle your hair. He was always touching your hair, because it was his. You looked like a family.

'I stopped her going, but that wasn't the end of it. You were always there, you were going to inherit everything. I thought if you went for a soldier you might be killed, then everything would be the way it should be. The Seigneur didn't need you, he had a boy of his own. Nobody wanted you. You should have died.'

His voice was all conversational, like this was just a story he was telling me. I suppose that was natural, I mean it wasn't new to him. Just to me.

He said 'When the Spaniards came, I thought you really had, and for the first time I was free. I'd picked up a few bits and pieces at the Manor, I was going to take my wife and children, walk out of the Gate, and find somewhere we could start again. Then suddenly there you were. All those good men who died that day, but you came out of it without a scratch. If you'd been alone, I don't know, I might have killed you myself, but you brought that boy with you, and the whole nightmare began again.'

'It was your idea,' I said. 'You can't blame me for that, you wanted him.'

'Oh, I did, I really did. And not just the money. That man's son reduced to living in my barn and dressing in your old clothes, depending on me for the very food he ate. I liked that. I wanted to watch him going under, I wanted him degraded, just as I'd degraded you. I used to take a lot of pleasure with you in the old days, I'd let your father see you spitting and swearing and filthy, with the marks of my fist on your face, because you were my lad now. I thought I'd do it with André too. But you didn't degrade him, you looked up to him, and the brat didn't spit on you, he started to lift you up.

'And you got more like him every day. You started to talk like him, act like him, think like him. The bastard was dead, but I had two of his sons right in my house, looking down on me, treating my own son like a servant. I'd come home and there you'd be, the two of you with Nell like you were the family, and I was the outsider.

'It was better when you left. Then that day at the church. You walked in wearing clothes like your father's, your hair dressed like his, I saw the expression on Nell's face. Then in came the other one, same clothes, same walk, same arrogance, and he went and sat in the Seigneur's place. Her face then. When she looked at you, she saw Antoine's son. When she looked at him, she saw Antoine. I should have killed him years ago. He was dangerous, he always was, I needed to put a stop to it right away.'

I remembered that day. I remembered him being nice to me in the churchyard after the service, and how happy I'd been.

'You were planning this even then?'

'Of course,' he said, looking at me in surprise. 'That's when I decided. I knew I'd got to make it up with you, and persuade you to come and visit, I was prepared to say and do anything, but I didn't need to, you fell for it right away.'

'And that's why you wanted me at Christmas? And those other times? All those things you said, they were all lies?'

'That's right,' he said patiently. 'I did hesitate at times, don't think it's been easy, but it had been so good that last year, just the four of us, I had to protect that. I still do.'

I looked up then, because his voice had changed, and I saw he'd picked up the pistol from my side. I never even saw him do it.

Jean-Marie Mercier

There were six soldiers, and they all went into the cottage, we watched them from the paddock. They didn't draw their swords or make any attempt to cover the back entrance, they simply walked in, and Stefan called them a disgrace to a fine army. André was less sure. He said it looked as if the Spaniards couldn't believe we were really here yet, and were planning to sit and wait for us to arrive. When five minutes passed and they still hadn't come out, we thought he must be right.

We set off at once for the Ancre stables. There wasn't a great deal of urgency, because Jacques quite obviously knew the danger already, but we did need to intercept him before he could walk back into the ambush at the cottage.

André led us up a little track to a slope from which you could look down on the Manor. We peered rather carefully round the last bend, and saw them sitting out in the open in front of the stables, but the older man had a pistol in his hands, and it was pointed straight at Jacques.

All the tension was back in André's face. 'Can you take him, Jean?'

I had to say no. I could make the shot, but I'd have to step clear round the bend to do it, and Jacques' father needed less than a second to pull the trigger.

'All right,' said André. 'We'll go round the other way.'

He led us off the track and through the wooded under-growth towards a copse on the other side of the stables, where I could shoot without coming out of cover.

As long as Pierre Gilbert didn't shoot first.

Jacques Gilbert

I said 'What do you want with that?'

'Think about it from my point of view. I wouldn't want this story getting about.'

'I'm not going to tell anyone,' I said bitterly. 'Why would I? The Rolands don't want me, do they?'

He laughed. 'You'd have liked that, wouldn't you? To be a noble bastard? Poor Jacques. You even ask them, they'll drown you like a farmyard cat.'

'I'm not going to ask them, am I?' I said fiercely. 'Do you think I want to be somewhere I'm not wanted?'

'Then this is the kindest thing, isn't it?' He pulled the dog back into the firing position, and I realized the gun must be already primed. I could still flick up the sword in time, but there was this awful kind of lethargy coming over me, like the sword would be just too heavy to lift.

He said 'You do understand, don't you?'

The awful thing was I did. I could see how dreadful it must have been for him all these years. When he was speaking, I almost forgot it was me he was talking about, it felt like someone else, someone it was all right for him to hate.

I said 'It wasn't my fault.'

'Wasn't mine either,' he said. 'Neither of us asked for you to be born.'

'No,' I said. I wished I hadn't been. I sat there with fat tears rolling down my chin, and wished I'd never been born at all. I rubbed my sleeve across my eyes, and the sword slipped and ran down his arm.

'Careful,' he said mildly, and put it aside.

I said 'I'm sorry,' and laid the sword down on the grass.

He watched me. 'What's the matter, don't you want to kill me any more?'

I shook my head.

'What do you want then?'

I wanted him to comfort me.

He said 'Look at the state of you. My Pierre never cries.'

'He never needed to cry, you were always nice to him.'

A little flash of anger flared up in his eyes. 'You resented that, did you? You were going to inherit everything that should have been my son's, and you wanted me to like you as well? I hated you from the moment you were born.'

Everything was very quiet. There weren't even any birds.

I said 'You should have told me.'

'Why?'

'At least I'd have understood. I thought it was my fault, I thought it was me.'

'It was you.'

'It was my father.'

'Same thing,' he said.

I felt something strange washing inside me, like a kind of relief.

I said 'It's not. That's why you didn't kill me, isn't it? When I was a baby? Because you couldn't blame a baby for something its father did.'

'You're not a baby now.'

'It was my father you really hated. When you beat me, it was my father you wanted to hurt, not me.'

'Was it?'

'Yes.' I was suddenly so sure. I could see my whole life all in one piece, and for the first time everything in it made sense. 'You didn't want to hurt me at all. I remember times you were nice to me. When we started working in the stables together, and you showed me how to do it, we were close then, weren't we?'

He ran a hand through his hair and stared at me. 'Jesus Christ. You don't understand a word I've said.'

'But I do, that's what I'm saying. All these years I thought you didn't love me, but you did, you proved it by not killing me. You didn't even want to kill me this time, did you? You said it yourself, you thought they'd let me go. You don't hate me at all.'

'Poor Jacques,' he said. 'Do you know why I gave you that name? Because that's all you were, the extra one I never wanted. I saved my own name for my own son. I never gave a fuck what happened to you.'

'You must have. I couldn't be wrong about my whole life, could I?' I knew that, I *knew* that, it was singing inside me like a bird. 'There were loads of times you cared. When I was tiny, and you used to throw me up in the air and catch me, don't you remember? Then later, you'd put me on your shoulders and run with me, '*Bransle des Chevaux*', you must remember that. You can't tell me you never loved me. You can't.'

'Is that what you really want?'

'I want you to be honest,' I said. 'No one's ever going to know about any of this, we can say what we like. Can't you just admit you loved me?'

He looked up, and an extraordinary expression came

over his face. I don't know how to describe it except it was happy.

'Did you love me, Jacques?' he asked.

'Yes. I always did.'

'The Seigneur's son, and he loves me. Now there's a thing.'

'Tell me,' I said.

His shoulders moved, I leant forward for the hug, then there were two shots one after the other, and a scorching pain at my waist and I fell back. I scrambled up, and there was my Father lying on his side, half his face just a mess of blood and bone, and he was dead.

Jean-Marie Mercier

With the pistol where it was, it had to be a head shot. We so hoped it wouldn't be necessary, but I'm afraid it was. Jacques's father suddenly gave him this awful, evil, triumphant look, then I saw him bringing up the gun. Jacques wasn't even looking. André said 'Now!' and I fired.

I was only just in time. His finger must have been already pressing the trigger, but my shot knocked him sideways and the pistol ball only just grazed Jacques' side, instead of going into his stomach where his father had aimed it.

Jacques screamed 'Daddy!' and grabbed his father up from the ground, but I knew he was dead, I must have shot half his face away.

I think it's the worst thing I've ever had to do in my life.

Poor Jacques, down in the dust cradling his worthless father in his arms and howling like Martin Gauthier's dog. André ran down to him straight away, but Jacques turned to him almost gibbering, saying 'It's my dad, it's my dad, it's my dad,' over and over again, his voice getting higher and higher until André got his arms round his neck to quiet him. Then Jacques laid the body down carefully as if it was precious, and screamed at him 'Why?'

I didn't hear what André said, but it seemed to have some effect, and at least that awful howling stopped. André knelt and took him in his arms, and after a while Jacques was silent, and there were just those two dark heads close together, and the faint murmur of André's voice, the words indistinguishable in the distance.

Marcel was speaking. 'We have to move, that shot will bring the dons out of the cottage.'

I expect they'd heard the screaming too, it was certainly loud enough. I hauled myself up out of it, left Mercier twitching in shock, and the two of us went to join the happy little party in front of the stables.

Jacques heard us coming, and wrenched away to huddle over the body. André was left kneeling alone in the dirt, but he lifted his head when Marcel spoke, nodded obediently and climbed to his feet. His eyes were red, and his face wet with tears, but he didn't hesitate and went loping off at once towards the bend.

There was the tramp of boots coming up the track. Marcel said 'Get him out of it,' and ran after André. The kid peered round the bend, signalled 'Two,' and drew his sword.

Jacques seemed quite content to crouch in the open

clutching his dead father and not caring if he got killed or not, but there wasn't time to fuck about, so I grabbed up his sword then wrestled him back to the trees. I slung him down on the grass beside Mercier and drew my pistol. I'd lent my sword to Marcel, who seemed to have mislaid his own, but I can't say I was worried. Only two of them, and Marcel and André lying in wait, it didn't look a problem.

And there I was wrong, dear Abbé, which goes to show how even the most experienced soldier needs to be reminded not to underestimate the enemy. There was only a rustle to warn me, and then they were on us, another two of the bastards. They'd done exactly what we'd done, and crept round the other way.

I had my pistol levelled and fired in one movement, bringing the first man down. Beside me Mercier jerked up his musket for the other, but there was only that horrible little click which is all you can expect when you've forgotten to reload your bloody gun. I couldn't believe it. After all the training I'd given him, he'd forgotten that most basic thing.

It was too late now, the bastard was already on us, sword slicing down at Mercier. I parried him with the pistol barrel, then ducked my head and charged him, there was nothing else to do. The bastard jumped back to bring his sword up, which would have been the end of me if Jacques hadn't come to himself and stuck his own blade up and in the don's thigh. He crashed down on one knee, and Jacques slashed out at him, all but severed the man's throat with one blow, then slashed again the other way, he was for cutting the poor sod to ribbons. I pulled him back after the second cut, because the man was more than dead, and I didn't see the need for mutilation. He turned and glared as if he couldn't remember who I was.

I turned to look down to the track, where Marcel and André were engaged sword to sword with the other pair, but

it looked all right, André was in beautiful form, he was sending his man's blade spinning and was ready to lunge. Beside
me, Mercier was furiously reloading his musket, just a little
too late to be any good to anyone. Jacques looked blankly at
him, then suddenly seemed to realize the significance of what
Mercier was doing.

'It was you,' he said. 'You shot my Father.'

Mercier fumbled the powder, and spilt it on the ground.

'You did, didn't you?' said Jacques.

His voice was rising. I glanced down to the track. André's
man was down, and he and Marcel were fighting the other.
He was left-handed, that one, and his blade got an unexpected
slash down André's arm before the kid twisted and stuck
him through the middle.

Mercier said 'I'm sorry.'

'Sorry?' said Jacques. He was swinging his sword and looked
rather dangerous.

I said 'Leave him alone, he was obeying orders.'

The sword stopped swinging, and he turned his head to
me. His eyes were almost boiling. 'Orders? Whose orders?'

I remembered André down there holding Jacques in his
arms, and the sound of his voice.

I said 'Mine.'

Jean-Marie Mercier

Stefan was absolutely glaring at me, so I knew I was meant
to keep quiet.

He tried to explain we'd had no choice, but Jacques quite
refused to believe it, and insisted his father's gun only went
off by accident when I shot him. At last Stefan said 'Have it
your own way, but it was your bloody life we were saving,

remember that,' then turned away to reload his pistol. Jacques went on staring at his back, and after a moment he said 'I won't forget, Stefan. I'll never forget what you've done.'

I was rather relieved when André appeared through the trees, asking what the shooting had been about. Jacques turned to him at once, then stared in consternation at the long scratch down his arm.

André shrugged. 'I'm getting old and slow. That last man was very good.'

Jacques examined it. 'This is bad, you've got to be more careful.'

André opened his mouth to protest, then hesitated and said instead 'I'm sorry, it was stupid.'

'Got to be more careful,' said Jacques gruffly. He ripped off the sleeve of his shirt and bent to bandage André's arm with it.

André looked down at the top of his head and said very quietly 'I know.'

Stefan watched them a moment, then turned away.

Jacques Gilbert

My Father would never have tried to kill me, he'd already made that clear, he only pointed the gun in self-defence. I know he did mean to kill André, obviously I know that, but anyone could understand why. We'd all survived, no harm was done. If Stefan hadn't murdered him we could have talked it all through properly, he could have told me he loved me, and then I'd always know it deep down, instead of having stupid doubts in my head making me not sure.

I wanted at least to take his body back to Mother, but André explained there were two soldiers at the cottage, and we mustn't do anything to implicate her. He said the soldiers would find the body, and when they'd gone I could go and explain. He even offered to come with me, but I didn't want him hearing what I said to Mother, it was all stuff he must never know. I'd promised my Father I wouldn't tell. It was the only thing I'd ever be able to do for him again.

We set off to collect the horses. Marcel wouldn't let us use the track in case more soldiers came, so we climbed down the bank and walked round by the Manor itself.

I remember that walk very clearly. The grass of Ancre was still bright in the sun, but I had no father, I never had had, and it all looked black, like it did that night I came running out of the stables with a mad coachman waving a scythe. We were actually crossing the lawn where it all happened. I looked up at the window, the one where I'd seen the soldier and thought for a moment it was the Seigneur. I remembered feeling if the Seigneur was there then everything could still be all right. He wasn't, of course, but that didn't change the fact I'd had that feeling. I'd had it as long as I could remember.

I felt a little tingling somewhere inside.

I looked at those blackened walls, and thought of André's burnt wooden horse, then I remembered the one the Seigneur gave me, and knew quite suddenly he'd carved it himself. They take time, things like that, it must have taken him several evenings, and every minute he put into it was for me. I remembered him putting it into my hands and saying 'There you are, Jacques, now you've got a horse of your own.'

The tingling started to grow inside me. It was glowing.

I remembered other things. I remembered the Seigneur being angry at the stables the first time I'd been there with a black eye. I remembered the kind way he used to look at me, and knew that when I talked to my Mother she'd tell me my father, my real father had loved me.

The glow was all over, it was warming me. The green grass looked gold again, like a shining tapestry.

The sunlight was real. It lit up the boy's hand in my arm, and gleamed softly in the gold of his ring with the Roland crest. It was strange to look at it, because of course I was a Roland myself now, whether anyone knew it or not. Then I remembered that someone did know, my other Father had said the Comtesse came down to sort it out. I thought of how I'd always liked her, and the way she had of really looking at me, and realized she didn't just know, she actually cared. Of course she did, she was my grandmother.

The grass was almost humming with light. I could hear little sounds now too, there were bees in the grass, and a blackbird calling, everything was coming back to life.

I remembered I'd walked behind the biers at my father's funeral, and knew he'd have been pleased. I hadn't been in the vault when André took the ring, but I had one of my own, the ring on my finger that was splintering the sunlight into sparkles of bright colour. That ring had been my father's too. He hadn't given it to me himself, how could he? But his son had. He'd put it into my hand right here in the grounds of Ancre. His son had wanted me to have it.

And that was a new thought that sent the whole lot dancing like bubbles in a glass of Champagne wine.

This boy walking beside me. This boy, who knew nothing of any of this, but loved me anyway, not because he was obliged to, but just because he did. This boy, who was mine to love and to tease and to teach and protect and to love, this boy.

He was my brother.

Twenty-Five

André de Roland

Extract from a letter to Elisabeth, Comtesse de Vallon,
dated 20 June 1639

Dear Madame,

Forgive this hasty note, but I must not lose a moment in contradicting any reports you may have of my impending execution. These, as you can see, are slightly inaccurate. Rest assured I am quite safe, and so is my dear J.

I would be grateful if you could find an opportunity of conveying this reassurance to the family of the Baron de Verdâme, who might otherwise be alarmed at what they have heard. I am especially anxious you should see Mlle Anne, whom I hold in the highest regard. You would like her, Grandmother, truly you would. She has endured dreadful hardships with great courage, and I should tell you she saved my own life.

Perhaps, however, you will feel this no great recommendation now you have heard other accounts of my activities. It is true I have been a little reticent as to their nature, but it has not been possible to write a great deal with security in letters that must pass through enemy territory. Please believe there is considerable exaggeration in the rumours, and that I have indeed passed the Occupation in as safe and careful a manner as is consistent with my duty.

There is at least this advantage in these latest events: that now the identity of my beloved J is known to the enemy there can be no further reason to conceal it in my letters. His name is Jacques Gilbert, and he is son to the Ancre ostler, whom you may remember from your visits here. He is grieving at present, for his father died as a result of our escape, but he remains my closest, best and dearest friend, and I know you too well to imagine you will allow the circumstances of his lowly birth to make the slightest difference to your reception of him when we join you at last . . .

Jacques Gilbert

He was worried she wouldn't want me because my father was a groom, I was worried she wouldn't want me because he wasn't. In fact she wrote back to say she remembered me very well and was looking forward to seeing me, so I understood she was going to keep on pretending.

Mother said she wouldn't be able to do it for ever, it was bound to come out soon. She said it wouldn't have mattered if the Spaniards hadn't come, I'd have gone for a soldier and probably never seen André again, but now we were together every day and sooner or later someone was going to look at us and notice. She said 'Wouldn't it be better to tell him yourself, my darling, before he finds out some other way?'

I didn't think it would actually, I was dreading him knowing. His family didn't want to acknowledge me, and it would put him in a horrid position. He'd probably go feeling guilty and wanting to do things to make up for it, and I didn't want that, I liked him loving me when he didn't have to. So I said we couldn't tell him without the Comtesse agreeing, I'd wait till I saw her in Paris, and Mother accepted that in the end. I think she was disappointed though, she wanted to be done with the lying for good and all. She must have had a miserable time all these years, all those feelings squashed up inside her and no one to talk to at all.

Still, we thought we'd get away with it a bit longer. I didn't look nearly so much like André these days, not now I'd got that scar and my hair was longer than his. No one knew about Father either, we put it about he'd been murdered by the enemy, and André allowed him to be buried in the Ancre graveyard with the others. People just accepted it, and gradually things got back to normal.

Only actually they weren't. Nothing was the same after that June, not even André himself. Killing that officer made a big difference to him, like he was ready to put some of the horror behind him and think about other things. He said it couldn't make up for what happened, nothing could do that, but whenever he got the memory of that awful grinning face swimming up in his mind he'd got another picture he could stick over it instead, of that same face screaming in agony, and it made the first a lot easier to bear. He certainly didn't thrash about and talk in his sleep any more, or if he did it was about Mlle Anne and something else entirely. She was all he thought about now. He kept writing her unbelievably long letters which he couldn't possibly send, her father would have killed him, but he said it made him feel better just to write them. One night I even found him sitting by the stream chewing one of his precious pencils, and he said he was writing poetry.

He still wanted to fight, of course, we all did, but that was maybe the biggest difference of all. We weren't content with little hit-and-run raids any more, we'd tasted the blood of real battles and we wanted more. We wanted to go the whole way and take back the Saillie.

It felt like the right time. There were hardly any reinforcements coming out of Artois these days, and we guessed Don

Francisco's superiors had got pissed off with his lack of success. Even his own men were fed up, and I couldn't blame them. On the morning we were supposed to be hanged, half Dax turned up just to annoy them, and the soldiers were really curling up with embarrassment. The sergeant did his best, he said 'You want a hanging, you can have one, I'll hang the last two people left in this Square,' but people only ran away laughing till there was no one left but a dog and Mlle Tissot, who was about a hundred and deaf.

They were ready to fall, we just knew they were, but we still needed outside help to drive them out. André said we'd get it, he said France was bound to help now and I thought he was right. Our armies were busy in Artois already, they were still dug in at Hesdin, and it seemed likely they'd think about us next, especially when word got round what we'd achieved.

I don't know much about politics, or I'd have known that was bollocks. What made the difference in the end wasn't anything to do with the armies or Hesdin or us. What made the difference was Mlle Anne.

Anne du Pré

Extract from her diary, dated 18 September 1639

I was dreading today, because everyone says the Comtesse de Vallon is terrifyingly eccentric, but now I know they only mean she *says what she thinks*. It is extraordinary, but I think I rather like it. At least I know where I stand.

The Hôtel de Roland is in the Marais and very grand. The salon must have had a hundred candles sparkling in crystal chandeliers, and the ceiling was painted to resemble a summer sky. Papa and I felt quite intimidated, but the Comtesse led us into her own apartment for a private audience, really almost in the style of a *ruelle*. Her bedroom is grand in a different way, intimate but beautifully furnished, and everything upholstered in pale blue or silver. I found myself wishing I had not worn yellow.

The Comtesse herself must be nearly fifty, but still looks exquisitely beautiful. Her hair is quite, quite silver, and so immaculately coiffed I could not help wondering how it stayed in place. She is very tiny, and André would tower over her if only he were here, but she has something Papa calls 'presence', and I certainly found her most alarming. After only two minutes of pleasantries she turned to Papa and said 'So, Monsieur, what is this I hear about your daughter being betrothed to my grandson?'

Poor Papa was covered in confusion. He said quickly that nothing had been formally agreed, and the Comtesse said at once 'Gracious heavens, man, I know *that*. I ask only because I hear rumours of an attachment, of which I am bound to say I know nothing. My servants say it is the talk of the taverns that on hearing the news of M. de Roland's projected execution this young lady actually fainted.'

Her voice is very pretty, like the tinkling of silver bells, but I felt she mocked me, and when her eyes slid round and pierced me I knew she expected me to lie. Well, I would not. I looked her in the face and said composedly 'That is quite true.'

She regarded me a moment, then sat back in her chair and said 'Ah.' I never knew so short a word could sound so long. Then she said 'Your acquaintance was very brief. Will you tell me what occasioned such a reaction?'

I saw she thought the worst, so I explained the circumstances of our rescue as best I could. She gave a little sigh, then said

'You will not believe this, Mademoiselle, but I had no idea of the life he was leading. I think perhaps I had better order him home.'

I remembered André saying 'I have responsibilities here,' and the way he looked when he said it. I said hesitantly 'I do not think he will come.'

She laughed, a wonderfully beautiful sound, and said 'I see you do know him after all. Perhaps your father might like to return to the company so you can share your confidences with me.'

Papa hesitated, but when she mentioned casually that Monsieur le Prince had said he might send 'young d'Enghien', my poor father could scarcely contain himself and rushed from the room with embarrassing haste. The Comtesse only smiled, and took up a sheaf of ragged papers from a table.

'Now, Mademoiselle, you will wonder at my needing to hear from you about my own grandson, so let me explain. When did this happen, this bad wound you mention?'

I told her, and she flicked dextrously through the pile of letters, extracted one and read it with a smile. She said 'He apologizes here for his long delay in writing by saying he has been rather unwell, then goes on to describe the thanksgiving service for the Dauphin. Now do you understand?'

Quite suddenly I did. She seems supremely self-possessed, but now I saw for the first time the anxiety in her blue eyes and the restlessness of her hands. He is her only grandson and she loves him. One of her sons is dead, the other might as well be. André is all she has left.

So I told her everything I could, and she was interested in every detail. She even asked about André's friends, and in particular the man he had called Jacques, as if everything dear to him is now dear to her too.

When I finished she was silent a long time, then stood and paced silently about the room like a tiny doll on wheels. At length she stopped and said 'Well, I cannot leave him there, Mademoiselle, he is our only heir. If he will not come until Dax is free, why then we must free Dax.'

I began to see the family resemblance with André. I said cautiously 'How?'

'It will not be easy,' said she. 'I have tried many times, but the Saillie is of little strategic value and no economic importance, it holds no more interest for Richelieu than my own back gardens. But he is no fool. He needs popular successes to keep the money flowing and Hesdin is exciting no one. If we can make Dax-Verdâme a popular cause, then M. le Cardinal might look on it with more favour.'

I reported eagerly that Jeanette's stories have been well received everywhere, and the song of *'Le Petit Oiseau'* is now to be heard in every alehouse in Paris.

The Comtesse sniffed. 'The alehouses, yes, but we must lift it into the salons, that is where the real business is done. And that is where I hoped you might help.'

I was puzzled, and when she came and sat beside me I became also a little apprehensive, but she only laughed and patted my hand.

'Paris loves a love story, Mademoiselle. That is how I have heard of this famous faint. It is a romantic little tale, and comes at just the right time. Paris adores *L'Astrée.* It goes to *Le Cid* and longs for a hero, it needs something to stir its passion, and we can give them that, you and I. I might, for example, take you to the Hôtel de Rambouillet tomorrow and ensure the story reaches a few of the right ears. The place is positively stuffed with poets, and we ought to inspire a sonnet or two, or perhaps a *canard.* What do you think, Mademoiselle? Will you play my game?'

I said cautiously that there was no betrothal.

'That is unimportant,' she said. 'That is a matter of business, this is an affair of the heart. But people will talk of you, Mademoiselle, and if nothing should happen when André returns then I am afraid you may look foolish. Indeed, it may harm your chances of making another match elsewhere. What do you say to that?'

I knew what Papa would say. Then I thought instead of André, and the way he had fought all those men just to save me. I remembered his voice when he said 'Anne,' and how it felt when he kissed me.

I said 'Do you really think this will help him?'

She shrugged. 'It will certainly reach the King. The pretty Monsieur le Grand will see to that, if I can manage to have speech with him. Yes, I think it will help.'

I took a deep breath. 'In that case, Madame, I will play your game.'

She was silent a moment, her fingers tapping on the back of my hand. 'You are a good child,' she said. 'Perhaps I should ask your father what he thinks.'

I knew what his answer would be. I said 'There is no need for that, Madame. I know the risk, and am quite content to proceed.'

She gave another peal of that delightful laughter. 'Bravo, Mademoiselle!' she said. 'You are quite right. We have left this war for too long in the hands of men, and it is time to see what the women can do.'

Stefan Ravel

Oh yes, Abbé, that's how it's done. There's nothing like a little popular appeal to reconcile people to a war and keep their minds off the price of bread. God knows how the old woman managed it, but there were tasteful little poems circulating in no time, along with a few *canards* that weren't, and an acrostic that was frankly obscene. The couriers used to bring them with our letters, and poor André didn't know where to look. Some grovelling scribbler even wrote a play about him, I believe, though I can't say I ever saw it. I doubt I was in it myself, Abbé, from all accounts it was young André de Roland fighting the whole war single-handed, and all for the love of a 'Mlle Celeste' who apparently looked strikingly like Mlle Anne.

I didn't grudge it him. He was still André back then, he never came the big hero with me. Marcel insisted on him taking over the leadership, saying he'd only done it himself till the kid had enough experience, but even that didn't go to his head. He wanted my advice more than ever, he'd sit and listen to me for hours, his eyes on my mouth as if he didn't want to miss a single word.

No, I saw the purpose of it all well enough, and a couple of days before Christmas it finally looked like paying off. I was sitting by the stream with Marcel that afternoon, skinning a brace of rabbits for the pot. He was much more relaxed these days, Marcel, though I can't say I felt the same about him after what he'd done. Oh yes, I knew what he was, Abbé, I'd suspected it for some time, but I'd never pretended to return his strange little passion, and I'd certainly never asked him to start driving away my friends. Still, it's hard to hate someone for giving you affection, and the man was a soldier and a comrade. Something else you might remember, Abbé, while you're sitting there with a face like a dead fish, is that the lad had no one else at all.

So there we were stripping away with frozen fingers when we suddenly heard the most extraordinary sounds. There were hooves, which meant nothing, we were expecting a courier back from Lucheux, but there was a delicate jingling mixed in with it, and above it all a light tenor voice singing '*Enfin la Beauté*' as if we were in a concert in the Louvre. We looked at each other, and stood to face the apparition that burst into the clearing in front of us.

The courier was Baudet, which was enough of an apparition in itself in my opinion, if the man got any hairier someone was going to use him to stuff a mattress. But beside him came a young man in scarlet and mauve astride a dazzlingly white horse, his sword clinking merrily against his spurs. His fair hair bounced under his plumed hat, and about his face was a dirty white bandage to cover his eyes. He was the one singing, carolling away as carelessly as a blind bird.

We blinked.

Baudet reined to a stop and jerked the bridle of his companion, who obediently halted beside him. 'Oh,' he said, peering from side to side as if hoping to see through the blindfold. 'Are we there?'

Baudet untied the bandage, explaining gruffly the man had been waiting at the Poulet Noir with a letter for André but would only deliver it into his own hands. The youth gazed at us with eyes of astonishing innocence, dismounted elegantly and bowed to us both, announcing himself as Crespin de Chouy, aide-de-camp to M. le Maréchal de la Meilleraye.

Meilleraye. I didn't know they'd given him a baton, but it made sense. A year ago he was just a mediocre soldier and famous only for being related to the Cardinal, but things were very different now. Charles de la Porte, Duc de la Meilleraye, Duc de Rethel and all the bloody rest of it, was the man who'd just taken Hesdin, and put France back on the map of Artois.

I wondered if he might be thinking of doing the same with Dax-Verdâme.

He was thinking about it all right, the letter told us that straight off, but it was only a vague idea, and de Chouy was meant to report back on the easiest way to do it.

Only there weren't any easy ways, which is why we were so valuable to the Spaniards in the first place. A siege was out of the question because we backed on to Artois, which meant the Spaniards could get supplies and reinforcements while our own troops sat outside and starved. Sneaking them in by the *gabelle* road wasn't going to work either, I mean no invading army wants to come in single file, not to mention having to leave their artillery and baggage behind. The only possible way was a straight frontal assault, but when de Chouy saw the cannon at the Gates he didn't seem to think they'd like that idea either.

'What if we hold one of the Gates?' said André in desperation. 'If we take the Dax Gate and spike the cannon, surely your troops could charge it then?'

De Chouy seemed to think that was a wonderful idea, but then he thought everything about André was wonderful, I think he'd been reading some of that awful guff the Comtesse had been circulating. He was taken aback by the hair at first, but obviously assumed it must be all right because this was the famous André de Roland. I even saw him looking doubtfully at his own long curls, like he was worrying he might be behind some new fashion. He was very young, of course, and probably on his first campaign. He found everything very exciting, even the Hermitage, he thought it must be wonderful fun to live like that. I didn't think he'd like it so much after two years.

But he was wonderful to us too, because he was something

from the outside world. We hadn't seen anybody like him in years, he was something we'd forgotten even existed. He stayed for supper, talked mysterious rumours about a lady called Ninon and asked us our opinions on *La Belle Alphrède*, and even André looked blank. We got him drunk as quickly as we could, but he only sang '*Chanson d'Amour*' with lots of dramatic gestures, and Stefan stared like he was an exotic animal in a show.

The most incredible thing was just him being here at all. It made us feel people outside were thinking and talking about us, and something might really be going to happen at last. I remember him leaving that night, just casually riding out of the Saillie and back to Paris like it was nothing. I remember the brave little tinkling of the bells on his harness that sounded in an odd kind of way like hope.

Stefan Ravel

Me, I was a little sceptical. A battle's something you plan when you know who's in charge for the season, how many men they've given you, and what the enemy are up to on their own account. You don't sit down and plan it six months in advance unless you've got a much deeper scheme going on somewhere, of which this is only a part. And with apologies for being tedious, I'm afraid I was right again.

We made a plan anyway, just to make sure it was possible. Taking the Gate wasn't difficult, the problem was holding the fucking thing against a thousand angry dons while our troops strolled up to join us. But once we'd got our heads round the fact this was actually a defensive action to hold that small strip of land by the Gate, then it became a whole lot simpler. We'd have a distraction at Verdâme to draw a load of the bastards off, then a barricade on the Dax-Verdâme Road and archers and musketeers in the woods to stop them coming back. We'd have a screen of pike and shot across the bottom of the Square to deter any stray dons around Dax, which left only the little matter of the three hundred in the barracks itself. And after a little thought we came up with a way to deal with that too.

It wasn't going to be easy. It was certainly going to take more men than our humble army could boast of, but we'd used civilians the night the Spaniards came and were quite ready to do it again. This time we'd have months to prepare and train them. This time we were going to do it right.

Or so we thought. At the end of January young de Chouy came trotting back, with a hook-nosed companion he intro-duced as de Saussay, a senior official on Châtillon's staff. Well, la Meilleraye was one thing, Châtillon quite another, and I started to get an uneasy feeling right then. De Chouy didn't seem so happy this time either, he had a rather subdued air about him and wouldn't stay for supper.

We soon found out why. When the visitors had bowed themselves off, André called the four of us together and broke the news with a face as white as his shirt. Châtillon loved the idea of us taking the Gate, unsurprisingly enough, but wanted us to hold it for an hour.

'Impossible,' said Marcel, his face even paler than André's. 'Civilians against trained troops, it would be murder.'

'I know,' said André wretchedly. 'But they need to minimize their losses, because they've got an onward battle to fight. Apparently we're just the start.'

'Arras?' I said. There'd been rumours about it for ages, it was the obvious target.

'They wouldn't bother with us for Arras,' said Marcel. 'They'd cross the border further east, we're miles out of the way. It'll be Béthune or Aire.'

'Good luck to them,' I said. 'If our troops come through here first, the dons will see exactly where they're headed, and it'll be St Omer all over again. They'll just send troops from Arras to reinforce Béthune.'

A flush of colour returned to André's face. 'Yes, that's exactly what they'll do – then we'll march east and invest Arras instead. That's it, Stefan, we're a distraction.'

Well, it's always nice to know where one stands in the scale of things. I said 'If they're worried about their losses taking this little patch they won't have enough men to take Arras.'

'Oh, they'll have another army about somewhere,' he said loftily, trying to look like Gustavus and Wallenstein rolled into one. 'We'll only be a tiny bit of it.'

'Yes,' I said. 'We'll be a small pile of corpses that need burying. An hour, little general. How can they possibly justify that?'

He grimaced. 'They're afraid the Spaniards will see them coming from that watchtower. There'll be no glacis, no earth-works to hide behind, they'll be riding in the open. The cannon could wipe them out before they get halfway across the fields.'

'The dons could wipe us out even quicker than that.'

He was silent.

'Lot of casualties, kid,' I said. 'We hold this for an hour you'll win your battle, but it might be the end of the Saillie.'

He knew it, my little general, he knew exactly what choice he had to make. He looked at me in sudden anguish, but I only shook my head. He was in command now, and that meant making the hard decisions for himself. I'd trained him for it over the years, and I'll admit I was interested to hear the result.

He screwed up his eyes, rubbed his hands over them, then slowly let them drop. 'Yes,' he said. 'I've got to order it, that's my duty. But I've also got to do all I can to limit the casualties and keep the people safe. That's my responsibility.'

Well, yes, I'm bound to say I agreed. Pity a few more officers haven't worked that one out, but that's not the kind of education a nobleman usually gets. This one I'd taught myself.

'All right,' I said. 'But the only way to do that is to reduce the time we need to hold the Gate.'

'I know,' he said. 'And the only way to do that is to take the watchtower.'

Colin Lefebvre

Seigneur told us straight. We were going to be relieved in the summer, but we'd got to fight like we'd never fought before, he needed every volunteer he could get. Wasn't a raid he was talking about, this was a battle, second Battle of Dax, and this time we'd got to win.

He got his volunteers all right, could have had everyone in the Saillie. We were up for it too, we Lefebvres, we were all in it. My dad was to lead the archers, there being no one to touch him now Durand was gone. Simone was on the barricade, my mum with the alley teams, and I was loading for the top marksmen. Not all we were doing neither, my dad and me had pike-heads to make for over a hundred, and that's a tall order with your regular work on top. An art to it, you know, pike, getting the crescent perfect so it won't impede the spear when it's sliding in but give you a good barb for disembowelling when you're coming out. I'm telling you, Forge was the busiest place in the Saillie that year, fire was working all night.

We were training all through the spring. André's friends on the outside sent us arms and powder, and we used to go over the Wall and practise on the plains of France so the Spaniards wouldn't be drawn by the sound of our fire. I had a whole marksmen's team of my own now, and Giles, Jacob and I used to have contests against each other, which my team nearly always won. I don't mean to boast about it, because Jacob was over seventy now and perhaps a little slower than he had been, while Giles had been very generous in giving me so many top men. I had Simon as my second, and I'd promoted Georges too, who was turning out a far better marksman than he'd ever been a loader. I'd have liked Margot as well, but André wanted her on the barricades with Roger. Roger was a little doubtful whether people like the senior famers would take orders from a woman, but André smiled and said 'Oh, I think they'll listen to Margot.'

They certainly did. The civilians were often training at the same time as us, and we could hear Margot's voice all over the fields. We went to talk to her about it once, because it really was very difficult trying to give our own instructions over Margot shouting 'That's the way, ladies, let the bastards have it where it hurts!' Giles was very charming, but Margot only laughed, and told him to save it for his floozies and let her get on with her job. Giles seemed a little distracted the rest of the afternoon. He kept looking over at Margot and fingering his moustache.

The whole army trained in those fields. Sometimes we even had the cavalry, so they could gallop in the open without trees in the way, and that was a splendid sight. We'd never had a full cavalry section before, and all kinds of people volunteered for it, even Bettremieu. Georges thought that was tremendously funny, he said being on a horse still wouldn't stop Bettremieu being wounded, but Marcel gave him a simply enormous animal to take his weight, and he honestly looked quite terrifying.

We were all out there. There were archers and crossbow-men, there was Bruno's knife team, and even a section of pike to protect the Gate. Stefan was training the pike with Pinhead, and sometimes he made them work with us to learn how long we needed for a reload. Stefan hadn't really changed very much. Watching him yelling at those pikemen brought back memories of him teaching our unit all those years ago, when we were a groom, a farmer's son, a black-smith, a merchant, and a child.

Now we were soldiers, and it was up to us.

Stefan Ravel

It might have been fun if only we hadn't got Châtillon in charge. I knew what the army thought about Châtillon even back then, and they were right. He couldn't make a decision to save his life, and more importantly he couldn't make one to save ours.

He wasn't even going to be there, he was crossing the border somewhere else. We were being left to some ambi-tious nobleman called the Comte de Gressy, who'd obviously bought himself the honour, since I'd never heard of him, and never met anyone who had. It still didn't stop Châtillon meddling. Come the spring, we got dispatches from the idiot every week.

It had to be very precise timing now. The troops would emerge from the cover of the beech forest about half an hour before dawn, then advance to just over a mile's distance of the Wall. This, of course, kept them nicely out of cannon range, because naturally they didn't want anyone getting hurt, or at least no one important. They'd wait there nice and safe till five o'clock, which is when we were meant to stage our attack, spiking the cannon and getting rid of those inconvenient guards on the Wall, who just might have noticed a whole French regiment thundering towards them over the plain. By ten past, they reckoned we'd be keeping the Gate Guards and cannon occupied, and it would be safe for them to go the last mile. If the theory worked we'd only have to hold that Gate for twenty-five minutes, but of course it all depended on the watchtower not spotting them coming at half past four and manning the Gate with the entire garrison before we even started. In other words, it all depended on our little Chevalier. He and Jacques were taking that one themselves.

That, at least, was the plan. I thought you might as well know it, Abbé, since it's not what happened, it's only what we poor innocents were expecting. We were expecting it a long time too. Spring crawled into summer, and all we had were endless picky messages from Châtillon. Young de Chouy came so often we actually got to know him quite well. He was a cheerful little beggar, always singing, we could hear him coming a mile off, and it was a sound we learned to dread.

He was singing that last day too. We weren't training that afternoon, we were all of us ready long ago, and becoming more than a little pissed off with the delay. We were lying about in the sun doing nothing, and André was actually asleep.

Then we heard it, the faint sound of someone singing in the distance, and a minute later the cheery jingle of light harness. André opened his eyes and groaned. I looked over to see de Chouy trotting happily towards us, waving a letter as if he expected us to be excited.

I said 'If it's another change of timing I'm going to stick it up his arse.'

Philippe d'Argenson, Comte de Gressy

Extract from plain text of letter to André de Roland, dated 2 June 1640

. . . It is quite definite. The Seigneur de Puységur returned from Soissons this afternoon, where he had speech with both His Majesty and M. le Cardinal, and the plan is finally approved. We are currently at Amiens, but M. le Maréchal desires the troops shall move within twelve days from this date. Our own force is to move sooner, and our intention is to be in Abbeville on 7 June, so that our assault will take place in the early hours of Friday 8th along the schedule of timing previously discussed.

Puységur is confident the ruse will work. As he told His Eminence, the Spaniards are convinced we dare not assault Arras. They have a saying to the effect that 'When the French take Arras, the mice will eat the cats!'

We will make them eat their own words, will we not? . . .

Stefan Ravel

So you've even got that, have you? My word, you are thorough. Fancy young André keeping it all that time. Still, I suppose it's reasonable, we'd been waiting for it long enough.

But do you know, it was almost a sad occasion in a way. Now the moment had finally come we all began to see what it was really going to mean. It was the end of the Occupation, the end of the army, we were suddenly going back to the real world. For one thing, I'd been eating at the expense of the Chevalier de Roland for some time now, but in just over a week I'd be back to worrying where my next meal was coming from.

I'm a soldier. A man like me, you don't get close to people, for the simple reason they're likely to get blown to fuck the minute you take your eyes off them, and sometimes even if you don't. Still, I'd been with this unit four years now, and that's a long time. I'll be honest with you, Abbé, I looked round that little bunch of men that afternoon and felt something almost like affection. Young André, perky, bright-eyed with excitement. Marcel, radiant with enthusiasm, eyes on my face, seeing the future as he wanted it to be, not the way it was. Even bloody-minded Jacques Gilbert and dopy Bernard Rouet, I almost felt as if I'd miss them. Sentimental balls, of course, but you know how it is, things seem different when you know you're going to lose them.

I wasn't the only one feeling that way. We had a little party on the last night to finish up our reserves of cider, but it was rather a subdued affair. Oh, people like Lefebvre were fine, the ones who'd only seen the war as a disruption of their routine, but there were one or two more thoughtful types who saw things differently. Mercier, who for the first time in his life had really been something. Libert, who'd been fully accepted as a Flamand among Frenchmen. Pepin, who most of us would normally have been chucking stones at. Leroux, who'd have to go back to doffing his hat and bowing to a master he'd always despised. Oh, there were a few of us, Abbé, a few.

I stuck it for as long as I could, then wandered outside for a little peace and privacy, the sound of singing following me out into the night air. I headed for that quiet spot behind the weapons outhouse, but heard movement as I approached it, and realized someone else had had the same idea.

It was André, and he was fencing all by himself in the dark. Thrust, parry, riposte, lunge in-out, and all against the empty air.

Well, I'd had a bit to drink, Abbé, maybe more than I should. I'd had a drink, there was unfinished business here, and the opportunity would never come again. I stepped out in front of him and drew my sword.

'Fancy a bout?'

He laughed politely.

'What's the matter? Think you're too good for me?' He was, of course, I've never denied it, but it wasn't everybody who'd risk fencing him at all.

He had the grace to look abashed. 'Well . . .'

'You beat me once, remember?' I said. 'This is my last chance at revenge.'

He grinned at me, the cocky bugger. 'Well, in that case . . .' He saluted and gave me *en garde*. 'But practice speed only, all right?'

'To start with,' I said, and smiled.

We plodded through the opening moves, and I was careful to give him my full attention.

'Why does it have to be your last chance?' he said, as we patted our blades against each other, civilized as little girls. 'There could be others.'

'Really?' I said, risking a thrust, and nipping back fast. 'Think you'll be up for an occasional afternoon's fencing with the local tanner, do you?'

He smoothly closed distance to engage me again. 'I might.'

'Not with this one, you won't,' I said. 'I'm giving up the tannery, I'm going to be a soldier.'

He did something complicated with his wrist and sent my sword flying harmlessly into the grass. 'So am I. We might be in the same regiment.'

I picked up my sword and wiped it on my breeches. 'That'll be nice. You can splash me as you gallop past.'

He waited patiently for me to resume position. 'It doesn't have to be like that.'

'Yes it does. I'll make appointé maybe, and anspessade if I live long enough, but that's as good as it gets.'

We resumed the bout. He was gentler for a moment, doubtless making allowances for my inferior skill, then said casually 'Yes, but if you come with us . . .'

I walloped his blade out of my face. 'I'm not coming with you.'

'Why not? You'd be much more independent. I'd be a Gentleman Volunteer, you'd only really be answering to me.' He was back on the attack again, dancing back and forwards, luring me out towards him.

I stayed right where I was. 'You want me to be your servant?'

'Of course not.' He kept distance, his blade tickling mine point-to-point. 'I'd still need your advice. You could do what you liked.'

I batted his blade away and stepped back. 'You don't know much about the army, do you, André?'

He bristled at once. 'My family has always been in the army.'

'Oh yes,' I said. 'You know what it looks like from horseback with a wagonload of servants following you around.

Come down in the mud sometime and I'll show you what it's really like.'

He was silent a moment, then offered his blade and we engaged again. 'Maybe that's why I need you. I'd like to understand those things, I'd be a better officer if I did.'

'Won't happen,' I said. 'Officers and men don't mix.'

'They can. We've proved that here, haven't we?'

'A year from now if you see me in the ranks you'll cut me dead.'

'Why would I do that?'

'You're a gentleman, aren't you?'

He came in hard at my chest. 'So? Why shouldn't a gentleman be friends with a soldier?'

I slammed my sword round and stopped him dead. 'Because.'

He stepped back, wiping the back of his arm across his face. 'I do wish you'd tell me.'

I looked at him seriously. 'No, you don't.'

He lowered his sword. 'I sometimes think you don't much like nobility.'

'I sometimes think you're right.'

'It's different in the army . . .'

'It's worse in the fucking army. There are more of the bastards to steer clear of, that's all.'

He sighed patronizingly. 'An officer has to give orders, it's his job . . .'

'All right,' I said, and touched his blade to draw him back into the bout. 'All right, here's a little story for you. A young man in the army at the siege of La Mothe, under heavy cannon fire all day. That night he got drunk.'

'You?'

'Not me,' I said, fencing him back to a safe distance. 'But

the lad got pissed enough to hit someone, and unfortunately it was his capitaine.'

'That's not so good,' he said. He was attacking again but his mind wasn't on it, he kept glancing up at my face.

'Not so good,' I agreed. 'So next day the capitaine made him run the gauntlet. You know what that is, my little officer?'

He nodded without looking up. 'You run between two ranks of men and they try to hit you as you pass.'

'Very good,' I said. 'You clearly have all the education an officer needs. This wasn't one of the worst either, no pike, only cudgels. The lad was popular, no one hit as hard as they might. The men either side of me never touched him at all.'

'You knew him?'

'A little,' I said conversationally. 'He was my brother.'

He stopped dead and stared at me. 'Stefan . . .'

I struck his blade hard with my own. 'We're bouting, damn you.'

He dropped his eyes and put his sword back into play. 'What happened?'

I fenced without speaking a moment, beating the memory down hard. 'He made it through. So the capitaine had him driven through again. And again. Until he died.'

I heard his intake of breath. 'I'm sorry. Oh, Stefan, I'm so . . .'

'You're not allowed to be sorry,' I said. 'You're an officer, remember? Your whole authority depends on it. So let's hear you justify what happened.'

'I can't, it's wrong . . .'

'It's legal. Justify it.'

'I won't.'

He stepped back, but I struck out hard at him, my point grazing right across his shirt. He stared at me in shock.

'Justify it,' I said, and lunged.

His sword smashed up to meet mine. 'You think I'd do something like that?'

'You'd have to. Discipline is all that stops the men tearing you in pieces. You'd do it, André, what makes you so fucking different?'

He didn't answer, he was too busy fighting me off. I lashed out again, but he was twisting away and back, his blade up square to block me, the impact jarring up my arm. I slid up close, driving hard against him, his feet slipping on the grass as he struggled to hold ground. I used my whole weight to shove him away, then swiped sharp after him. He ducked, but my guard glanced off his chin, sending him staggering backwards, out of control. I thrust forward at once, but he spun clean round for the parry, then leapt back, righting himself straight and shaking the hair out of his eyes. Then he was steady again, coming in fast, jabbing at me in sharp, crisp thrusts, I couldn't deflect quick enough, I was having to give ground. He was too good for me, the little bastard, he always was.

I backed off and half lowered my sword. 'Slow it down a little, will you?'

He was as into the fight as I was, his head jerked back in frustration, but he got a grip on himself, took a deep breath and slowed down.

I shot back up to combat speed and really let him have it. He stumbled in shock, his blade wavering on my outside line. I belted it right out and back, I opened him like a bloody butterfly and slammed him against the wall, forcing my guard up under his jaw, my left hand clamping on his wrist, twisting it hard until the sword fell out of his hand.

I held him there a moment, looking right into those disbelieving, furious eyes, but there was no satisfaction in it, Abbé, only a kind of sour disappointment. He was so easy to cheat, poor bugger, honour made him helpless as a child.

I said sadly 'You're no different, André. You're a gentleman all through.'

I sensed the movement just a second before the pain hit me, and next moment I was bent double on the ground, eyes screwed shut in the effort not to scream. It took me a moment to become aware of anything else, then I saw his feet step past my face and his hand reach down into the grass to retrieve his sword. I peered up and there he was above me, sword steady in his hand.

The little bastard had kneed me in the balls.

He looked down at me dispassionately. 'What was that about me being a gentleman?'

For a moment I'll admit to a twinge of alarm, then a little smile twitched the corners of his mouth, and I'm afraid I had to laugh. It was excruciating, but I couldn't help it. I coughed, retched, and said 'All right, so you're evil as well.'

He laughed too, the kid, he knelt down beside me and waited for my contortions to subside. 'I'm sorry. But you're wrong about me, Stefan, you really are.'

'Evidently.' I'd done the sensible thing and judged him by my experience, but the problem with André de Roland was he wasn't like anyone else I've ever known.

He said gently 'I'm sorry about your brother.'

I sat up rather gingerly and looked at him. There was a graze on his jaw where my guard had struck, but nothing in his eyes but concern.

I said 'I know,' and was surprised to find it was true.

We sat in silence a while. The singing from the Hermitage seemed to grow louder, accompanied by a rhythmic stamping of feet. I might have known it, they were at that stage of drunkenness, they'd started on that sodding '*Petit Oiseau*'.

I said 'They'll come looking for you in a minute.'

He nodded reluctantly and stood up. He sheathed his sword, turned half back towards me and said 'It's all right, I do understand.'

'What?'

He gave a tiny shrug. 'I can see why you won't want to know me in the army. I wouldn't either.'

I stood to brush myself down. 'Oh, I don't know, it might be entertaining.'

He was very still. 'You mean that?'

I said 'Yes, little general. I think I do.'

Twenty-Six

Père Gérard Benoît

The Second Battle of Dax took place on the morning of 8 June in the year of our Lord 1640.

There is little about the prosperity of our village to suggest the tragic conflict that once raged within its enclosing Wall, yet the signs are there if the patient visitor will look for them. The crosses either side of the Dax-Verdâme Road mark the place where the barricade once stood, and are a permanent memorial to the villagers who lost their lives there. Les Étoiles still stands, and its pockmarked walls bear witness to the savagery of the battle which raged in its environs, while two crossed pike take pride of place about the fireplace inside the Quatre Corbeaux. The stables where so many of our brave young men met their end have long since been pulled down, and a new alehouse to welcome travellers erected in their place, yet the sign above its door gives it the name Le Tireur d'Élite, and the painting is clearly recognizable as that of a marksman in the act of firing a musket.

Our village inn, Le Soleil Splendide, has been restored to its former condition, save only for the fine back gates, which are of decorated wrought iron, and represent the work of our own village smith, Colin Lefebvre. Of the infamous watchtower there is now no trace, and with it has gone the only tangible memorial to the achievements of our Seigneur on that most desperate morning. Neither is there anything to mark the scene of the last stand at our Gate. Nothing is there now but our own Wall, seemingly unmarked and unchanged by time. The embrasures which once housed mighty cannon now enclose only baskets of flowers, while the great Gate of Dax stands forever open, revealing the green plains of Picardie stretching away to the beech forest on the horizon. These things are all that remain to show how André de Roland, Sieur of Dax, fought alone against his enemies to win our freedom, and perhaps, in the end, they are the memorial that would have pleased him most.

Carlos Corvacho

Funny kind of mood there was those days, almost expectant, if you know what I mean, and people going quiet when they saw us coming. My Capitán took to nosing round the woods again, said he was hunting, but I guessed he thought the rebels might be back, and was keeping his eyes open for signs of activity.

That's what he was doing that last day too. The Thursday, this would have been, Señor, 7 June. I was with him that afternoon, and it happened we picked up the trace of a wild boar. We followed it all the way into the north-eastern corner of the Forest of Verdâme, then the beast broke cover right in front of us and went belting off towards this great rocky mound on our right.

'Now we have him, Carlos,' says my Capitán. 'He can't climb that.' So we go plunging after it, but when we get to the knoll it's completely disappeared. 'That's interesting,' says my Capitán, then suddenly he exclaims, and when I join him I see why. There were these two great rocks like cliffs, Señor, only over-lapping very slightly, like the two halves of a kissing gate, so there was actually a little path between them. A well-worn path, by the look of it, and wide enough to take a full-grown boar. There were hoof prints as well as boot tracks. Horses.

'Very interesting indeed,' says my Capitán, and guides his horse carefully through. And there it is, this distinct track, leading away bold as anything off towards the east Wall. So we follow it quite a way until we see the gorge coming up and think we're going to have to turn back, but that's when we get the really big surprise. Once we get to the brink, there's suddenly no gorge at all. There's been some kind of landslide at one time, Señor, and there's this one part of the ravine where it's almost filled in, you could ride a horse right across it. It was steep down and up again, and very narrow, a little like a single-track bridge if you take my meaning, but we rode over it with no trouble at all.

We knew what we'd found then. Once the gorge was crossed, there was nothing to stop a man riding on through the forest and out into France where the Wall stopped. The Capitán reckoned the rebels hadn't got a new base at all, they were simply living in France and nipping in and out when they felt like it.

'Not much we can do about that then, is there, Señor?' says I.

'Is there not?' says my gentleman, with a little smile. 'If we picket this road secretly, who knows what we might catch?'

And at that moment, Señor, at that very moment, we hear the sound of a horse approaching from the east, and faint in the air we hear a man singing.

Jacques Gilbert

The light died very slowly that day.

It was still warm in the early evening, and the sun was giving that sort of gentle, mellow light that colours everything like a stained-glass window. Stefan was wearing a deep-red shirt, and it blazed up and made him look like one of the rougher apostles. The grass was that kind of rich, golden green that almost hurts your eyes, and the trees glowed like dark fire.

Everything was quiet. There wasn't any more training going on, there wasn't any point, we were ready, and it was now. We were waiting in a half-hearted kind of way to see if Crespin was going to bring any last-minute instructions, but we didn't really expect him, it felt like that was over and done. People were spending last time with their families, or just sitting chatting with their friends, but all speaking in low voices, like we were in church.

A blackbird started up singing when the light began to fade. It stuck itself high in a beech tree where everyone could see it, and sang and trilled away for ages like it was giving us a concert. The boy was sitting hunched over a last letter to Anne, and I remember him lifting his head to listen, the glow of the sun warm on his face. A bit of me wondered if I oughtn't to be telling him the truth, and how I'd feel if he died without ever knowing I was his brother, then I told myself if he died I was bloody well going to die too, and not worry about any of that old stuff, the things that happened before we were either of us born. What mattered was what was happening now, these summer evening moments that felt like the last there'd ever be.

Some of the men were strolling into the woods with women, and Stefan actually took two. I remember Marcel looking after them, something sad in his eyes. Giles was away longer than anyone, and when he emerged again he hadn't got his usual smug expression, he was looking sort of dazed, and holding Margot's hand. I could have done the same thing myself, I suppose, but I somehow didn't fancy it. I'd got this strange kind of peaceful feeling coming over me, like when you've just come out of Confession, feeling you never want to do anything bad ever again. Normally that only lasts about two minutes, but this evening I felt like it might last for ever, however long for ever was going to be.

After a while, people started to drift off to their homes, or where they needed to be for the start of the action, until in the end there was nobody left but us, and the light was gone at last. It's funny, I kept feeling the others were somehow still there with us. I could almost hear the ghost of that blackbird singing in the dark.

Carlos Corvacho

It's the letter gets my Capitán most excited, Señor, but it's all in code, and the courier in no state to tell us anything, being deep unconscious from being knocked off his horse by my boar-spear. It's coming on dark too, and no time to hang around, so we bundle him up on my horse and ride back fast as we can to the barracks.

My gentleman locks himself away with the Colonel, and they spend hours poring over that cipher with no result at all. Then the courier starts stirring at last, so we douse him with cold water till he starts to mumble, then our officers take turns at him, demanding to know who the letter was for and what was in it. We were sure he knew something, Señor, the use of the code told us that. A code's no good unless you've got people writing to each other regular; it had to be one of a series. The courier had to be regular too, he knew exactly where he was going, he should be able to tell us all we wanted to know.

Well, able he may have been, but willing he was not. A

very young man he was, very frightened, but very brave. He claimed he was only a courier, he knew nothing of what was in the letter or how to find the recipient, he said they always came to meet him on the road, which we didn't believe for a moment, Señor, the timing would have been impossible. So the Capitán keeps on asking, until at last the man says 'I tell you, I don't know, I'm not important enough, the Maréchal would never confide in someone like me.'

'The Maréchal?' says the Colonel.

The man shuts his mouth fast, but now we know it's serious. There's an army out there somewhere in communication with our rebels, and that can only be bad for us.

'Put him to the question,' says the Colonel. 'Now.'

Jacques Gilbert

We were in the Forge by midnight. The wagons were already in place, one laden with barrels outside Les Étoiles, and two filled with pitch and straw standing innocently by the bakery. Everything looked ready.

We were just sitting down to eat when Arnould Rousseau came shambling in. He scrabbled on his wig at sight of Mme Lefebvre, refused an offer of lentil soup with a sort of shudder, and said 'Rope's in place, and the password's San Isidoro of Sevilla. Bloody silly, but there it is. I picked it up twice, I'm quite sure.'

He was a miracle, Arnould, he really was. He'd spent the last months wandering all over the south wing of the barracks to get the information we needed, he'd gone everywhere bringing food to people who'd never asked for it, but the Spaniards just thought he was mad and left him alone. I could understand that actually, I mean when someone cooks as well as Arnould you don't bother about little things like him being insane.

There was nothing to do after he'd gone, so we changed into our Spanish dress and sat in the Forge to wait. It was warm in there, and I was feeling almost drowsy as I watched Colin hammering. The Spaniards might not buy the spit he was making for them but someone would, people will always want iron.

The boy was staring into the fire without blinking; it made my eyeballs feel dry just to watch him. The light was flickering over his face, and I found myself remembering a night four years ago, and a twelve-year-old boy watching the burning of his home. I realized he'd made a promise all the way back then, and tonight was the night we were going to make it good.

Carlos Corvacho

My gentleman never could bear torture, especially the rack, he'd a real horror of it. He came striding into his office, and I only just got a basin to him in time.

He wiped his face, clenched the sides of the basin, and said 'He is crying for his mother.'

I said 'Why don't you go to bed now, Señor? The Colonel's in charge, isn't he? '

The Colonel never missed an interrogation, Señor, he'd quite a fascination with them. He wrote a poem once called 'The Mastery of the Body', all about the dialogue during torture between the soul and body. I'm told it's very moving.

My gentleman went to the mirror to adjust himself and smooth his moustache.

'There are nearly four hundred men in this garrison, Carlos, two at the Château, and two more at Verdâme, to say nothing of those billeted around the villages, and the wives and followers. Would you have them all die because I had not the stomach to hurt an enemy soldier?'

He was a very fine officer, my Capitán. A fine man.

I said 'No, Señor.'

He said 'No.' He straightened his ruff, pulled down his sleeves, and patted down his hair, carefully arranging it to hide that hateful little scar.

The village clock struck half after three. My gentleman took one step to the door, and then the whole floor seemed to shake, Señor, it juddered and went still. The little vase of lilies went down bang on his desk, spilling water all over his papers. In the distance we heard something like a great boom.

Jacques Gilbert

We were waiting in the little back yard when it came. There was this distant rumbling, the ground trembled, and the sky lit up in a purple flash from the direction of Verdâme. It must have been a belter of an explosion for us to feel it this far away, but then I suppose it would be. We'd blown up the Verdâme barracks.

M. Lefebvre hoisted me so I could scramble on to the roof, then the boy after me. We crept to the barracks wall, keeping low so as not to make an obvious lump against the sky. The knotted rope was there, hanging down just as it ought to be, practically invisible next to the decorative stone piping. It smelt of rotten cabbage too, which wasn't surprising since we'd smuggled it in to Arnould by tying it round a cartload of vegetables. We crouched beside it, waiting.

A crash below told us the courtyard gates were opening, and a minute later the first horsemen came galloping out. There were more even than we'd hoped, maybe even a hundred, all heading for Verdâme and safely out of our way. Better still, there was an imposing figure in bright blue at the head of them, so Don Francisco was leading them himself. It would have been nice if d'Estrada had gone too, but I suppose you can't have everything.

We waited till the first of them made a screen between us and the Gate Guards, then the boy was up and climbing, with me hard behind. It was only a short haul to the third storey from the Forge roof, and in ten seconds the boy's legs were vanishing through the window. Two more knots up, and I was at the sill myself and wriggling through to join him in the store-room. We hauled the rope inside, then paused a second to catch our breath and straighten our clothes.

We'd known about the storeroom, of course, but it still felt unfamiliar and frightening, especially in the dark. I remember getting a sudden panic this mightn't be the right room at all, we could be standing here brushing ourselves down in somebody's bedroom and they were watching us thinking we were mad. Then as my eyes adjusted to the darkness I saw drums piled on the floor, a rack of pipes and flutes, and a load of tall thin things wrapped in canvas I guessed were flags. Arnould had got it right this time, and we were safe.

We could hear noises on the floor below us, footsteps and doors opening and voices, and guessed a lot of people must have been woken by the explosion. There were company officers living all over that floor, clerks, barbers, surgeons, musicians, and it sounded like every one of them was up and about. At least it seemed quiet outside our own door, so after pressing our ears against it for a moment we pushed it open and stepped out.

The third floor was a barren sort of place, mainly stores and servants and defaulters' cells, and there was nothing to see but a landing of rough bare boards and a load of doors like the one we'd just come out of. There were a few windows on the courtyard side, all of that thick glass with swirly round bumps that make you think of women's breasts, but nothing else, just dirty walls. There wasn't much light either, just two sconces for the whole landing, but it was bright enough to see the boy's face. He was astonishingly calm, and I felt sort of shut out and on my own.

We started walking towards the tower room, our boots seeming to crash on the boards at every step. I was counting the doors we passed, waiting for the sixth, the one with the little grille. Third door, fourth, and a girl started up laughing in a room behind us and my heart jumped halfway into my throat, fifth door, but then the boy stopped in front of me and we were there. I suddenly didn't feel ready, I wanted more time, I needed to remember what we'd got to do, but the boy's hand was raised, he was knocking on the door and it was too late.

A gruff voice from the other side demanded '*Contraseña?*'

The boy's mouth opened, then I saw a curious desperation come over his face and realized he'd forgotten the password. It's funny, but that made me feel better, it's like he was human after all.

I said 'San Isidoro de Sevilla.' He grinned at me in relief, and I tried to grin back. My cheekbones felt stiff, like I hadn't used them in ages.

The voice said 'Fucking idiot, that was yesterday.'

The shock was awful, and I found myself thinking stupidly we ought to have thought of that, they probably changed it at midnight. The next second the door was being unlocked anyway, and a laughing soldier opened it to let us in.

I suppose it's just human nature. Officers forget about that when they come up with these rules for security, they forget it's ordinary people who've got to carry them out, and no one takes them seriously when it's stupid things like having a password inside your own barracks. So the man just said 'Idiots!' in a friendly kind of way, and that was it, we stepped inside and André closed the door with his left hand. His knife was in his right.

As he thrust up from under his cloak, I moved clear into the room, which is when I got my next shock, because there was a second guard sitting on the table, his grin fading as he took in what was happening. Arnould had guessed only one, because the soldiers used to moan what a lonely job it was, but there was this other man with his mouth opening to yell and I hadn't even got my knife ready. I punched him hard as I could on the jaw, and he crashed back against the wall. André jumped round in alarm, and a second later a voice called down from beyond the wooden steps. The guard in the watchtower was asking what was up.

I had a hand over my man's mouth now, and finished the job with my knife, while André called up in his gruffest voice 'Fucking idiot!' then laughed. The guard above us laughed in return and went quiet.

So did we. There wasn't even a door between him and us.

We bundled the bodies quickly under the table and stood staring at the door in silence, wondering how long before four o'clock when the relief came. My breathing seemed to take ages to slow down, I felt like the guard in the tower would hear it. I was hot too, we'd got those thick black Spanish coats on over our shirts, and I felt a line of sweat trickling down the side of my face. I glanced at André and saw he was the same, his chest was heaving and his upper lip damp.

He saw me looking, wiped it with the back of his hand and gave me a rueful little smile.

I smiled back, and suddenly it was just him and me again, waiting for an ambush like we'd done scores of times over the years. I got control of my breathing, wiped my palm down my breeches, adjusted my grip on the knife and stared firmly at the door. The wood was grey and scratchy and the knots black with age. One looked like the face of a man with a beard.

There were footsteps coming up the corridor, then a sharp knock on the door. André cleared his throat and asked for the password, and they actually said the same as we did, they said 'San Isidoro', so we laughed and called them idiots, then let them through the door and killed them. I don't want to say any more about that, because actually it was horrid. They were just ordinary people like us, they made mistakes and joked about it, they were men I'd have got on with. But we'd got no choice. There wasn't time to go tying them up and gagging them, we'd got no choice.

There was only the guard in the tower left. We went up the rickety steps that led to the roof and along the wooden tunnel, then there in front of us was the tower ladder, disappearing up into a round hole in the platform where the guard stood. On the other side of the ladder was the door on to the roof that had scared us so much when that man came out to piss.

I didn't use the password, it felt silly, I just called up '¡Hola!' and the guard called it back, and next minute his shoes and stockings appeared in the opening as he started to climb down. He was expecting it, of course, he knew it had gone four, he'd heard voices in the anteroom and thought it was his relief arriving, he wasn't thinking about anything except getting back to his mess, and maybe having a drink before grabbing a bit of sleep. He climbed down like you'd expect, facing the ladder and with his back to us, it was the easiest kill we'd ever made. Then the boy was swinging himself up like a monkey up a tree, and I unbolted the door on the other side and stepped out on to the roof.

The wind hit me at once. I sheltered behind one of those little mock towers to fumble the cords out of my pockets, then put my head down and walked quickly towards the rear, the bit looking down on the south end of the Backs. The stone lions were where we'd remembered, so I lowered the weighted cord into the dark. A minute later there was a tug on the end, I hauled it back up and there was the first rope ladder. There was something else attached to the top rung and that was a small flask, tied on by the neck. It was a lovely touch, that flask. It was Giles giving me a drink, like having him next to me saying 'Well done.' I had a quick slug and the spirit shot into my head, giving me a great rush of something as I realized what we'd achieved.

I looped the ladder round the first lion, tied the flask on to the cord and lowered it down again to Giles. I couldn't see him in the dark, but it made all the difference knowing he was there. We got the other two ladders up, I secured them on the last two lions, and that was our escape route in place. It was also the way up for Giles' men, and that was a good feeling too. They weren't coming till just before five, they couldn't do it till Bruno's team had taken out the back gate guards, but it made me feel help was on the way.

I set off back to the tower, but the boy was already out, he was standing by the door with his hands in his pockets and an odd little smile on his face. I went to him quickly, but he didn't say anything, he just took my arm and said 'Come and look, Jacques. Just look.'

I followed him up to the platform. It was a really rubbish

bit of work, that tower, with two of us on the ladder it felt like the whole thing was wobbling. I squeezed halfway through the hole at the top till I'd run out of ladder to stand on, then gripped the flagpole that went all the way up through the roof, and hauled myself on to the platform. The boy didn't even look round as I came up, he was pressed against the wall, staring through one of those tiny little slits of windows. I stood next to him, found another slit and peered through.

I couldn't see anything at first. It was still dark, of course, and it took me a minute to get my bearings and work out what I was seeing through a hole that small. Then I saw I'd got a view right over the plain and the beech forest on the horizon.

'Look,' said the boy. 'Look at the forest.'

It was moving. It's like the edges of it were spreading, the way a pool of ink does when you spill it on a table, it was sort of creeping out and towards us.

'They're coming,' said the boy.

There was a great body of men advancing towards us. There was one pool putting more and more distance between itself and the others every minute, and I guessed they'd be the cavalry. Behind them came the infantry, and that really sluggish sort of mass crawling along behind would be the artillery and baggage wagons and all that stuff. It was an army, a real French army, and it was coming for us.

I reached out my hand blindly into the space on my right, and somehow the boy found it, he grabbed and squeezed it tightly. We hadn't been forgotten. We hadn't been abandoned after all. We stood side by side in the dark and watched as our own country came for us at last.

I went through the Forge into the Backs to give Giles the flag. It had taken Mother weeks to make, but it was a proper regimental one, plain white with the arms of our Colonel-in-chief in red, and we wanted it to be a surprise for André. We knew the battle would be credited to the real French army, you see, but it didn't seem fair for some other regiment's flag to fly over Dax when we had a proper army of our own.

We honestly did feel like one that morning. I crossed the Backs to the south alley, went through the back gate into the Thibault farm, and found Simon and Georges already waiting. We crossed the farm to the far wall, where the rest of the team were standing by the siege ladders. There was one for my marksmen, which would take us directly on to the roof of the stables, and two next to it for the ground troops, who'd be hiding in the barn behind. We'd considered the barn for our own position, because it was bigger and a few feet higher, but the sight-lines to the Gate were no good, you see, we'd tried it.

There was a little stir in the crowd, then Stefan strolled to the front, returned safely from his mission in Verdâme. I think we all felt a little better at the sight of him. He looked expressionlessly at me, and said 'Fucking good bang, wasn't it?'

I always found it difficult to think of things to say to Stefan, but I had my team behind me, and didn't quite like to look feeble in front of them. I said 'And we're going to make some fucking good bangs of our own.'

He grinned and gave me a wink. I could see his face quite clearly. The sky was lightening, and dawn was on the way.

He broke just before dawn.

It often happens about then, Señor, it's a popular time, but of course my Capitán was in charge now, and he knew how to handle these things. What it is, Señor, things like the rack do a man so much damage that in the end his body's quite mashed up, and the pain doesn't stop even when the rack does. Now that's no good to us, there's no incentive to talk when it's like that, so as soon as the Colonel left we tried a little bout of *tortura del'agua* instead. Now, the water torture's much more effective, because your man goes through all the terror of drowning, then you give him a little break to think about it before you lay him back down and start pouring it in again.

So that's what we did here. A little after four the man fainted again, and the surgeon said the heart was in trouble, so we cleaned up the vomit, gave him wine and a priest, got a blanket over him, and let him rest. Then at maybe half past my Capitán said it was time to resume, and I took the blanket away.

That's what did it, Señor. He was clutching at that blanket like it was his mother, begging me not to take it, quite moving it was really. Muños comes for him, and he starts grabbing at the chaplain to protect him, and the priest gets out of it fast, but my Capitán makes us all stand back, then soothes the man and says no one will hurt him if he just tells us a few things we want to know.

So gradually he does. He gives his name as de Chouy, and says the letter's for de Roland himself, though he doesn't know where to find him, says he was to wait in the church until he was approached. My Capitán asks what the letter says, and the fellow says he doesn't know, but it's from someone called the Comte de Gressy, and he thinks there's a battle planned.

'When are they coming?' asks my Capitán. He's holding the man's hand, but he's clutching it tightly, Señor, I see he's on edge.

The man lies still a moment then says faintly 'What day is it?'

'Friday,' says my Capitán. 'When will they come?'

De Chouy actually gave us a little smile. 'Monday,' he said. Then he's gasping again, and his face turning blue, and the surgeon says we'd better have the priest back fast.

The Capitán swore like one of our own troopers, which was most unlike him, most. Then he's striding back fast to his office, snapping out orders on the way. He sends a cabo to Verdâme to alert the Colonel, and a clerk to prepare a dispatch for Béthune, then orders the whole barracks on to full alert immediately.

'It's not till Monday, Señor,' I point out.

'I don't believe it,' says the Capitán. 'If it were Monday, why the devil didn't he tell us before, and save himself the agony? It's sooner, Carlos, I'm sure of it. Get me that letter.'

I couldn't see the point in it myself, Señor, they'd already tried the cipher and got nowhere, but I fetched it for him, and he sat down at his desk to decode it.

'We know a lot more now,' he said. 'Now we'll crack it. See this first word? Nine letters. If the letter's for de Roland then that could be 'Chevalier', and if it is – oh, look here, Carlos, here's those same two 'Ch' letters again in a five-letter word. The man's name was de Chouy, wasn't it? If that's his name, and it looks like it, the 'e' matches for 'de', then we've got all the vowels, we've got the 'y', the 'l', the 'r', the 'v' and the 'd'. Then there's a single letter here, we know it's not 'a', it's not 'y', it'll be 'M' for Monsieur. We're off.'

He didn't say another word, just sat scribbling as if our lives depended on it, which perhaps in a way they did.

Philippe d'Argenson, Comte de Gressy

Plain text of letter to André de Roland, dated 6 June 1640

Chevalier,

Forgive the extreme lateness of this message, but M. le Maréchal has expressed further concern as to how we might guarantee the safety of our troops. I therefore desire that just before the hour of our final advance your men should dip the flag in order to show beyond doubt that your assault has commenced and it is safe for our cavalry to proceed.

Should there be any serious obstacle to this, please return de Chouy to us *immediately*, instructing him to ride hard through the night to ensure he reaches us before the appointed hour of our departure. Should we hear nothing, we will assume all is well and wait on your signal before the advance.

May God prosper us in our venture!

D'Argenson

Carlos Corvacho

I see you've got the letter, Señor, you know what it said. It didn't make a lot of sense at the time, but what troubled my Capitán was this de Gressy saying de Chouy needed to ride hard to reach them in time. Now that needn't mean much, because if the army was in Paris the attack might be days away. But, says my Capitán, what if they're in Doullens, what then? It could be this very morning.

Then this business about 'dipping the flag', that threw us completely. We couldn't think where the rebels would find to fly a flag that would be visible outside the Wall. The Capitán sent men off right away to look at the church towers, but those were the only places we could think of that could possibly be high enough.

'Unless,' says my Capitán suddenly. 'Unless . . .'

Jacques Gilbert

The army came to a halt at quarter to five, and we knew that must be the mile mark. It looked a lot further to me, but André said they must know what they were doing, and what mattered was they were in position for our attack to start at five. We were free to leave now. No one was due up to the tower again till eight, and Giles would be joining us on the roof in ten minutes.

We peeled ourselves away from the windows, then André started backwards down the ladder. I'd only gone a couple of rungs after him when I heard footsteps behind me, and twisted to see a soldier coming down the tunnel ahead of us, and the bastard already drawing his sword. Behind him was d'Estrada himself.

They'd been forewarned, of course, they'd have seen there were no guards in the anteroom, they didn't need to recognize us to guess we were the enemy. That servant of d'Estrada's, Corvacho, his sword was already clear of his belt, his arm starting back for the lunge.

And the boy hadn't heard them. I couldn't believe it, he was almost on the ground and still hadn't turned round. I let go the ladder and dropped down hard just as Corvacho lunged full at André's back. I deflected the blade all right, there was this awful, deep stabbing pain slicing into my thigh, the shock of it was frightful, my leg just crumpled under me and I crashed down hard on the floor. I heard André landing behind me, and had just enough sense to shove him back and away as I rolled aside from Corvacho's second thrust. He was coming in again, I was furiously trying to slide backwards, then the boy's sword flashed out from behind me and Corvacho flinched away, stepping back hastily into d'Estrada. I was huddled uselessly on the floor between them and hadn't even been able to draw my sword.

For a second we all stared at each other, and no one moved. André stood firm behind me, his sword levelled at the Spaniards over my body, and Corvacho didn't dare come any nearer. I expect d'Estrada would have, but he couldn't get past Corvacho, the space between ladder and wall was only wide enough for one man at a time. I worked myself up on to my knees, but didn't think I could stand yet, my left leg was throbbing, and there was blood oozing thickly through my breeches. I crawled backwards another foot, forcing André towards the door to the roof.

'Get out,' I said to him. 'The door, now!'

Corvacho thrust forward again, but André drove him back. They were fighting over my body, and I realized that as long as I stayed there the boy was safe. Even if I died, they'd have to climb over me before they could touch him.

'Get on the roof, André,' I said. I clutched the side of the ladder above my head and hauled myself somehow to my feet. 'I'll hold here.' I leant against the wall and drew my sword.

I heard his intake of breath behind me, but felt the cold air on my back as he opened the door. I moved back towards it, my sword still directed against Corvacho, but he came on after me, and behind him d'Estrada.

The edge of the doorway banged into my shoulder, and I knew I mustn't go any further. André was on the roof, he could get to the ladders if I stayed here one more minute. I squared myself in the doorway and kept my blade levelled. I wasn't very steady, to be honest, the pain was terrible, but I'd got a strange kind of elation pumping through me, I felt sort of big and heroic.

Then there was André's hand on my shoulder, and he jerked me right back and out on to the roof. I stumbled at the step and my leg just gave up and folded underneath me, dumping me down hard on the stone. He yanked me clear of the doorway, but Corvacho was coming through after me and the boy threw himself at him at once, the blades clashing together as Corvacho flung up a parry just in time. It was weak, though, *faible* to *faible*, and André disengaged smoothly for the lunge, but Corvacho had had enough, he was backing away in panic. I screamed at the boy to run, but he wasn't going to leave me, he was just standing there, then d'Estrada was through the doorway with his own sword drawn and it was all too bloody late.

D'Estrada looked at André, then took a step forward, gently guiding Corvacho out of his way with his blade. He might as well have said 'Mine,' and be done with it. André stepped back clear to give him more space.

Corvacho turned on me, but d'Estrada said sharply 'No!' and actually gave me a little nod. Maybe it's because I was down already, maybe he thought he owed me my life because of last time, but he obviously didn't feel the same about André, and as he turned to follow him his eyes sort of glittered.

André moved deeper on to the roof, and they started

circling round each other like wrestlers at a fair. I pulled out my handkerchief and started binding my leg. The sword had come out clean, there was a neat flap of skin I could stick back over the wound and hold with the bandage.

'In false colours, Chevalier?' said d'Estrada.

The boy looked down at his black coat with its red Burgundy cross, then actually lowered his sword to remove it. D'Estrada smiled, then took off his cloak and flung it carelessly to Corvacho. In their shirtsleeves, they weren't a Spaniard and a Frenchman any more, they were just two gentlemen who were going to fight a duel to the death. Corvacho actually came and leant against the parapet to watch. He folded his arms, looked down at me, and said pleasantly 'Now we shall see.'

I thought 'You'll see all right, you smug bastard, you haven't the smallest idea what the boy can do,' then I looked over at André, and felt an odd flutter of panic. He still had that sort of suppressed eagerness he always had before a bout, but he looked nervous, there was a sense of alarm like he knew something I didn't. He went ahead anyway, he saluted, tapped d'Estrada's blade lightly with his own, and said '*En garde.*' D'Estrada took up position, and then of course I finally saw.

We'd never seen d'Estrada with a sword in his hand before, except that once when I'd watched him on the drive at Ancre. I'd known there was something odd at the time, but never understood why, it didn't seem important back then. I'd had another chance on the Back Road two years later, when I'd seen him facing André and thought he looked like a mirror image. Of course he bloody did. André wore his sword on his left hip, but d'Estrada wore his on the right. The bastard was left-handed.

I felt really sick. We hadn't known, we'd never even tried fencing that way, whereas d'Estrada must have fought right-handed men every day, it's what he was used to. All those years of the boy's training were suddenly useless.

Corvacho was smiling.

Carlos Corvacho

Oh yes, Señor, I thought it would all be over in a minute, it often was when an opponent was surprised by my gentleman's little peculiarity. Still, my Capitán had been looking forward to this a long time, and I hoped your Chevalier wasn't going to disappoint him.

In fairness, I have to say he didn't. My Capitán was gentle to start with, giving him a nice sense of security, but the Chevalier came straight in at him, fast and furious, trying to disarm my gentleman before he had time to build an attack. That's not a bad ploy when you're up against a better swordsman than yourself, but of course my Capitán was ready for that. Oh yes, he took a wee bit of a step back to collect himself, but that was only him thinking, Señor, he did a lot of that in a bout, he fought with his mind as well as his blade. Then he came in himself, Señor, none of that wild slashing with my Capitán, it was all in the wrist, tight into the body, quick, light jabs, but all the while he was closing distance, dancing forward inch by inch and the Chevalier backing further and further away. Then it was stamp and in, a nice clean body lunge -

Jacques Gilbert

– and the boy twisted away, did a full turn and his blade zipped straight at d'Estrada, touched him too, just the inside of his arm, but a real touch and close to the chest. D'Estrada's face was quite something, and I wondered how long it had been since anyone actually did that.

I daren't get too hopeful. André was fencing well, but he couldn't do his best stuff. He was fine with defence, he'd deflected left-handed angles every time he'd fought more than one man at once, but a good attack is all about forcing the other man to make a move you can predict, and the boy couldn't predict d'Estrada at all. How could he? Every attack he'd built up was designed to work the other way round, and you can't just switch that stuff round in your head, it's like trying to do something by looking in the mirror. His only hope was defence, and a chance that d'Estrada's over confidence would leave him open to a riposte like that last one. But the look on d'Estrada's face told me there weren't going to be any more of those.

I took off my stocking and bound it tightly round my leg to numb the pain and slow the bleeding. I'd got to get to my feet somehow, I'd got to be ready to save the boy. Corvacho was actually licking his lips.

D'Estrada was coming in faster now, they both were. The blades were in almost constant contact, they sounded like something rattling, and then it suddenly went quiet, and I looked up to see the boy was in there, he'd got a bind, and it doesn't matter what hand you're using when you're into contact that intimate. D'Estrada looked startled, and I knew he was feeling that subtle tug that tells you the other man's got control of your blade. He had to use all his skill to twist away, and only just got clear in time, André got the edge to him and his blade slashed d'Estrada's sleeve. I wanted to cheer. We knew the weakness now, we only needed real blade contact and the left-handedness wouldn't matter, another *envelopment* to confuse him, then maybe a turn into the *flaconnade* when he was off balance, we could beat him.

D'Estrada's mouth went all thin, and I knew he was thoroughly pissed off. He came forward again, and this time he was savage, stamping and thrusting, luring the boy's blade forward then striking up at the face, always doing that Spanish thing of going for the eyes. André defended, but it was like looking at me all those years ago, just beating the blade back, no time to riposte, it was *battement, battement,* lateral parry, *battement,* it was all defence, he was fucked.

Carlos Corvacho

I knew that desperate look, Señor, I'd seen it a few times when a man faced my Capitán. But the Chevalier wasn't giving in easy. There he was, all on the defensive, then suddenly did this little half-turn, a *demi-volte,* you might say, whipping my gentleman's blade out with him, then he was in and under it, going for the leg in my opinion, a very underhand trick, very French, but my Capitán's left hand on to it, he beats it off easy and now he's in for the attack. This was one of his own tricks, a sudden sharp jump forward, but the lunge twisting at the last second into a flick, and there was the Chevalier's sword in the air, jerked clean out of his hand –

Jacques Gilbert

– and landing a good six feet away. I remember the tinkle as it came slowly to rest on the stone.

And there was my brother standing helpless and disarmed, and d'Estrada's elbow already back for the lunge. It was too late for me to move. All I could do was close my eyes so I wouldn't have to see it. I knew I'd hear it anyway. I knew I'd hear it for ever.

But there was nothing, and after a second I opened my eyes. There was André standing waiting for the thrust, and that awful desolate look in his eyes, because he'd been beaten and knew it and wanted to die, but d'Estrada, facing him, hadn't moved.

Then d'Estrada said gently 'I'm sorry.'

André dropped his head. He didn't want pity.

'You're still young.'

'Old enough.'

D'Estrada cocked his head to one side and smiled. 'If you'd been prepared . . .'

'I wasn't.'

D'Estrada sighed. Then he said 'You owe me a life, Chevalier,' and sheathed his sword.

The boy stared helplessly at the ground, burning up with shame. After a moment d'Estrada walked slowly forwards till he stood right in front of him, looking down at his lowered head. He spoke very quietly, but I heard him just the same. He said 'Come, Chevalier. We don't cry.'

André's head shot up. He wasn't crying, of course he wasn't, but there was something else on his face now, something startled, almost shocked. For a second something like a memory was tweaking at me, but it sort of wriggled away, and there was only a Spanish officer looking at André with an almost sad smile on his face.

'We don't cry,' said d'Estrada. 'We get angry, then next time we fight better.'

André hesitated, then actually smiled back. I didn't understand, it was like d'Estrada was giving him something, he was bringing him back to life. I wondered what Corvacho thought, but he wasn't even looking, he was staring towards the back of the roof with his mouth half open, then he yelled out 'Capitán!'

Giles was clambering over the parapet. There were hands on the rung of the second ladder, and a curly head sticking up over the third that looked like Pepin. It sounds stupid, but I'd almost forgotten them, I'd almost forgotten everything but what was happening right here.

D'Estrada whirled round and snatched out his sword, but Giles was on the roof already, Pepin climbing over, and other men swarming up behind. D'Estrada spun back round to André, but the boy was still standing there, bound in honour not to move. D'Estrada wrenched his head away, and turned to the tower.

I got to my feet at last, with some confused idea of stopping them giving the alarm, but I was tottery, and d'Estrada pushed straight past me. He signalled Corvacho through the door, gave us one last wild glare, then turned and was gone. I heard his voice calling for guards as he went.

'André,' said Giles, calmly unslinging his musket.

'Giles,' said André, picking up his sword.

'All right?' He must have seen what had happened, but he wasn't going to mention it, not Giles, he knew we'd a battle coming and if ever the men needed to keep their faith in André it was now.

André didn't even seem bothered. It was extraordinary, he was himself again, like he'd never even thought about wanting to die. He said cheerfully 'Sorry, Giles, I've screwed up, the alarm's given.'

Giles shrugged. 'Minute early, if that. They'll know about us soon enough when we start shooting.'

'Do you want me to hold here?' asked André, gesturing towards the tower door.

'And leave the army without their capitaine?' said Giles.

'Bugger off, we're fine.' There were more of his men up now, and he whistled two of them over. They were probably loaders, but they had swords, and that was all that mattered. Giles said 'You two, guard that door. Anything tries to come through it, stick them, got it?'

They were used to Giles. They just nodded and went to the door.

André leant forward suddenly and grasped Giles' arms. Giles gripped him back, then they broke quickly, and Giles went to the parapet, where his men were starting to lie down with their muskets.

'Look at the spacing of you, for Christ's sake,' he said. 'Three feet, how many times have I told you? Stop bloody cuddling up to each other, where do you think you are?'

André helped me as far as the ladder, then went over first to support me if I got in trouble. The sky was lighter now, but it didn't seem like it when I looked down, I couldn't see the bottom. I waited a second to give the boy a start, then lowered myself after him into the dark.

Twenty-Seven

Jean-Marie Mercier

The sky was getting paler, and it was almost time. I eased myself into the firing position, and rested my first musket on the parapet like a stand. I remember how it felt lying there. The stable roof was tarred wooden lathes, but the sun hadn't warmed it yet, it was cold through my breeches. I remember how it felt against my legs.

I had already allocated the first targets. Mine was the furthest man on the firing step, a large, rather jolly-looking soldier, who was pacing up and down, flapping his arms against the cold. He leant forward for a casual look through his embrasure, and I took careful aim between his shoulders.

The clock started to strike five. At the same instant my man stiffened, turned, and said something to the soldier next to him, who at once looked through his own embrasure as if to see what my man had described. I didn't wait for the clock to finish. I adjusted my aim, and fired.

Stefan Ravel

It was stifling in that barn with the whole assault team squashed in together. At the first crack of Mercier's musket I yelled 'Go!' and we burst the doors and were out.

Those poor dons never knew what hit them. By the time I reached the Gate, the Guards on the firing step were already dead, cut down in that first volley, and those on the ground hadn't time to turn before arrows came pelting at them from the woods on the other side. I hacked one down by the first cannon, Pinhead took out another with his sledgehammer, Mercier's lot unleashed their second volley and that was the Gate Guards gone.

Which only left the little matter of the men in the barracks a hundred yards away. Not my business, of course, I was one of the mules hauling back that first cannon for Pinhead to hammer the spike in, but I could hear a great roar going up from the Square and knew the civilians were doing their stuff. I did glance round to check our infantry running across to screen us, but they did it all right, and so they should, God knows I'd drilled them long enough. Two rows of pike, with musketeers on each wing to provide sleeves of shot, just as we'd planned it all those months ago. It was a good plan, Abbé.

Given a chance, it might even have worked.

Jacques Gilbert

André shot through the empty Forge, me limping speedily after him, and there we were in the shelter with the horses. I was giddy and sick after the climb, but he helped me up on Tonnerre, and the relief of taking the weight off my leg was wonderful. I felt safer on horseback anyway, and there were my pistols loaded and ready in the holsters, everything just where it ought to be. The boy opened the half door and mounted Tempête, and I ripped off my Spanish coat. André hadn't fought under false colours today, and neither would I.

It was just starting as we rode out. It was a shock even for us, so God knows what it did to the Spaniards. There was a terrific howl of people shouting, and a rumbling crash right next to us as the wagon with barrels was heaved to slam against the courtyard gates. The guards on our side tried to resist, but were overwhelmed in the rush of people pouring out of the Corbeaux and Les Étoiles, all armed with clubs and pikes and scythes and axes and reaping hooks, and screaming like madmen. One went down with a pike deep in his stomach, and the woman wielding it was Mme Laroque, Pierre's mother, her face wild with hate. Another was scrambling over the barrels in the wagon, hooking his hands over the courtyard gate and scrabbling with his feet, trying to climb back inside, but a dozen hands were reaching for him, then a reaping hook came sweeping across the cart and yanked his legs from under him, and M. Poulain was dragging him down on the ground to the mob. There was a flash of steel as pikes and scythes were all raised in the air at once, and I turned away fast so as not to see them slicing down.

The second wagon was hurtling forward to block the south alley, propelled by the sheer weight of people shoving it, ordinary people like old Gabriel the sexton and Robert's sister Agnès, only they didn't look ordinary any more, they looked frightening. The wagon by the north alley was already in place, and as we urged our horses through the mêlée, there was a great *whoomph* of flame as the straw flared up, setting fire in an instant to the pitch underneath. There were a couple of soldiers on the other side, but the flames drove them back and they turned to run towards the mill. Old Mlle Tissot actually leant over the wagon to shake her fist and scream 'Cowards!' as they ran. She needn't have worried. Bruno's men were guarding the bridge over the mill stream, and no one was getting out that way.

We were out and in the clear. I turned in my saddle to see

574

M. Thibault's men blocking the main door to the barracks, but the crashing inside sounded like the soldiers were actually trying to barricade it shut, like they thought we were trying to get in. Looking at the mob by the courtyard, who'd run out of soldiers to kill and were climbing on the wagon to take pot-shots over the gates, I began to think they might even be right.

Carlos Corvacho

We went down those corridors like cannon shells, Señor, banging on doors and yelling the French were on us. We thought the rebels were trying to get in, you understand, we thought they were attacking us through our own roof.

We'd hardly touched ground on the bottom floor when we learned different. There's young de Medina panting up saying our front door's held against us, the guards dead and marksmen on the other side, there's a wagon against the courtyard gate and rebels simply swarming up it, he says they're not after attacking us, they're trying to keep us in.

'The back,' says my Capitán, and round we turn to head the other way, but now there's Alférez Calante coming up the corridor in a panic, saying the back gate's shut and the guards killed. My Capitán's for breaking out anyway, but Calante says we can't, the gates are locked. They're wrought iron, you see, Señor, and it seems somebody's stuck a chain through the bars and padlocked the whole bloody lot shut.

It didn't look good, Señor. There's men shouting in alarm all round us, and glass breaking where they're trying to escape out the windows, and gunfire and screaming coming from outside. Shocking sound, that screaming, it sounded like women to me, and that's no joke in a battle, you don't want to come up against a female when her blood's up, and certainly not a French one. Our men are trying to fire at them through the windows, but they're below us or out of sight at our own doors, we can't get at them at all. So I'm looking at our officers, and there's Calante shaking like a fever, and young de Medina licking his lips and looking as if he's about to bolt.

It's times like that you can tell the real gentleman, Señor, that's when you know you've got the real thing. My Capitán gives a little laugh and says 'All right, Calante, round up a couple of *escuadra*, we're going out the side windows.'

'No good, Señor,' says Calante. 'The alleys are blocked by fire, and the back yard's suicide, there are marksmen on our roof picking off anyone who gets out. I tell you we're trapped.'

My Capitán laughs again. He's still flying a little, seeing as he's just beaten the Chevalier de Roland blade to blade, he's maybe a little light-headed. 'It's not as desperate as that, Fernando,' says he, clapping the alférez on the back. 'There's a third way out of the south alley, and we might just give the rebels a little surprise.'

Jacques Gilbert

We met up with Marcel's cavalry north of the church, hunting down the soldiers who'd emerged from the out-billets. There weren't many actually, I think most had decided to stay quietly indoors. We chased a few running out of the cottages by the Almshouses, but it felt really strange doing it, like these were our streets again, and they were the fugitives. It felt sort of wonderful.

The clock was striking the quarter and our troops would be here any minute, so we galloped back down to the Gate, people cheering as we passed. Edouard was climbing on to the firing step to open the top bolt of the Gate, Pinhead was hammering a spike into the last cannon, and I remember thinking it was all safe no matter what happened, nothing could stop our troops now. But Pinhead had this awful strained expression on his face, and Stefan was actually hurrying towards us, he was almost running.

He said 'They're not coming.'

'What?' said André.

Stefan was speaking quickly and quietly like he didn't want the others to hear, it was hard to get what he was saying. 'We can see them through the embrasures. They're not moving, they're just sitting there a good mile away, I tell you they're not fucking coming.'

I couldn't take it in. Our troops ought to be at the Gates right now, but he was saying they hadn't moved, they were still twenty minutes away, we were right back where we'd started and everything we'd done had been for nothing. As we stared at him in horror, there came the thunder of hoofbeats pounding towards us down the Dax-Verdâme Road.

Stefan Ravel

André snapped out of his trance. 'Get the Gates open,' he said. 'Help Edouard and get the bloody Gate open, we'll damn well *make* them come.' Then he turned to Marcel and said 'Take men from the screen and reinforce the barricade. It's got to hold now, it's our only hope.'

Whatever I may say about that kid, he knew how to take control when we needed it, and what's more he was right. There were mostly civilians on that barricade, Abbé, we'd never thought they'd have to deal with more than a few messengers before our troops relieved us. Now they'd got Don Francisco and what sounded like half the Verdâme garrison coming at them and would need all the help they could get. At least we could spare the men here, it was still nice and quiet on the Square. There was musket fire from the barracks roof, so I knew we'd got soldiers breaking out somewhere, but no one seemed to be attempting to come down the alleys. They might make it into the Thibault farm, but that was walled and we held the gate.

All of which was true, Abbé, and it wasn't till we heard the shouts from Market Street that I realized the one little flaw. We'd left our ladders up in the farm, and we weren't the only buggers who knew how to climb.

Jean-Marie Mercier

They came swarming over the farm wall on our own siege ladders. One led directly on to the stable roof, and there were soldiers up it and on us in seconds.

I tried to swing my musket round, but we were packed too close to bring it to bear. The soldiers were swiping viciously down at our loaders, blades against ramrods and bare hands, scarlet blood spattering over us in a great spray. But Colin was on his feet, swinging his musket like a huge club, he smashed the nearest soldier off the roof, then reached out to our ladder, seized its hooks and heaved it out and away, spilling the soldiers off the rungs and thrusting it back down into the farm with one mighty shove. Georges managed to turn his musket on one still up, while Simon fired a pistol into the last, but then I heard them both cry out in alarm, and turned to see the worst nightmare a marksman can possibly face.

There were soldiers on the roof of the barn behind us. The barn was higher than we were, and there were loaded guns pointed directly down at us, at a range of less than six feet.

They fired together in one great deafening volley. I think I'll always remember the sound of it. Something like a great hammer smashed into my knee, and I think I may have screamed, but there were so many people crying out at once I'm hardly sure. There was choking blue smoke all about us, and suddenly a tremendous weight crushing against me and cracking my head against the parapet, and I think I must have fainted.

Jacques Gilbert

I remember hearing somebody screaming in sheer fury, then realizing it was me.

Then we were charging straight into them, because that's what cavalry's for, you bloody charge the bastards, and I was hacking down like I've never hated anyone so much in my life. It wasn't exciting, the way it had been by the Almshouses, that was all over, it had never been real, our troops weren't coming and we were all dead. Only that bloody shambles on the stable roof was real, that and these black and red bastards suddenly in amongst us like being invaded all over again.

It was d'Estrada, of course, no one else could have kept his head and led a counter-attack like that. I could see him keeping a bunch of his men tight together, they'd somehow got past our first rush and were heading towards the Gate. I reined in Tonnerre to wheel after them, but André was pounding up behind me with infantry at his heels, shouting 'The barn! The men on the barn!' and of course he was right.

I could see them ahead of me, reloading frantically, and the boy was right, they'd make bloody ribbons of us if they fired that lot, we'd got to take them down.

We turned on them, all of us. They were too high to reach, even on horseback, but André fired one of his pistols into them, I did the same, then Bettremieu snatched a pike from an infantryman, stood up in his stirrups and swung it like a scythe, sweeping half the men back across the roof in a struggling mass, back to where our infantry were climbing up behind. The bastards stopped even thinking about reloading, they just tried to get the hell out before our infantry tore into them. Some jumped off the roof, but André was waiting with his sword drawn and bloody, he was half hanging off his stirrups to reach more of them, slashing about as if to cut them all into shreds. I didn't blame him. I could see the mess of flesh and bone that had been our men on the stable roof, there was blood trickling down the whitewashed walls into the dust.

I took the last one myself, then turned to ride back through the men who'd got past us. There weren't many left now, but d'Estrada was nearly at the open Gate and a handful of men with him. Stefan and the infantry screen moved forward to meet them, I saw Dom thrust his pike at one, his face savage as I'd never seen it, and Pinhead faced up to d'Estrada himself, swinging that great sledgehammer he'd been using for the spikes. D'Estrada whirled on his feet and whipped down with his blade, and there was Pinhead falling across the barrel of the cannon, his neck gaping open in one huge red gash, but the sledgehammer struck as he fell, and d'Estrada was down too, rolling over like a rabbit, then lying still. The rest of his men scattered at sight of us, running blindly for the Square, where Jacob's muskets picked them off from Les Étoiles.

Edouard's voice was calling down from the firing step. He was looking out of the embrasure towards the fields, but we heard him shout 'They're moving, André. Our troops are starting to advance.'

The boy turned at once to the Square and yelled out 'They're coming, we can see them, our troops are on the way!'

A great cheer went up from the people by the alleys, by the courtyard gates, on the roofs, all over Dax people were cheering and throwing their hats in the air. André's head came back to mine, the smile still fixed on his face, but his eyes were anguished. He was doing his best, but he knew as well as I did it could be another ten minutes before our army got here, more if they waited for the infantry.

'We'll hold,' I said desperately. 'André, don't worry, we'll hold.'

There came another crash of gunfire from the Dax-Verdâme Road.

'Cavalry to the barricade!' cried André. 'Come on, we're finished here.' He turned to rally our horsemen down the road, then hesitated by the remains of the infantry screen.

'Take them,' said Stefan. He was struggling to wedge a chock under the first leaf of the Gate, but seemed calmer than he had. 'Take them, it's all quiet here.'

André nodded gratefully and sent the last of our infantry charging after the cavalry. Even Edouard jumped down from the Wall to join them. But Marcel was already running up from the barricade, grazed and dusty with being unhorsed. He panted 'We need more shot. Roger's down, there's only Margot holding them together. The middle wagon's gone, we've no time between charges to push it back, I've got to have more shot or we can't hold.'

'Take Jacob's marksmen,' said André desperately. 'I'll hold it till you're back.'

Marcel ran on towards the Square, and we wheeled again to ride down the Dax-Verdâme Road, but we'd only got as far as the corner when firing broke out from the woods, a shot cracked past my face, and a horse screamed. Tempête was rearing and stamping, André jerked up in the air, flopped back, slipped clear out of the saddle and crashed down heavily on the stones. Behind me I heard M. Lefebvre and Bernard calling their bowmen and realized soldiers were trying to break through the trees.

I threw myself down off Tonnerre, then crumpled to my knees as the shock opened up my leg, but the boy was rolling clear and Tempête collapsing harmlessly next to him, kicking and screaming in agony. André scrabbled in the holster for his pistol and tried to bring it up to the poor beast's head, but Tempête was thrashing to and fro, and the boy's hands were shaking, he was still half stunned, and it was hard to do it, to kill this horse that had saved his life on this same road three years ago. I crawled over, grabbed Tempête's mane, put my own last pistol against his forehead, and pulled the trigger. The gelding shuddered, and was still.

The boy gave a kind of terrified sob, then turned away to grope for his sword. I struggled to stand, though it felt like I'd got a roll of blanket instead of a leg, and I had to put all my weight on the other. Then something drew my eye back to the Wall, something was moving between the second and third cannon. Someone was getting up.

'The barricade,' said the boy, climbing shakily to his feet. 'We have to help Margot. Can you take me on Tonnerre?'

D'Estrada was still alive. Pinhead's dying blow must have glanced off him and knocked him out for a moment, because he was getting slowly to his feet, his sword still in his hand. I wasn't totally sorry. The Gate was right next to him, and I didn't think I'd mind if d'Estrada escaped. We owed it him, after all.

But he didn't go for the Gate. He went for Stefan. He was totally alone, and Stefan was no threat, he was just trying to wedge the second leaf open, there was no sense in it at all, but he threw himself at Stefan with a kind of howl.

Stefan Ravel

It was lucky for me the bastard was already injured. He was half mad with rage, and that first swipe should have done for me, but his aim was off, and I got my sword up just in time. We were face to face then, the two of us, and I saw in his eyes what it was all about. That's nobility for you, Abbé. Men dying all round him, fucking French army charging towards him across the plain, and all he's thinking about is the man who marked his pretty face.

It was likely to prove serious enough for me. He was a swordsman, that one, I knew it right off, and what's more he was a left-hander. I belted him off and away a couple of times, but that was as good as it was going to get, and I doubt I'd have done even that if he hadn't got a stiff shoulder from Pinhead's hammer. I was dead in a minute if someone didn't settle him, but they'd all gone rattling off to the barricade and I was on my own.

But not quite. I slid my sword up guard to guard, in the hope of getting my other hand to him and throttling the bastard off, but even as he ducked and twisted away, I got a view over his shoulder, and there was André himself at the corner of the woods. He looked shaky as all hell, but he was on his feet, he'd got Jacques next to him, and more to the point he'd got a pistol in his hand.

I've no time for pride, Abbé, I'd rather stay alive any day. I walloped d'Estrada away again, and used the second's respite to shout to the kid. Nothing dramatic, just the old call one soldier makes to another when he needs a hand, the way he'd called me himself that night at the Château.

I called 'André!'

Jacques Gilbert

We couldn't reach them in time, and there was no one else. André had the pistol, but he couldn't use it, he was only alive at d'Estrada's gift. He did the only possible thing. He stopped, brought his left arm up fast in a fist, bent it at the elbow, levelled the pistol across it, and shouted 'Stop, or I shoot!'

It was all quiet around us, there even seemed to be a lull at the barricades. There were just the four of us standing there.

D'Estrada stepped back from Stefan, kept him at length with the blade of his sword, then turned his head towards us.

He shouted 'Private matter, Chevalier! Affair of honour!'

Stefan Ravel

Oh, fuck his honour, I went straight for him when his back was turned, but he'd known I would, the bastard, he was twisting even as I lunged, then he was round again and attacking furiously, I'd never seen anything so fast. He was dancing up close, and I knew he could take me any time, he was only toying with me, I could see it in his smile.

I shouted again 'André!'

The boy stiffened all over, then jerked the pistol back up. He was going to shoot a man in the back, a man in the middle of a duel of honour, a man who'd spared his own life. He was ruined, he was shamed for ever, he was really going to do it.

I screamed 'André, no!'

His face whipped round to me, desperate, hardly recognizable.

'André, you can't!'

He blinked, then a shock of despair passed over his face. He flung down the pistol, snatched up his sword and started to run towards d'Estrada.

I tried to follow, but my leg kept going dead, I couldn't do much more than hobble. It didn't matter, it was too late anyway. D'Estrada had finished playing with Stefan, he was forcing hard forward, then Stefan stumbled, falling back against the open Gate.

I suppose I must have heard the footsteps before that, but I didn't take them in. The first I knew was a great cry, then someone rushing forward into the picture I was looking at. Marcel leapt full at d'Estrada, knocking him back with his sword, forcing himself in front of Stefan's fallen body, then lunging out at d'Estrada's face. D'Estrada didn't hesitate, his blade came in fast and clean, Marcel never even saw it coming. He was as unbalanced by the left-handedness as the boy had been, he parried in the wrong place, and d'Estrada's sword whipped in, taking him full in the chest and punching right into the Gate on the other side.

Marcel hung there a second, impaled on the blade, and he didn't make a sound, the dreadful cry I was hearing must have been Stefan. Blood poured out of Marcel's mouth, all down his white shirt, and I knew he was dead, he must have died instantly. D'Estrada pulled out, and Marcel's body crumpled and collapsed on top of Stefan. The sound of gunfire rose again from the Dax-Verdâme Road.

The boy was nearly up to them, but d'Estrada took his time. He looked down at Stefan, brought the point of his sword right up to his face, then gave the tiniest flick of his wrist and stepped back. I thought he'd killed him at first, then saw the trickle of blood on Stefan's cheek, and all at once I understood. I remembered how much d'Estrada had wanted the 'Tanner of Verdâme', and now I understood the whole bloody thing, and that Stefan had brought it on himself.

André came panting up, and d'Estrada faced him, blade levelled, but at that moment there came a great crash from the Dax-Verdâme Road. The shooting intensified, but there was shouting and screaming, some obviously women, then the pounding of hoofbeats getting louder as they galloped towards us. D'Estrada sketched a tiny salute with his sword, then turned and ran up the road, and I knew the barricade had broken at last.

Jean-Marie Mercier

There was something blocking my mouth and I couldn't breathe. I tried to brush it away, but the weight was too much, I had to push out my arms and heave. I opened my eyes but had to close them again instantly, because I was looking right into Simon's face. He was lying on top of me, and he was dead.

I rolled clear, and found I could see sky. My knee still felt as if something were lying on it, but I could see there wasn't. I expect it was just because I'd been shot there. I could see it bleeding. It was bleeding quite a lot.

A voice said 'Jean?'

Colin was kneeling up on the roof and obviously very much alive. His arm had a gash running along it, as if a musket ball had scored him as it passed, but otherwise he seemed unhurt.

'Can you shoot? Georges doesn't think he's up to it.'

I rolled back on to my stomach. My knee made a strange kind of sensation that was a little like screaming as I rested it on the roof, but it didn't seem much to do with me. What was real was Georges' face next to mine, and he was alive too. His face was grey, almost pale blue, and when I looked down his body I nearly vomited. His lower back and legs were dark, dark red, and I've no idea how many bullets he'd taken. But he'd been at the front with me, and Colin just behind us, so I suppose the men at the back had taken the worst of the volley and we had all survived.

I said 'I can shoot.'

'Lots of guns,' said Colin, passing me one. 'No one else here needs any.'

He was very brave, Colin. He must have been every bit as upset as I was at the death of the rest of us, but honestly no one would have known. He gave the impression he was happy to be there with all those loaded muskets at his disposal.

'Better be quick,' he said. 'Look.'

I focused my eyes over the parapet. The space before the Gate was curiously empty. I could see only two men standing there, and they were the two men I'd most have wanted to see, they were André and Jacques, with Stefan climbing to his feet just beyond them. But there was a tremendous crashing and firing coming from the Dax-Verdâme Road, and when I turned my head that way, I saw a mass of horse-men pouring down it. Some were our own, I could see the unmistakable figure of Bettremieu fighting on horseback, but most seemed to be the enemy, and they were all heading for the Gate.

'Quick as you like, Col,' I said, and fired.

He passed me another, even as my first man was toppling off his horse. But too many were through and fighting our men for possession of the first leaf of the Gate. Our own cavalry couldn't get past them, and there was no one to defend the second except André and Jacques.

I said 'Faster.'

Jacques Gilbert

I felt so bloody tired, and my leg was nagging at me. I leant back against our leaf of the Gate to take my weight off it.

'Good idea,' said André, and came and stood next to me. 'If they want to shut this Gate, they'll have to kill us first.'

I didn't think in my case it would take very much, but it didn't seem to matter any more. Even as I watched, the lead-ing Spanish cavalry broke away from our men at the first leaf and came galloping towards us.

A shot rang out from the direction of Market Street, then seconds later another, and the cavalrymen both dropped to the stones.

André said 'There's men alive up there.'

I looked back to the stable, as yet another shot cracked, then another. It sounded like two men, even three, but the flashes were coming from a single position. I felt a funny kind of prickling behind my eyes.

'Just one,' I said. 'And I bet I know who.'

Next to me a voice said 'Is Bettremieu wounded yet, Jean-Marie?'

Dear Georges. I shut out the memory of what I'd seen of his lower body and kept firing. I aimed for the cavalry, because no one on foot would have a hope against them, not even André. Colin was wonderful, he had the next gun ready every time, pressing them into my hands, all I had to do was point and shoot.

Georges' voice was very slurred now. 'They're coming, Je'm'rie, our army, I can see them.'

I didn't dare stop to look. André and Jacques had three or four men on foot to deal with, I couldn't afford to let any more reach them. Stefan could have gone to help, but he was fighting alongside our men at the other leaf, and I suppose he was too hard pressed. There was another knot of cavalry breaking through, I fired at the leading horse and reached for another musket.

It was only as I was squeezing off the next shot that I recognized the man I'd unhorsed. It was Don Francisco himself, and he was running straight for André.

Jacques Gilbert

I was pulling out from my last man when I saw Don Francisco. My sword was free, I lunged straight at him, but his guard crunched into my jaw, I spun off balance and crashed against the Gate. He was bloody strong, it wasn't just fat in that great frame of his, there was a lot of muscle too. His sword came plunging in at my belly, but another blade shot underneath and sprang it back up, and that was André, of course, it was the boy. He thrust at the Colonel, driving him outward from the Gate, forcing him into leaving me alone and fighting with himself.

It was ridiculous, Don Francisco was huge, he was nearly a foot taller and a whole lot broader, his sword looked like a child's toy in his hand. I kept my feet and launched myself after them, but there was another coming in, probably the Colonel's page, certainly not much of a swordsman, but he had to be dealt with all the same, and it drove me mad because I wanted to get to the boy.

But there was a fury about André I'd never seen before. There was no defending about him now, he was straight at the Colonel, attacking, attacking, footwork flawless, blade darting in and out so fast I could hardly even see it. Don Francisco couldn't either, he didn't seem to believe it was happening, he just sort of blinked and gave back, retreating, retreating, his polished boots slipping on the stones.

I finished off the page, and saw three more riders hurtling towards us, but Bettremieu shot out from behind the first leaf of the Gate and practically took the head off the nearest with his sabre, while a bolt from the woods had another. The third got nearly as far as Don Francisco before a musket shot from the stables caught him, and he toppled at André's feet. André never even turned, he just went on driving that big bastard further and further back till his guard was all to fuck, his sword just dangling from its lanyard, he was trying to ward off the attack with his fat white hands. Then the boy started to hit him. He whipped his blade right down his chest, scoring down his red sash, then drew back and slashed down the other side, slicing right through the padded doublet, and Don Francisco was crumpling, he was falling on his knees, and still the boy was hitting him. He was saying stuff under his breath, and I couldn't catch it, then I heard the words 'Robert Thibault' and knew he was saying names of all the people who'd been killed, he was making them sort of real again, then last of all he said 'Martin Gauthier,' and drove his sword right into Don Francisco's throat, drove it all the way through until his guard was under that fat chin, and only then did he pull out.

Jean-Marie Mercier

Georges' voice came very faint now. 'Is my brother there?'

I couldn't see Dom, but Georges' eyes were glazing in that drained face, and I said 'He's fine, he's with André, he's fine.'

Georges' contented sigh was lost in a triumphant roar below us, and I saw the Spaniards had won control of the first leaf, scattering our men and slamming it shut. More were getting through from the Dax-Verdâme Road, and I couldn't see our own cavalry any more, they were all unhorsed, even Bettremieu. We still had some infantry fighting, there were archers firing steadily from the fringes of the woods, and some of our civilians were running down from the Square, but we were hopelessly outnumbered. A great rush of soldiers broke clear and ran for the second leaf, where there were only André and Jacques with Bettremieu.

I fired at the first, got him, and reached for another musket. I shot the second, and reached for another. Beside me Georges' eyes were still as glass and I knew he'd died. I fired, and reached for another gun.

Never seen anything like it, never. It was hand out, next gun, bring it up and fire, hand out again, next gun. Hardly even seemed to be looking where he was shooting, but he must have been, never saw him miss. Leg smashed to pieces, must have ground something terrible against the roof, but it never stopped him. Wincing with the pain, have to say that, face white as dead Georges', and blood on his chin where he was biting his lip, but he never stopped firing, not for a second.

Couldn't afford to, neither. Right old mess down there, would have been a massacre if it hadn't been for us. Left Gate shut now, nothing to be done about that, though our people still fighting the dons for it, trying to get it back. André was holding the other, him and that Libert, and we'd a couple more of our infantry managed to reach them, but a sorry little force all the same. My poor old Jacques in the thick of it too, standing himself up by holding on to the Gate, didn't look good for anything much.

Jacques Gilbert

The boom of the first leaf closing felt like the end of the world. It drove the boy frantic, he was fighting wilder than ever, and that scared me, he'd got too far away from our own leaf, he was wide open. A couple of infantry had broken through to join us, but there were loads of Spaniards coming at us now, too many even for Jean-Marie to deal with. Not that the boy seemed to care, he was taking all comers, he was whirling about, ducking and sidestepping, the best fencing

I'd ever seen him do, but his back was exposed and someone was going to get him in the end.

I peeled myself away from the support of the Gate, and got behind André so we could fight back to back. He knew it was me, he just said 'Thanks,' but it came out in a kind of breath and I knew he was exhausted. For a second he even leant against me for support, and my leg hurt so much I nearly fainted, but I wasn't going to say a word, because he needed me now, my brother, and if taking his weight was all I could do, then at least I was going to do that.

A shot blazed past my head. Some of the enemy were unhorsed cavalry with pistols, and another aimed right at André, but one of our infantrymen leapt on him just as the pistol went off. It must have shot our man right in the stomach, he creased in agony and slumped to the ground, and I saw it was Dom, my patient Brother Shoveller, writhing and choking his life out on the stones. The thought flashed through me that this would kill Georges, but then I remembered Georges was on the stable and must be dead already, and that was a final blow I couldn't bear. I came hurtling round with my sword and stuck that bastard Spaniard right through the neck, and if I could have killed him again I would.

But I'd left the boy, and turned frantically to see him surrounded, three against him, and one going for his back. Bettremieu roared and charged them, scything down with his sabre, opening up the first from shoulder to navel, but the second turned and thrust his sword full into Bettremieu's side. With an ordinary man it would have come out the other side, but Bettremieu swung his sabre one last time and brought it down on the neck of the man who'd stabbed him, then collapsed quite gently to the cobbles, and fell on his side. Bettremieu, indestructible Bettremieu, was down.

André saw it, he was crying out, he whipped his sword out of the third man, and made to kneel down by Bettremieu, but there were more coming and our last infantryman down in the rush, and now it was just him and me again, just me and the boy, and everyone dying round us, and now it was our turn to die too. I made a last desperate effort to get to him, whirling round with my sword to keep the bastards at bay, but my leg buckled, it just folded up like a handkerchief, then someone crashed into me, my head smacked hard against the Gate, and everything went totally black.

Carlos Corvacho

I saw it all.

I was in the charge with the Capitán, made it all the way to the Gate. I was fighting side by side with him till he fell, and in a manner of speaking that's what put me out of it too. I'd taken a ball in the shoulder from somewhere, so I was already on the ground when the big man who'd downed my Capitán came sliding off a cannon dead on top of me, and there I was, pinned under the weight of him. Totally trapped I was, Señor, I couldn't move at all.

But I was conscious all through, I saw the lot. It was a fine display your Chevalier gave at that Gate, I've never seen a better by a Frenchman. Young Gilbert went down at last, and de Roland simply stepped astride him to protect his body, kept his back to the Gate and took on everyone who came near. He held that leaf all by himself, Señor, held it for whole minutes against a great press of our men, held it all alone till the end. No one could take him front on, no one, my Capitán being engaged down the road, but he couldn't move position without abandoning his friend, so three of our men got round behind the leaf, and started to push it closed.

That was it, Señor. The weight smashed into him from behind, knocked him clear off his feet and down on his knees. He was still blocking the Gate, him and the body of his friend, so our men pressed forward to kill him and drag him out of the way, only he still somehow got his sword up to parry, parry and riposte, Señor, and him on his knees. He was about all in, I'd say, kneeling half forward, hair in his face, fighting half-blind, but he took two hands to his sword and drove the front men back, a third leapt forward, then horses came charging through the open Gate, a rush of French cavalry hurtling in amongst us, screaming and slashing down with their sabres, and I'd enough sense to keep my head down and my eyes closed and try to look as dead as a man can be.

Jean-Marie Mercier

It was a wonderful moment.

The soldier attacking André was spitted like a boar on the first Frenchman's sword and driven right back by the momentum of the charge. Our cavalry were simply pouring in, more and more of them. Some turned to their left to finish off the Spaniards by the Gate, some charged straight on up towards the Square, but most of them turned right to the Dax-Verdâme Road where the fighting was thickest. I saw Spaniards throwing down their weapons in panic, and dropping to the ground in surrender, while others simply turned and ran for the woods. They were scattering, they were routed, they were beaten. Capitán d'Estrada lowered his sword and was looking for someone to receive his surrender.

Even Colin was swept away by the excitement. When I didn't reach back for the next gun, he smacked himself down beside me and fired it into the air like a salute.

He said 'Battle of Dax, isn't it? Can't have it said I didn't fire a single shot, can I?' Then he laughed.

It was a totally natural sound, that laugh. I think that's when I fully understood it was really over at last. I remember resting my last gun against the parapet, and I think perhaps I cried.

Carlos Corvacho

My Capitán had no choice, Señor. Left to himself he'd have fought to the death, but with the Colonel dead he was senior officer, and the men to think of. We were outnumbered ten to one, and more streaming in every minute. The Capitán yelled to our men to lay down their arms, then turned to find an officer to surrender himself to, but it didn't seem there was such a thing, this being a peasant army and mainly composed of rabble. His shout brought some bowmen out of the woods, and in despair my Capitán offered his surrender to the first of them, a vacant-looking peasant with a crossbow under his arm and an extraordinary floppy hat on his head.

Things quietened down a little when the proper French officers arrived to keep their men in order and take the surrender of the garrison. The curé had stretchers improvised to carry the wounded from the barricade to the church, and there were women among them, Señor, women and what I'd call children, a right bloody mess and no mistake. There was this great hush descending on us all as we saw these people carried out, you could only hear little whimpers of the wounded, and here and there maybe a child crying.

All this while the Chevalier's stayed at the Gate, sat back on his knees, holding the hand of his fallen friend and staring ahead at nothing, but now he climbs to his feet and watches the procession with what looks like anguish. One of the women sees him and walks over, she salutes him like a soldier, Señor, and this a barefoot peasant woman. She says 'Any orders, Sieur?' and he looks away and says 'I'm sorry, Margot. Margot, I'm so sorry.' She sticks her hands on her hips, regular Amazon this one, and says 'Well they're not bloody sorry, none of them, cost is little enough for what you've done.' He looks at her then, takes her hand, kisses it, and presses it hard against his cheek, but doesn't say another word.

Into this quiet rode a little group of what looked like senior officers. They wore those huge, wide-brimmed hats with enormous plumes, you know the ones, Señor? We don't go so much for that in Spain, you understand, we'd rather win a battle than look good losing it. So there they are clip-clopping past the Gate, colourful as peacocks, when your Chevalier catches sight of them, puts the woman aside, and stands himself in front of their horses. The leader's looking down at him in some disdain, but a tall dark fellow with a beaked nose has a word in his ear, which I'd guess is telling who he is, Señor, then there's a lot of bowing and doffing of hats and the leader announcing himself as this Comte de Gressy whose messages we've been tampering with. They're maybe expecting some courtesies in return, but the Chevalier's just staring at them in disbelief and not saying a word. Then he takes a step towards them and says 'Where were you?', and it comes out with this dreadful bitterness we could hear all round the Gate. People stop what they're doing, Señor, stop and turn to look.

The Comte starts making indignant noises, he's saying

'What do you mean, where were we?' but the Chevalier takes no notice, I doubt he even hears. My Capitán understands all right, and he's getting his escort to bring him to explain, but it's too late, the Chevalier's got hold of the Comte's bridle, and now he's almost shouting.

'Where were you?' he cries, and there's this crack in his voice as if he's ready to break down with despair. 'Where the bloody hell were you?'

Everyone's looking at them now, every soul in the village, and the Comte's in a right old huff, but my Capitán reaches him and explains we intercepted his letter, and the Chevalier never knew he was supposed to dip the flag at all. The Comte goes pale at that, and I can see him thinking that's his career over, and I'm guessing that's no more than truth, Señor, seeing as I never heard of him again.

He starts up quick with 'I'm sorry . . .' but never gets any further.

'Sorry?' says de Roland. 'Damn the signal, man, you could see the Gate was open, you must have known we were fighting, look at us, look!' His arm sweeps out and gestures at the bodies of his comrades, and the civilians being carried from the Dax-Verdâme Road. 'Sorry?' he says.

'There has clearly been some misunderstanding,' says the Comte stiffly. 'I am blameless in this matter. You gave the signal, and we came at once. Now if you will excuse me . . .' He turns away fast as he can, and sets off towards the barracks, his officers cantering quickly after him.

De Roland stands looking desolate and lost, not at all what you'd expect of a victor. He says miserably to my Capitán 'I don't understand. We gave no signal.'

My gentleman explains about the tower, and the Chevalier turns his head absently in that direction, but then he stops, and his face becomes quite still, as if all expression's been wiped off with a handkerchief. As he stares, I see just the trace of a tear slowly marking a little white path through the grime of gunsmoke on his cheek.

I looked at the tower myself, just to see what the fuss was about. There was still a flag there right enough, and it wasn't dipped either, it was streaming high and proud in the morning breeze. Then I saw with a shock there wasn't any Burgundy cross, it wasn't our own flag at all. It was one I'd never seen before, but the coat of arms on a white background told me what it had to be all the same.

It was the flag of a regiment of France.

Twenty-Eight

Jacques Gilbert

I wasn't dead, obviously, it was only my leg and a biff on the head. M. Pollet bandaged my leg like a huge sausage and told me to rest, so André put me to bed in our old cell at the barracks, and I'd never felt anything so comfortable. I was kind of floating on waves of relief at everything being all right, and drifted off to sleep in minutes.

When I woke it was lunchtime and the boy was back with bread and cheese. He'd brought me a stick too, so I hobbled up and down like Mlle Tissot while he told me the news. It was better than we'd feared. Lots of the casualties were only wounded and had a good chance of recovery. Jean-Marie was the worst, the doctor had been forced to take his leg off, but we'd got a proper surgeon looking after him and André was quite hopeful. Colin had survived the roof massacre with only a scratch, and Giles' team were untouched. The Spaniards hadn't been able to break through the tower door, and as things got hotter downstairs they'd abandoned it altogether, and Pepin had nipped in and actually raised a flag of our own.

'It's just as well he did,' said André. 'It's only when he lowered the Spanish flag that our troops thought we'd given the signal and started their attack.'

I didn't really understand that, but I was pleased about the flag. He said it was a regimental one with the Roland arms in the centre. The boy's crest. His and mine.

I said 'I wish I'd seen it.'

600

'It's still there,' said the boy, and smiled. 'These are our barracks now.'

I hopped over to the window and peered out into the courtyard. At first glance it seemed much the same as before. There were soldiers milling about with horses, and the same noises of men shouting and steel jingling, and hooves clattering on the cobbles. But these weren't Spaniards, they were real French soldiers, there wasn't a red cockade or a Burgundy cross anywhere. Some of our own people were down there too, I saw Pepin helping the cavalry water their horses, and Bruno leading a bunch of infantry into the other wing, while Stefan leant lazily against a wall with his arms folded, talking to a laughing group of troopers and looking totally at home. I found myself searching round for Marcel and Pinhead and Simon and Roger and Dom and Georges, before my brain reminded me I wasn't going to find them, I was never going to find any of them again.

Something angry stirred inside me. So many of us had died, but standing next to the real French Army, our men didn't even look like soldiers any more. We'd never had the proper gear, of course, but we'd still been an army, we'd been real proper soldiers, and the fact that Dax was free was proof of it. Now our people were waiting on the regular French soldiers like ordinary peasants, and with a sense of shock I realized that's exactly what they were.

I said 'It's not fair.'

André joined me at the window, and we looked down together at the French troops. I found I was really resenting them, their bright clean clothes, their well-fed bodies, their sleek horses and polished weaponry, I resented the lot of them. I said 'They didn't do bloody much, did they?'

'Their battle is ahead of them, Jacques,' said André gently. 'Ours is over.'

The anniversary of the Battle of Dax is marked each year with a service in which the dead are recalled aloud by name. Some of our most prominent local citizens figure in this roll of honour, among them our esteemed blacksmith, Henri Lefebvre, who fell to a musket ball in the last defence of the Gate. For some years afterwards our May Day archery contests were muted occasions, yet his son Colin now carries the bird as regularly as his father, while rumour has it a young butcher from Verdâme has grown up to pull a pretty bow himself, and the conflict this year between Lefebvre and Durand is once more keenly awaited.

I myself undertook nothing of a martial nature in the battle, but assumed the direction of a dressing station, which on the cessation of hostilities passed into the hands of military surgeons from both sides. The number of our injured who recovered their ordeal stands as a living testament to their dedication. Most remarkable among these was the case of a Flemish labourer named Libert, who had not only suffered gross internal injuries, but bore so many marks of previous violence upon his body as to render his very existence a matter of wonder. His condition appeared hopeless, and I administered Extreme Unction on two separate occasions, yet the days passed and still he lingered, until at last he rose from his bed and returned calmly to his work. He is to be found to this very day caring for the poultry on the Roland Home Farm, where he rejoices in the soubriquet of Bettremieu 'l'Immortel'.

Yet in all the chaos of these first hours of freedom I could not but feel sympathy for our erstwhile adversary, the Don Miguel d'Estrada. He had ever been an honourable opponent, and in the event proved a formidable one as well. M. le Comte de Gressy accordingly offered him the same terms as those given Spanish forces in other occupied forts, namely that if he would give his word not to engage in further hostilities for the period of a year, he and his men would merely be escorted to the borders of Artois with full honours of war. To this Don Miguel agreed, save only that he requested the courtesy of speech with the commanding officer of the forces who had defeated him, as was customary with an officer of his rank.

M. le Comte appeared confused, and said haughtily 'You are speaking with him now, Señor.'

Don Miguel smiled politely, and said 'I think not.'

Jacques Gilbert

We were drinking wine in the courtyard when that vulture-faced Chevalier de Saussay strode in, bringing d'Estrada himself to see the boy.

It was all weirdly polite, with lots of complimenting each other on what wonderful opponents we'd been, like it hadn't really been about killing each other at all. They weren't polite about de Gressy, though, and I've got to say I agreed. It didn't matter about the letter and the signal, he must have seen we were fighting and still did nothing but sit chewing his nails at the mile mark while women and children got slaughtered. I bet it wasn't a mile anyway, it took them ages to get here, I bet it was more like two.

Then d'Estrada asked for a private word with André, so de Saussay and I both backed off a little distance and tried to look like we weren't listening, which obviously we were. It wasn't easy actually, they were speaking very quietly, and de Saussay and I both ended up sort of leaning like weather-cocks to hear.

D'Estrada said 'I have to release you from your bond, Chevalier.'

'I know,' said André sadly. 'Another man has paid it for me.'

D'Estrada said stiffly 'I had to fight that duel, Chevalier, and I think you understand why.'

'I think so, Señor, but you must believe we had no knowledge of it.'

'Your friend made that clear to me,' said d'Estrada. I had to look away fast because I knew he was going to glance towards me, and he did too, I saw him out of the corner of my eye. 'Had it been otherwise, I would have acted very differently on the roof.'

The boy flushed. 'Had it not been for your magnanimity I would have acted very differently at the Gate.'

'Indeed,' said d'Estrada, smiling, 'for you would not have been there at all.'

It was a touch, but the boy deflected it gracefully. 'Then I must thank you for your generosity.'

D'Estrada matched him courtesy for courtesy. 'My folly might be a better word. Had it not been for that, your army would have arrived too late. Next time there will be, shall we say, less generosity.'

The boy's eyes flashed. 'Next time, Señor, there will be no need for it.'

D'Estrada actually laughed, and after a second André joined him. Over their heads my eyes met de Saussay's for a moment, and we both looked away hastily, because of course he wasn't listening, and neither was I.

'Oh, Chevalier,' said d'Estrada, 'I look forward to it.'

'So do I,' said André.

They bowed gravely to each other, then de Saussay took d'Estrada back to the gate.

It was only then I caught sight of someone in a brown coat leaning against the barracks wall, picking his teeth and watching us with a sour expression on his face. It was bloody Stefan, and I knew he'd seen the whole thing.

Stefan Ravel

Oh yes, I saw them, André and his little friend d'Estrada, chatting away in the open courtyard as if there was nothing to be ashamed of. The man was responsible for the deaths of half our men, but he was a gentleman, you see, Abbé, which made it perfectly all right. It turned my stomach.

André didn't even see me till his new friends had gone and he was free to notice such a thing as a lowly tanner. I can't say he looked ashamed even then. He simply said something to Jacques and came strolling over, certain I'd be pleased at his notice. I let him be quite sure I'd seen him, then walked away.

He came after me, of course. He followed me right the way to my room, which I guessed must have been Don Francisco's once, judging by the scarlet silk on the bed and the clutter of looted ornaments. I wasn't keen on the stink of lavender, and the bear grease on the pillow was rather unsavoury, but it was private, and that's all I was interested in. Not that that bothered André, naturally, he came straight in after me and said he wanted to talk.

Oh, I won't weary you with it, Abbé, it bored me quite enough at the time. He was giving it a lot of yap about honour and d'Estrada sparing him, but I can't say I gave a toss. I already knew the important thing, which is he wouldn't fire a pistol to save my life, and Marcel was dead as a result.

He said 'I can't tell you how sorry I am about Marcel. I couldn't know he'd do what he did.'

I started rummaging through the clothes press to see if there was anything worth looting. 'What else would he do? What kind of bastard puts the life of an enemy above the life of a friend?'

'It wasn't like that. You and d'Estrada, that was a personal fight, a duel.'

'In the middle of a battle?'

His face hardened. 'You know what I'm talking about. That cut on your face proves it.'

I might have known he'd bring it back to that. 'All right, so what?'

'You cut him when he was helpless. He was our prisoner.'

I found a rather nice fur-lined cloak and chucked it on the bed. 'Young de Chouy was theirs. Seen him yet, have you?'

He shook his head, eyes wide.

'They tortured him half to death. That's how your honourable friend treats prisoners.'

He sat down abruptly on the bed and put his face in his hands. At last he said 'It's different. They needed information, I can see that. You had no reason to hurt d'Estrada at all.'

'Didn't I?'

'All right then,' he said, lifting his head and looking at me. 'Why did you?'

How can you answer something like that? You do what you do, you don't always work out the reasons for it first.

I turned back to the press. 'It shouldn't matter why, we should still be on the same side.'

'Not in this. I couldn't shoot a man in the back who was engaged in a duel.'

I chucked a couple of embroidered baldrics on the pile next to him. 'Come on, I've stabbed dozens of men in the back in this war, and so have you. I saw you at the Château. And how many did you get last night in that tower?'

'That was war.'

'And so is this, André! It's war! You and d'Estrada, saving each other's lives all over the place, what the fuck do you think this is, a game? War's war, and you fight the enemy until they're dead or you are. That's what Marcel did.'

'Not for that,' he said quietly. 'He did it for you.'

I didn't need telling that. Poor, lonely Marcel. I'd never felt for him the way he wanted, but he gave me his life just the same.

'Well, maybe,' I said. 'Maybe he was stupid enough to care.'

'So do I,' he said miserably. 'That's why I'm so sorry.'

You know, I actually pitied him. I said 'You can't have it both ways. You want to be honourable, go ahead, but you can't care about anyone if you do.'

He got wearily to his feet. 'It's what we did in the battle. We did our duty, but we tried to look after people too.'

'And look what happened to them.'

He struck out savagely, scattering a row of toy soldiers all over the floor. 'That was that bastard de Gressy.'

'There'll always be other bastards,' I said, and bent to pick up the soldiers. 'If you want to care about people, you've got to be prepared to lie and cheat and grovel, yes and kill when you have to, otherwise you're fucked. It's a rotten world, André. A man with humanity can't afford honour as well.'

He saw me struggling with an armful of soldiers and held my knapsack open so I could shove them in. 'Well, I'm going to try, that's all.'

It was tragic really. 'Then I'm looking at a dead man.'

He met my eyes. Clear, green eyes, I never saw any like them in my whole life, Abbé. Never until now.

I said 'Ah, Christ, André, couldn't you just have pulled that fucking trigger?'

He turned away abruptly and began fiddling with some miniatures on the dresser. He was fumbling and ill at ease, and after a moment I guessed why.

'It was Jacques, wasn't it?'

His hands stilled.

'I heard him yell at you. You know why he really did it. He blames me for killing his father.'

He kept staring down at the miniatures. 'I tried to tell him. I said it was my order, but he won't believe me.'

'If it hadn't been for Jacques, you'd have fired.'

There was a long silence. Then he turned round at last, but his eyes were weary and defeated. 'I don't know. Yes, Jacques stopped me, but he was right, and I hope I'd have seen it for myself.'

Well, you can't say I didn't give him a chance. I said 'Then we've got nothing left to say to each other, have we?'

I turned back to the clothes press, and rooted through what was left.

'But if we're going into the army . . .'

I laughed. 'Oh, I'm joining the army. But for your own sake you'd better pray I never meet you there.'

I heard him step towards me. I heard him say 'Stefan.' I just went on flicking through the shirts. After a moment I heard the floorboards creak, then the soft closing of the door.

Anne du Pré

As soon as we stepped out of the house I knew.

My nice old water-vendor threw his hat in the air at sight of me and cried 'Good luck, Mademoiselle!' Antoinette the flower-seller ran up and pressed a bunch of forget-me-nots into my hand, saying 'For love, Mademoiselle,' and gave me the most beautiful smile. When we left the Place Dauphine for the Pont-Neuf there were two painters squabbling beneath the statue, but they stopped as we appeared and both cried 'Good luck, Mlle Celeste!' They only call me that because it is the name of the character in that silly play, but Colette does not like it, she says I should not let people be so famil-iar. I do not care at all. For all these months I have missed my home, but today for the first time I understood something of what makes Paris what it is, and why there is nowhere like it in the world. The full length of the Pont-Neuf it was the same, 'Good luck, Mademoiselle! Good luck!' Tonight I shall hear it in my dreams.

We had the news officially from a crier outside the Tuiler-ies, who announced the Saillie was free and the Chevalier de Roland alive and well. I wished at once to rush to the Hôtel de Roland, but Colette said I should not dream of it until the Comtesse invited us herself. She said 'You must be very careful, Anne, there has been no word of a betrothal, and you will be exposed to ridicule if she does not offer one now.'

I know very well she may not, she has been scrupulous in making no promises, but I did not say so, for Colette seemed quite cross enough already. Florian was kinder, and said 'Ah but when André comes it will be a different story. He will surely persuade his grandmother to do whatever he wishes.'

Colette quite snapped at him. 'When André comes he will be seventeen and a hero who could have any woman he wishes. Why should he remember a childish flirtation with our poor sister?'

Poor Colette. I know she is worrying about her own impending marriage. Last night she came to my room and said she thought it would be all right, because she had heard of something one could do with fish skin so one's husband would never know. I would like to have said that at the Baron's age he should consider himself lucky she was even female, but she seems set on him so I didn't.

I still feared she might be right about André, and tried very hard to stay calm and sober all through the walk back, but when we arrived home and saw a horseman at the *porte-cochère* I could not help a ridiculous hope it might be one of his men after all. Of course it was not, it was only a military courier, but he said he had ridden post all the way from the Saillie, and leant down to put a little packet into my hands.

Florian at once became very dignified on my behalf, and said 'Is that really all there is, fellow? Surely there is a letter to accompany it?'

The courier turned to him a face lined with sweat and dust, but otherwise blank of any expression. He said wearily 'My apologies, Monseigneur. The Chevalier had just fought a battle, he may have had one or two other things on his mind.'

I knew what at least one of them had been, and did not need a letter to tell me so, for when I opened the packet I saw he had sent me a rose. It was a little soft with the travel and faintly brown at the edges, but it was the same salmon-pink as the one he had sent me before, and I knew it had come from the same garden and been cut by the same hand. I knew the meaning as clearly as if he had stood beside me and spoken it.

He is coming for me. And this time, please God, he will stay.

Jacques Gilbert

By late July we were ready to go.

Lots of people came to say goodbye to us in the barracks, and the boy found it really depressing. It wasn't like he wouldn't see them again, loads were joining the Ancre staff when the Manor was rebuilt, but for him it was never going to be the same. The Occupation was over, he was the Seigneur, and no one called him 'André' any more, they called him 'Sieur', and stood respectfully with their heads down, because he was nobility and they weren't supposed to look in his face. I knew that was right, that was the way it had to be, but I felt him hating it all the same.

What was upsetting him most was that Stefan didn't come. We hadn't really expected it, they hadn't spoken to each other for weeks, but I think deep down André was disappointed. So was I in a way. I'd like to have kicked his head in for upsetting the boy.

But none of that was going to matter now, we were off to Paris and a completely new life. I was desperately excited, and André kept telling me new things to expect, like beds with all feathers in the mattress instead of straw, a little room one actually went to piss in, and food like Arnould cooked every single day. I told my Mother all about it when I went to say goodbye, and she smiled and agreed it sounded wonderful, like the Manor in the old days, only better.

Then she brought me my omelette and said 'What about the Comtesse, darling? You haven't forgotten you're going to ask her about telling André the truth?'

I looked down at my plate, but my appetite was suddenly shrivelling. 'I don't have to right away, do I? It'll be better once she's got to know me, so she doesn't think I'm after anything.'

Mother was silent.

I said 'Maybe it's best if I don't even tell her I know. She wants it kept quiet, doesn't she? She's looking forward to seeing me, André says so, I don't want to spoil things.'

There was a sound of whistling from the back yard and the creak of the well rope as the bucket came up. Little Pierre had obviously finished in the stables for the day and was come home to wash.

Mother said 'You'll have to tell them both, my darling, you won't be able to hide it.'

'She's kept it secret nineteen years, hasn't she? Why can't I?'

'Because of this,' she said, and reached out and touched my face.

Something in my stomach started flapping about with nerves. I said 'But it doesn't show much now, not with my moustache.'

There were splashing noises from outside and Mother rose quickly to make Pierre his omelette. She said 'You will still tell the truth, my darling, because that is what is right.'

She was funny, my Mother. She couldn't make a decision about anything, she even used to stare at the eggs in anguish and ask me which I thought I'd like, but when it came to something as big as knowing what was right or wrong she didn't seem to need anyone else's help at all.

She was right this time too, and I knew it really, I was

thinking about it all the way home. It was going to be bad enough telling André the truth, but if he found out I knew and hadn't told him he was going to go mad. I told myself I'd talk to the Comtesse the very first chance I had.

Home was that little room at the top of the barracks, but it was all right actually, we'd got old Bertrand from the Steward's household looking after us, and he'd found us feather pillows and a basin to wash in, he'd put red curtains over the window and stuck a looking glass up on the wall, he'd made it almost grand.

André was packing when I got in, and from the slump of his shoulders I knew Stefan hadn't been. He wasn't going to talk about it though, he just asked brightly how Mother was, and if she'd got enough money till we got back. I said we'd left her plenty, but couldn't help a slight pang of guilt when I saw him packing into a small bag all that was left of the jewellery that had once bulged out of two great boxes. I knew how little he'd spent on himself.

It was the same with his clothes. I watched him carefully draping his good shirt over a chair for the morning, and thought how worn and shabby it looked now. He'd thought to get new dresses for Mother and Blanche, but it never occurred to him to get something made for himself. I said so, but he only shrugged and said 'We can get better things made in Paris. I'll need something really special for when I call on Anne.'

He looked in the mirror, and I knew from his dopey expression he was seeing himself in a splendid new outfit with Mlle Anne on his arm. Then his smile faded, his shoulders drooped again, and I heard him say 'Shit.'

'What?'

He was looking at his hair, stretching at it to try and make it seem longer.

I stood beside him to look. I said 'It's not bad now, André,' and really it wasn't, it at least reached his shoulders, but of course it wasn't what it had been, not when Mlle Anne had seen him.

'No,' he said, fingering it doubtfully. 'No.'

I scooped up my own, scrunched it back behind my neck and said 'Look, if you tied it back, no one would know . . .'

'Maybe,' he said, brightening and pushing his own hair back. 'Maybe it's long enough for . . .'

His voice trailed off, and I looked sharply from my reflection to his.

The colour was draining from his face, but not so much I couldn't see what he was seeing. Not when it was literally staring back at me, something we'd never, ever seen before, the two of us side by side.

Colin Lefebvre

So there we all were, right, sitting outside the Corbeaux, having a quiet drink, discussing how we were going to send off the Seigneur next day. Mercier's first day out and about since the battle, as it happened. Hadn't got his wooden leg yet, nothing but a stump and a stick, had to be carried about in a chair, but he was doing all right, Mercier, lot of respect on account of what he'd done that day, people coming and clapping him on the back all the while. Doing all right in other ways too, Seigneur getting his family business set up again good as new. Marin Aubert said Mercier's leg must have been the most expensive in Picardie.

Someone else perky that day was Leroux. Going to be verderer at Ancre now, and well pleased about it too, him never being able to stand the Baron. Not so pleased with the state of old Gauthier's cottage, if you ask me, filled with rotting animals from all accounts, old Jacques said he could still hear Leroux's shout of 'Jesus *Christ!*' when they opened the door. Not that he'd need to clean it himself, that was plain enough. There he was, hand in Big Margot's, and expression on him like a cow with bloat. Told us they were getting married, and about time too in my opinion, a man couldn't so much as cross a field without falling over those two at it somewhere, about time they did it regular and with the bed shriven.

Still no one feeling much like celebrating now the Seigneur's going. Knew he'd be off some time, stood to reason, but him gone, we'd have a new Steward in, they'd be wanting the *cens* again, say nothing of the *taille* and the *gabelle*. Naturally we'd miss him himself, not saying we wouldn't, done a fair old lot for Dax one way or another, everyone sorry to see him go. Then we heard someone laughing behind us, and there was Ravel, dressed up like a soldier on account of being off to Arras in the morning, and finding us all very funny.

'Just listen to yourselves,' he said, sitting down on the last chair and spreading his boots right under the table. 'Fawning over a sprig of the nobility who's probably already forgotten you exist. The sooner we're shot of him the better.'

Bit of a nasty silence after that one. We all knew Ravel had taken against Seigneur for some reason, but he could be a right touchy bastard if you'll forgive my language, so no one said nothing, just watched as he lit his pipe. Then there was this odd rumbling sound, and there was that Bernard Rouet looking constipated, and we suddenly realized he was going to speak. Didn't happen often, so we all looked at him expectantly, then he looked right at Ravel and said 'Why don't you just fuck off?'

Ravel was that startled he bit clean through his pipe, sat

looking at the pieces as if he couldn't see how it happened. Leroux started laughing, and Margot, she put her meaty great arm round Rouet's shoulders and looked at Ravel like to say 'Argue with that if you dare.'

Did dare though, this was Ravel. He said 'With which intellectual contribution to the discussion I think we can consider the subject closed. Now is it worth my staying for a drink, or are you just going to witter on about André?'

Silence again, with nothing but that Rouet still rumbling 'fuck off' like he'd got stuck and couldn't get any further, then Mercier pulled himself upright in his chair, looked Ravel smack in the eye and said 'You didn't think so little of him by the gorge,' he said. 'Have you forgotten that?'

Ravel didn't flicker so much as an eyelash. He said 'Blessed are the meek?' he said, which is the Bible, as you know. He said 'I took your advice, Mercier. I asked, and I didn't get.'

Meant bugger all to Mercier, looked quite confused to me, but he held his ground for all that, kept his head high and said 'Well, it can't have been possible, that's all.'

'Oh, it was possible,' said Ravel, standing himself up to go. 'No, that debt's paid. The next time I meet André de Roland we'll be on equal terms. And you know what? I'm quite looking forward to it.' Crammed his hat on his head, nodded at us under its filthy old brim, then turned and took himself off, jaunty as a magpie, swaggering away to war.

Best thing that could have happened, you ask me. Jacques said there'd been talk of him joining them in the army, and he could see as well as me that wouldn't do. Under Occupation's one thing, real life quite another. Sieur of Dax being friends with a tanner, well, I ask you. In the Bible, isn't it? Everyone in their place.

He leant against the wall with his hands in his pockets, and I told him everything.

He was kind about it, he didn't blame me at all. When I said about Father telling me, he looked up and said 'That must have been an awful shock,' and I said eagerly 'Yes, it was, that's why I was so upset,' but he just repeated 'an awful shock', and went quiet to allow me to go on. When I'd finished there was just this silence.

At last he jerked himself away from the wall and started to finish his packing. There wasn't much of it, just the few bits and pieces we'd brought from the Hermitage, his old things from the barn.

He said 'I should have known really. I knew my father loved you, he always said I should be more like you. He used to ask if I'd seen you, and how you were. He was always asking that.'

His voice was trailing a little, and I saw he'd picked up his picture, the one of his parents that opened like a little book. 'Sometimes, when you weren't at the stables, I used to pretend you had been, because he always liked it if I could say I'd seen you.' He looked at the picture a moment, shut it gently, and put it in his pack. 'It wasn't really lying, more like telling a story.'

'Was that why you used to come round so often? Ask me all those questions?'

'No,' he said, and looked at me in surprise. 'No, I did that for me. I liked to watch you. I wanted to see what you were doing right and I wasn't.'

I closed my eyes. That poor lonely little boy, following me round to find out my secret, and never knowing it wasn't his fault, any of it, only that his father didn't love his mother and never could, not the way he loved mine. The whole thing was so bloody unfair.

I said 'He did love you, André, anyone could see that.'

'Oh yes,' he said vaguely, as if it didn't matter. 'He was fond of me.' He picked up his wooden horse and stroked its nose, showing it to me with something like pride. 'He made this for me himself, did I tell you that?'

I felt a hard lump coming up in my throat. I knew I must never, ever tell him he'd made one for me too.

I said 'That's right. And I wasn't that important to him really, I mean he gave me away, didn't he?'

He packed away the horse. 'He couldn't very well do that with me. They needed an heir to inherit the title.' He looked up at me suddenly, and I saw his eyes were shining wet, but he didn't cry, he was André, Chevalier de Roland, and he didn't cry. 'It could have been you, don't you realize that? If he'd married your Mother, it would have been you.'

'He couldn't, it was his duty . . .'

'It was his duty to do what was right,' said André. He blinked away the tears, and reached for his books. 'We can't have needed the money that badly, he loved your Mother, he ought to have married her. None of this need have happened.'

'But then you wouldn't have been born at all.'

'No,' he said, and there was something funny in his voice. 'I wouldn't, would I?'

I sat on the bed and watched helplessly as he started to shove his books into the pack, just stuffing them in like they didn't mean anything any more. It's an awful feeling when you know something's done that can't ever be undone, it felt like my whole insides were sinking slowly to the floor. I'd have given anything just to go back an hour and not stand beside him in that mirror, not let any of it happen at all.

I said miserably 'I'm sorry, it's a bloody mess.'

André started to close up his pack. 'Well, we'll just have to put it right, that's all.'

'What?'

'We've got to acknowledge you for a start, anything else is just wrong.'

'But your grandmother won't do it, they wanted it hushed up.'

'She'll do it,' he said grimly. 'She must. My mother's dead now, there's no reason to keep it secret any more.'

I felt panic tightening me up inside like indigestion. 'We can't tell anyone, your grandmother would hate me for it, there isn't any need . . .'

'Of course there's a need.' He put his pack on the chair, then saw he'd left his tennis ball out, hesitated, then picked it up. 'You can't have the title of course, but you're the oldest son, you've got to have rights.'

It was mad, I mean things aren't done that way, it was as stupid as saying his father ought to have married my Mother. I said 'André, bastards don't have rights.'

He threw the ball up in his hand and caught it. 'This isn't about the law, it's a matter of honour, you should know that.'

I said 'I do bloody know that, that's why I didn't tell you. But there's nothing we can do, and that's all right, I don't blame anybody, I just want things to go on like they are.'

'I don't,' he said. His face had an odd, pinched look like it did when he was so ill. 'I don't want anything that's not morally mine.'

I felt like he'd stabbed me. 'And you think I do?'

He looked down at the ball in his hand and started squeezing it like it was somebody's neck. 'All these years you've been mucking out stables when you should have been living like me. It's only right for you to want it.'

The panic was almost choking me, I had this stupid urge to keep moving my head, twisting my neck to make it go away. 'Well, I don't. Why would I? I've never wanted it.'

He went on squeezing that bloody ball. 'You don't want to be a gentleman?' For a moment he almost sounded like my Father.

I said 'You're already making me that, aren't you? I'm your aide, and that's a gentleman's job, isn't it?'

He shrugged. 'Well, yes, but . . .'

'You're giving me a nice house to live in, and proper clothes to wear, what else could I possibly want? You've even given me the best horse in your stable, you've given me Tonnerre. What could I possibly have if you went and acknowledged me that I haven't already got?'

He stopped squeezing the ball and started picking at the bit of rag sticking out. 'You don't understand, it's about status. I'm talking about people recognizing you as a gentleman in your own right.'

'I know what you're talking about!' I said, and suddenly I couldn't sit any more, it's like I was getting angry. I got up and tried to pace about the room, but it was too small, I just ended up with my head in the curtains and had to turn round. 'I know about being a proper gentleman, I've heard all about it from M. Gauthier.'

'Have you?'

'Don't you dare laugh at that,' I said. 'He loved you, M. Gauthier, he knew what it took to be real nobility, and he said you'd got it all.'

'I'm not laughing,' he said, and actually he wasn't. He chucked the tennis ball on the bed and said 'What did Martin say I needed?'

I felt a bit stupid suddenly. 'Honour, courage, and the use of the sword.'

He stared down at the bed. 'And that was just for me, was it?'

'Well, it wasn't bloody me. How could it be? I can't live up to that stuff, people will laugh at me if I even try. Please, can't we just stay as we are? I mean nothing's really changed . . .'

'Everything's changed,' he said, and looked me right in the face. 'You're my father's son. I can't just pretend you're not.'

There was something distant in his voice I couldn't bear, something cold in his face that was worse. I sat down again and felt my world sort of cracking around me.

'All right, then you can't. But it's just between us, isn't it, no one else needs to know.'

He sighed, and ran his hands through his hair. 'For the moment, maybe. We can't do anything till we've talked to my grandmother, and there's your Mother, she needs to be warned. But I can't just leave it, you must understand that.'

I did really, I could see it would be unbearable for him if he didn't. I'd never have been able to take over Father's old job knowing it really ought to be Little Pierre's.

I said unsteadily 'As long as we're still together, that's all.'

He reached out for his cloak, and started to sling it round his shoulders.

I said 'Where are you . . . ?'

'I'm just going out for a while,' he said. 'Just some fresh air.'

Somewhere away from me. I said miserably 'Are you angry with me?'

He paused at the door. 'How could I be? It's not your fault, is it?'

He opened the door and went out.

I don't know how long he was gone, but it felt like hours.

I had time to pack up my own stuff, and I did it slowly and carefully, folding everything properly, trying to pretend everything was normal and nothing had really changed at all. I had time to go and have a last drink with Colin, I had time to come back and be nervous outside the door and hope the boy was feeling better, then come in and see he still wasn't back. I had time to put myself to bed and lie there feeling miserable and angry with my Mother and the Comtesse and even André himself, because it's like they were all blaming me for being who I was, and it wasn't my fault at all.

I'd been doing it a long time when I heard him come back in. He was creeping about in the dark like he didn't want to talk, so I tried to breathe regularly and pretend to be asleep. I felt him climb under the blankets beside me, but he didn't rest against me as usual, he just lay turned away and stayed very still. His back felt sort of rigid, and his shirt was cold. There was a strange, dank smell on it too, it tingled in my nose, then slowly opened into a memory of a day four years ago, the squelch of mud under my shoes and the crack of an open door beside me, a glimpse of white stone shelves stretching back into darkness, and two shrouded bundles being laid side by side. He'd been back to the Ancre vault. He'd been to see his father.

For a moment I felt a stab of jealousy, because I'd like to have seen him too, I'd never been allowed in the vault at the funeral, and that wasn't fair, because he was my father too. Then I caught myself actually grudging the boy the last tiny thing he'd got left for himself, and a wave of self-loathing went over me like cold water. He'd given me everything. He shared everything he had with me, he'd been doing it for years. He'd made sure I had new clothes when he did, he'd even got me a rapier like his own so I could wear a dress sword like a gentleman. Even now Tempête was dead he was only taking the colt so I could keep his father's warhorse for my own. He hadn't held back a single thing, all he had was being who he was, and now I'd even taken that too.

It had to stop. I'd got to do something to show him it didn't have to be like that, he didn't owe me anything, I wasn't trying to take his place. I knew he'd never feel the same about me, there was nothing to be done about that, but I lay awake all night trying to think how to put the rest of it right.

There was one thing I could do straightaway, which was tiny and trivial but at least would be a start. I waited till the curtains began to look red instead of black, then got up quietly by myself and went out to knock up M. Pollet. It took longer than I'd thought, he insisted on doing it all properly, and by the time he'd finished I was terrified I was going to be late. The horses would be waiting in the Square at nine, and the clock was already striking when I came running through the back entrance into the barracks.

André was up and dressed, of course, and looked in a totally filthy mood. I didn't mind that, actually, it was more like himself, and anything was better than that cold politeness he'd given me last night. He certainly wasn't polite now, he started snapping as soon as I got in. He was saying 'Where the *hell* have you been, don't you know we've got people waiting, I've been worried sick, where the *hell* have you been?' then he saw my hair and stopped dead.

His face seemed to curl up in distress and his voice dropped into a whisper. He said 'Oh, Jacques, what have you . . . ?' then shut his mouth again, because it was obvious what I'd done, I could see it in the mirror behind him. My hair was nice and neat, but M. Pollet had judged it beautifully, and it was at least an inch shorter than André's.

I said quickly 'I had to do something. I don't want to be

better than you, I never have, I just want us to be together.'

His eyes looked huge. 'But, Jacques, I don't want . . .'

'But I do. I'm still your aide, aren't I? You said I could be, you're not going to go back on it now, are you?'

He hesitated. 'Not if it's really what you want.'

I said firmly 'It is.'

There was a little tap at the door.

André pulled himself together and said 'Come in,' but he was still looking at me.

Bertrand crept in nervously and wondered if we wanted to delay our departure.

André dragged his head round to look at him, then said 'No. No, we're coming directly.'

Bertrand looked at me, because of course we ought to be going down first, so I grabbed the bags, turned to André, said formally 'We'll be five minutes,' and shot out the door before he could change his mind.

My confidence was rising as I went outside. It could still be all right, I was going to be allowed to stay with him, I was his aide after all. The courtyard was empty, but I could guess why, I could hear the rumble of the crowd in the Square even through the gate, and knew the whole of Dax was out there to see the boy off. That was right really, that was how it should be, he was the Seigneur.

Bertrand took the baggage through the gate, and I stationed myself beside it, ready to open it for André. I'd seen M. Chapelle do that stuff so often it felt strange to be doing it myself, like I was a character in a play. I brushed down my clothes and smoothed my hair, and wished I'd got a mirror to check what I looked like.

The side door to the barracks opened and André came out. He looked round the empty courtyard, straightened his hat and began to walk towards me. I remembered him making that walk the other way when he gave himself up to save my life, I remembered him looking up at my window and giving me that little wave. He didn't wave now.

I watched him getting nearer, and suddenly there was a window back between us and I was seeing the Chevalier de Roland approaching his aide. His clothes were scruffy and his hair too short, but he held himself upright, he seemed sort of tall. My eyes went all by themselves to his sword, it was clearing the stones by inches, and with a stupid pang I found myself remembering a black night and a little boy running towards me, a long sword trailing behind him in the wet grass. The loss was suddenly so unbearable I felt my knees start to shake.

I squashed it down, I stamped it out dead and ignored the fact it made me feel dead too. I got my chin up to face my master, took off my hat and bowed.

I said 'Chevalier.' I said it beautifully.

He stepped up beside me and said 'No.'

My mouth went dry. 'André, you said I could . . .'

'No,' he said. 'Like this.' He held out his hand.

I stared blindly at it. It was empty of course, only it wasn't, because in it was the one last thing he had to give, and it was the one thing I really wanted. I looked up at his face, afraid I'd got it wrong, scared he was going to hurt me, but it was just the boy, it was André, like no one in the world ever saw him but me.

'Come on, brother,' he said, and smiled.

I took his hand, and opened the gate wide. The rumble of the crowd swelled into a sudden great roar as we walked out together into the sunshine.

They were all out there, all of them, people from Verdâme as well as Dax, we'd got the whole bloody Saillie to see us off. They were all bright in Sunday clothes, rows of cheering

625

faces, and a great flurry of hats flying up into the air. I shoved my head down quickly to show I knew the cheers weren't for me, but André jerked my hand to keep me close, and the noise actually got louder.

I risked a look up. Père Gérard was standing on the church steps beaming right at me, and Mother beside him, shining with pride. Colin was there too, Jean-Marie, Giles, all waving and calling out, and no-one looked disapproving or like I oughtn't to be where I was. As I mounted Tonnerre I got a sudden dizzying feeling that they might be right. M Gauthier always said 'The seed of honour's in every man,' and at last I understood it, what André had seen at once: that it might even be inside me.

The bells started ringing, a wild, joyous clanging that hurt my ears, and I turned to see André drawing his sword. I took a deep breath, and drew my own.

We rode out like that together. The crowd opened to let us through, and we galloped down the road, through the Gate and onto the fields of France. There was no Wall in front of us, the grass stretched all the way to the beech forest on the horizon. It loomed in front of me like the dark blur of a world I'd never been in and didn't know, but the sun was flashing on our blades like white fire, and the shadows seemed to part before us as we came.

Historical Note

While it is natural for our narrators to be most concerned with their own little world of the Saillie, the events outside may need clarification for the non-historian.

The Thirty Years War of 1618–1648 was fought between the great Catholic powers of Spain and the Holy Roman Empire on the one side, and the predominantly Protestant nations on the other. Its division along essentially religious lines in part accounts for the extraordinary mix of nations to be found in each army, where mercenaries were drawn from all countries, and the man charged with holding Arras against the French was actually a Scot. The predominance of mercenaries was also a factor in the extreme brutality of this war, in which context the behaviour of even Don Francisco appears impeccably restrained. Atrocities were committed by all sides, usually against a helpless civilian population, and the infamous Sack of Magdeburg by Catholic forces in 1631 remained a byword for centuries in the expression 'Magdeburg justice', as used in these pages by Ravel.

Although Catholic herself, France refused at first to be drawn in, for she held a policy of limited toleration towards Protestants, enshrined in the Edict of Nantes, and was moreover inclined to favour any side that might impose a curb on dangerous Habsburg domination. However, in 1635 Louis XIII's First Minister Cardinal Richelieu finally declared openly against Spain, and France entered the war with offensives in the Rhineland. The empire hit back decisively with the invasion of Northern France with which the Abbé Fleuriot's narrative opens. Lefebvre's account of the fall of the forts in the Year of Corbie is remarkably accurate, although none of our narrators seem to have been aware of the full extent of the danger. The Spanish offensive was but part of the invading force, and the outstanding Bavarian general Johann von Werth won a cavalry action which brought Imperial troops to within twenty miles of Paris itself. Only the rapid formation of a new French army under Louis XIII and the help of France's ally Bernard of Saxe-Weimar saw the Imperial troops driven back from Compiègne. Even then, Lefebvre is likely right in his assumption that the withdrawal of the enemy from Corbie had less to do with the success of French counter-attack than with the need to retire on winter quarters. If this military division of a year into specific campaign seasons seems incomprehensible to us today, we should perhaps remember the importance to an invading army of pasture for the horses as well as food in the fields for the men. The hard winter of 1639–1640 was one reason la Meilleraye anticipated such difficulty in the assault on Arras – and was, in the event, proved right.

France was a long time recovering from the shock of the *Année de Corbie*. The commanders of La Capelle, Le Câtelet and Corbie were all condemned to death for allowing their forts to be taken, an attitude which may help us understand André's personal sense of shame at having failed to prevent his territory falling into enemy hands. The recovery of ground was slow too, and as Père Gérard says, La Capelle was not retaken until 1637, nor Le Câtelet until 1638. By 1640, Richelieu was desperate for significant victories in Artois, and his generals were warned they would answer with their heads if they failed to take Arras. This may excuse some of the caution mentioned by our narrators, although most historical commentators appear to share Ravel's rather dim view of the abilities of Gaspard III de Coligny, the Maréchal de Châtillon. I can, however, find no further reference to a 'Comte de Gressy' and am inclined to suspect the tactful Abbé Fleuriot of using a pseudonym in this single case.

The little-known march on Aire and Béthune was also a matter of fact, and André seems to have been right in his conjecture as to its purpose, for an account of the meeting with Louis XIII and Richelieu can be found in Puységur's own memoirs, where the ruse to draw men out of Arras is in fact credited to Châtillon rather than la Meilleraye. Its success appears, however, to have been limited, for while the two French armies did indeed combine to invest Arras on 13 June, the city had by then been reinforced and the siege endured until 8 August.

The role played by the Comtesse de Vallon in the liberation of the Saillie may appear extraordinary to modern readers, but we should not underestimate the influence of women in the French political arena at this time. The salons held in the great town houses (or 'hôtels' in the parlance of the day) held enormous sway over society, especially the famous literary *coterie* established round that of Madame de Rambouillet. Neither does Ravel exaggerate the power of the written pamphlets and canards, for it was scurrilous publications of this kind directed against Mazarin that provided the fuel for the later Fronde, just as a hundred and fifty years later they would inflame the populace against Marie Antoinette.

Many of the other personages mentioned in Paris figure prominently in the Abbé's later papers, so I shall write no more of them here. The reader need only note that I have preserved the contemporary titles accorded princes of the blood, so that when no other name is offered 'Monsieur le Comte' can only refer to the Comte de Soissons, and 'Monsieur le Prince' to the Prince de Condé. 'Young d'Enghien' is of course his son, later known to history as 'the great Condé', while 'Monsieur le Grand' was the title given to the King's favourite and Master of the Horse, the Marquis de Cinq Mars, whose conspiracy was later to have such tragic consequences for our hero.

The only one of these notables whom André never met was the kindly Governor of Doullens who returned Jacques' ring. This would have been the celebrated François de Jussac d'Ambleville, Sieur de Saint-Preuil, who was executed in 1641 for attacking the garrison at Baupaume when nobody told him they had already capitulated. His real crime may have been involvement in the Soissons rebellion, but the injustice of his death provides a timely reminder that the world André was now entering was fraught with more danger than the one he was leaving behind.

Edward Morton
Cambridge, April 2010